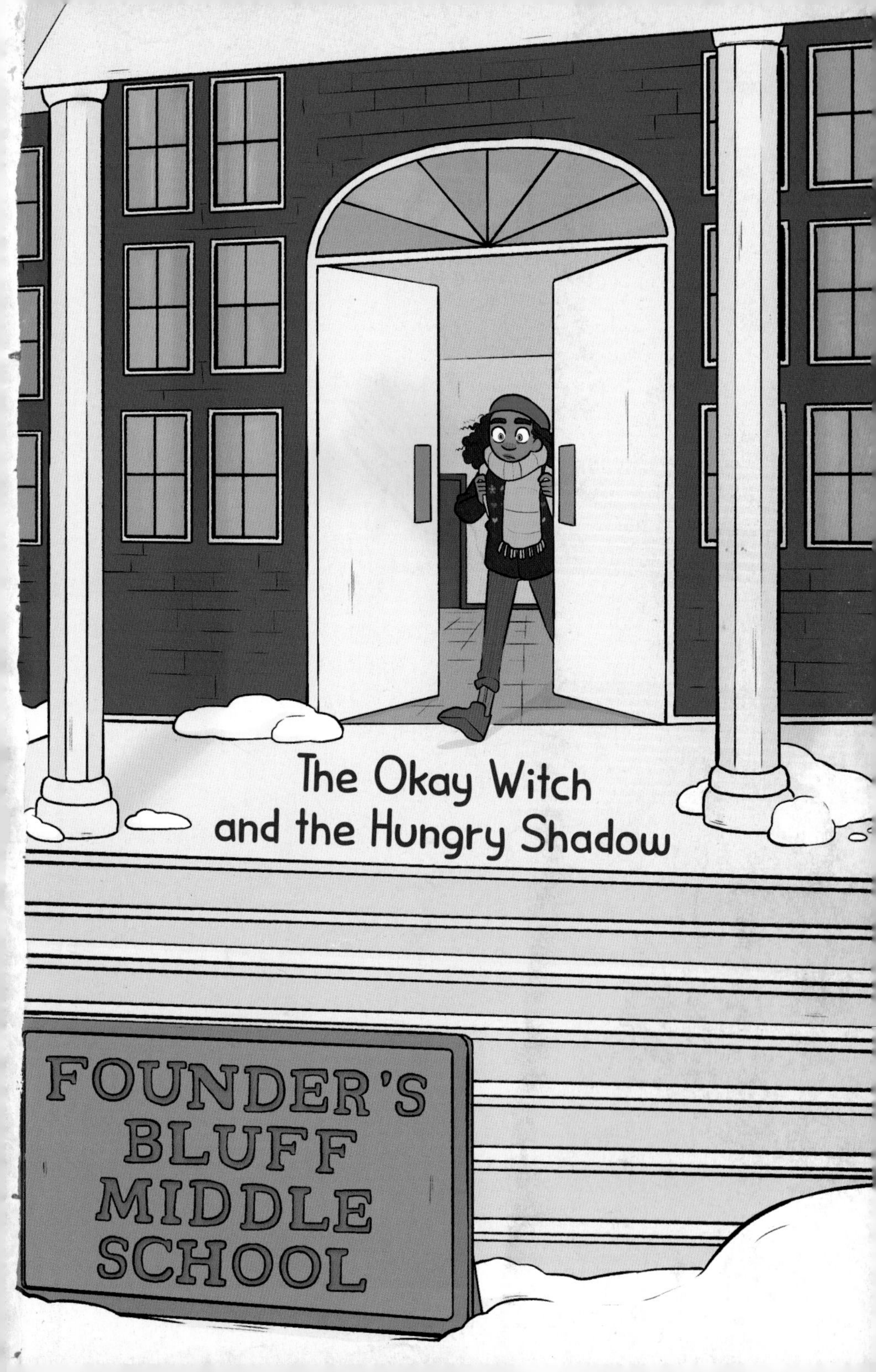
The Okay Witch
and the Hungry Shadow
FOUNDER'S
BLUFF
MIDDLE
SCHOOL

To Team Steinkellner.

I love this family of ours.

Also by Emma Steinkellner

The Okay Witch

FOUNDER'S
BLUFF
EST. 1676

ALADDIN | An imprint of Simon & Schuster Children's Publishing Division | 1230 Avenue of the Americas, New York, New York 10020 | First Aladdin edition July 2021 | Copyright © 2021 by Emma Steinkellner | All rights reserved, including the right of reproduction in whole or in part in any form. | ALADDIN and related logo are registered trademarks of Simon & Schuster, Inc. | For information about special discounts for bulk purchases, please contact Simon & Schuster Special Sales at 1-866-506-1949 or business@simonandschuster.com. | The Simon & Schuster Speakers Bureau can bring authors to your live event. For more information or to book an event contact the Simon & Schuster Speakers Bureau at 1-866-248-3049 or visit our website at www.simonspeakers.com. | Designed by Karin Paprocki and Emma Steinkellner | The illustrations for this book were rendered digitally. | The text of this book was set in Minou Regular. | Manufactured in China 0421 SCP | 10 9 8 7 6 5 4 3 2 1 | Library of Congress Control Number 2020931412 | ISBN 9781534431492 (hc) | ISBN 9781534431485 (pbk) | ISBN 9781534431508 (eBook)

THE OKAY WITCH AND THE HUNGRY SHADOW

By Emma Steinkellner

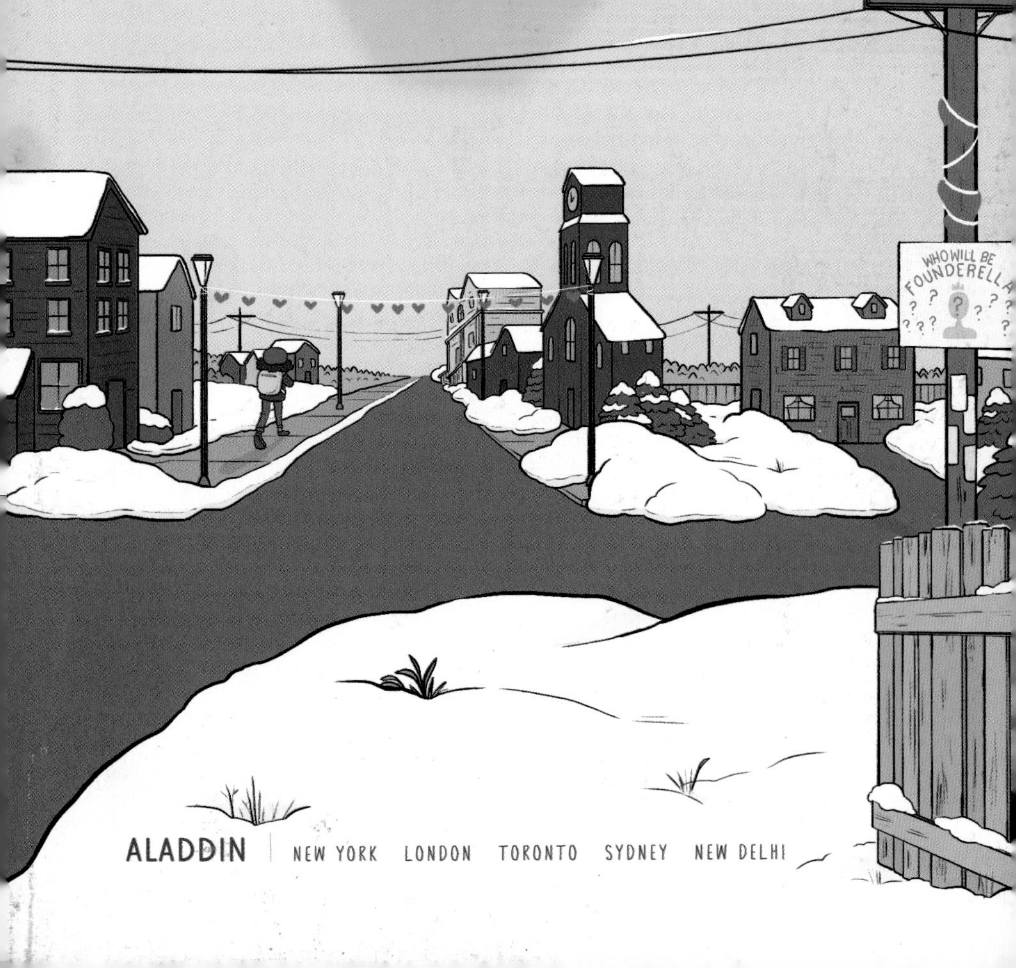
WHO WILL BE FOUNDERELLA

ALADDIN | NEW YORK LONDON TORONTO SYDNEY NEW DELHI

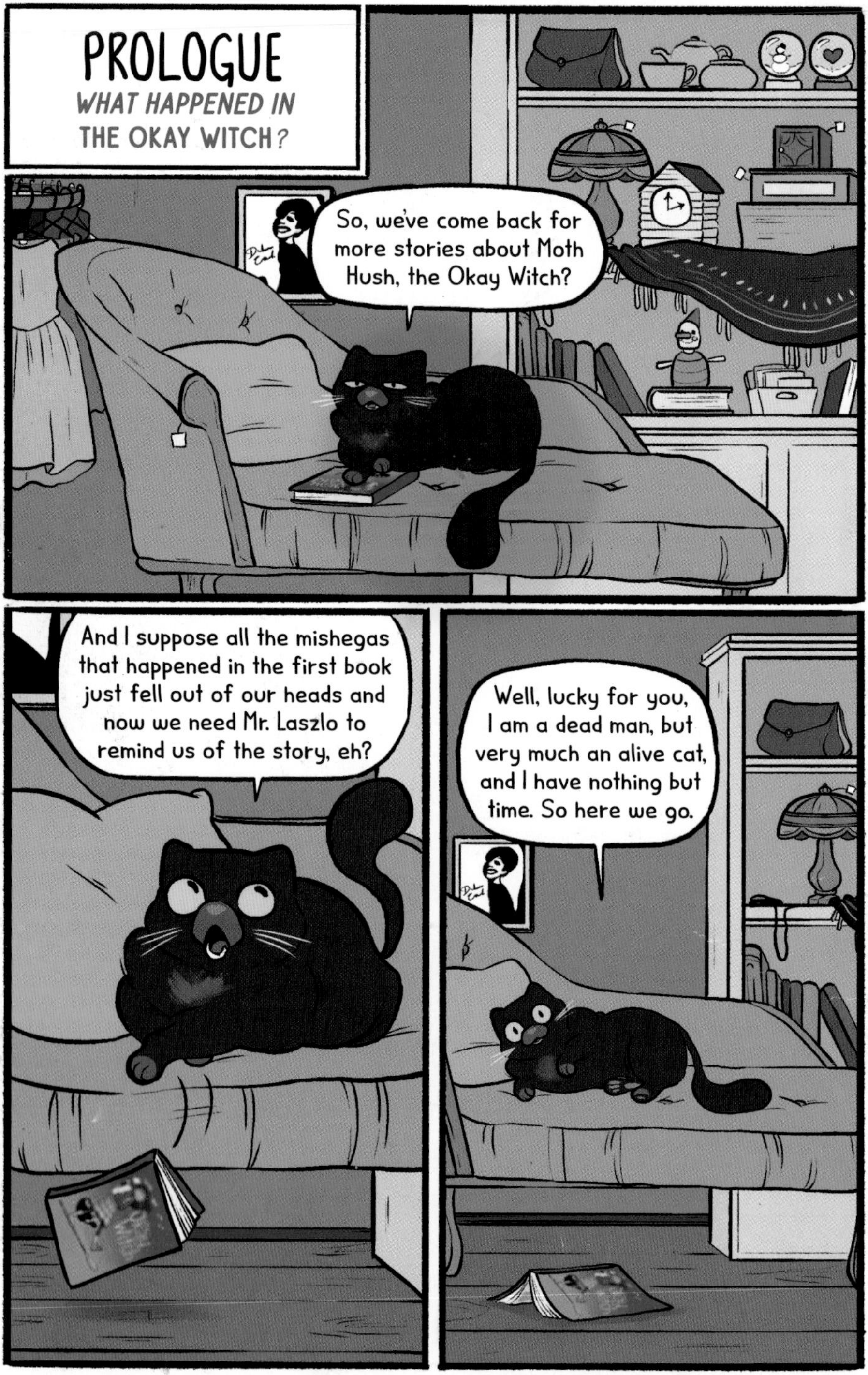
PROLOGUE
WHAT HAPPENED IN THE OKAY WITCH?
So, we've come back for more stories about Moth Hush, the Okay Witch?
And I suppose all the mishegas that happened in the first book just fell out of our heads and now we need Mr. Laszlo to remind us of the story, eh?
Well, lucky for you, I am a dead man, but very much an alive cat, and I have nothing but time. So here we go.

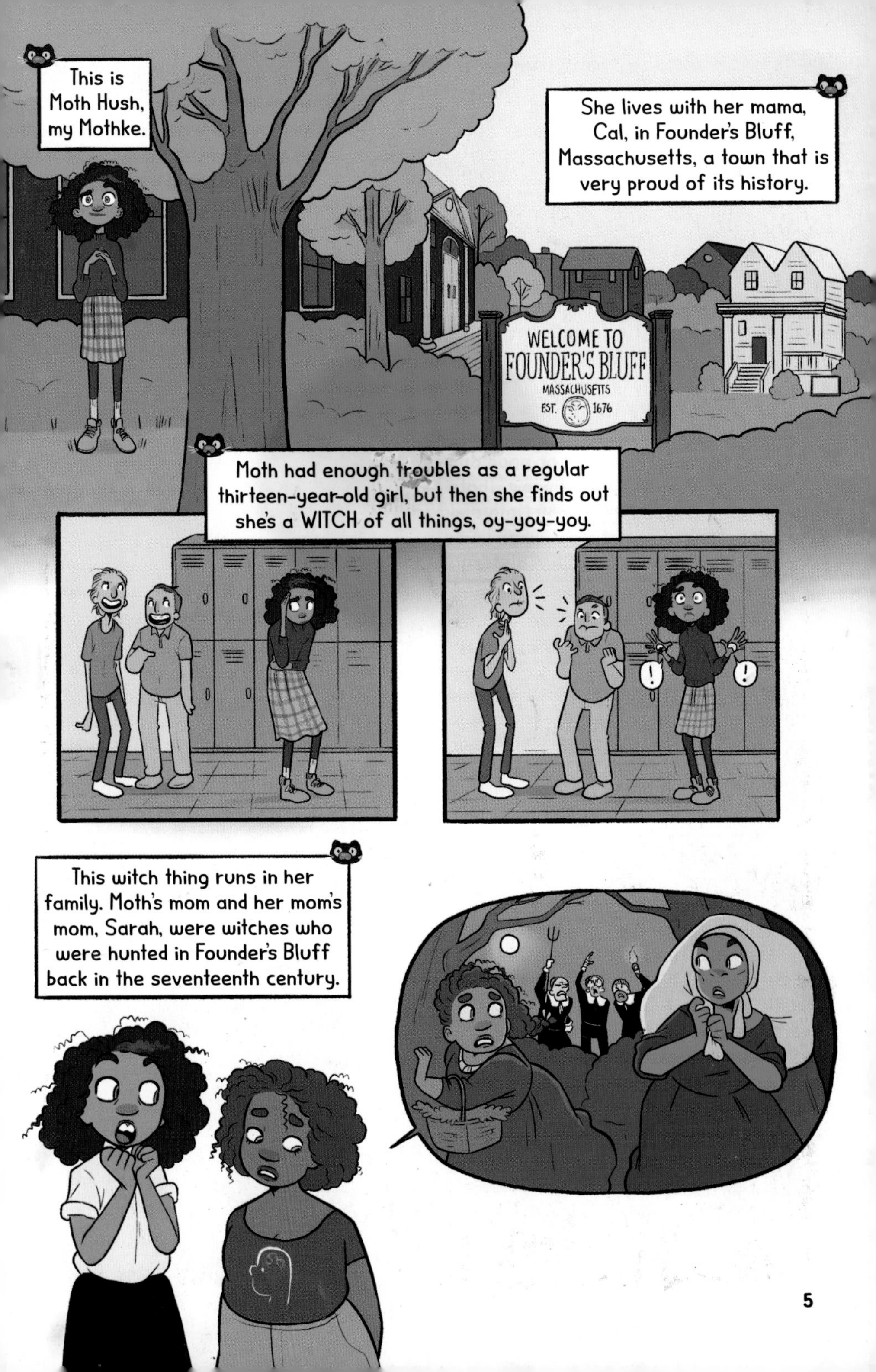
This is Moth Hush, my Mothke.
She lives with her mama, Cal, in Founder's Bluff, Massachusetts, a town that is very proud of its history.
WELCOME TO
FOUNDER'S BLUFF
MASSACHUSETTS
EST. 1676
Moth had enough troubles as a regular thirteen-year-old girl, but then she finds out she's a WITCH of all things, oy-yoy-yoy.
!
!
This witch thing runs in her family. Moth's mom and her mom's mom, Sarah, were witches who were hunted in Founder's Bluff back in the seventeenth century.

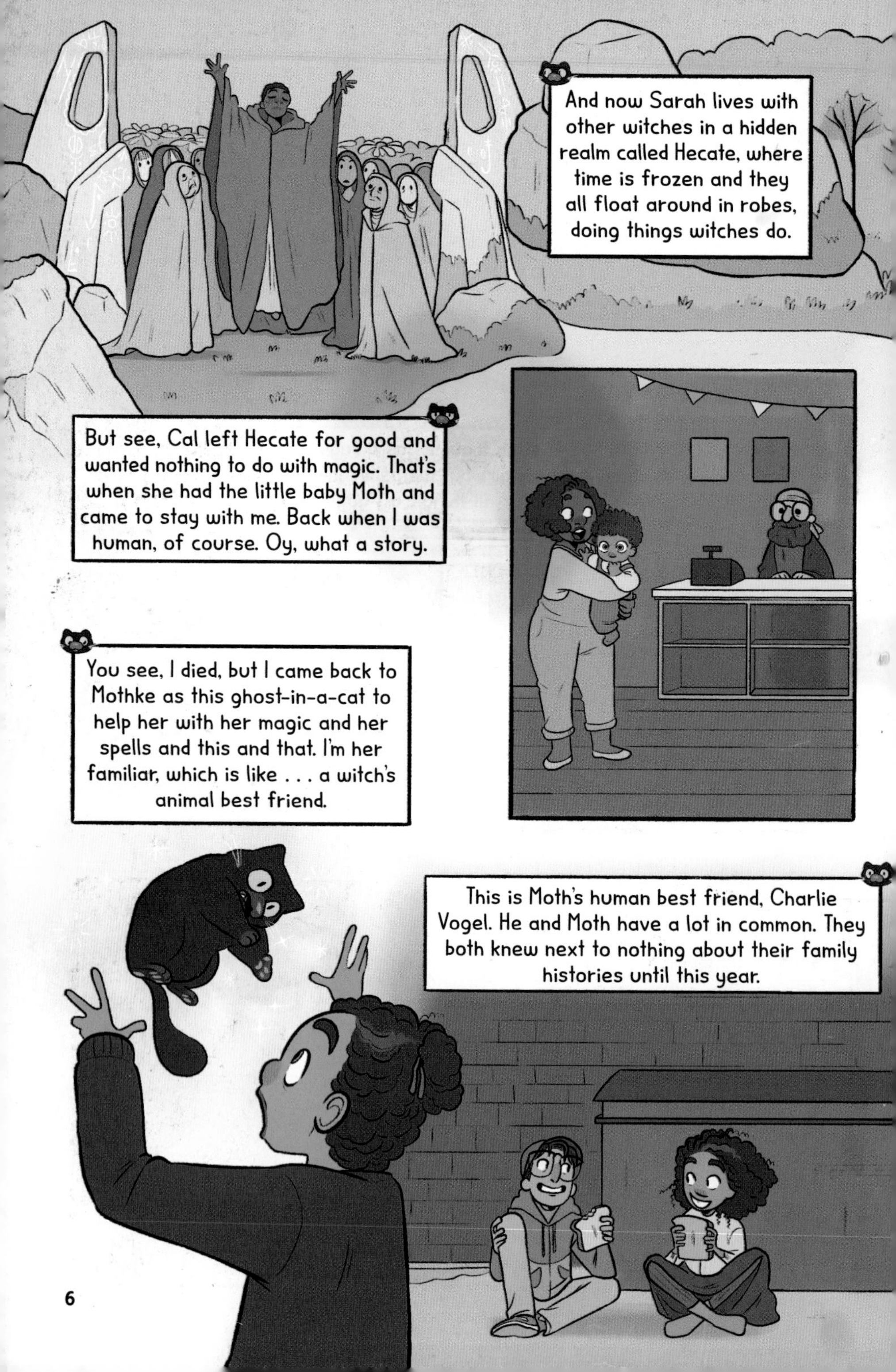
And now Sarah lives with other witches in a hidden realm called Hecate, where time is frozen and they all float around in robes, doing things witches do.
But see, Cal left Hecate for good and wanted nothing to do with magic. That's when she had the little baby Moth and came to stay with me. Back when I was human, of course. Oy, what a story.
You see, I died, but I came back to Mothke as this ghost-in-a-cat to help her with her magic and her spells and this and that. I'm her familiar, which is like . . . a witch's animal best friend.
This is Moth's human best friend, Charlie Vogel. He and Moth have a lot in common. They both knew next to nothing about their family histories until this year.

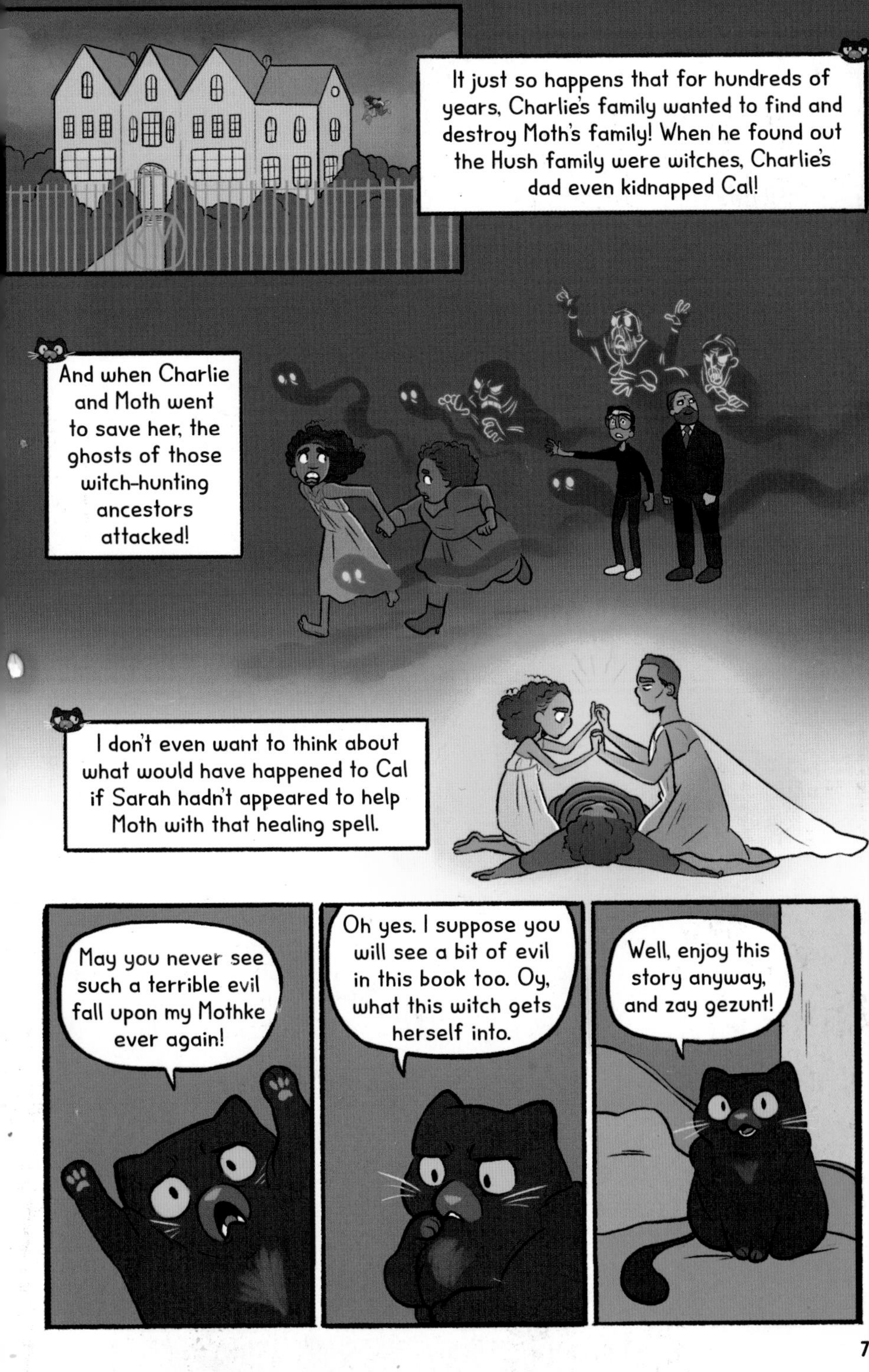
It just so happens that for hundreds of years, Charlie's family wanted to find and destroy Moth's family! When he found out the Hush family were witches, Charlie's dad even kidnapped Cal!
And when Charlie and Moth went to save her, the ghosts of those witch-hunting ancestors attacked!
I don't even want to think about what would have happened to Cal if Sarah hadn't appeared to help Moth with that healing spell.
May you never see such a terrible evil fall upon my Mothke ever again!
Oh yes. I suppose you will see a bit of evil in this book too. Oy, what this witch gets herself into.
Well, enjoy this story anyway, and zay gezunt!

CHAPTER 1
Her Greatest Enemy

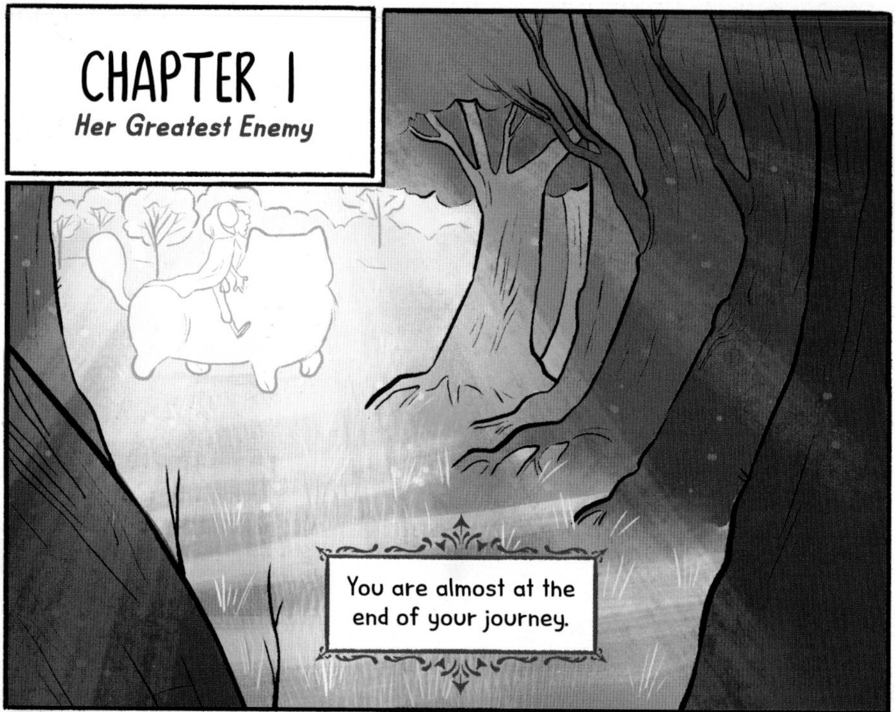
You are almost at the end of your journey.

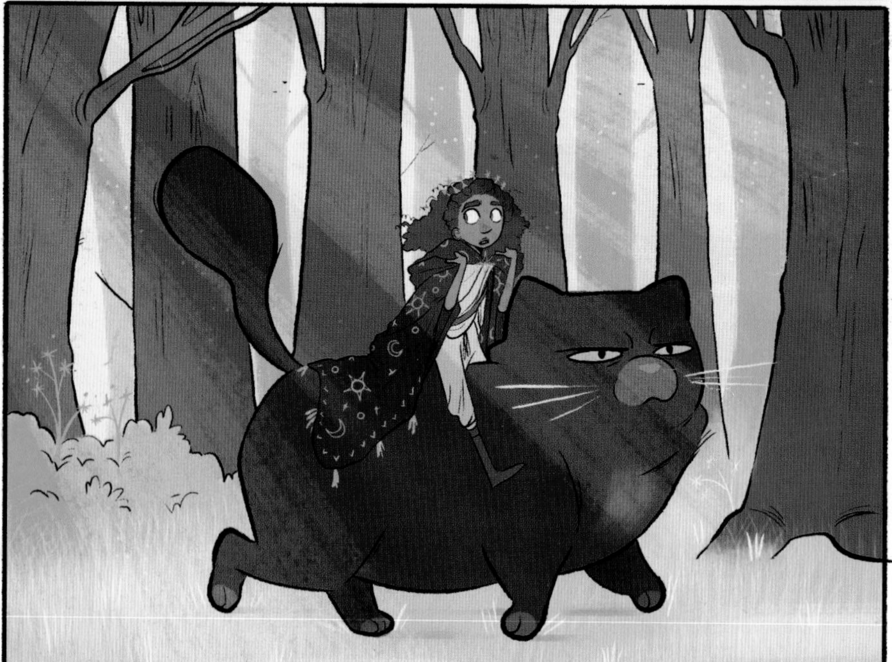

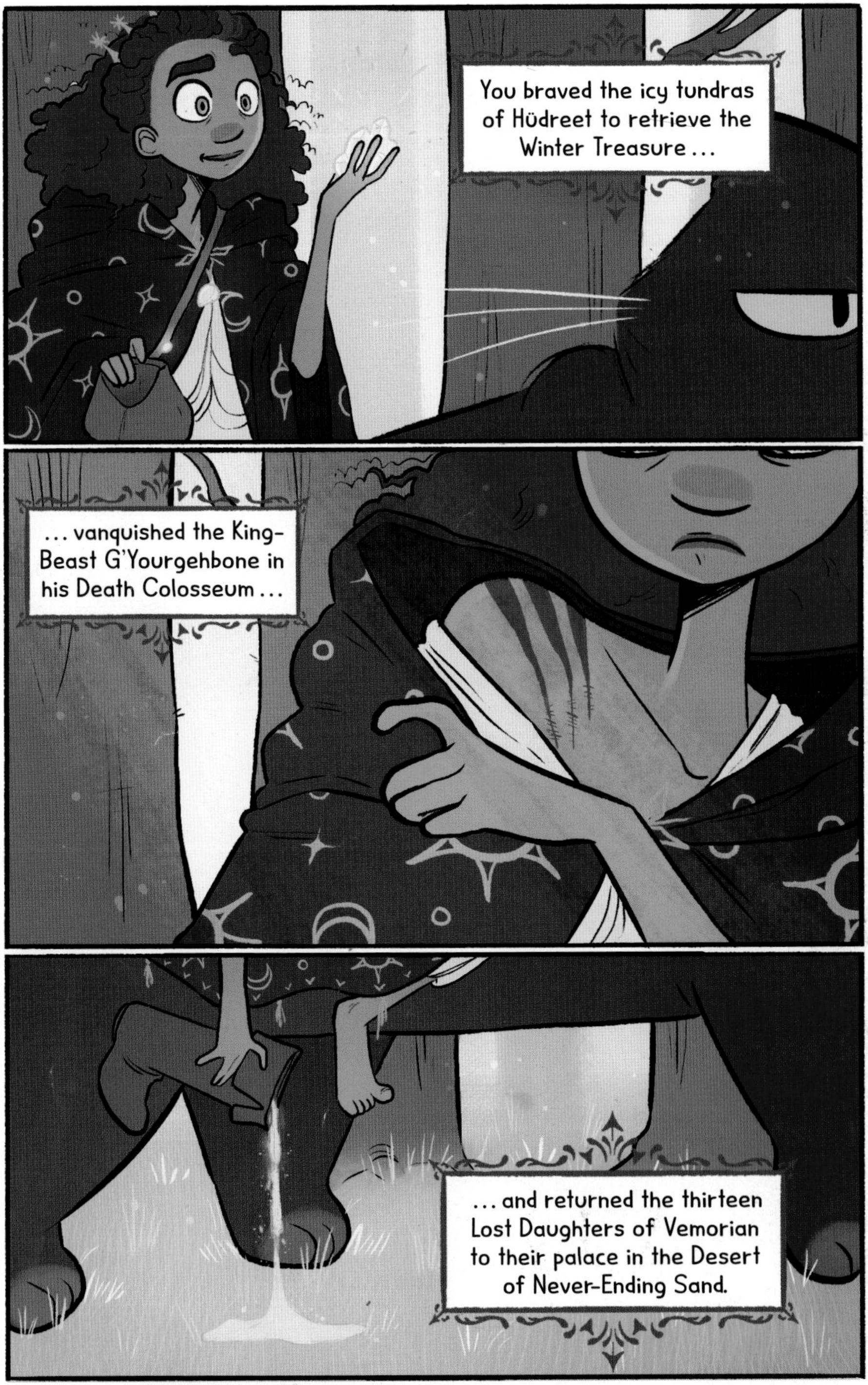
You braved the icy tundras of Hüdreet to retrieve the Winter Treasure . . .
. . . vanquished the King-Beast G'Yourgehbone in his Death Colosseum . . .
. . . and returned the thirteen Lost Daughters of Vemorian to their palace in the Desert of Never-Ending Sand.

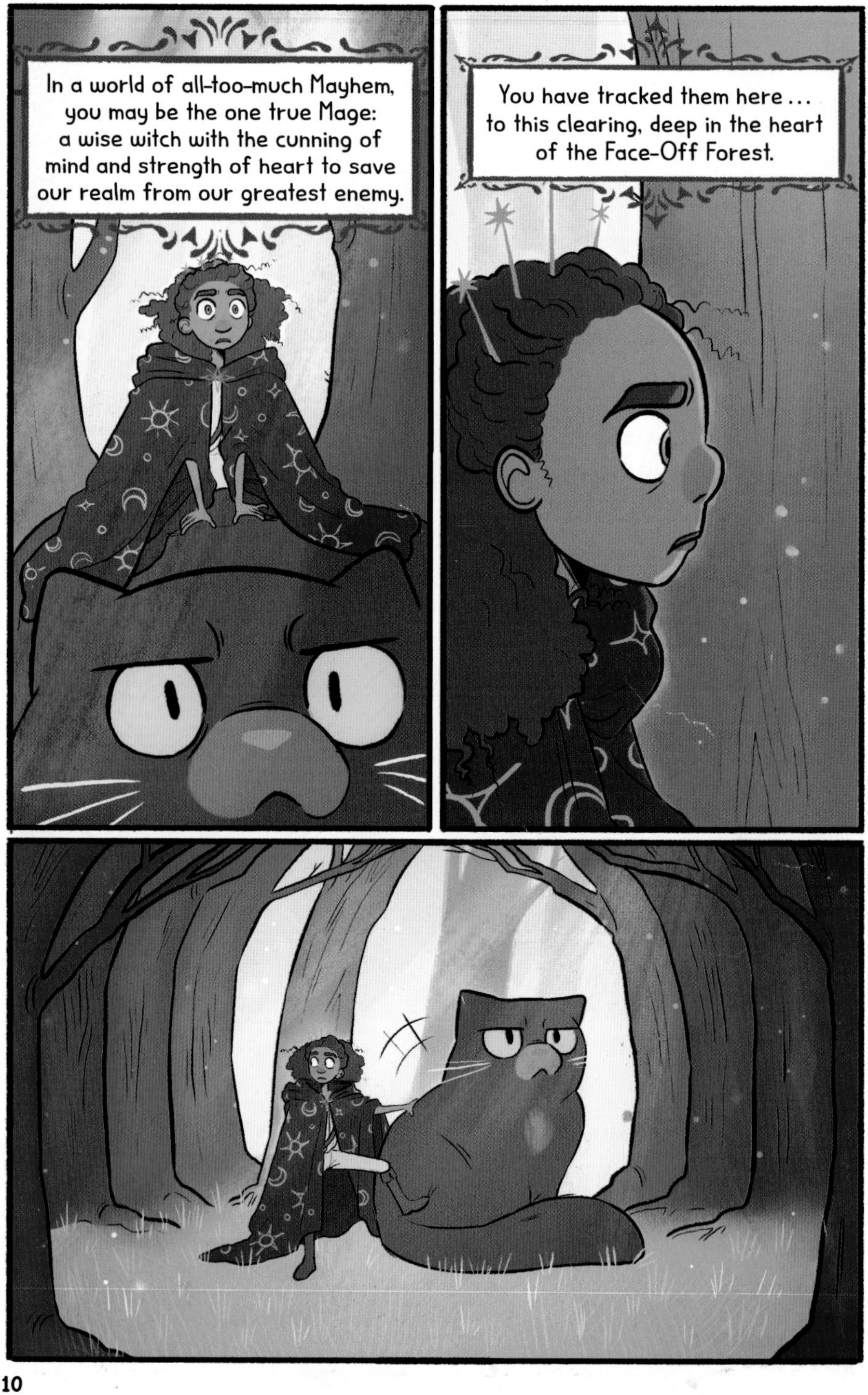
In a world of all-too-much Mayhem, you may be the one true Mage: a wise witch with the cunning of mind and strength of heart to save our realm from our greatest enemy.
You have tracked them here ... to this clearing, deep in the heart of the Face-Off Forest.

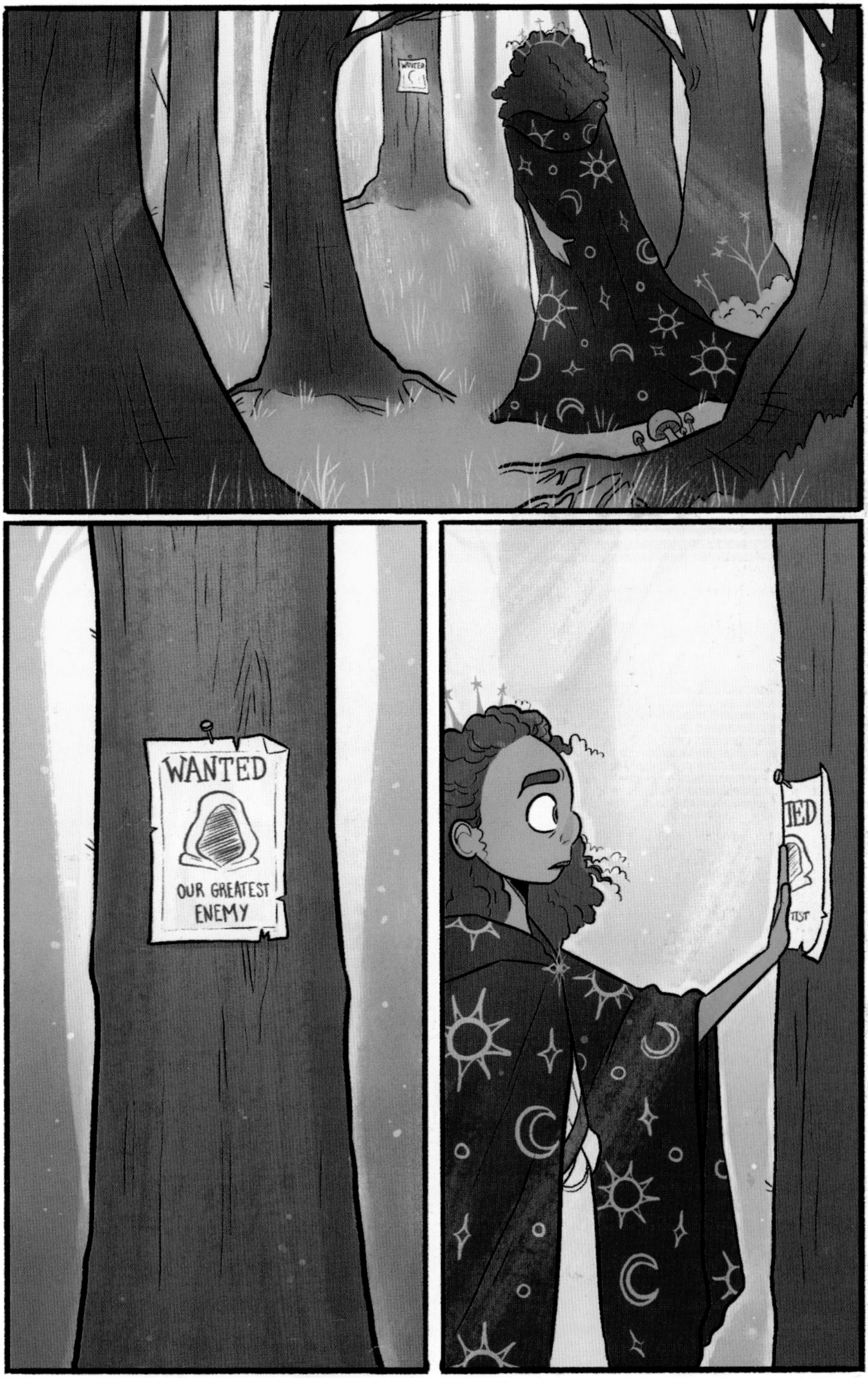
WANTED
WANTED
OUR GREATEST ENEMY

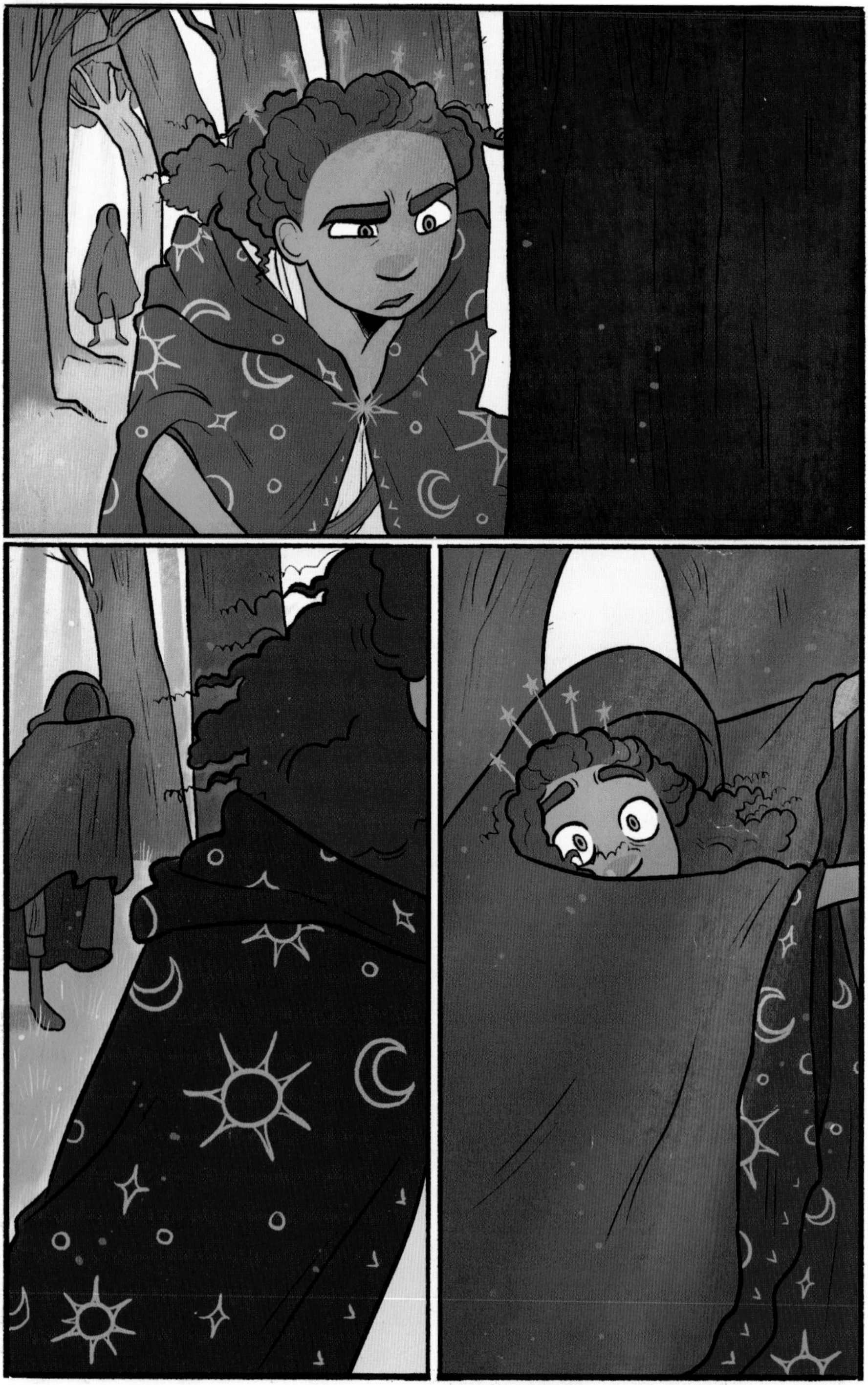

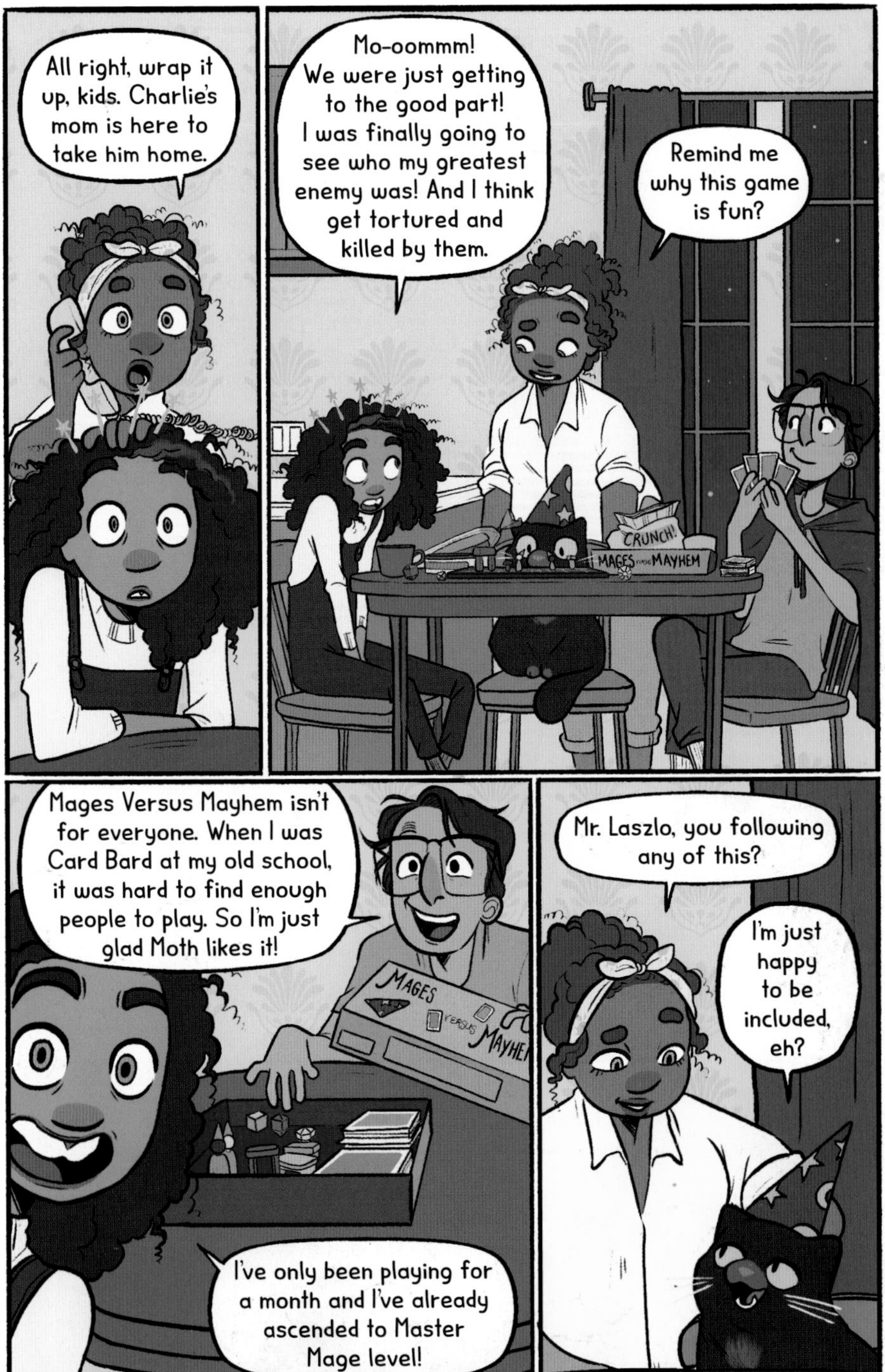
All right, wrap it up, kids. Charlie's mom is here to take him home.
Mo-oommm! We were just getting to the good part! I was finally going to see who my greatest enemy was! And I think get tortured and killed by them.
Remind me why this game is fun?
CRUNCH!
MAGES VERSUS MAYHEM
Mages Versus Mayhem isn't for everyone. When I was Card Bard at my old school, it was hard to find enough people to play. So I'm just glad Moth likes it!
MAGES VERSUS MAYHEM
I've only been playing for a month and I've already ascended to Master Mage level!
Mr. Laszlo, you following any of this?
I'm just happy to be included, eh?

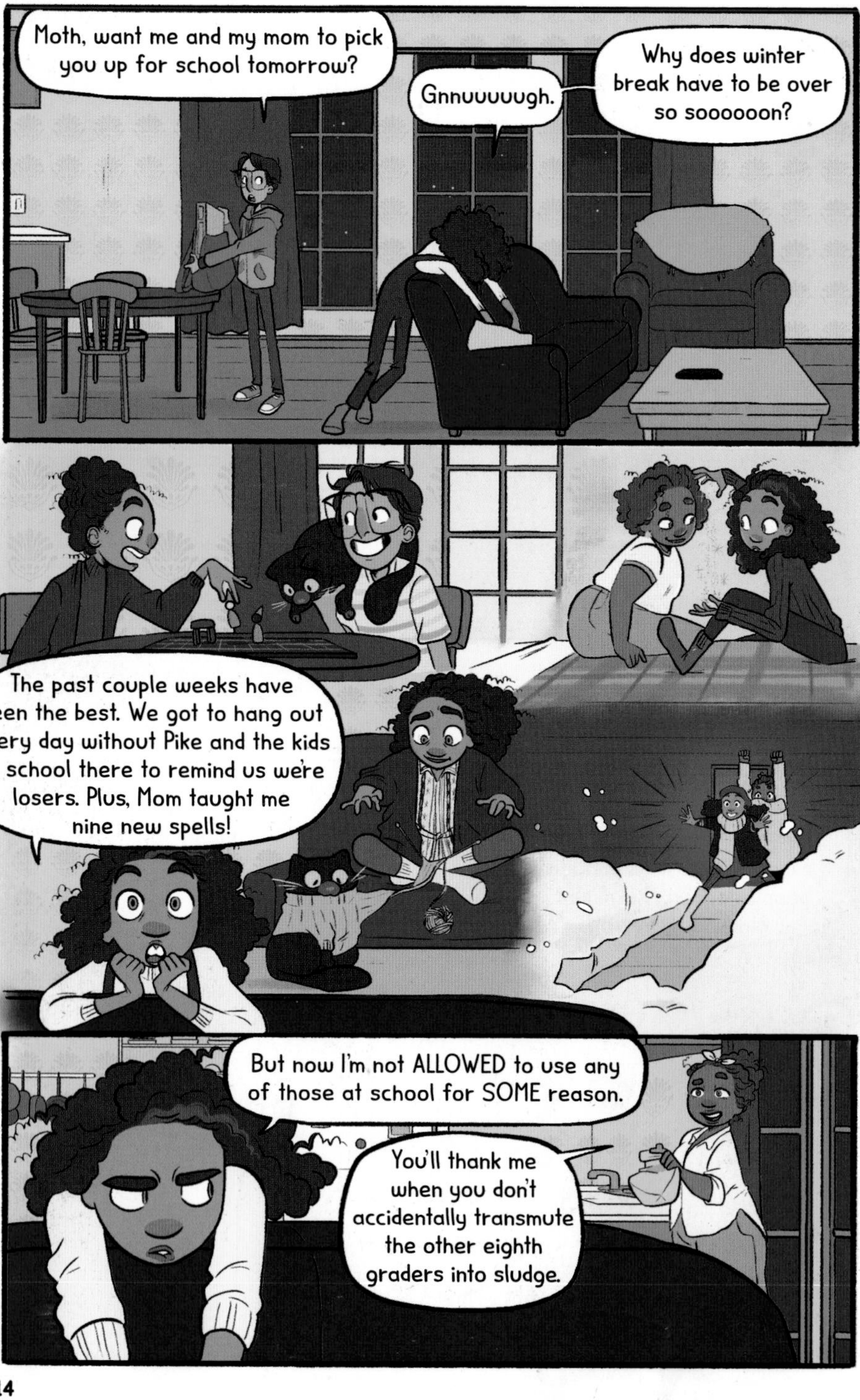
Moth, want me and my mom to pick you up for school tomorrow?
Gnnuuuuugh.
Why does winter break have to be over so soooooon?
The past couple weeks have been the best. We got to hang out every day without Pike and the kids at school there to remind us we're losers. Plus, Mom taught me nine new spells!
But now I'm not ALLOWED to use any of those at school for SOME reason.
You'll thank me when you don't accidentally transmute the other eighth graders into sludge.

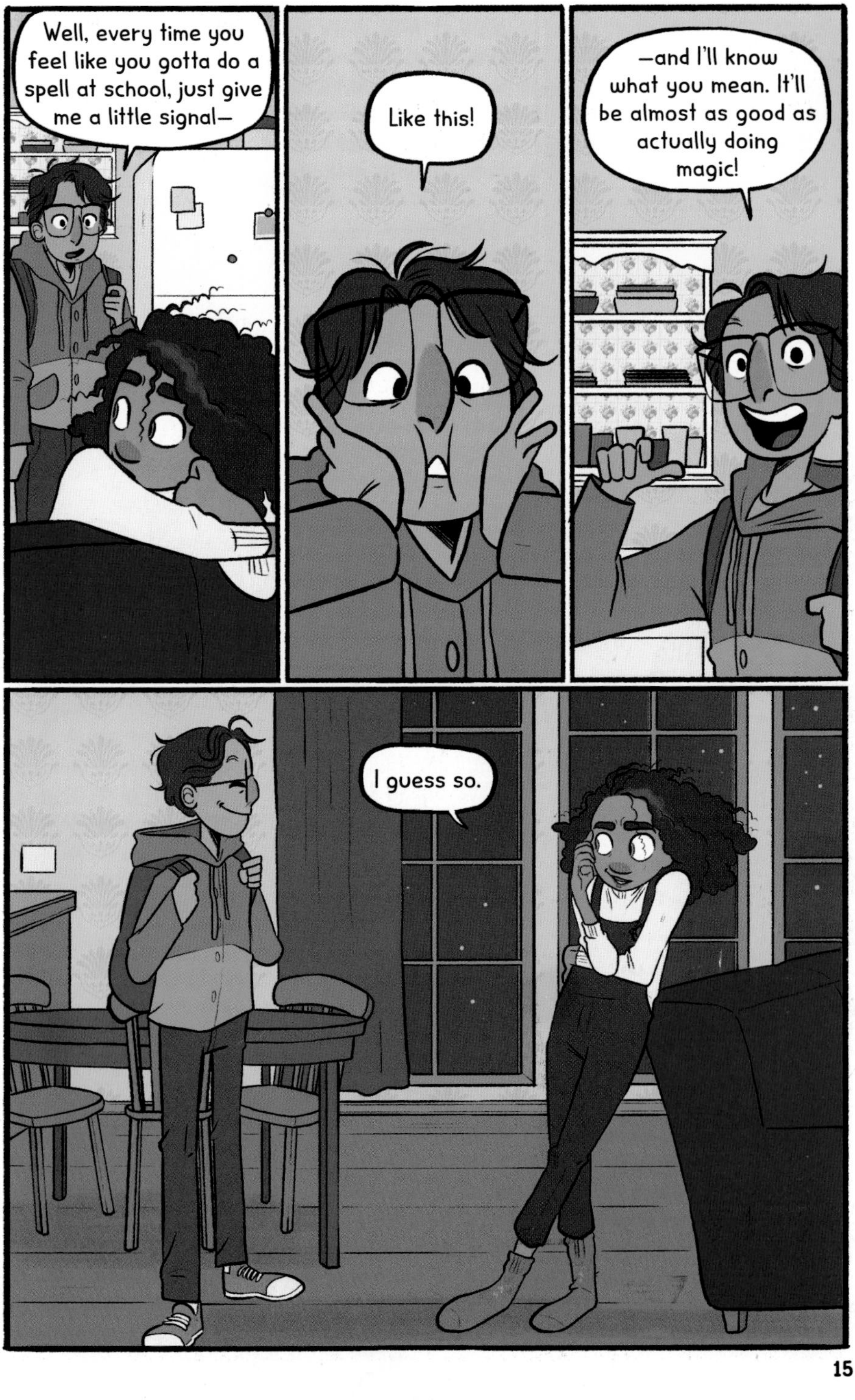
Well, every time you feel like you gotta do a spell at school, just give me a little signal—
Like this!
—and I'll know what you mean. It'll be almost as good as actually doing magic!
I guess so.

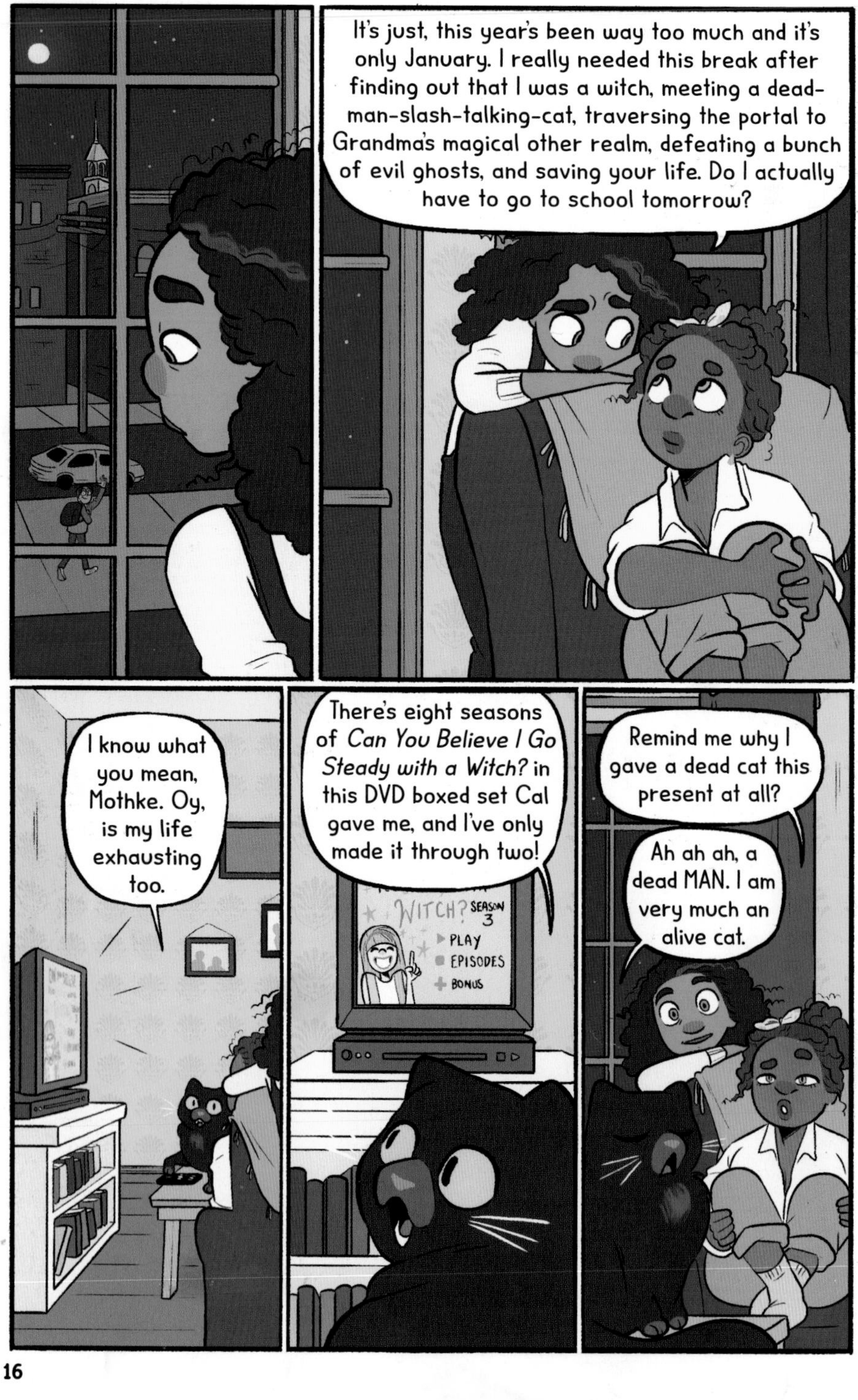

It's just, this year's been way too much and it's only January. I really needed this break after finding out that I was a witch, meeting a dead-man-slash-talking-cat, traversing the portal to Grandma's magical other realm, defeating a bunch of evil ghosts, and saving your life. Do I actually have to go to school tomorrow?
I know what you mean, Mothke. Oy, is my life exhausting too.
There's eight seasons of *Can You Believe I Go Steady with a Witch?* in this DVD boxed set Cal gave me, and I've only made it through two!
WITCH? SEASON 3
PLAY
EPISODES
BONUS
Remind me why I gave a dead cat this present at all?
Ah ah ah, a dead MAN. I am very much an alive cat.

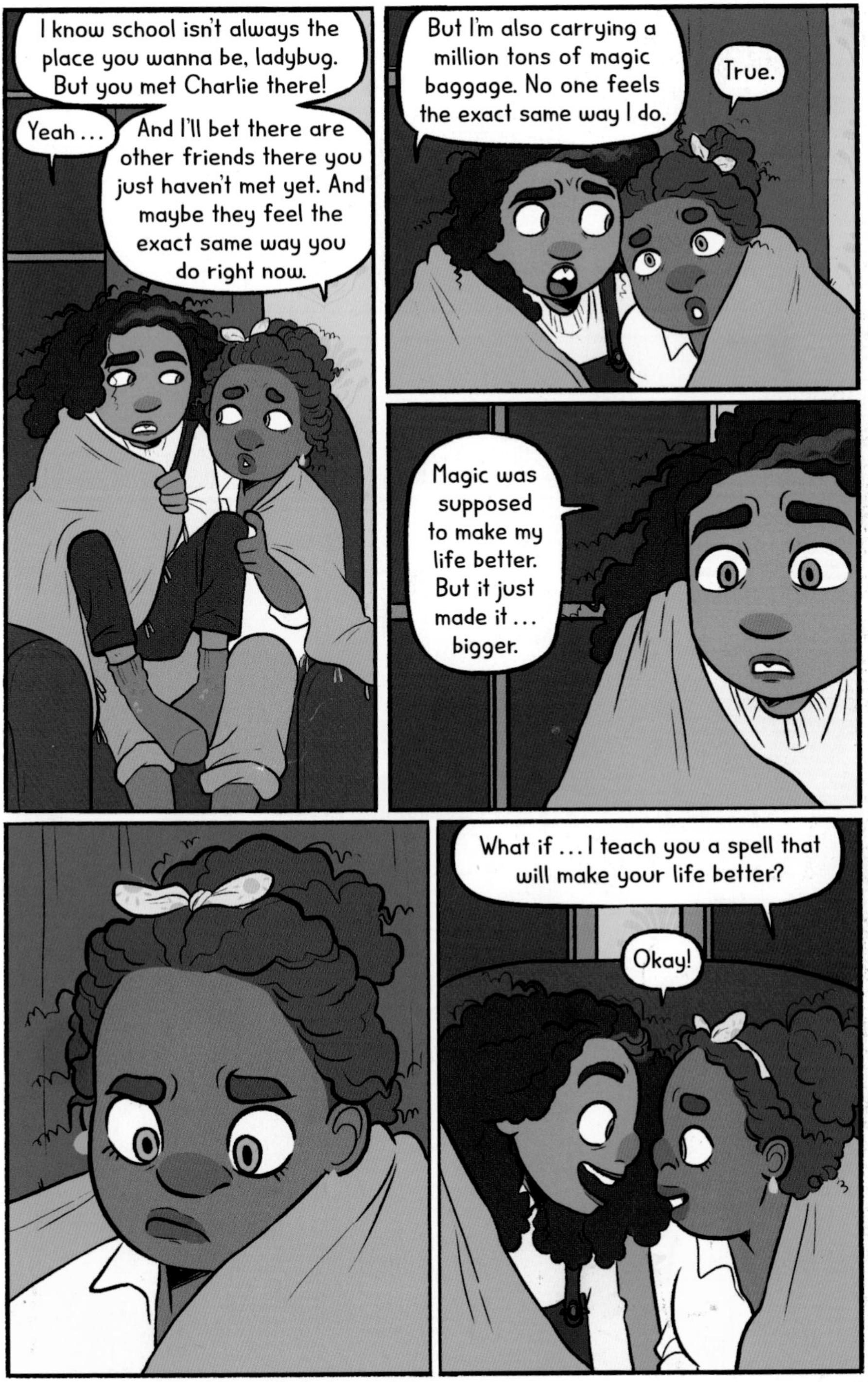

I know school isn't always the place you wanna be, ladybug. But you met Charlie there!
Yeah ...
And I'll bet there are other friends there you just haven't met yet. And maybe they feel the exact same way you do right now.
But I'm also carrying a million tons of magic baggage. No one feels the exact same way I do.
True.
Magic was supposed to make my life better. But it just made it ... bigger.
What if ... I teach you a spell that will make your life better?
Okay!

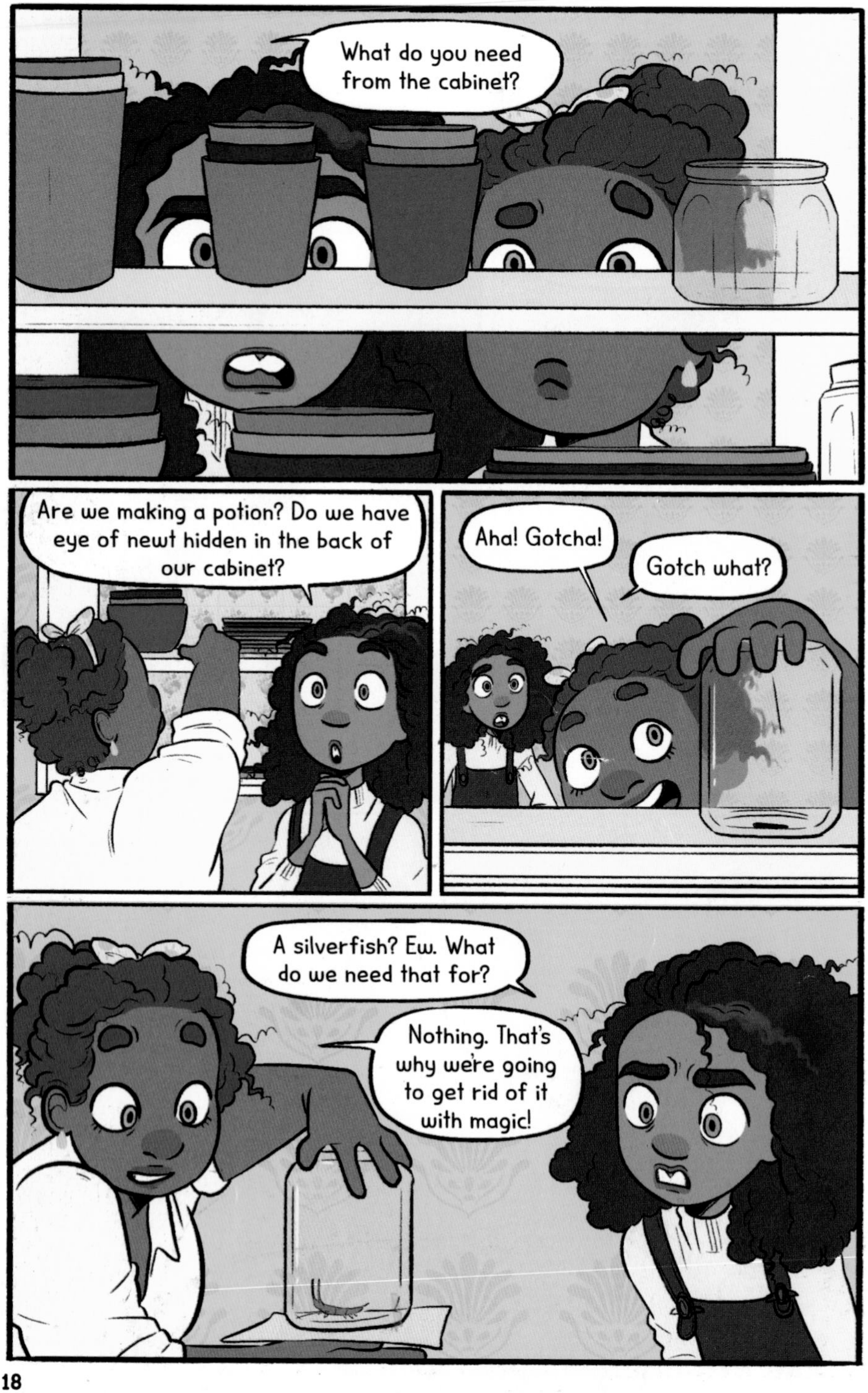
What do you need from the cabinet?
Are we making a potion? Do we have eye of newt hidden in the back of our cabinet?
Aha! Gotcha!
Gotch what?
A silverfish? Ew. What do we need that for?
Nothing. That's why we're going to get rid of it with magic!

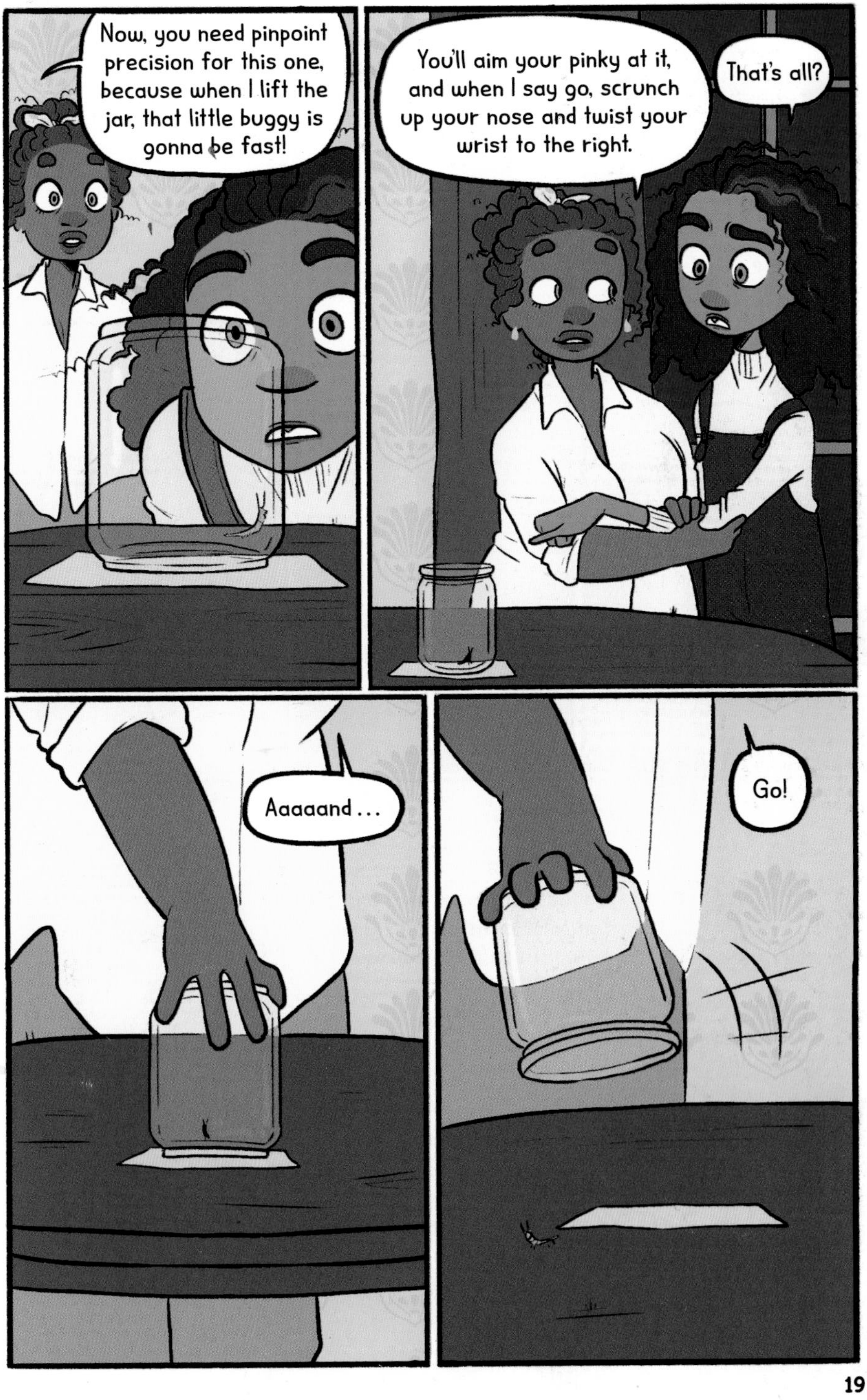

Now, you need pinpoint precision for this one, because when I lift the jar, that little buggy is gonna be fast!
You'll aim your pinky at it, and when I say go, scrunch up your nose and twist your wrist to the right.
That's all?
Aaaaand . . .
Go!

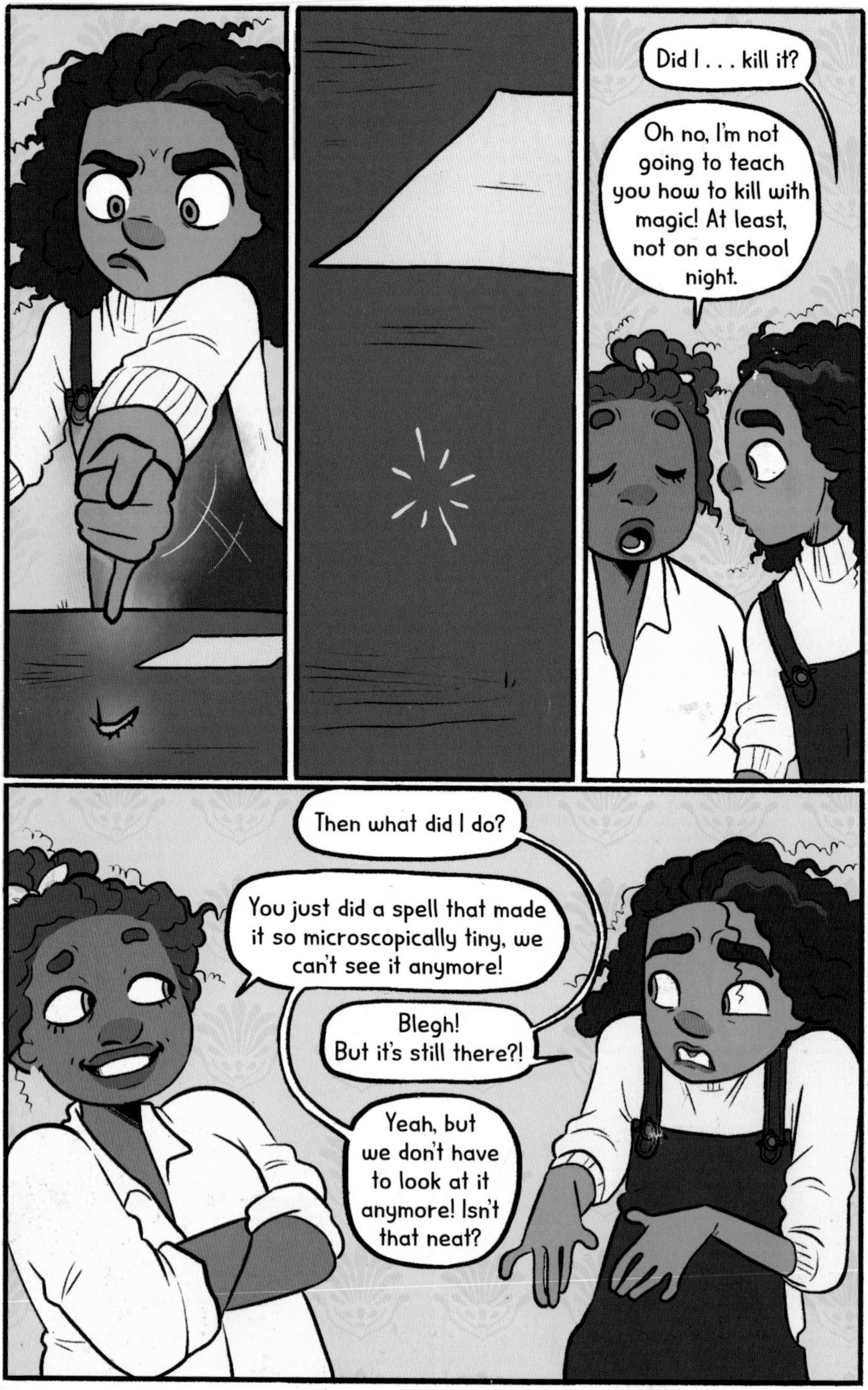
Did I . . . kill it?
Oh no, I'm not going to teach you how to kill with magic! At least, not on a school night.
Then what did I do?
You just did a spell that made it so microscopically tiny, we can't see it anymore!
Blegh! But it's still there?!
Yeah, but we don't have to look at it anymore! Isn't that neat?

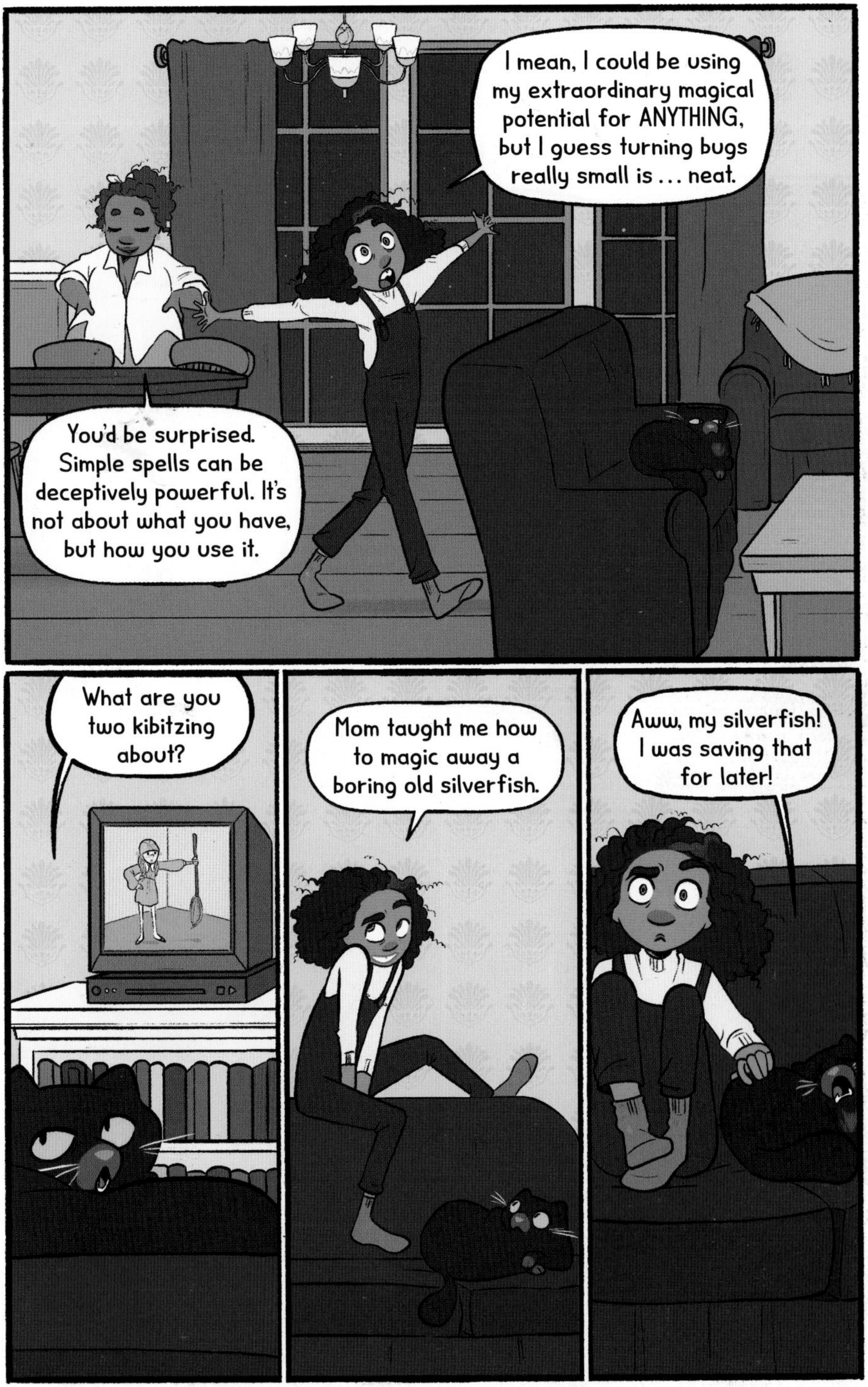
I mean, I could be using my extraordinary magical potential for ANYTHING, but I guess turning bugs really small is . . . neat.
You'd be surprised. Simple spells can be deceptively powerful. It's not about what you have, but how you use it.
What are you two kibitzing about?
Mom taught me how to magic away a boring old silverfish.
Aww, my silverfish! I was saving that for later!

CHAPTER 2

Moth, the Meme

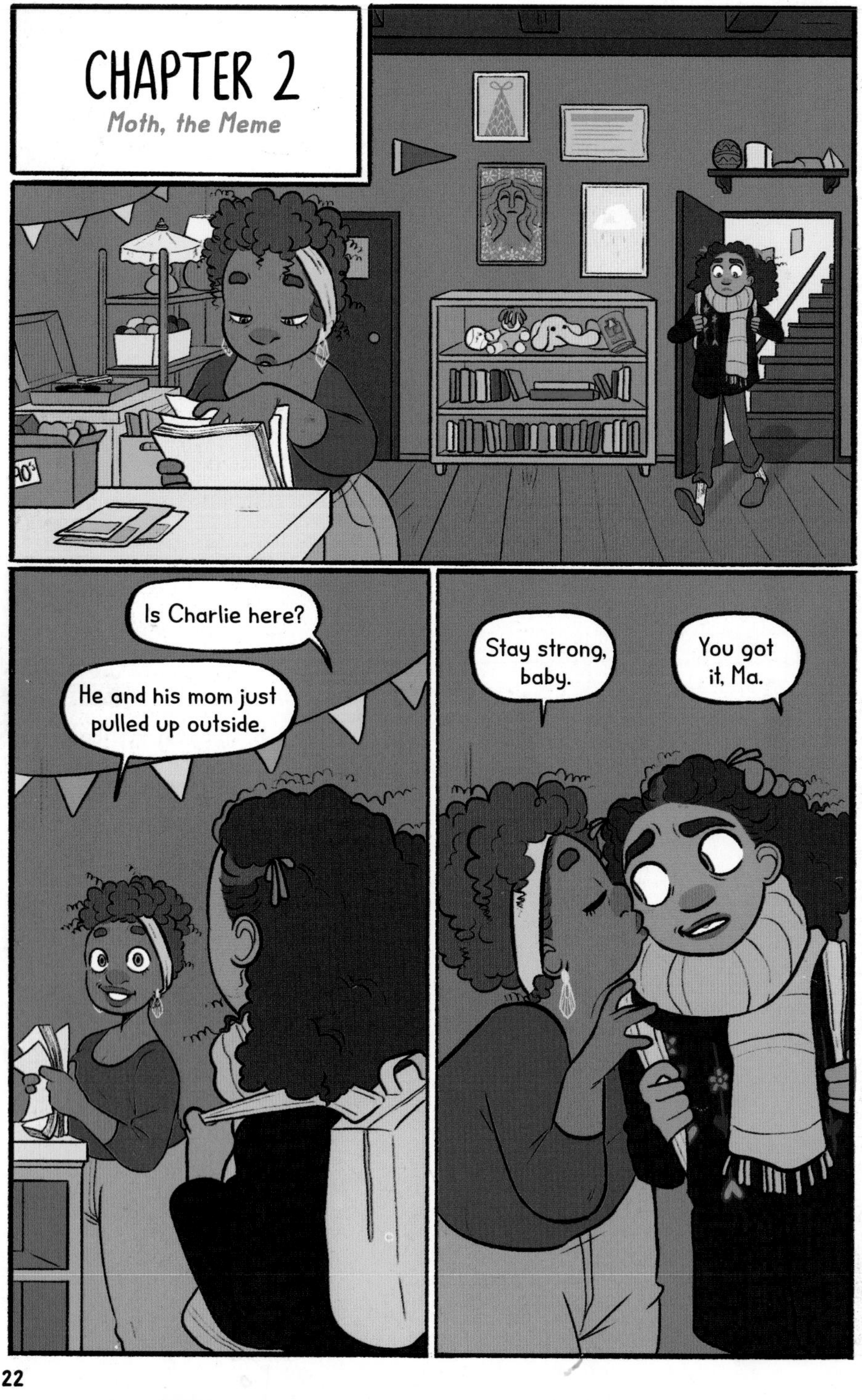

90's
Is Charlie here?
He and his mom just pulled up outside.
Stay strong, baby.
You got it, Ma.

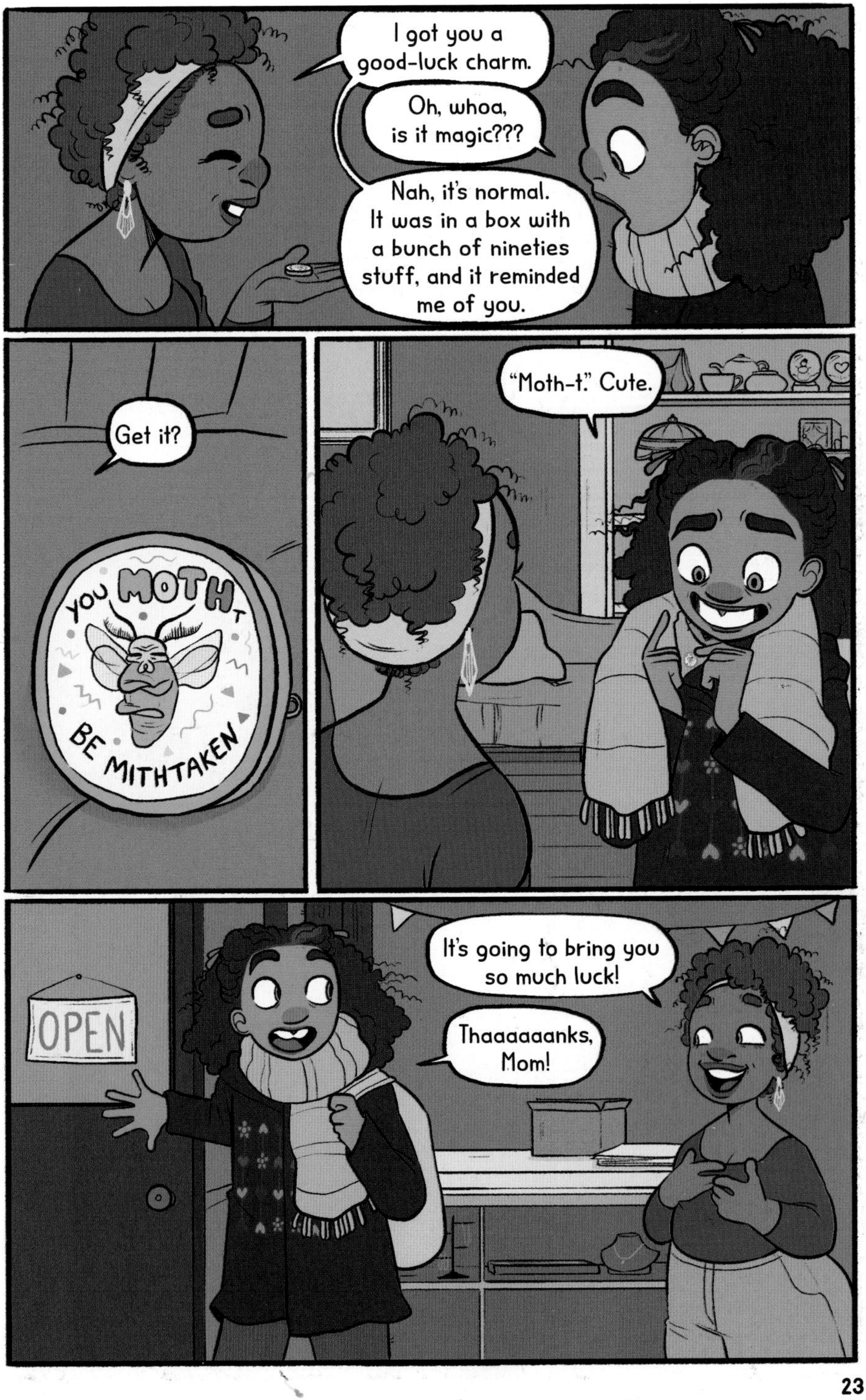
I got you a good-luck charm.
Oh, whoa, is it magic???
Nah, it's normal. It was in a box with a bunch of nineties stuff, and it reminded me of you.
Get it?
YOU MOTHT BE MITHTAKEN
"Moth-t." Cute.
OPEN
It's going to bring you so much luck!
Thaaaaaanks, Mom!

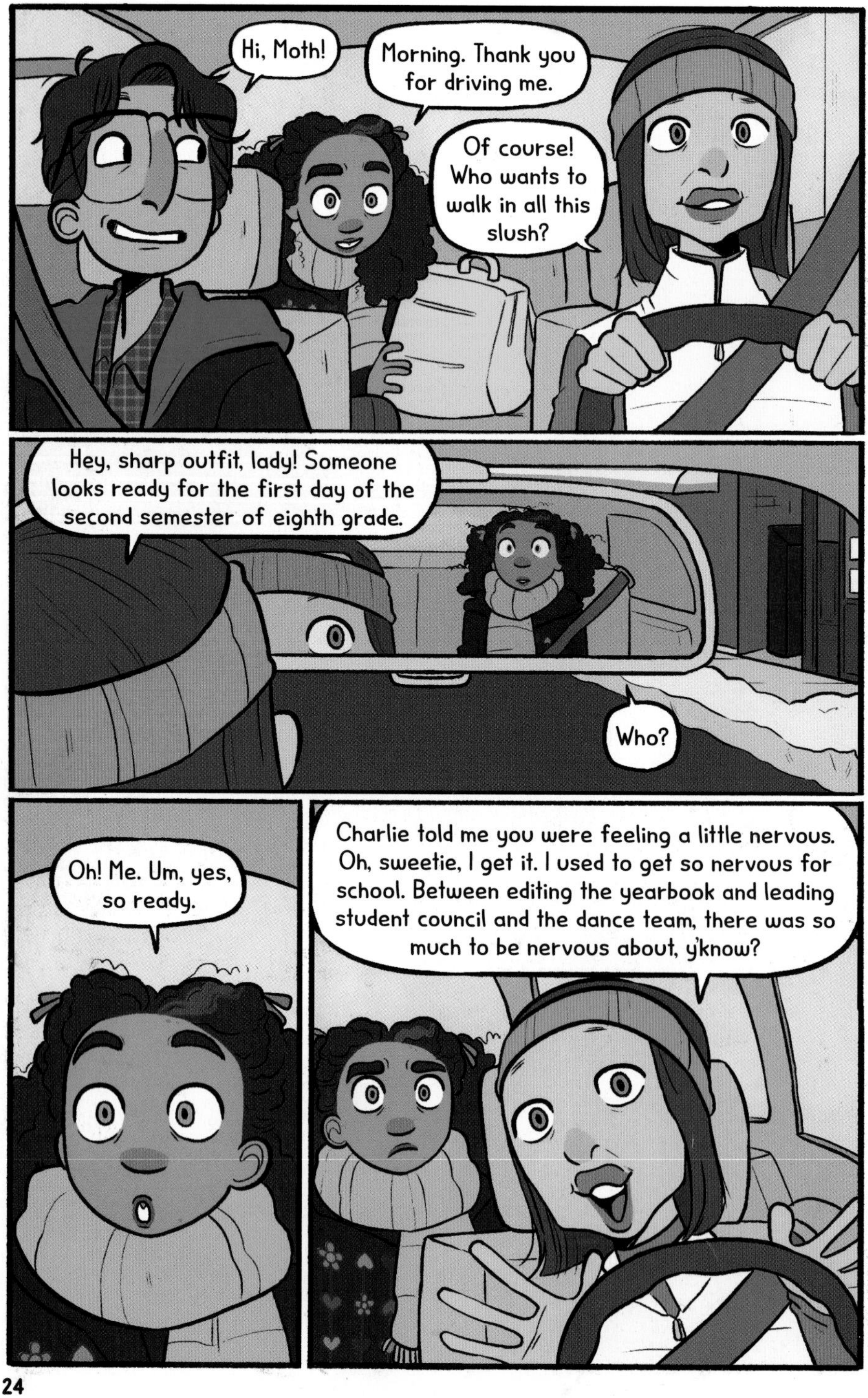
Hi, Moth!
Morning. Thank you for driving me.
Of course! Who wants to walk in all this slush?
Hey, sharp outfit, lady! Someone looks ready for the first day of the second semester of eighth grade.
Who?
Oh! Me. Um, yes, so ready.
Charlie told me you were feeling a little nervous. Oh, sweetie, I get it. I used to get so nervous for school. Between editing the yearbook and leading student council and the dance team, there was so much to be nervous about, y'know?

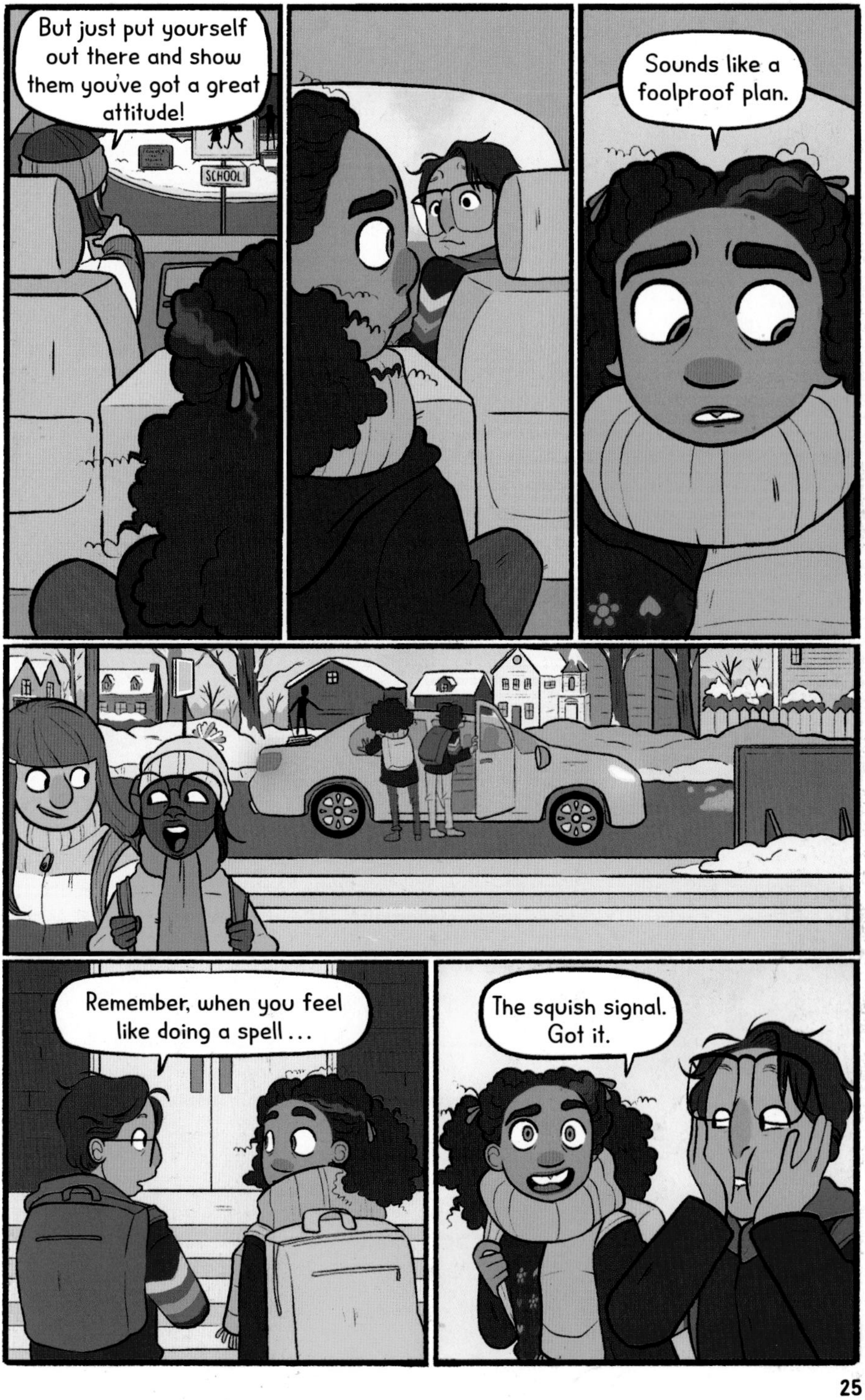
But just put yourself out there and show them you've got a great attitude!
SCHOOL
Sounds like a foolproof plan.
Remember, when you feel like doing a spell . . .
The squish signal. Got it.

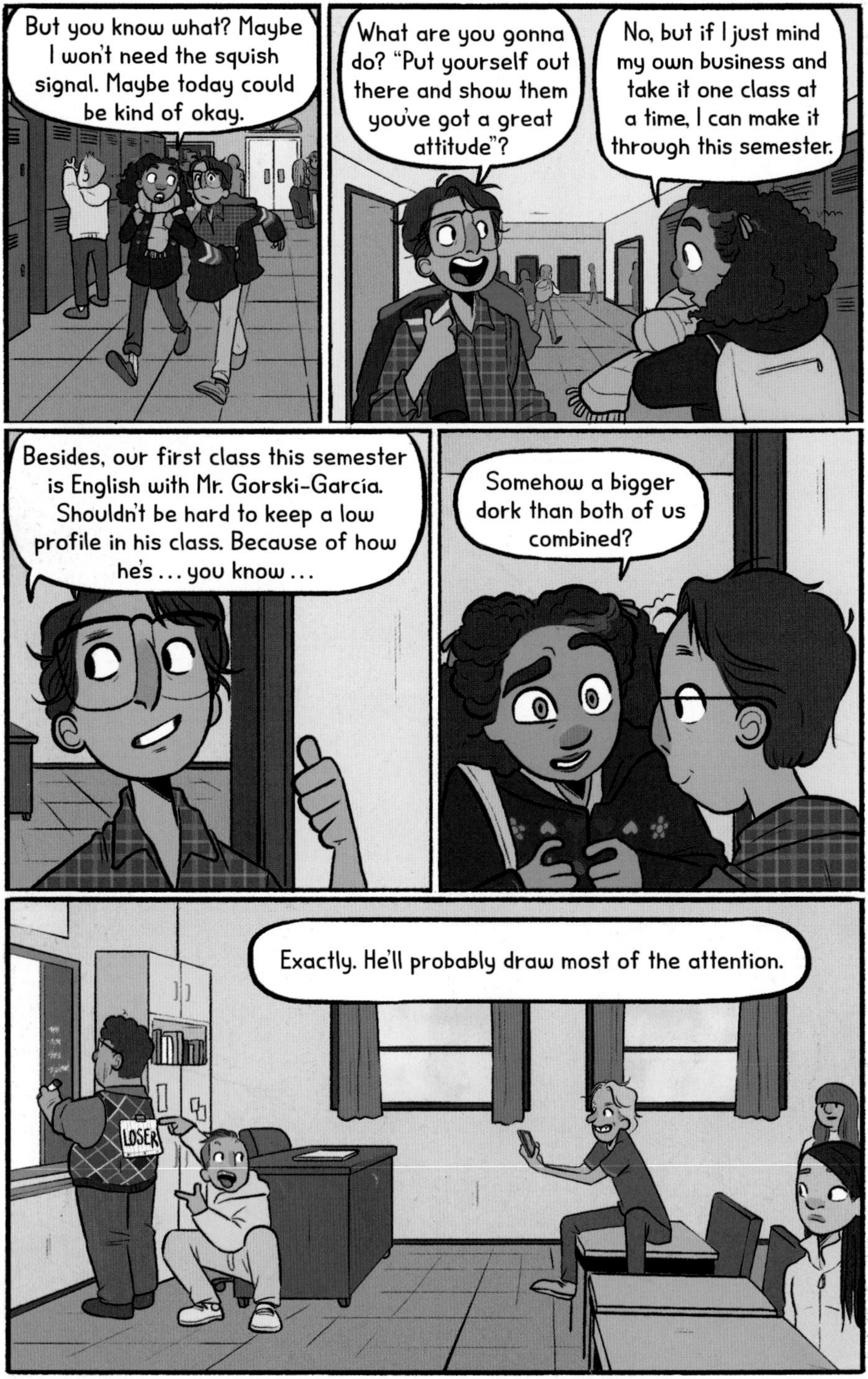
But you know what? Maybe I won't need the squish signal. Maybe today could be kind of okay.
What are you gonna do? "Put yourself out there and show them you've got a great attitude"?
No, but if I just mind my own business and take it one class at a time, I can make it through this semester.
Besides, our first class this semester is English with Mr. Gorski-García. Shouldn't be hard to keep a low profile in his class. Because of how he's . . . you know . . .
Somehow a bigger dork than both of us combined?
Exactly. He'll probably draw most of the attention.
LOSER

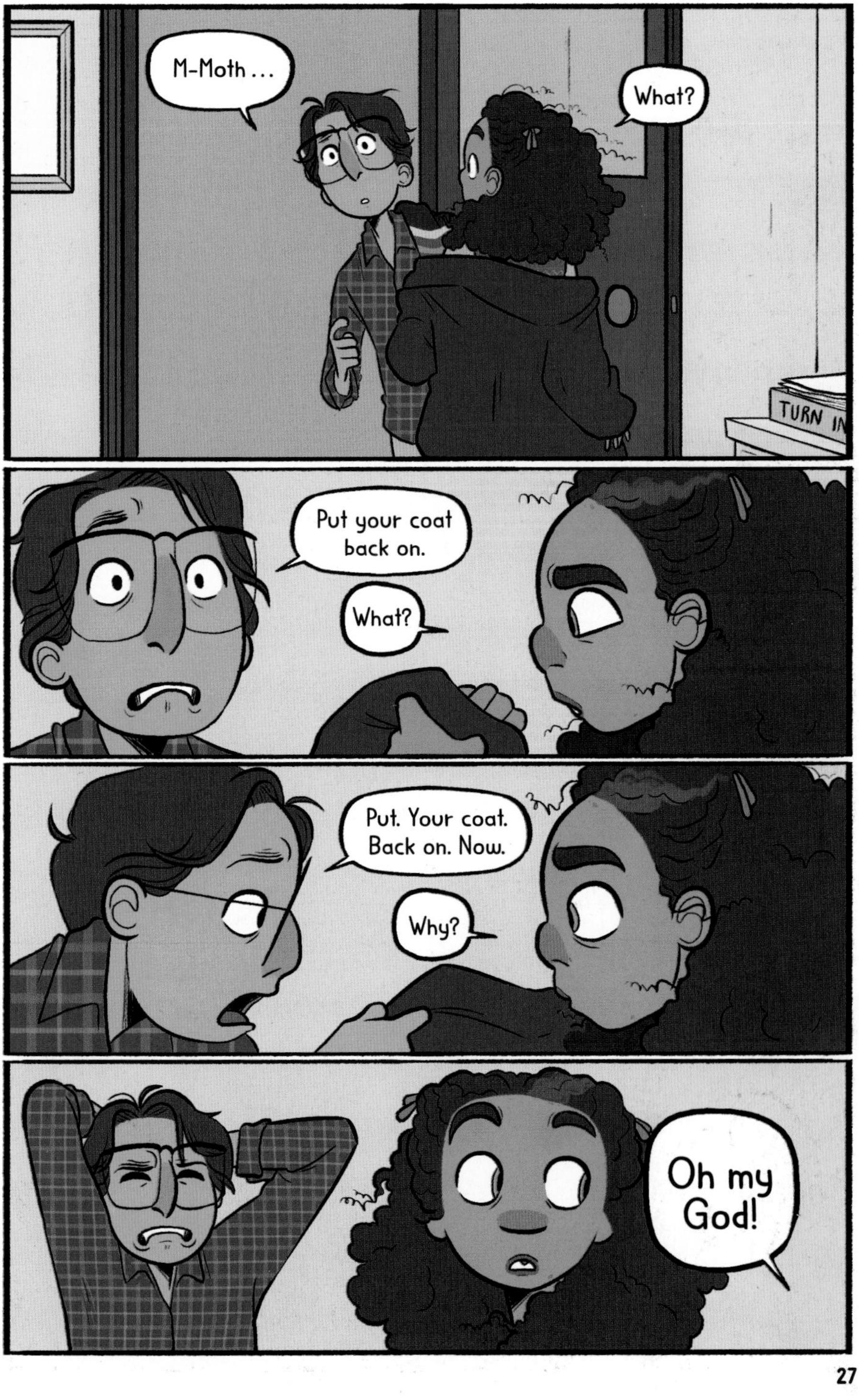
M-Moth . . .
What?
TURN IN
Put your coat back on.
What?
Put. Your coat. Back on. Now.
Why?
Oh my God!

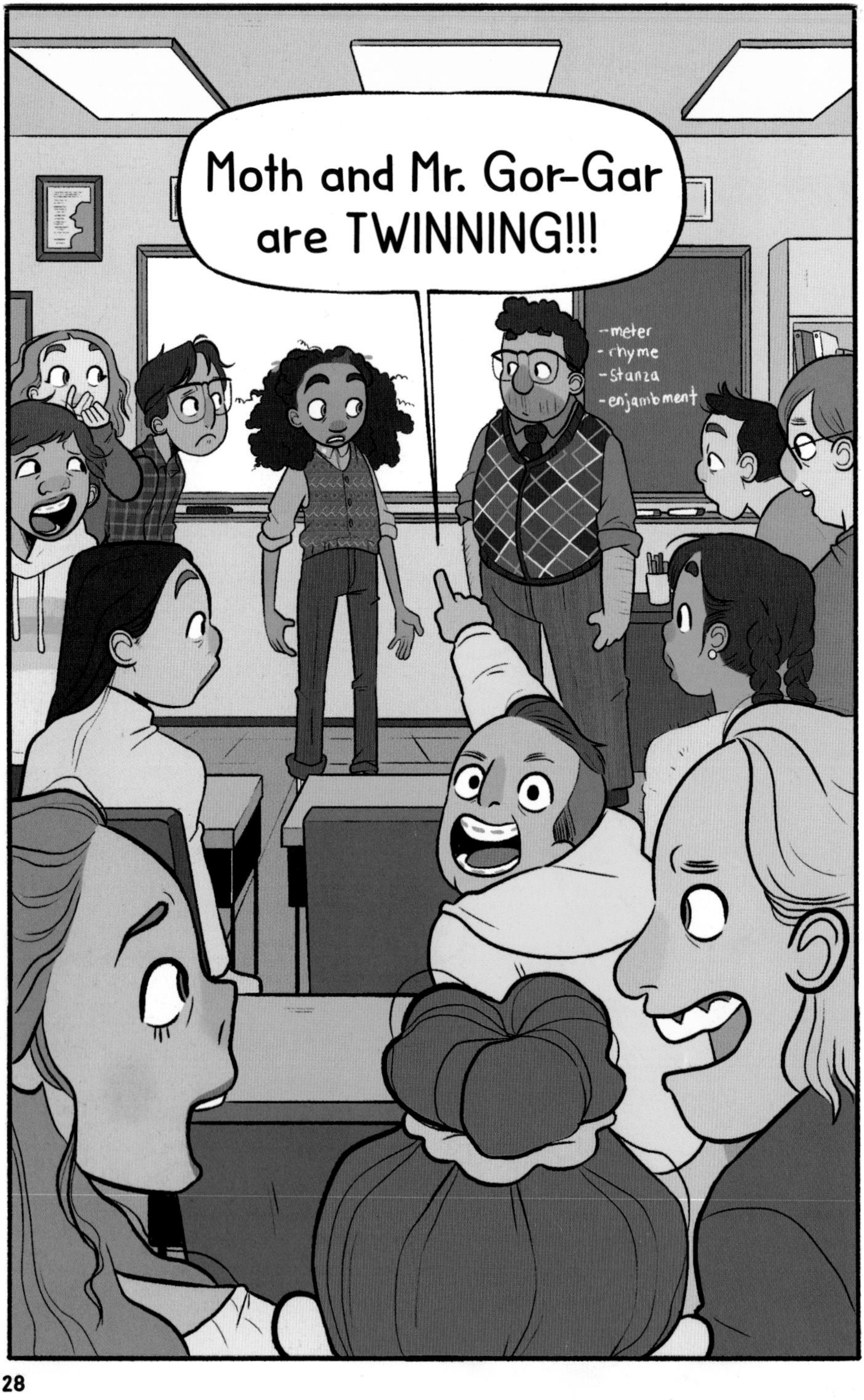
Moth and Mr. Gor-Gar are TWINNING!!!
-meter
-rhyme
-stanza
-enjambment

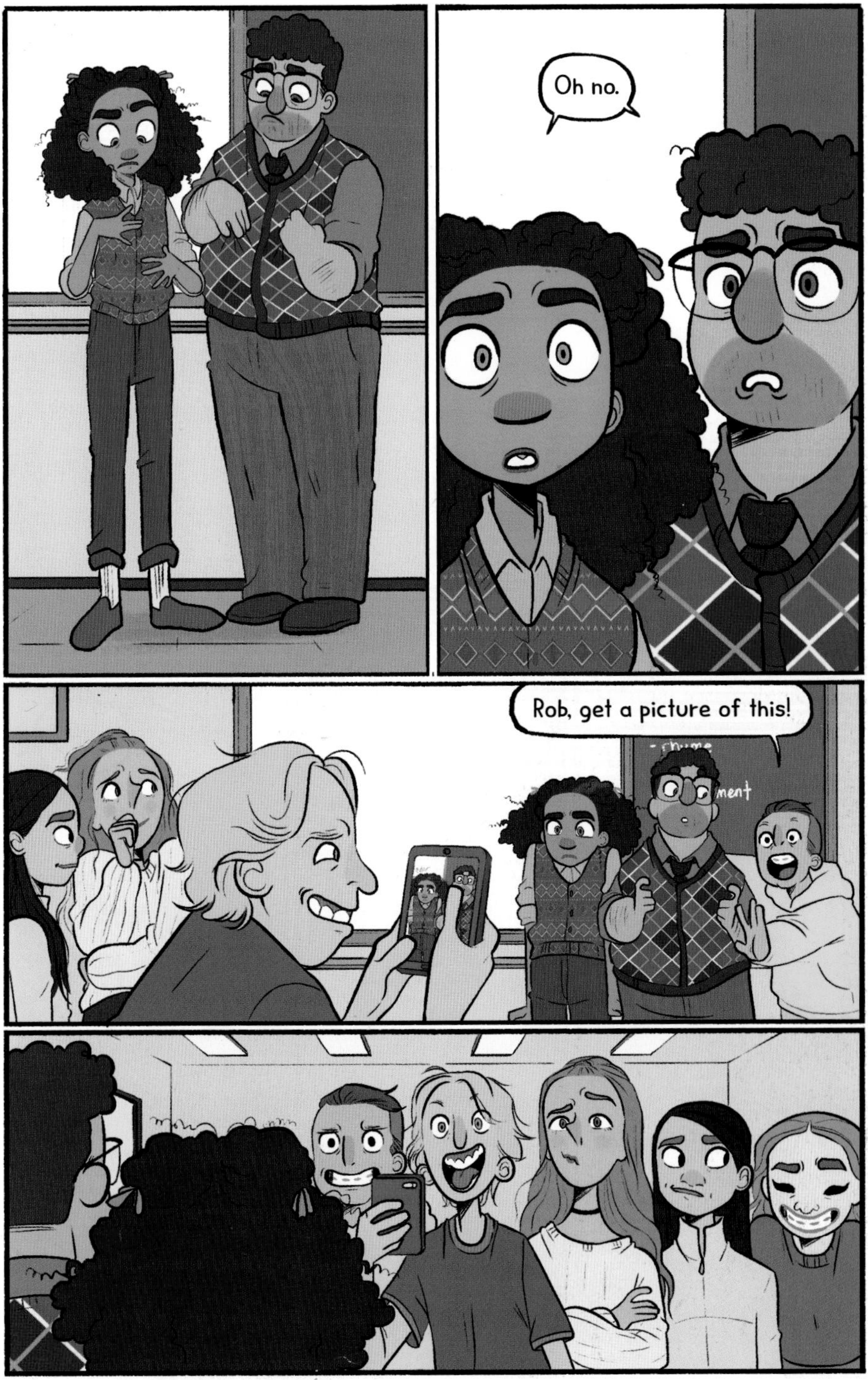
Oh no.
Rob, get a picture of this!

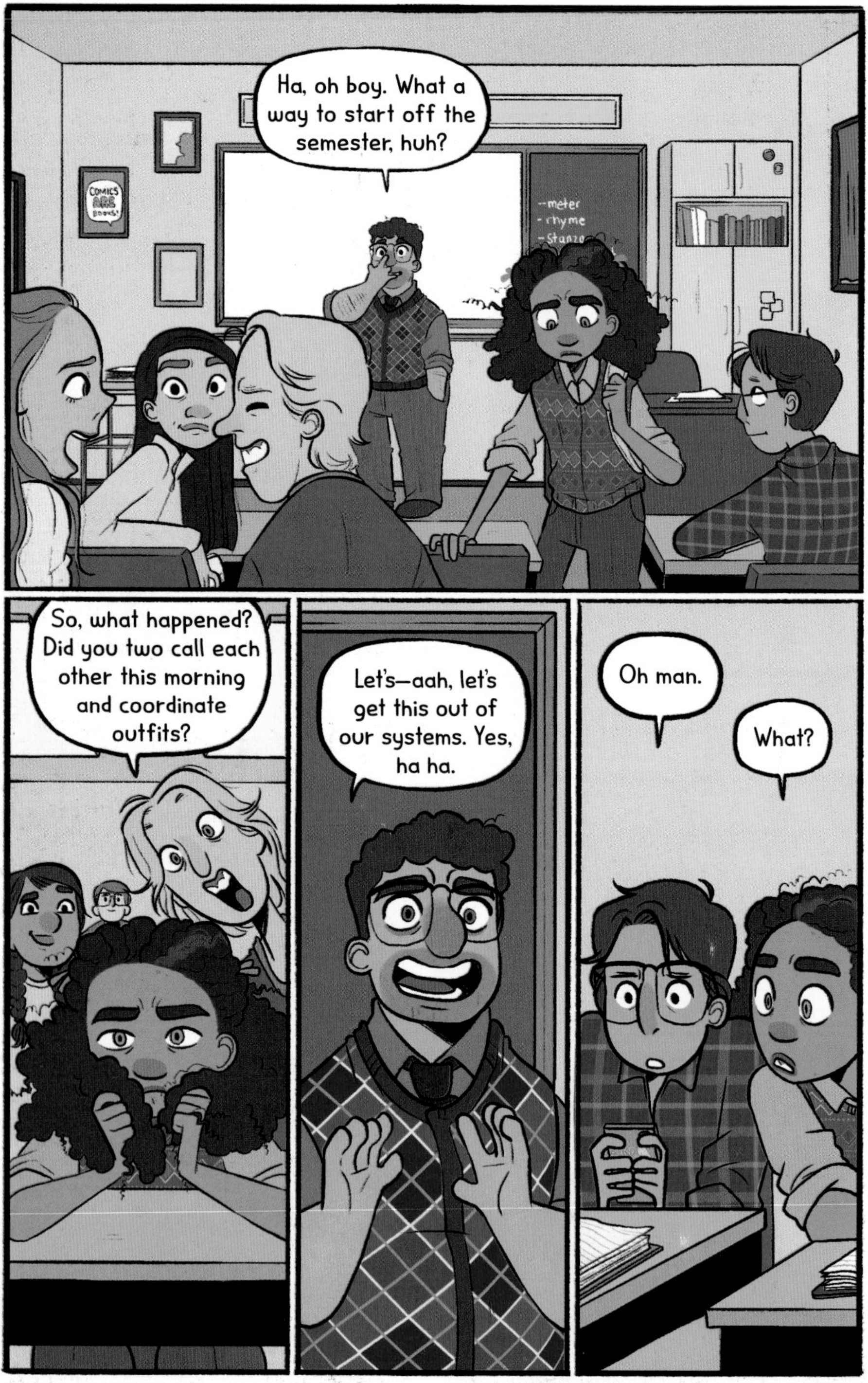
Ha, oh boy. What a way to start off the semester, huh?
COMICS ARE BOOKS!
-meter
-rhyme
So, what happened? Did you two call each other this morning and coordinate outfits?
Let's—aah, let's get this out of our systems. Yes, ha ha.
Oh man.
What?

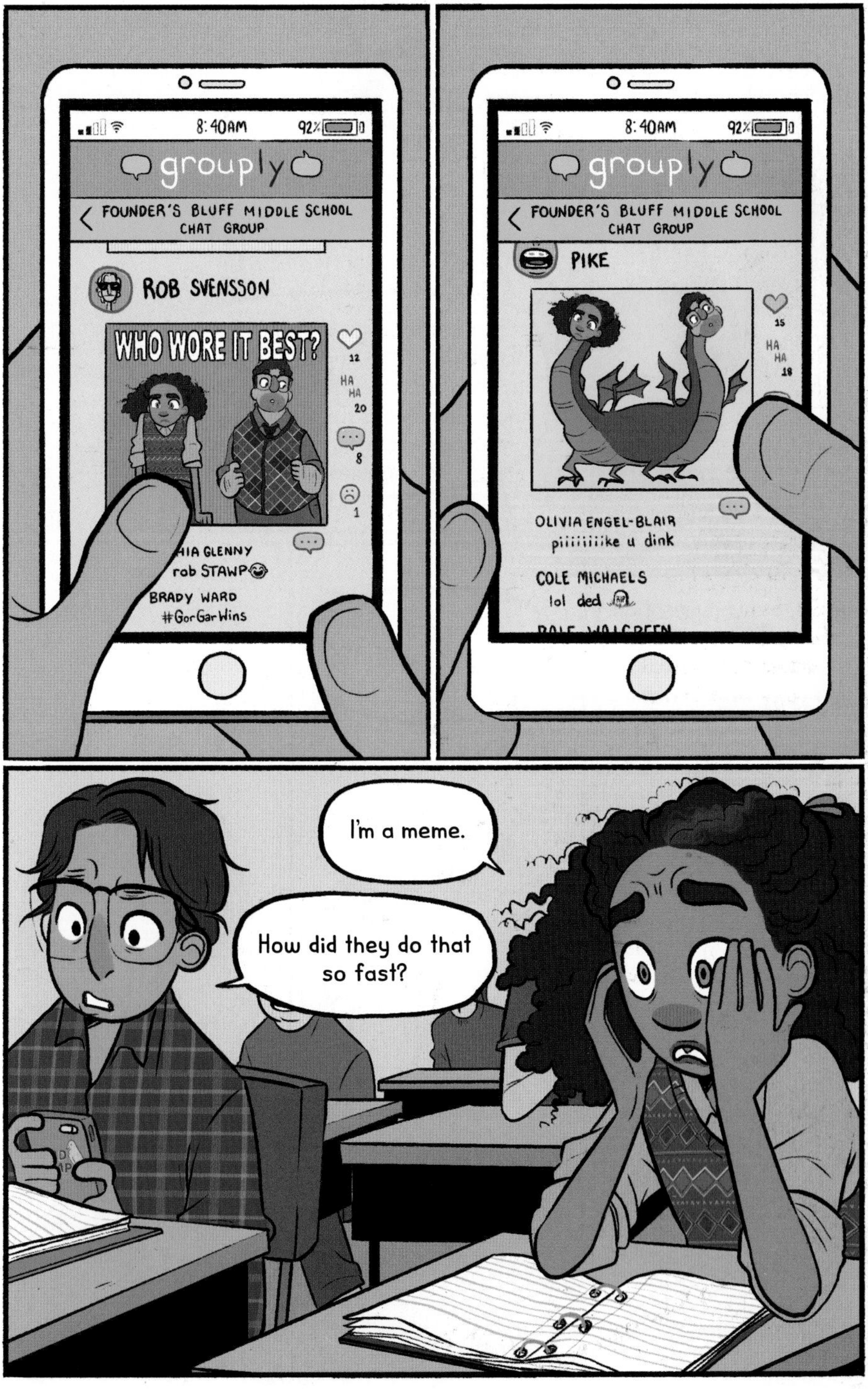

8:40AM
92%
grouply
FOUNDER'S BLUFF MIDDLE SCHOOL CHAT GROUP
ROB SVENSSON
WHO WORE IT BEST?
rob STAWP
BRADY WARD
#GorGarWins
8:40AM
92%
grouply
FOUNDER'S BLUFF MIDDLE SCHOOL CHAT GROUP
PIKE
OLIVIA ENGEL-BLAIR
piiiiiiike u dink
COLE MICHAELS
lol ded
I'm a meme.
How did they do that so fast?

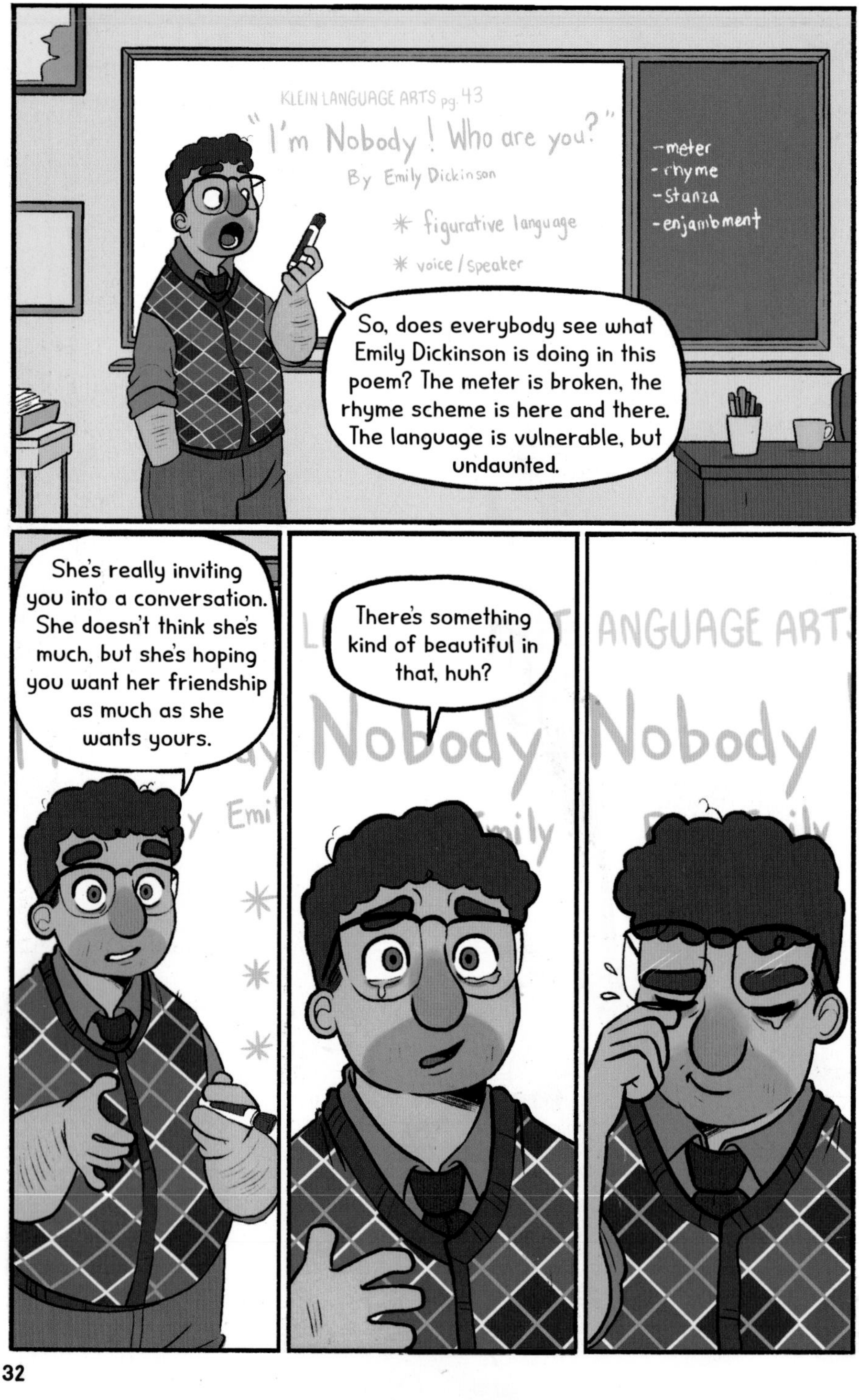
KLEIN LANGUAGE ARTS pg. 43
"I'm Nobody! Who are you?"
By Emily Dickinson
* figurative language
* voice / speaker
-meter
-rhyme
-stanza
-enjambment
So, does everybody see what Emily Dickinson is doing in this poem? The meter is broken, the rhyme scheme is here and there. The language is vulnerable, but undaunted.
She's really inviting you into a conversation. She doesn't think she's much, but she's hoping you want her friendship as much as she wants yours.
There's something kind of beautiful in that, huh?

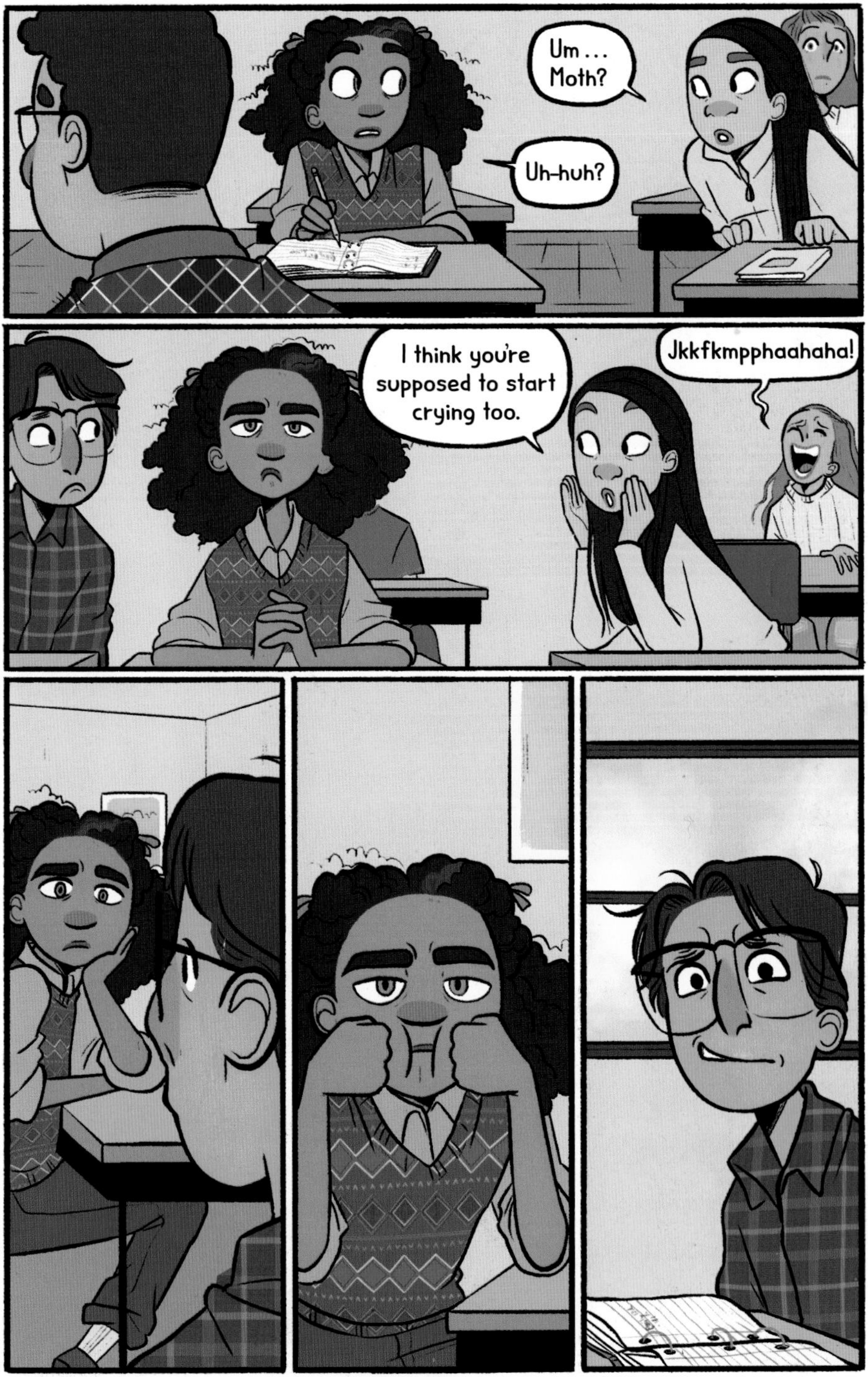
Um... Moth?
Uh-huh?
I think you're supposed to start crying too.
Jkkfkmpphaahaha!

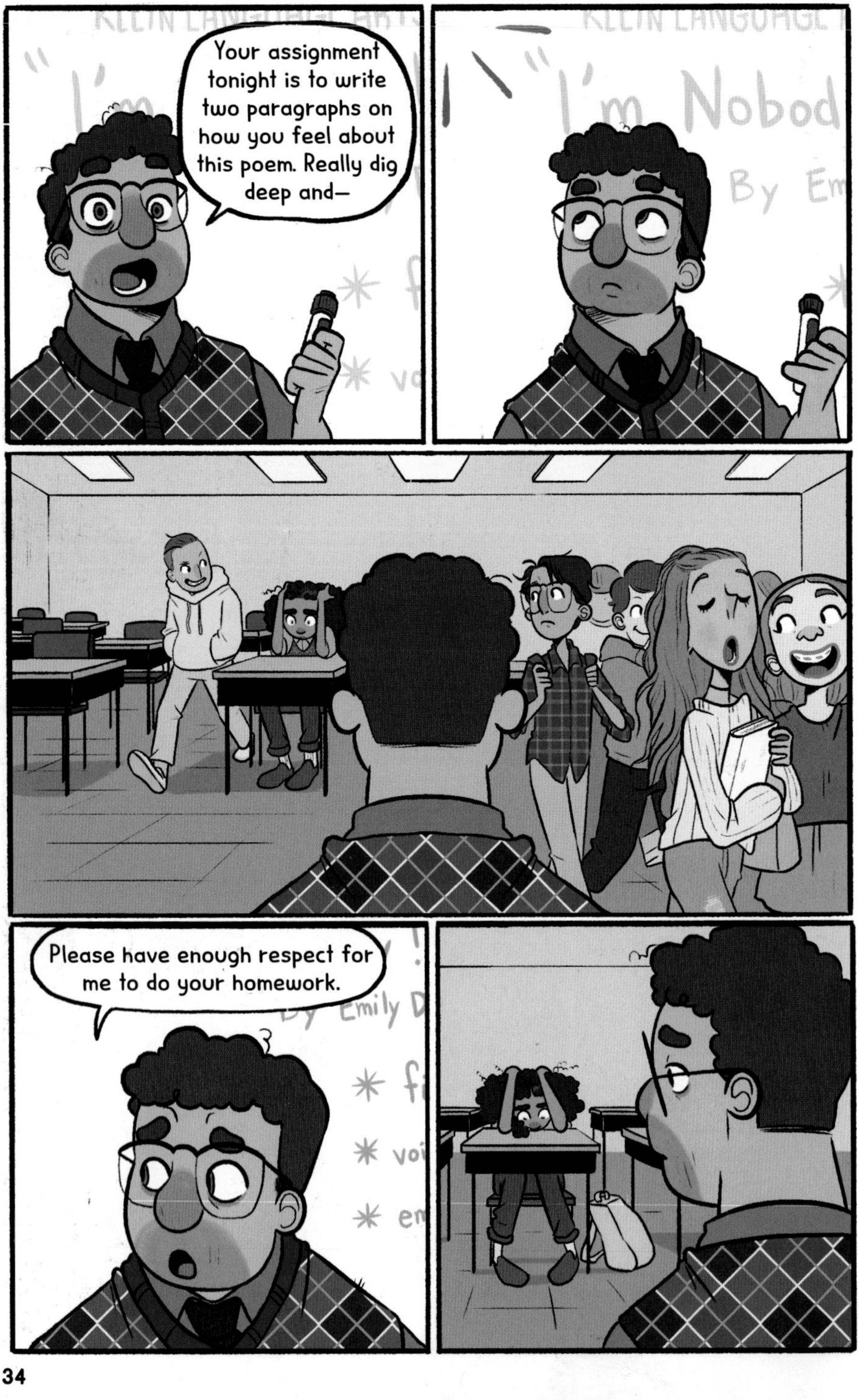
Your assignment tonight is to write two paragraphs on how you feel about this poem. Really dig deep and—
Please have enough respect for me to do your homework.

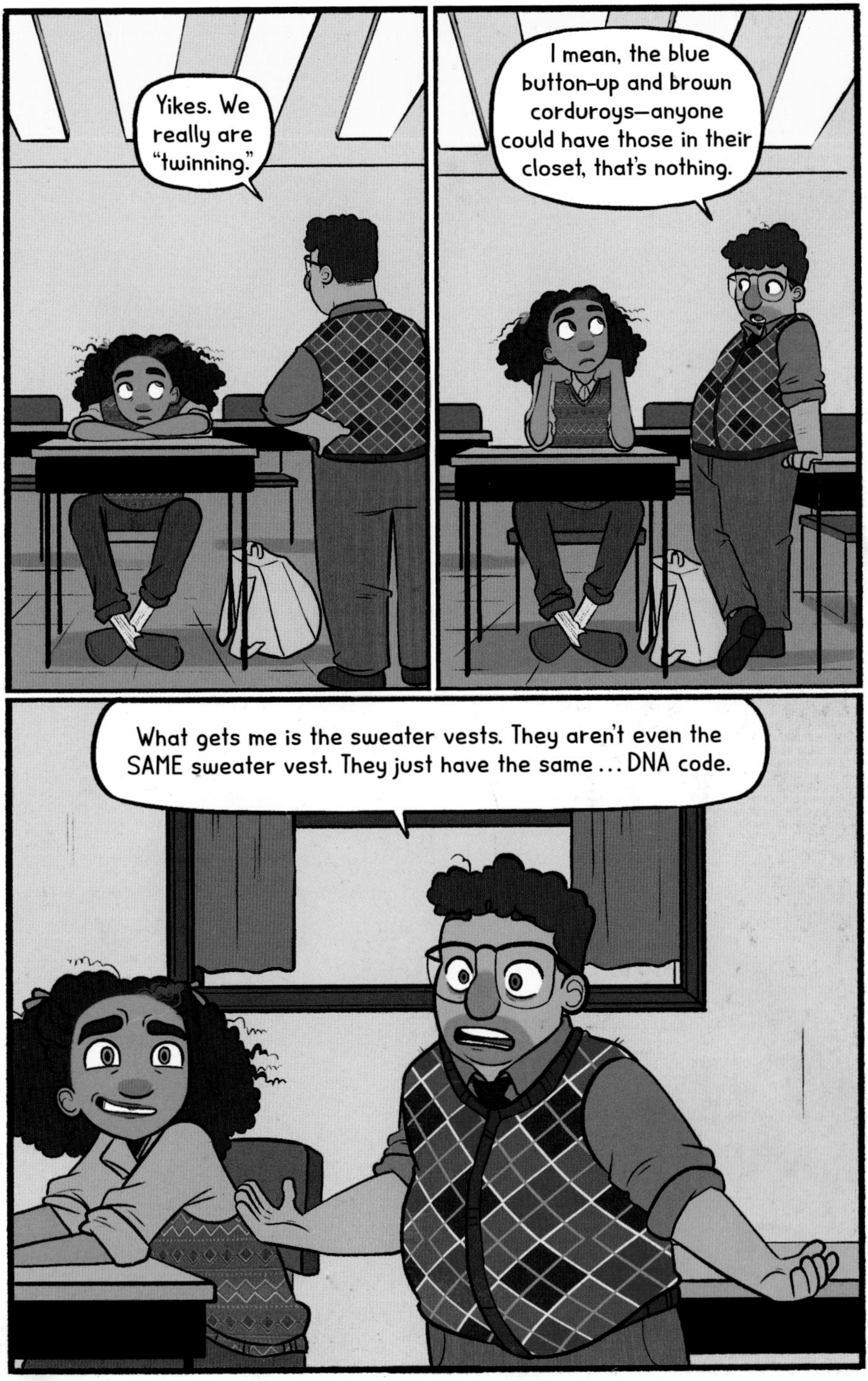
Yikes. We really are "twinning."
I mean, the blue button-up and brown corduroys—anyone could have those in their closet, that's nothing.
What gets me is the sweater vests. They aren't even the SAME sweater vest. They just have the same . . . DNA code.

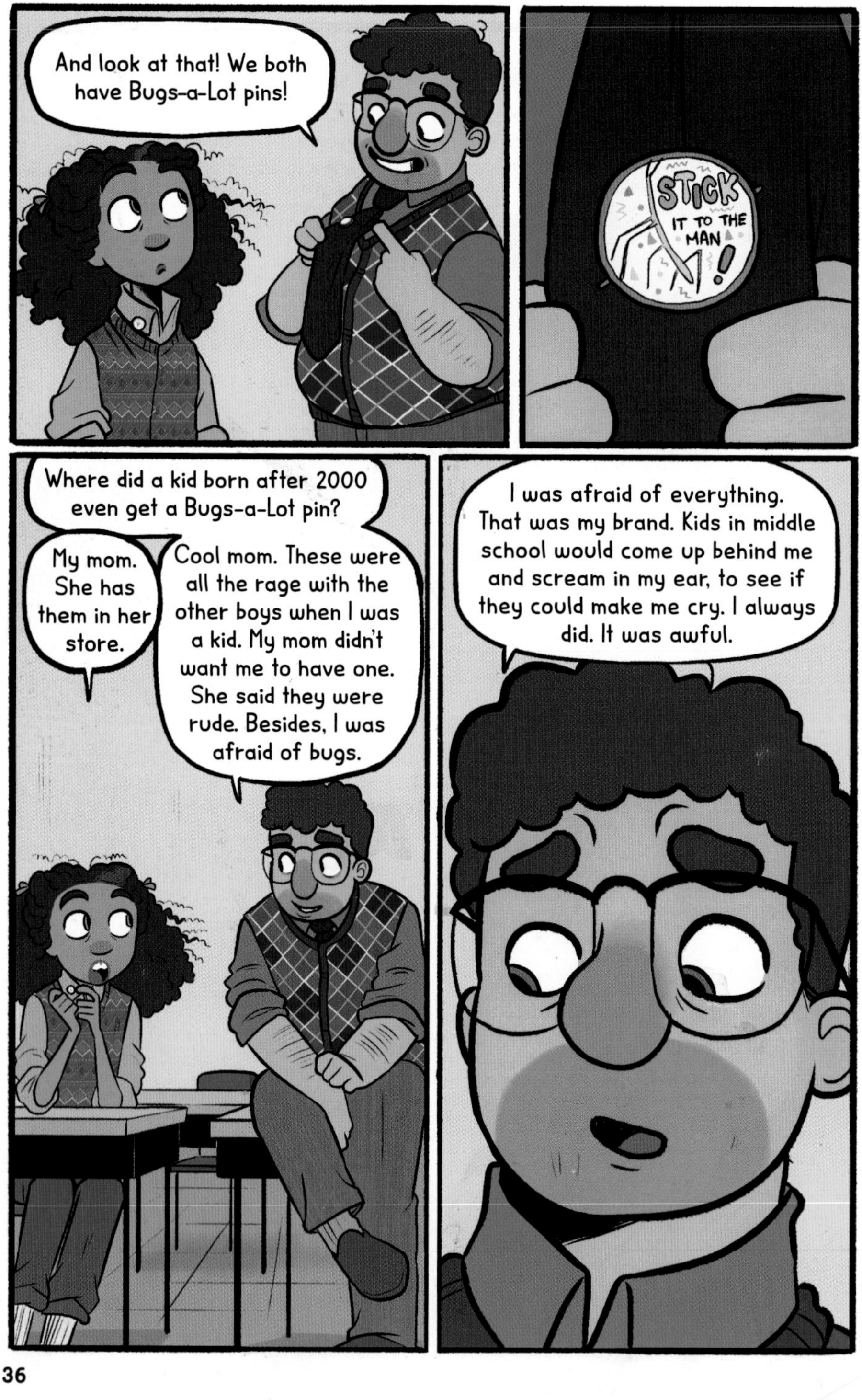
And look at that! We both have Bugs-a-Lot pins!
STICK IT TO THE MAN!
Where did a kid born after 2000 even get a Bugs-a-Lot pin?
My mom. She has them in her store.
Cool mom. These were all the rage with the other boys when I was a kid. My mom didn't want me to have one. She said they were rude. Besides, I was afraid of bugs.
I was afraid of everything. That was my brand. Kids in middle school would come up behind me and scream in my ear, to see if they could make me cry. I always did. It was awful.

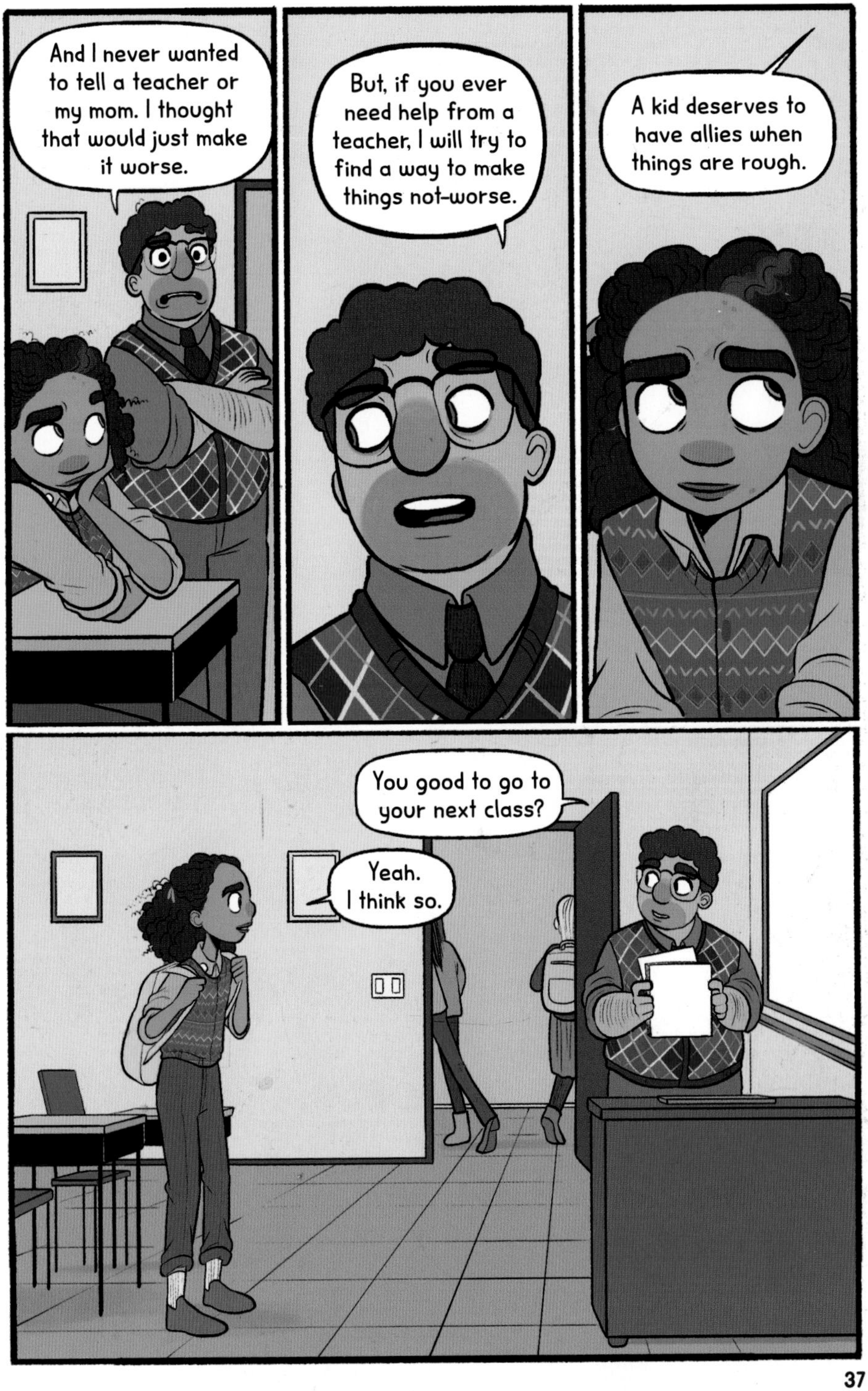
And I never wanted to tell a teacher or my mom. I thought that would just make it worse.
But, if you ever need help from a teacher, I will try to find a way to make things not-worse.
A kid deserves to have allies when things are rough.
You good to go to your next class?
Yeah. I think so.

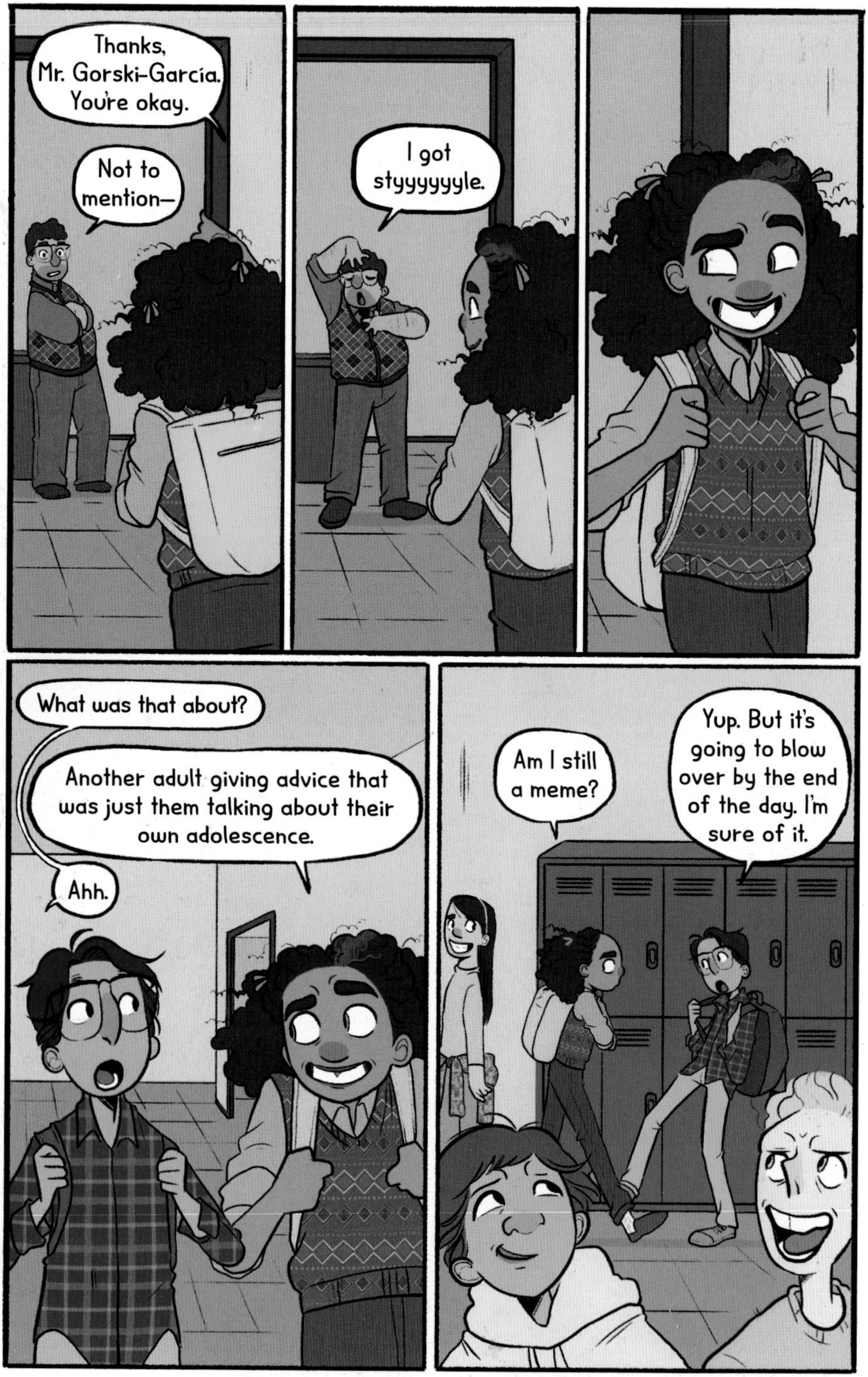
Thanks, Mr. Gorski-García. You're okay.
Not to mention—
I got styyyyyyle.
What was that about?
Another adult giving advice that was just them talking about their own adolescence.
Ahh.
Am I still a meme?
Yup. But it's going to blow over by the end of the day. I'm sure of it.

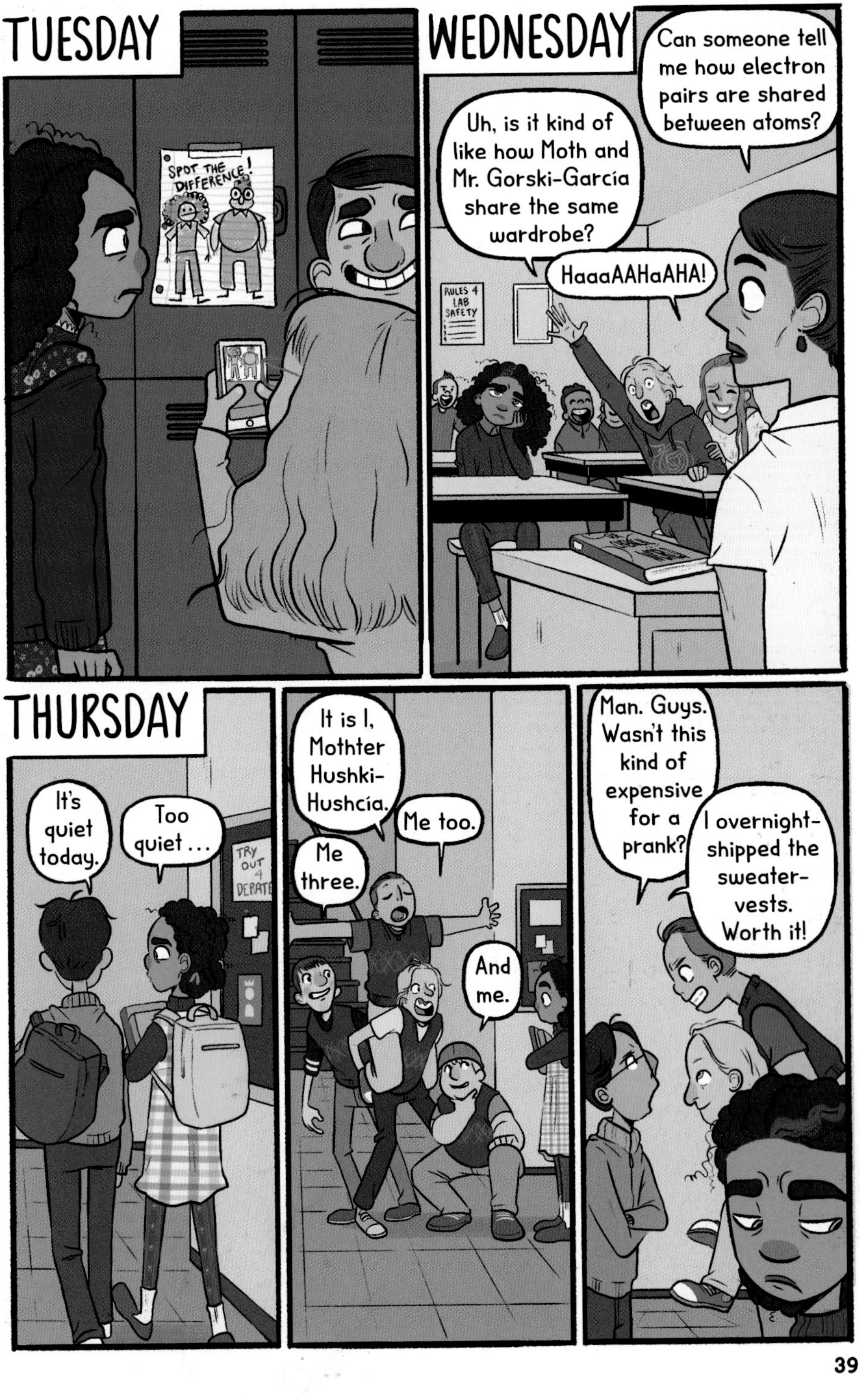

TUESDAY
SPOT THE DIFFERENCE!
WEDNESDAY
Can someone tell me how electron pairs are shared between atoms?
Uh, is it kind of like how Moth and Mr. Gorski-García share the same wardrobe?
HaaaAAHaAHA!
RULES 4 LAB SAFETY
THURSDAY
It's quiet today.
Too quiet . . .
TRY OUT 4 DEBATE
It is I, Mothter Hushki-Hushcía.
Me too.
Me three.
And me.
Man. Guys. Wasn't this kind of expensive for a prank?
I overnight-shipped the sweater-vests. Worth it!

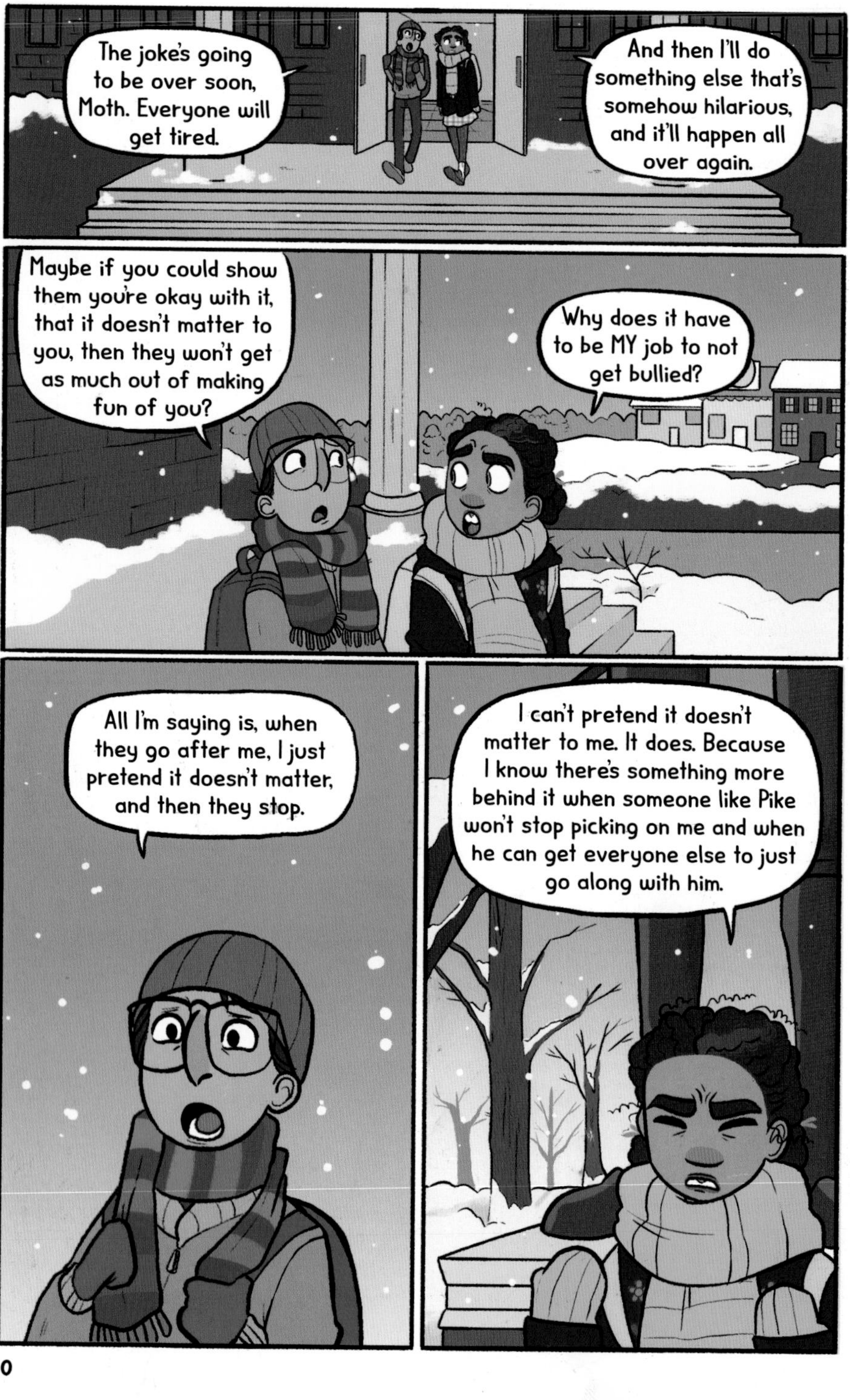
The joke's going to be over soon, Moth. Everyone will get tired.
And then I'll do something else that's somehow hilarious, and it'll happen all over again.
Maybe if you could show them you're okay with it, that it doesn't matter to you, then they won't get as much out of making fun of you?
Why does it have to be MY job to not get bullied?
All I'm saying is, when they go after me, I just pretend it doesn't matter, and then they stop.
I can't pretend it doesn't matter to me. It does. Because I know there's something more behind it when someone like Pike won't stop picking on me and when he can get everyone else to just go along with him.

Panel 1: I know you get picked on, too. But, come on, Charlie. We're not exactly the same.

Panel 2: One of us is descended from the most powerful guy in Founder's Bluff history, and it isn't me. While your ancestors were all buddy-buddy with Pike's ancestors, my family was getting hunted by them.

Panel 3: But I'M not friends with—

I know that was hundreds and hundreds of years ago. But it doesn't just go away. You know that.

Panel 4: Every day, I have to walk past this statue of a guy who tried to destroy my family. He's still treated like some hero.

And I have to walk into that super-white school where I'm treated like a complete outcast, no matter what I do.

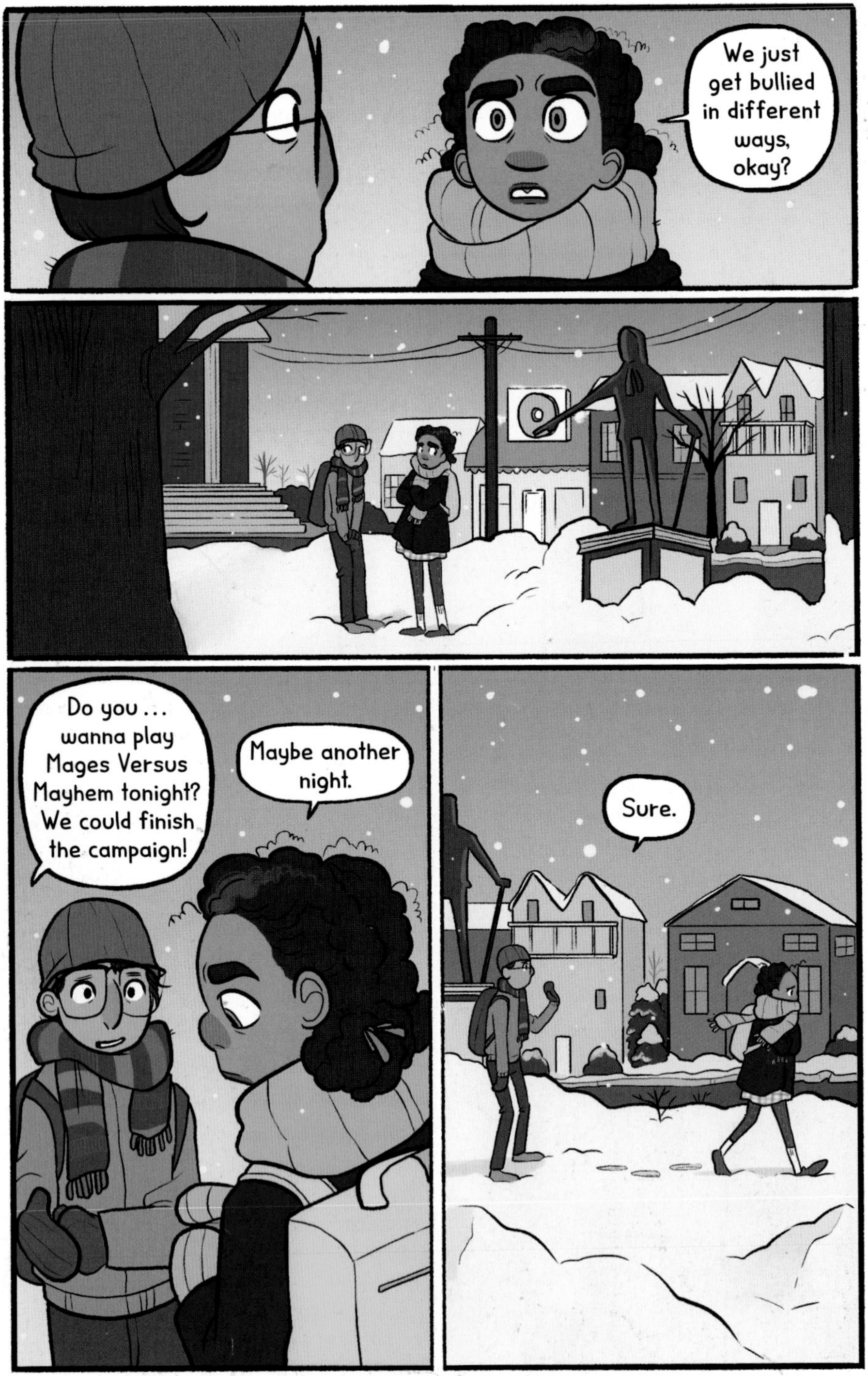
We just get bullied in different ways, okay?
Do you... wanna play Mages Versus Mayhem tonight? We could finish the campaign!
Maybe another night.
Sure.

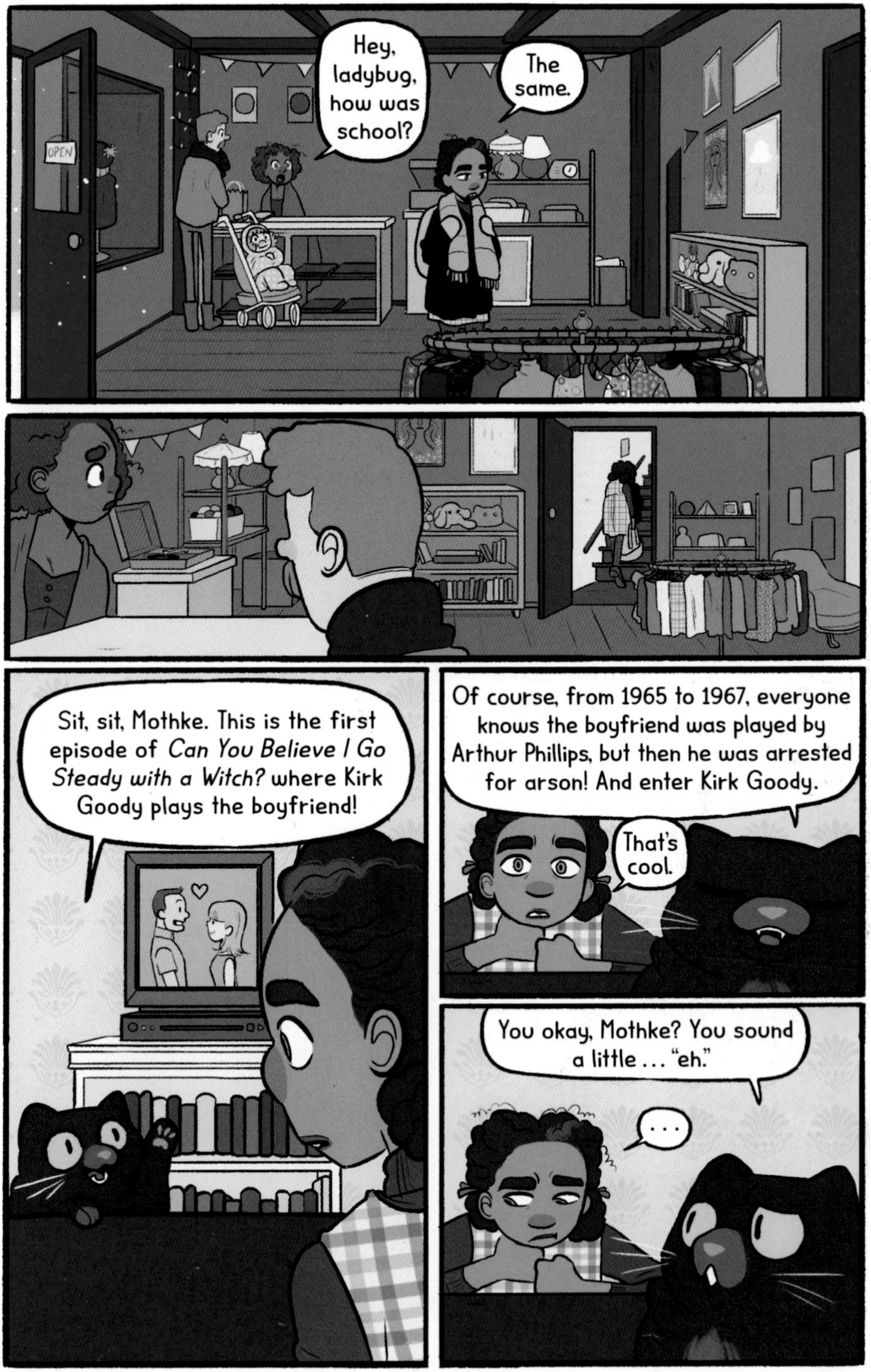
Hey, ladybug, how was school?
The same.
OPEN
Sit, sit, Mothke. This is the first episode of *Can You Believe I Go Steady with a Witch?* where Kirk Goody plays the boyfriend!
Of course, from 1965 to 1967, everyone knows the boyfriend was played by Arthur Phillips, but then he was arrested for arson! And enter Kirk Goody.
That's cool.
You okay, Mothke? You sound a little . . . "eh."
. . .

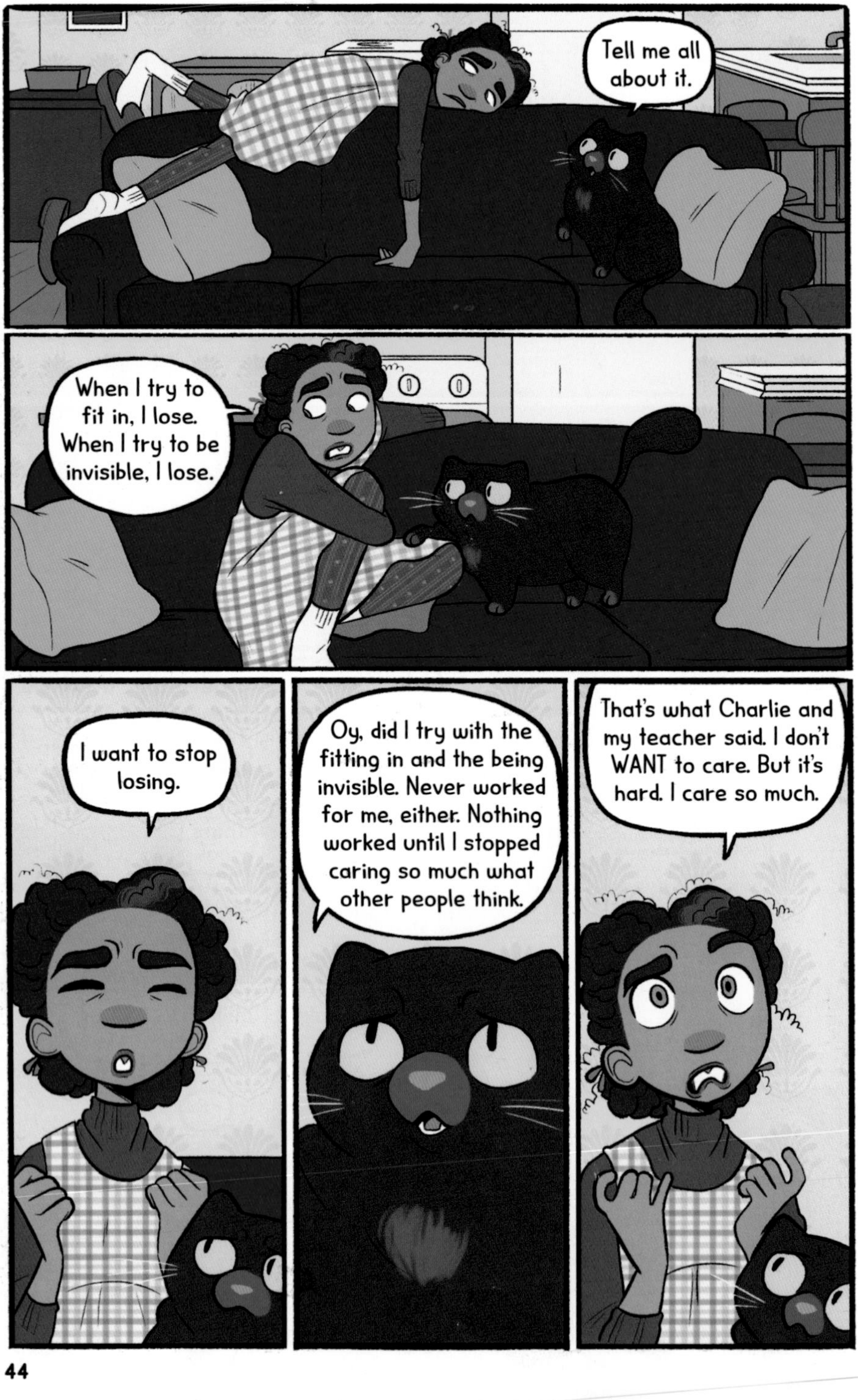
Tell me all about it.
When I try to fit in, I lose. When I try to be invisible, I lose.
I want to stop losing.
Oy, did I try with the fitting in and the being invisible. Never worked for me, either. Nothing worked until I stopped caring so much what other people think.
That's what Charlie and my teacher said. I don't WANT to care. But it's hard. I care so much.

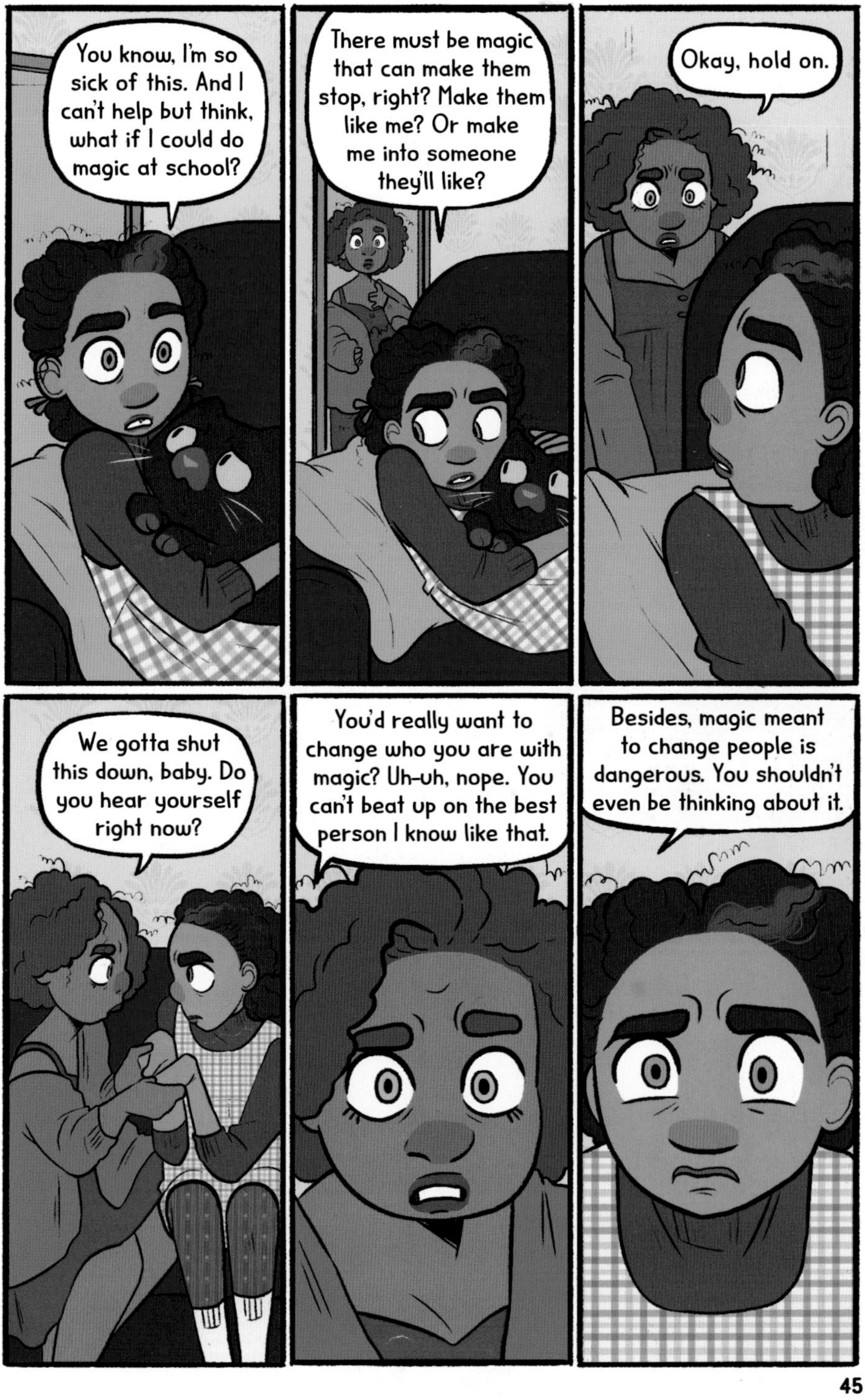
You know, I'm so sick of this. And I can't help but think, what if I could do magic at school?
There must be magic that can make them stop, right? Make them like me? Or make me into someone they'll like?
Okay, hold on.
We gotta shut this down, baby. Do you hear yourself right now?
You'd really want to change who you are with magic? Uh-uh, nope. You can't beat up on the best person I know like that.
Besides, magic meant to change people is dangerous. You shouldn't even be thinking about it.

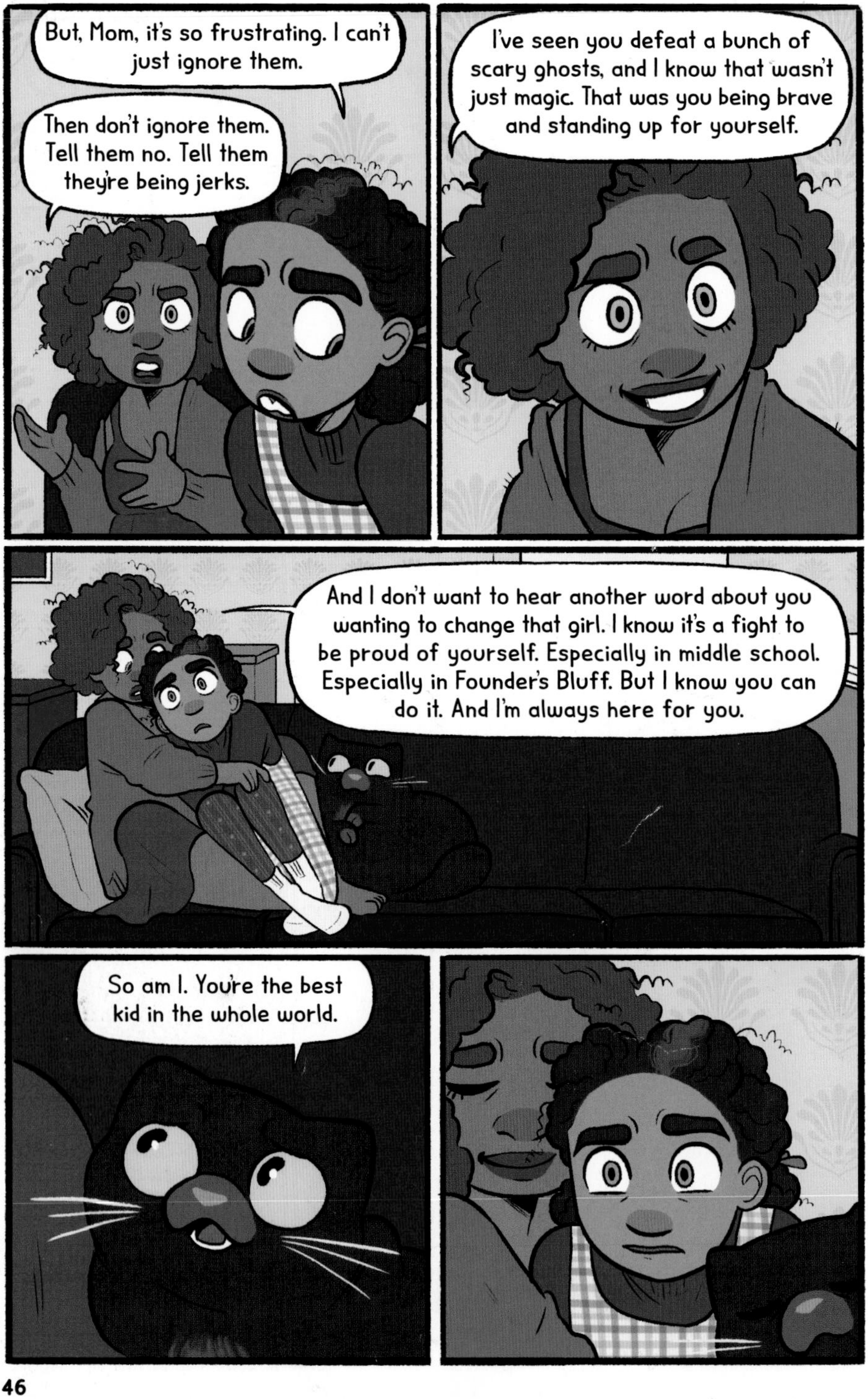
But, Mom, it's so frustrating. I can't just ignore them.
Then don't ignore them. Tell them no. Tell them they're being jerks.
I've seen you defeat a bunch of scary ghosts, and I know that wasn't just magic. That was you being brave and standing up for yourself.
And I don't want to hear another word about you wanting to change that girl. I know it's a fight to be proud of yourself. Especially in middle school. Especially in Founder's Bluff. But I know you can do it. And I'm always here for you.
So am I. You're the best kid in the whole world.

CHAPTER 3

Sarah's Bask

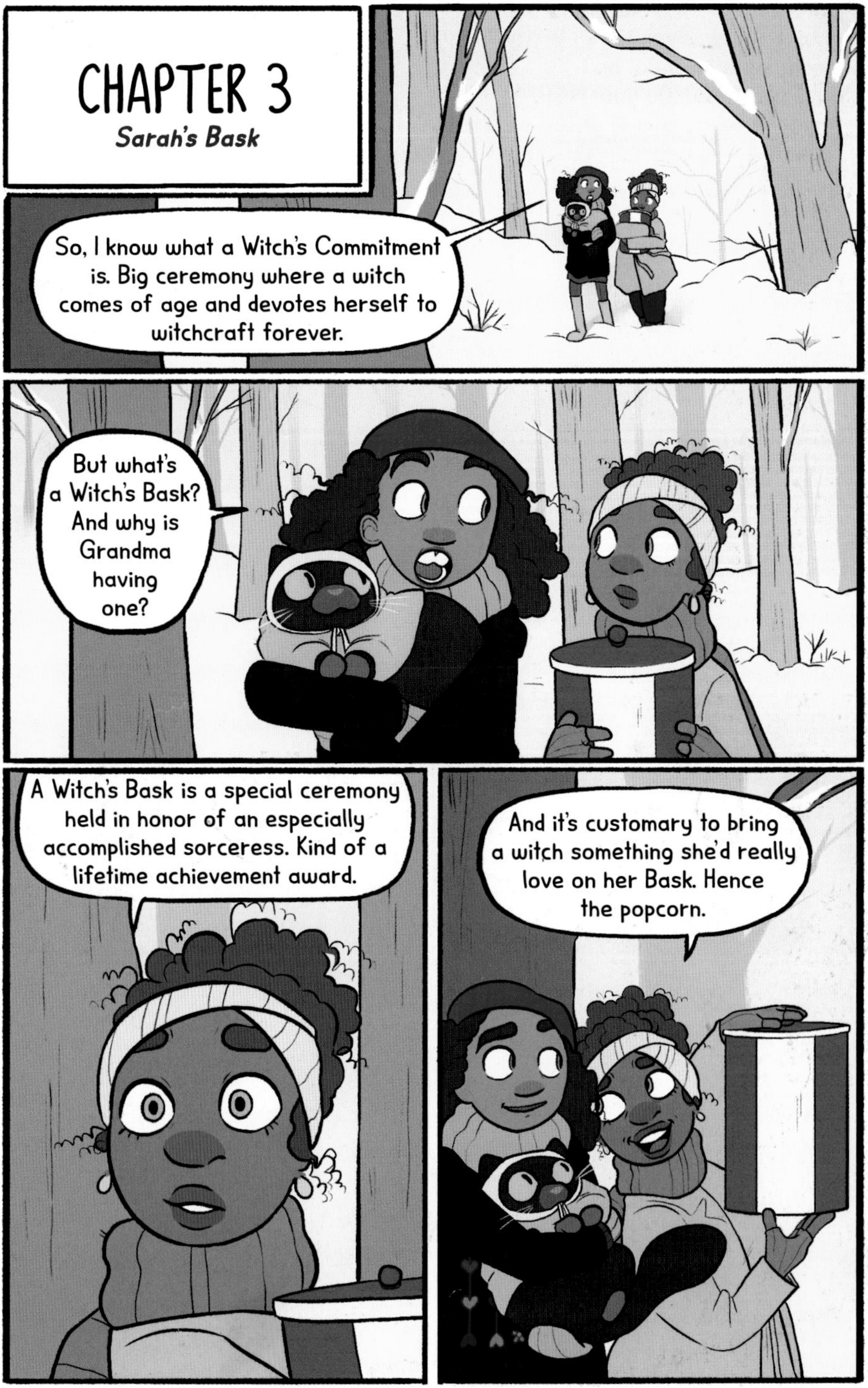
So, I know what a Witch's Commitment is. Big ceremony where a witch comes of age and devotes herself to witchcraft forever.
But what's a Witch's Bask? And why is Grandma having one?
A Witch's Bask is a special ceremony held in honor of an especially accomplished sorceress. Kind of a lifetime achievement award.
And it's customary to bring a witch something she'd really love on her Bask. Hence the popcorn.

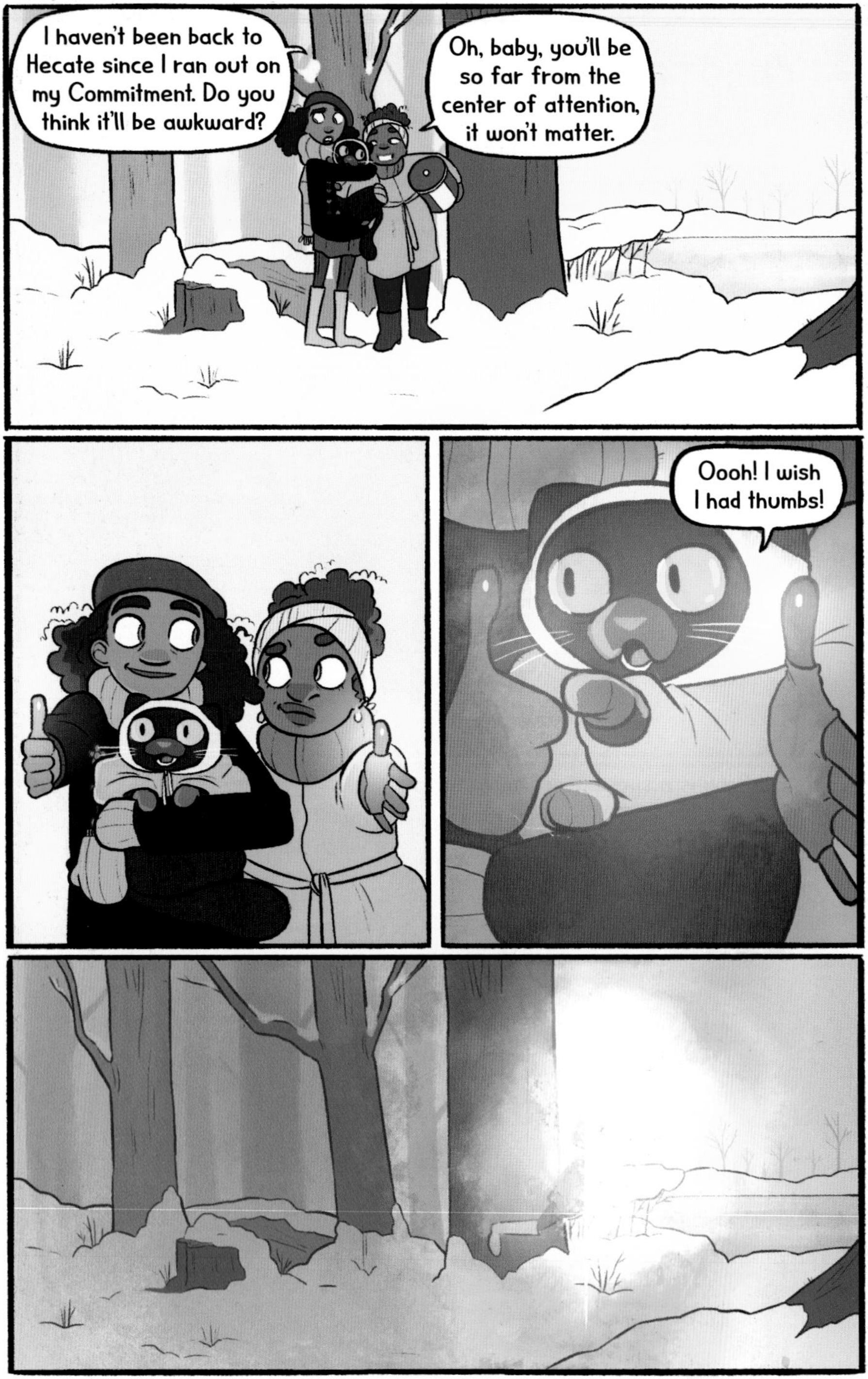
I haven't been back to Hecate since I ran out on my Commitment. Do you think it'll be awkward?
Oh, baby, you'll be so far from the center of attention, it won't matter.
Oooh! I wish I had thumbs!

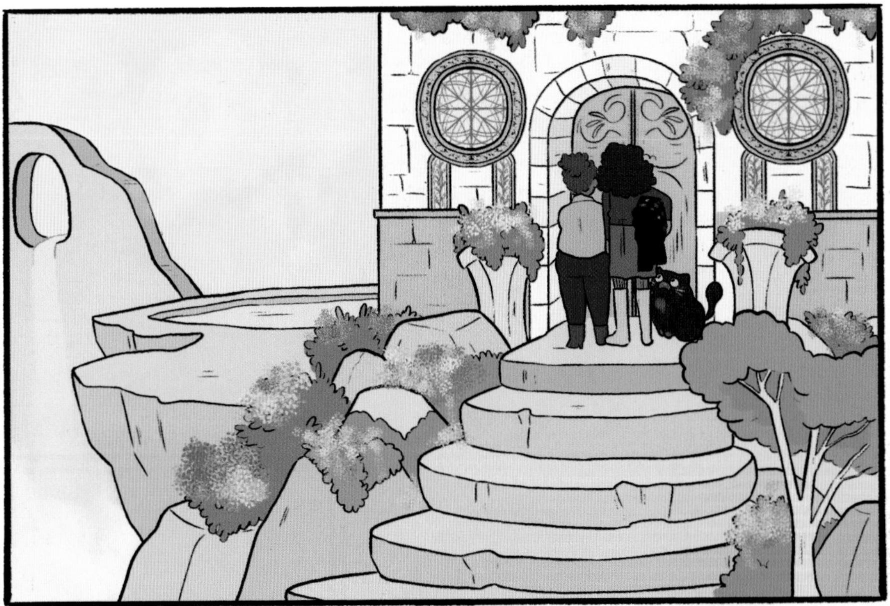

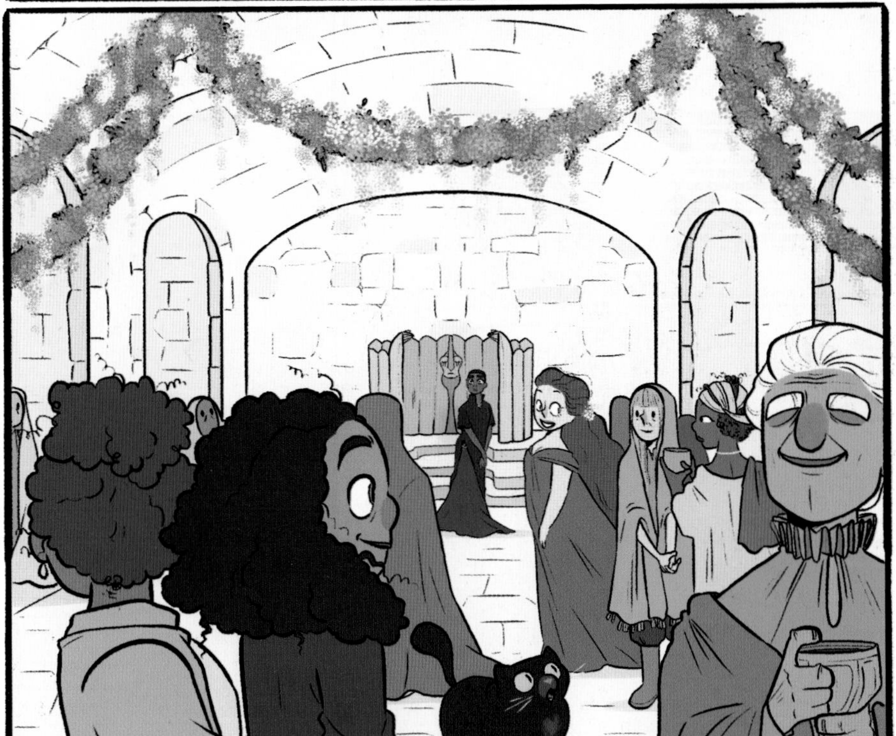

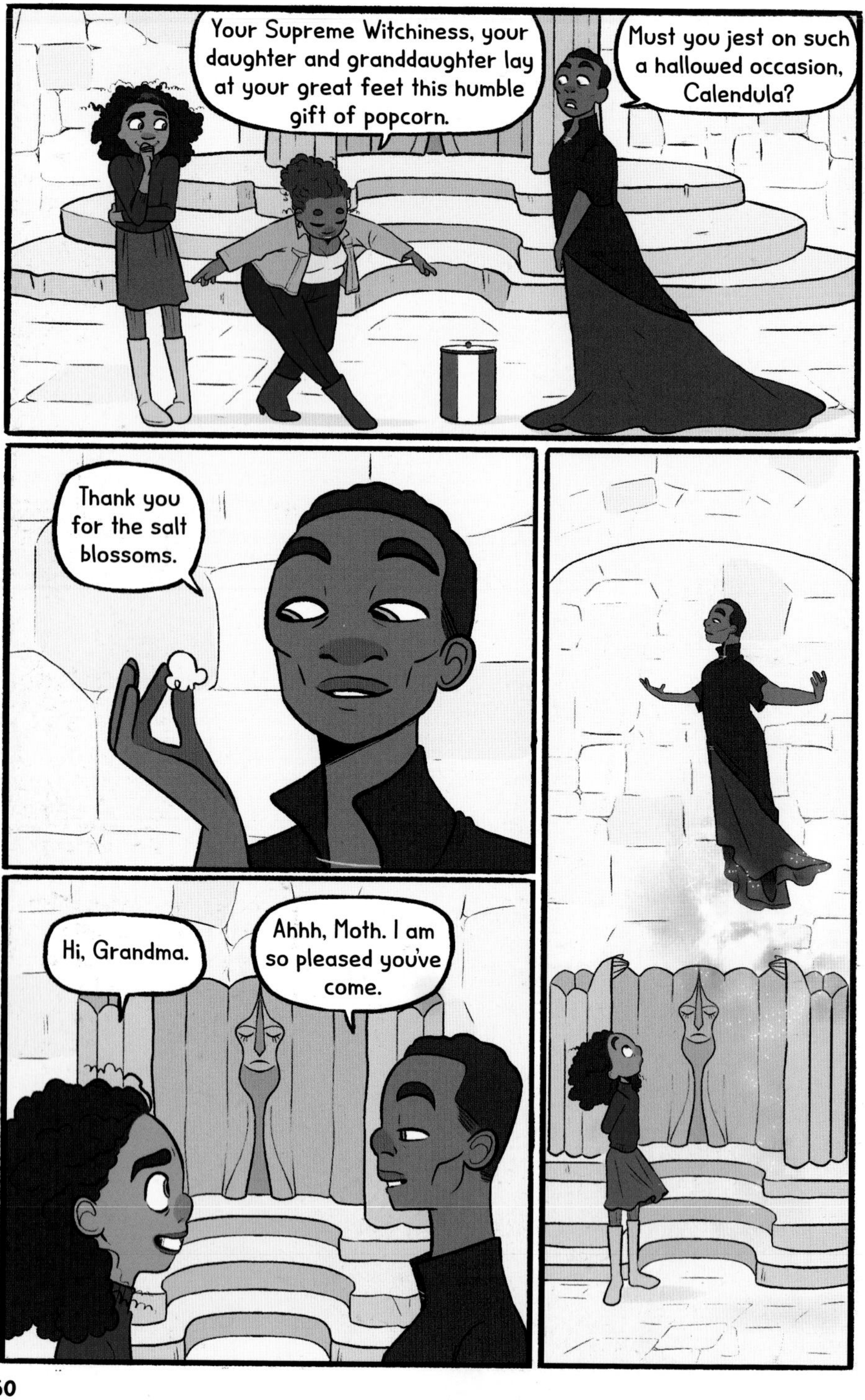
Your Supreme Witchiness, your daughter and granddaughter lay at your great feet this humble gift of popcorn.
Must you jest on such a hallowed occasion, Calendula?
Thank you for the salt blossoms.
Hi, Grandma.
Ahhh, Moth. I am so pleased you've come.

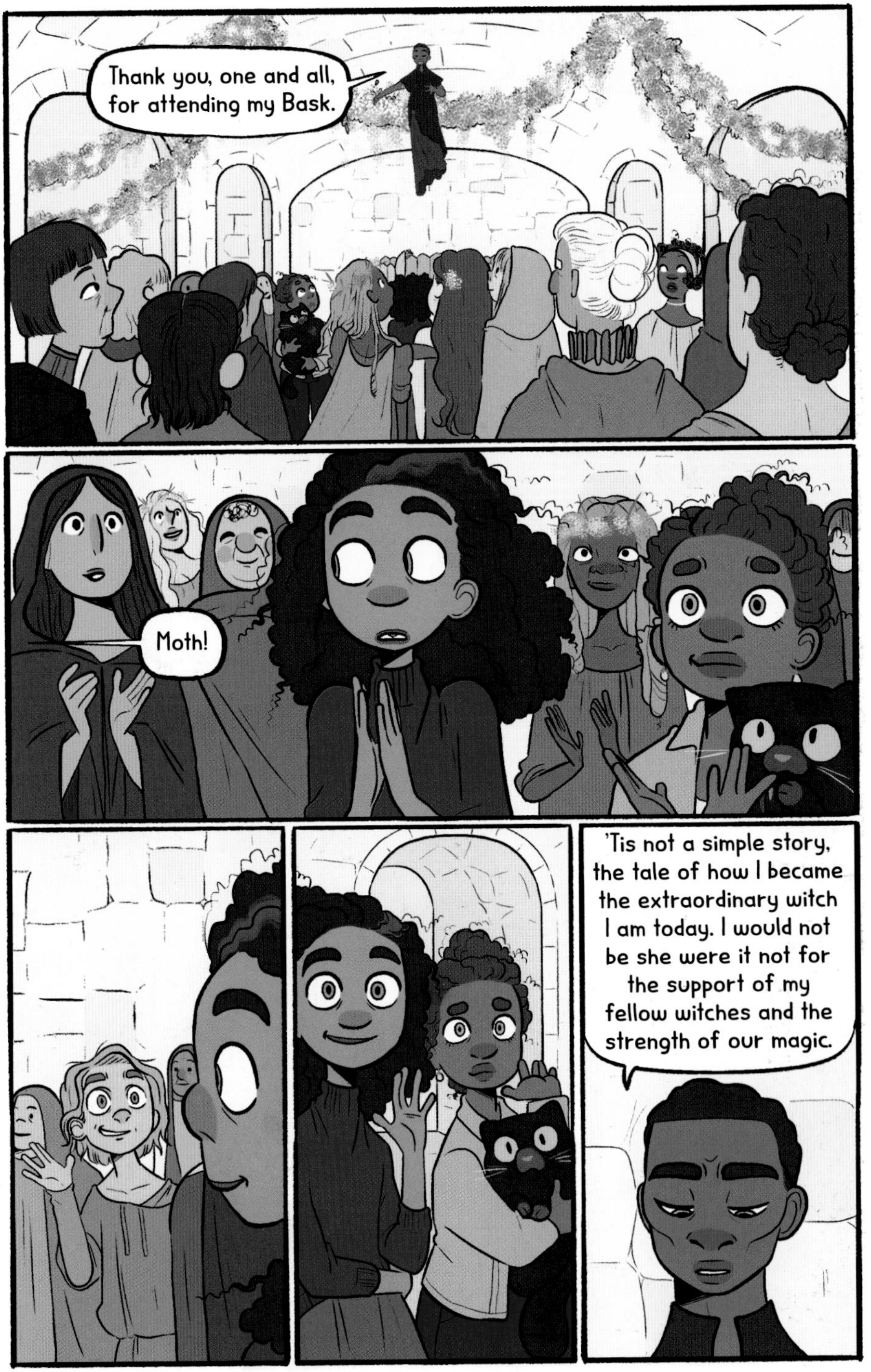
Thank you, one and all, for attending my Bask.
Moth!
'Tis not a simple story, the tale of how I became the extraordinary witch I am today. I would not be she were it not for the support of my fellow witches and the strength of our magic.

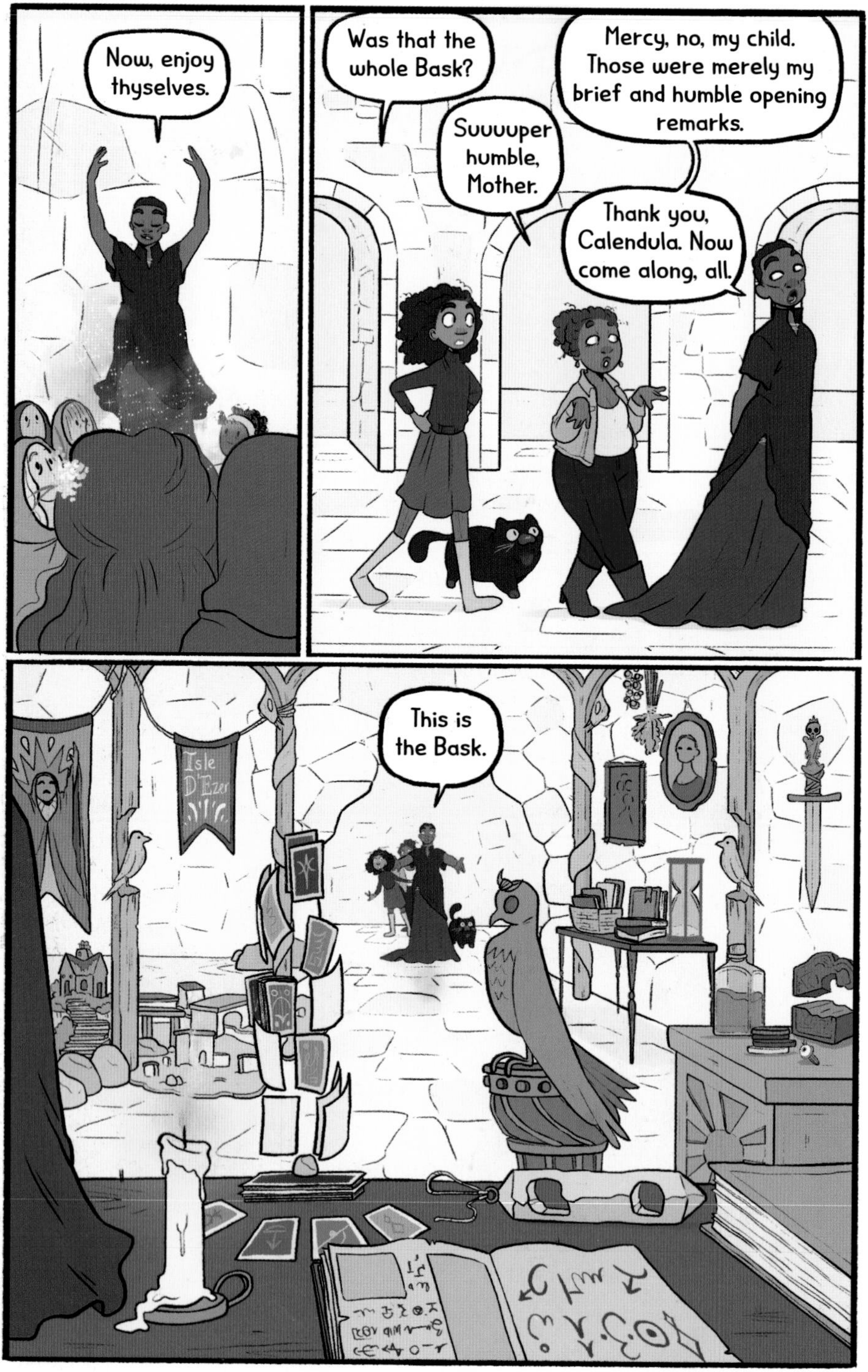
Now, enjoy thyselves.
Was that the whole Bask?
Mercy, no, my child. Those were merely my brief and humble opening remarks.
Suuuuper humble, Mother.
Thank you, Calendula. Now come along, all.
This is the Bask.
Isle D'Ezer

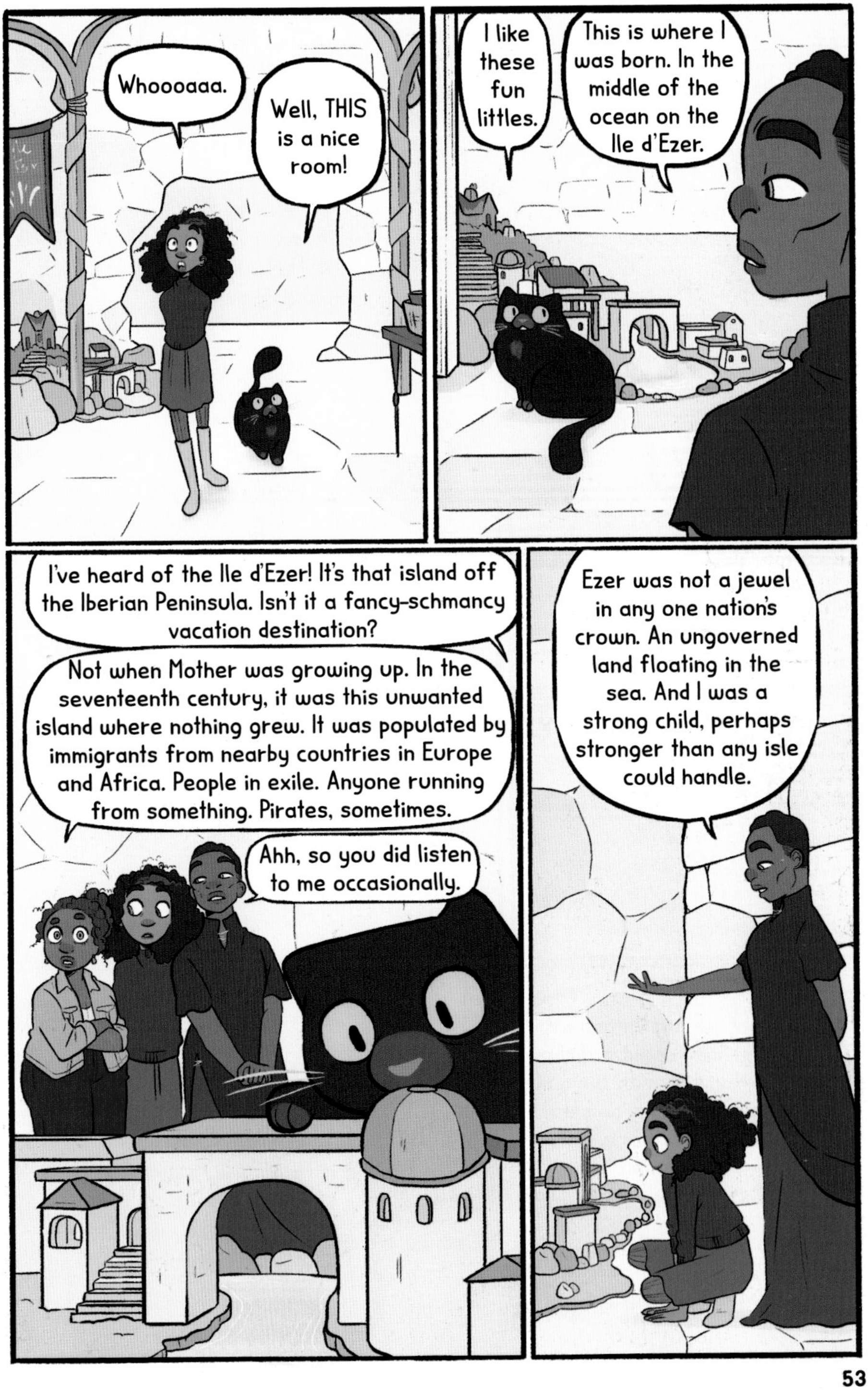
Whoooaaa.
Well, THIS is a nice room!
I like these fun littles.
This is where I was born. In the middle of the ocean on the Ile d'Ezer.
I've heard of the Ile d'Ezer! It's that island off the Iberian Peninsula. Isn't it a fancy-schmancy vacation destination?
Not when Mother was growing up. In the seventeenth century, it was this unwanted island where nothing grew. It was populated by immigrants from nearby countries in Europe and Africa. People in exile. Anyone running from something. Pirates, sometimes.
Ahh, so you did listen to me occasionally.
Ezer was not a jewel in any one nation's crown. An ungoverned land floating in the sea. And I was a strong child, perhaps stronger than any isle could handle.

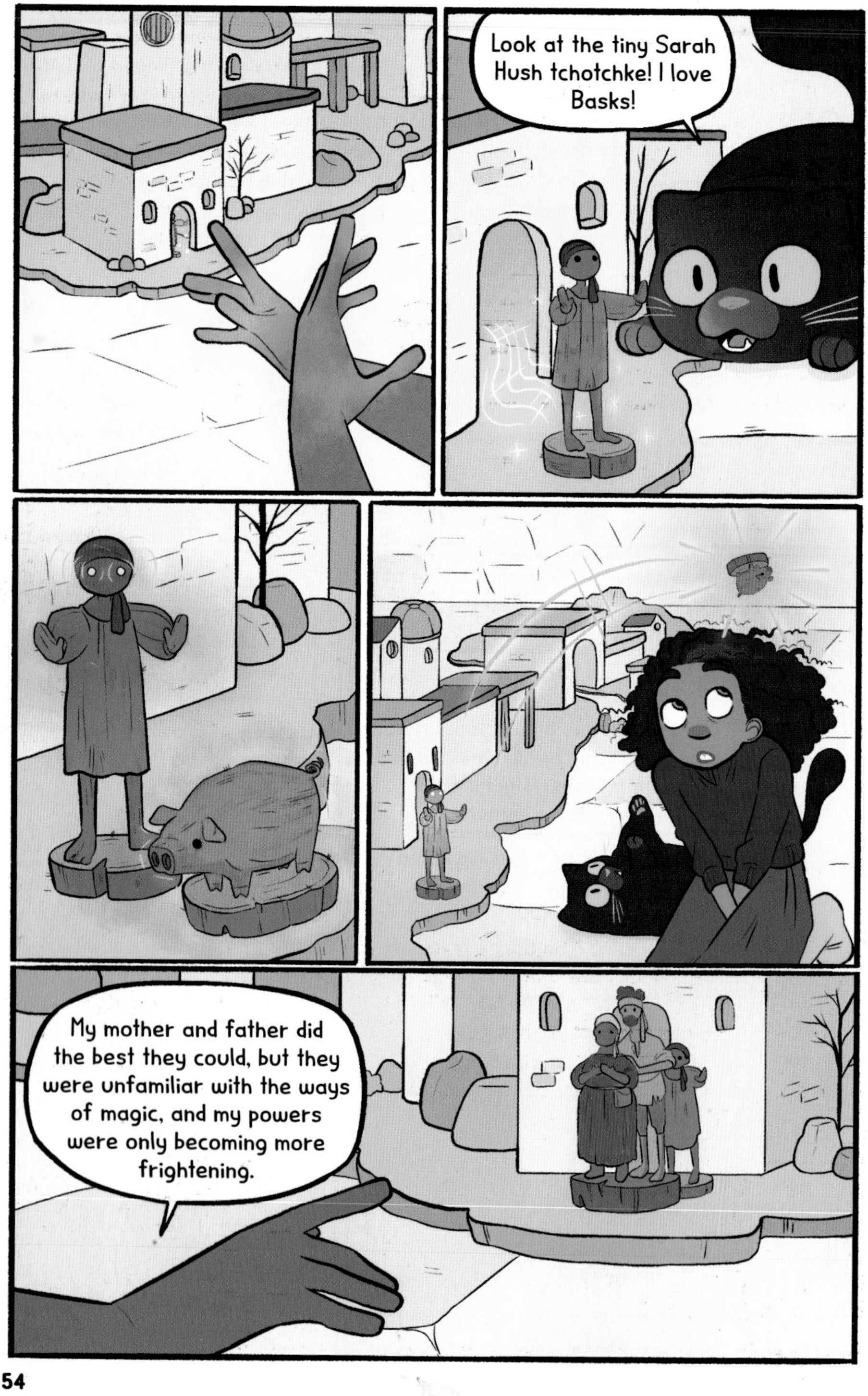
Look at the tiny Sarah Hush tchotchke! I love Basks!
My mother and father did the best they could, but they were unfamiliar with the ways of magic, and my powers were only becoming more frightening.

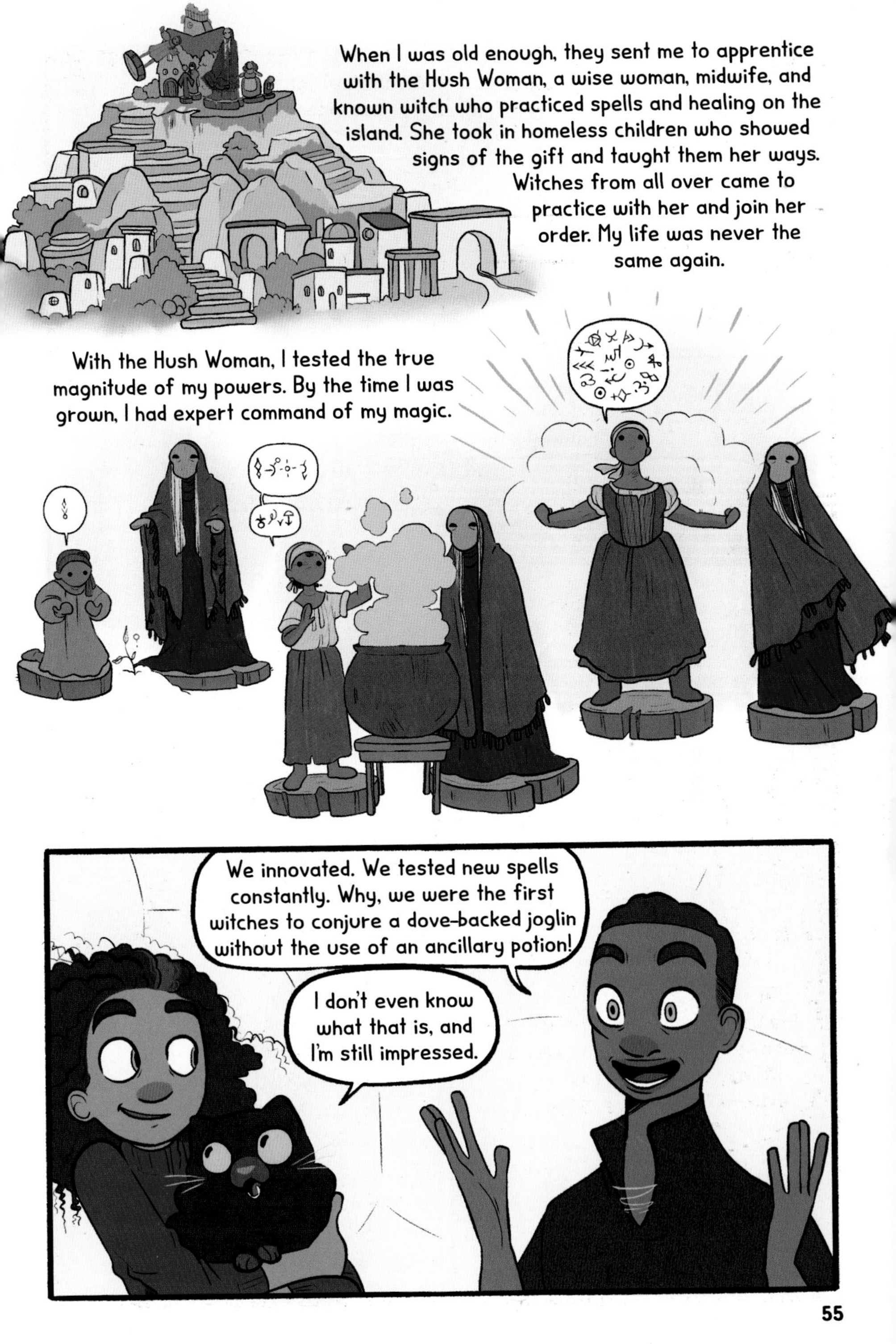
When I was old enough, they sent me to apprentice with the Hush Woman, a wise woman, midwife, and known witch who practiced spells and healing on the island. She took in homeless children who showed signs of the gift and taught them her ways. Witches from all over came to practice with her and join her order. My life was never the same again.
With the Hush Woman, I tested the true magnitude of my powers. By the time I was grown, I had expert command of my magic.
We innovated. We tested new spells constantly. Why, we were the first witches to conjure a dove-backed joglin without the use of an ancillary potion!
I don't even know what that is, and I'm still impressed.

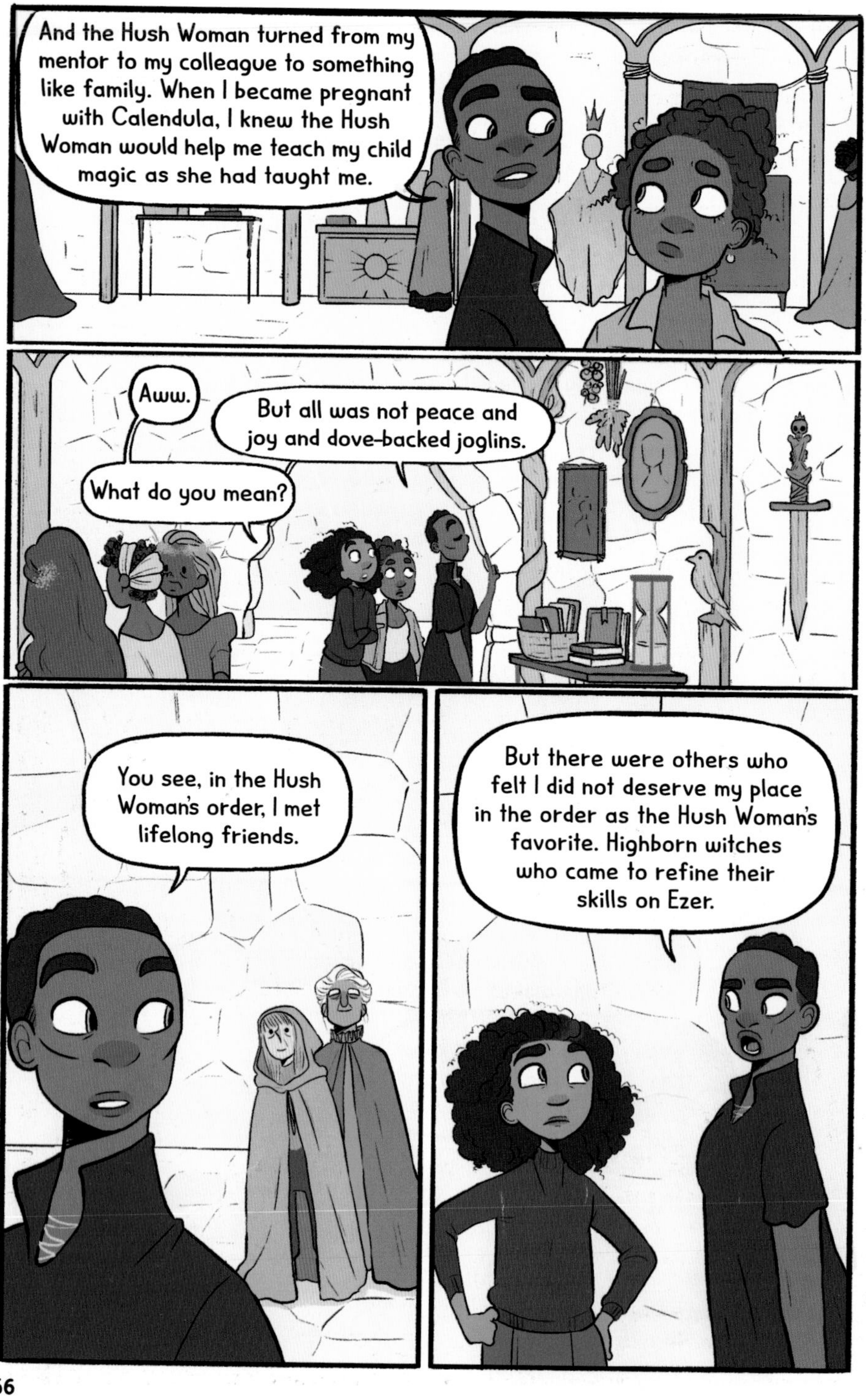
And the Hush Woman turned from my mentor to my colleague to something like family. When I became pregnant with Calendula, I knew the Hush Woman would help me teach my child magic as she had taught me.
Aww.
What do you mean?
But all was not peace and joy and dove-backed joglins.
You see, in the Hush Woman's order, I met lifelong friends.
But there were others who felt I did not deserve my place in the order as the Hush Woman's favorite. Highborn witches who came to refine their skills on Ezer.

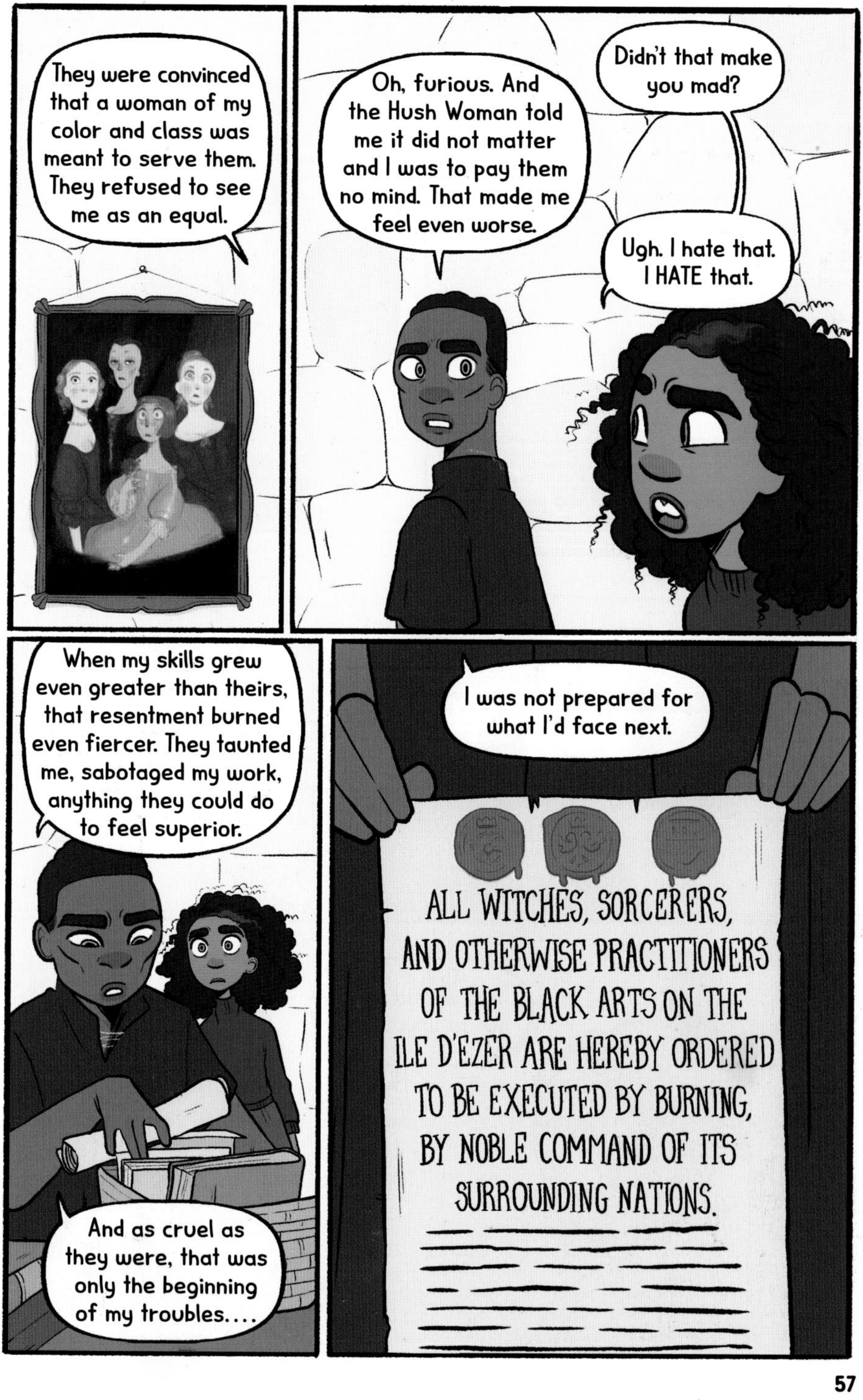
They were convinced that a woman of my color and class was meant to serve them. They refused to see me as an equal.
Oh, furious. And the Hush Woman told me it did not matter and I was to pay them no mind. That made me feel even worse.
Didn't that make you mad?
Ugh. I hate that. I HATE that.
When my skills grew even greater than theirs, that resentment burned even fiercer. They taunted me, sabotaged my work, anything they could do to feel superior.
And as cruel as they were, that was only the beginning of my troubles....
I was not prepared for what I'd face next.
ALL WITCHES, SORCERERS, AND OTHERWISE PRACTITIONERS OF THE BLACK ARTS ON THE ILE D'EZER ARE HEREBY ORDERED TO BE EXECUTED BY BURNING, BY NOBLE COMMAND OF ITS SURROUNDING NATIONS.

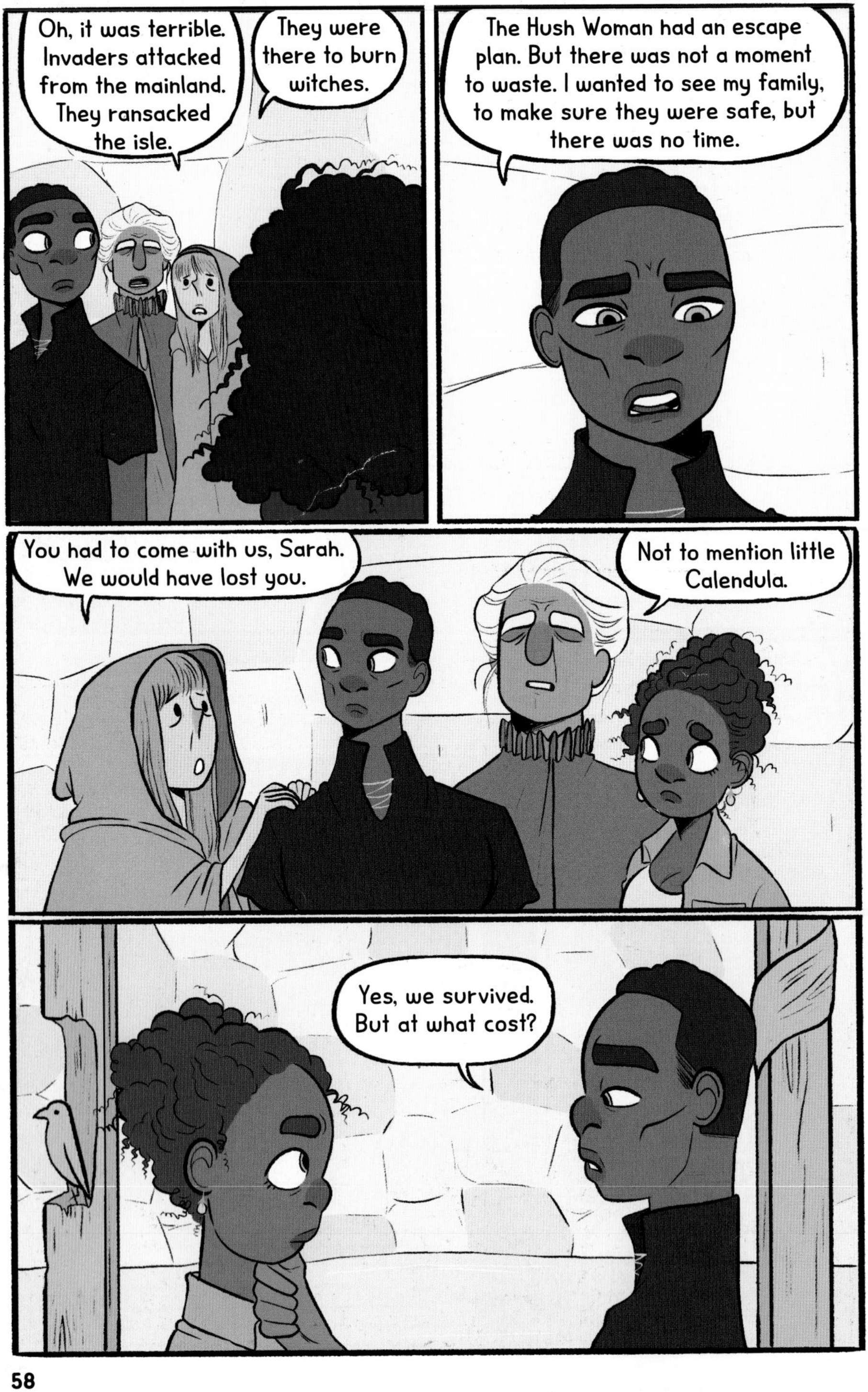
Oh, it was terrible. Invaders attacked from the mainland. They ransacked the isle.
They were there to burn witches.
The Hush Woman had an escape plan. But there was not a moment to waste. I wanted to see my family, to make sure they were safe, but there was no time.
You had to come with us, Sarah. We would have lost you.
Not to mention little Calendula.
Yes, we survived. But at what cost?

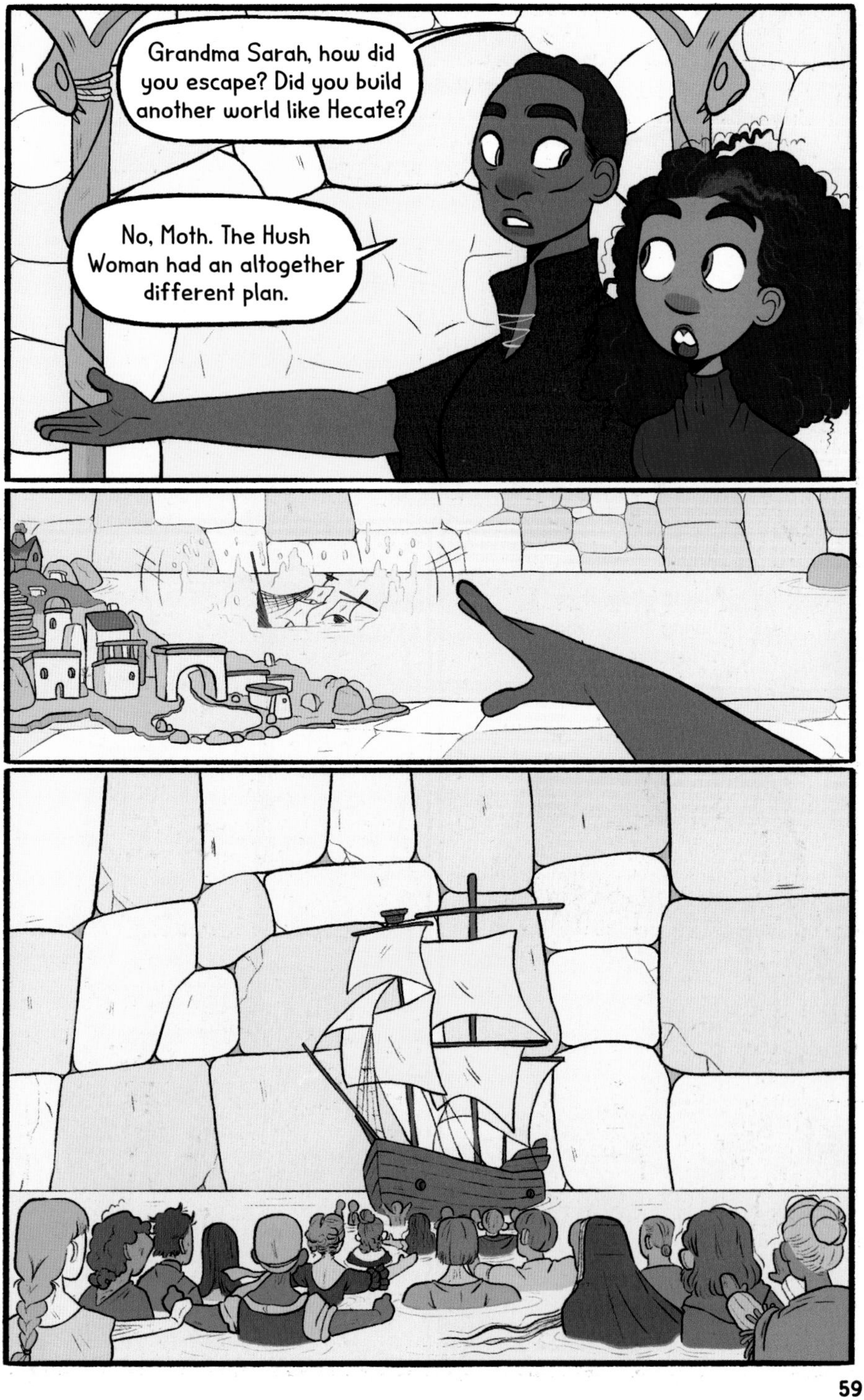
Grandma Sarah, how did you escape? Did you build another world like Hecate?
No, Moth. The Hush Woman had an altogether different plan.

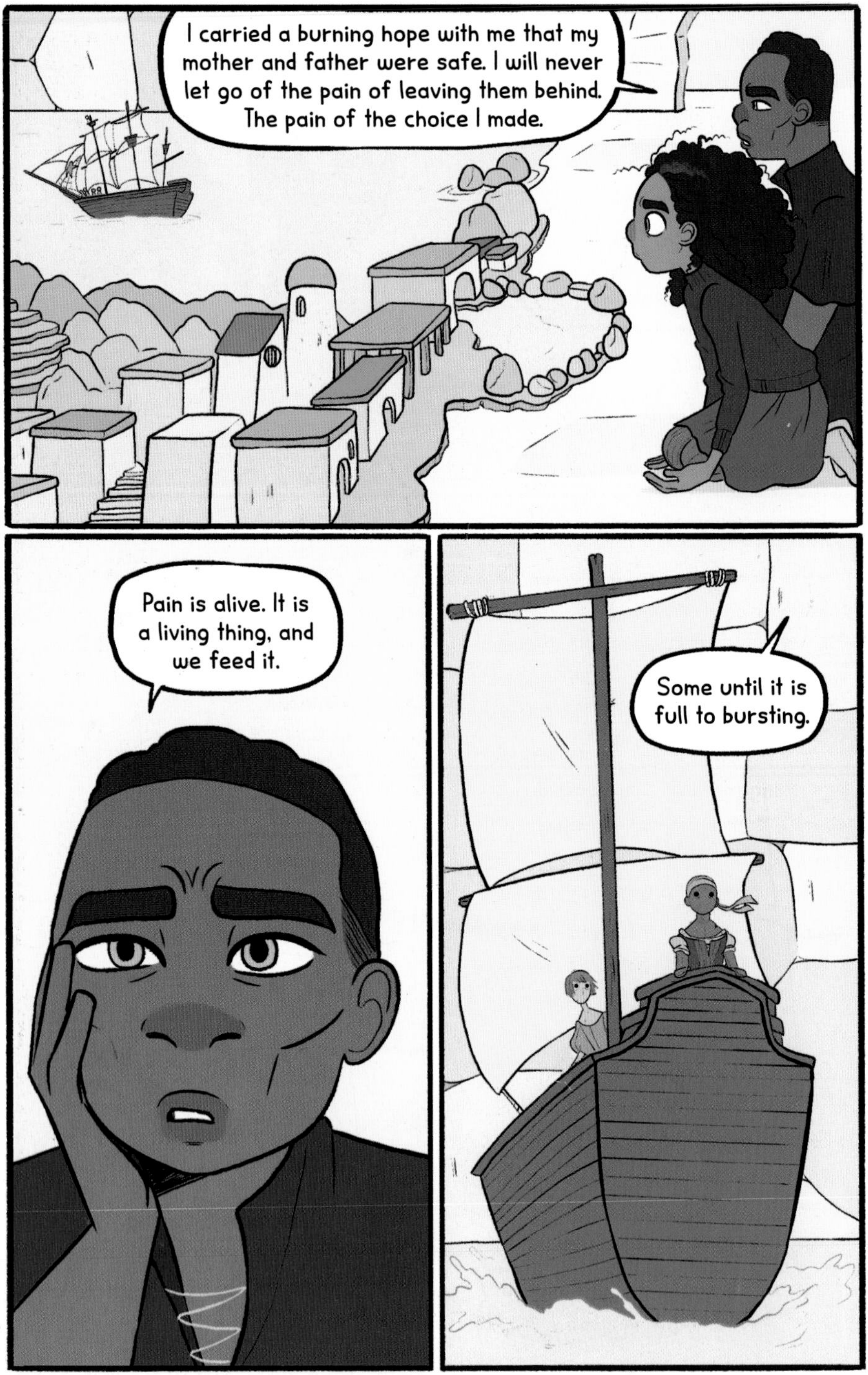
I carried a burning hope with me that my mother and father were safe. I will never let go of the pain of leaving them behind. The pain of the choice I made.
Pain is alive. It is a living thing, and we feed it.
Some until it is full to bursting.

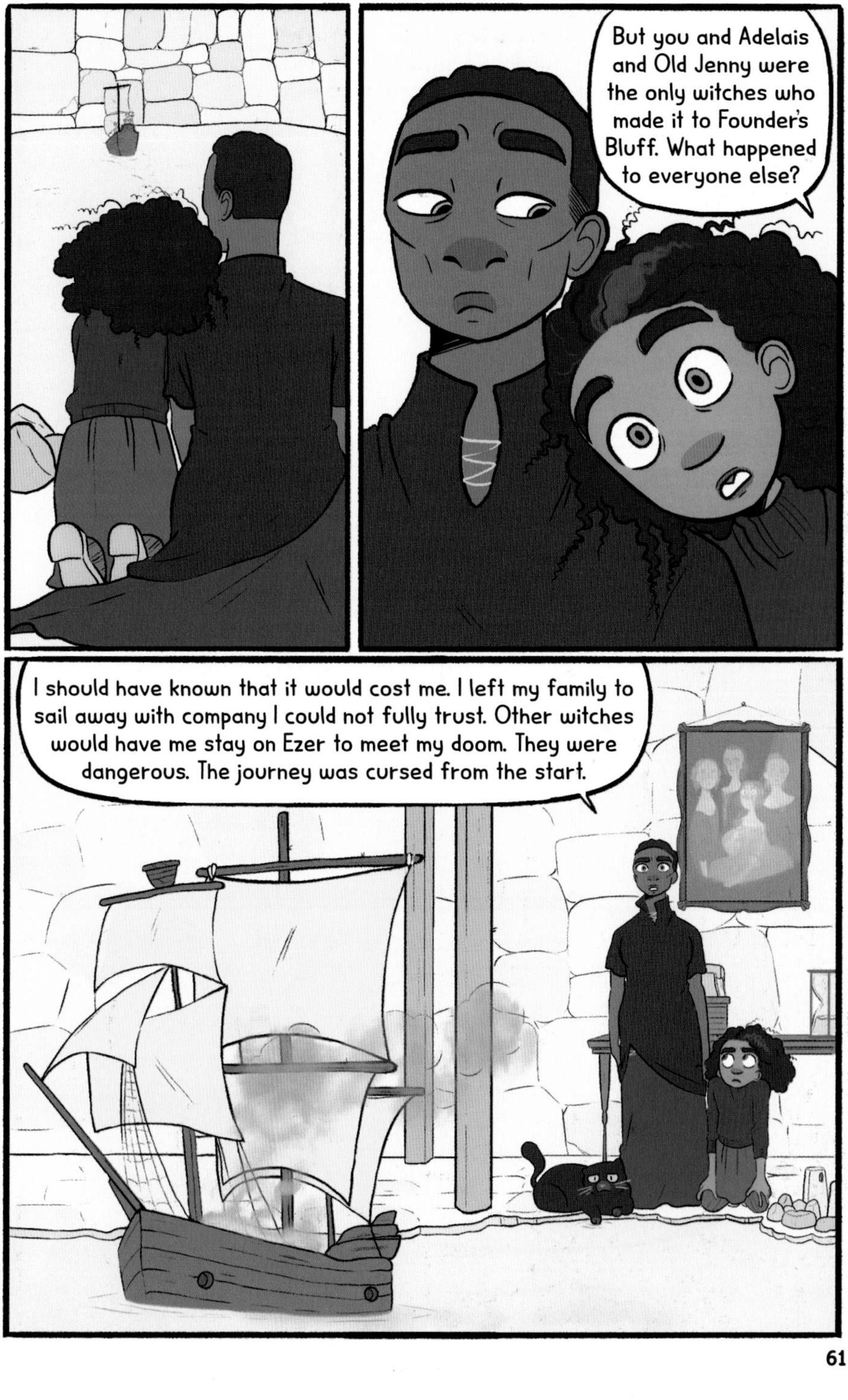
But you and Adelais and Old Jenny were the only witches who made it to Founder's Bluff. What happened to everyone else?
I should have known that it would cost me. I left my family to sail away with company I could not fully trust. Other witches would have me stay on Ezer to meet my doom. They were dangerous. The journey was cursed from the start.

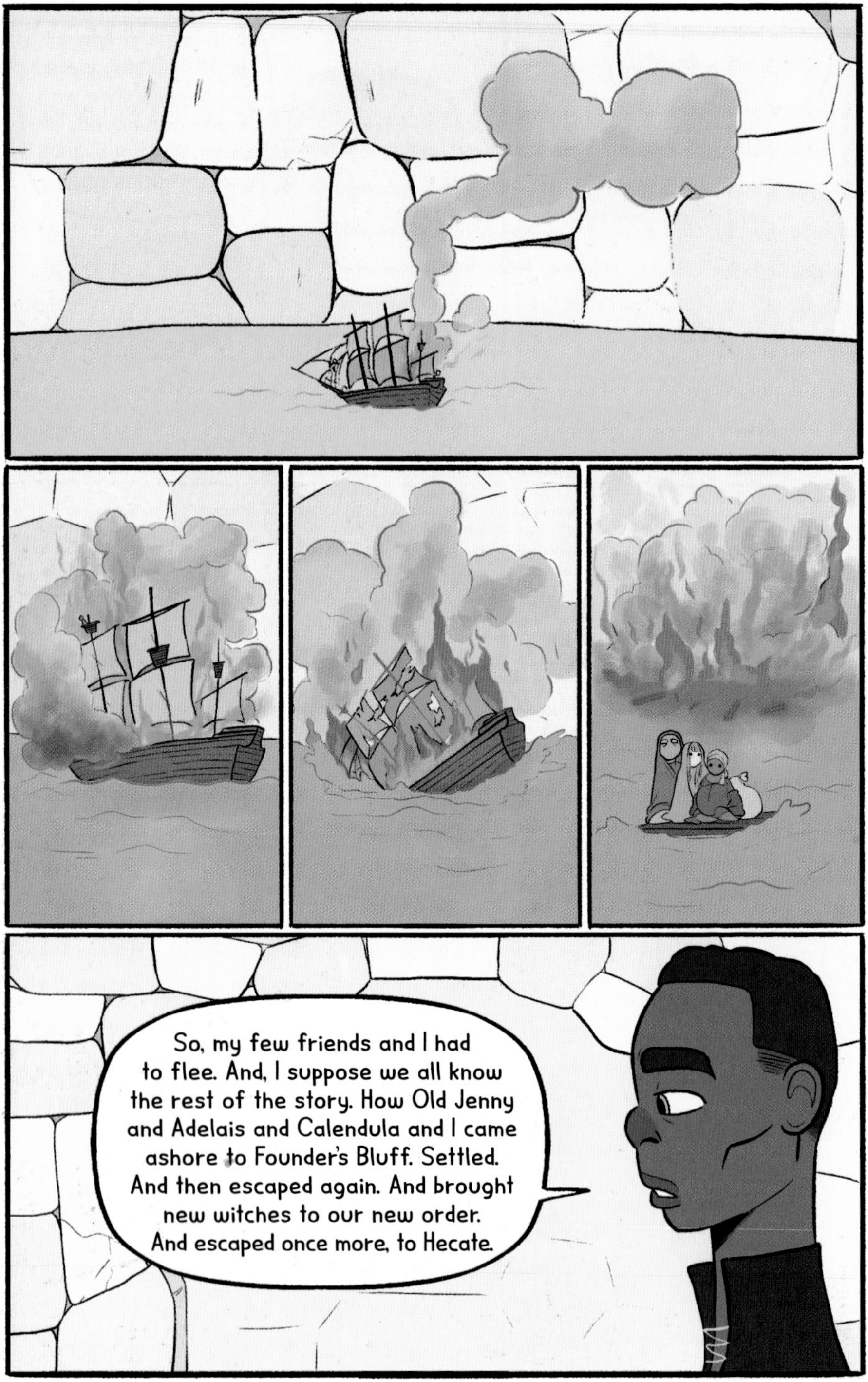
So, my few friends and I had to flee. And, I suppose we all know the rest of the story. How Old Jenny and Adelais and Calendula and I came ashore to Founder's Bluff. Settled. And then escaped again. And brought new witches to our new order. And escaped once more, to Hecate.

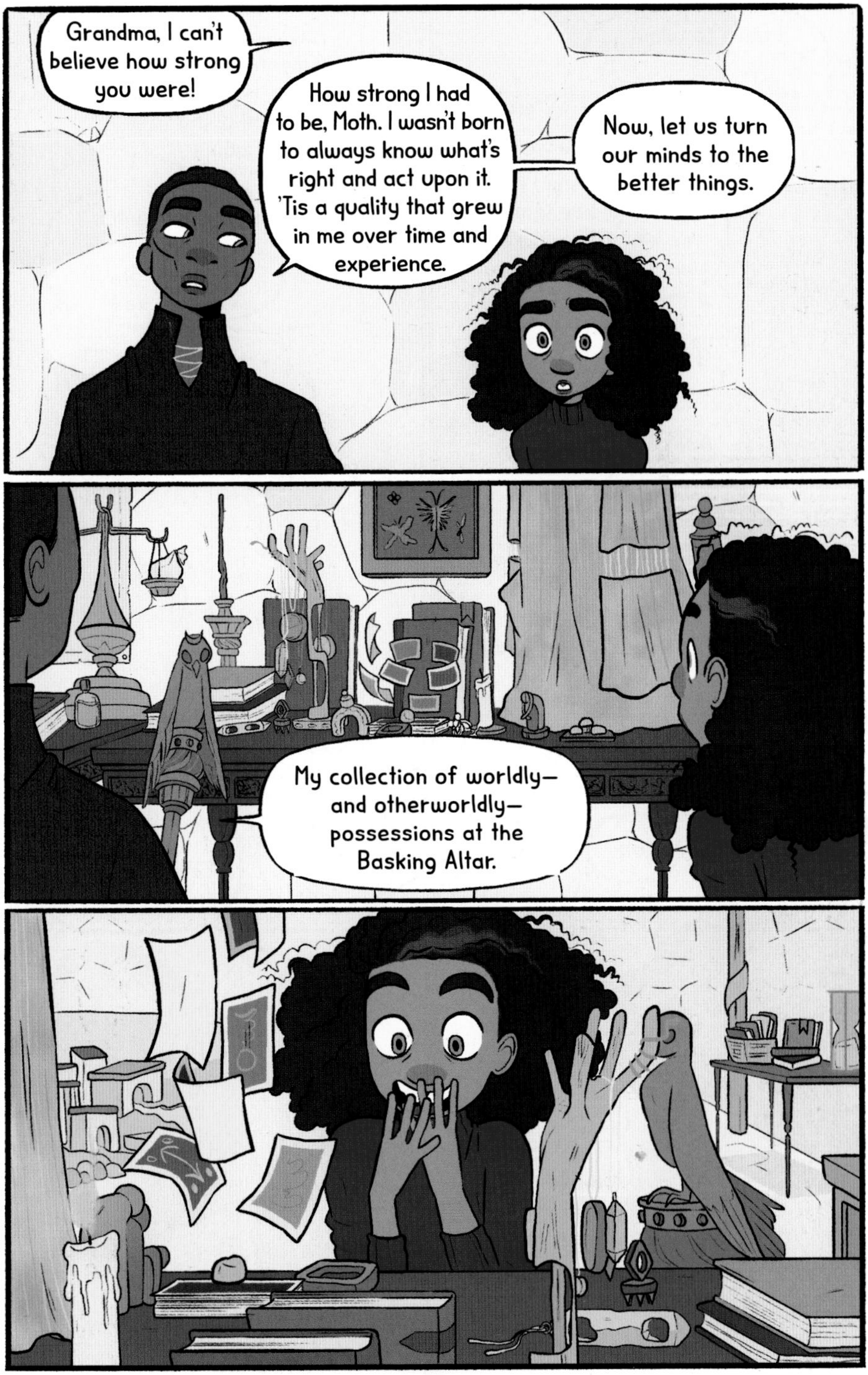
Grandma, I can't believe how strong you were!
How strong I had to be, Moth. I wasn't born to always know what's right and act upon it. 'Tis a quality that grew in me over time and experience.
Now, let us turn our minds to the better things.
My collection of worldly—and otherworldly—possessions at the Basking Altar.

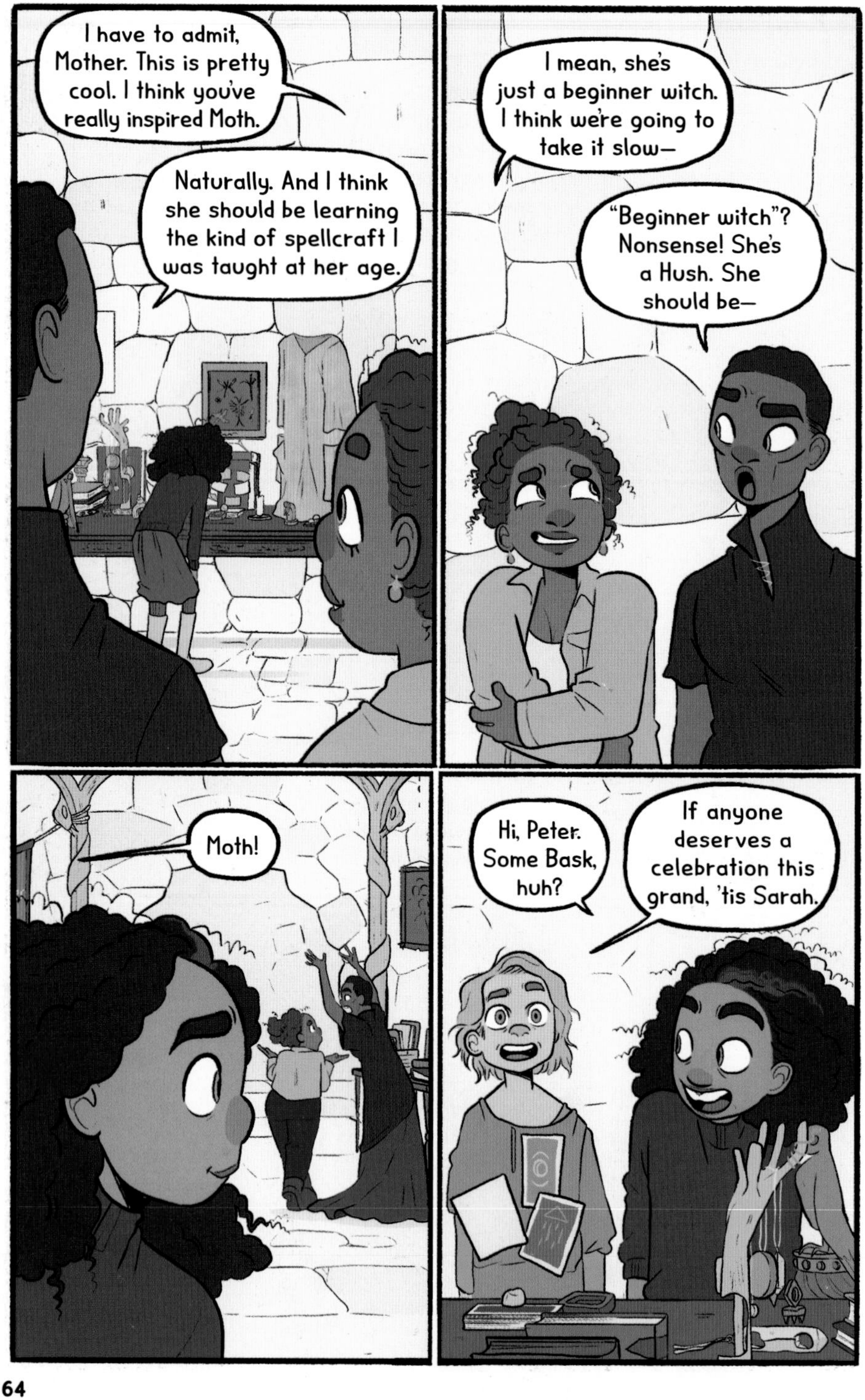

I have to admit, Mother. This is pretty cool. I think you've really inspired Moth.
Naturally. And I think she should be learning the kind of spellcraft I was taught at her age.
I mean, she's just a beginner witch. I think we're going to take it slow—
"Beginner witch"? Nonsense! She's a Hush. She should be—
Moth!
Hi, Peter. Some Bask, huh?
If anyone deserves a celebration this grand, 'tis Sarah.

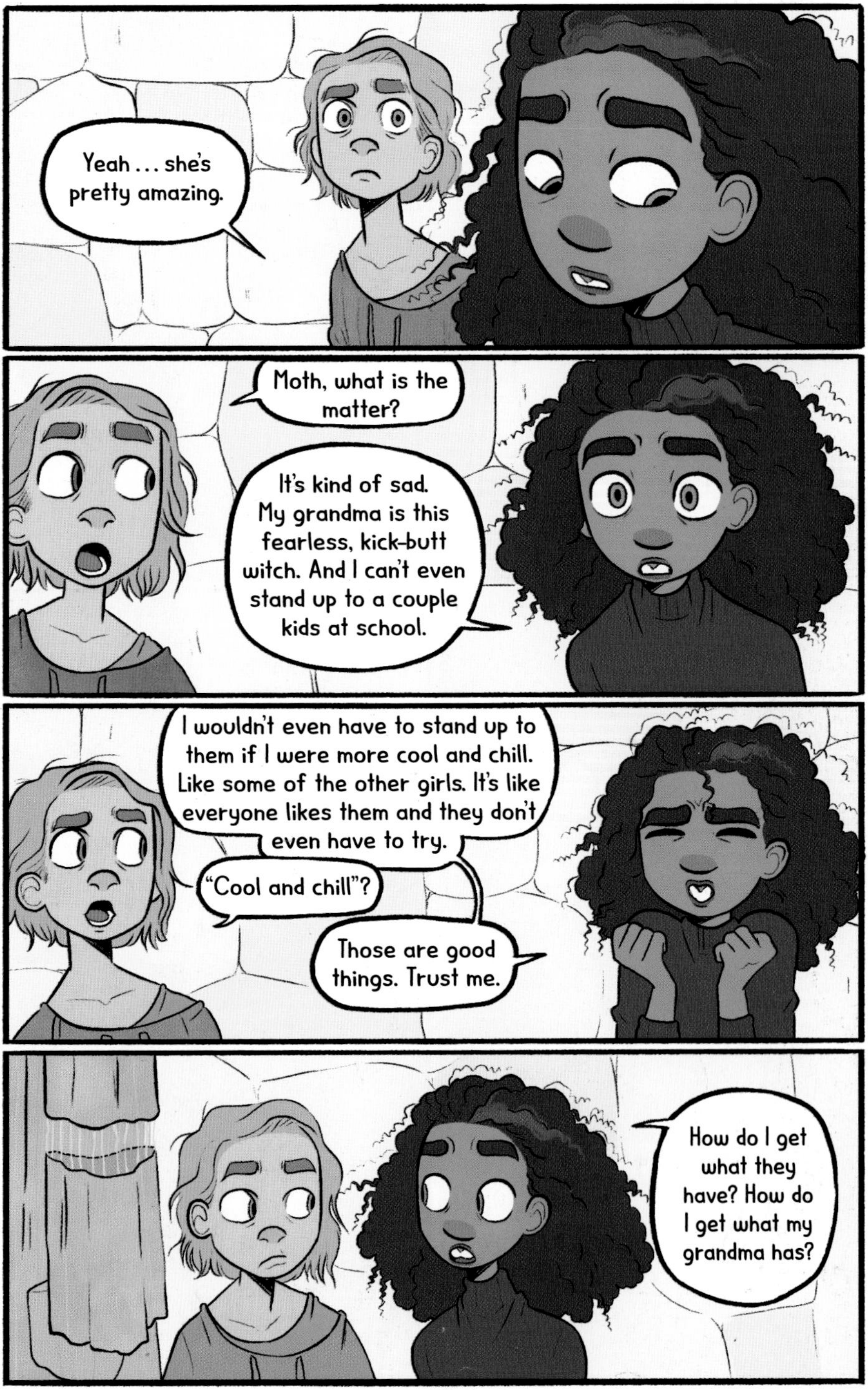

Yeah . . . she's pretty amazing.
Moth, what is the matter?
It's kind of sad. My grandma is this fearless, kick-butt witch. And I can't even stand up to a couple kids at school.
I wouldn't even have to stand up to them if I were more cool and chill. Like some of the other girls. It's like everyone likes them and they don't even have to try.
"Cool and chill"?
Those are good things. Trust me.
How do I get what they have? How do I get what my grandma has?

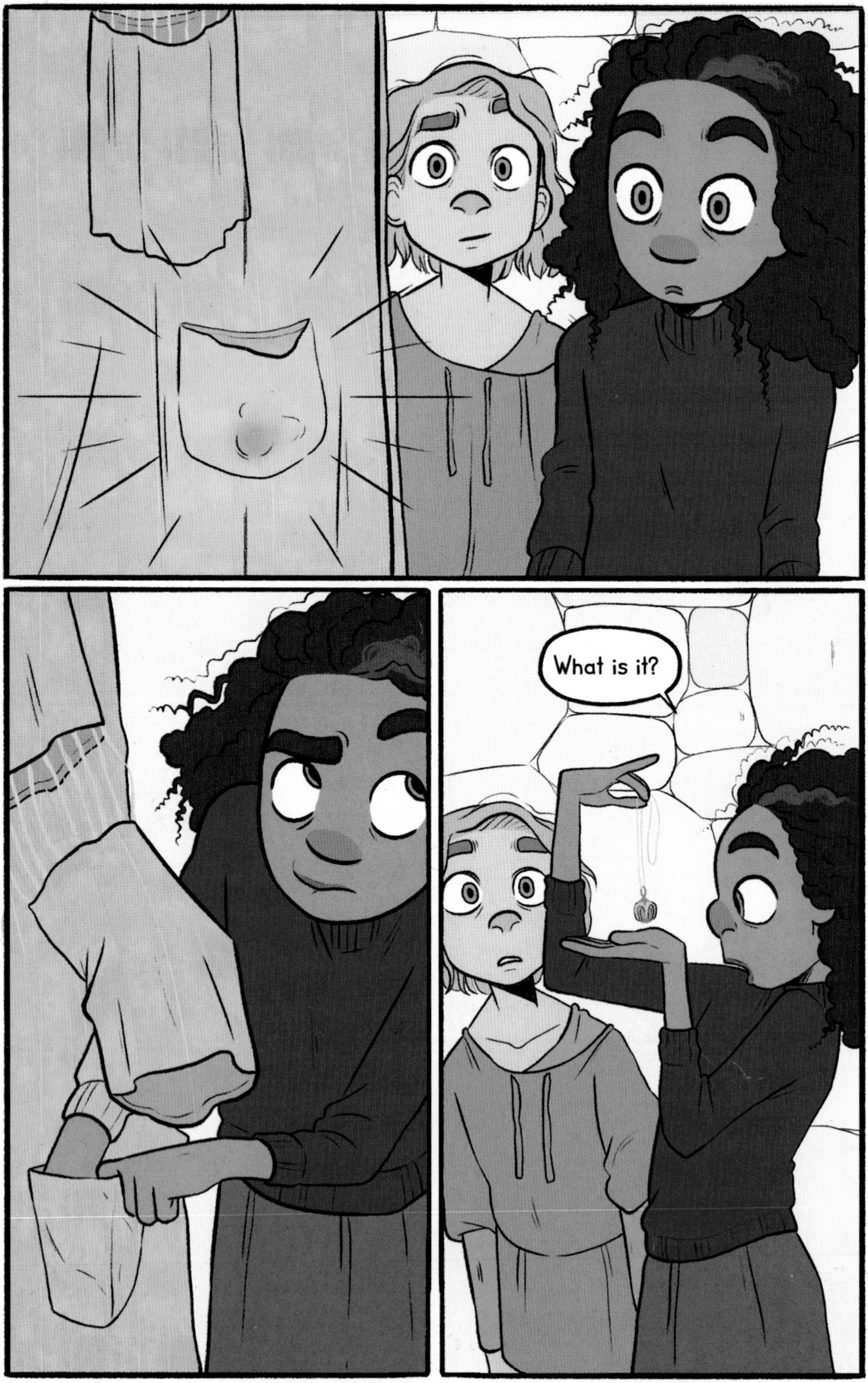
What is it?

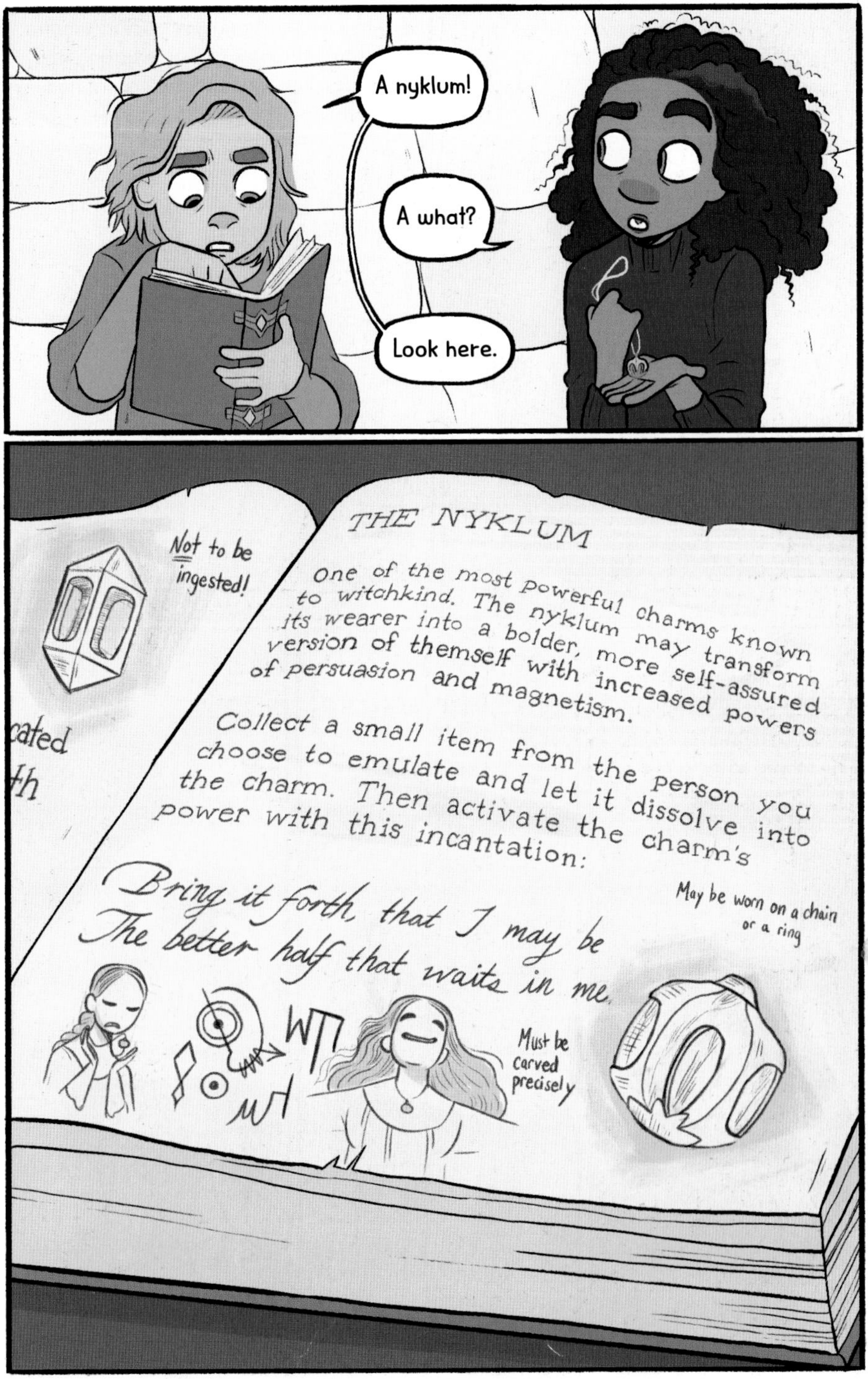
A nyklum!
A what?
Look here.
Not to be ingested!
cated
th
THE NYKLUM
One of the most powerful charms known to witchkind. The nyklum may transform its wearer into a bolder, more self-assured version of themself with increased powers of persuasion and magnetism.
Collect a small item from the person you choose to emulate and let it dissolve into the charm. Then activate the charm's power with this incantation:
Bring it forth that I may be
The better half that waits in me.
May be worn on a chain or a ring
Must be carved precisely

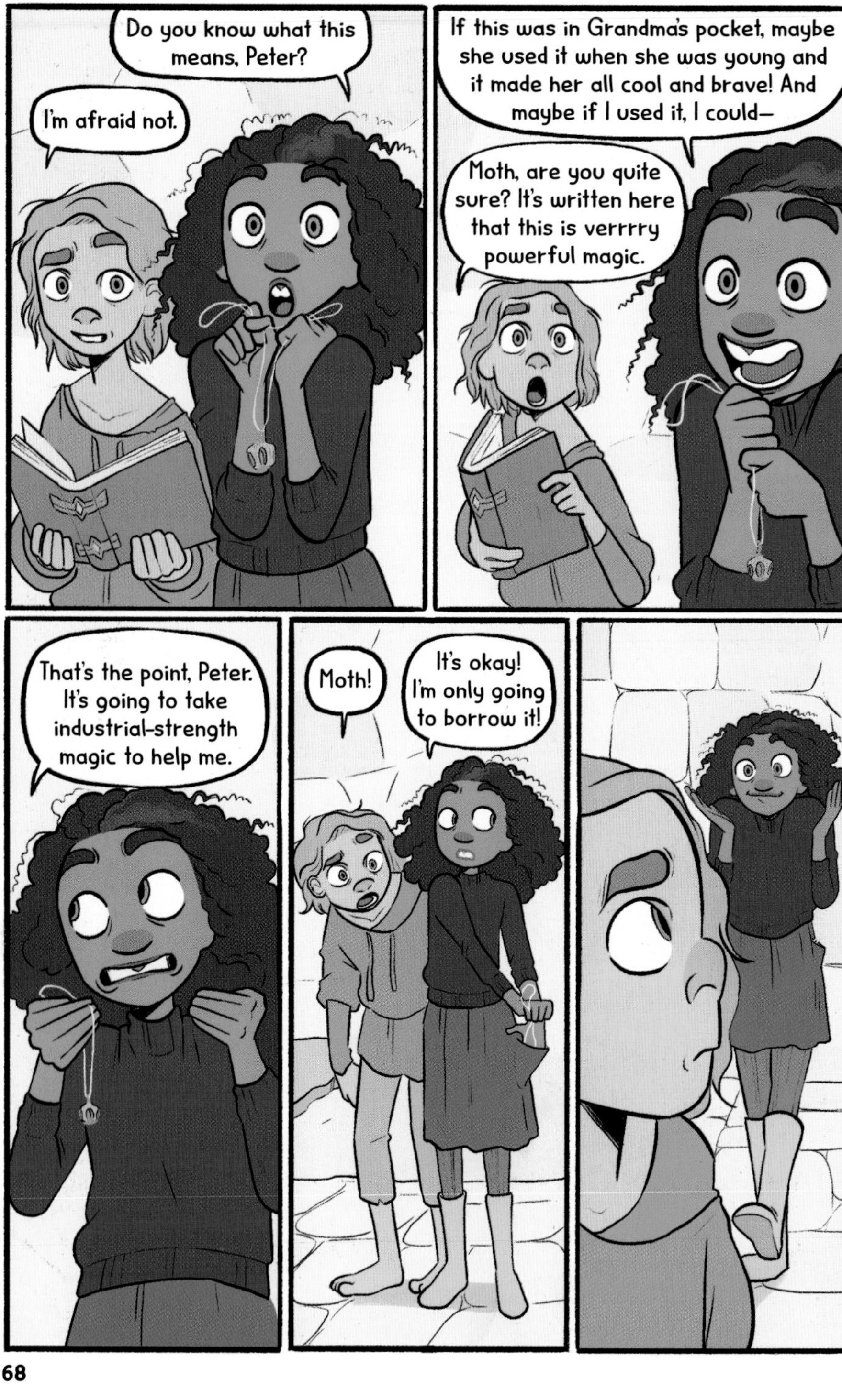
Do you know what this means, Peter?
I'm afraid not.
If this was in Grandma's pocket, maybe she used it when she was young and it made her all cool and brave! And maybe if I used it, I could—
Moth, are you quite sure? It's written here that this is verrrry powerful magic.
That's the point, Peter. It's going to take industrial-strength magic to help me.
Moth!
It's okay! I'm only going to borrow it!

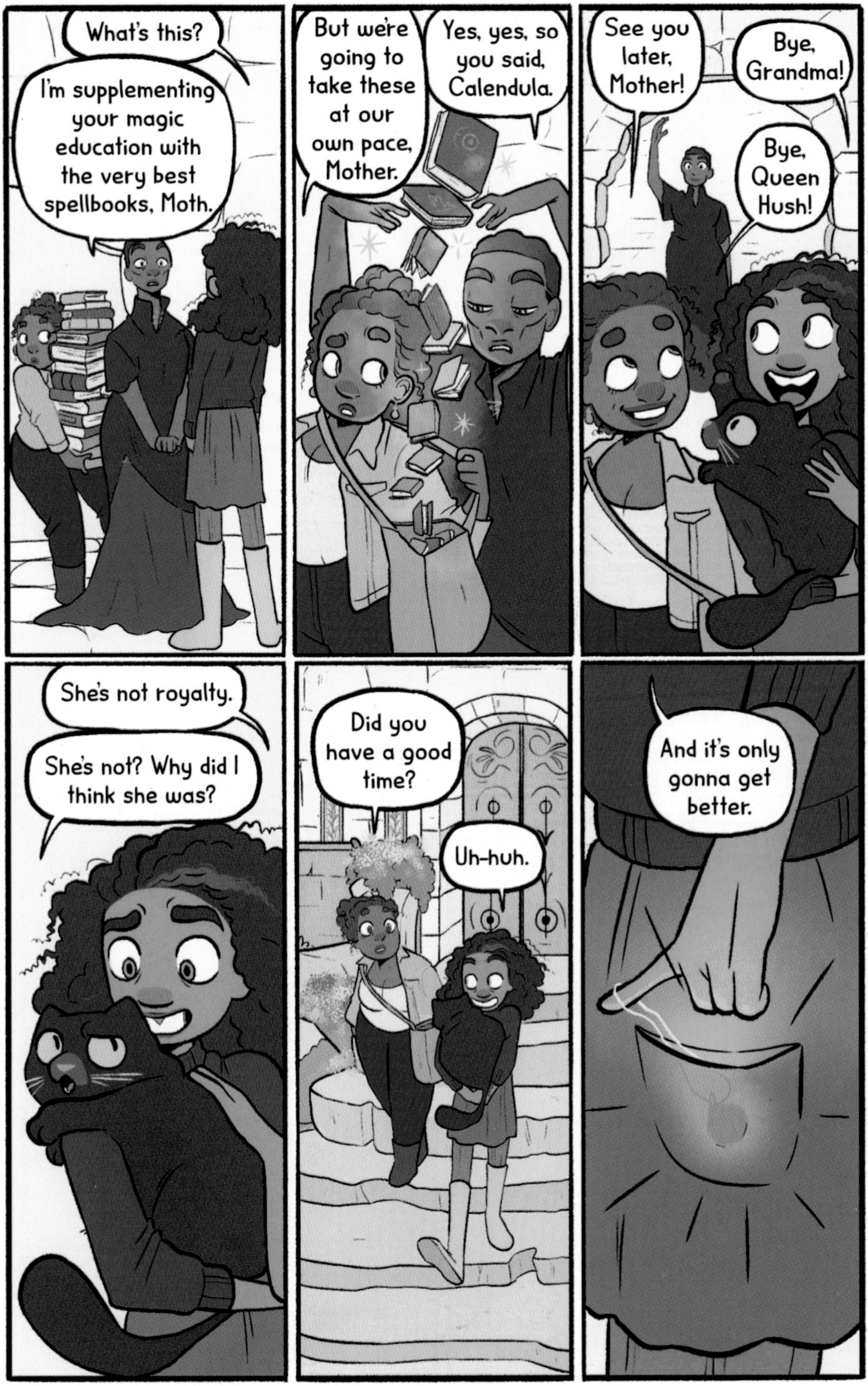
What's this?
I'm supplementing your magic education with the very best spellbooks, Moth.
But we're going to take these at our own pace, Mother.
Yes, yes, so you said, Calendula.
See you later, Mother!
Bye, Grandma!
Bye, Queen Hush!
She's not royalty.
She's not? Why did I think she was?
Did you have a good time?
Uh-huh.
And it's only gonna get better.

CHAPTER 4

The Most Popular Girls

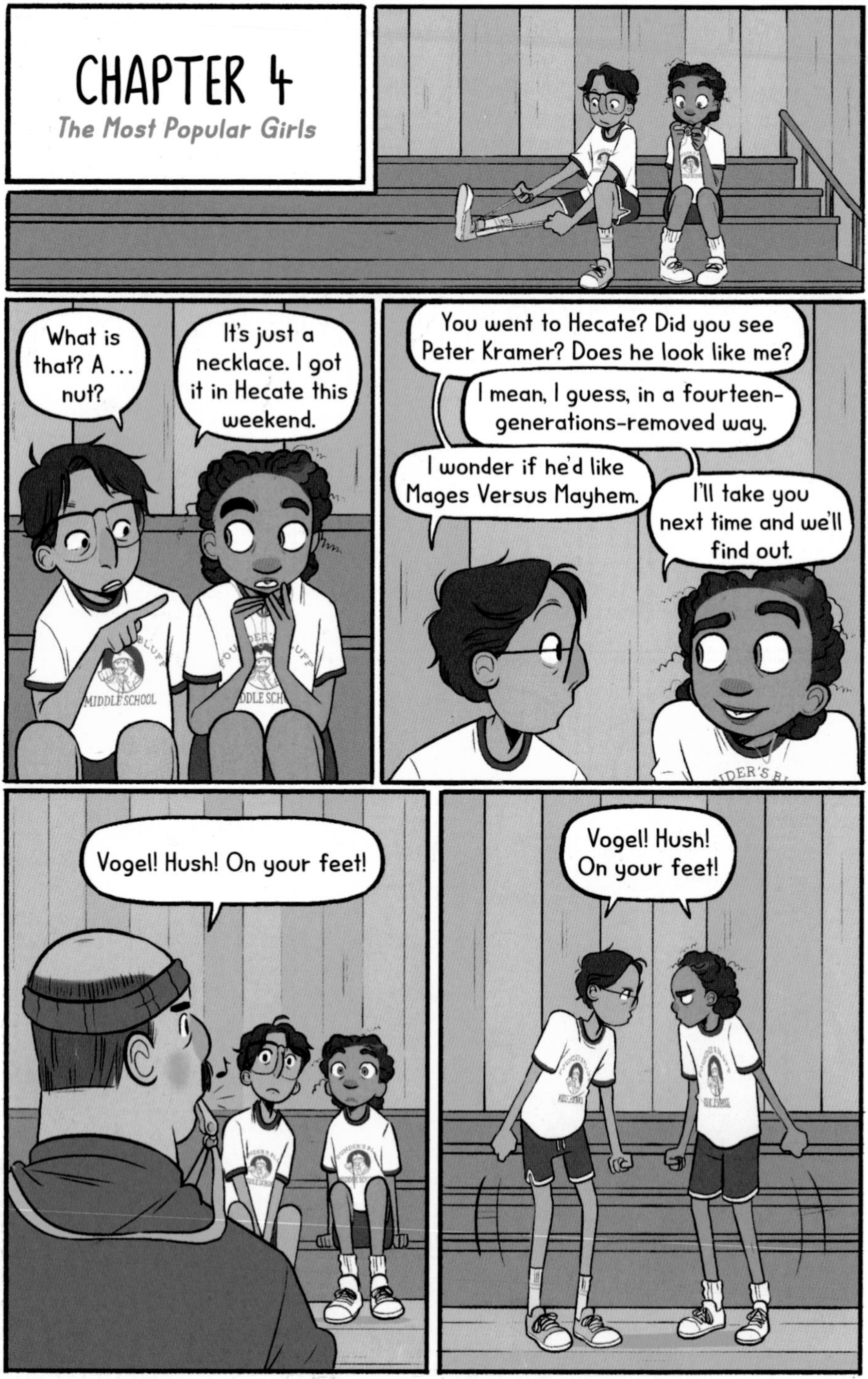

What is that? A . . . nut?
It's just a necklace. I got it in Hecate this weekend.
MIDDLE SCHOOL
You went to Hecate? Did you see Peter Kramer? Does he look like me?
I mean, I guess, in a fourteen-generations-removed way.
I wonder if he'd like Mages Versus Mayhem.
I'll take you next time and we'll find out.
Vogel! Hush! On your feet!
Vogel! Hush! On your feet!

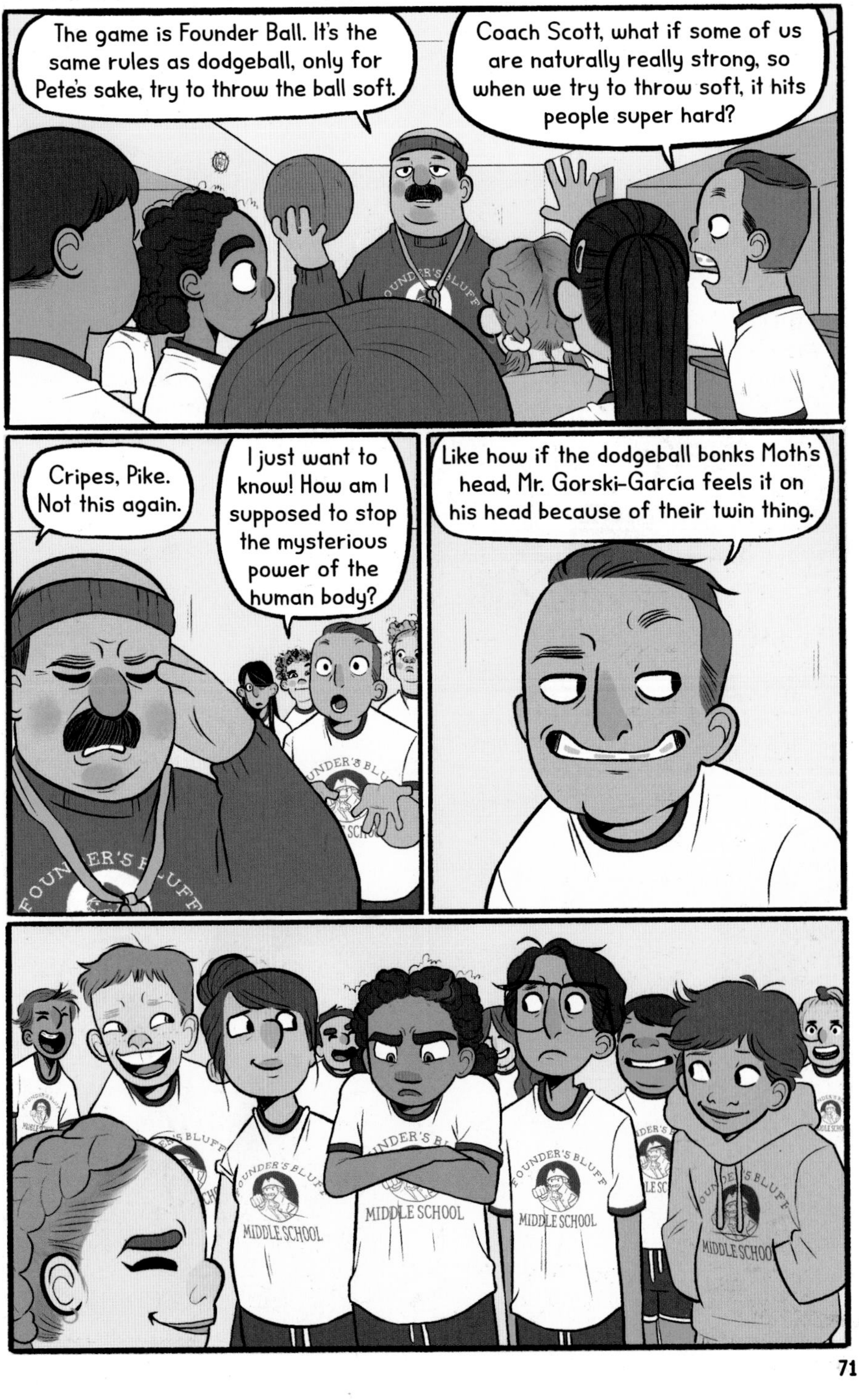
The game is Founder Ball. It's the same rules as dodgeball, only for Pete's sake, try to throw the ball soft.
Coach Scott, what if some of us are naturally really strong, so when we try to throw soft, it hits people super hard?
FOUNDER'S BLUFF
Cripes, Pike. Not this again.
I just want to know! How am I supposed to stop the mysterious power of the human body?
Like how if the dodgeball bonks Moth's head, Mr. Gorski-García feels it on his head because of their twin thing.
FOUNDER'S BLUFF
MIDDLE SCHOOL

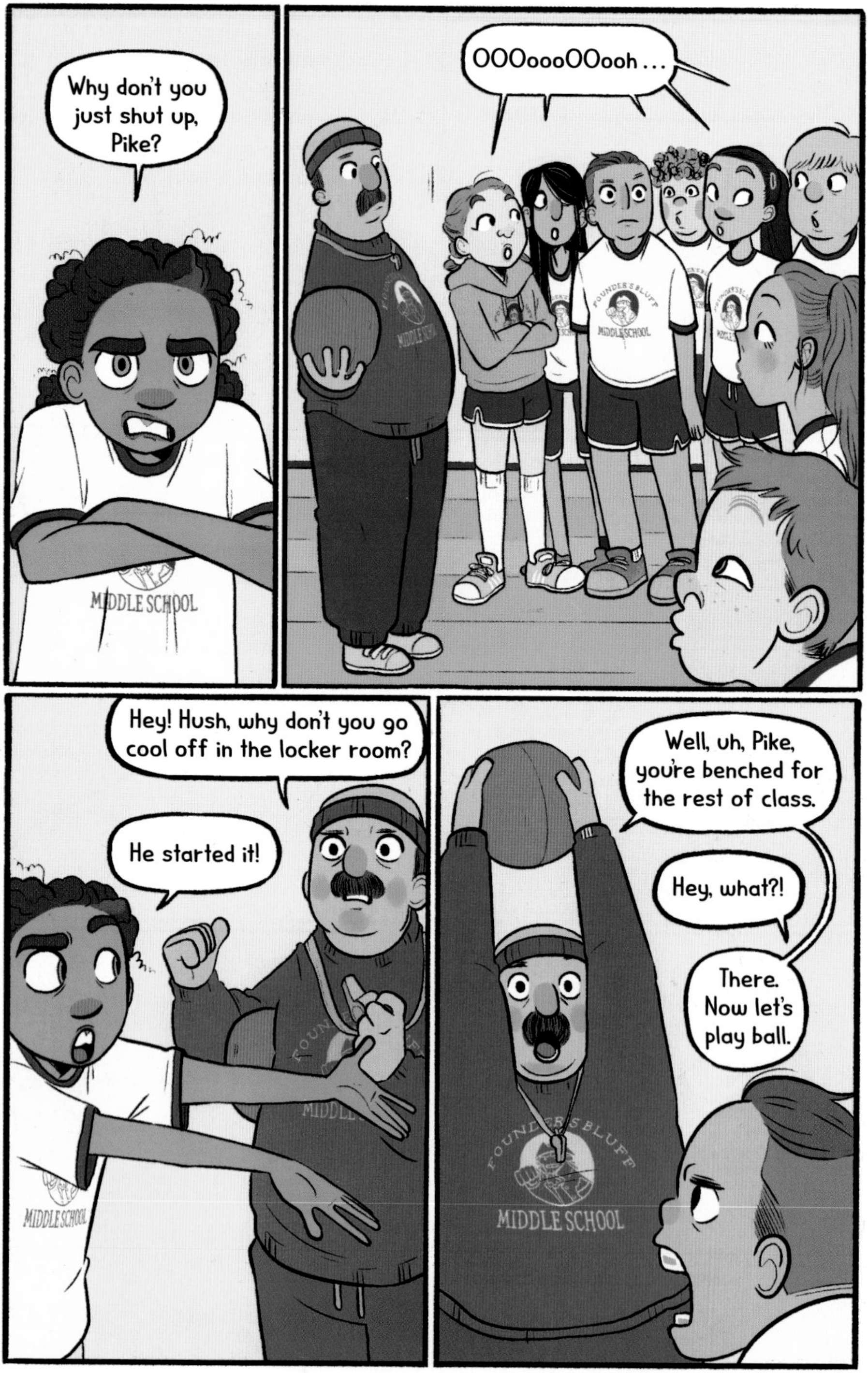
Why don't you just shut up, Pike?
OOOoooOOooh...
MIDDLE SCHOOL
Hey! Hush, why don't you go cool off in the locker room?
He started it!
Well, uh, Pike, you're benched for the rest of class.
Hey, what?!
There. Now let's play ball.
FOUNDER'S BLUFF
MIDDLE SCHOOL

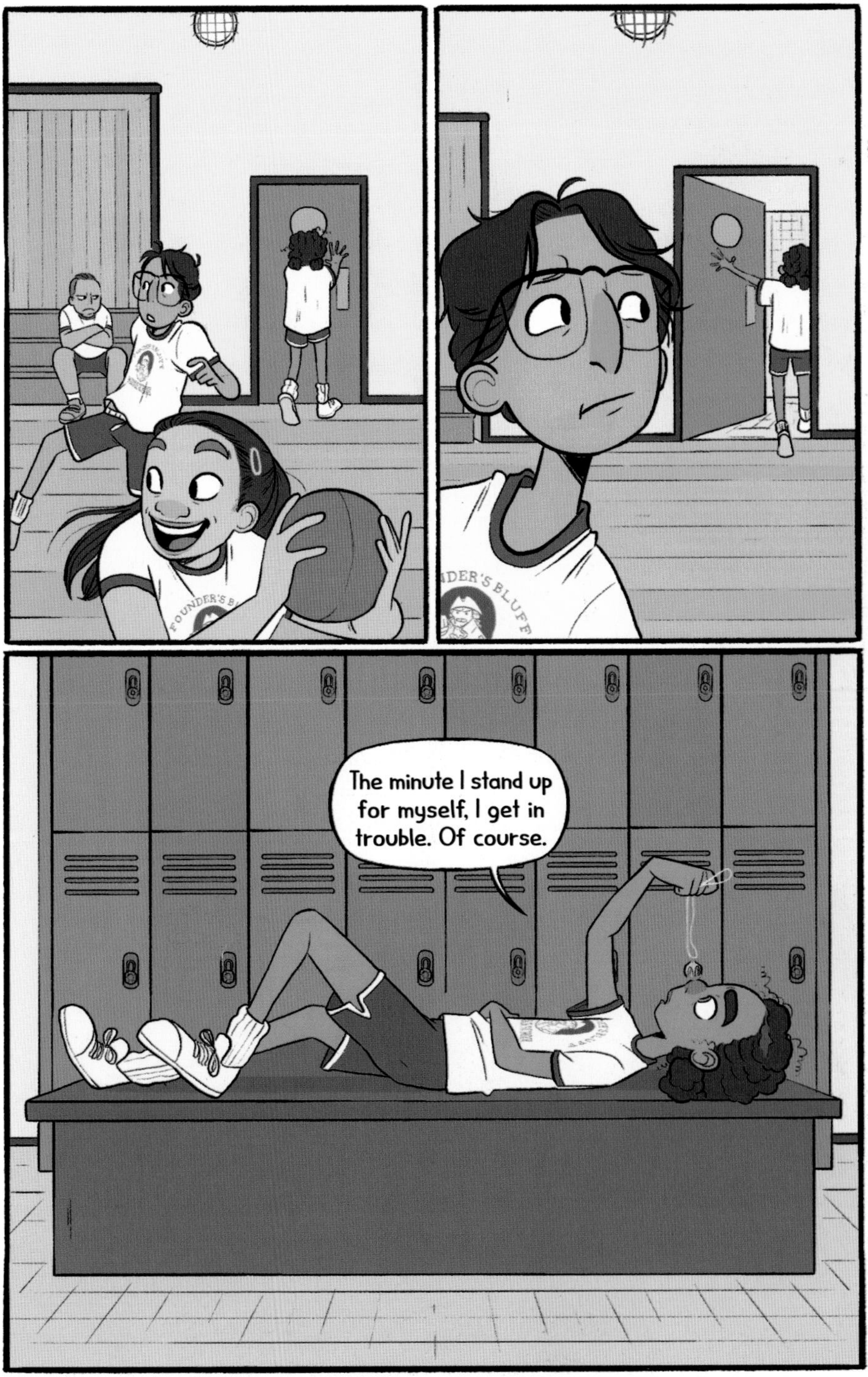
The minute I stand up for myself, I get in trouble. Of course.

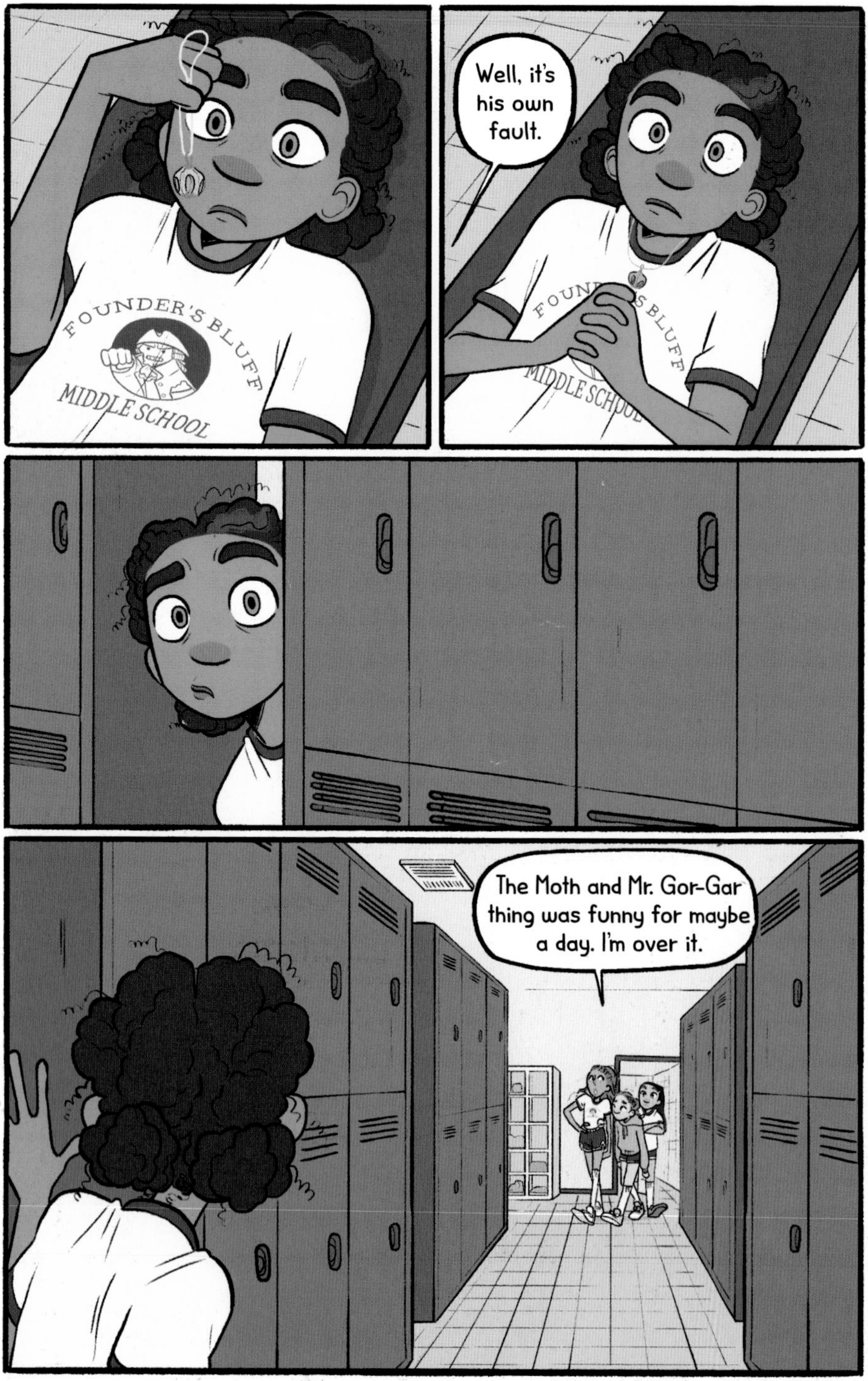
FOUNDER'S BLUFF MIDDLE SCHOOL
Well, it's his own fault.
The Moth and Mr. Gor-Gar thing was funny for maybe a day. I'm over it.

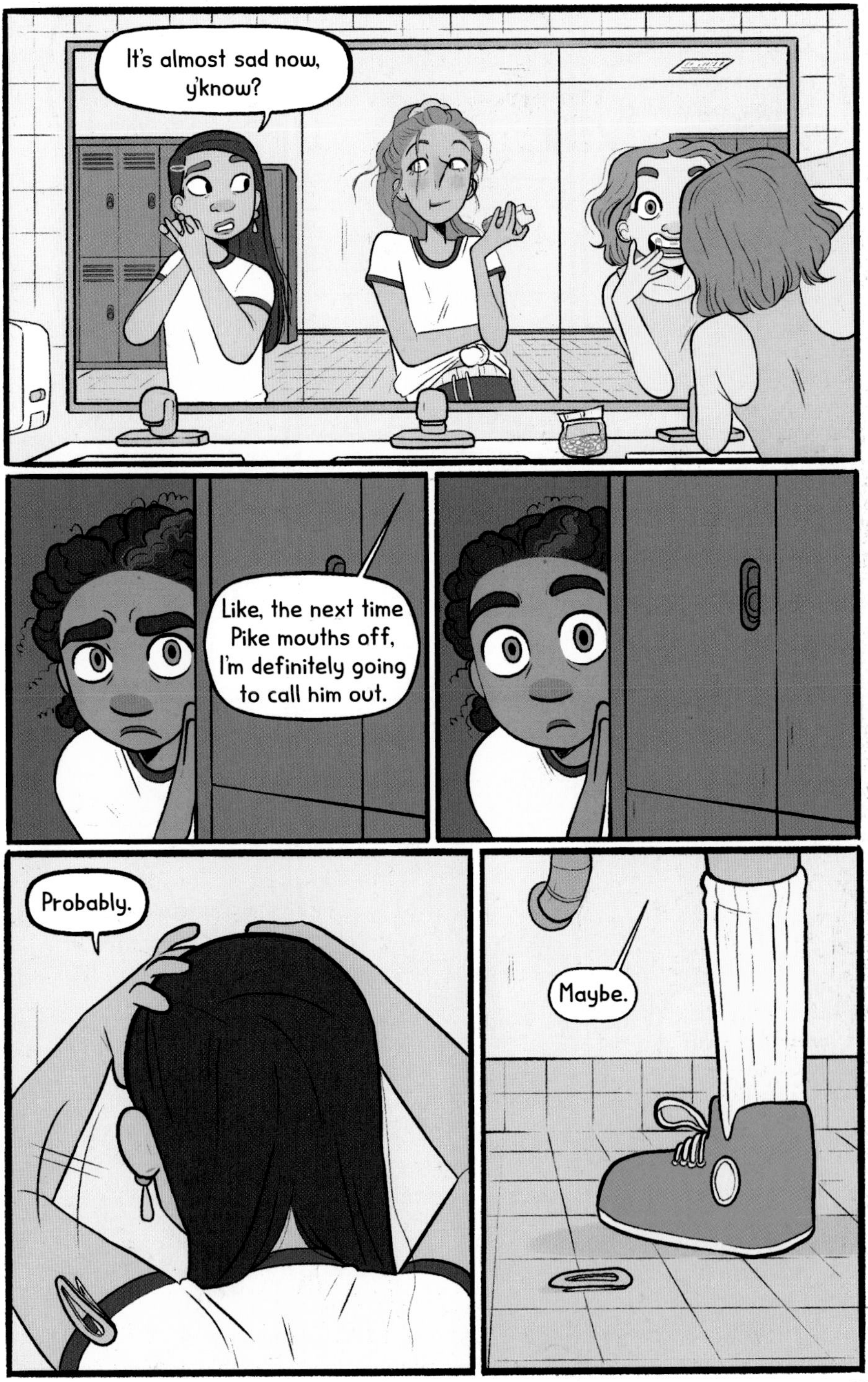

It's almost sad now, y'know?
Like, the next time Pike mouths off, I'm definitely going to call him out.
Probably.
Maybe.

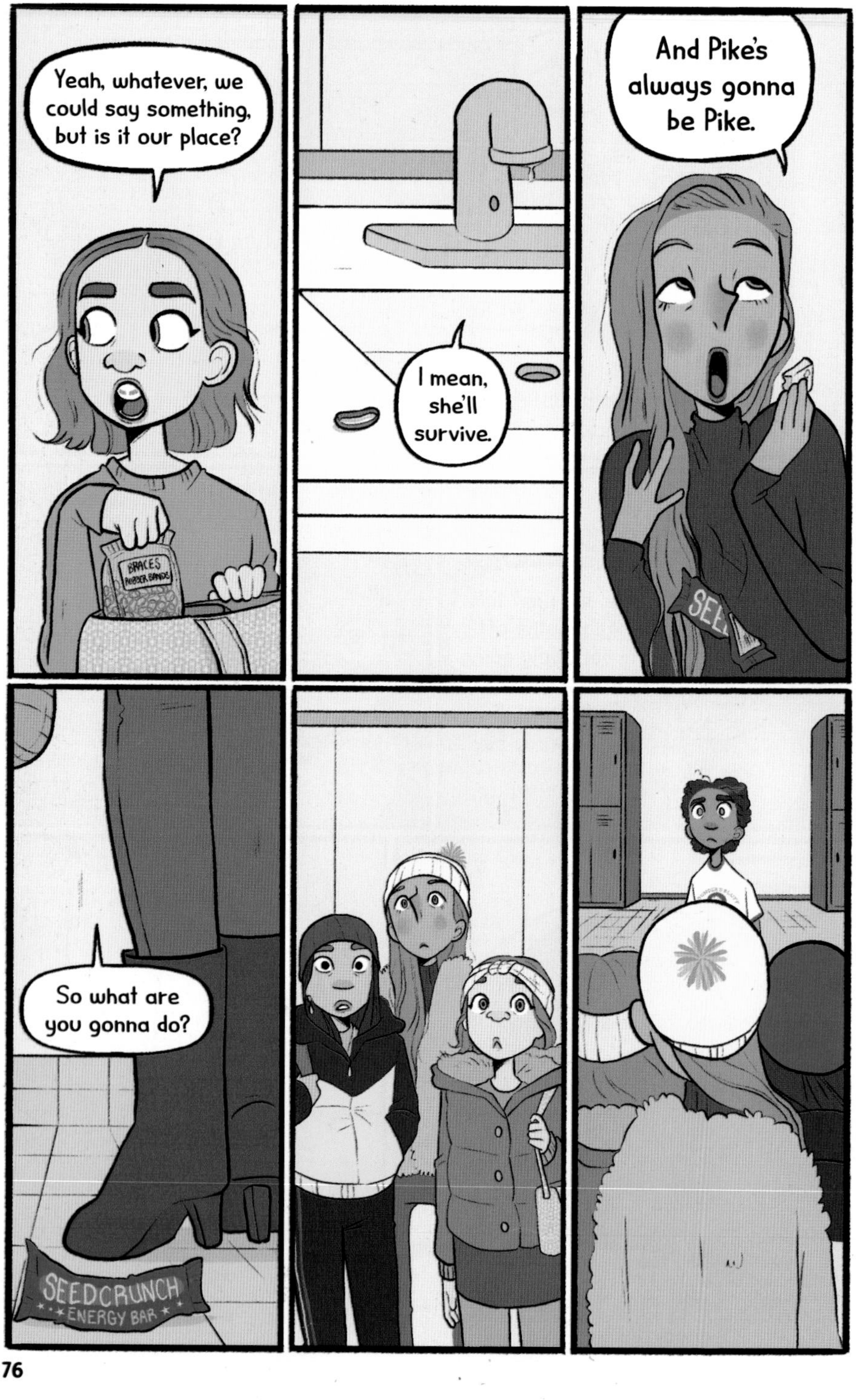
Yeah, whatever, we could say something, but is it our place?
BRACES RUBBER BANDS
I mean, she'll survive.
And Pike's always gonna be Pike.
So what are you gonna do?
SEEDCRUNCH
ENERGY BAR

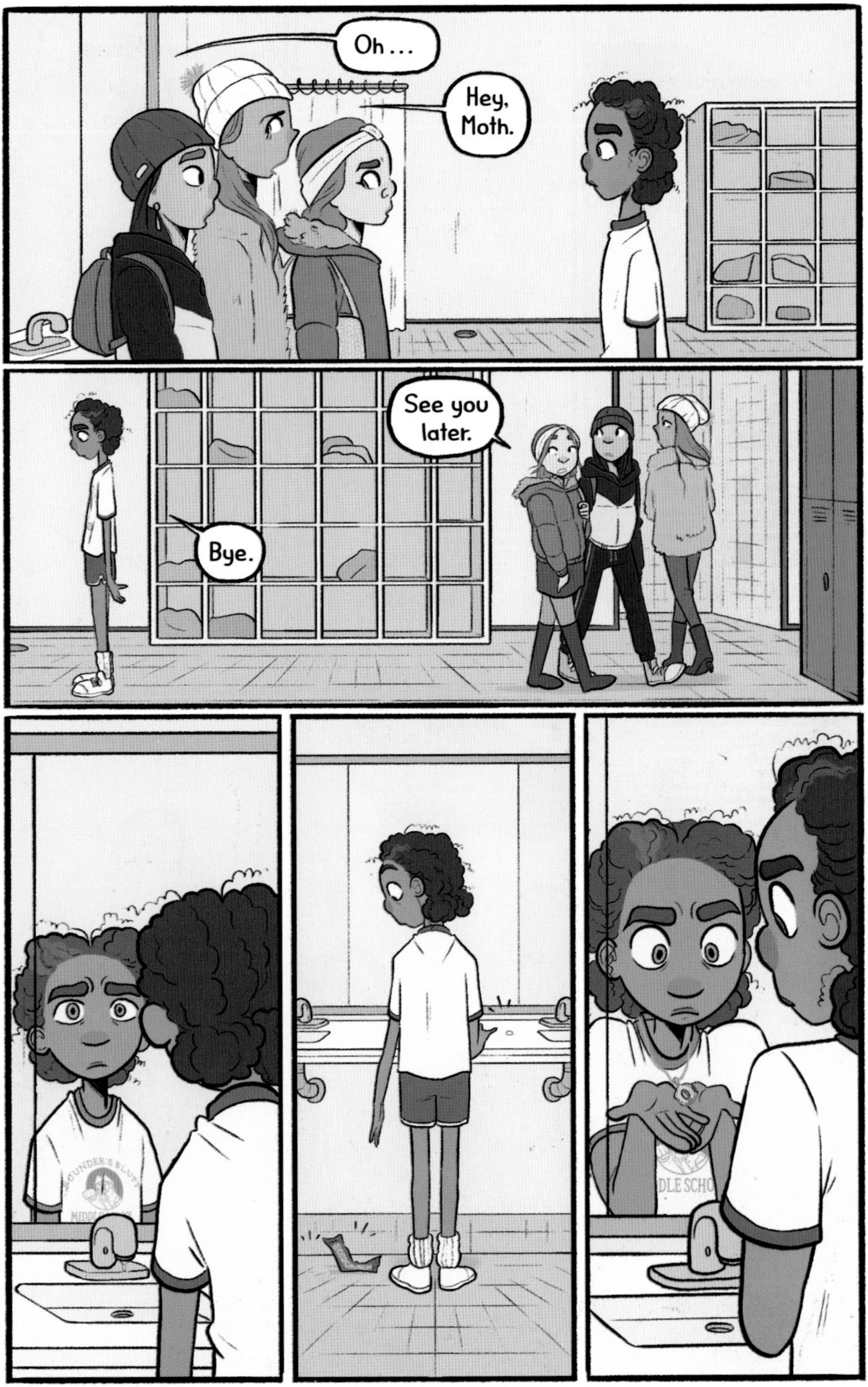
Oh...
Hey, Moth.
See you later.
Bye.

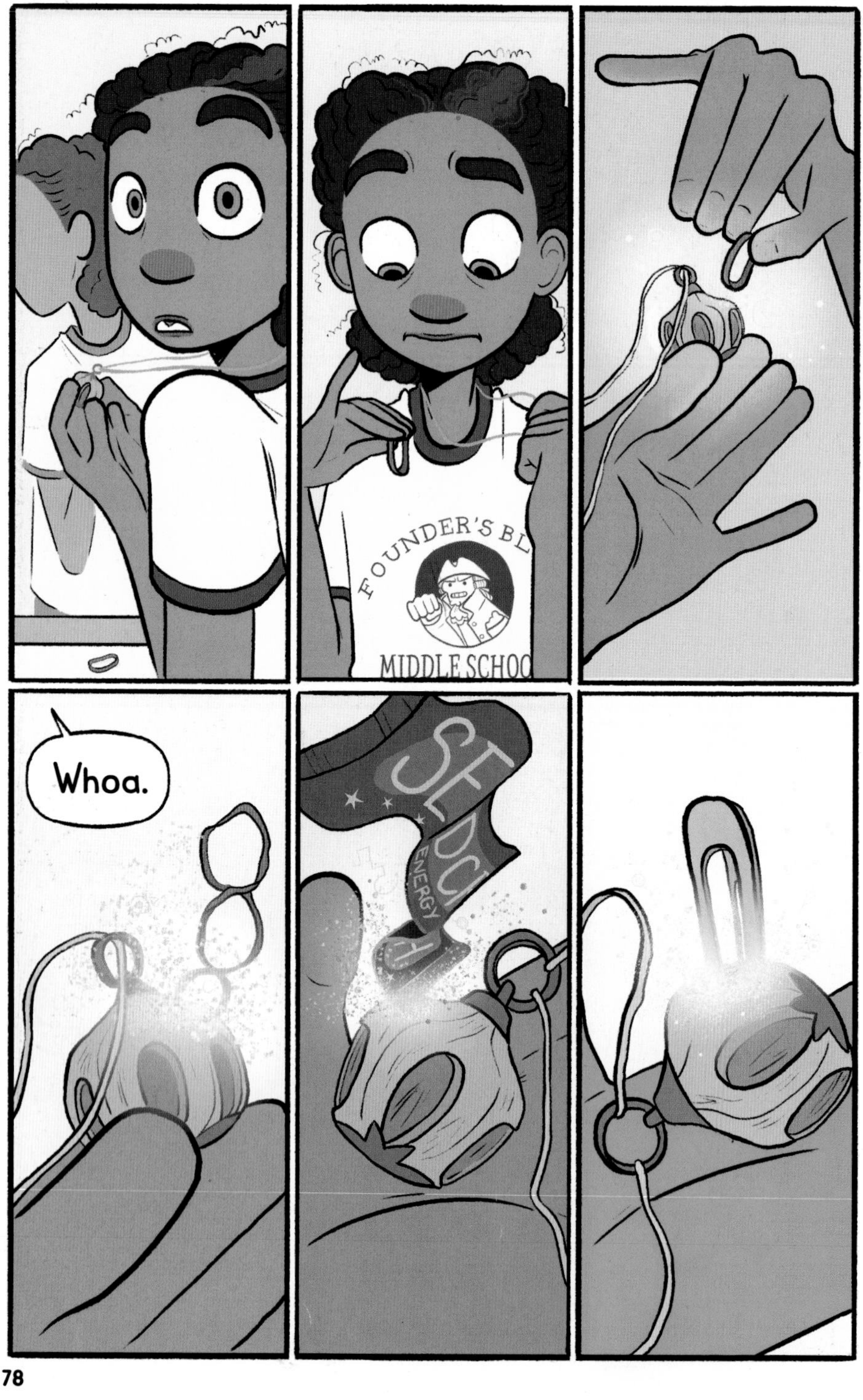
FOUNDER'S BL
MIDDLE SCHOO
Whoa.
SE
DCI
ENERGY

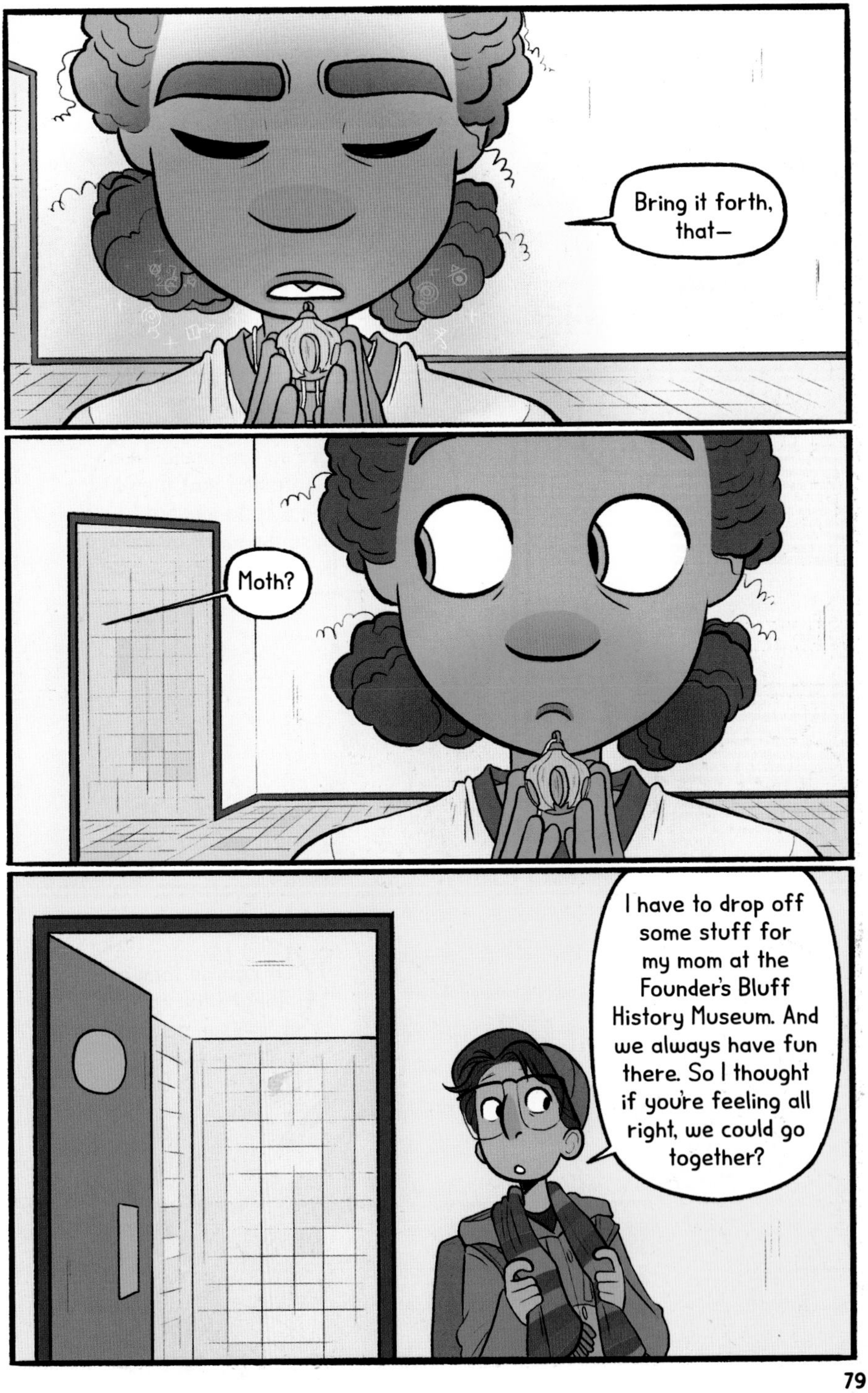
Bring it forth, that—
Moth?
I have to drop off some stuff for my mom at the Founder's Bluff History Museum. And we always have fun there. So I thought if you're feeling all right, we could go together?

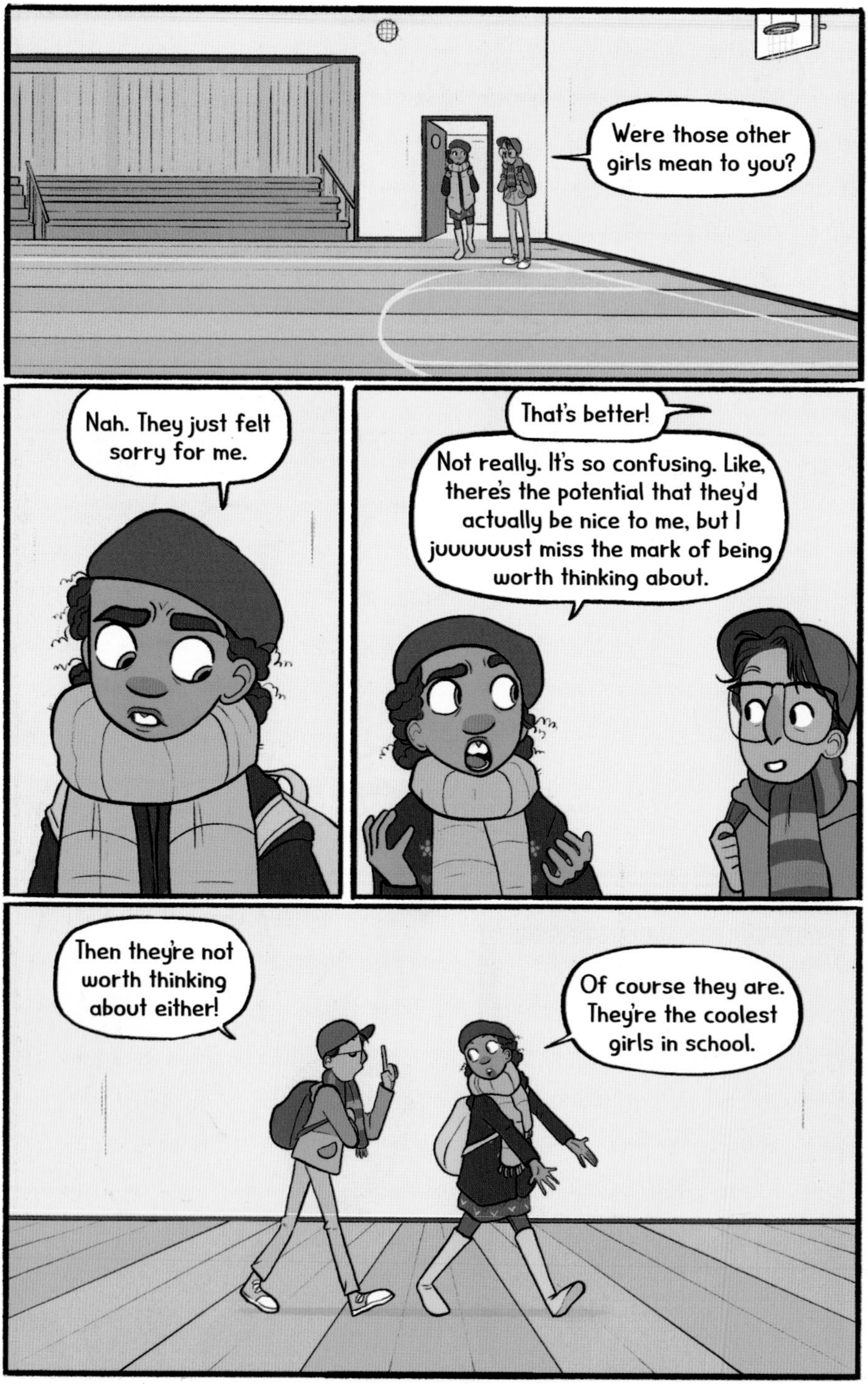
Were those other girls mean to you?
Nah. They just felt sorry for me.
That's better!
Not really. It's so confusing. Like, there's the potential that they'd actually be nice to me, but I juuuuuust miss the mark of being worth thinking about.
Then they're not worth thinking about either!
Of course they are. They're the coolest girls in school.

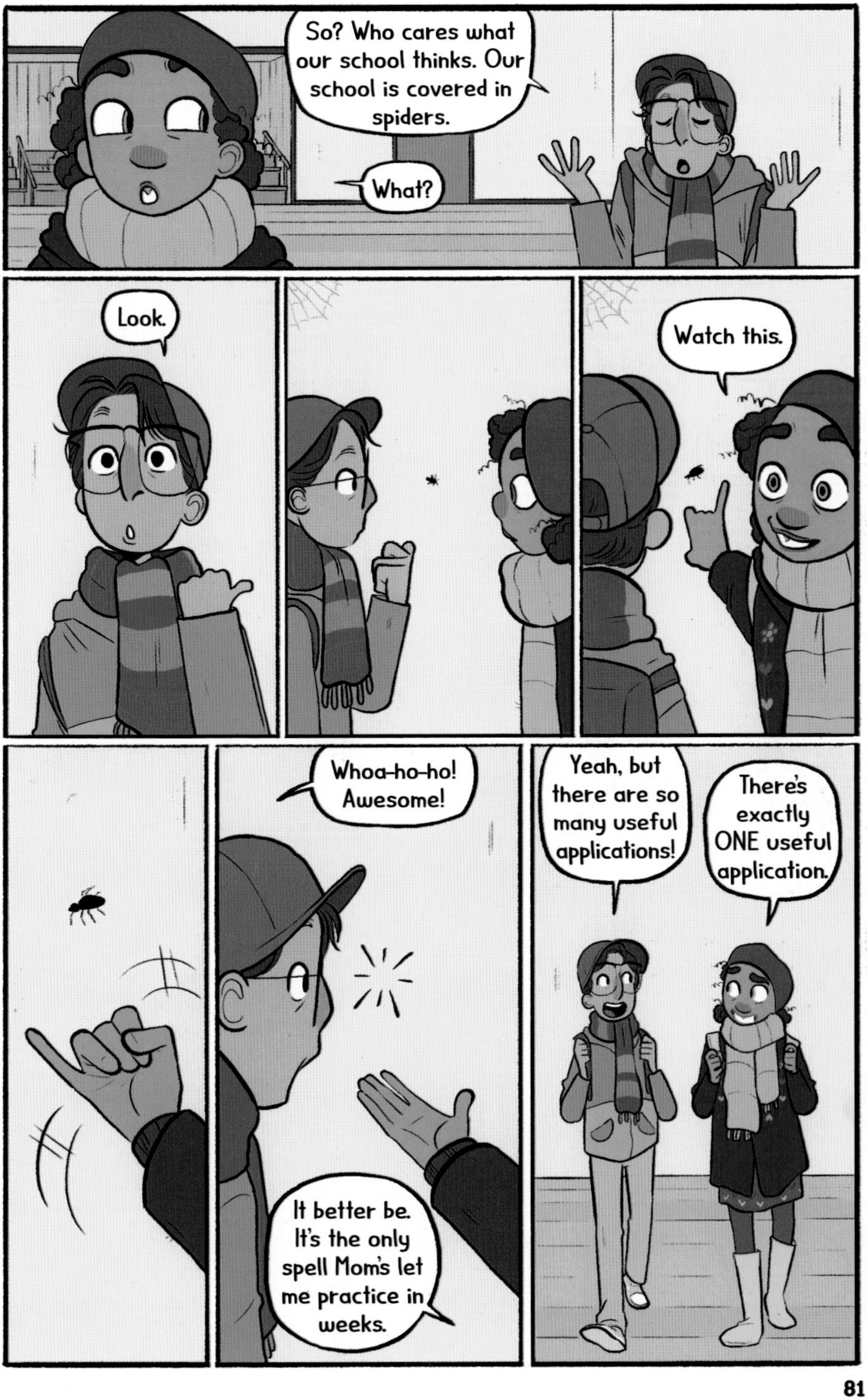
So? Who cares what our school thinks. Our school is covered in spiders.
What?
Look.
Watch this.
Whoa-ho-ho! Awesome!
It better be. It's the only spell Mom's let me practice in weeks.
Yeah, but there are so many useful applications!
There's exactly ONE useful application.

CHAPTER 5
Founderella

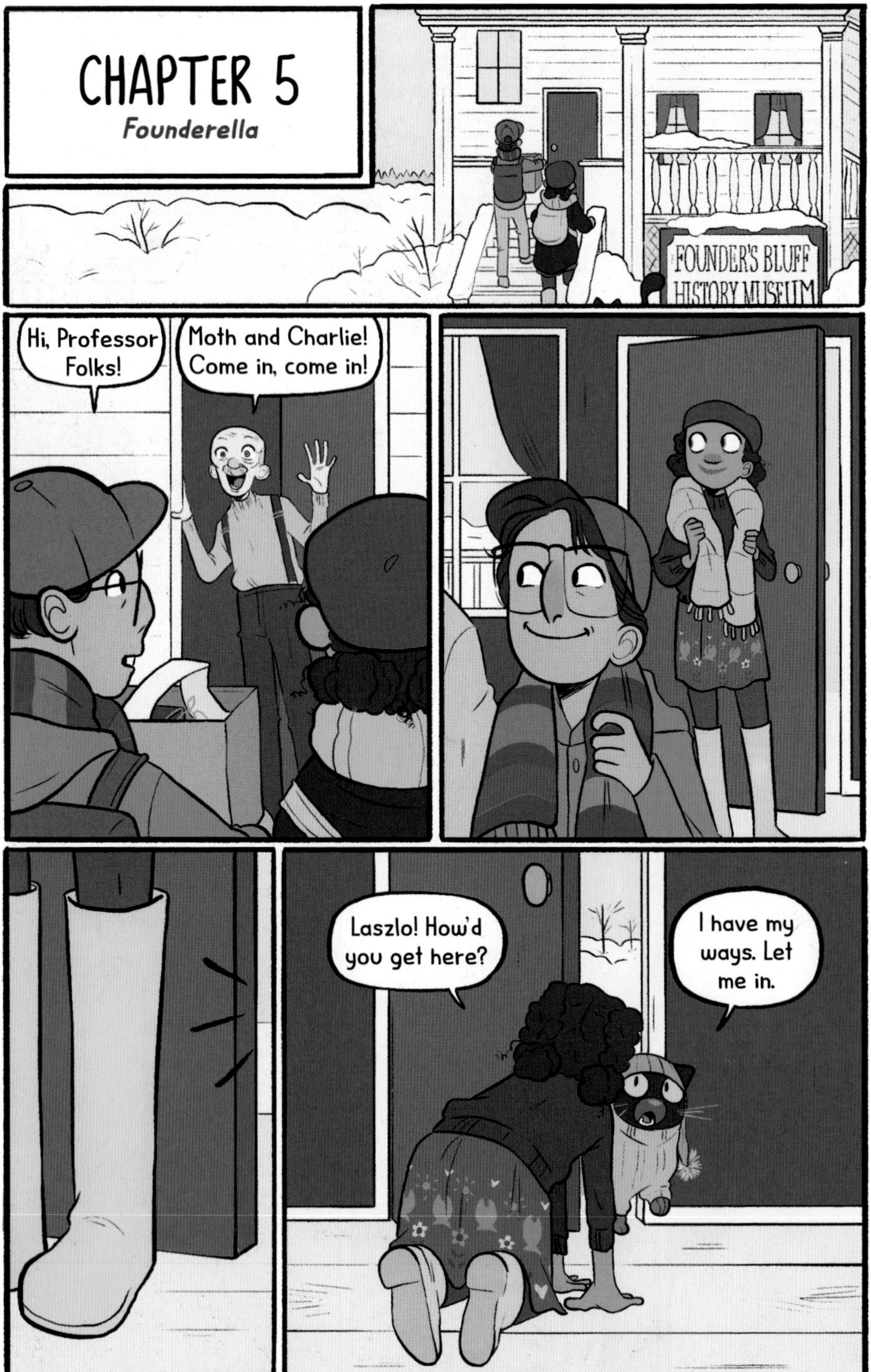
FOUNDER'S BLUFF HISTORY MUSEUM
Hi, Professor Folks!
Moth and Charlie! Come in, come in!
Laszlo! How'd you get here?
I have my ways. Let me in.

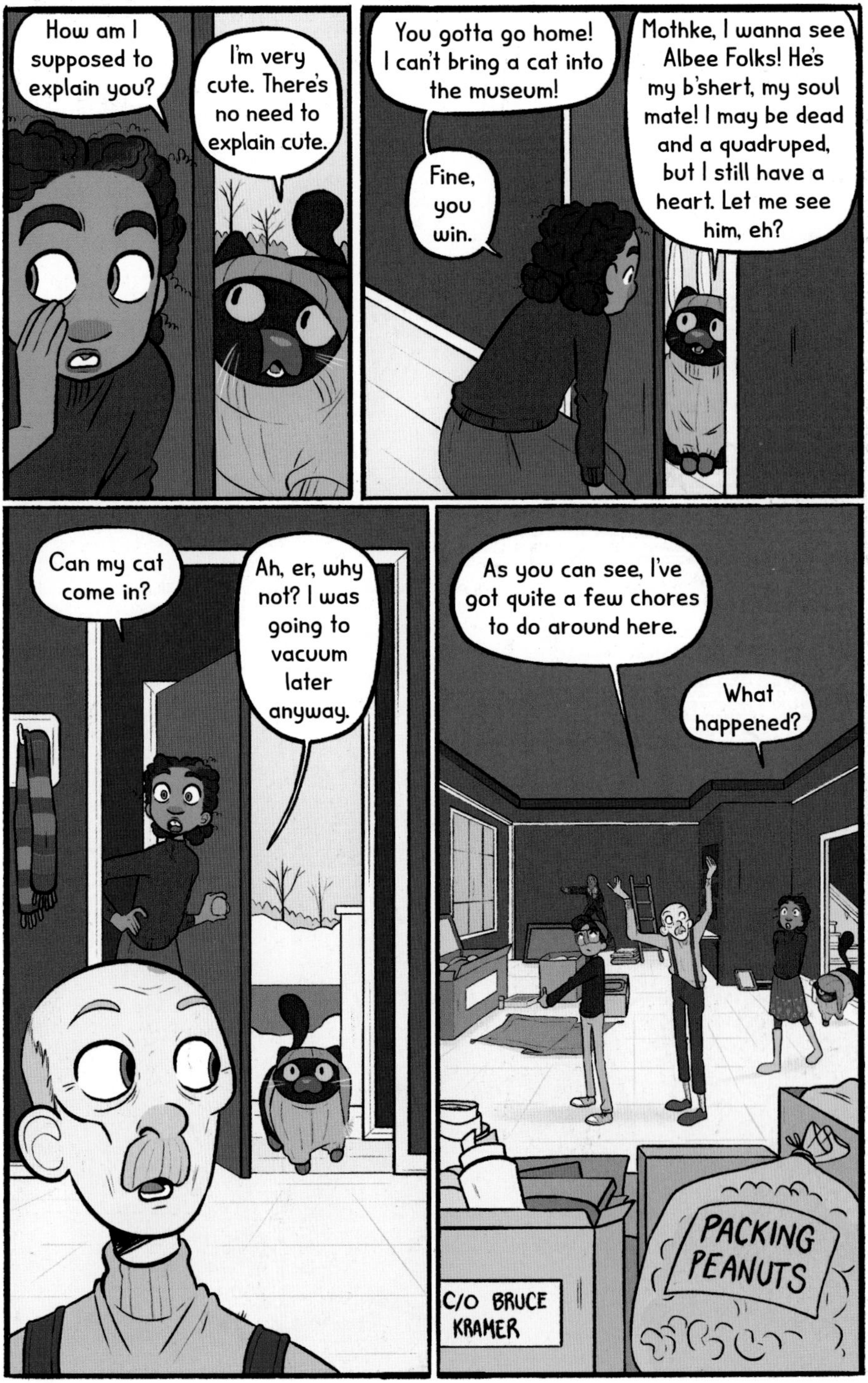
How am I supposed to explain you?
I'm very cute. There's no need to explain cute.
You gotta go home! I can't bring a cat into the museum!
Fine, you win.
Mothke, I wanna see Albee Folks! He's my b'shert, my soul mate! I may be dead and a quadruped, but I still have a heart. Let me see him, eh?
Can my cat come in?
Ah, er, why not? I was going to vacuum later anyway.
As you can see, I've got quite a few chores to do around here.
What happened?
PACKING PEANUTS
C/O BRUCE KRAMER

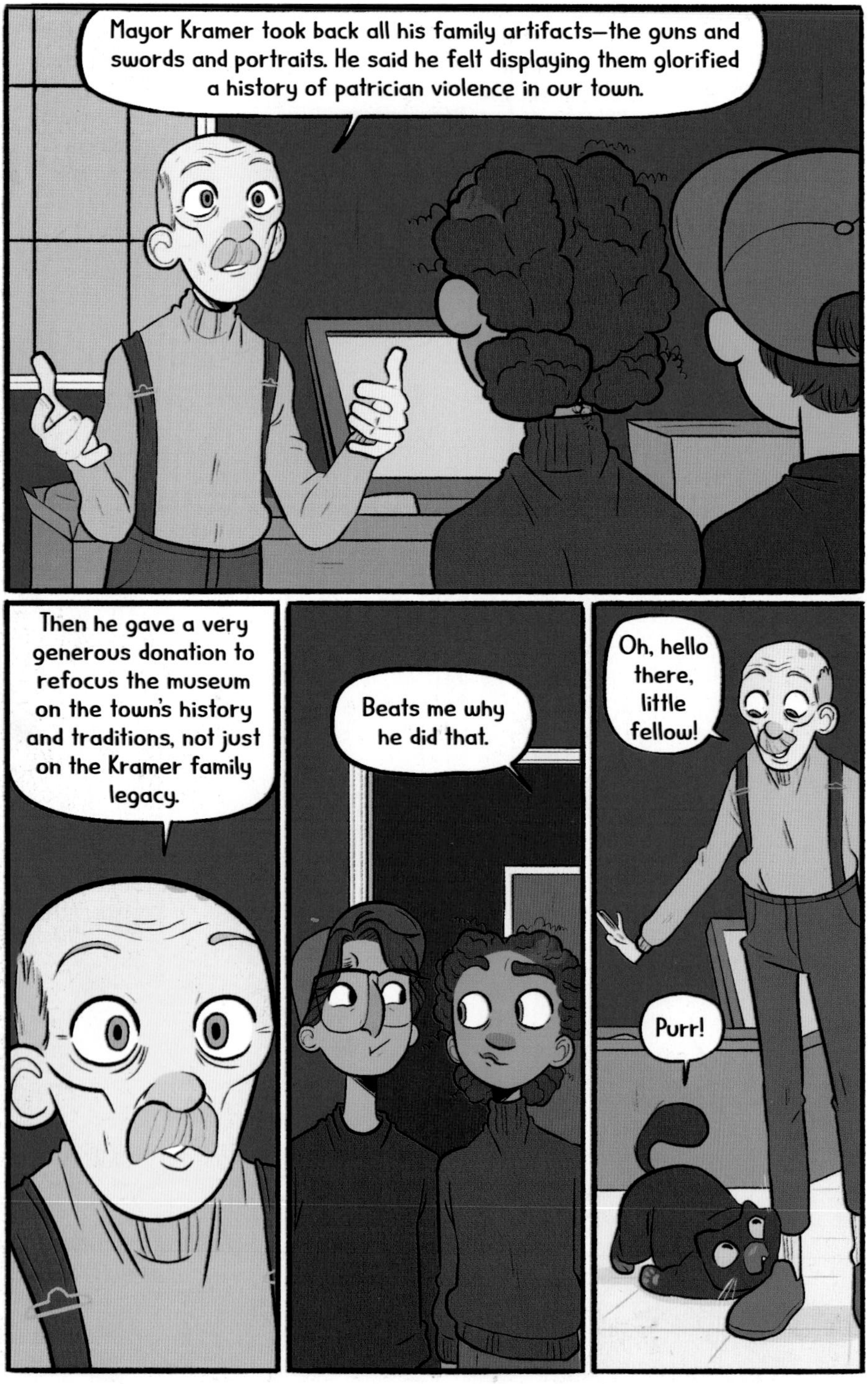
Mayor Kramer took back all his family artifacts—the guns and swords and portraits. He said he felt displaying them glorified a history of patrician violence in our town.
Then he gave a very generous donation to refocus the museum on the town's history and traditions, not just on the Kramer family legacy.
Beats me why he did that.
Oh, hello there, little fellow!
Purr!

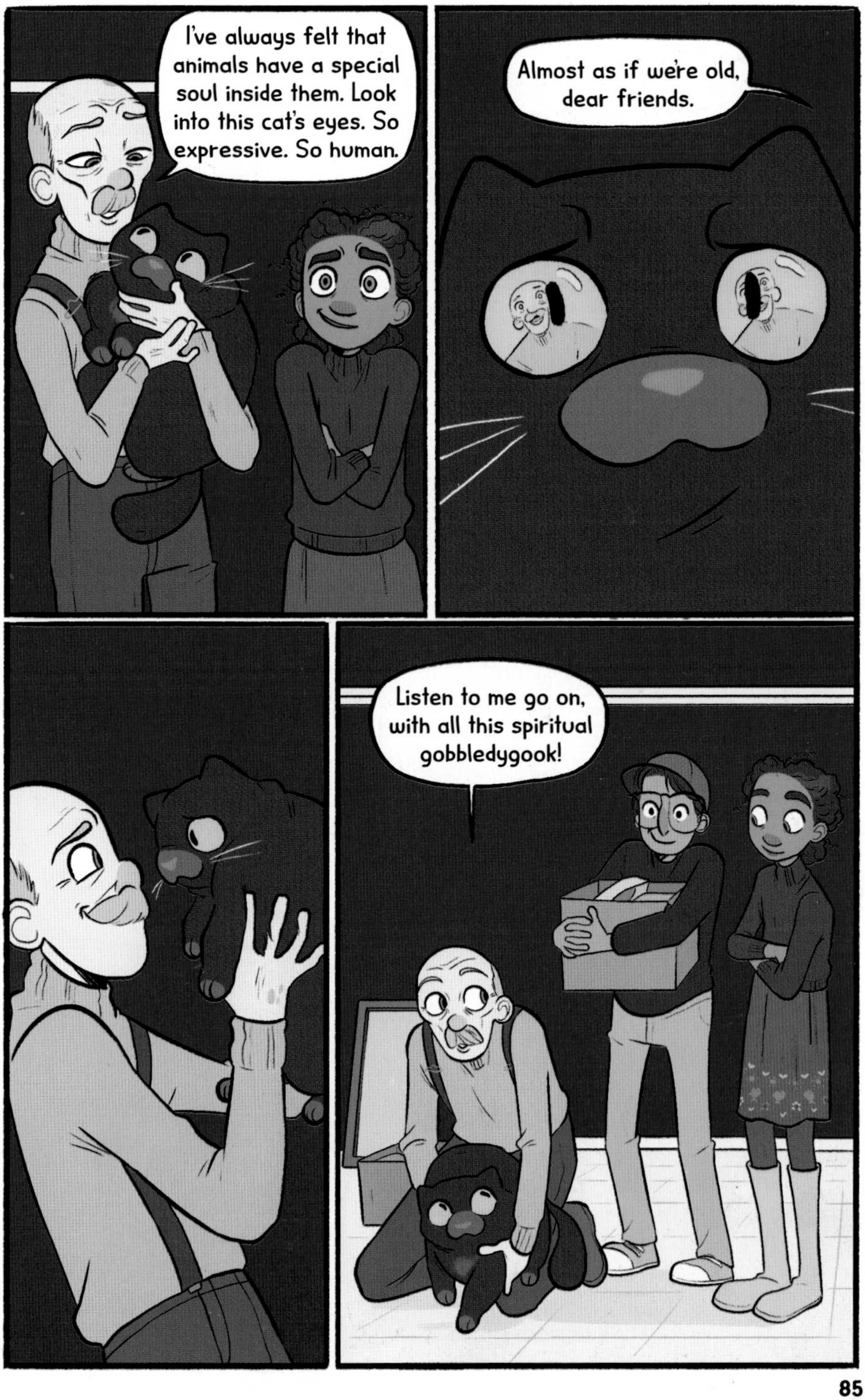
I've always felt that animals have a special soul inside them. Look into this cat's eyes. So expressive. So human.
Almost as if we're old, dear friends.
Listen to me go on, with all this spiritual gobbledygook!

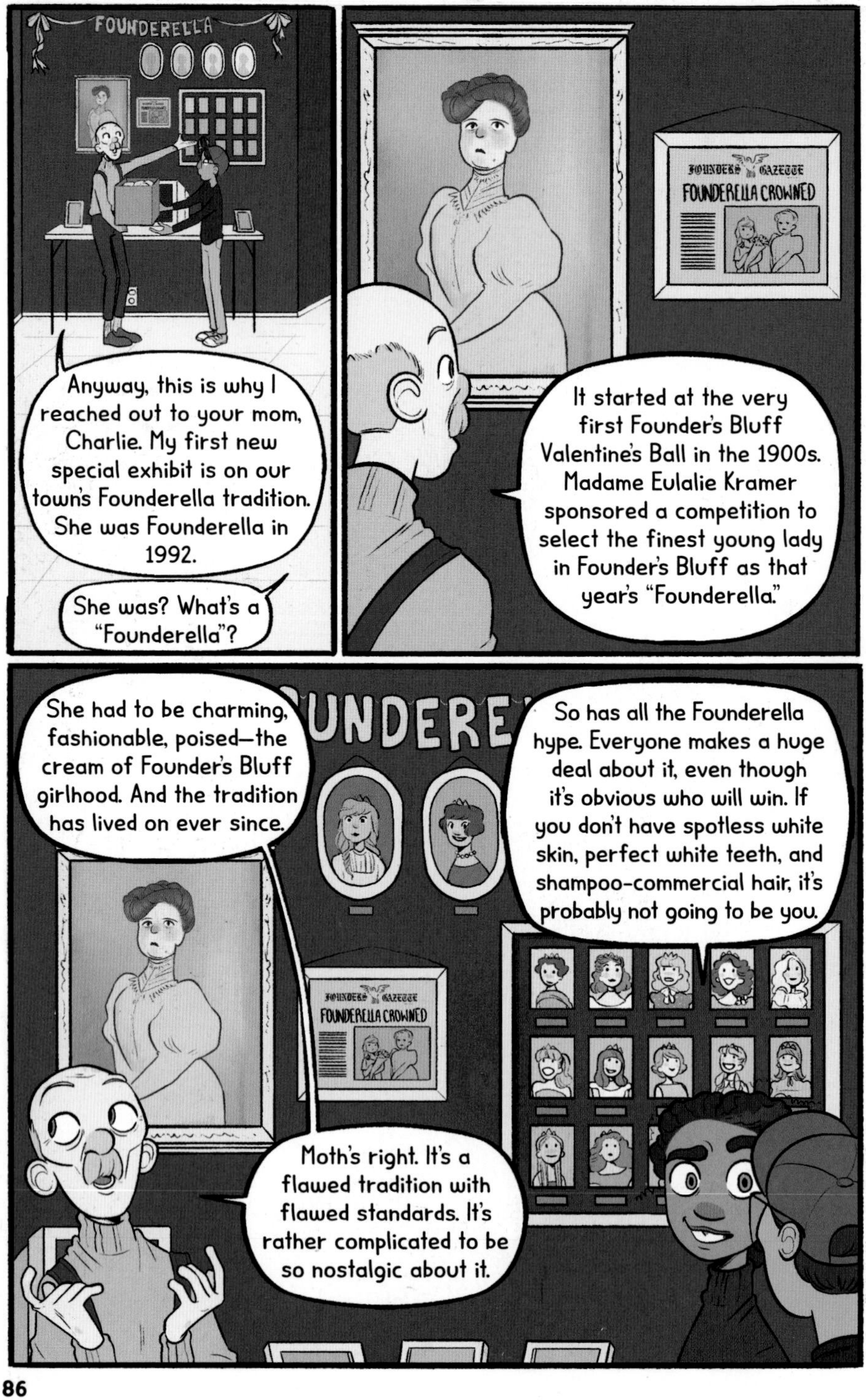
FOUNDERELLA
Anyway, this is why I reached out to your mom, Charlie. My first new special exhibit is on our town's Founderella tradition. She was Founderella in 1992.
She was? What's a "Founderella"?
FOUNDERS GAZETTE
FOUNDERELLA CROWNED
It started at the very first Founder's Bluff Valentine's Ball in the 1900s. Madame Eulalie Kramer sponsored a competition to select the finest young lady in Founder's Bluff as that year's "Founderella."
She had to be charming, fashionable, poised—the cream of Founder's Bluff girlhood. And the tradition has lived on ever since.
So has all the Founderella hype. Everyone makes a huge deal about it, even though it's obvious who will win. If you don't have spotless white skin, perfect white teeth, and shampoo-commercial hair, it's probably not going to be you.
FOUNDERS GAZETTE
FOUNDERELLA CROWNED
Moth's right. It's a flawed tradition with flawed standards. It's rather complicated to be so nostalgic about it.

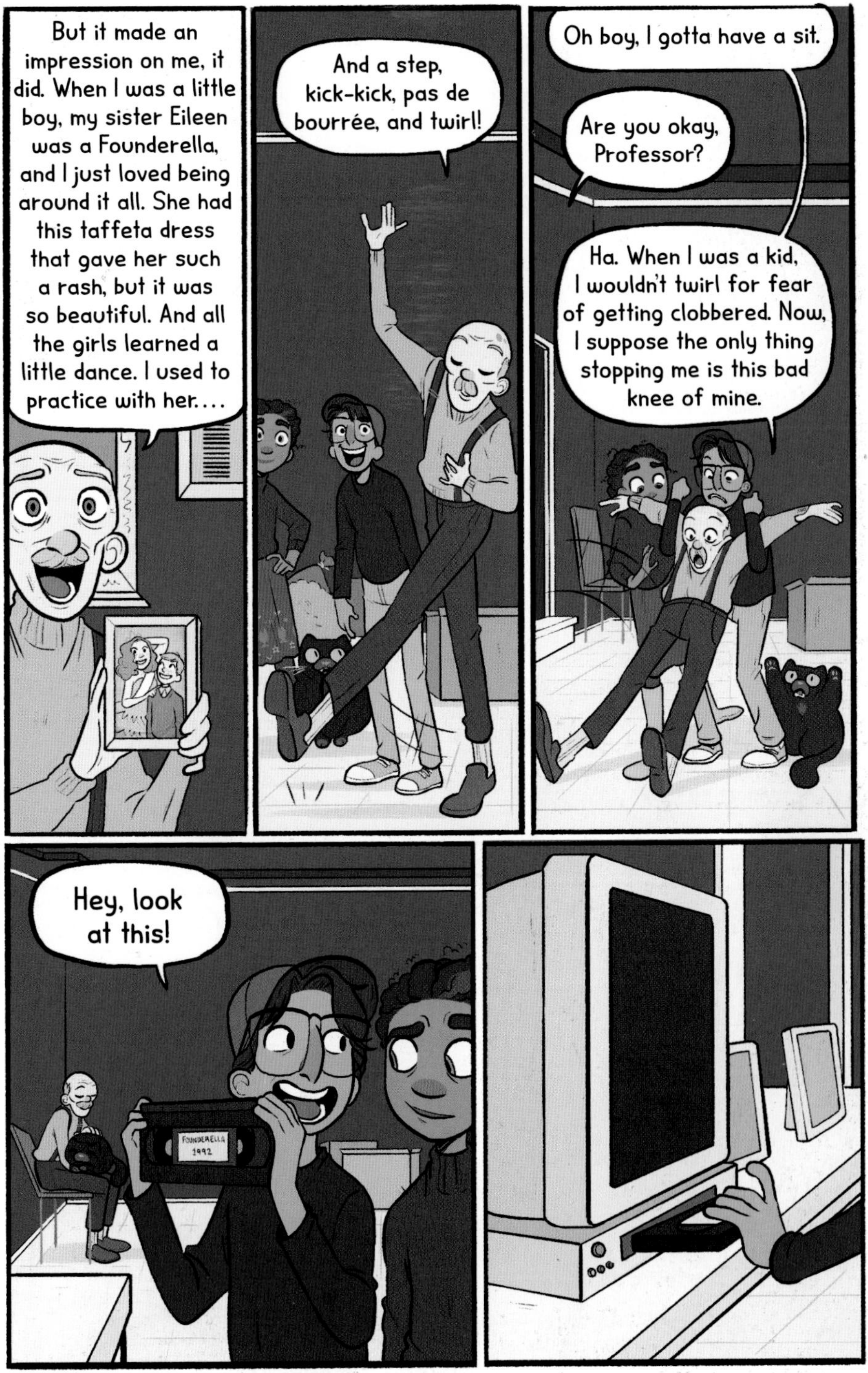
But it made an impression on me, it did. When I was a little boy, my sister Eileen was a Founderella, and I just loved being around it all. She had this taffeta dress that gave her such a rash, but it was so beautiful. And all the girls learned a little dance. I used to practice with her....
And a step, kick-kick, pas de bourrée, and twirl!
Oh boy, I gotta have a sit.
Are you okay, Professor?
Ha. When I was a kid, I wouldn't twirl for fear of getting clobbered. Now, I suppose the only thing stopping me is this bad knee of mine.
Hey, look at this!
FOUNDERELLA 1992

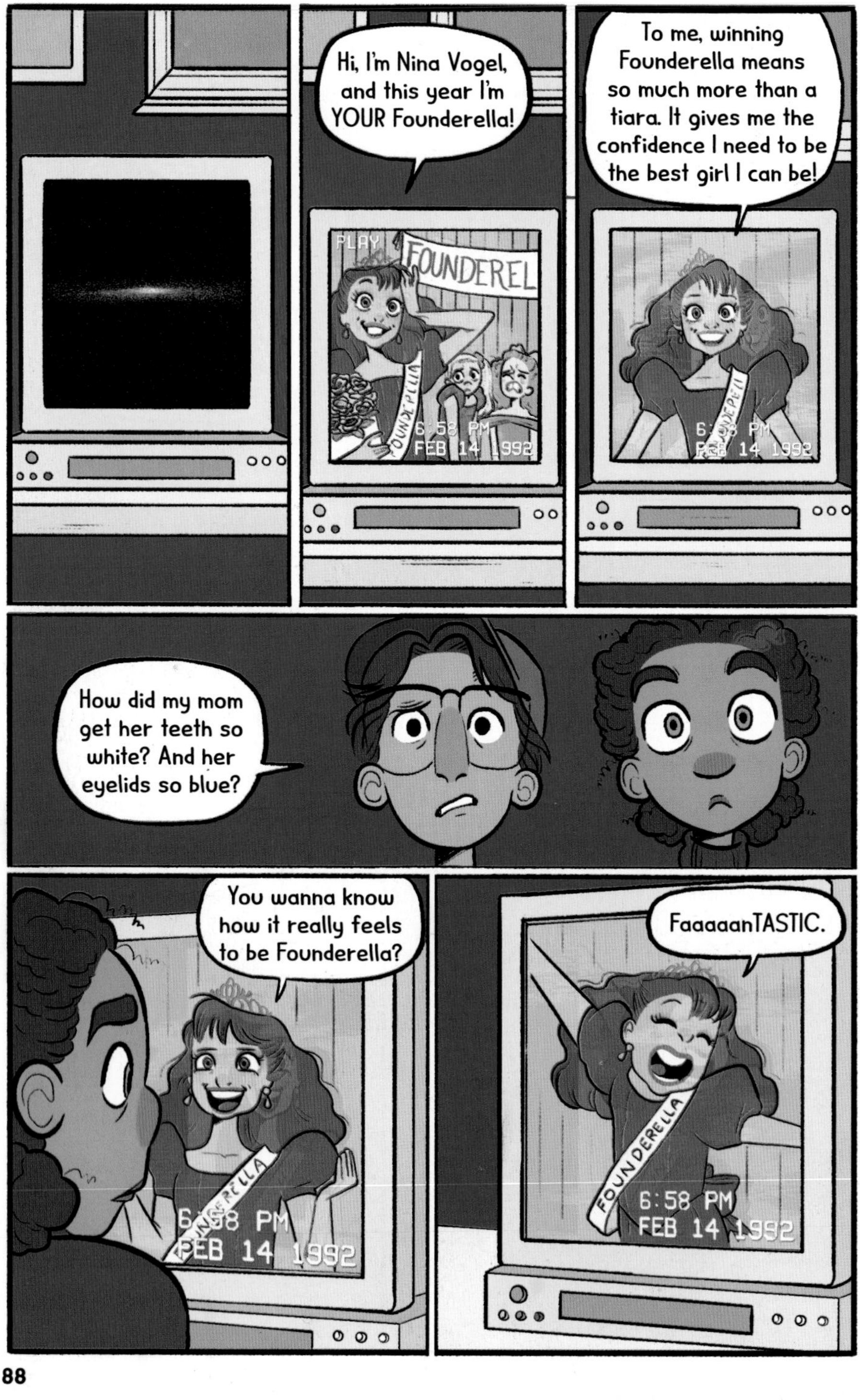
Hi, I'm Nina Vogel, and this year I'm YOUR Founderella!
PLAY
FOUNDEREL
FOUNDERELLA
6:58 PM
FEB 14 1992
To me, winning Founderella means so much more than a tiara. It gives me the confidence I need to be the best girl I can be!
How did my mom get her teeth so white? And her eyelids so blue?
You wanna know how it really feels to be Founderella?
6:58 PM
FEB 14 1992
FaaaaanTASTIC.
FOUNDERELLA
6:58 PM
FEB 14 1992

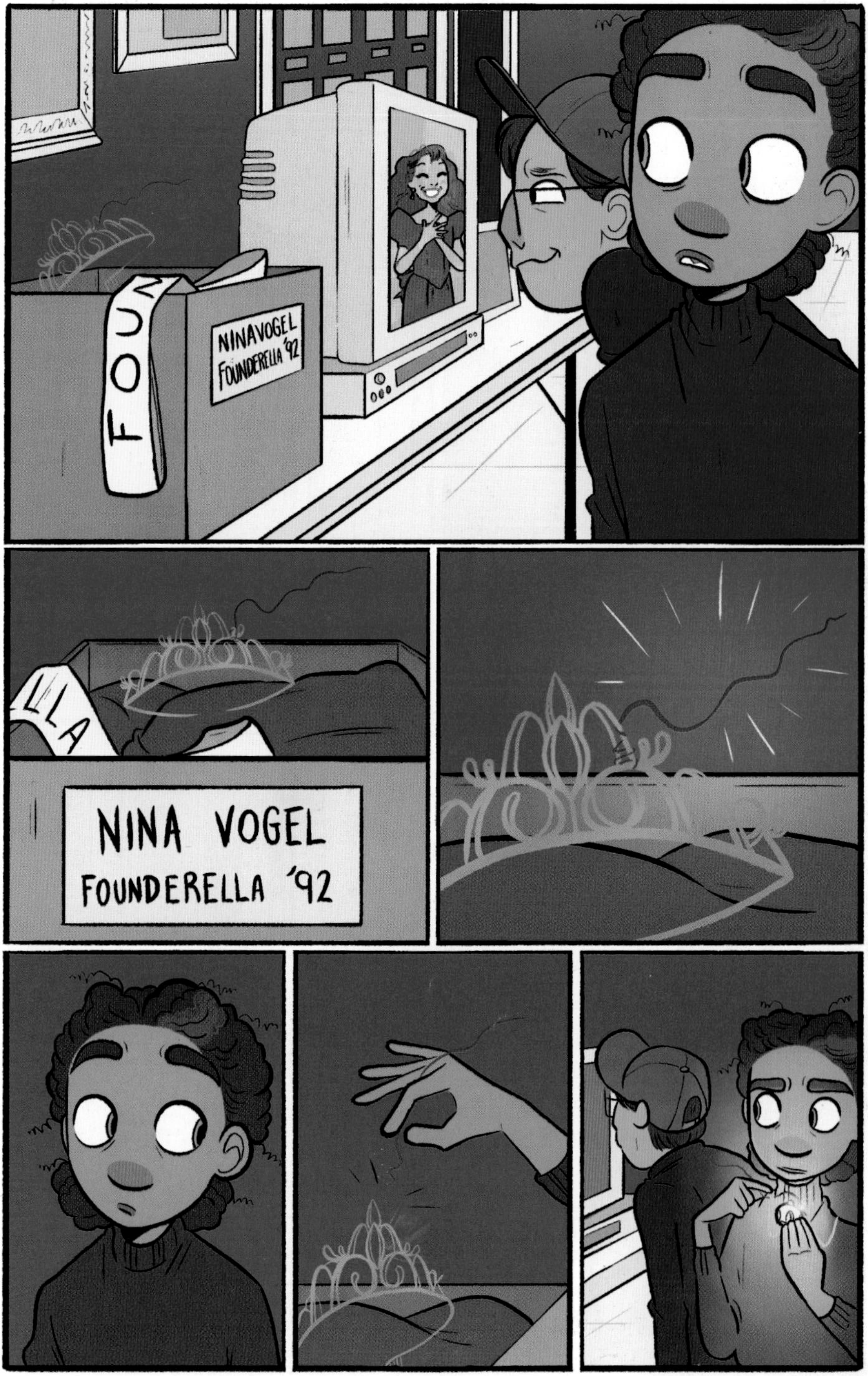
FOUN
NINAVOGEL
FOUNDERELLA '92
LLA
NINA VOGEL
FOUNDERELLA '92

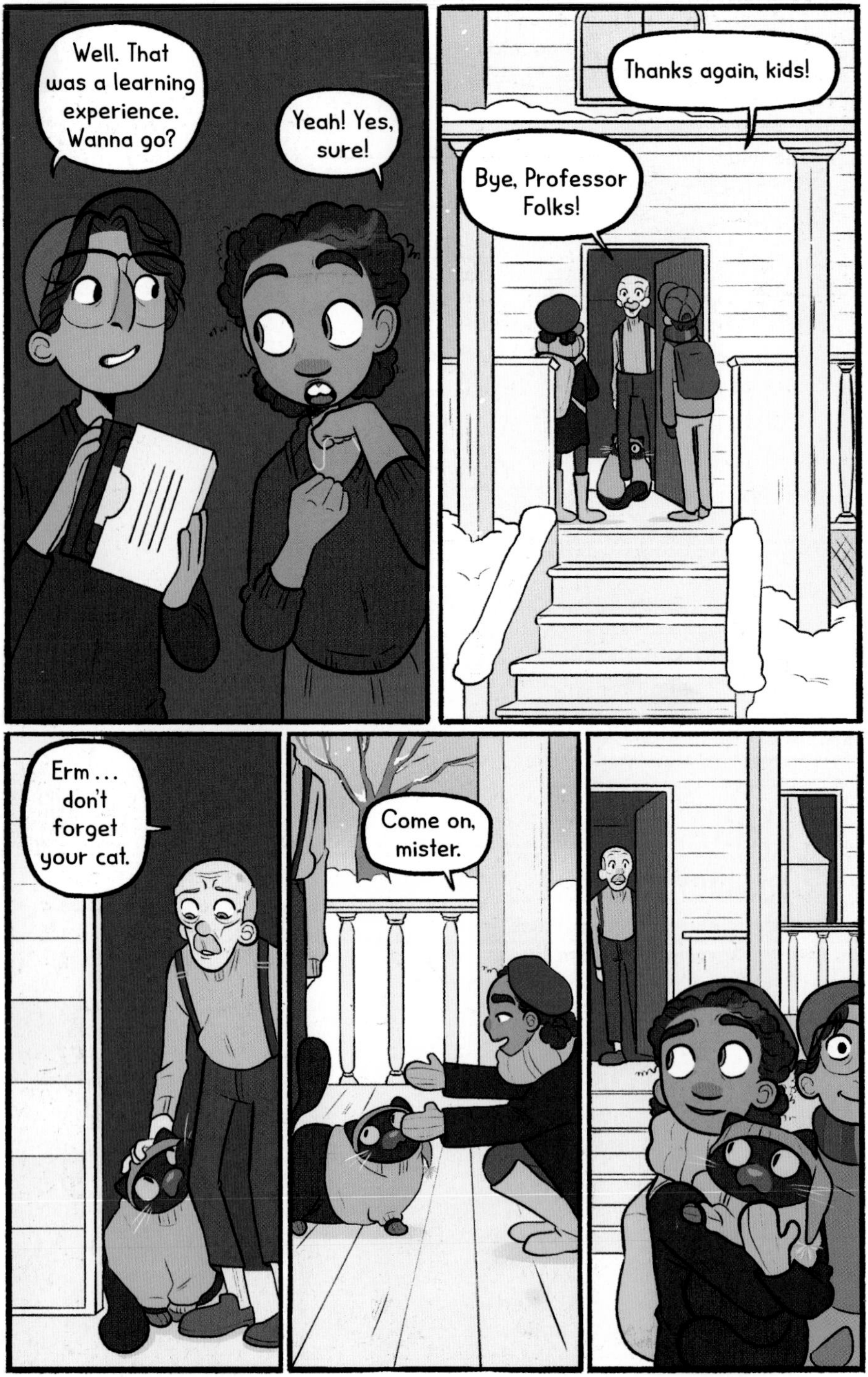
Well. That was a learning experience. Wanna go?
Yeah! Yes, sure!
Thanks again, kids!
Bye, Professor Folks!
Erm . . . don't forget your cat.
Come on, mister.

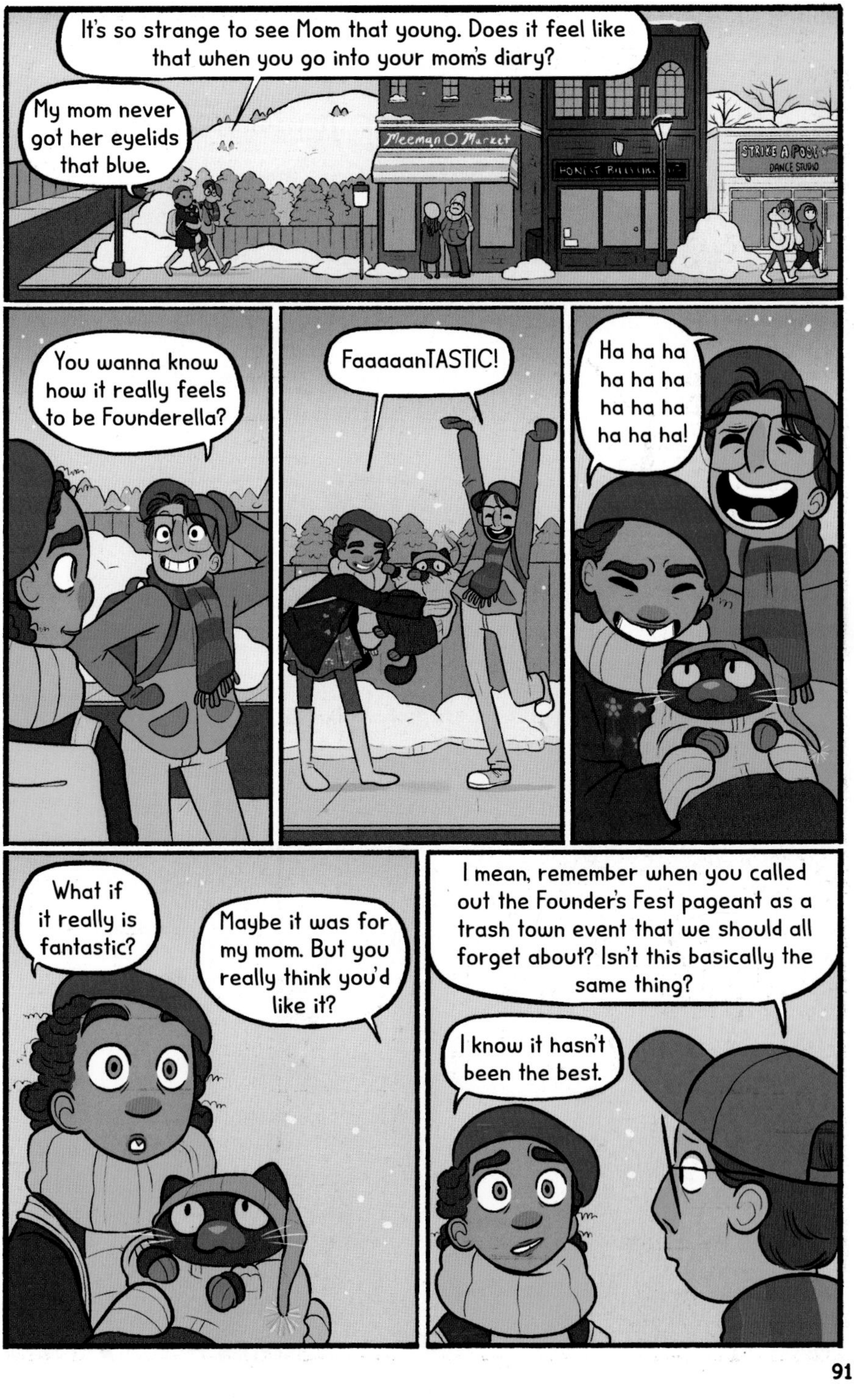
It's so strange to see Mom that young. Does it feel like that when you go into your mom's diary?
My mom never got her eyelids that blue.
Meeman Market
STRIKE A POSE
DANCE STUDIO
You wanna know how it really feels to be Founderella?
FaaaaanTASTIC!
Ha ha ha ha ha ha ha ha ha ha ha ha!
What if it really is fantastic?
Maybe it was for my mom. But you really think you'd like it?
I mean, remember when you called out the Founder's Fest pageant as a trash town event that we should all forget about? Isn't this basically the same thing?
I know it hasn't been the best.

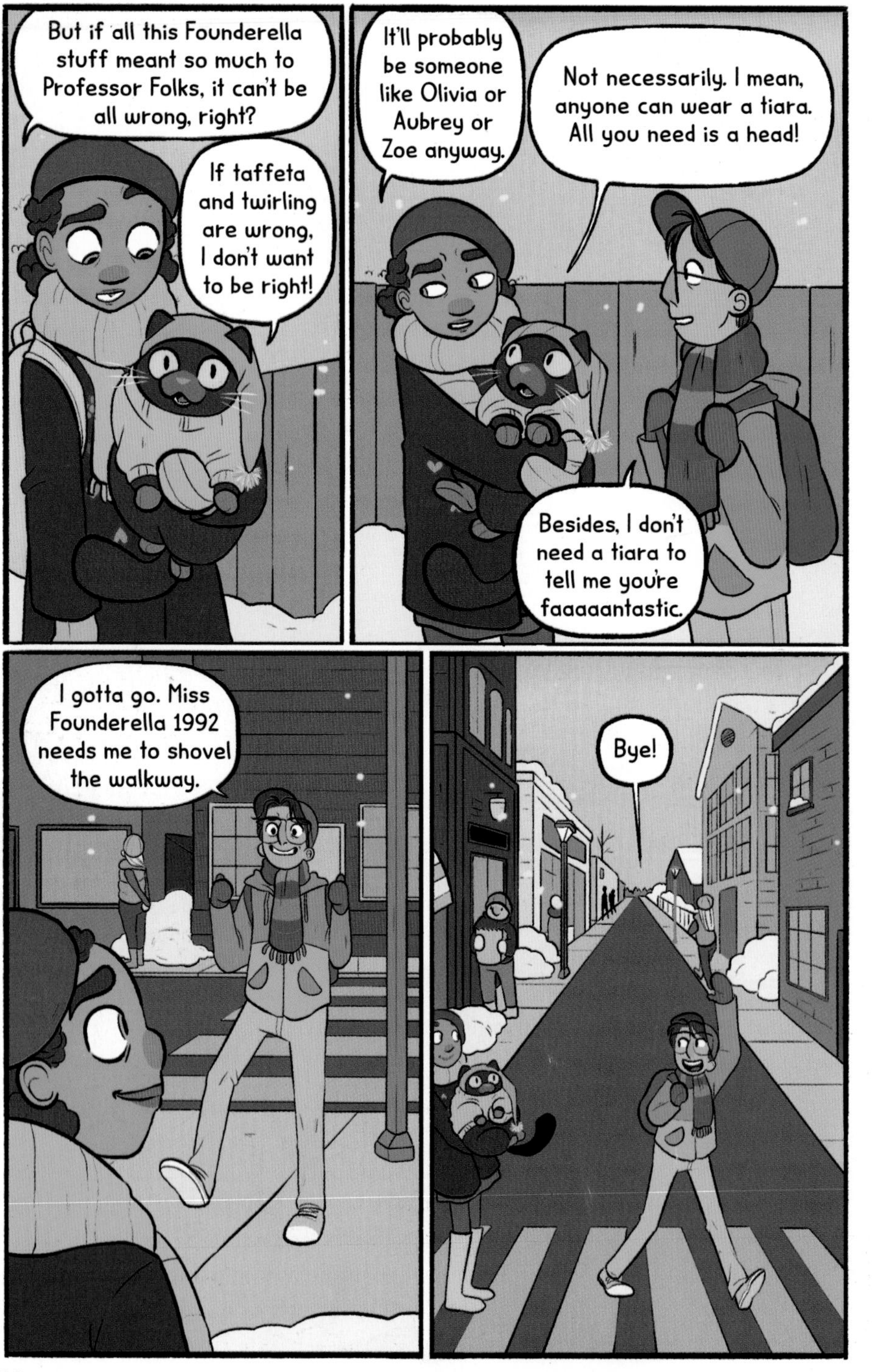
But if all this Founderella stuff meant so much to Professor Folks, it can't be all wrong, right?
If taffeta and twirling are wrong, I don't want to be right!
It'll probably be someone like Olivia or Aubrey or Zoe anyway.
Not necessarily. I mean, anyone can wear a tiara. All you need is a head!
Besides, I don't need a tiara to tell me you're faaaaantastic.
I gotta go. Miss Founderella 1992 needs me to shovel the walkway.
Bye!

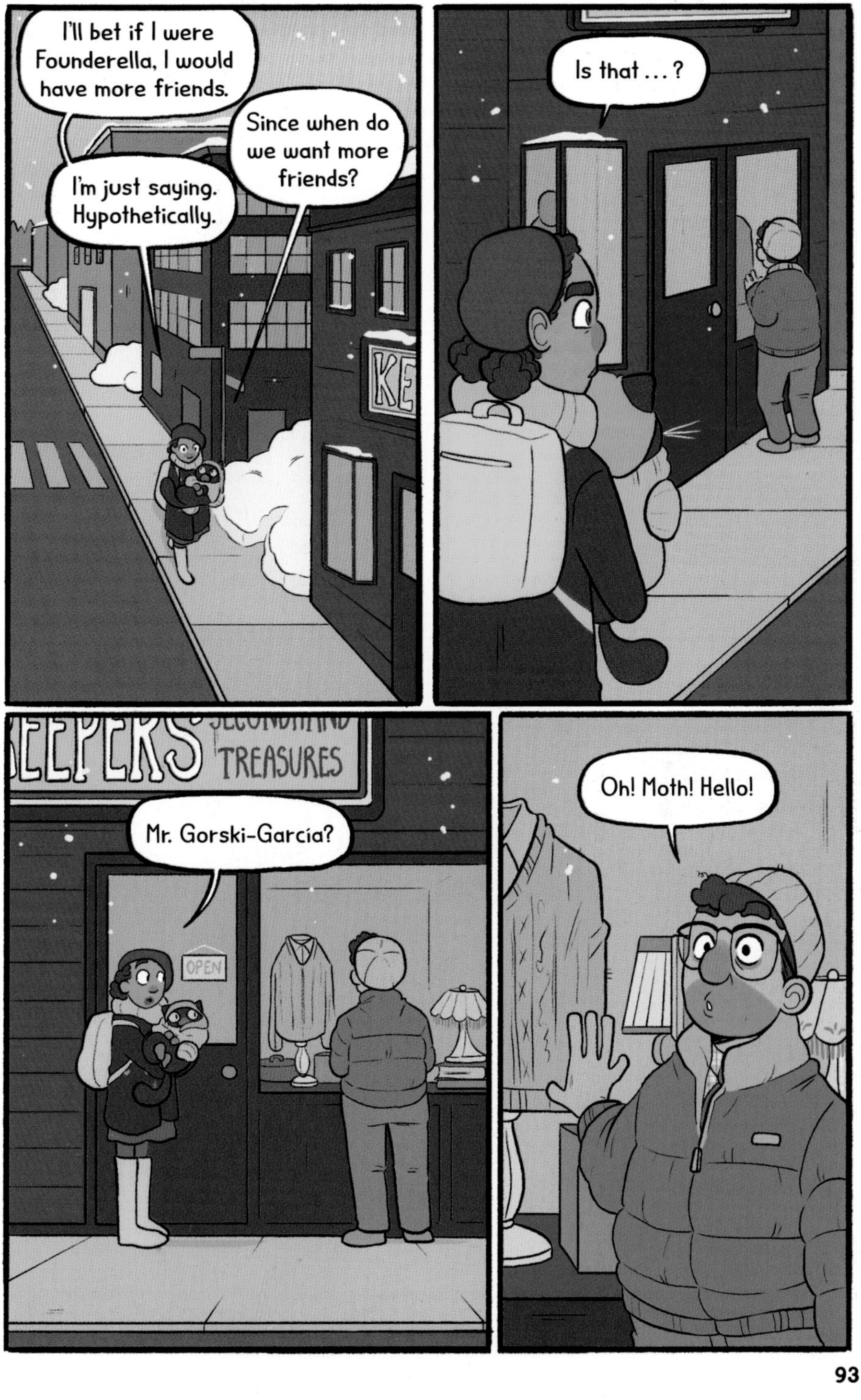

I'll bet if I were Founderella, I would have more friends.
Since when do we want more friends?
I'm just saying. Hypothetically.
KE
Is that . . . ?
EEPERS' SECONDHAND TREASURES
Mr. Gorski-García?
OPEN
Oh! Moth! Hello!

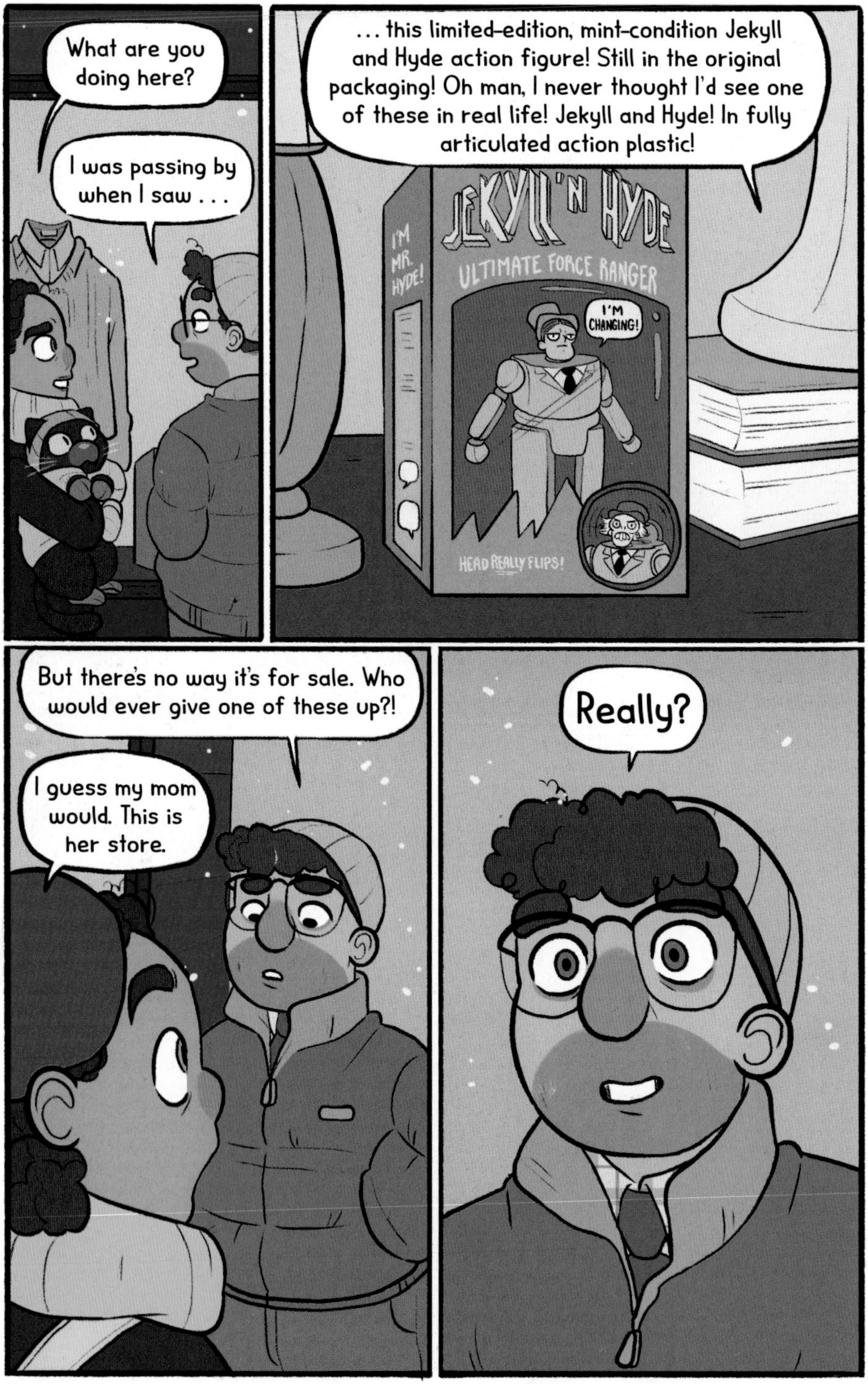
What are you doing here?
I was passing by when I saw . . .
. . . this limited-edition, mint-condition Jekyll and Hyde action figure! Still in the original packaging! Oh man, I never thought I'd see one of these in real life! Jekyll and Hyde! In fully articulated action plastic!
JEKYLL 'N HYDE
ULTIMATE FORCE RANGER
I'M MR. HYDE!
I'M CHANGING!
HEAD REALLY FLIPS!
But there's no way it's for sale. Who would ever give one of these up?!
I guess my mom would. This is her store.
Really?

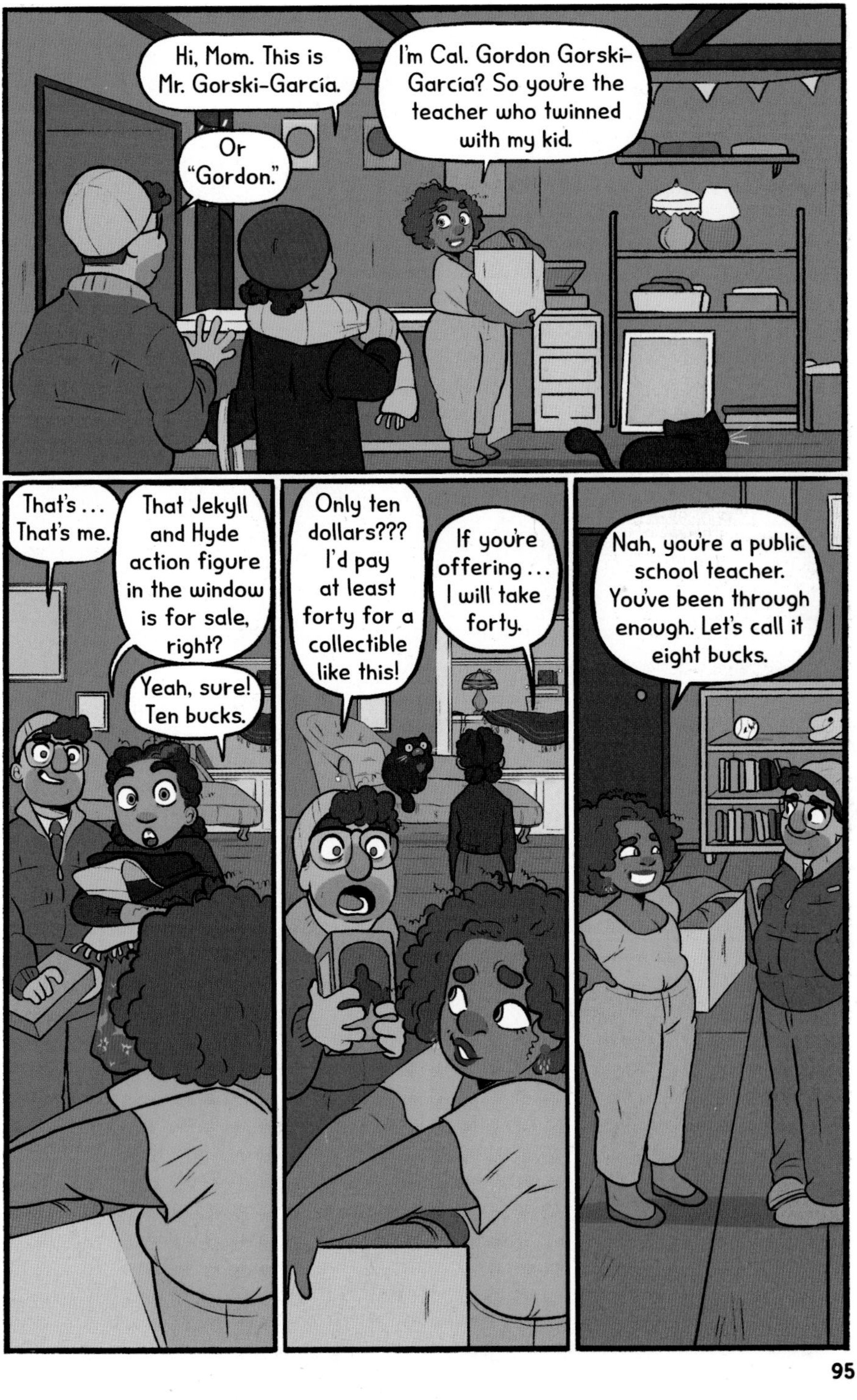
Hi, Mom. This is Mr. Gorski-García.
Or "Gordon."
I'm Cal. Gordon Gorski-García? So you're the teacher who twinned with my kid.
That's . . . That's me.
That Jekyll and Hyde action figure in the window is for sale, right?
Yeah, sure! Ten bucks.
Only ten dollars??? I'd pay at least forty for a collectible like this!
If you're offering . . . I will take forty.
Nah, you're a public school teacher. You've been through enough. Let's call it eight bucks.

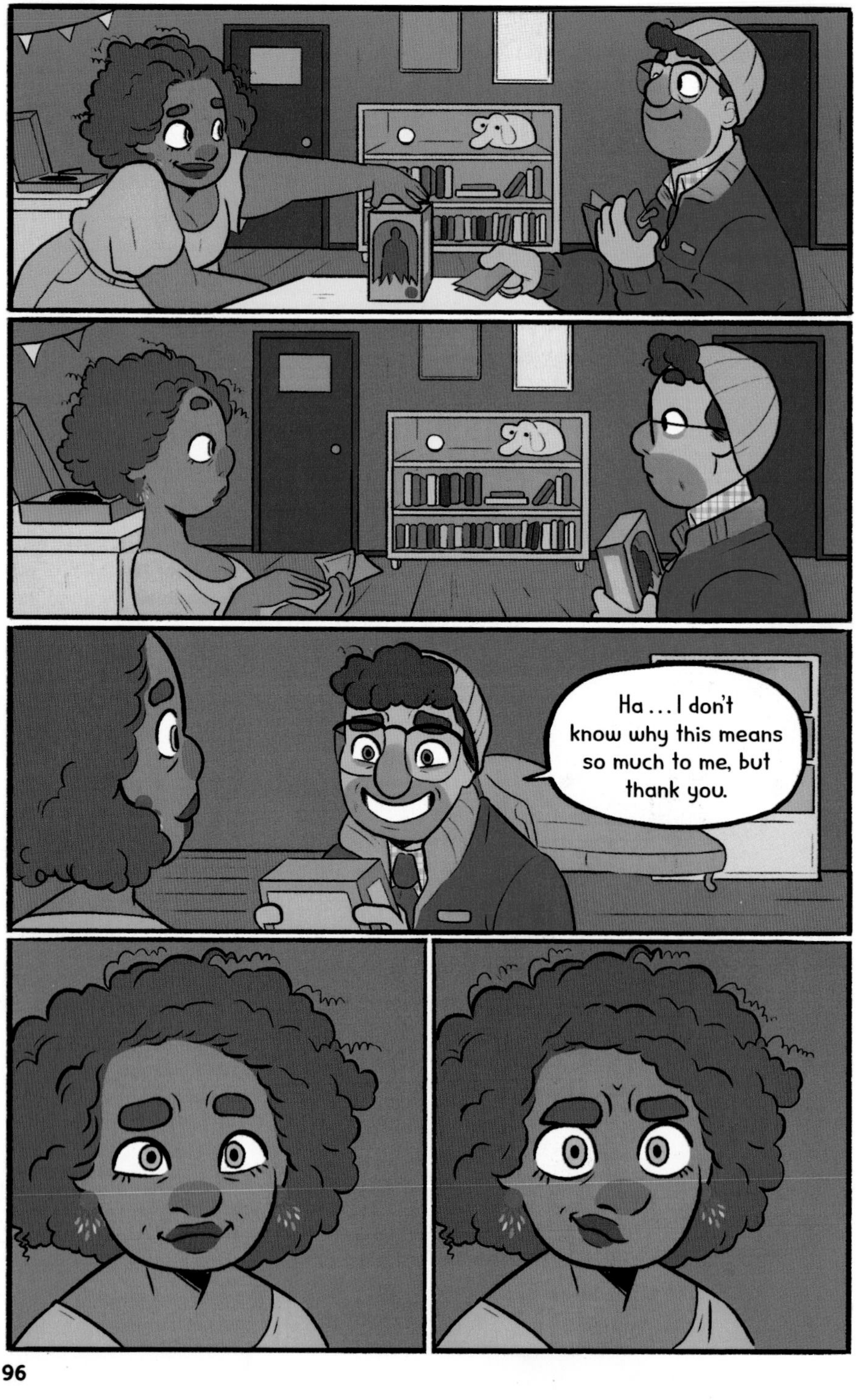
Ha . . . I don't know why this means so much to me, but thank you.

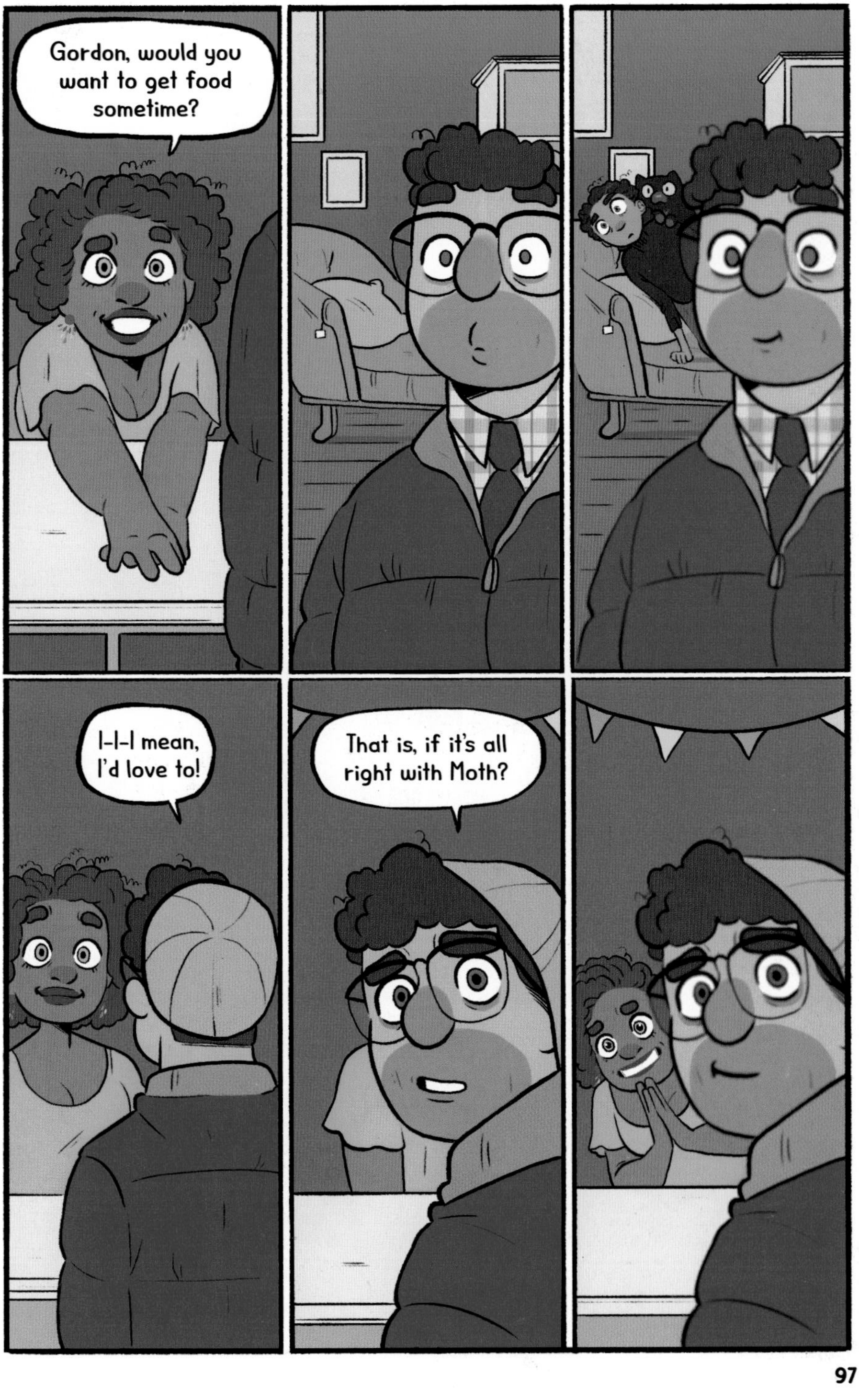
Gordon, would you want to get food sometime?
I-I-I mean, I'd love to!
That is, if it's all right with Moth?

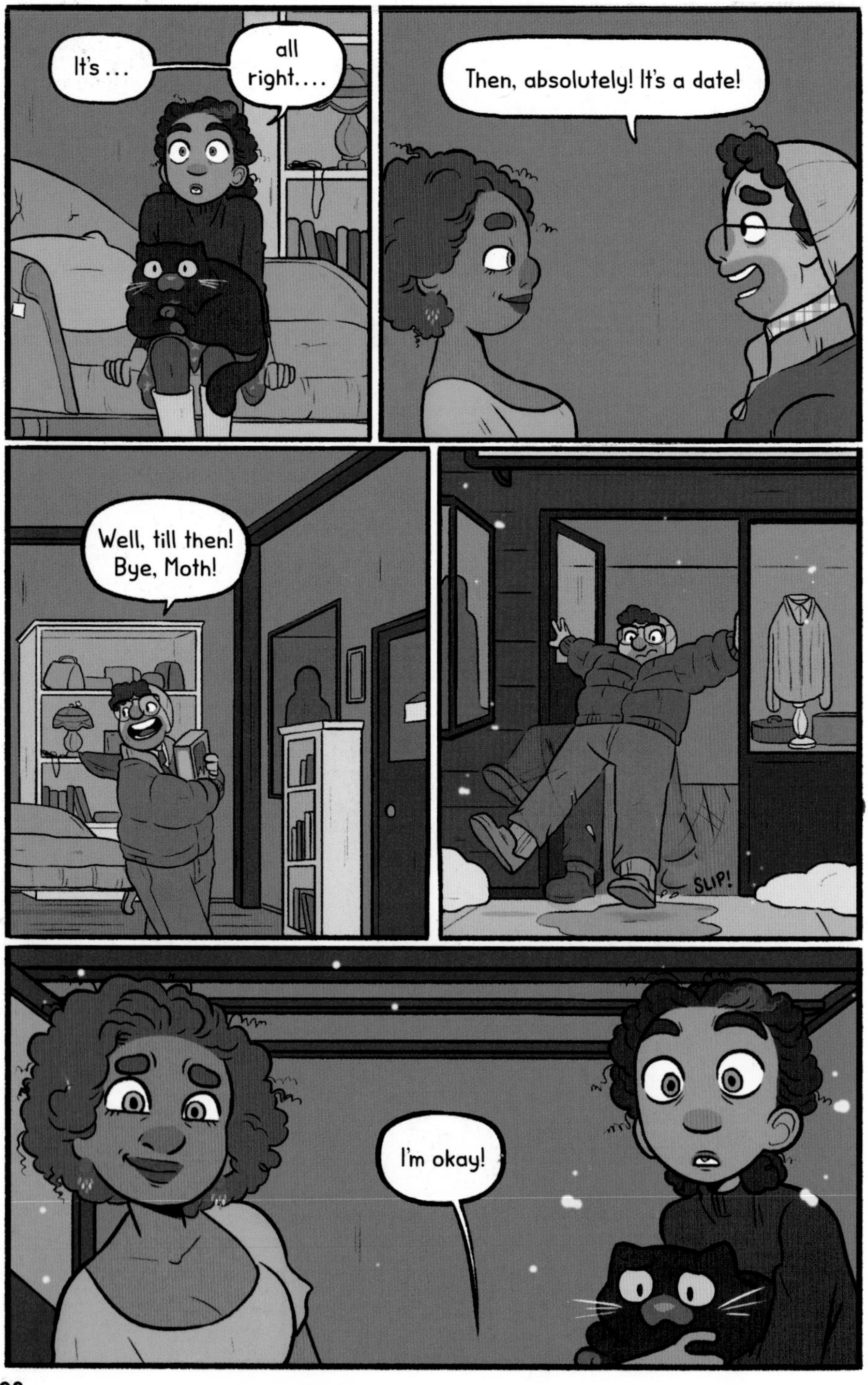
It's . . .
all right. . . .
Then, absolutely! It's a date!
Well, till then! Bye, Moth!
SLIP!
I'm okay!

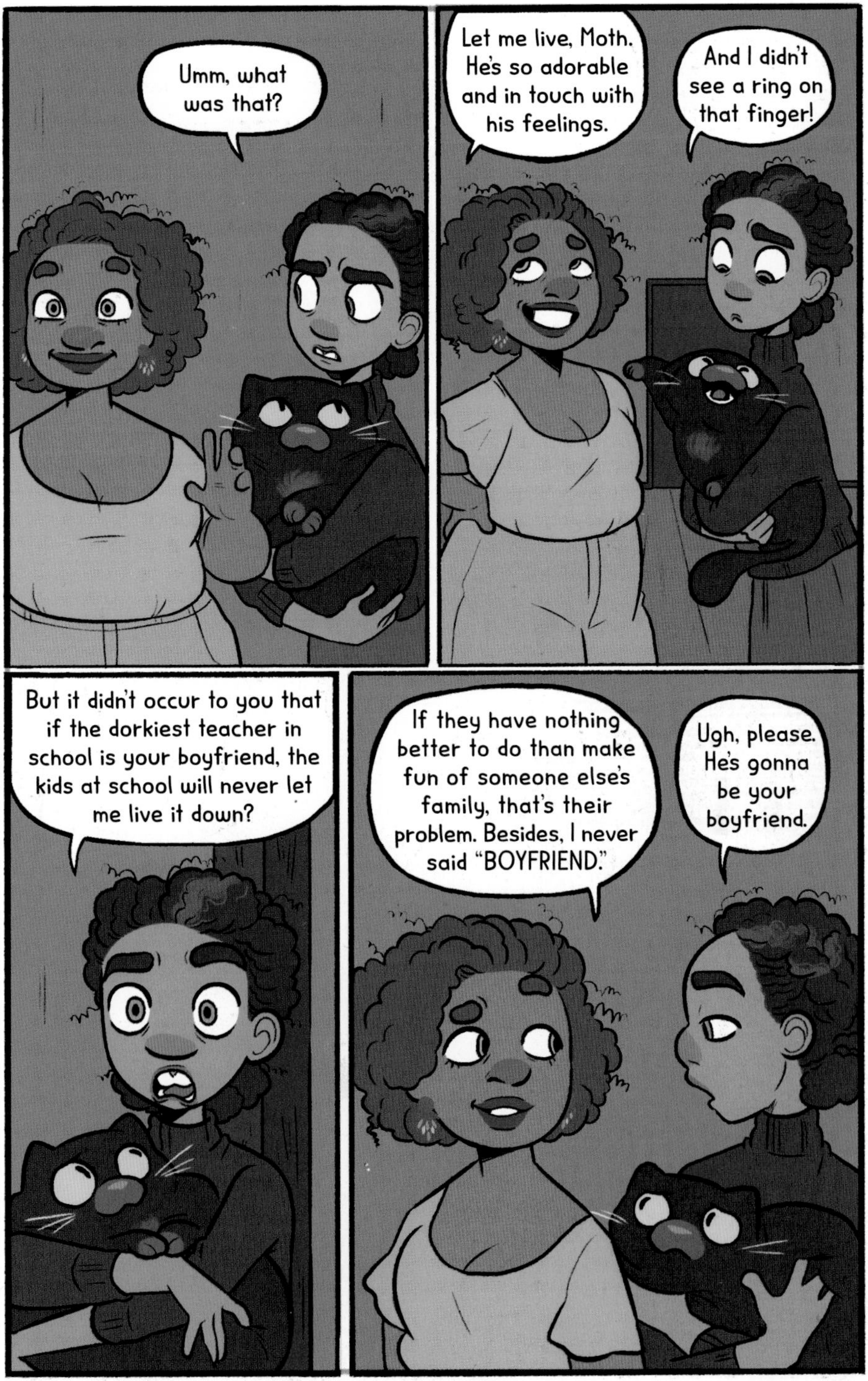
Umm, what was that?
Let me live, Moth. He's so adorable and in touch with his feelings.
And I didn't see a ring on that finger!
But it didn't occur to you that if the dorkiest teacher in school is your boyfriend, the kids at school will never let me live it down?
If they have nothing better to do than make fun of someone else's family, that's their problem. Besides, I never said "BOYFRIEND."
Ugh, please. He's gonna be your boyfriend.

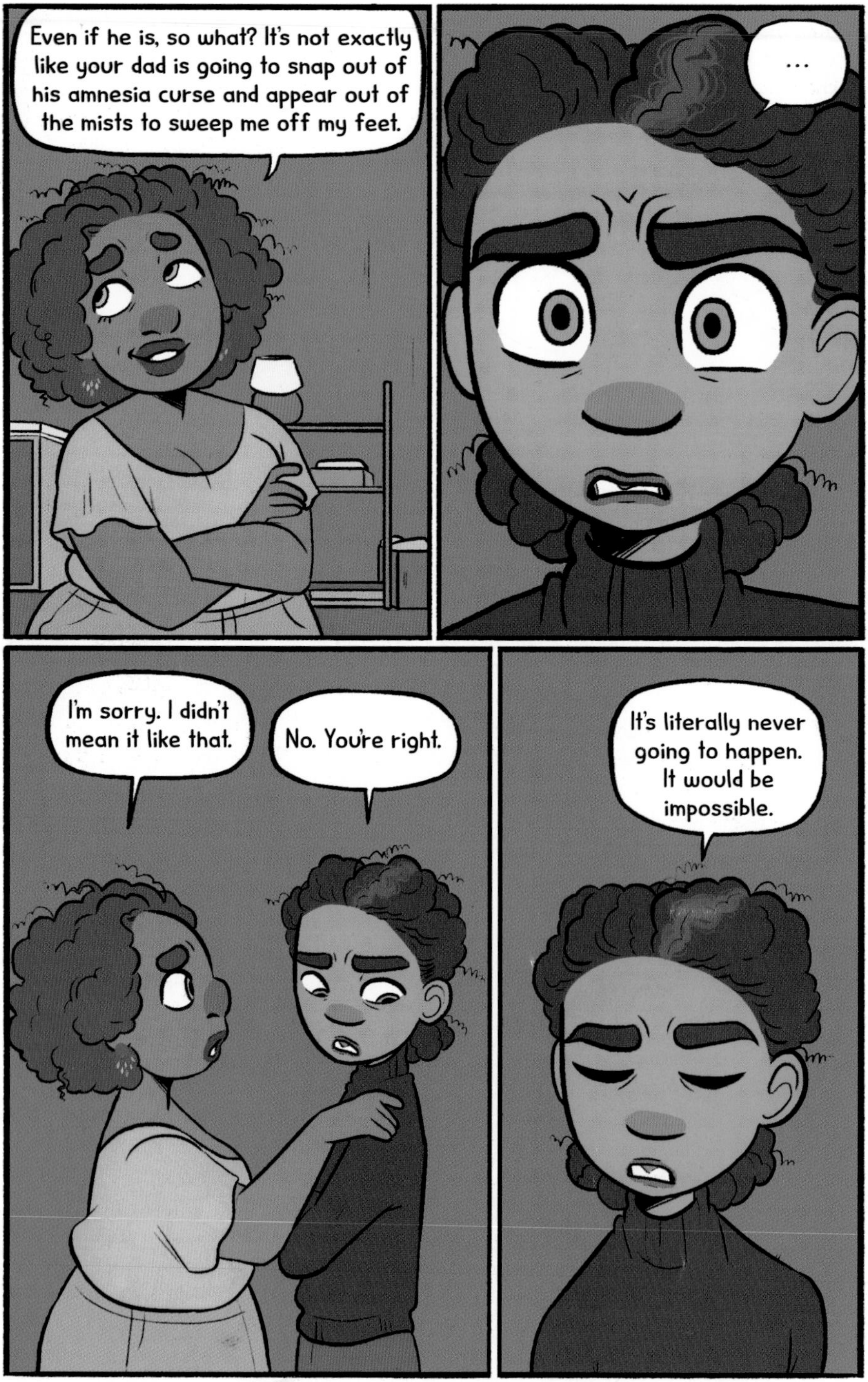
Even if he is, so what? It's not exactly like your dad is going to snap out of his amnesia curse and appear out of the mists to sweep me off my feet.
...
I'm sorry. I didn't mean it like that.
No. You're right.
It's literally never going to happen. It would be impossible.

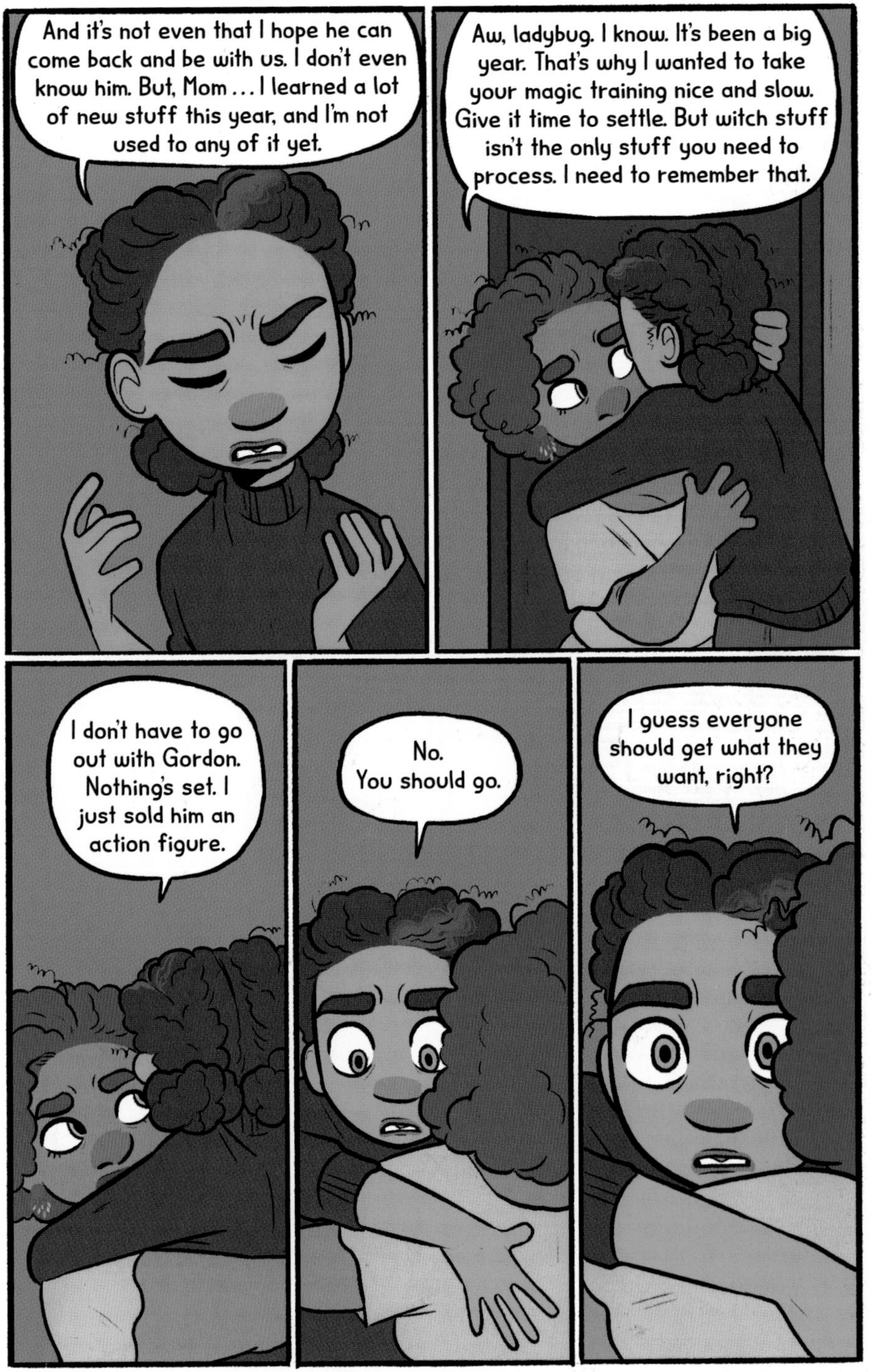
And it's not even that I hope he can come back and be with us. I don't even know him. But, Mom . . . I learned a lot of new stuff this year, and I'm not used to any of it yet.
Aw, ladybug. I know. It's been a big year. That's why I wanted to take your magic training nice and slow. Give it time to settle. But witch stuff isn't the only stuff you need to process. I need to remember that.
I don't have to go out with Gordon. Nothing's set. I just sold him an action figure.
No. You should go.
I guess everyone should get what they want, right?

CHAPTER 6

Wait, Do We Like Moth?

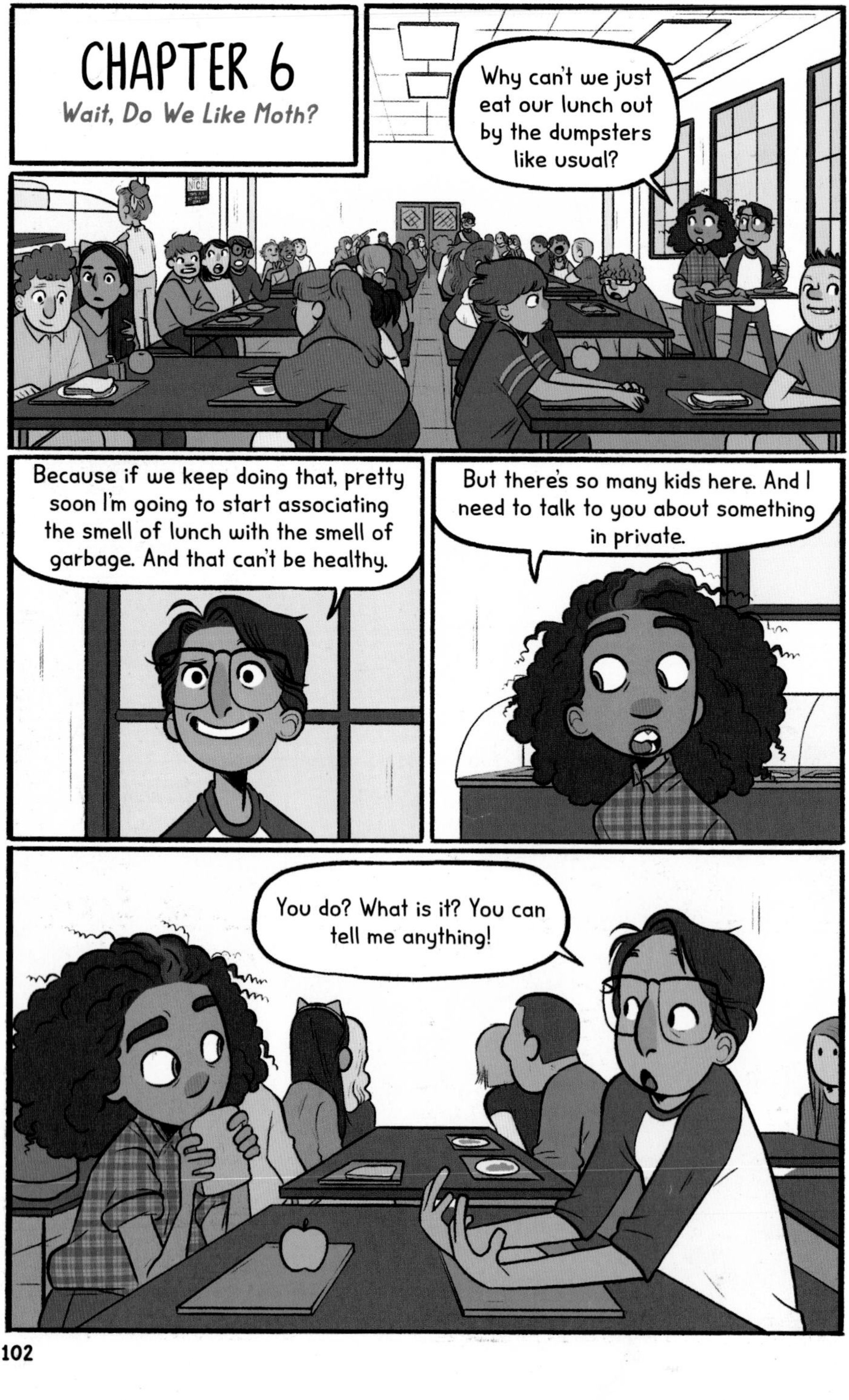

Why can't we just eat our lunch out by the dumpsters like usual?
Because if we keep doing that, pretty soon I'm going to start associating the smell of lunch with the smell of garbage. And that can't be healthy.
But there's so many kids here. And I need to talk to you about something in private.
You do? What is it? You can tell me anything!

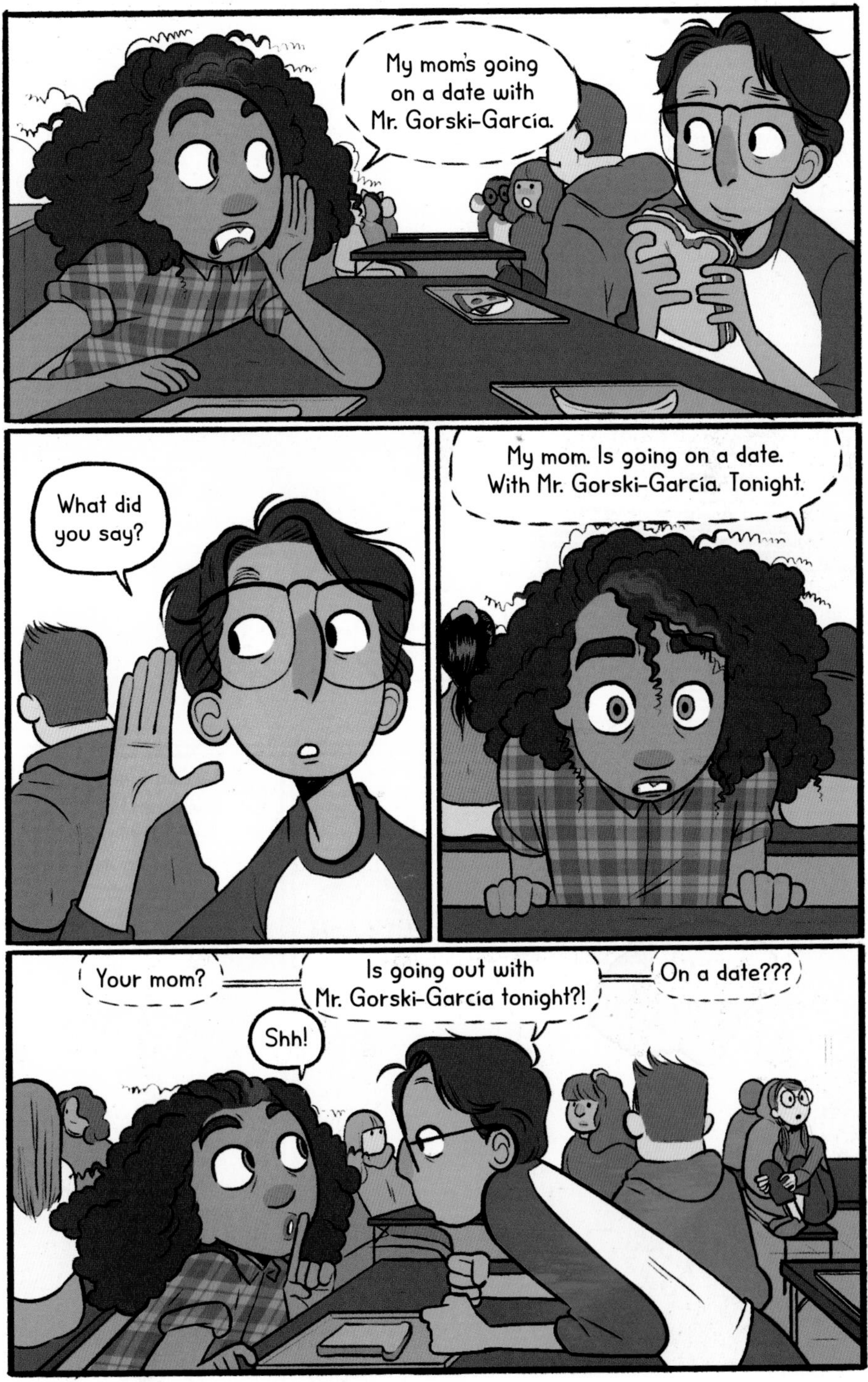

My mom's going on a date with Mr. Gorski-García.
What did you say?
My mom. Is going on a date. With Mr. Gorski-García. Tonight.
Your mom?
Is going out with Mr. Gorski-García tonight?!
On a date???
Shh!

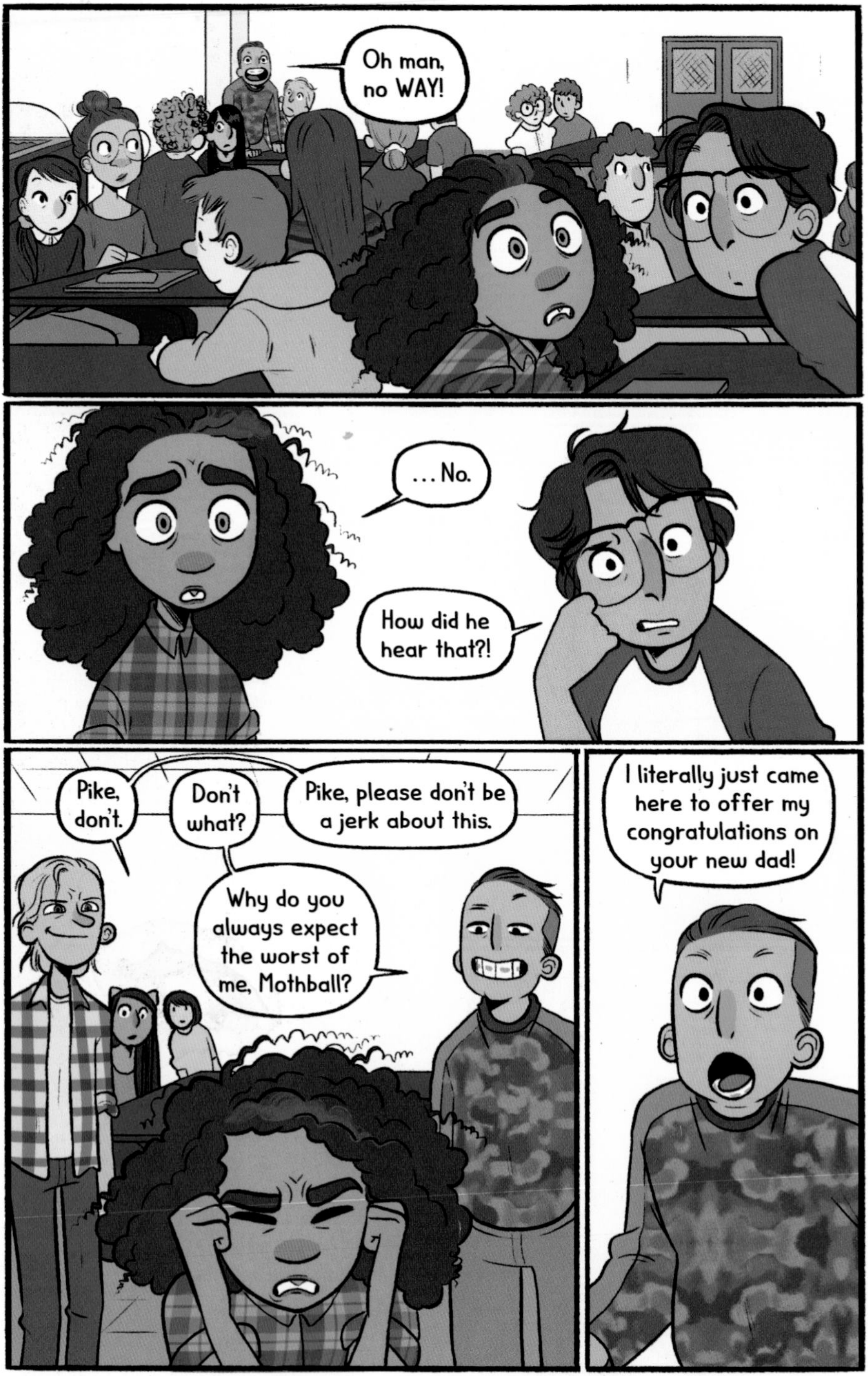

Oh man, no WAY!
...No.
How did he hear that?!
Pike, don't.
Don't what?
Pike, please don't be a jerk about this.
Why do you always expect the worst of me, Mothball?
I literally just came here to offer my congratulations on your new dad!

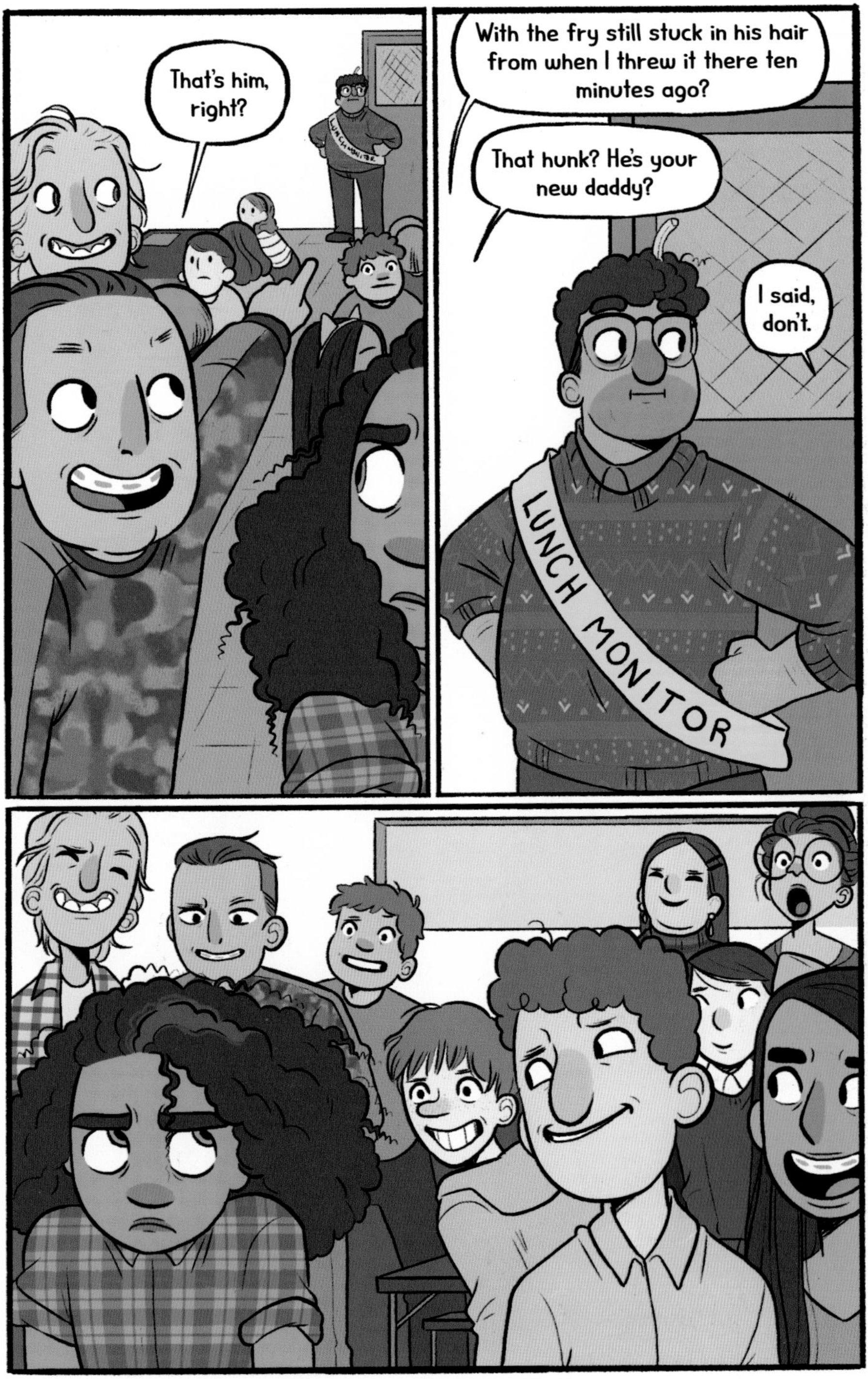
LUNCH MONITOR
That's him, right?
With the fry still stuck in his hair from when I threw it there ten minutes ago?
That hunk? He's your new daddy?
I said, don't.
LUNCH MONITOR

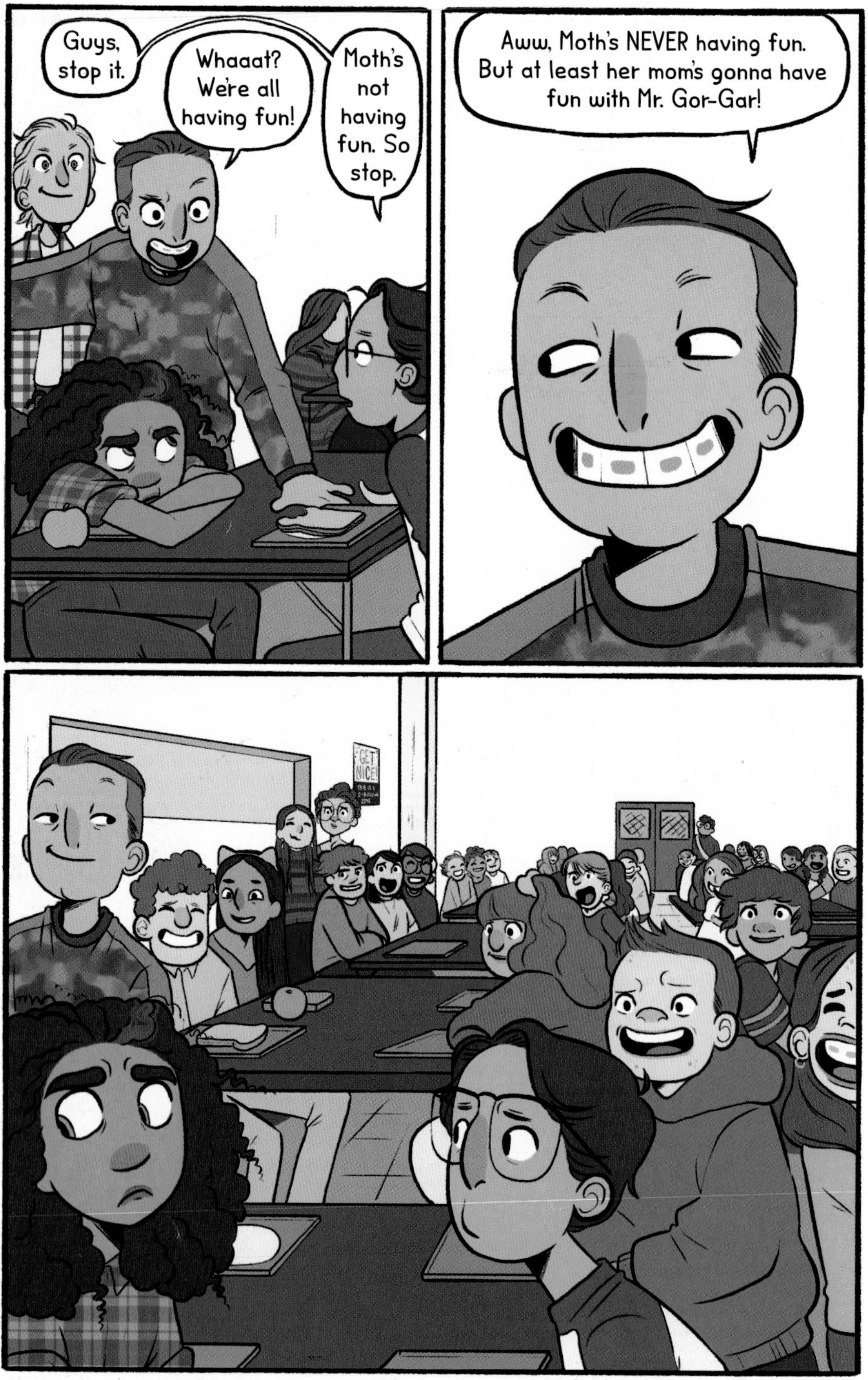
Guys, stop it.
Whaaat? We're all having fun!
Moth's not having fun. So stop.
Aww, Moth's NEVER having fun. But at least her mom's gonna have fun with Mr. Gor-Gar!
GET NICE!

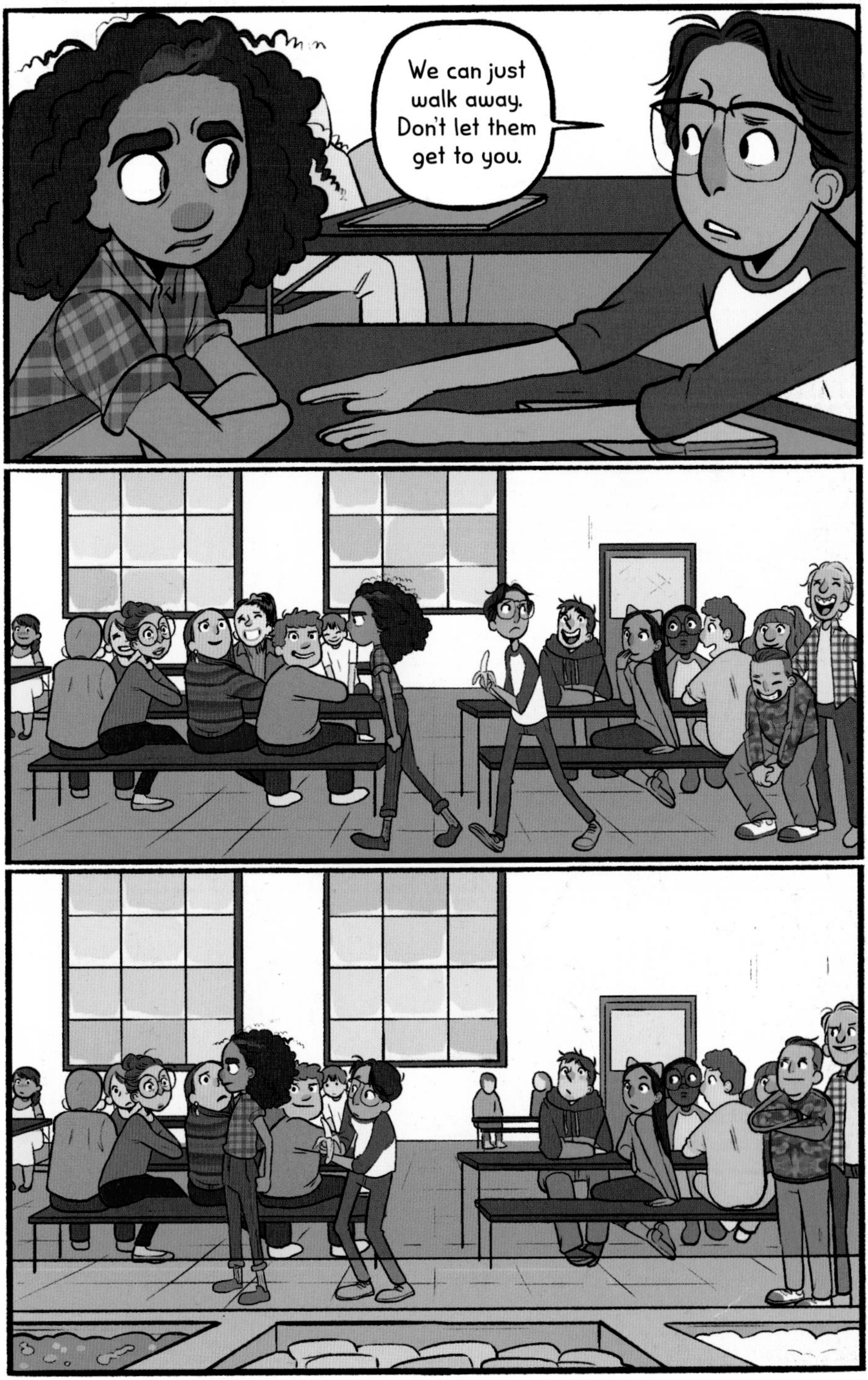
We can just walk away. Don't let them get to you.

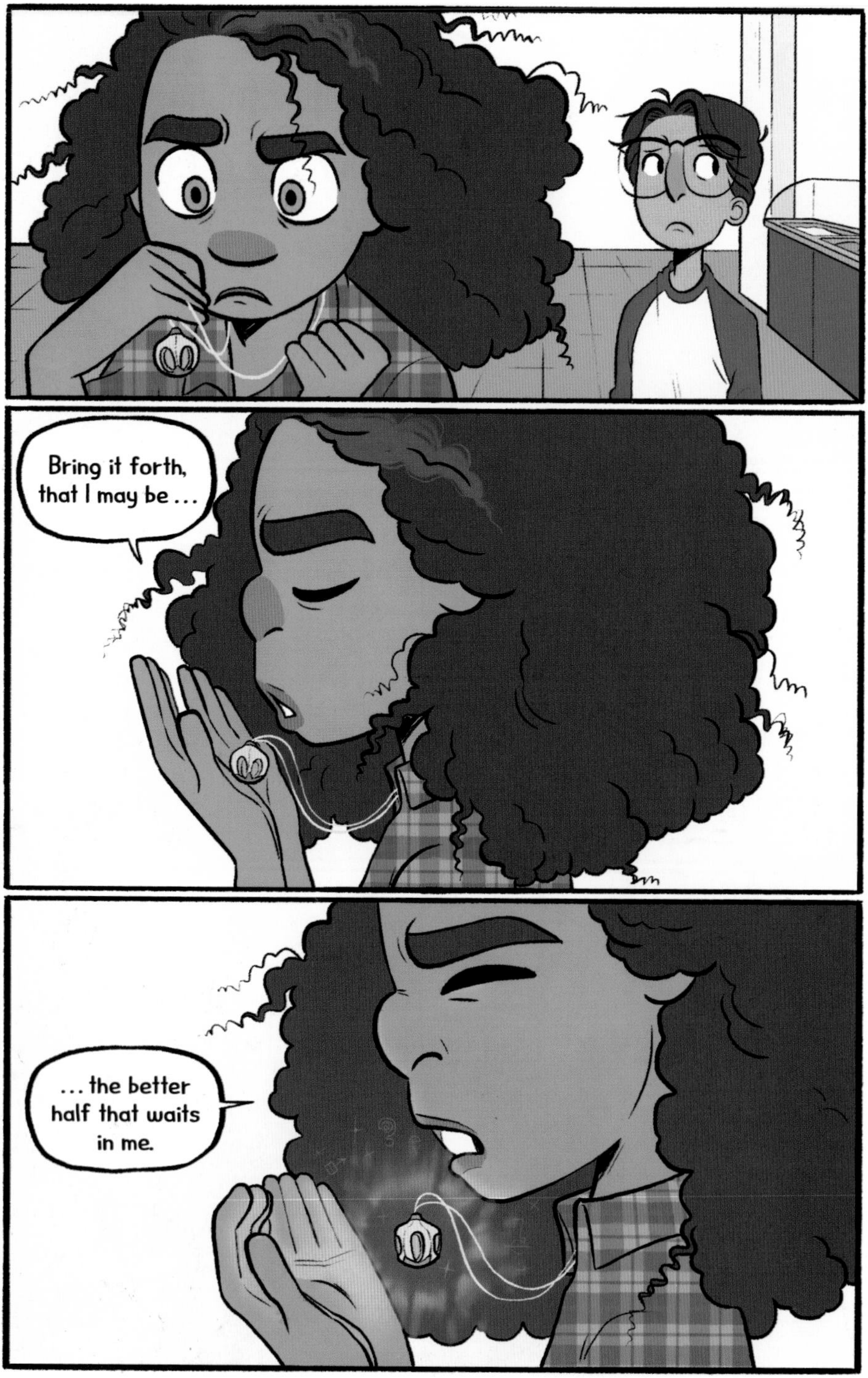
Bring it forth, that I may be . . .
. . . the better half that waits in me.

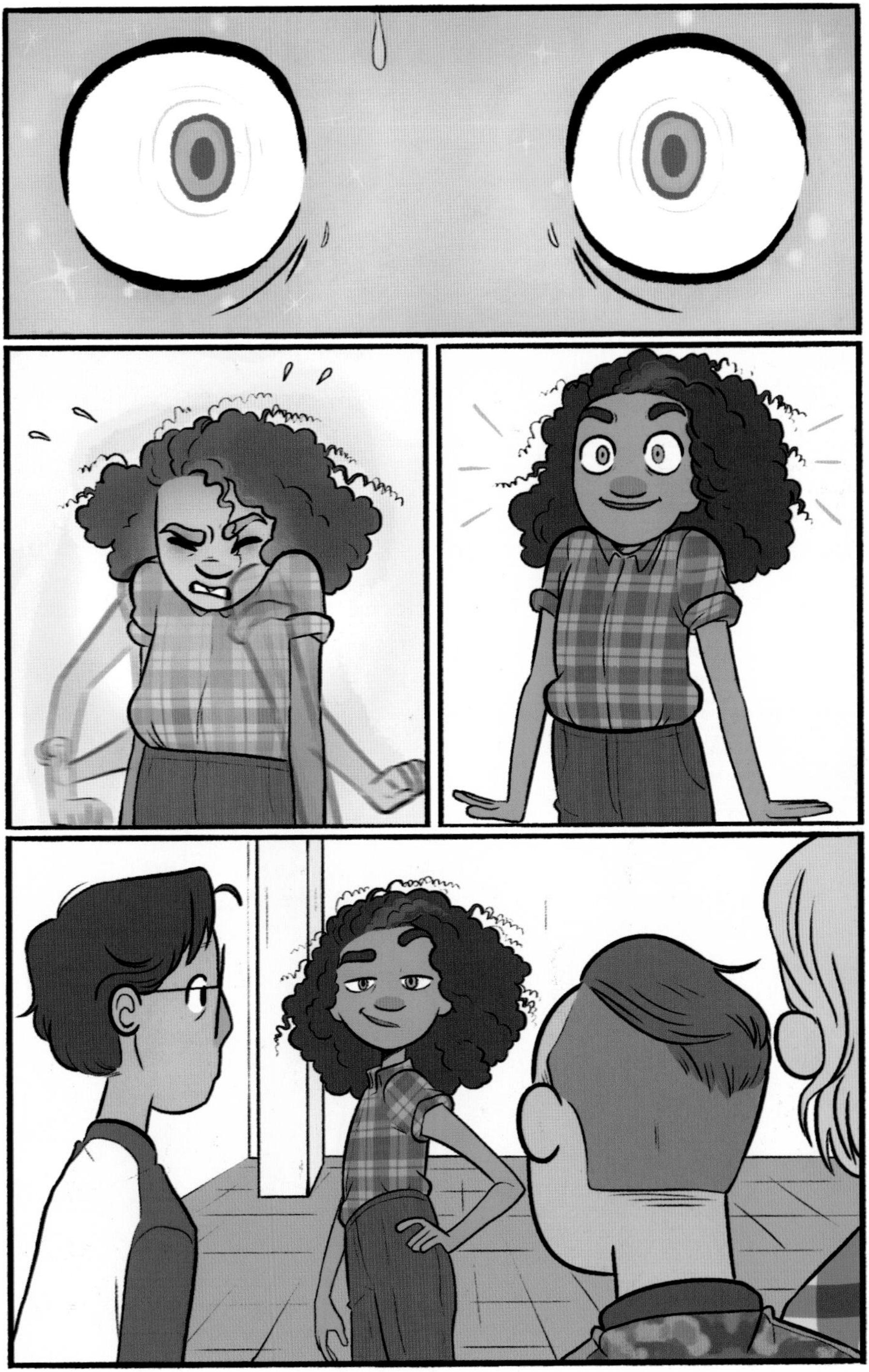

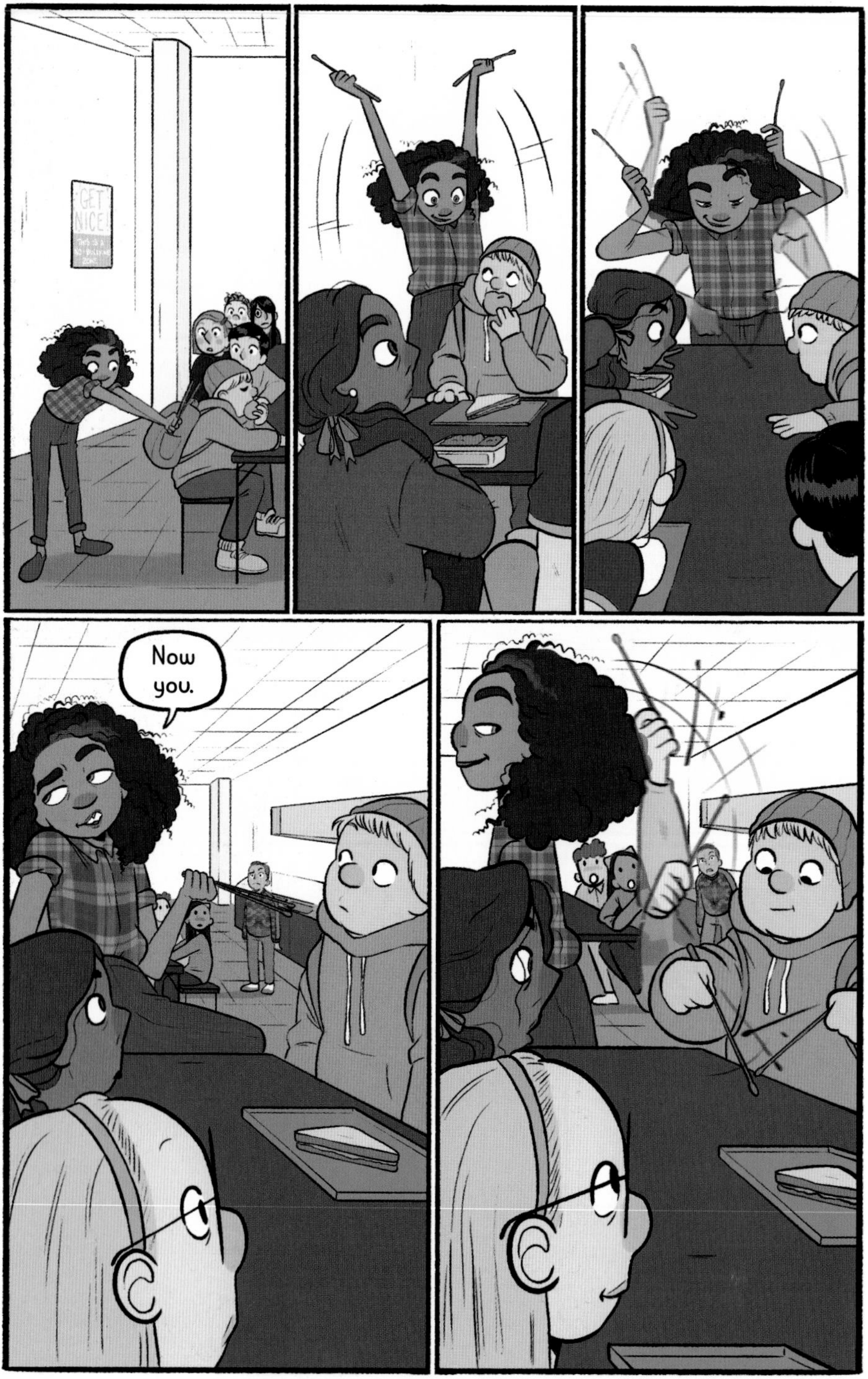
GET NICE!
Now you.

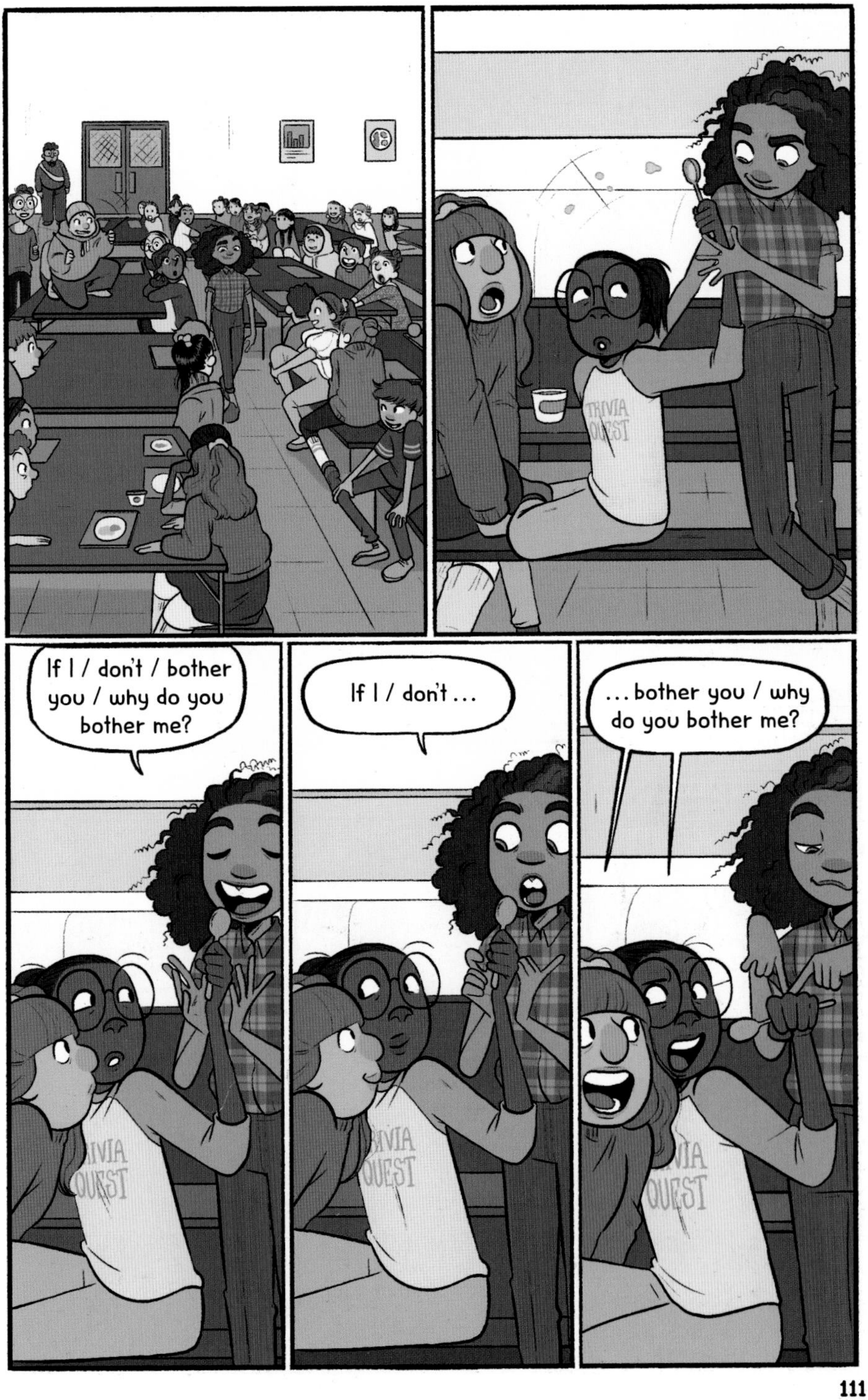
TRIVIA QUEST
If I / don't / bother you / why do you bother me?
If I / don't . . .
. . . bother you / why do you bother me?

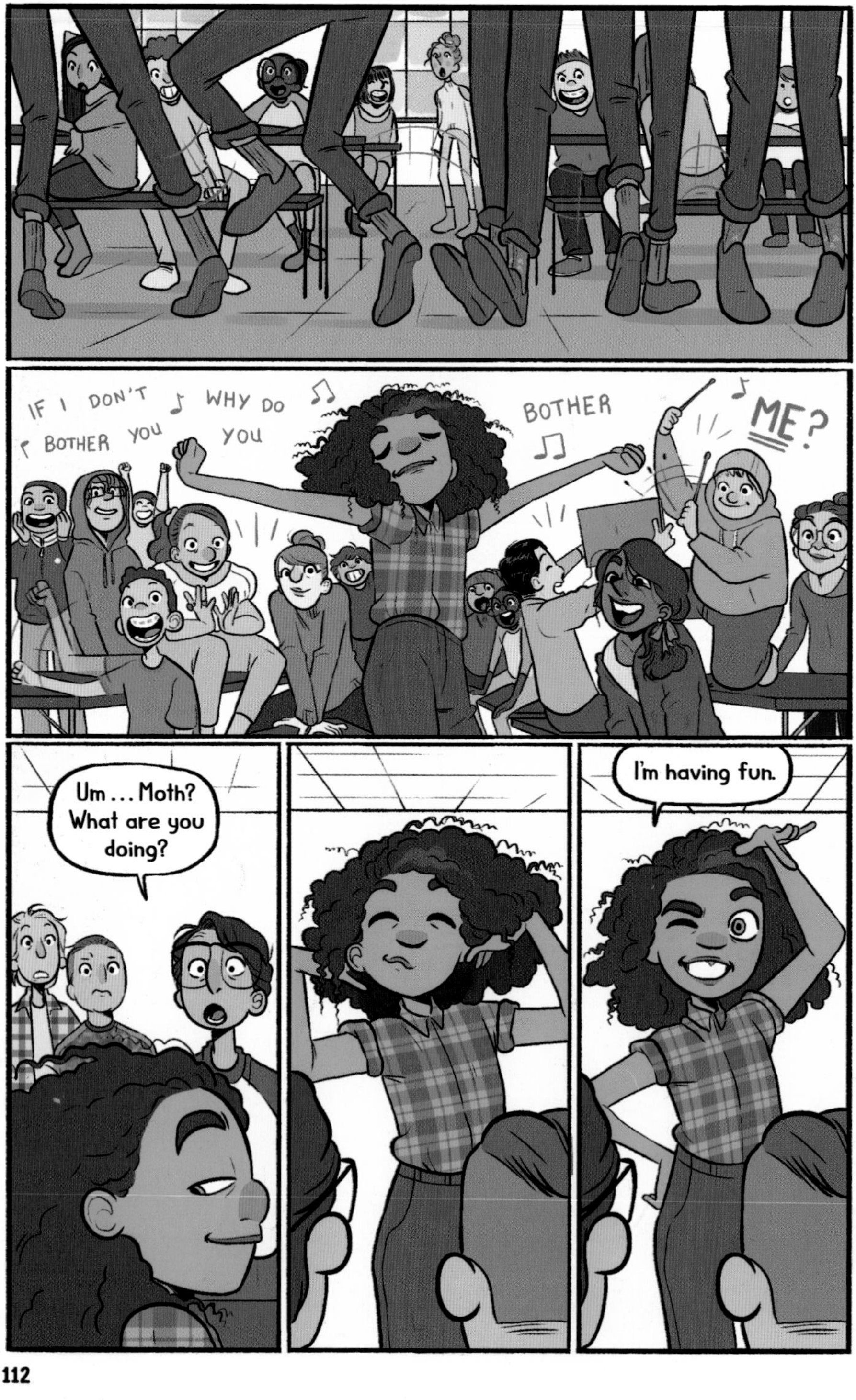
IF I DON'T BOTHER YOU
WHY DO YOU BOTHER
ME?
Um . . . Moth? What are you doing?
I'm having fun.

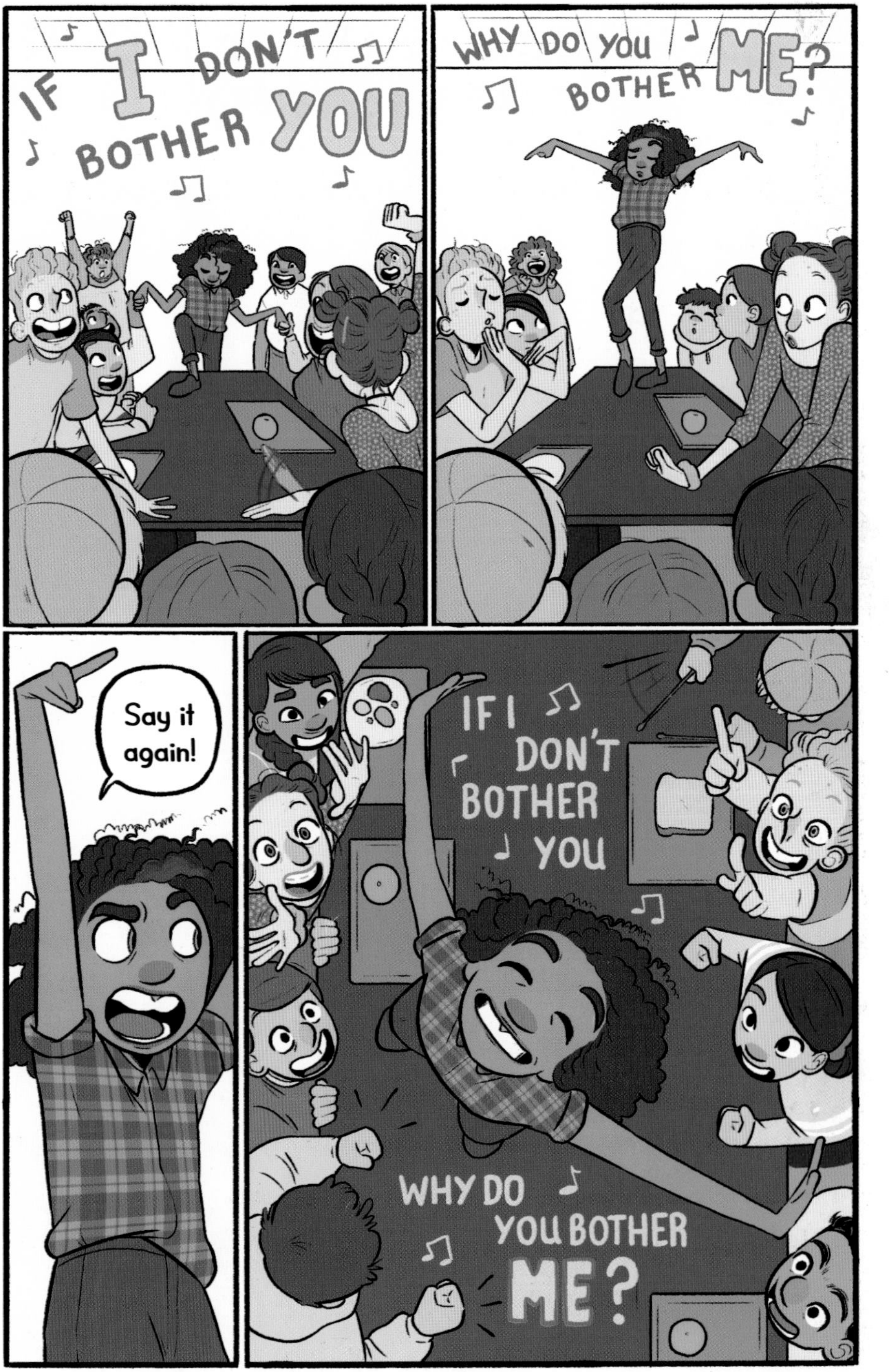
IF I DON'T BOTHER YOU
WHY DO YOU BOTHER ME?
Say it again!
IF I DON'T BOTHER YOU
WHY DO YOU BOTHER ME?

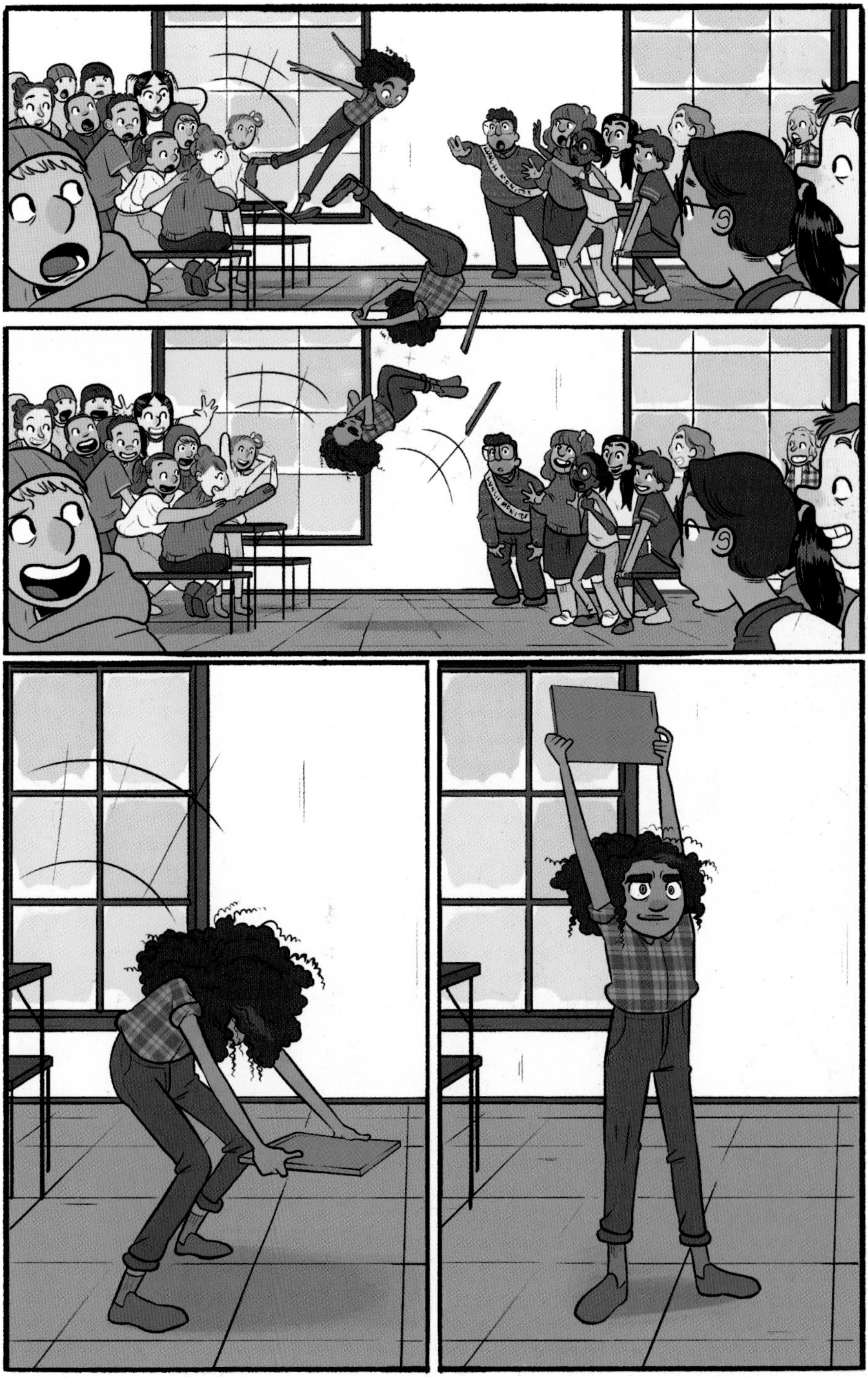
LUNCH MONITOR
LUNCH MONITOR

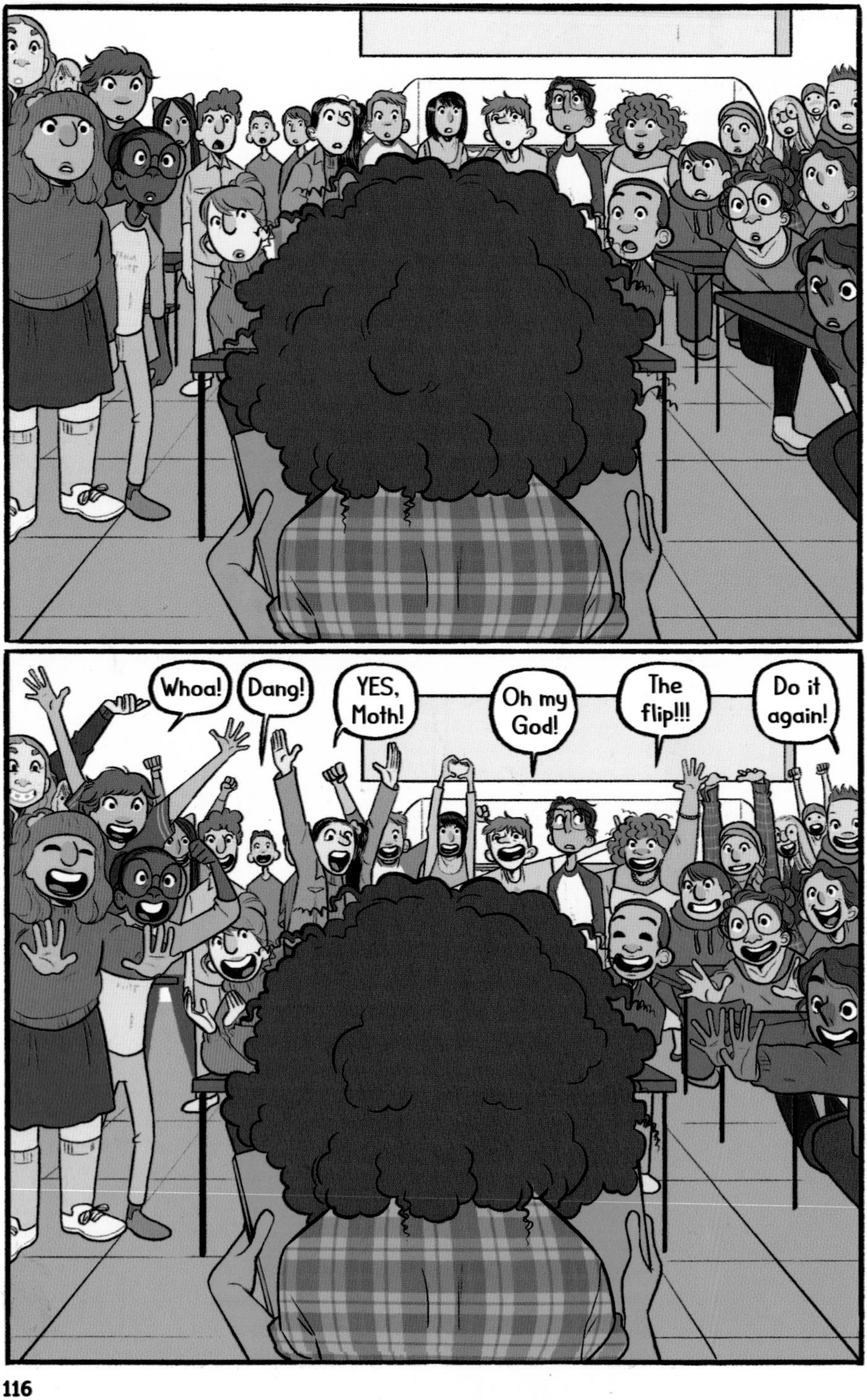
Whoa!
Dang!
YES, Moth!
Oh my God!
The flip!!!
Do it again!

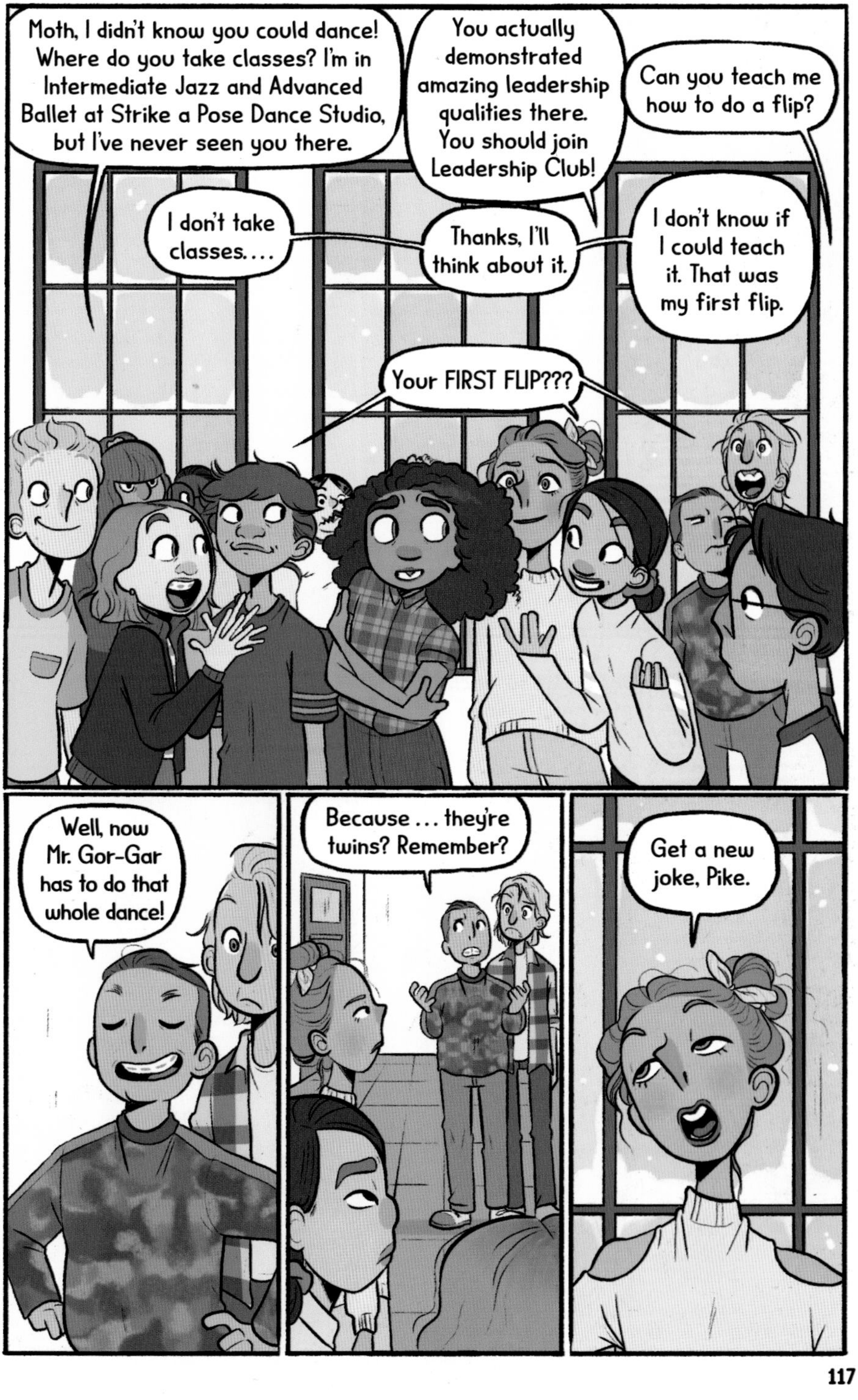
Moth, I didn't know you could dance! Where do you take classes? I'm in Intermediate Jazz and Advanced Ballet at Strike a Pose Dance Studio, but I've never seen you there.
You actually demonstrated amazing leadership qualities there. You should join Leadership Club!
Can you teach me how to do a flip?
I don't take classes. . . .
Thanks, I'll think about it.
I don't know if I could teach it. That was my first flip.
Your FIRST FLIP???
Well, now Mr. Gor-Gar has to do that whole dance!
Because . . . they're twins? Remember?
Get a new joke, Pike.

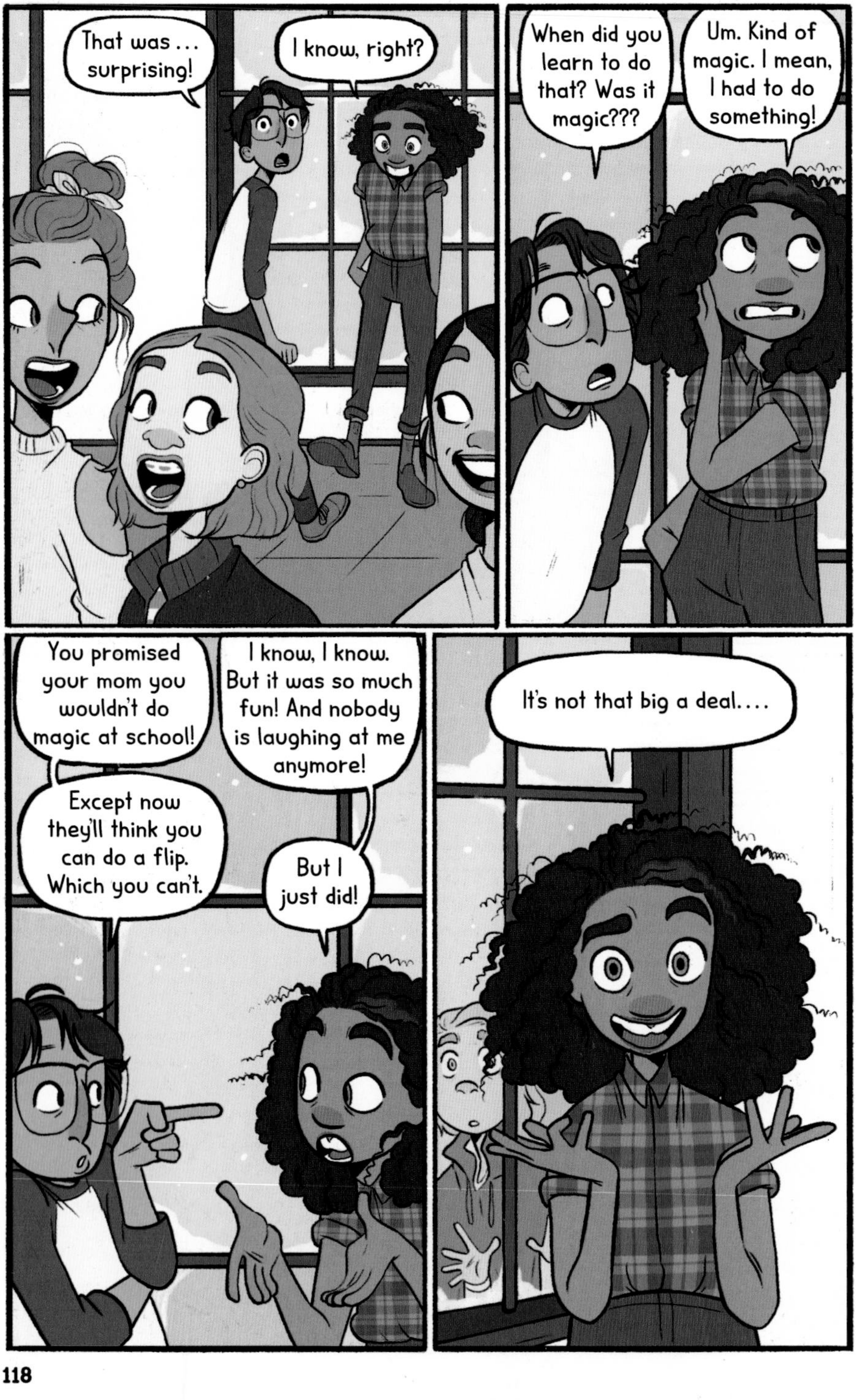

That was . . . surprising!
I know, right?
When did you learn to do that? Was it magic???
Um. Kind of magic. I mean, I had to do something!
You promised your mom you wouldn't do magic at school!
I know, I know. But it was so much fun! And nobody is laughing at me anymore!
Except now they'll think you can do a flip. Which you can't.
But I just did!
It's not that big a deal. . . .

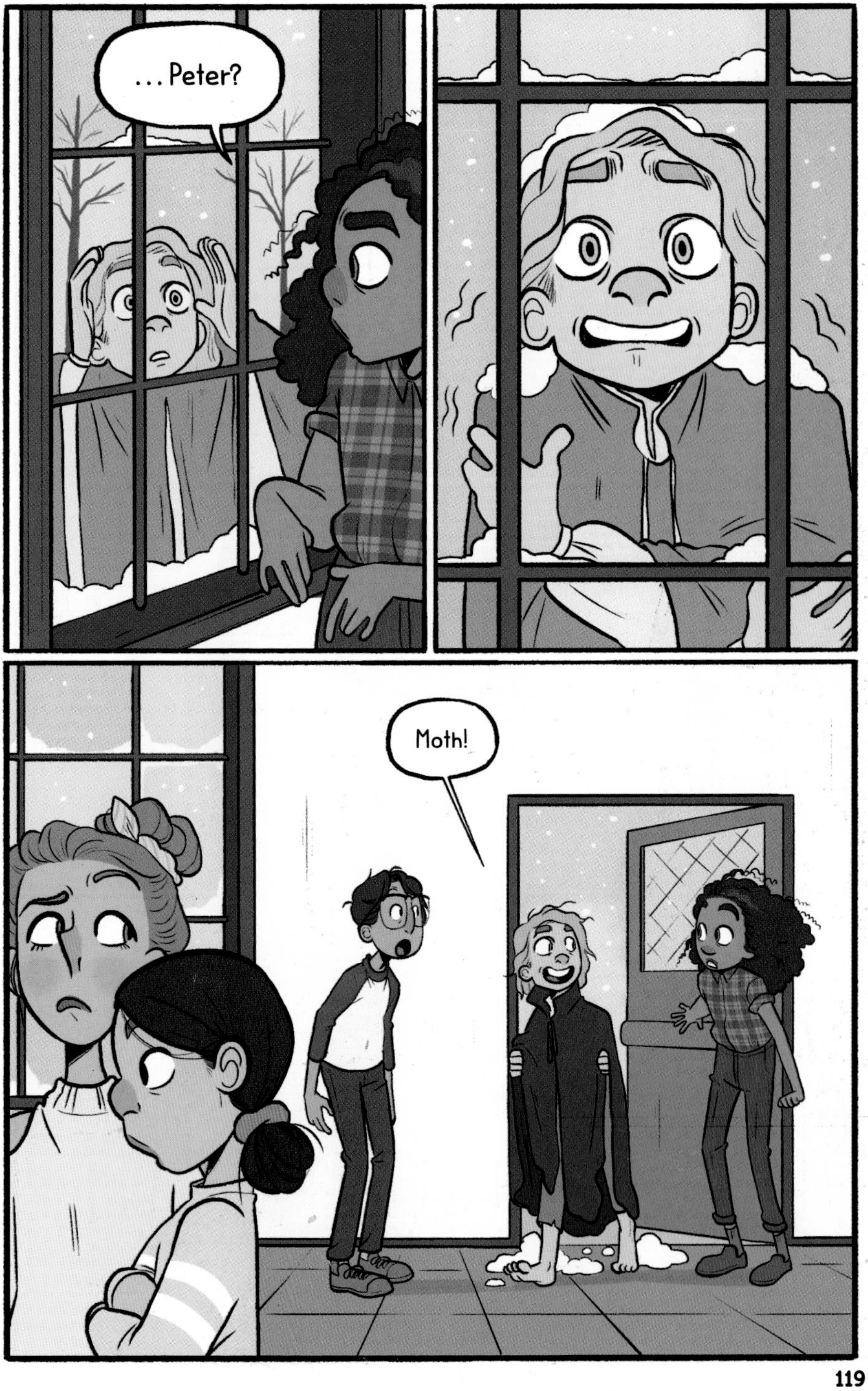
...Peter?
Moth!

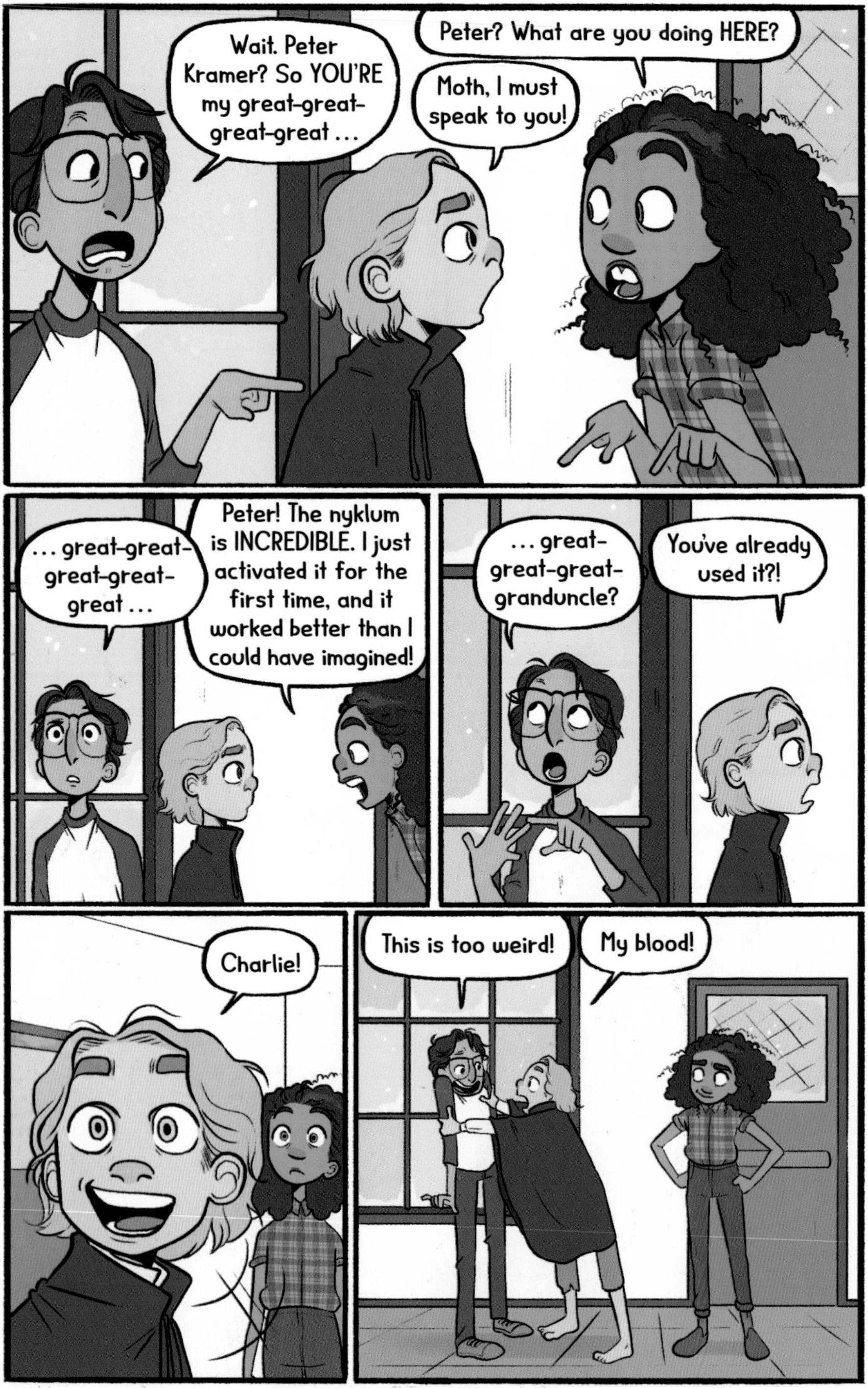
Wait. Peter Kramer? So YOU'RE my great-great-great-great . . .
Peter? What are you doing HERE?
Moth, I must speak to you!
. . . great-great-great-great-great . . .
Peter! The nyklum is INCREDIBLE. I just activated it for the first time, and it worked better than I could have imagined!
. . . great-great-great-granduncle?
You've already used it?!
Charlie!
This is too weird!
My blood!

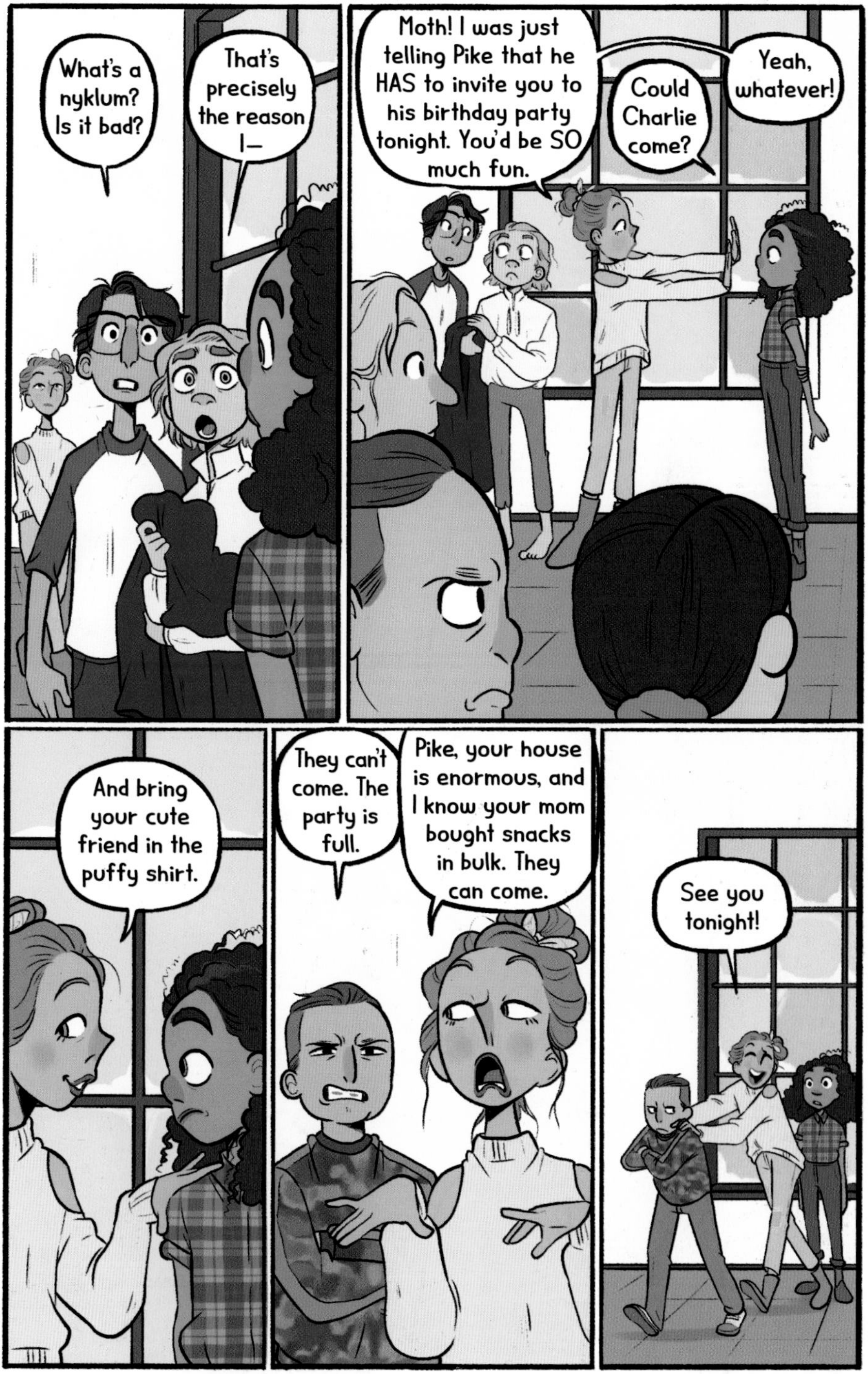

What's a nyklum? Is it bad?
That's precisely the reason I—
Moth! I was just telling Pike that he HAS to invite you to his birthday party tonight. You'd be SO much fun.
Could Charlie come?
Yeah, whatever!
And bring your cute friend in the puffy shirt.
They can't come. The party is full.
Pike, your house is enormous, and I know your mom bought snacks in bulk. They can come.
See you tonight!

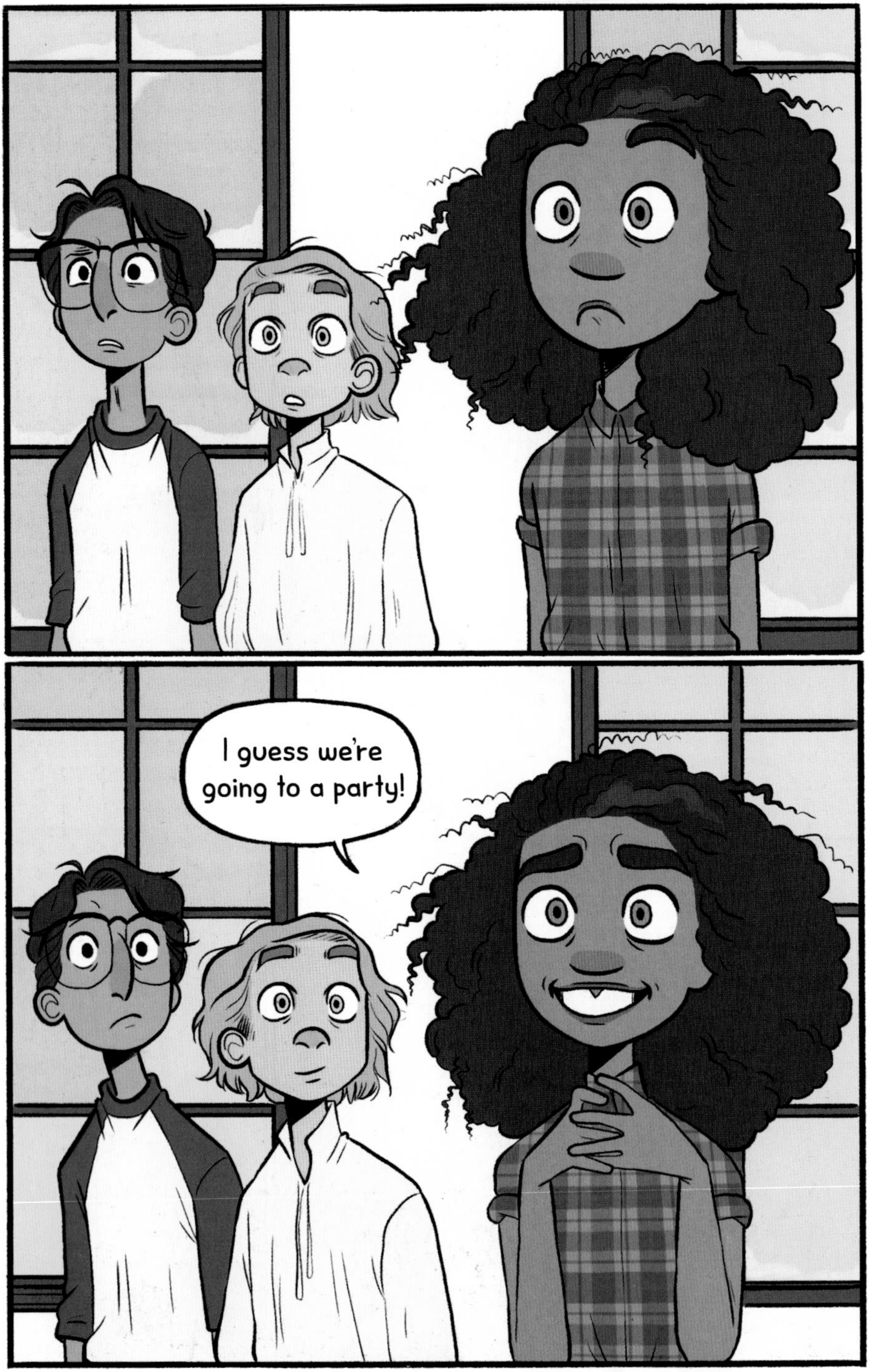
I guess we're going to a party!

CHAPTER 7

Mass Pike

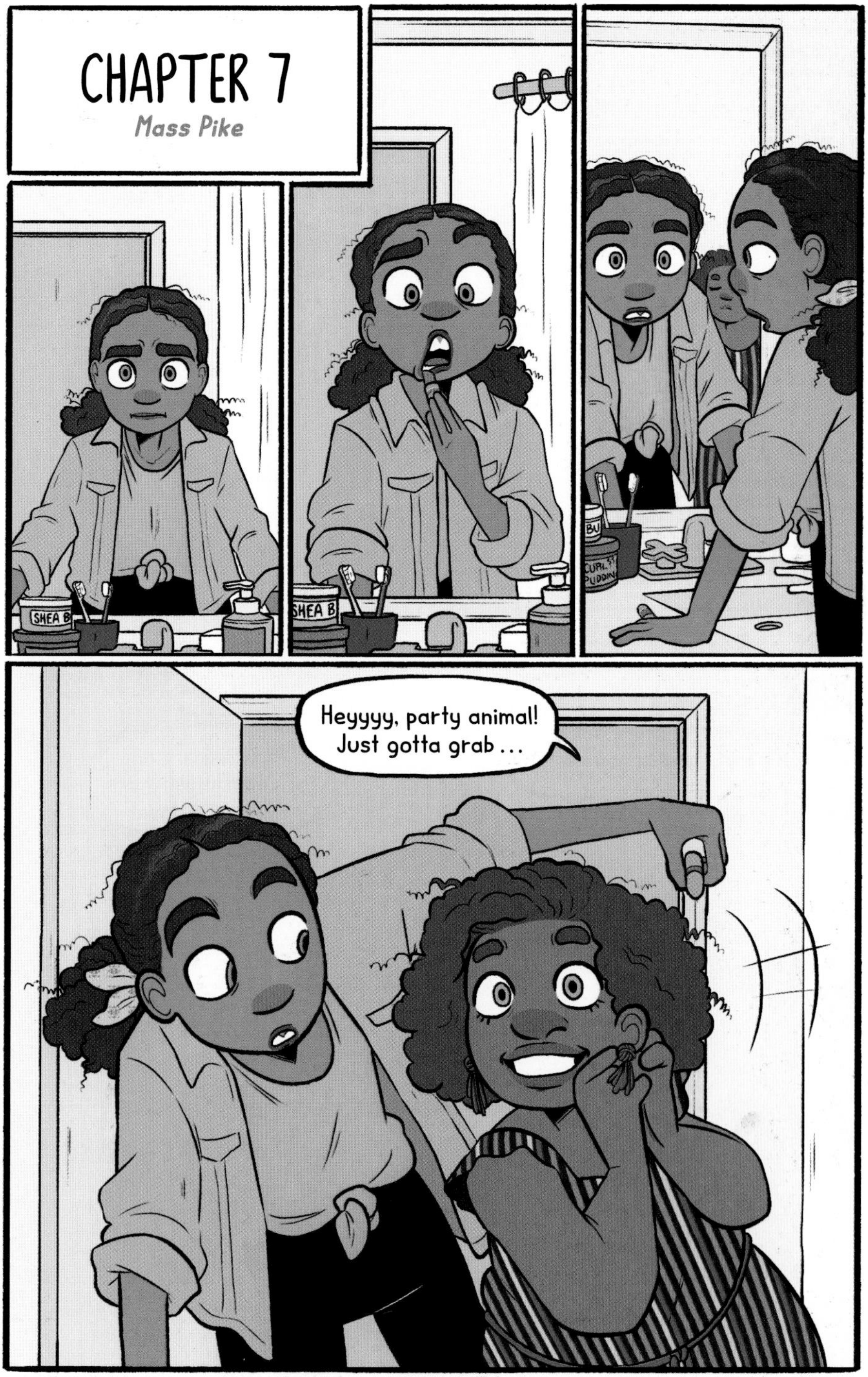
SHEA B
SHEA B
Heyyyy, party animal! Just gotta grab . . .

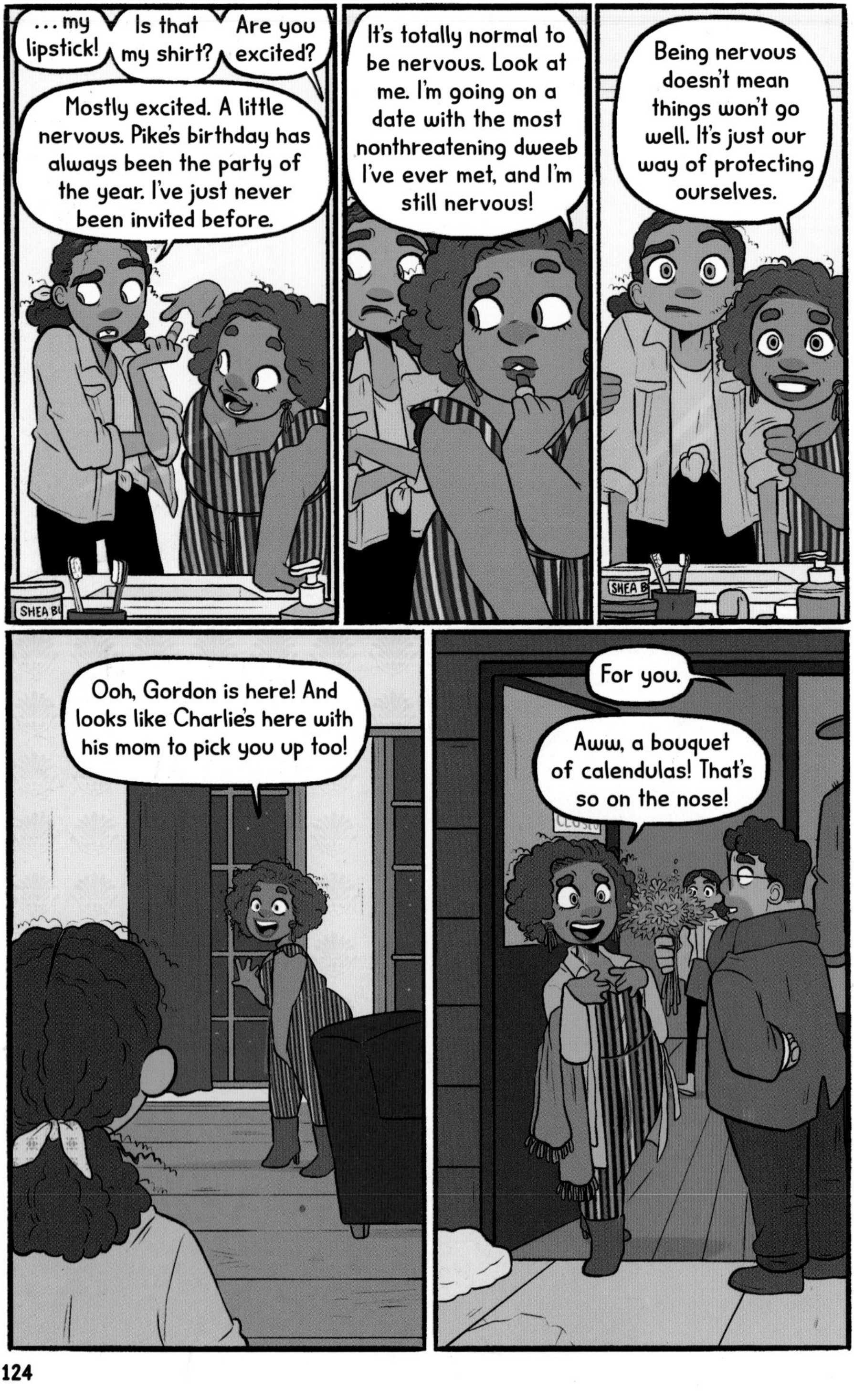

... my lipstick!
Is that my shirt?
Are you excited?
Mostly excited. A little nervous. Pike's birthday has always been the party of the year. I've just never been invited before.
It's totally normal to be nervous. Look at me. I'm going on a date with the most nonthreatening dweeb I've ever met, and I'm still nervous!
Being nervous doesn't mean things won't go well. It's just our way of protecting ourselves.
Ooh, Gordon is here! And looks like Charlie's here with his mom to pick you up too!
For you.
Aww, a bouquet of calendulas! That's so on the nose!

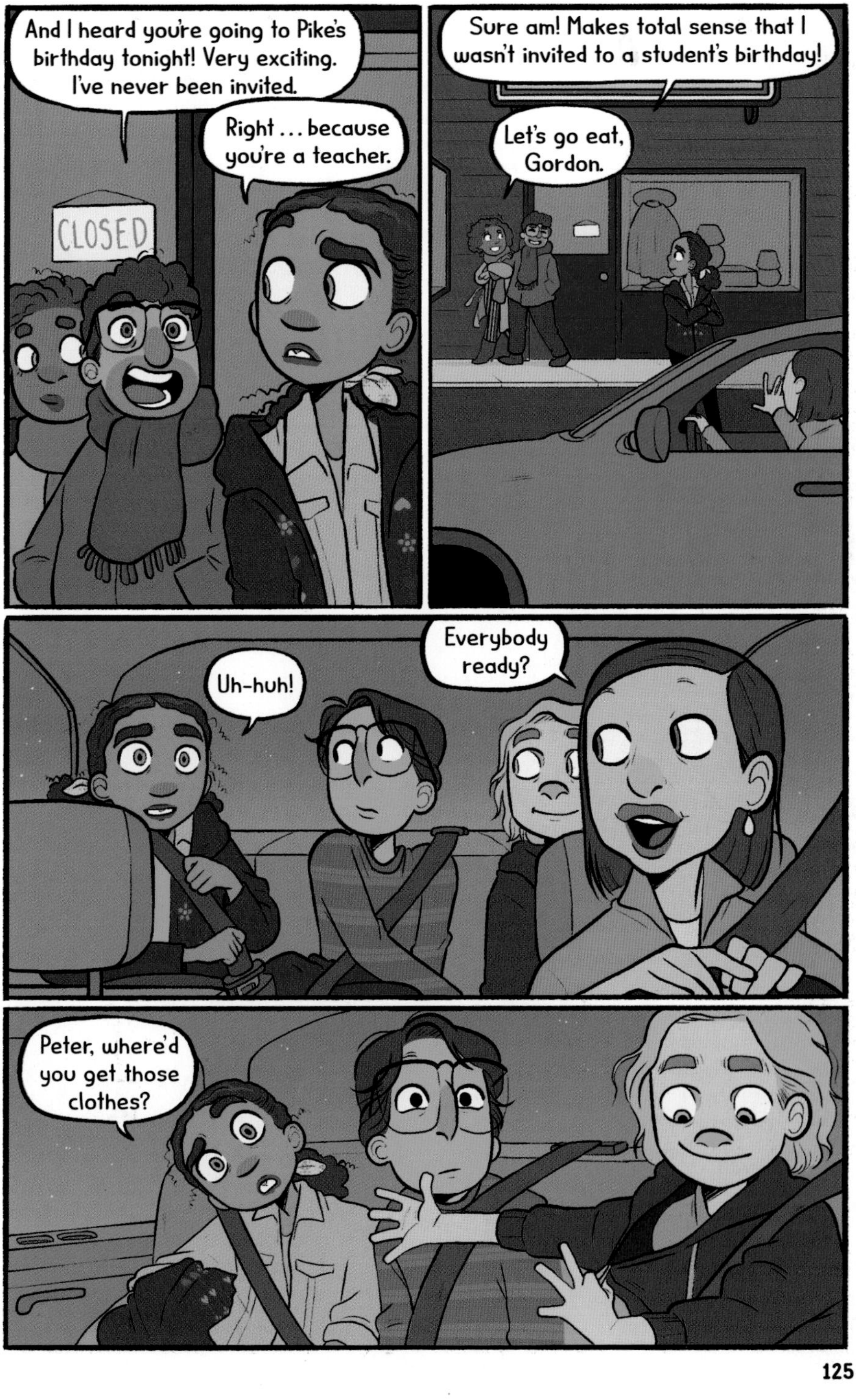
And I heard you're going to Pike's birthday tonight! Very exciting. I've never been invited.
Right . . . because you're a teacher.
CLOSED
Sure am! Makes total sense that I wasn't invited to a student's birthday!
Let's go eat, Gordon.
Everybody ready?
Uh-huh!
Peter, where'd you get those clothes?

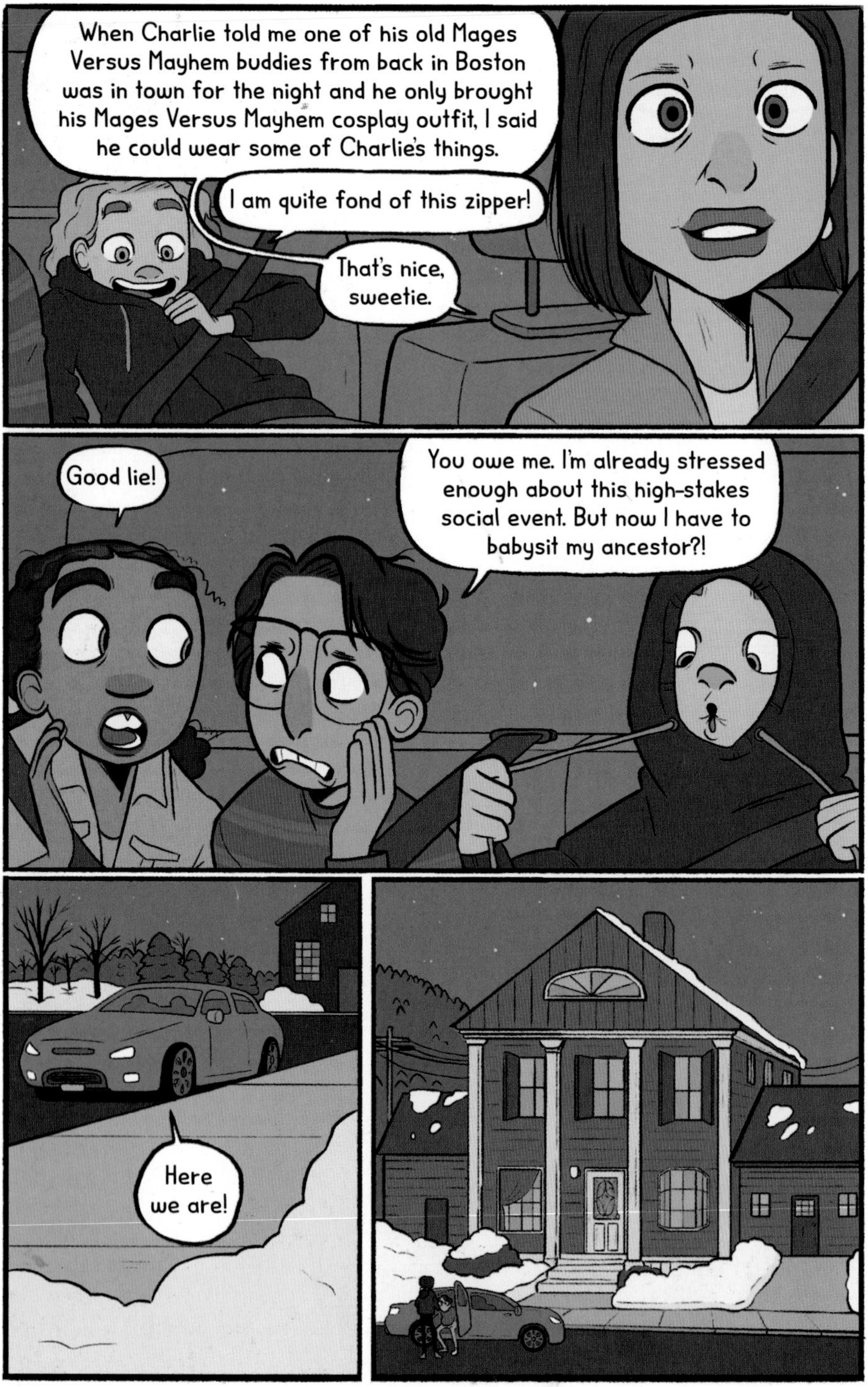
When Charlie told me one of his old Mages Versus Mayhem buddies from back in Boston was in town for the night and he only brought his Mages Versus Mayhem cosplay outfit, I said he could wear some of Charlie's things.
I am quite fond of this zipper!
That's nice, sweetie.
Good lie!
You owe me. I'm already stressed enough about this high-stakes social event. But now I have to babysit my ancestor?!
Here we are!

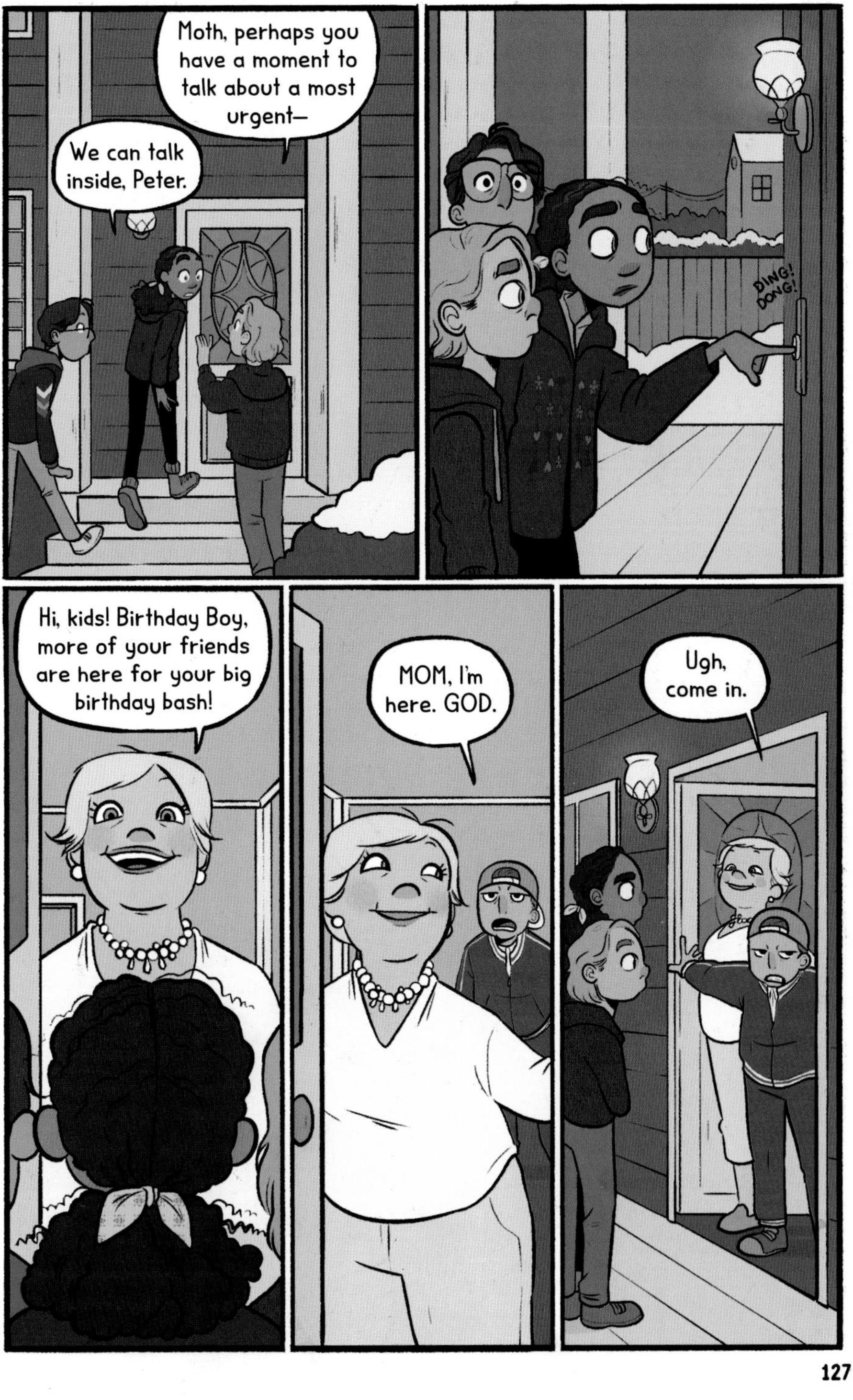
Moth, perhaps you have a moment to talk about a most urgent—
We can talk inside, Peter.
DING! DONG!
Hi, kids! Birthday Boy, more of your friends are here for your big birthday bash!
MOM, I'm here. GOD.
Ugh, come in.

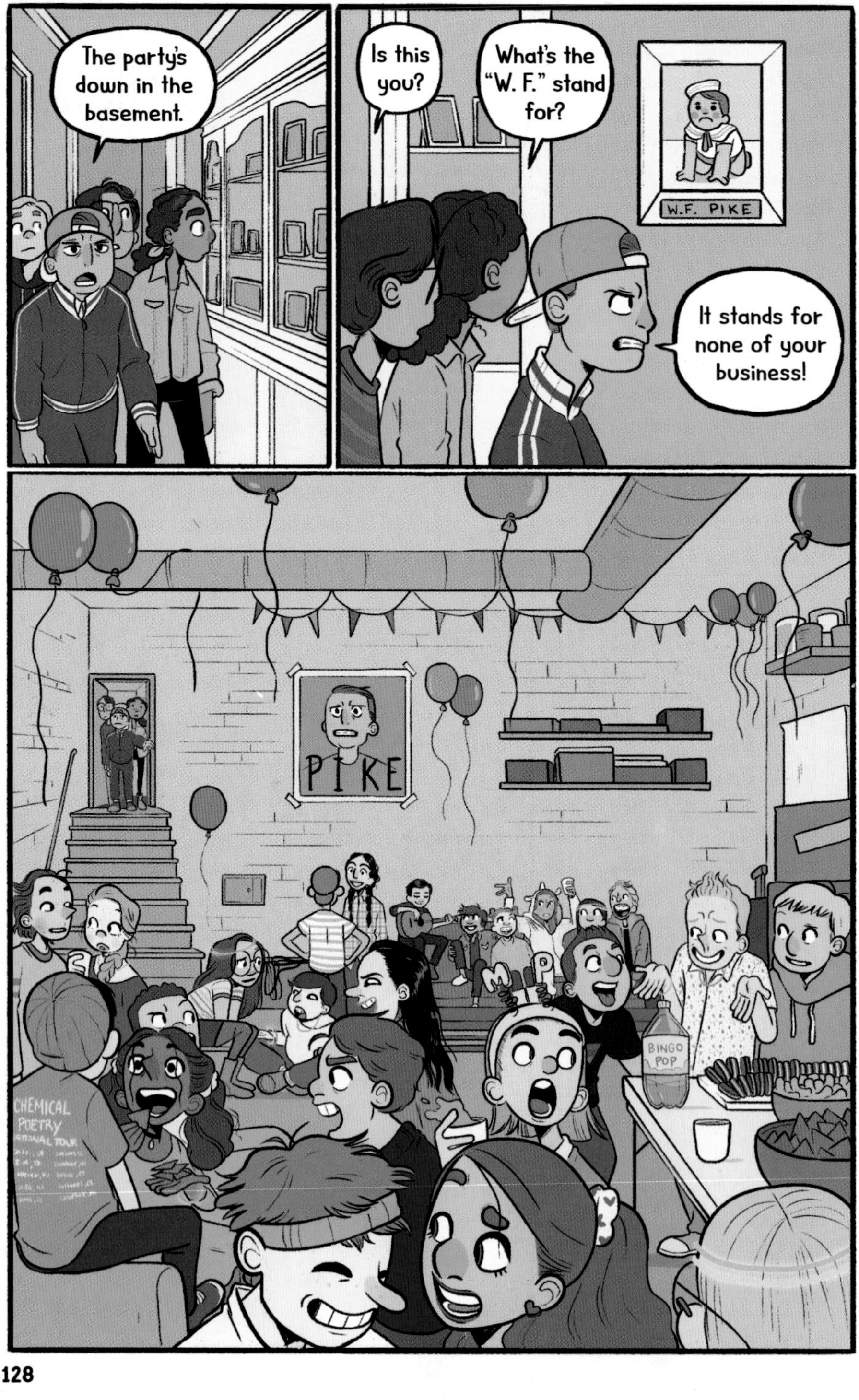
The party's down in the basement.
Is this you?
What's the "W. F." stand for?
W.F. PIKE
It stands for none of your business!
PIKE
BINGO POP
CHEMICAL POETRY

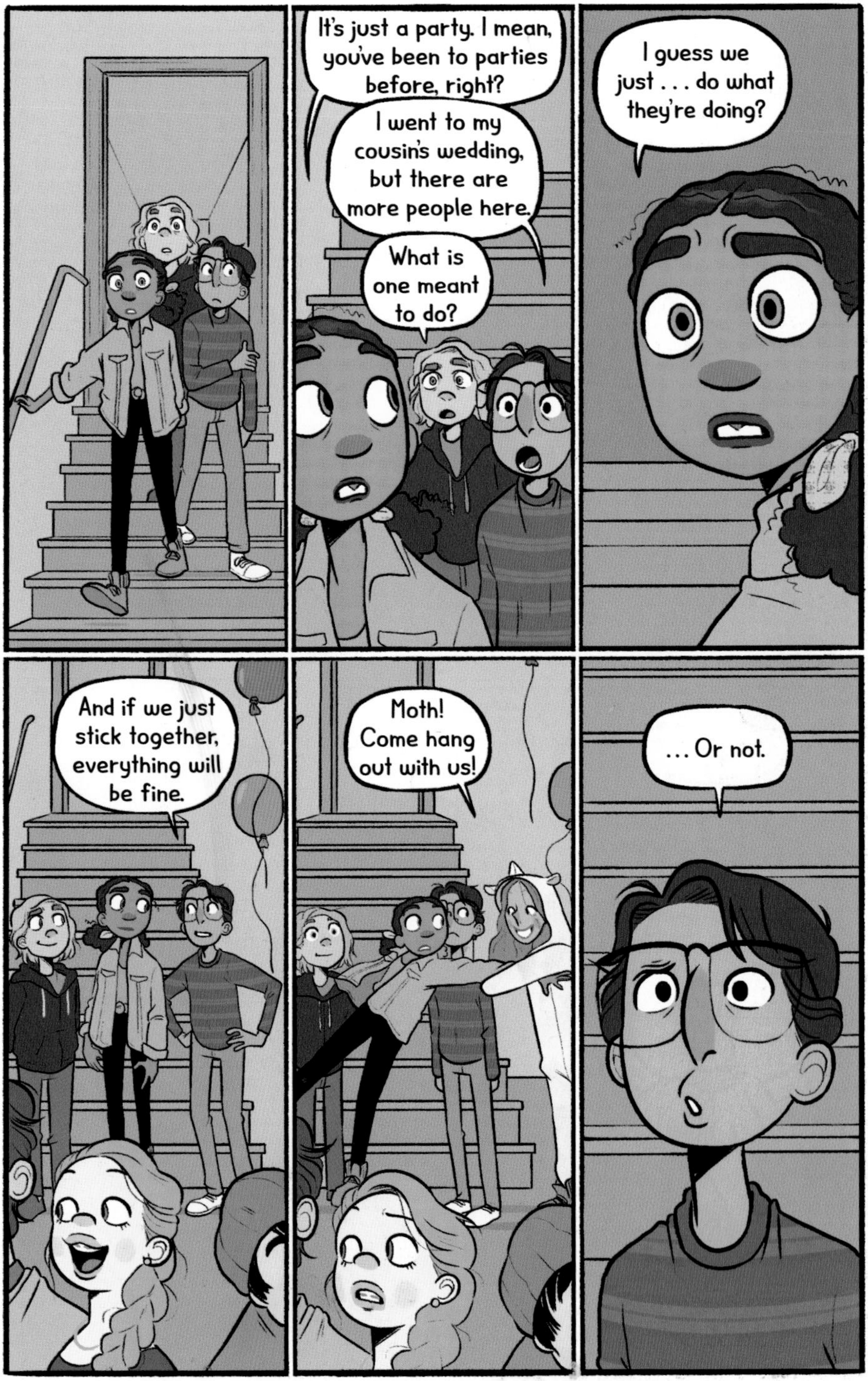
It's just a party. I mean, you've been to parties before, right?
I went to my cousin's wedding, but there are more people here.
What is one meant to do?
I guess we just . . . do what they're doing?
And if we just stick together, everything will be fine.
Moth! Come hang out with us!
. . . Or not.

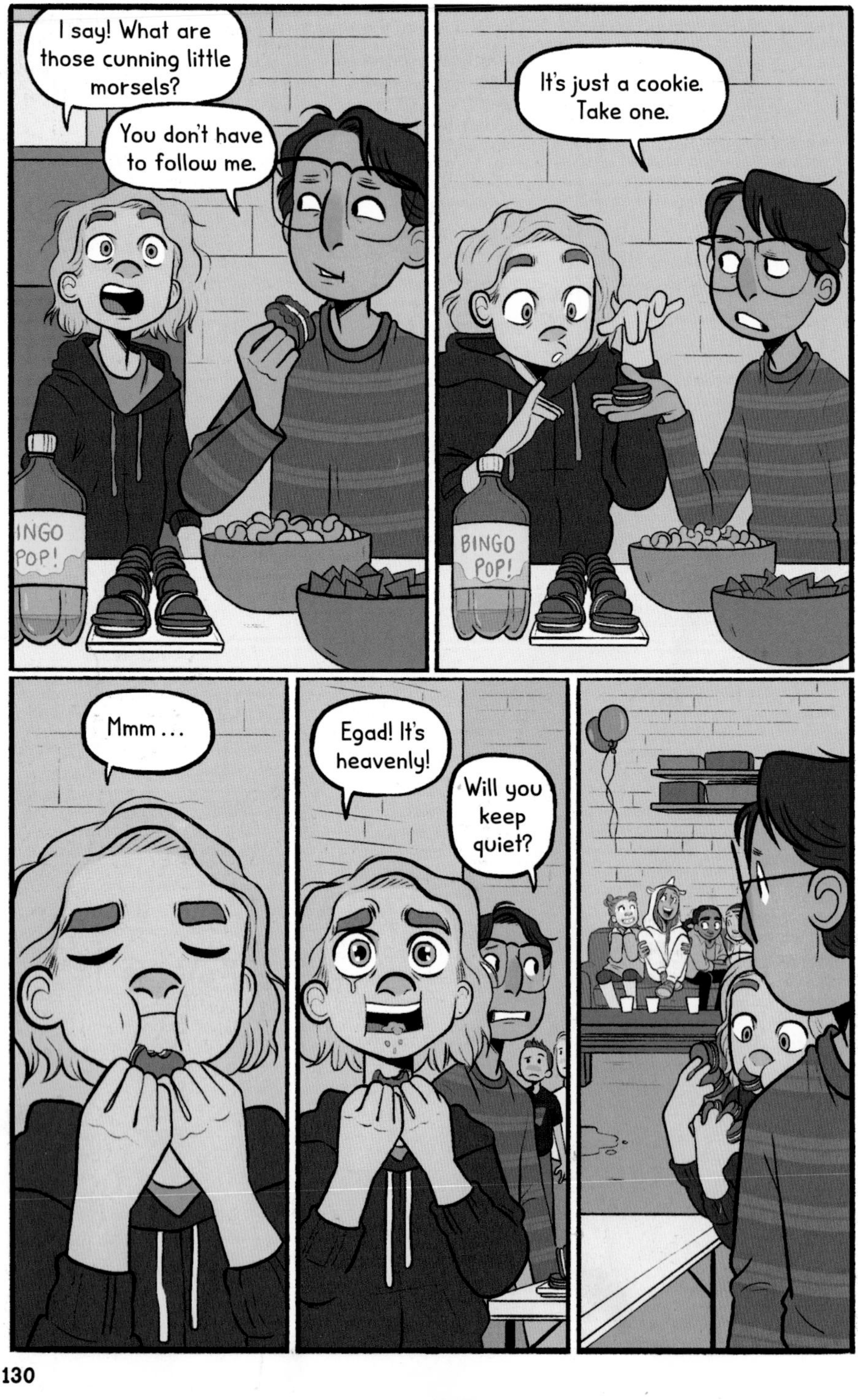
I say! What are those cunning little morsels?
You don't have to follow me.
BINGO POP!
It's just a cookie. Take one.
BINGO POP!
Mmm...
Egad! It's heavenly!
Will you keep quiet?

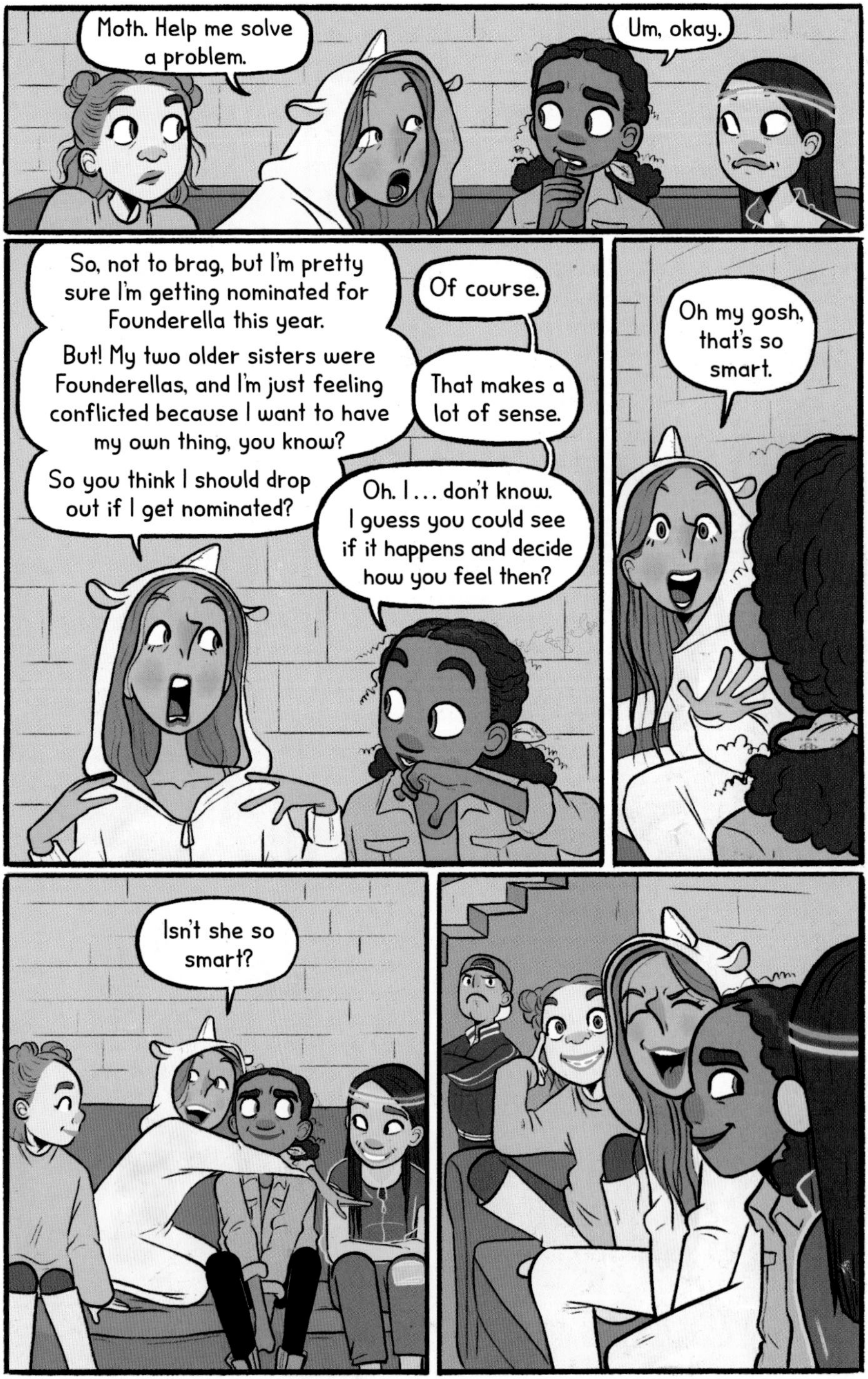
Moth. Help me solve a problem.
Um, okay.
So, not to brag, but I'm pretty sure I'm getting nominated for Founderella this year.
But! My two older sisters were Founderellas, and I'm just feeling conflicted because I want to have my own thing, you know?
Of course.
That makes a lot of sense.
So you think I should drop out if I get nominated?
Oh. I . . . don't know. I guess you could see if it happens and decide how you feel then?
Oh my gosh, that's so smart.
Isn't she so smart?

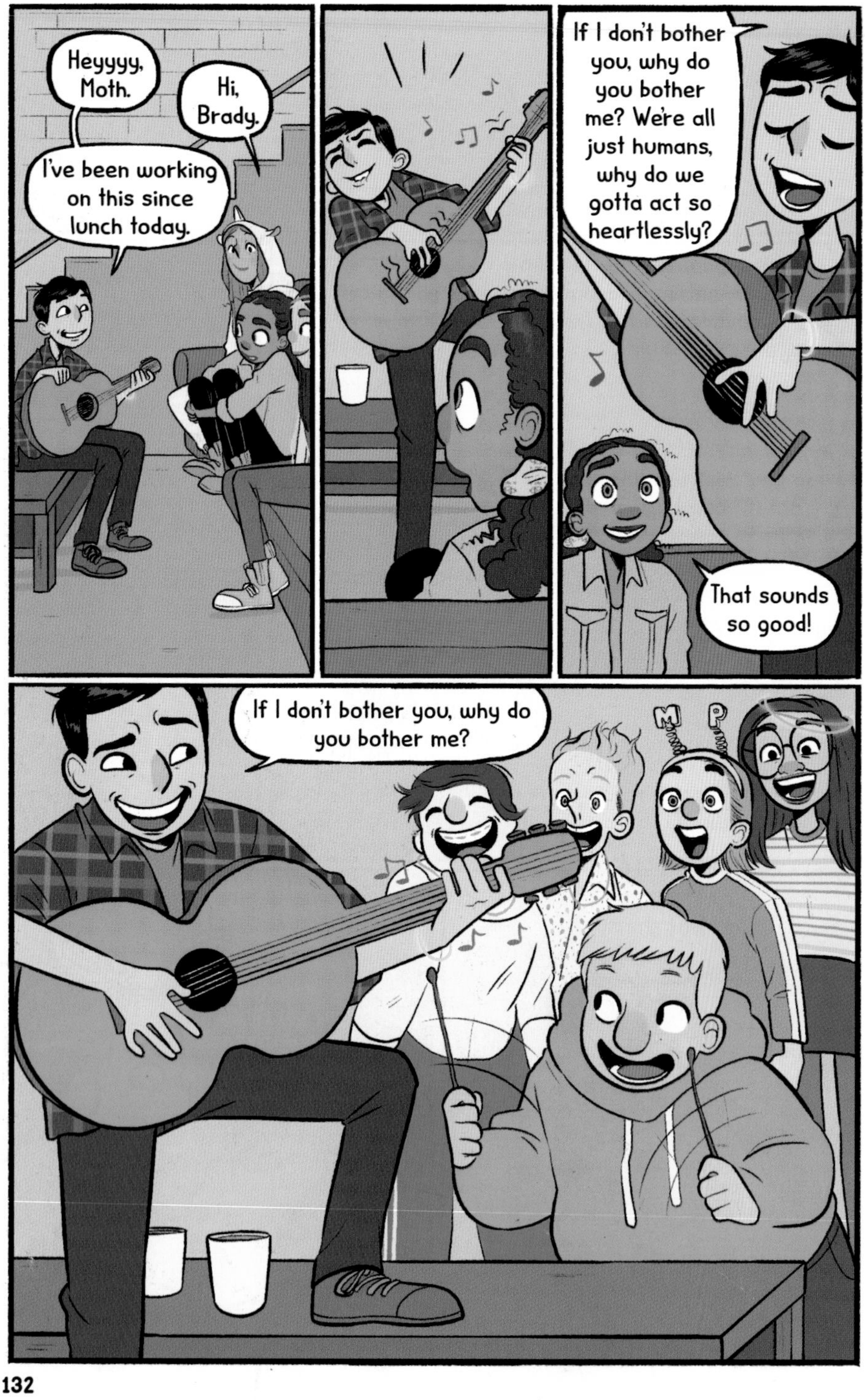
Heyyyy, Moth.
Hi, Brady.
I've been working on this since lunch today.
If I don't bother you, why do you bother me? We're all just humans, why do we gotta act so heartlessly?
That sounds so good!
If I don't bother you, why do you bother me?
M
P

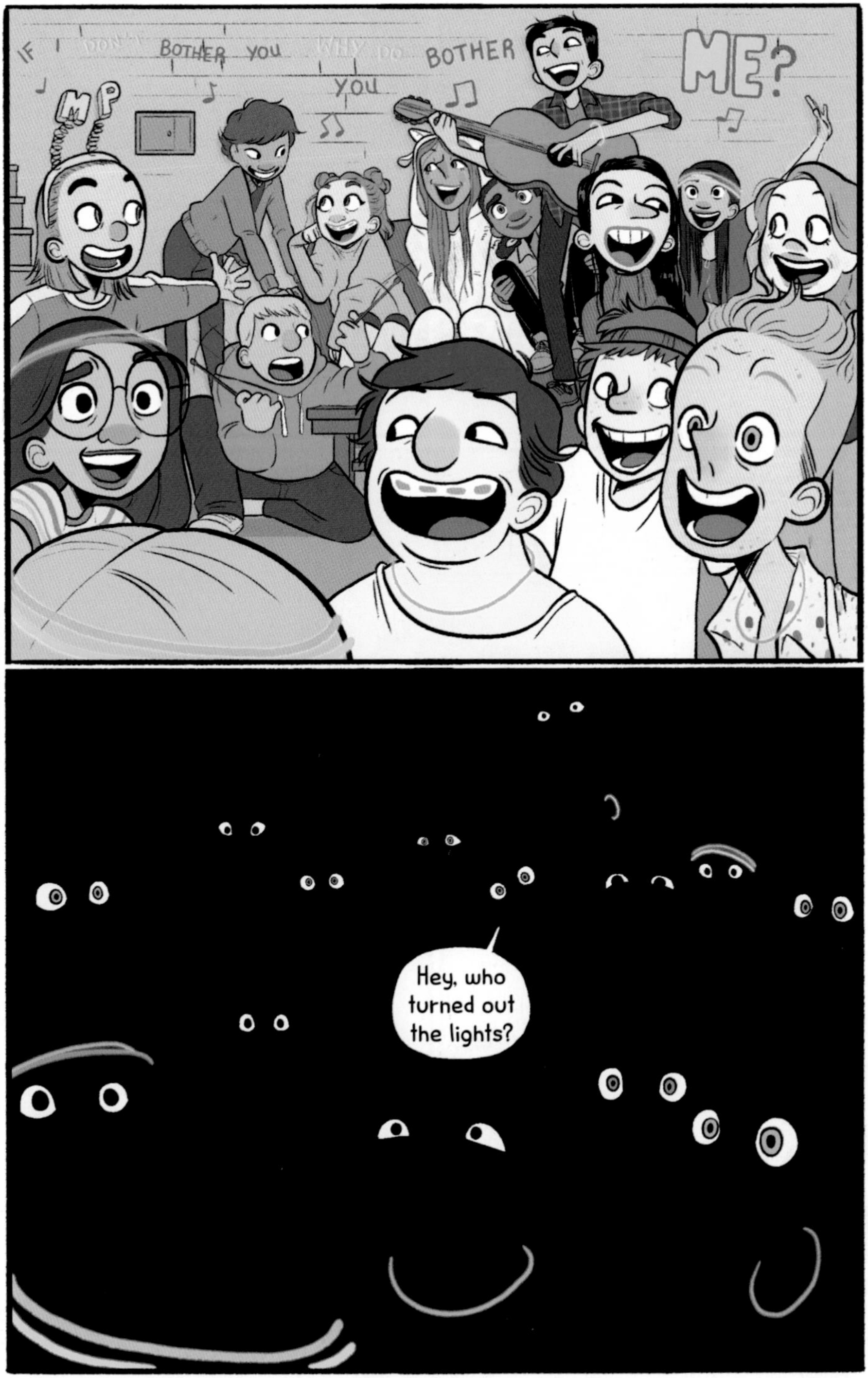
IF I DON'T BOTHER YOU WHY DO YOU BOTHER ME?
MP
Hey, who turned out the lights?

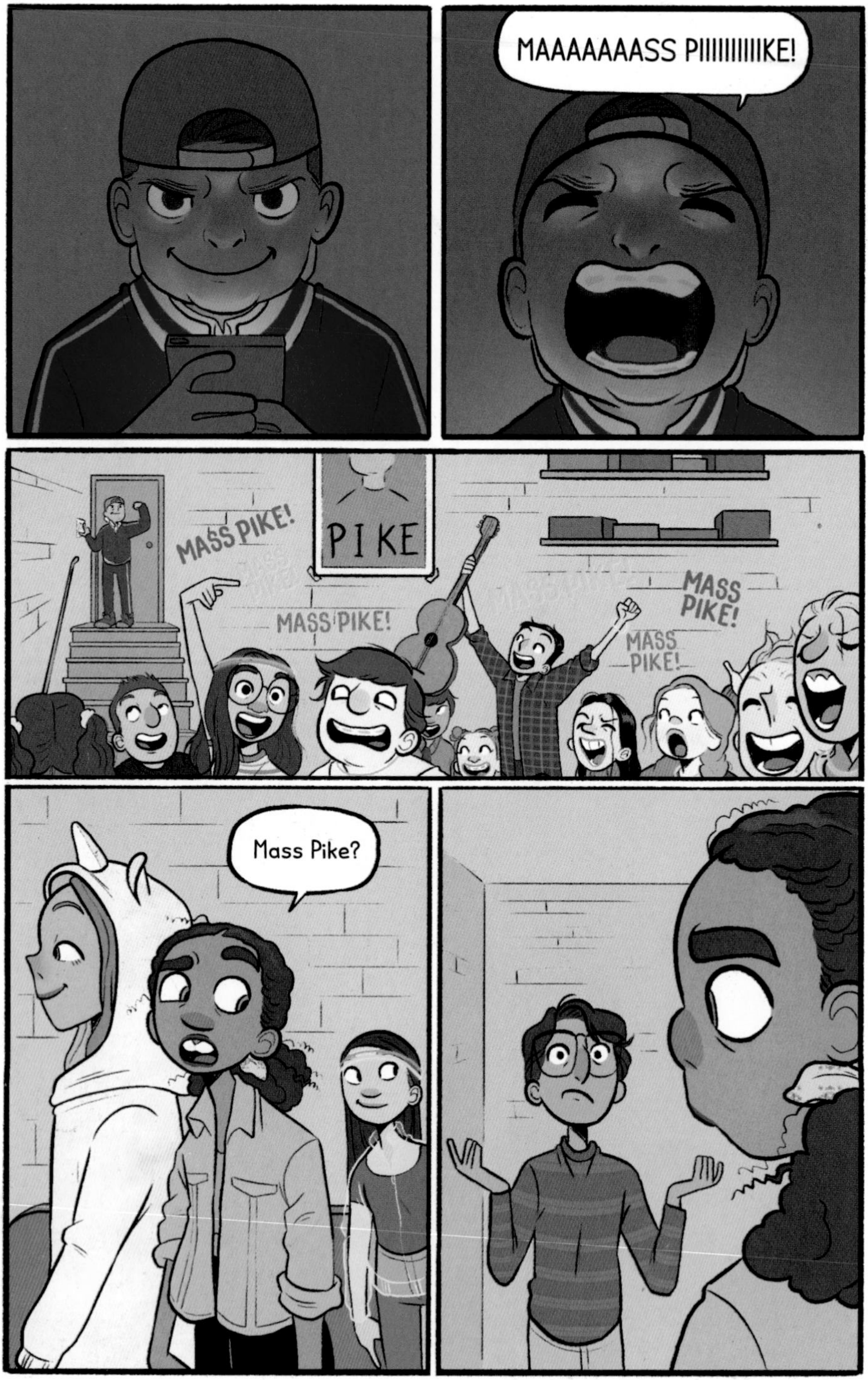
MAAAAAAASS PIIIIIIIIIKE!
PIKE
MASS PIKE!
MASS PIKE!
MASS PIKE!
MASS PIKE!
Mass Pike?

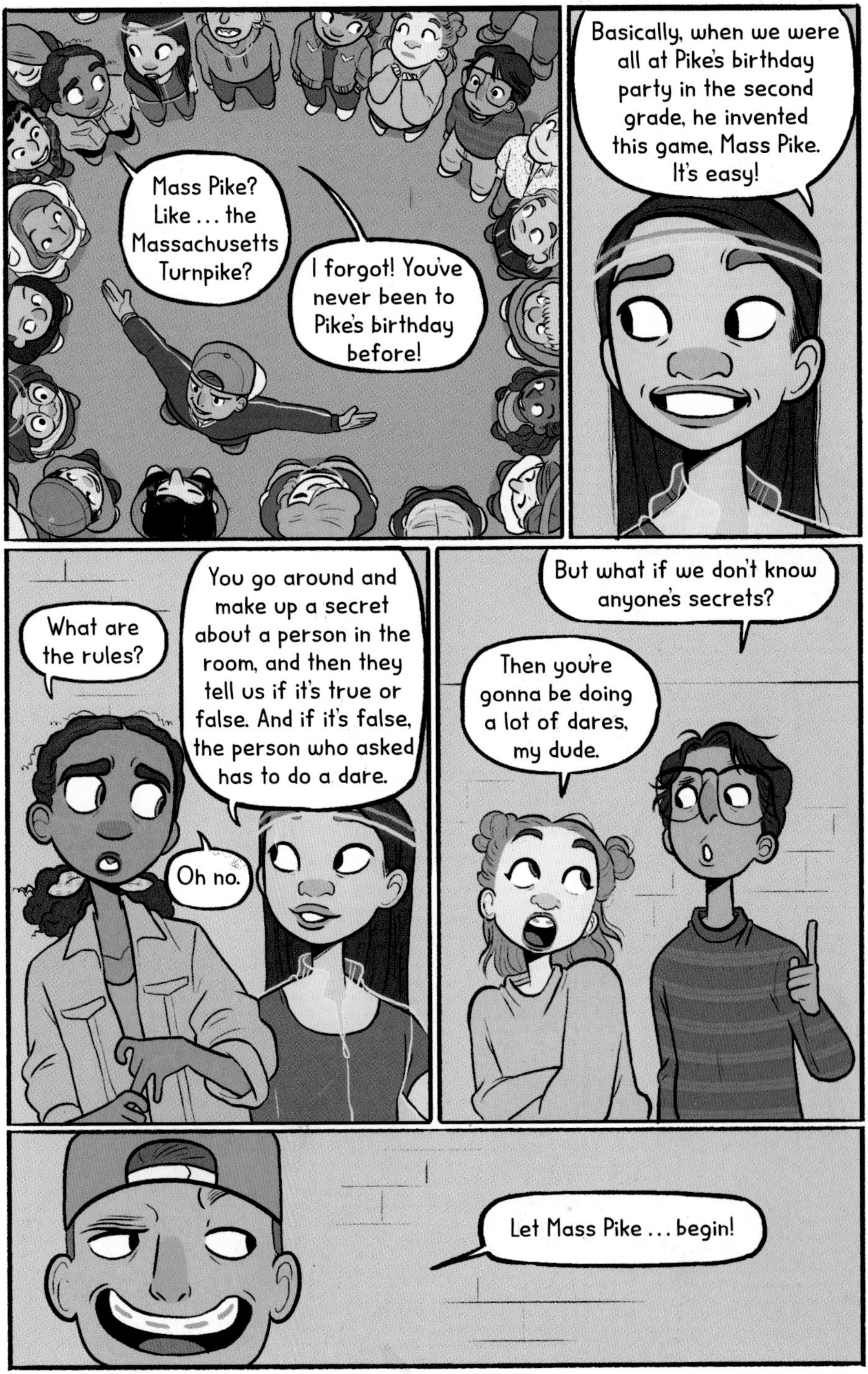
Mass Pike? Like . . . the Massachusetts Turnpike?
I forgot! You've never been to Pike's birthday before!
Basically, when we were all at Pike's birthday party in the second grade, he invented this game, Mass Pike. It's easy!
What are the rules?
You go around and make up a secret about a person in the room, and then they tell us if it's true or false. And if it's false, the person who asked has to do a dare.
Oh no.
But what if we don't know anyone's secrets?
Then you're gonna be doing a lot of dares, my dude.
Let Mass Pike . . . begin!

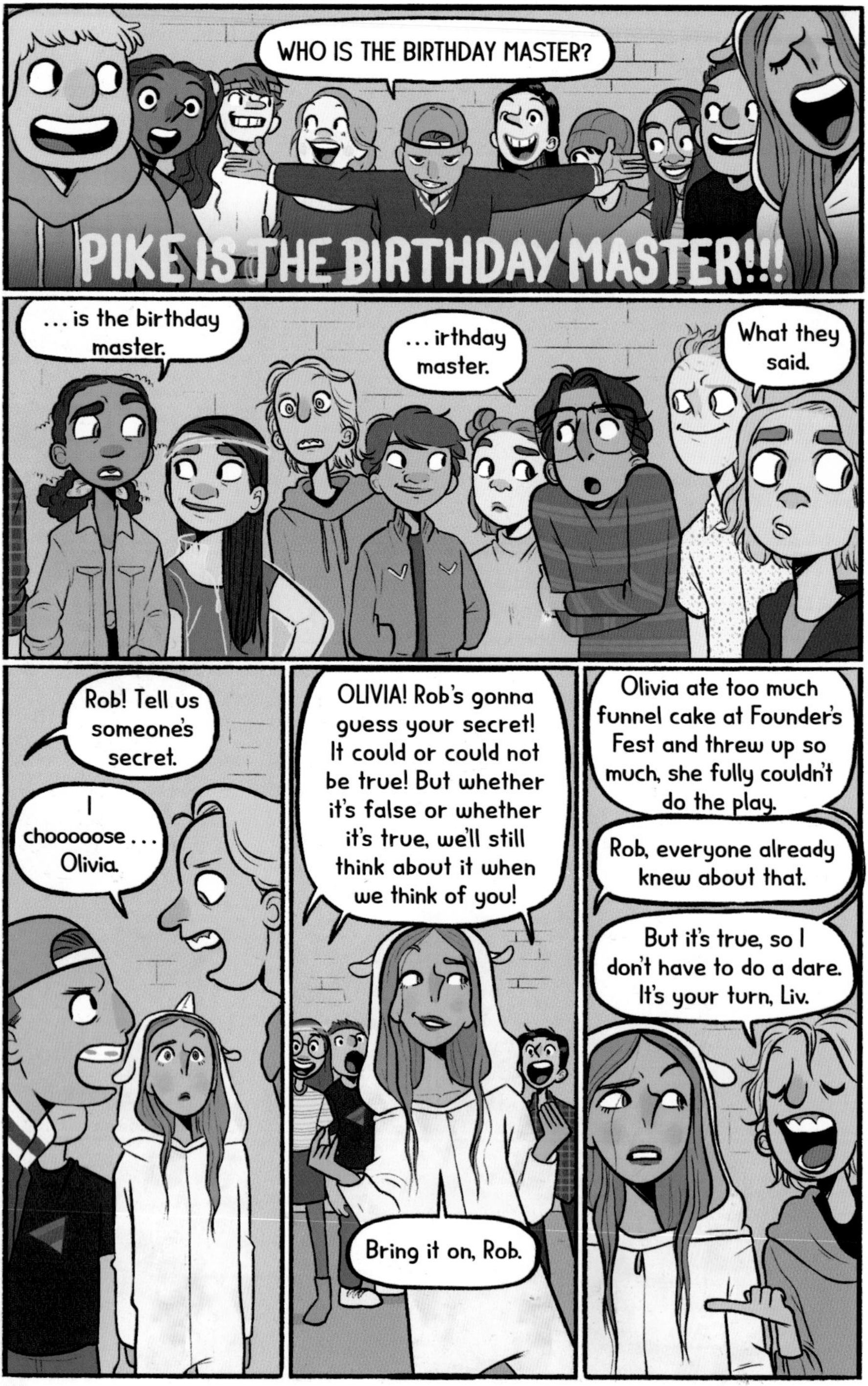
WHO IS THE BIRTHDAY MASTER?
PIKE IS THE BIRTHDAY MASTER!!!
. . . is the birthday master.
. . . irthday master.
What they said.
Rob! Tell us someone's secret.
I chooooose . . . Olivia.
OLIVIA! Rob's gonna guess your secret! It could or could not be true! But whether it's false or whether it's true, we'll still think about it when we think of you!
Bring it on, Rob.
Olivia ate too much funnel cake at Founder's Fest and threw up so much, she fully couldn't do the play.
Rob, everyone already knew about that.
But it's true, so I don't have to do a dare. It's your turn, Liv.

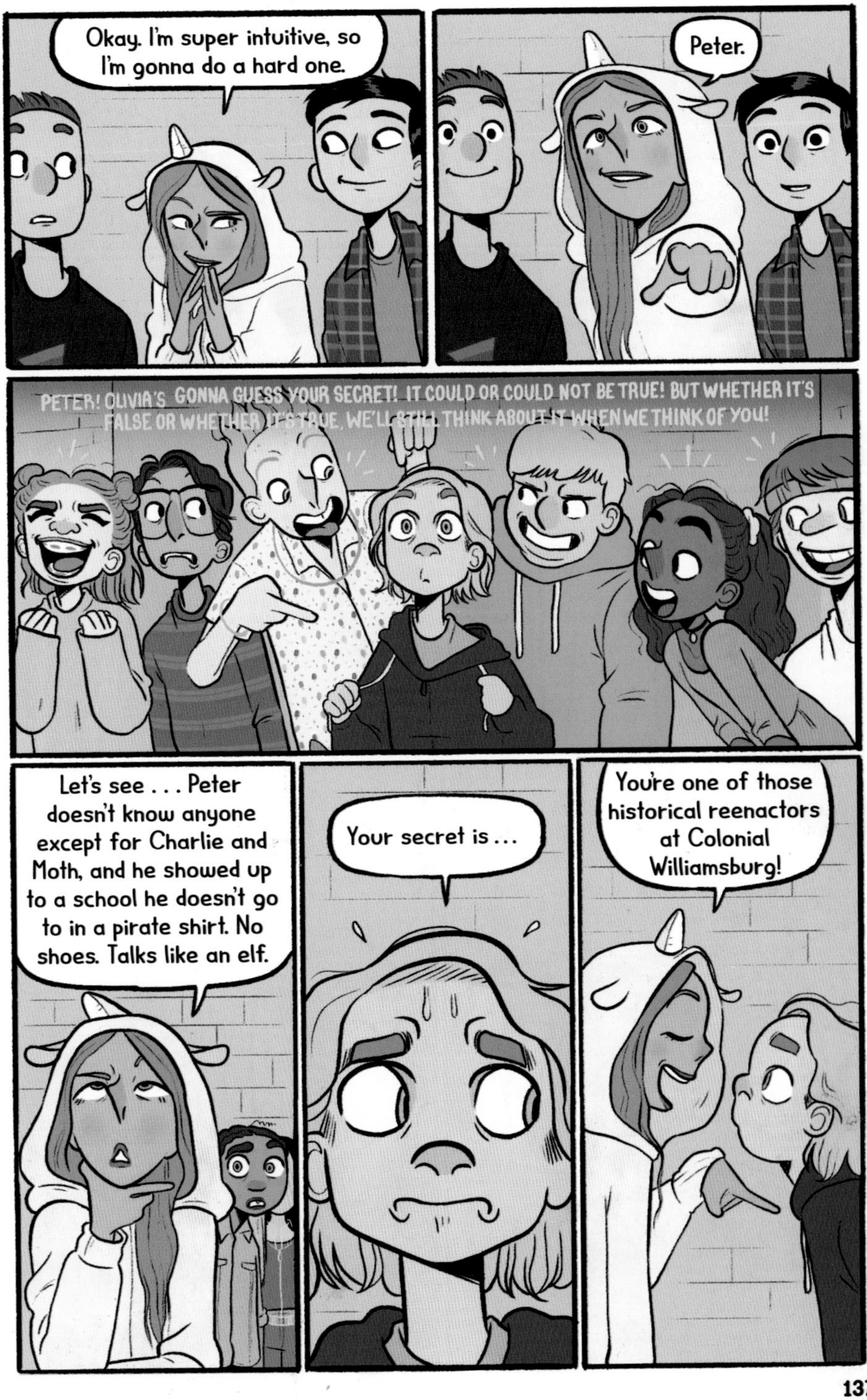
Okay. I'm super intuitive, so I'm gonna do a hard one.
Peter.
PETER! OLIVIA'S GONNA GUESS YOUR SECRET! IT COULD OR COULD NOT BE TRUE! BUT WHETHER IT'S FALSE OR WHETHER IT'S TRUE, WE'LL STILL THINK ABOUT IT WHEN WE THINK OF YOU!
Let's see . . . Peter doesn't know anyone except for Charlie and Moth, and he showed up to a school he doesn't go to in a pirate shirt. No shoes. Talks like an elf.
Your secret is . . .
You're one of those historical reenactors at Colonial Williamsburg!

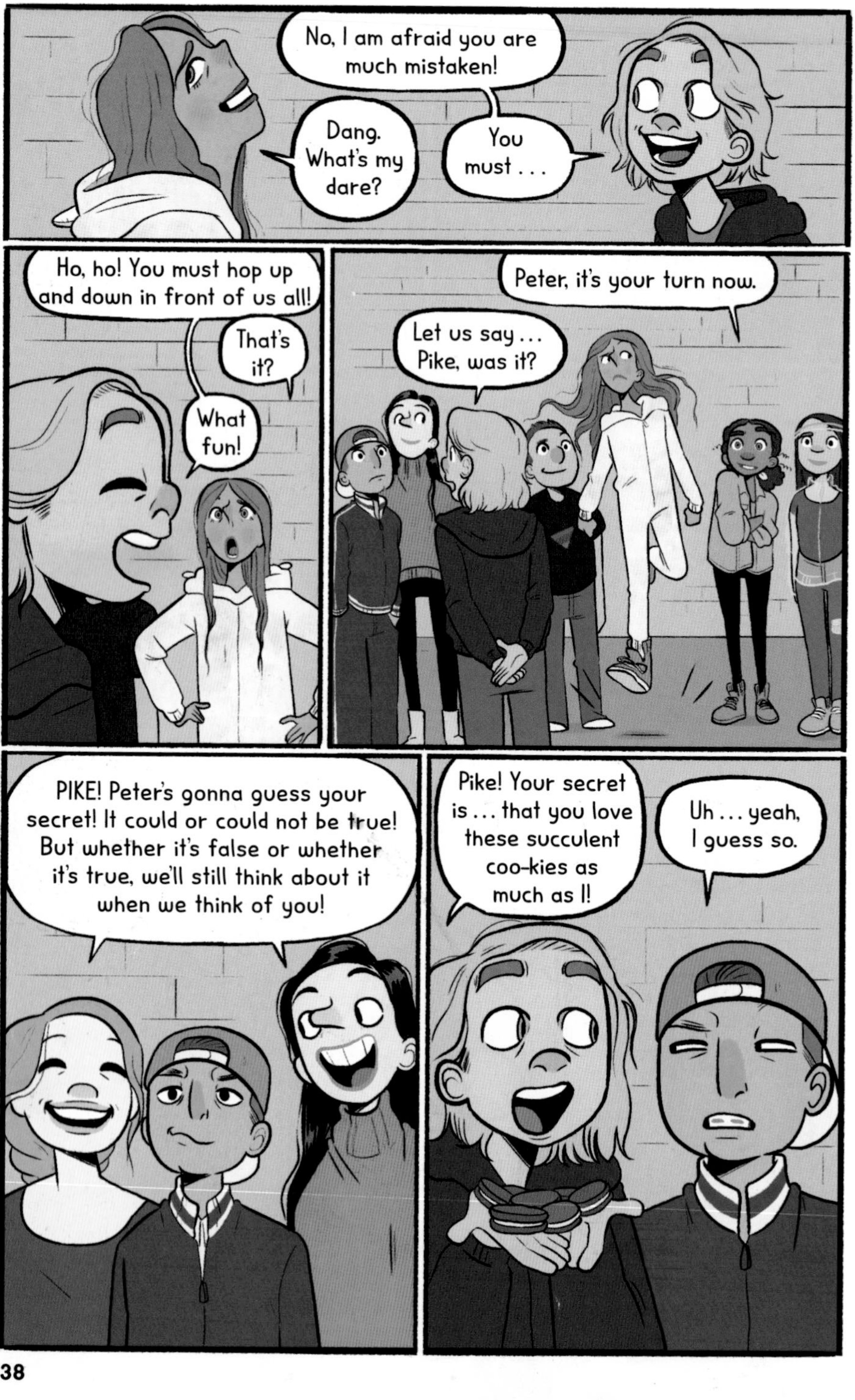
No, I am afraid you are much mistaken!
Dang. What's my dare?
You must . . .
Ho, ho! You must hop up and down in front of us all!
That's it?
What fun!
Peter, it's your turn now.
Let us say . . . Pike, was it?
PIKE! Peter's gonna guess your secret! It could or could not be true! But whether it's false or whether it's true, we'll still think about it when we think of you!
Pike! Your secret is . . . that you love these succulent coo-kies as much as I!
Uh . . . yeah, I guess so.

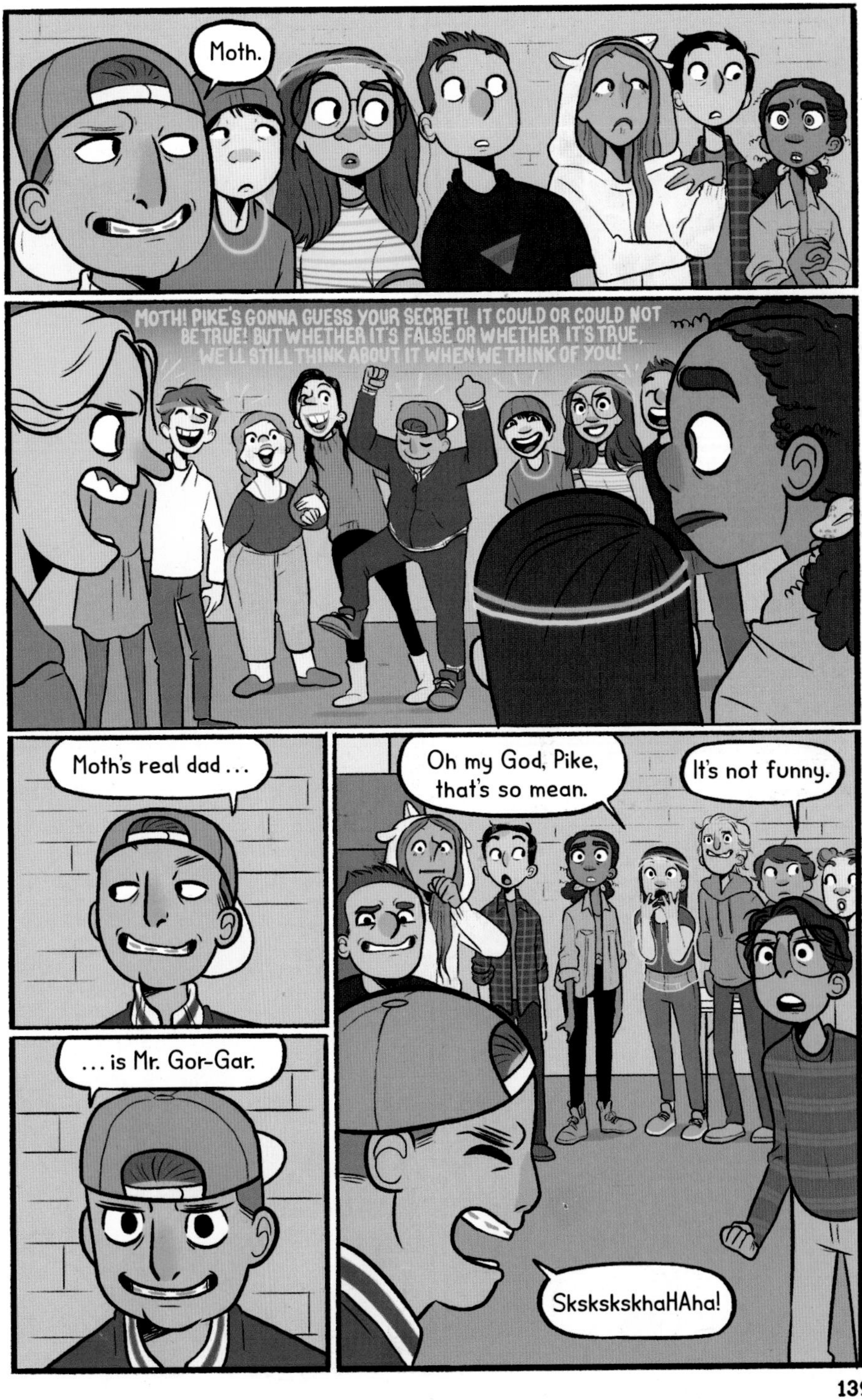
Moth.
MOTH! PIKE'S GONNA GUESS YOUR SECRET! IT COULD OR COULD NOT BE TRUE! BUT WHETHER IT'S FALSE OR WHETHER IT'S TRUE, WE'LL STILL THINK ABOUT IT WHEN WE THINK OF YOU!
Moth's real dad . . .
. . . is Mr. Gor-Gar.
Oh my God, Pike, that's so mean.
It's not funny.
SkskskskhaHAha!

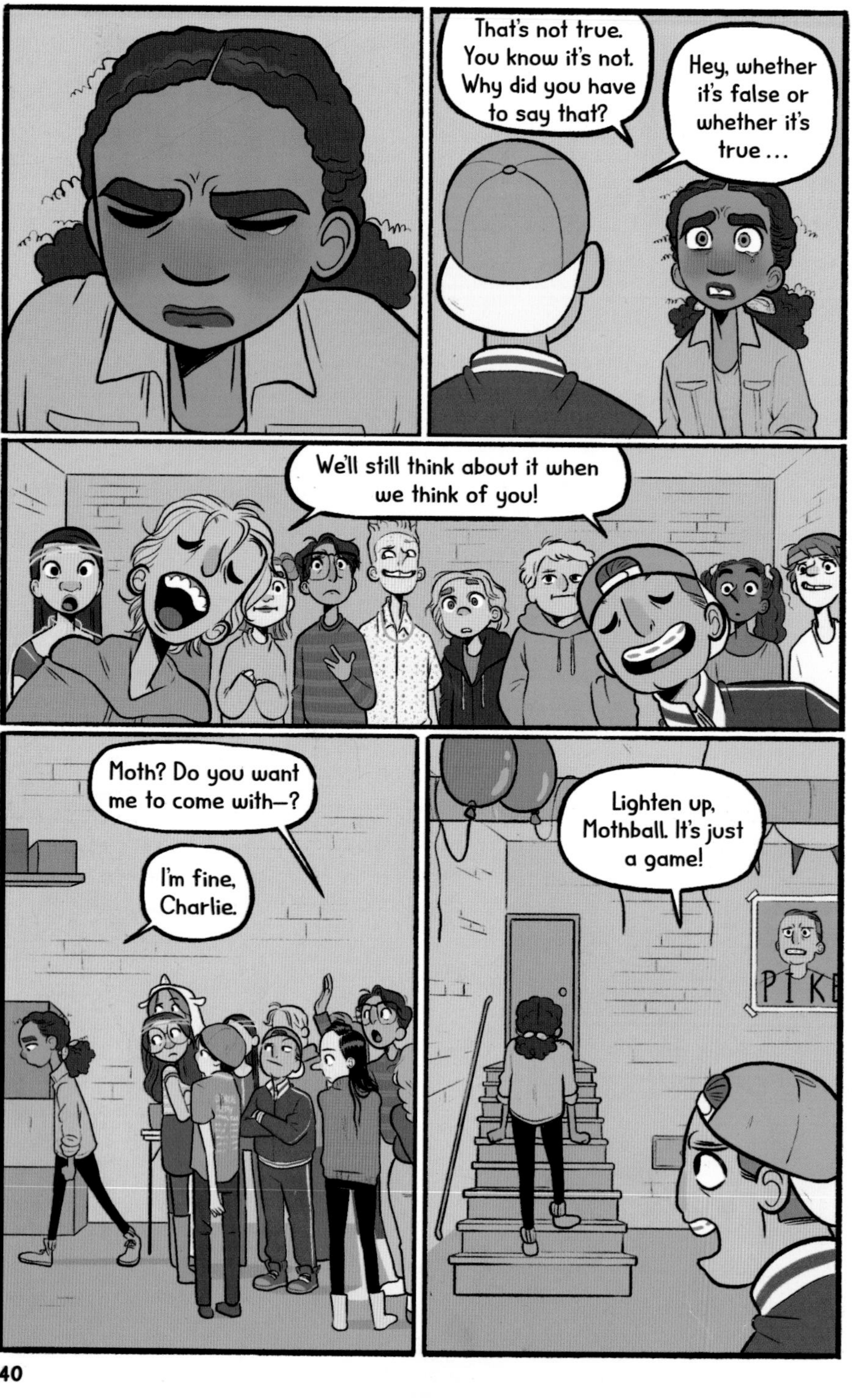
That's not true. You know it's not. Why did you have to say that?
Hey, whether it's false or whether it's true . . .
We'll still think about it when we think of you!
Moth? Do you want me to come with—?
I'm fine, Charlie.
Lighten up, Mothball. It's just a game!
PIKE

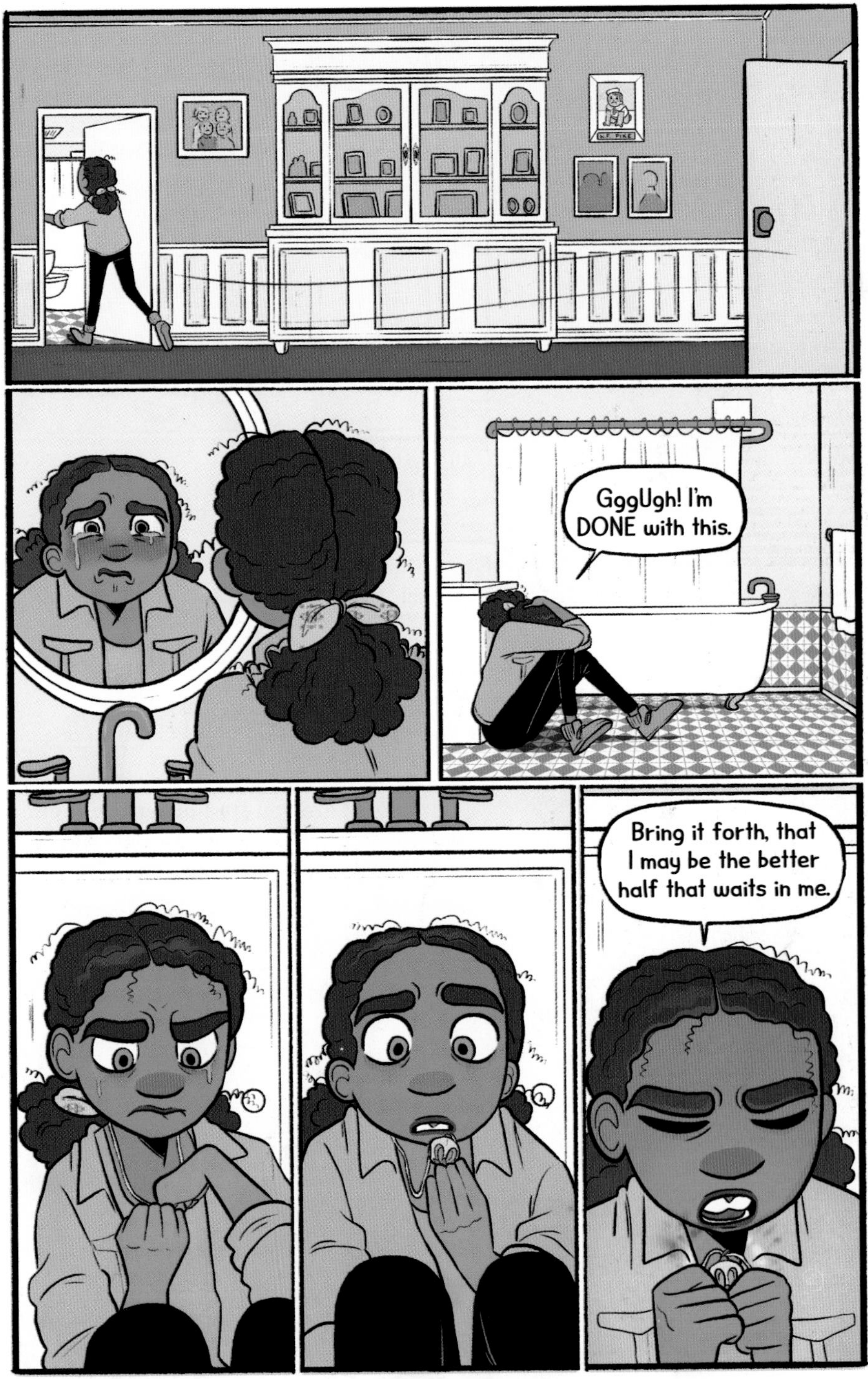
GggUgh! I'm DONE with this.
Bring it forth, that I may be the better half that waits in me.

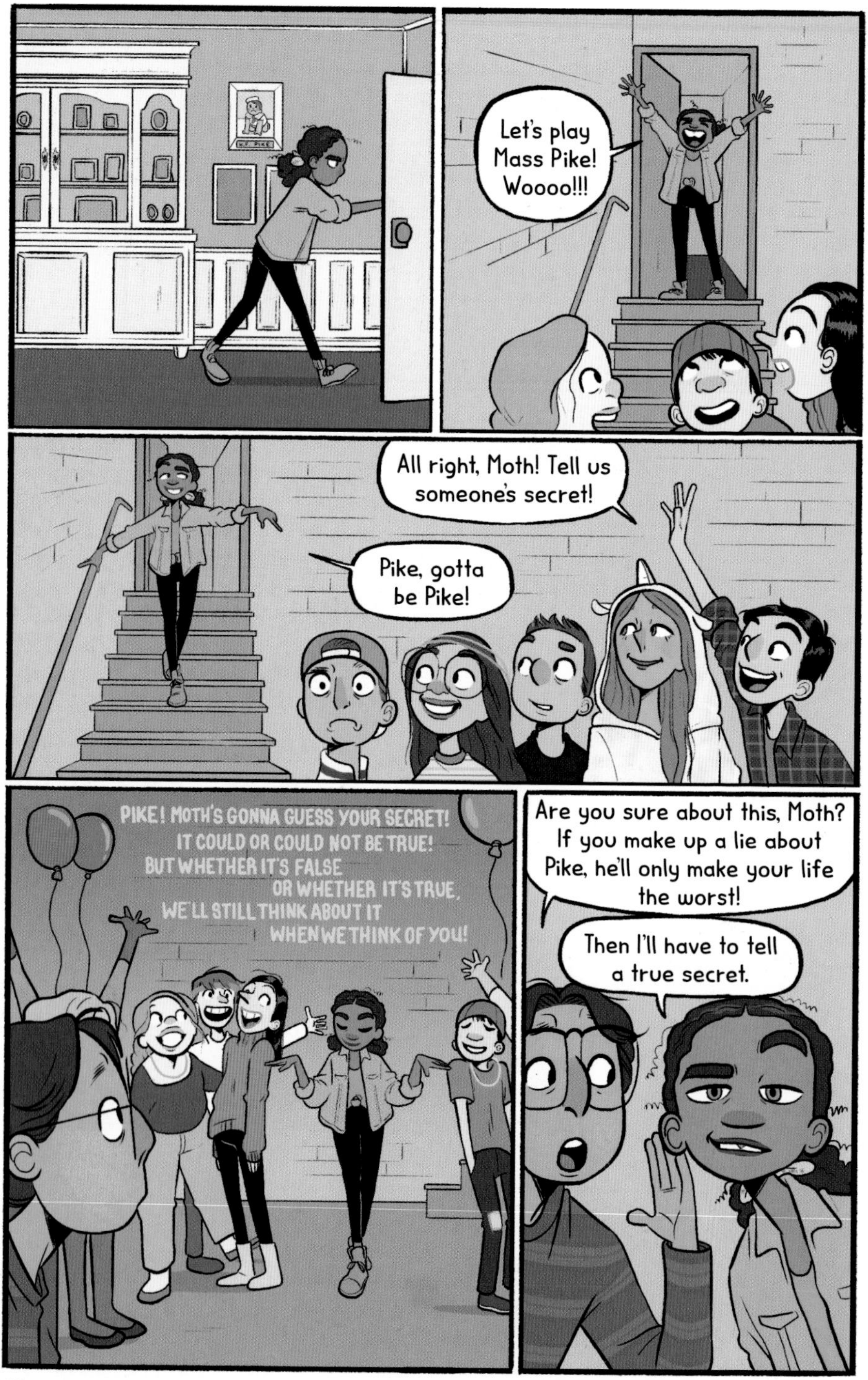
Let's play Mass Pike! Woooo!!!
All right, Moth! Tell us someone's secret!
Pike, gotta be Pike!
PIKE! MOTH'S GONNA GUESS YOUR SECRET!
IT COULD OR COULD NOT BE TRUE!
BUT WHETHER IT'S FALSE
OR WHETHER IT'S TRUE,
WE'LL STILL THINK ABOUT IT
WHEN WE THINK OF YOU!
Are you sure about this, Moth? If you make up a lie about Pike, he'll only make your life the worst!
Then I'll have to tell a true secret.

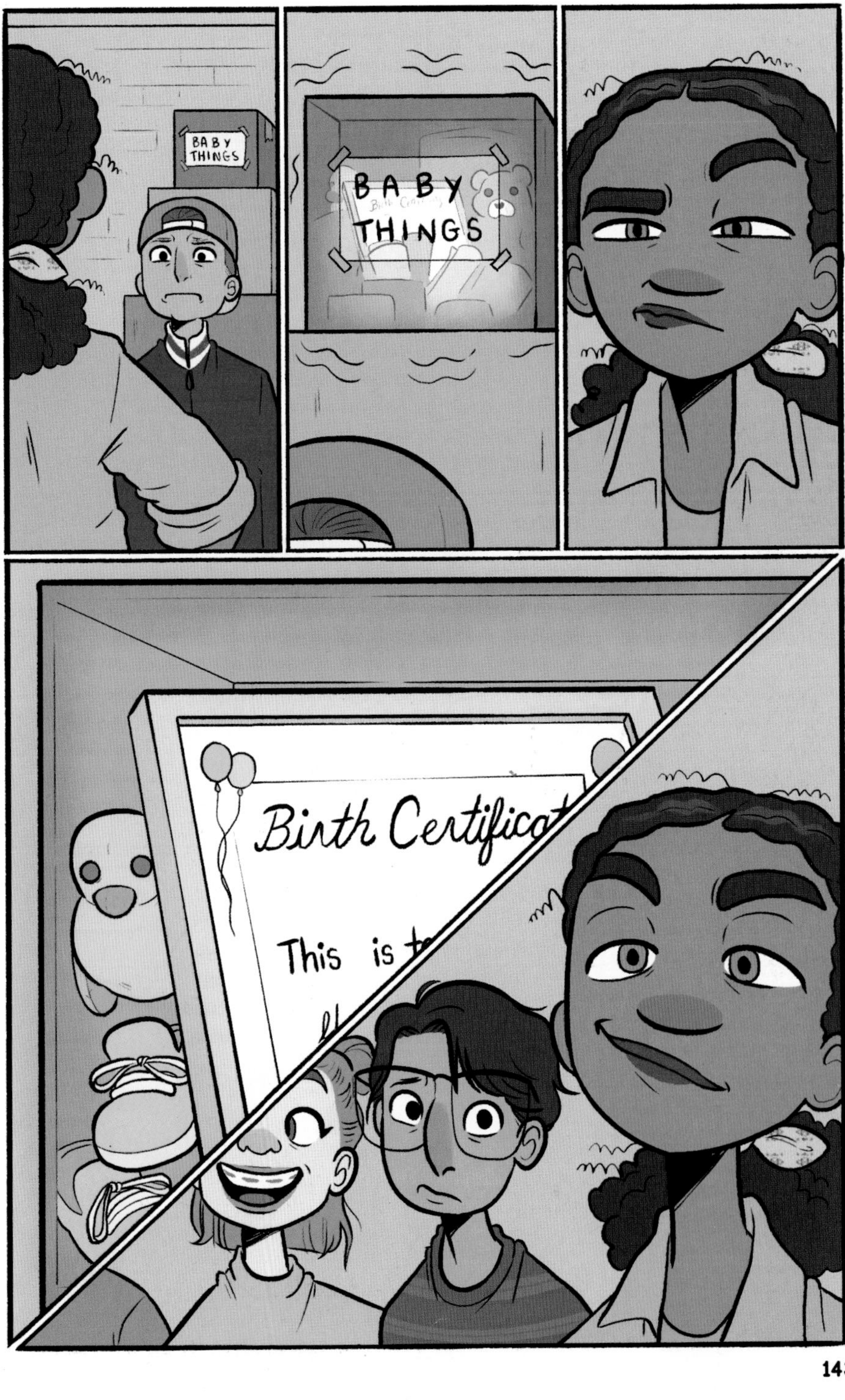
BABY THINGS
BABY THINGS
Birth Certificat
This is t

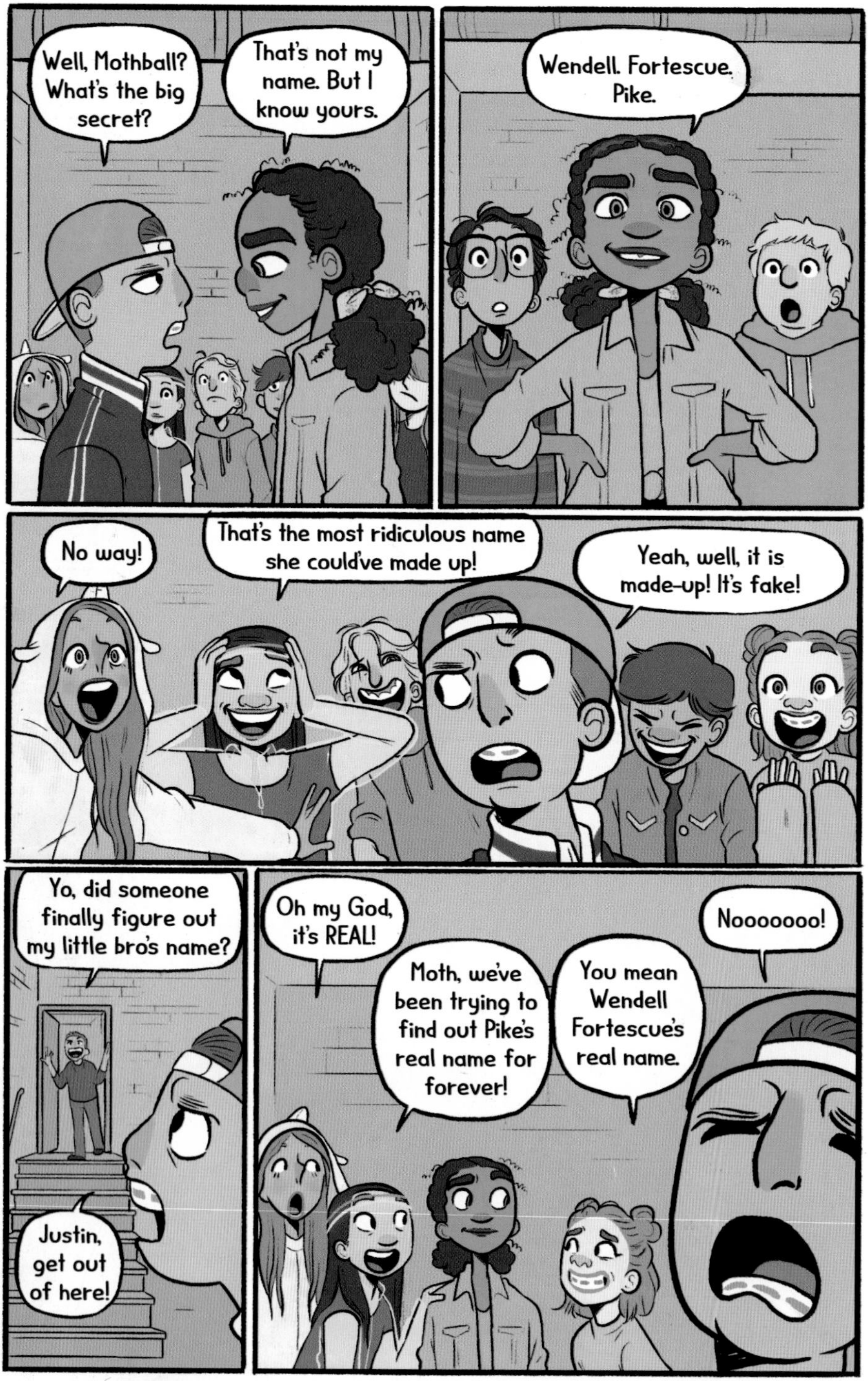
Well, Mothball? What's the big secret?
That's not my name. But I know yours.
Wendell. Fortescue. Pike.
No way!
That's the most ridiculous name she could've made up!
Yeah, well, it is made-up! It's fake!
Yo, did someone finally figure out my little bro's name?
Justin, get out of here!
Oh my God, it's REAL!
Moth, we've been trying to find out Pike's real name for forever!
You mean Wendell Fortescue's real name.
Nooooooo!

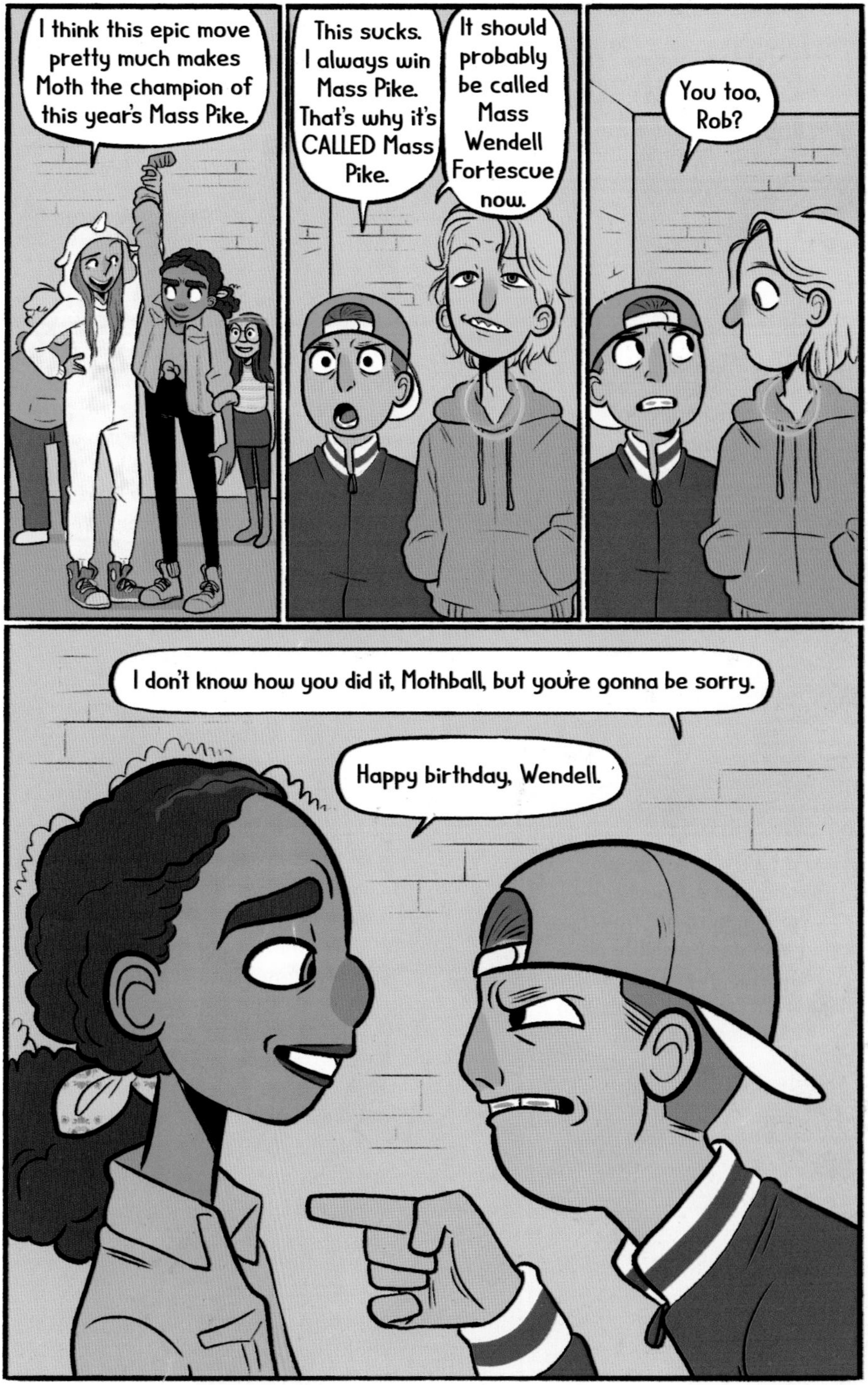
I think this epic move pretty much makes Moth the champion of this year's Mass Pike.
This sucks. I always win Mass Pike. That's why it's CALLED Mass Pike.
It should probably be called Mass Wendell Fortescue now.
You too, Rob?
I don't know how you did it, Mothball, but you're gonna be sorry.
Happy birthday, Wendell.

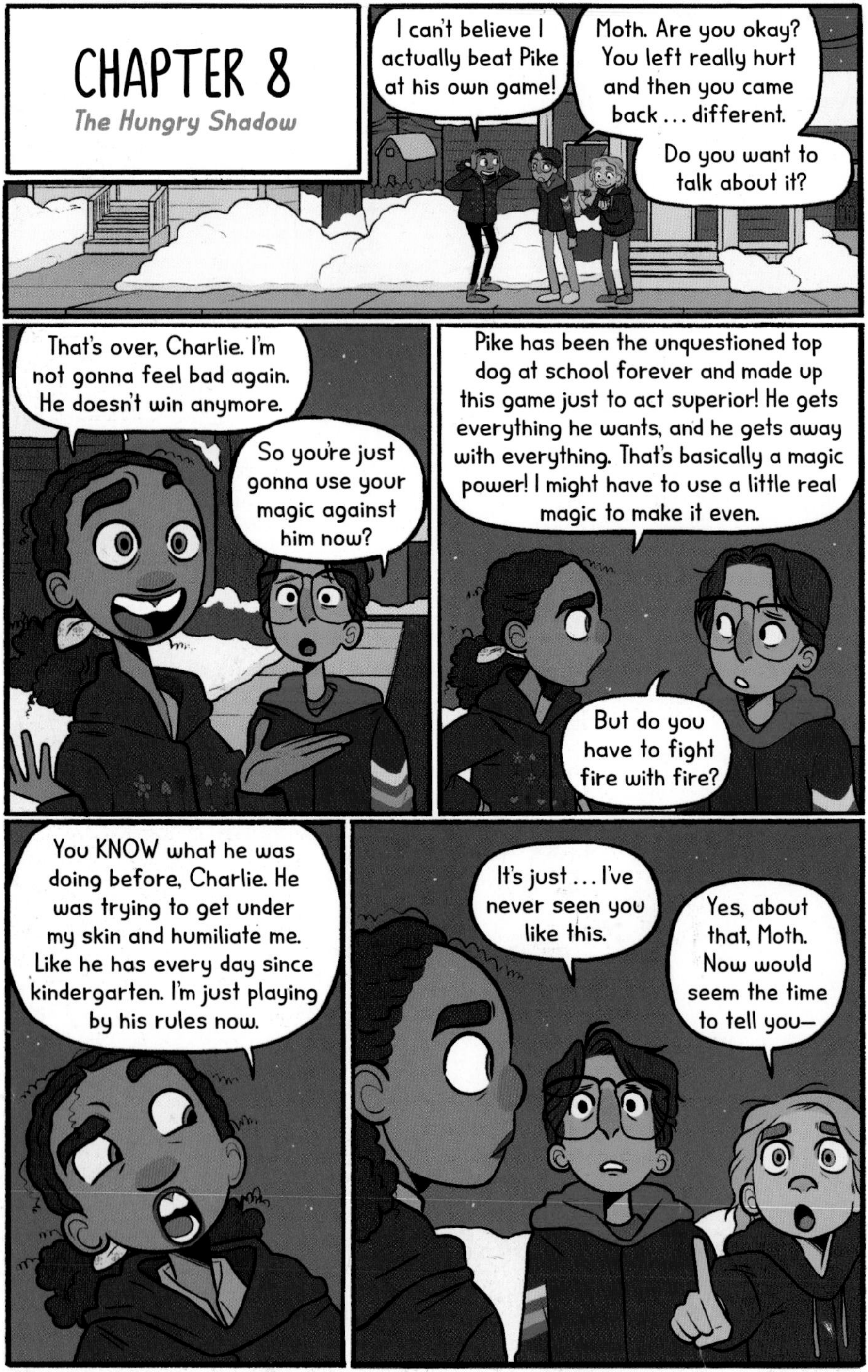
CHAPTER 8
The Hungry Shadow
I can't believe I actually beat Pike at his own game!
Moth. Are you okay? You left really hurt and then you came back . . . different.
Do you want to talk about it?
That's over, Charlie. I'm not gonna feel bad again. He doesn't win anymore.
So you're just gonna use your magic against him now?
Pike has been the unquestioned top dog at school forever and made up this game just to act superior! He gets everything he wants, and he gets away with everything. That's basically a magic power! I might have to use a little real magic to make it even.
But do you have to fight fire with fire?
You KNOW what he was doing before, Charlie. He was trying to get under my skin and humiliate me. Like he has every day since kindergarten. I'm just playing by his rules now.
It's just . . . I've never seen you like this.
Yes, about that, Moth. Now would seem the time to tell you—

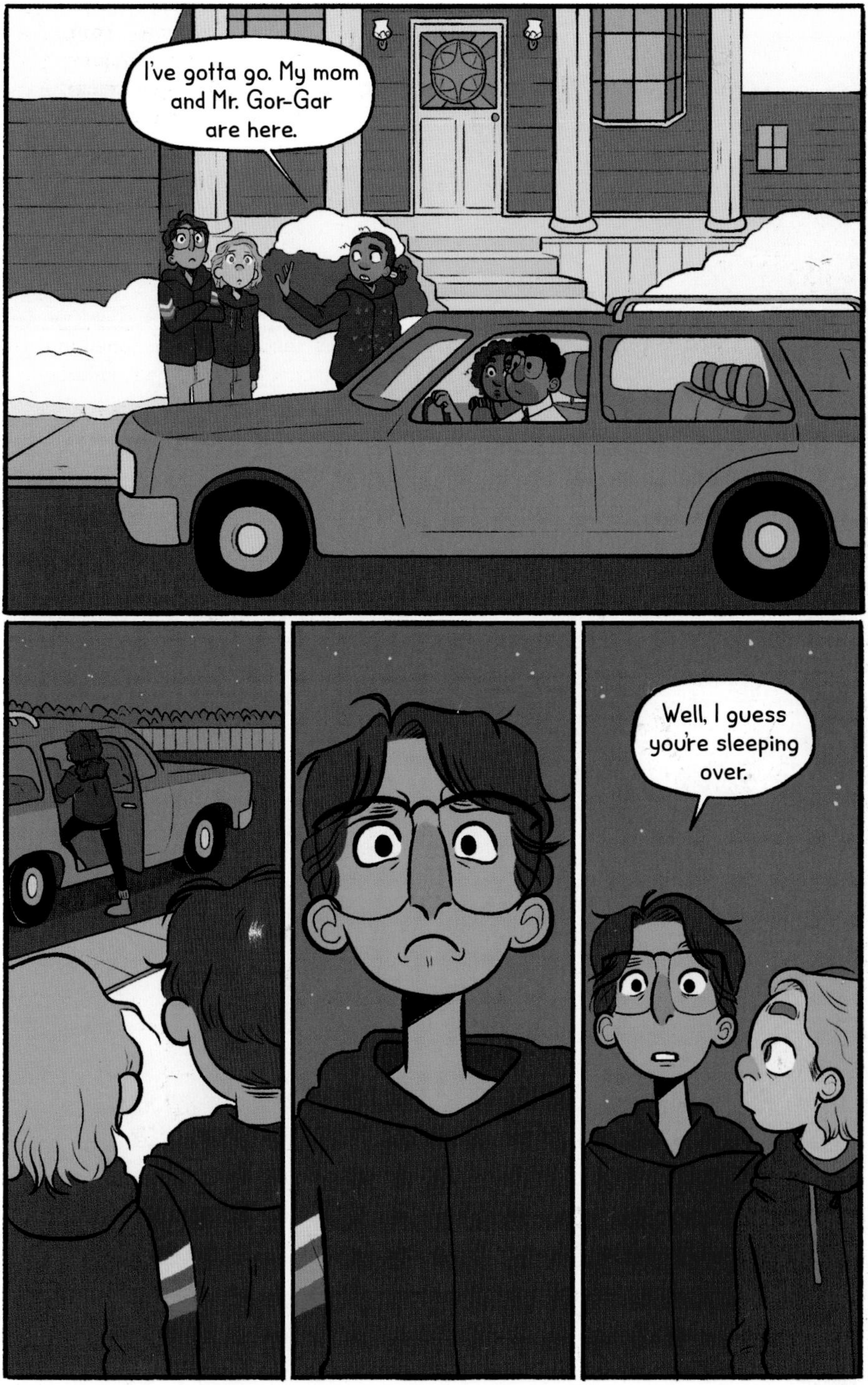
I've gotta go. My mom and Mr. Gor-Gar are here.
Well, I guess you're sleeping over.

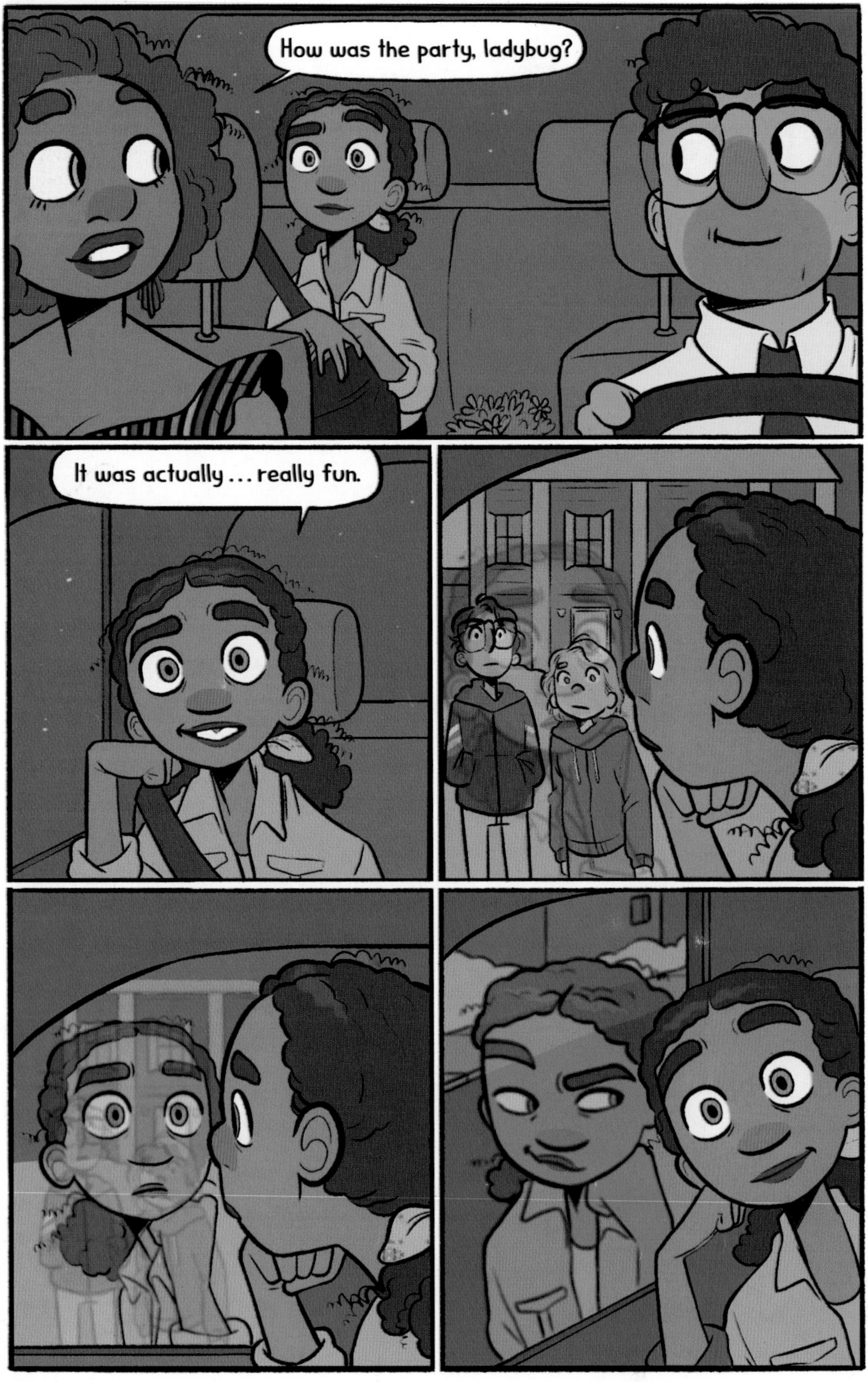
How was the party, ladybug?
It was actually . . . really fun.

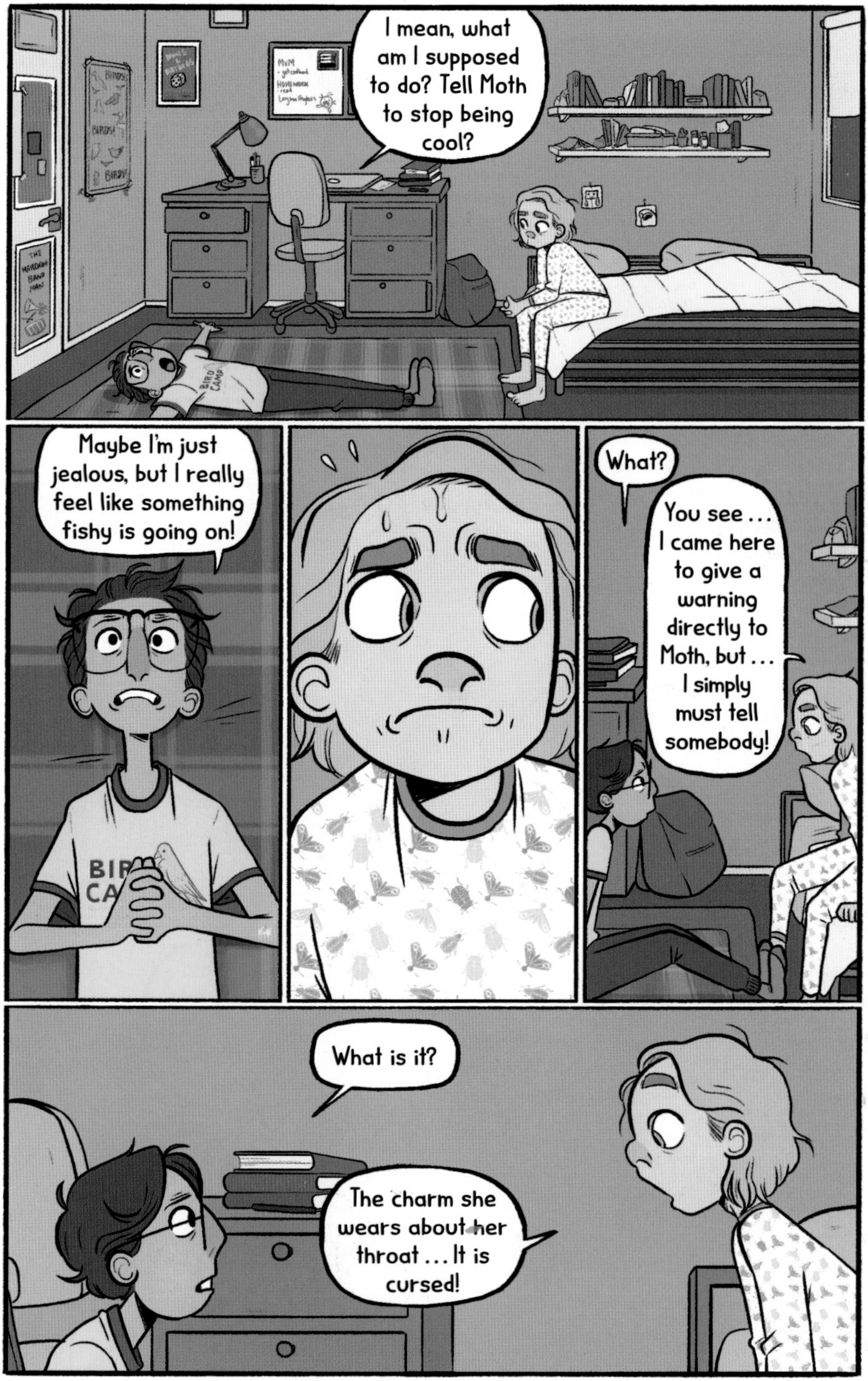
I mean, what am I supposed to do? Tell Moth to stop being cool?
Maybe I'm just jealous, but I really feel like something fishy is going on!
What?
You see . . . I came here to give a warning directly to Moth, but . . .
I simply must tell somebody!
What is it?
The charm she wears about her throat . . . It is cursed!

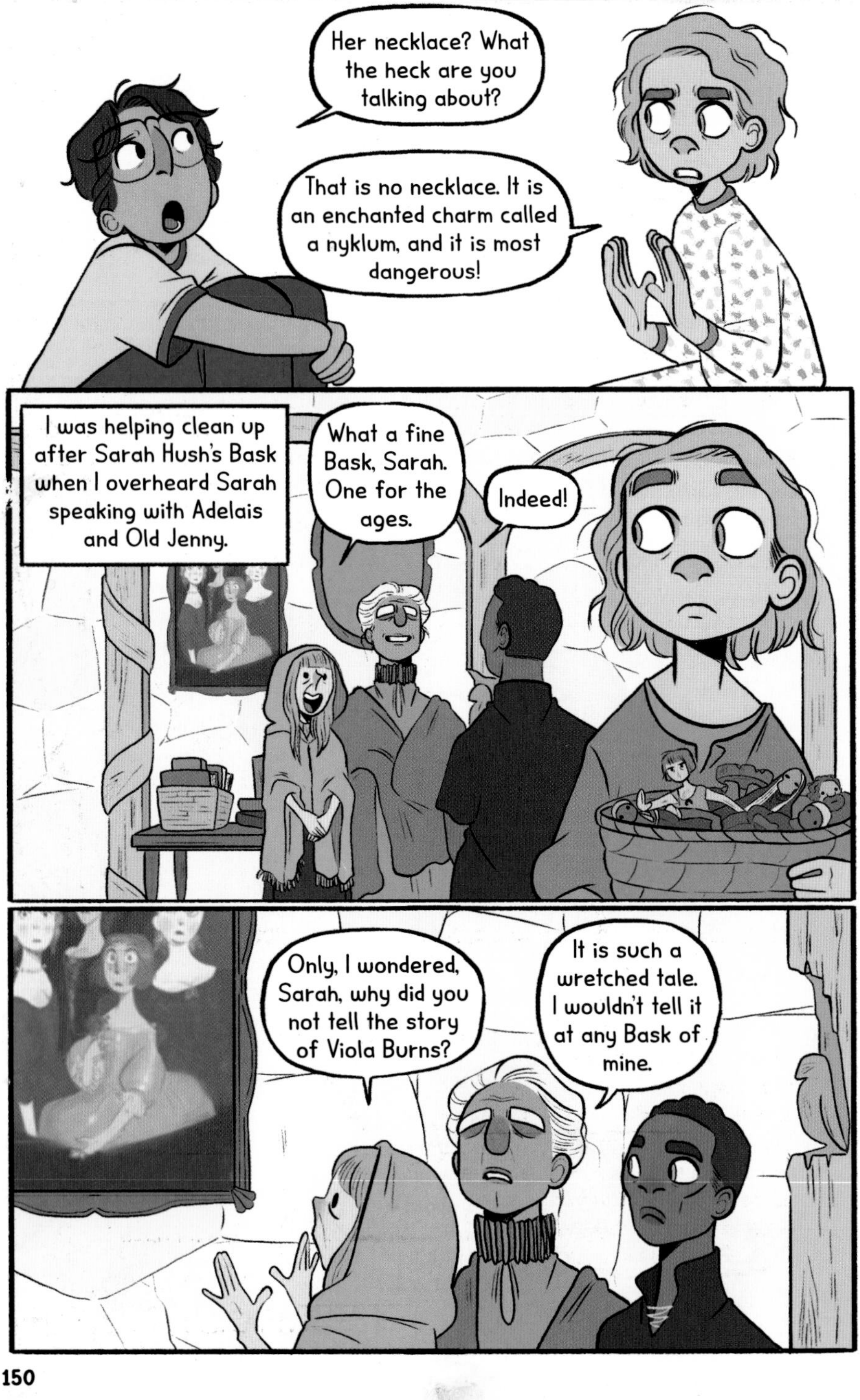
Her necklace? What the heck are you talking about?
That is no necklace. It is an enchanted charm called a nyklum, and it is most dangerous!
I was helping clean up after Sarah Hush's Bask when I overheard Sarah speaking with Adelais and Old Jenny.
What a fine Bask, Sarah. One for the ages.
Indeed!
Only, I wondered, Sarah, why did you not tell the story of Viola Burns?
It is such a wretched tale. I wouldn't tell it at any Bask of mine.

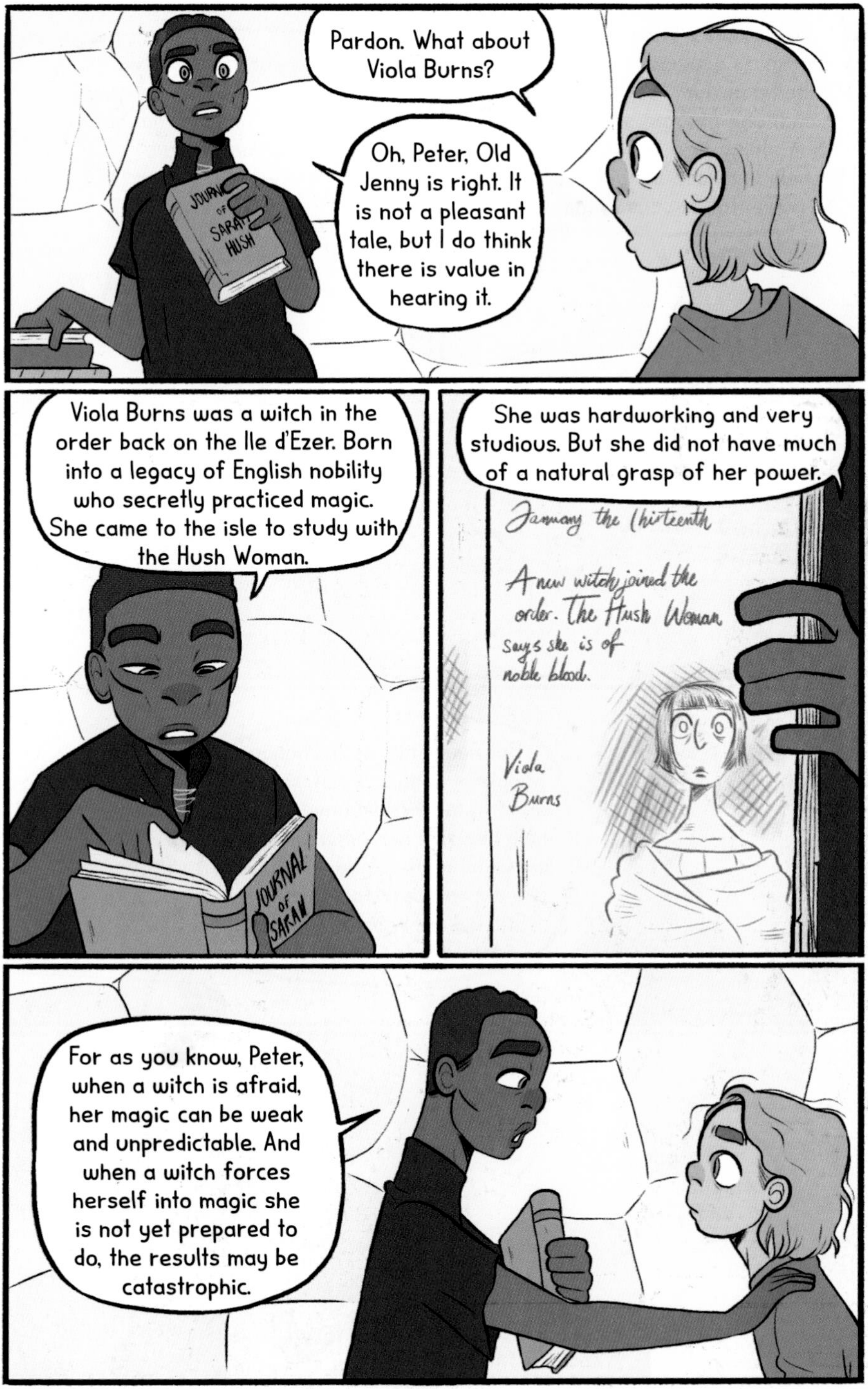
Pardon. What about Viola Burns?
Oh, Peter, Old Jenny is right. It is not a pleasant tale, but I do think there is value in hearing it.
JOURNAL OF SARAH HUSH
Viola Burns was a witch in the order back on the Ile d'Ezer. Born into a legacy of English nobility who secretly practiced magic. She came to the isle to study with the Hush Woman.
JOURNAL OF SARAH
She was hardworking and very studious. But she did not have much of a natural grasp of her power.
January the thirteenth
A new witch joined the order. The Hush Woman says she is of noble blood.
Viola Burns
For as you know, Peter, when a witch is afraid, her magic can be weak and unpredictable. And when a witch forces herself into magic she is not yet prepared to do, the results may be catastrophic.

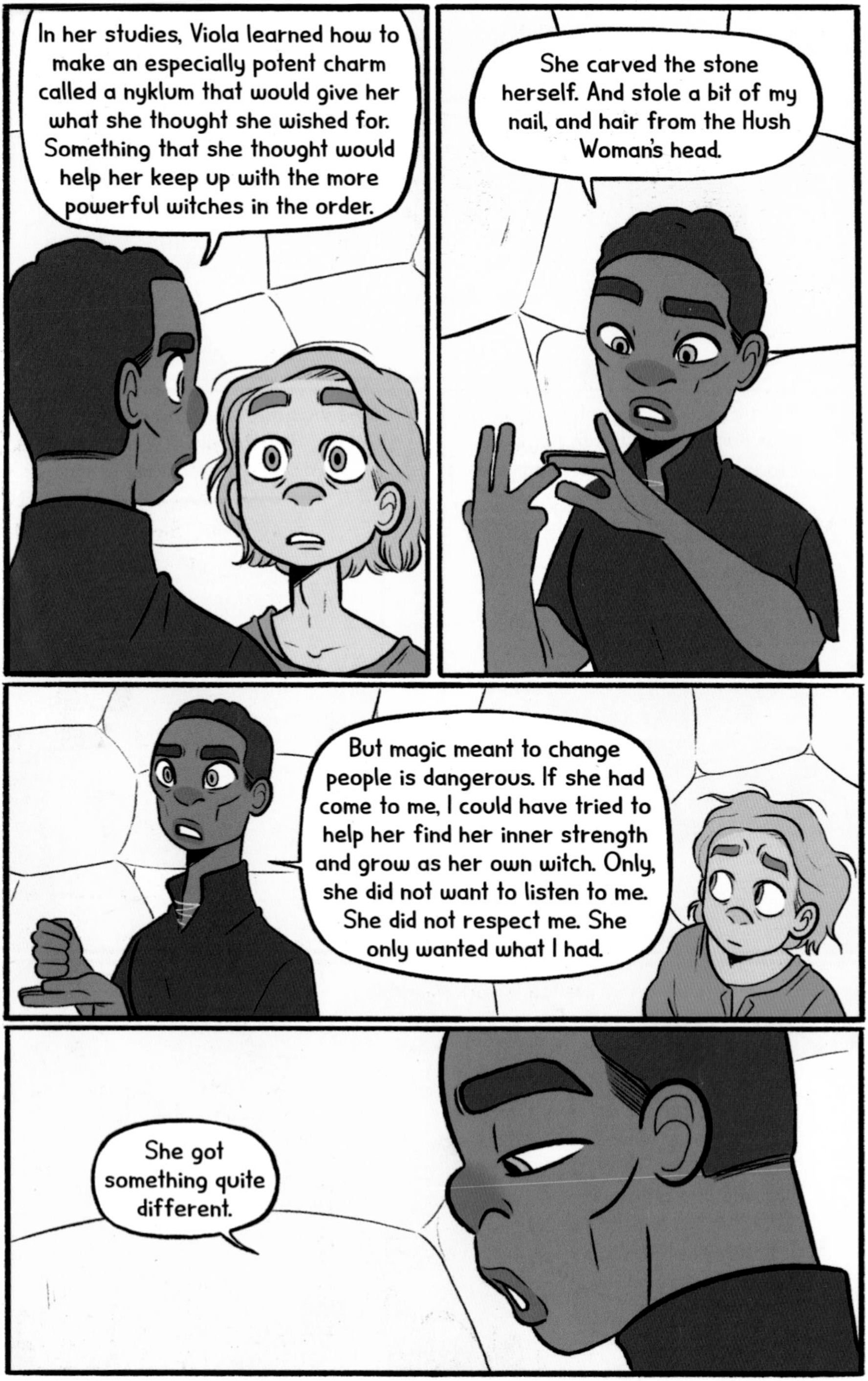
In her studies, Viola learned how to make an especially potent charm called a nyklum that would give her what she thought she wished for. Something that she thought would help her keep up with the more powerful witches in the order.
She carved the stone herself. And stole a bit of my nail, and hair from the Hush Woman's head.
But magic meant to change people is dangerous. If she had come to me, I could have tried to help her find her inner strength and grow as her own witch. Only, she did not want to listen to me. She did not respect me. She only wanted what I had.
She got something quite different.

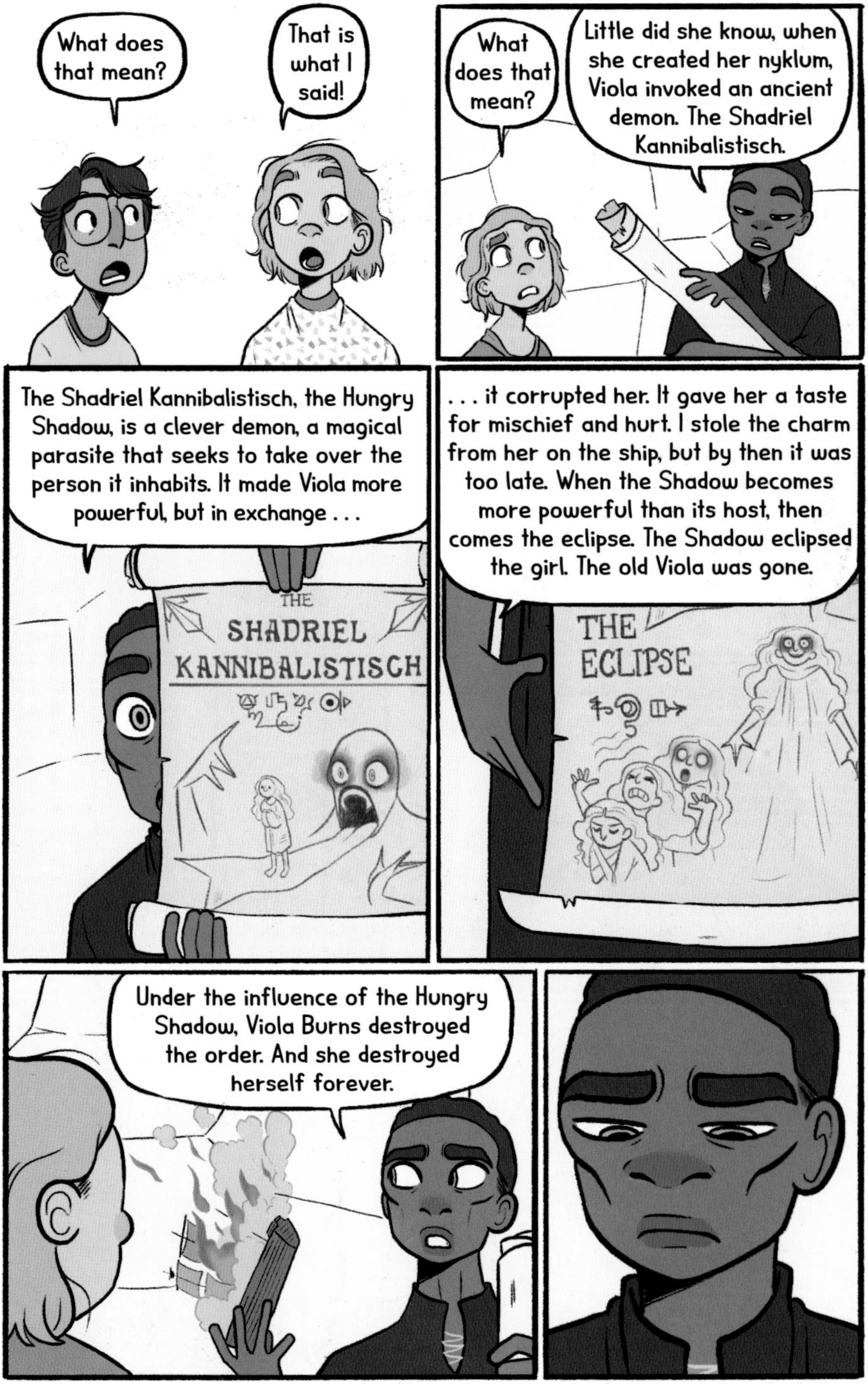
What does that mean?
That is what I said!
What does that mean?
Little did she know, when she created her nyklum, Viola invoked an ancient demon. The Shadriel Kannibalistisch.
The Shadriel Kannibalistisch, the Hungry Shadow, is a clever demon, a magical parasite that seeks to take over the person it inhabits. It made Viola more powerful, but in exchange . . .
THE SHADRIEL KANNIBALISTISCH
. . . it corrupted her. It gave her a taste for mischief and hurt. I stole the charm from her on the ship, but by then it was too late. When the Shadow becomes more powerful than its host, then comes the eclipse. The Shadow eclipsed the girl. The old Viola was gone.
THE ECLIPSE
Under the influence of the Hungry Shadow, Viola Burns destroyed the order. And she destroyed herself forever.

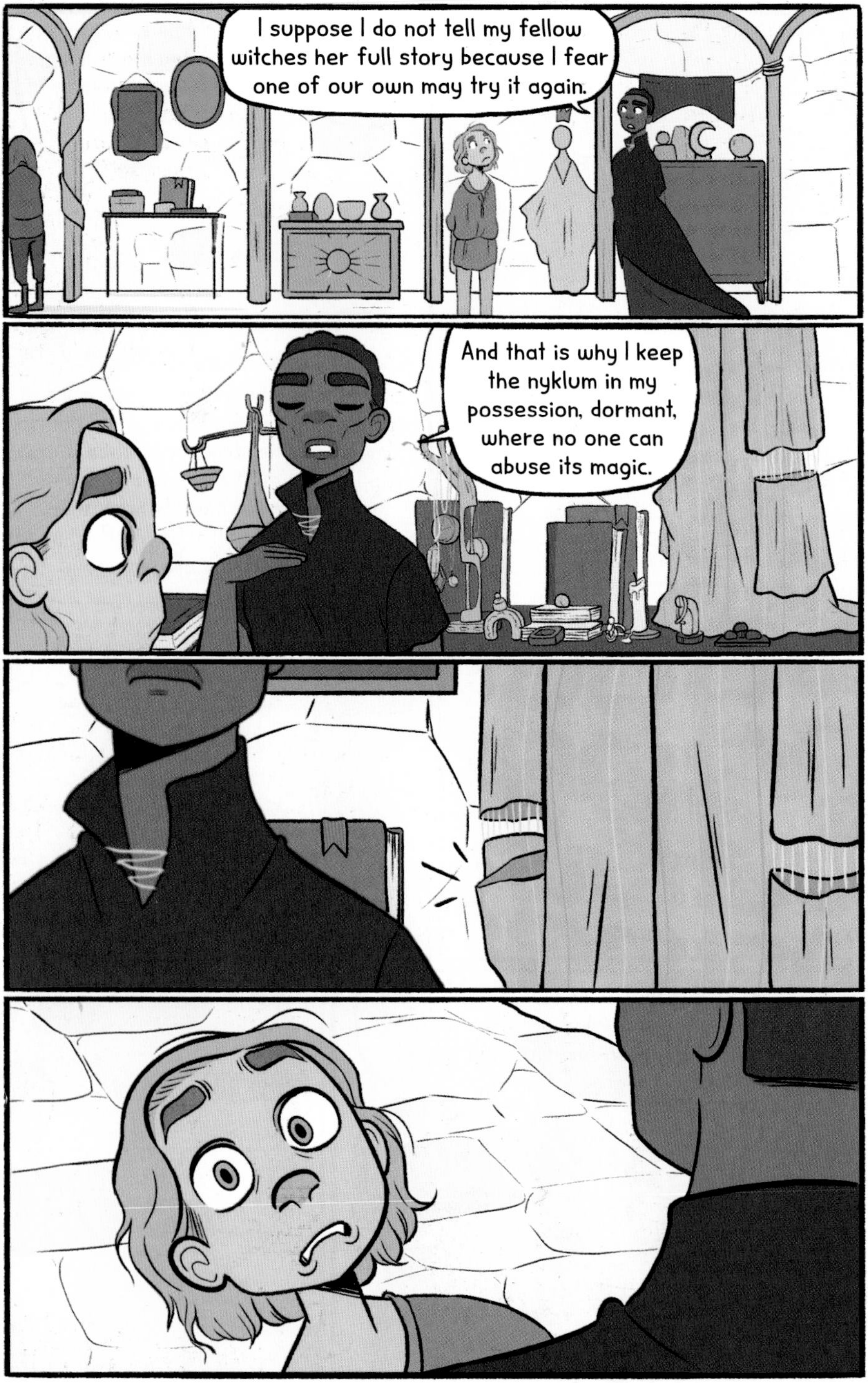
I suppose I do not tell my fellow witches her full story because I fear one of our own may try it again.
And that is why I keep the nyklum in my possession, dormant, where no one can abuse its magic.

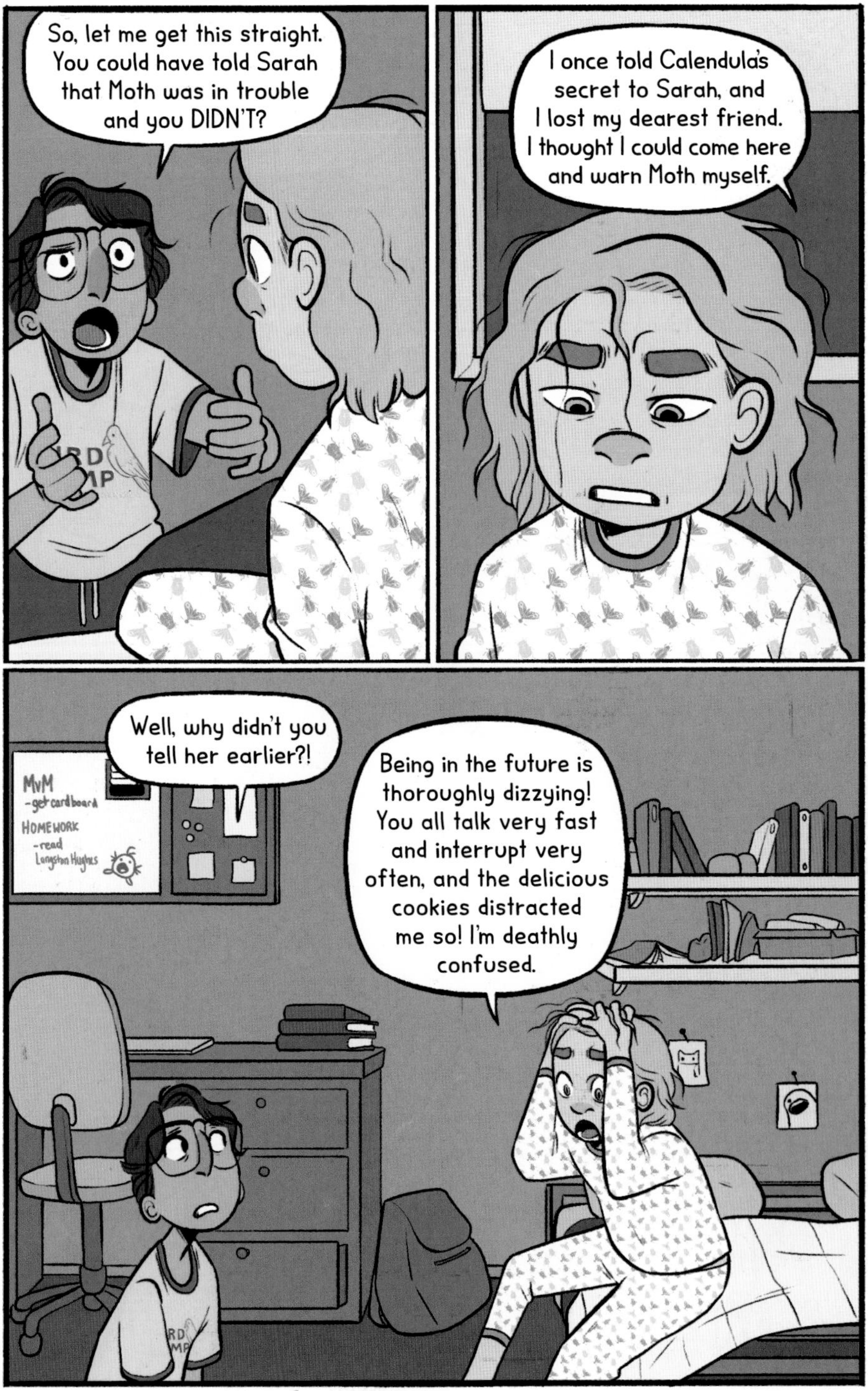
So, let me get this straight. You could have told Sarah that Moth was in trouble and you DIDN'T?
I once told Calendula's secret to Sarah, and I lost my dearest friend. I thought I could come here and warn Moth myself.
Well, why didn't you tell her earlier?!
MvM
-get cardboard
HOMEWORK
-read
Being in the future is thoroughly dizzying! You all talk very fast and interrupt very often, and the delicious cookies distracted me so! I'm deathly confused.

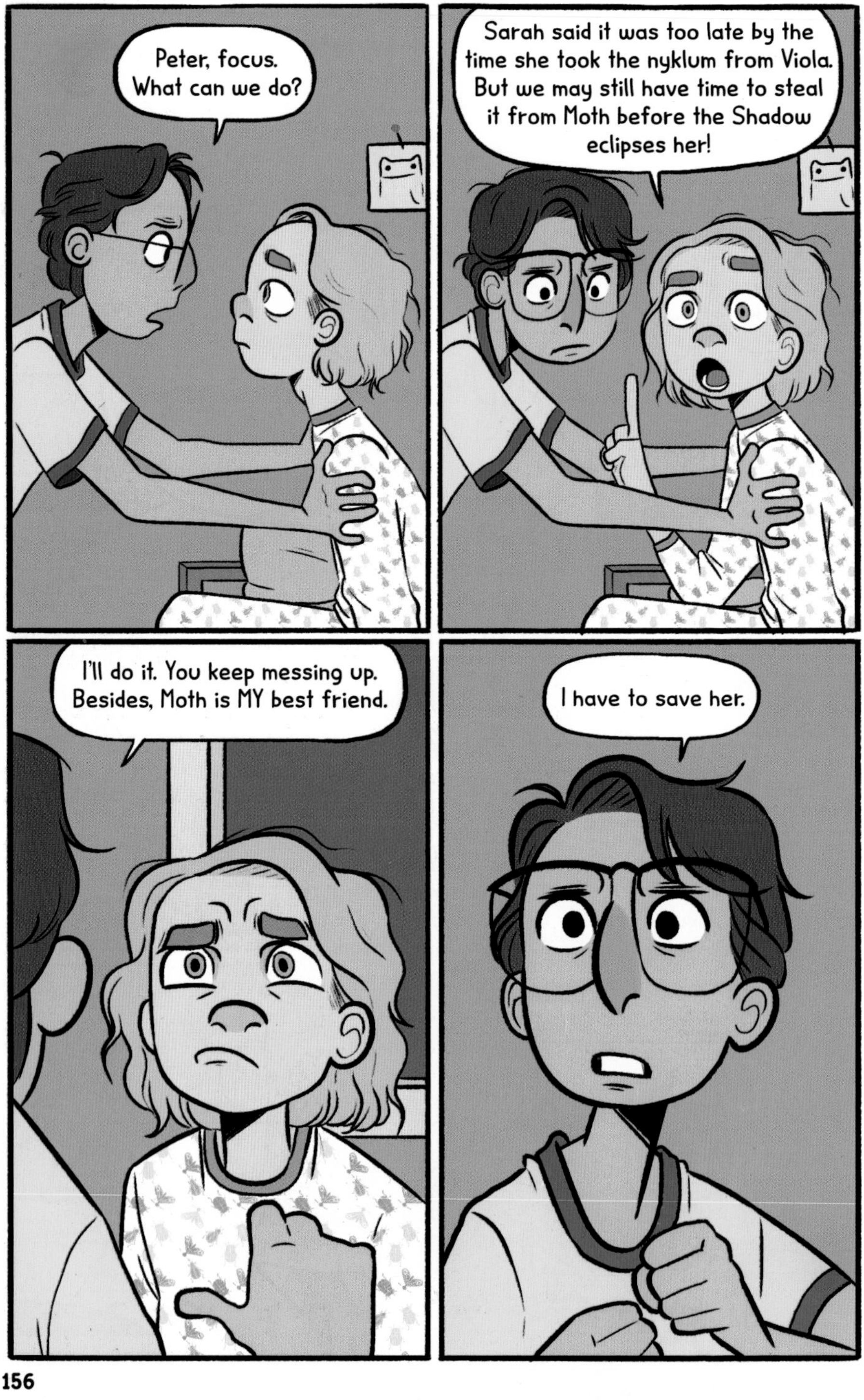
Peter, focus. What can we do?
Sarah said it was too late by the time she took the nyklum from Viola. But we may still have time to steal it from Moth before the Shadow eclipses her!
I'll do it. You keep messing up. Besides, Moth is MY best friend.
I have to save her.

CHAPTER 9

Goo-ed and Evil

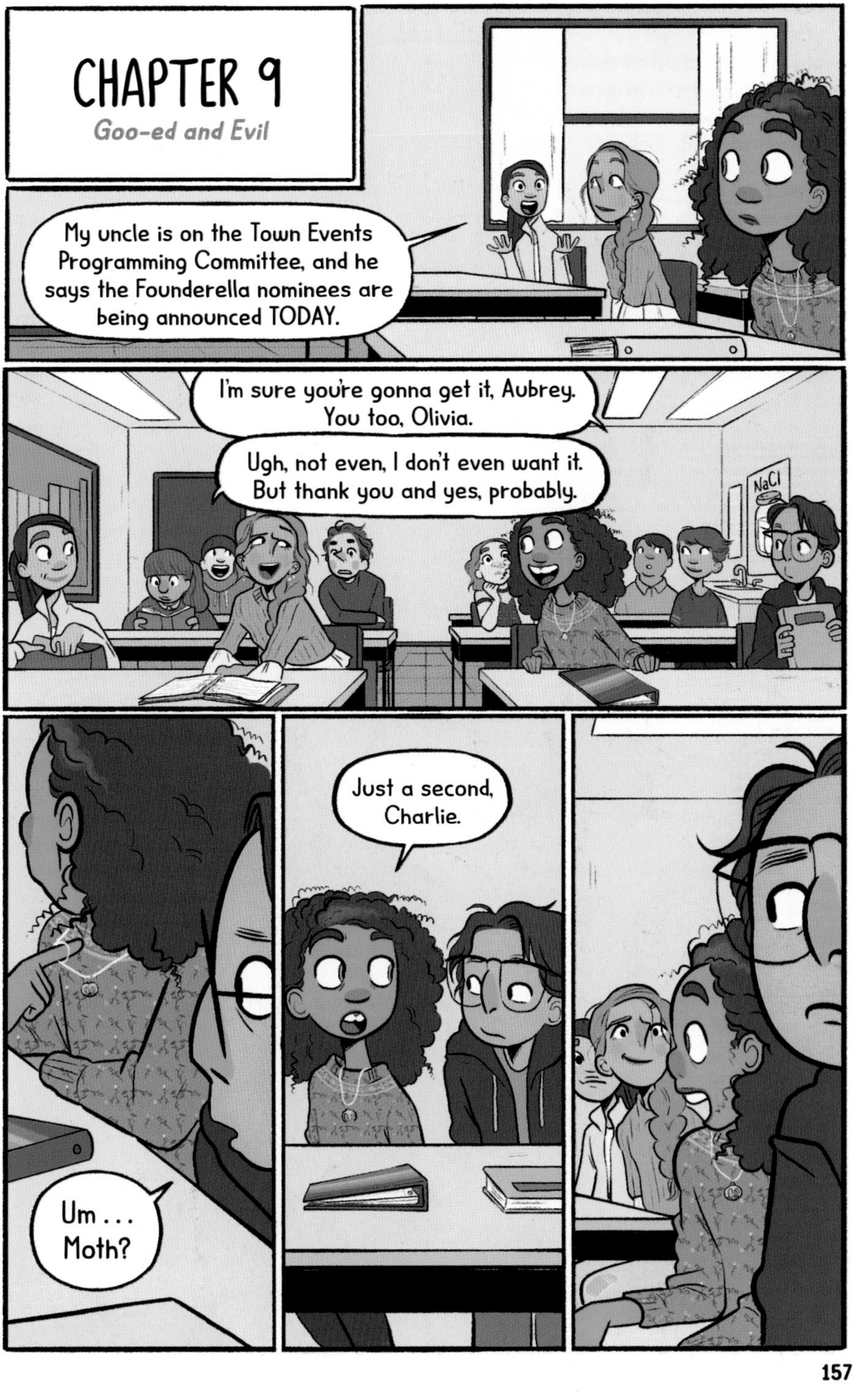

My uncle is on the Town Events Programming Committee, and he says the Founderella nominees are being announced TODAY.
I'm sure you're gonna get it, Aubrey. You too, Olivia.
Ugh, not even, I don't even want it. But thank you and yes, probably.
NaCl
Um . . . Moth?
Just a second, Charlie.

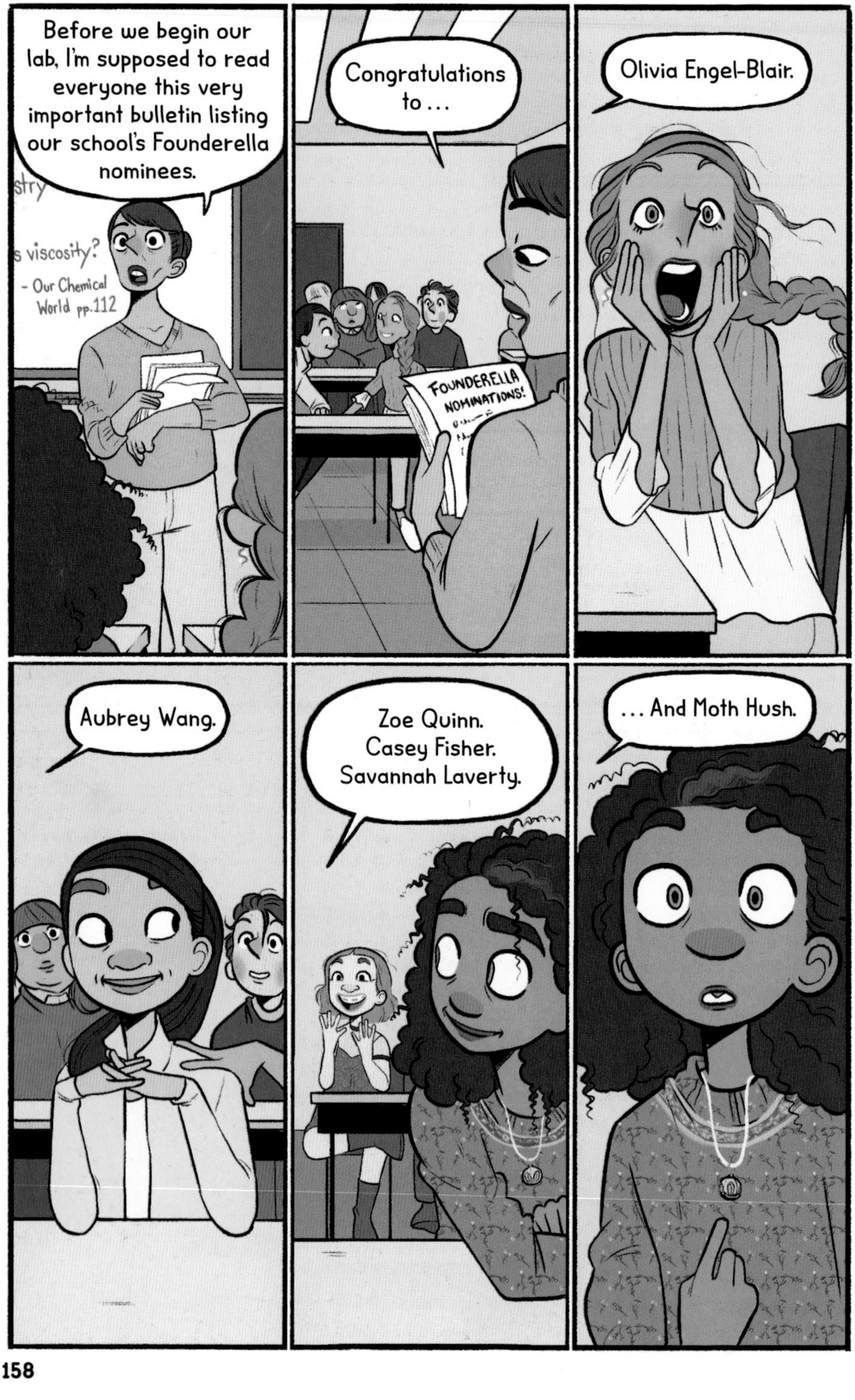
Before we begin our lab, I'm supposed to read everyone this very important bulletin listing our school's Founderella nominees.
stry
s viscosity?
- Our Chemical World pp.112
Congratulations to . . .
FOUNDERELLA NOMINATIONS!
Olivia Engel-Blair.
Aubrey Wang.
Zoe Quinn.
Casey Fisher.
Savannah Laverty.
. . . And Moth Hush.

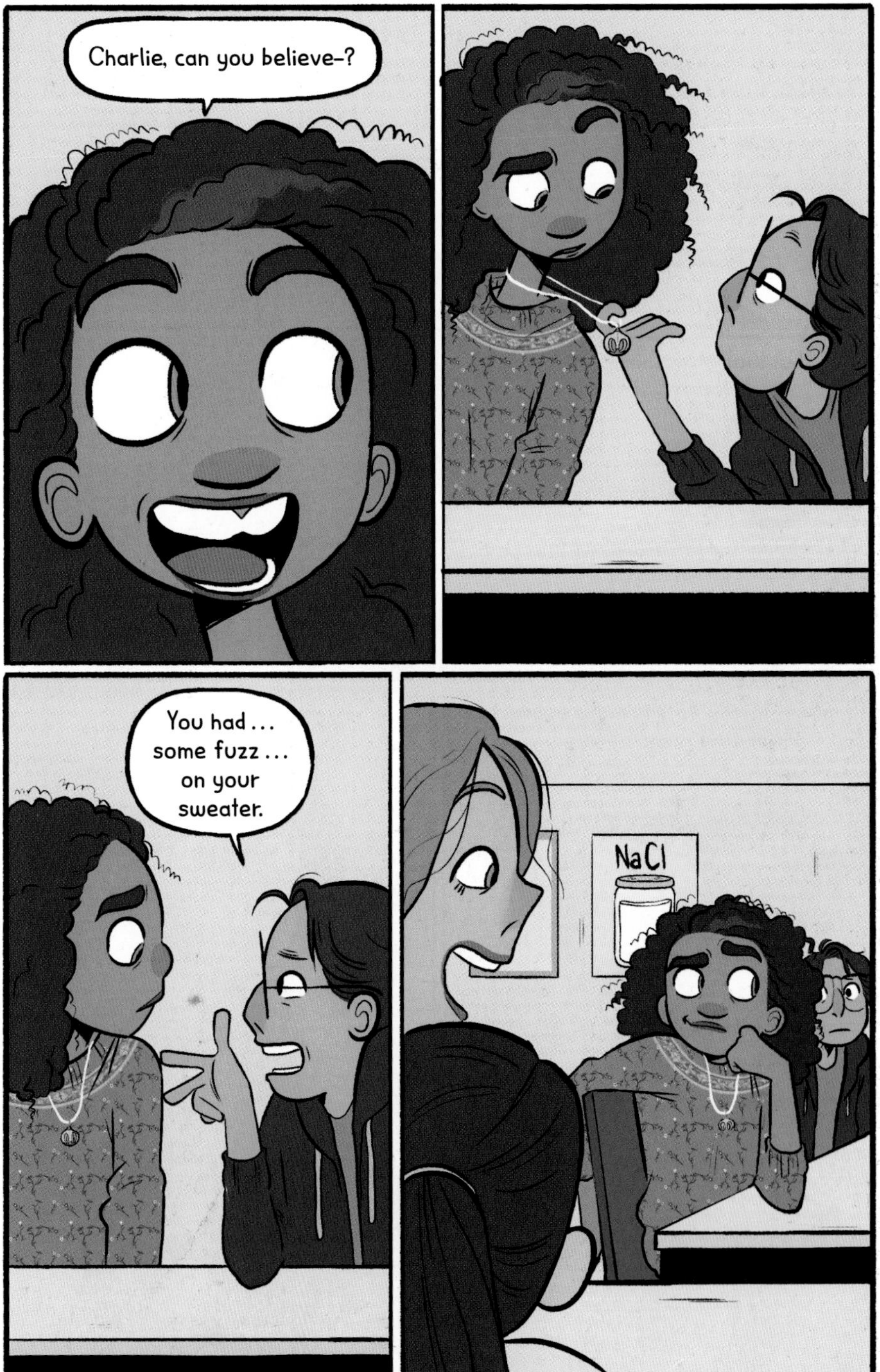
Charlie, can you believe–?
You had . . . some fuzz . . . on your sweater.
NaCl

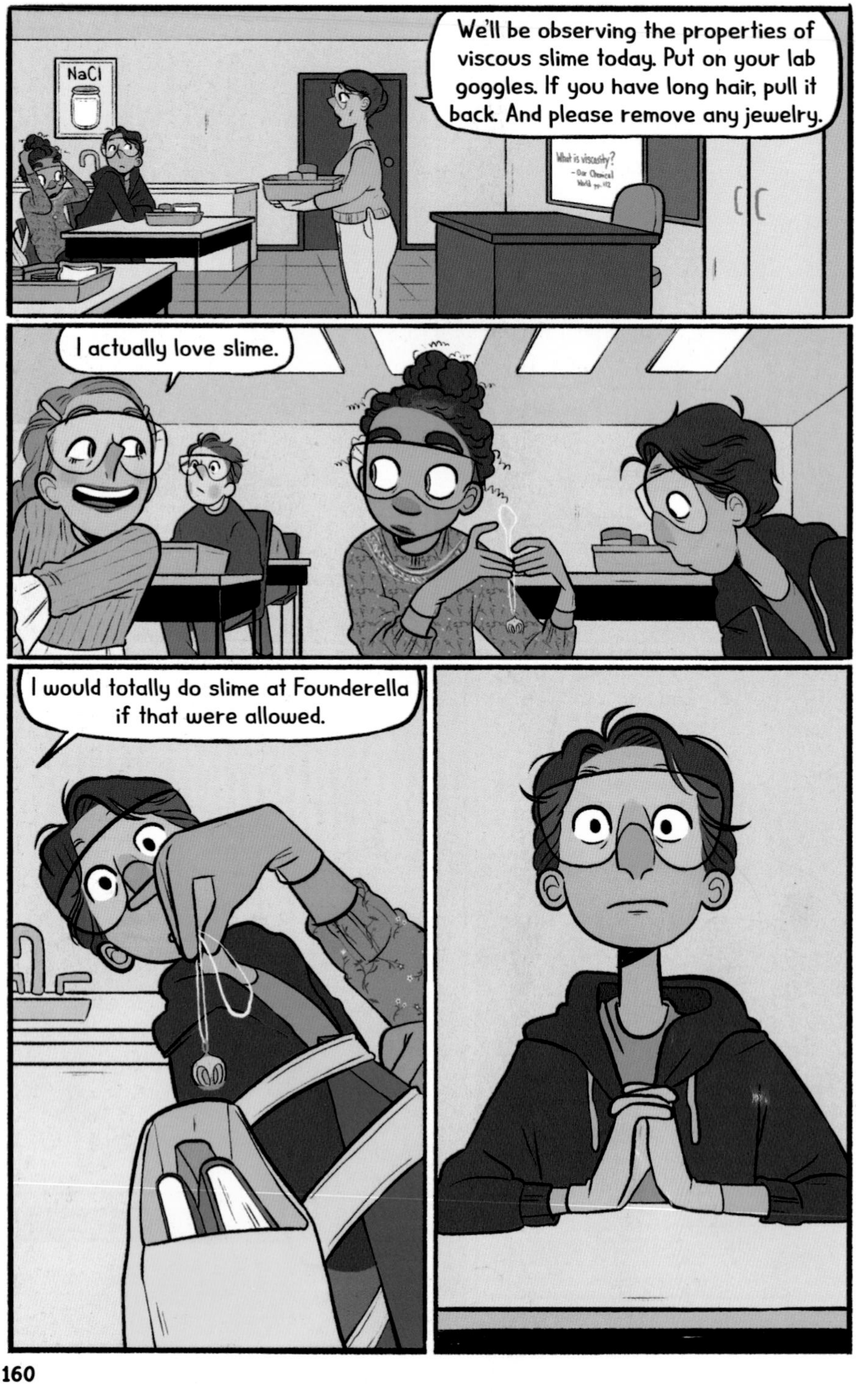
NaCl
We'll be observing the properties of viscous slime today. Put on your lab goggles. If you have long hair, pull it back. And please remove any jewelry.
I actually love slime.
I would totally do slime at Founderella if that were allowed.

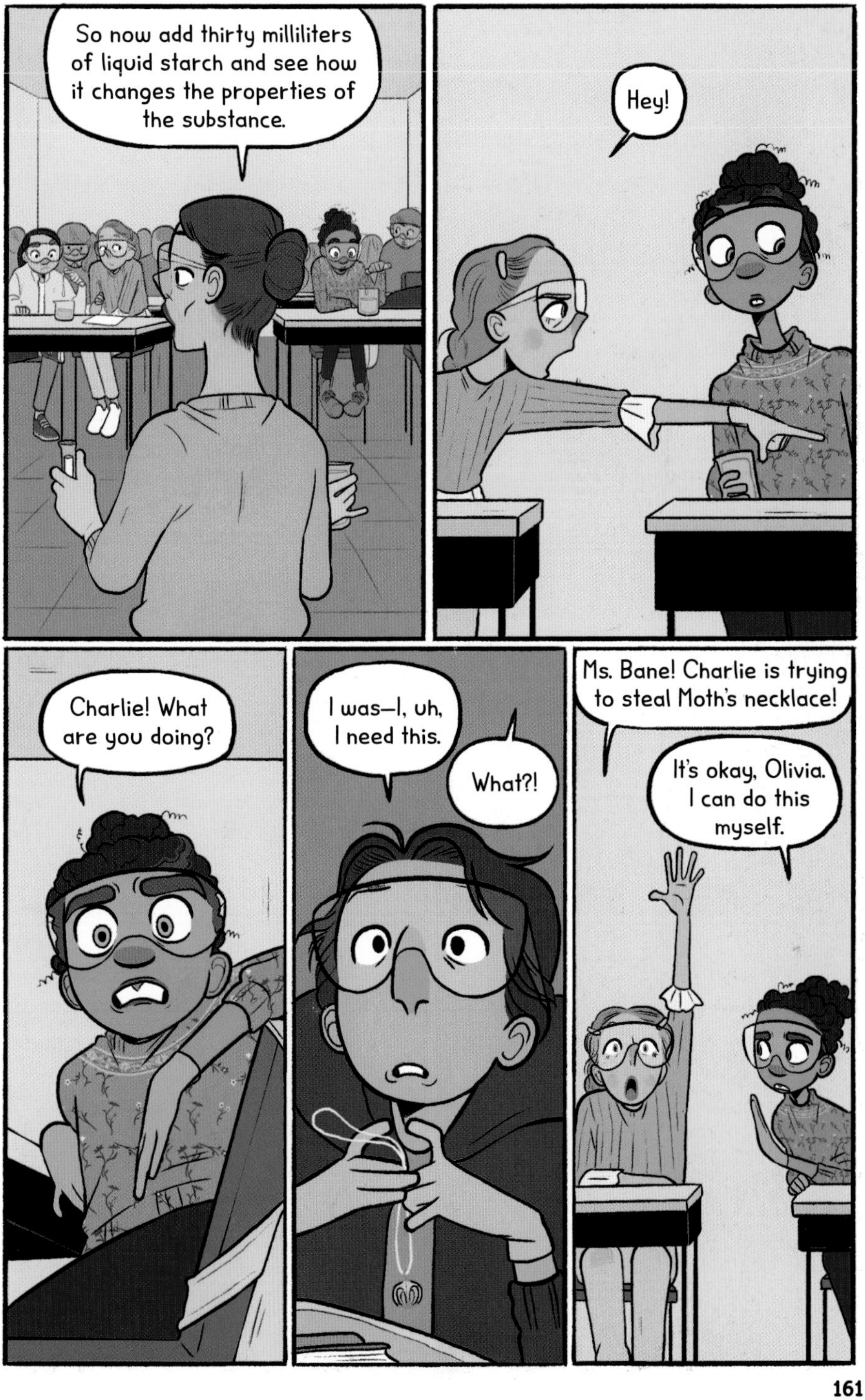
So now add thirty milliliters of liquid starch and see how it changes the properties of the substance.
Hey!
Charlie! What are you doing?
I was—I, uh, I need this.
What?!
Ms. Bane! Charlie is trying to steal Moth's necklace!
It's okay, Olivia. I can do this myself.

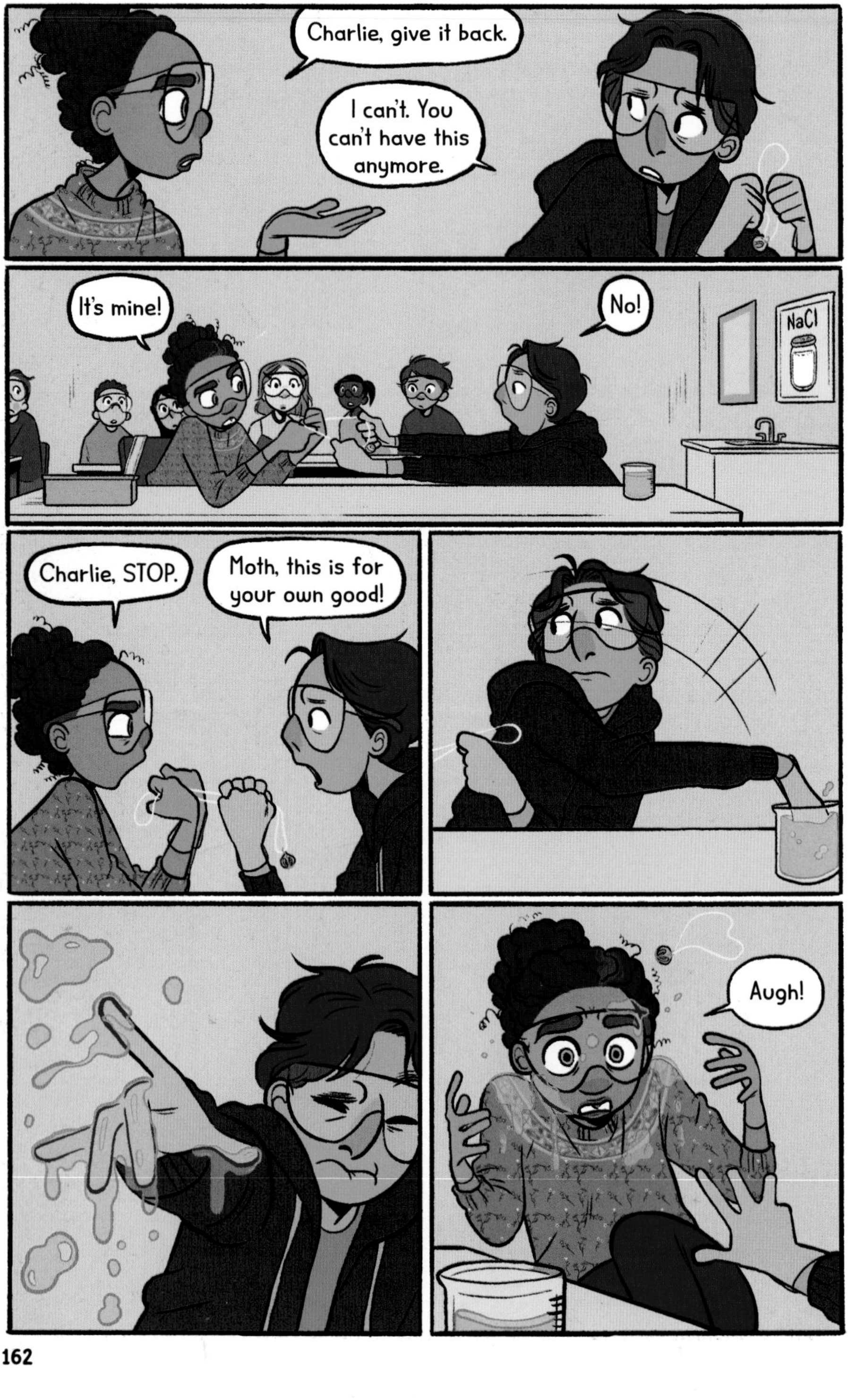
Charlie, give it back.
I can't. You can't have this anymore.
It's mine!
No!
NaCl
Charlie, STOP.
Moth, this is for your own good!
Augh!

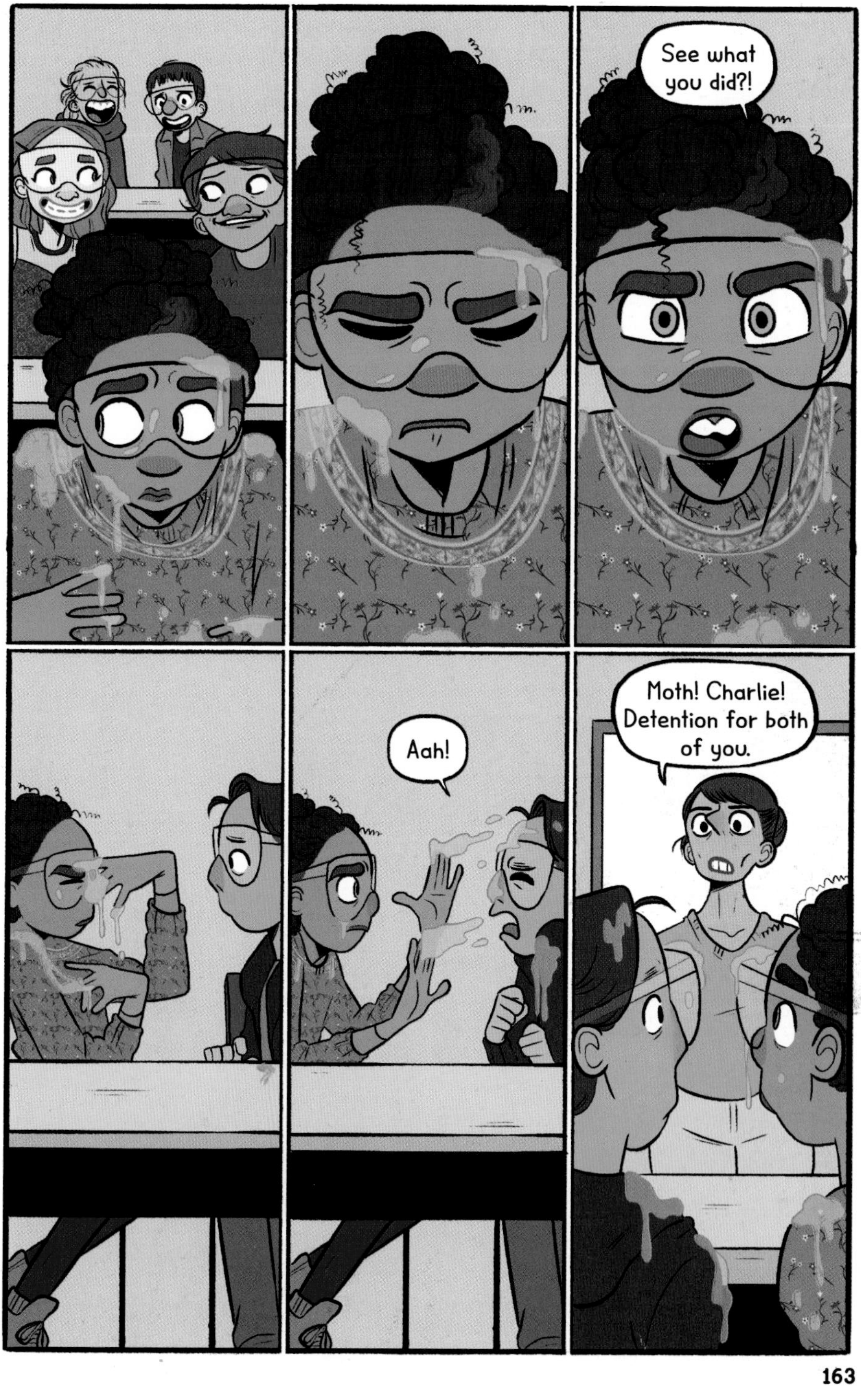
See what you did?!
Aah!
Moth! Charlie! Detention for both of you.

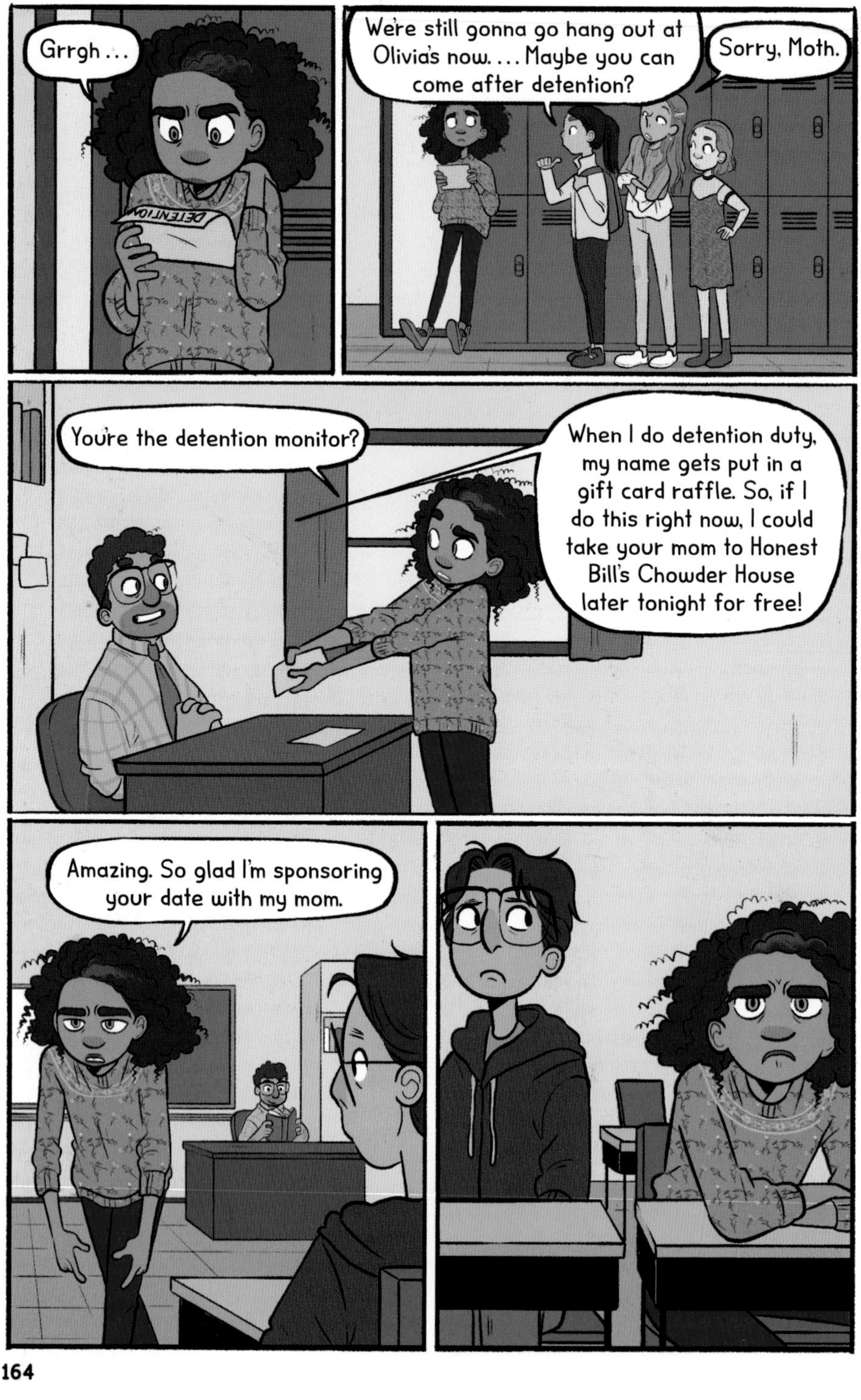
Grrgh . . .
DETENTION
We're still gonna go hang out at Olivia's now. . . . Maybe you can come after detention?
Sorry, Moth.
You're the detention monitor?
When I do detention duty, my name gets put in a gift card raffle. So, if I do this right now, I could take your mom to Honest Bill's Chowder House later tonight for free!
Amazing. So glad I'm sponsoring your date with my mom.

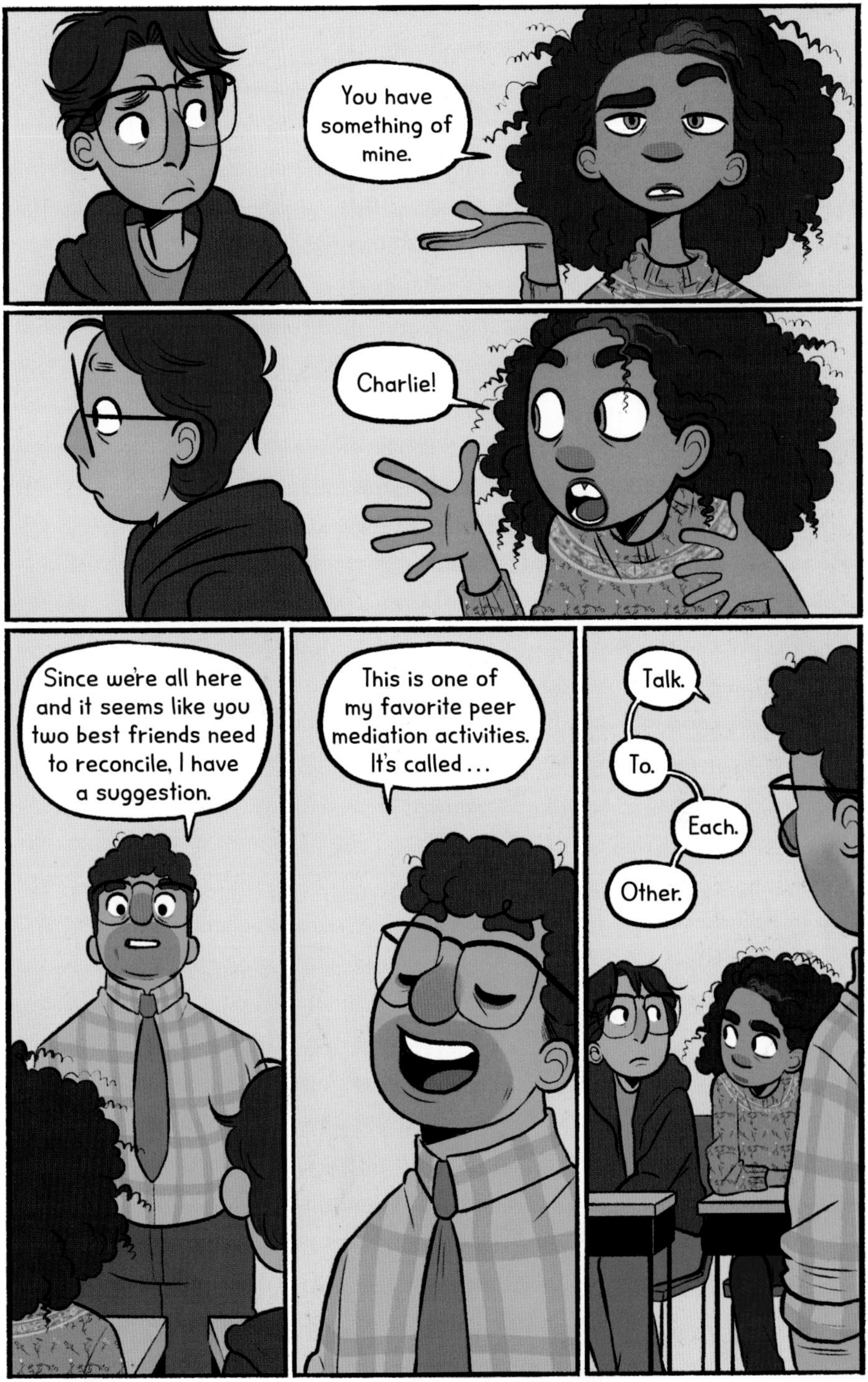
You have something of mine.
Charlie!
Since we're all here and it seems like you two best friends need to reconcile, I have a suggestion.
This is one of my favorite peer mediation activities. It's called . . .
Talk.
To.
Each.
Other.

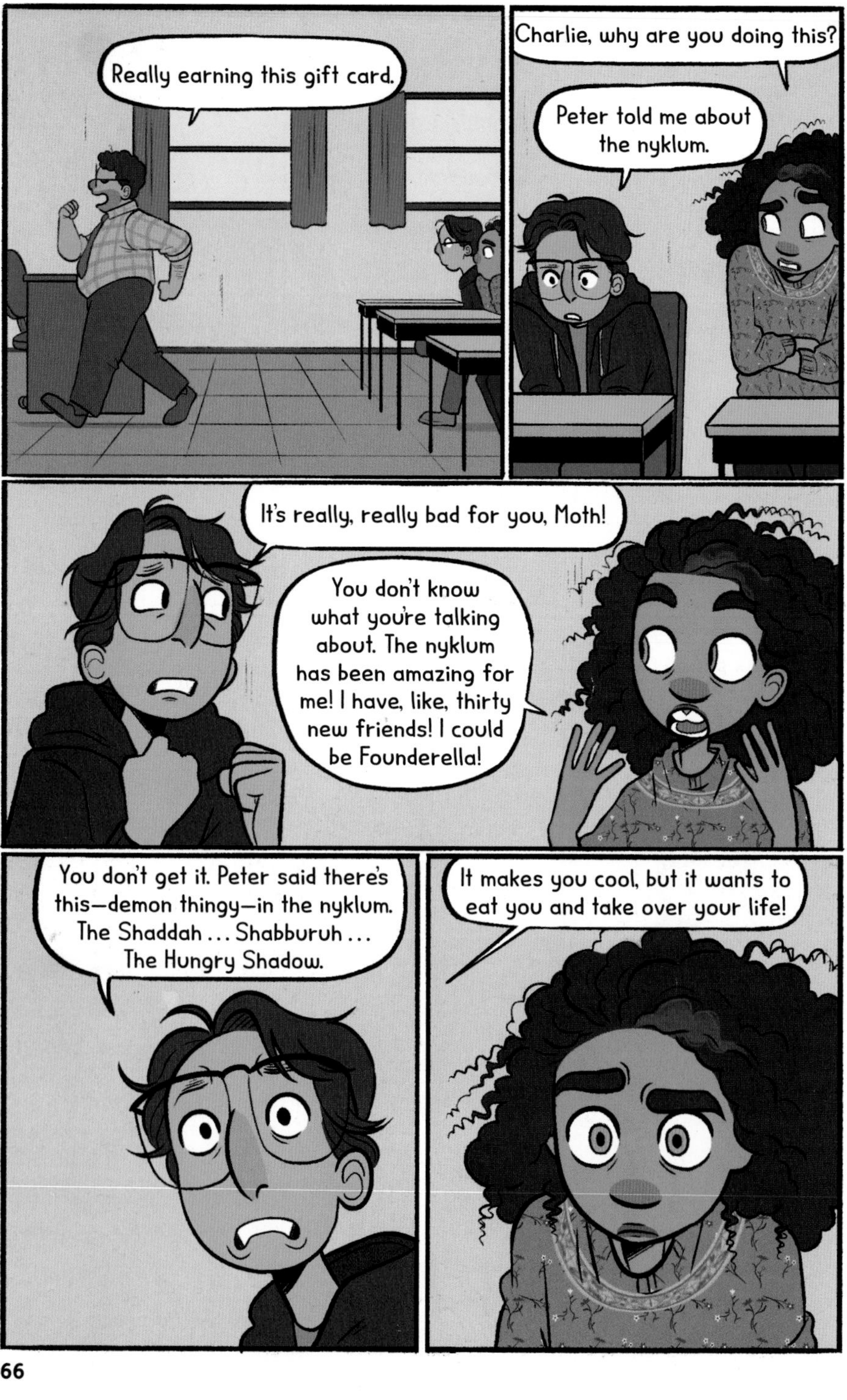
Really earning this gift card.
Charlie, why are you doing this?
Peter told me about the nyklum.
It's really, really bad for you, Moth!
You don't know what you're talking about. The nyklum has been amazing for me! I have, like, thirty new friends! I could be Founderella!
You don't get it. Peter said there's this—demon thingy—in the nyklum. The Shaddah . . . Shabburuh . . . The Hungry Shadow.
It makes you cool, but it wants to eat you and take over your life!

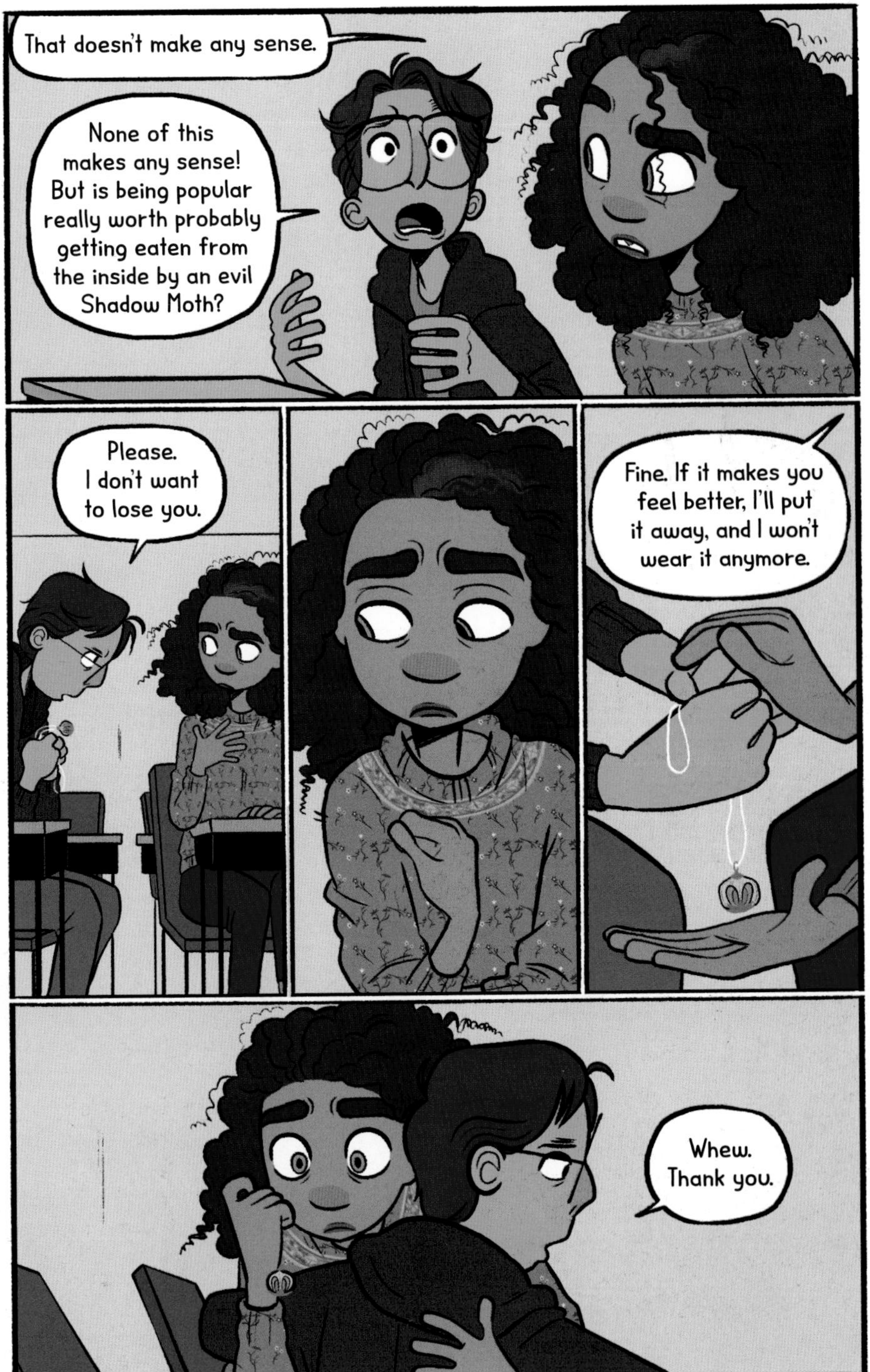
That doesn't make any sense.
None of this makes any sense! But is being popular really worth probably getting eaten from the inside by an evil Shadow Moth?
Please. I don't want to lose you.
Fine. If it makes you feel better, I'll put it away, and I won't wear it anymore.
Whew. Thank you.

CHAPTER 10
Nightmare

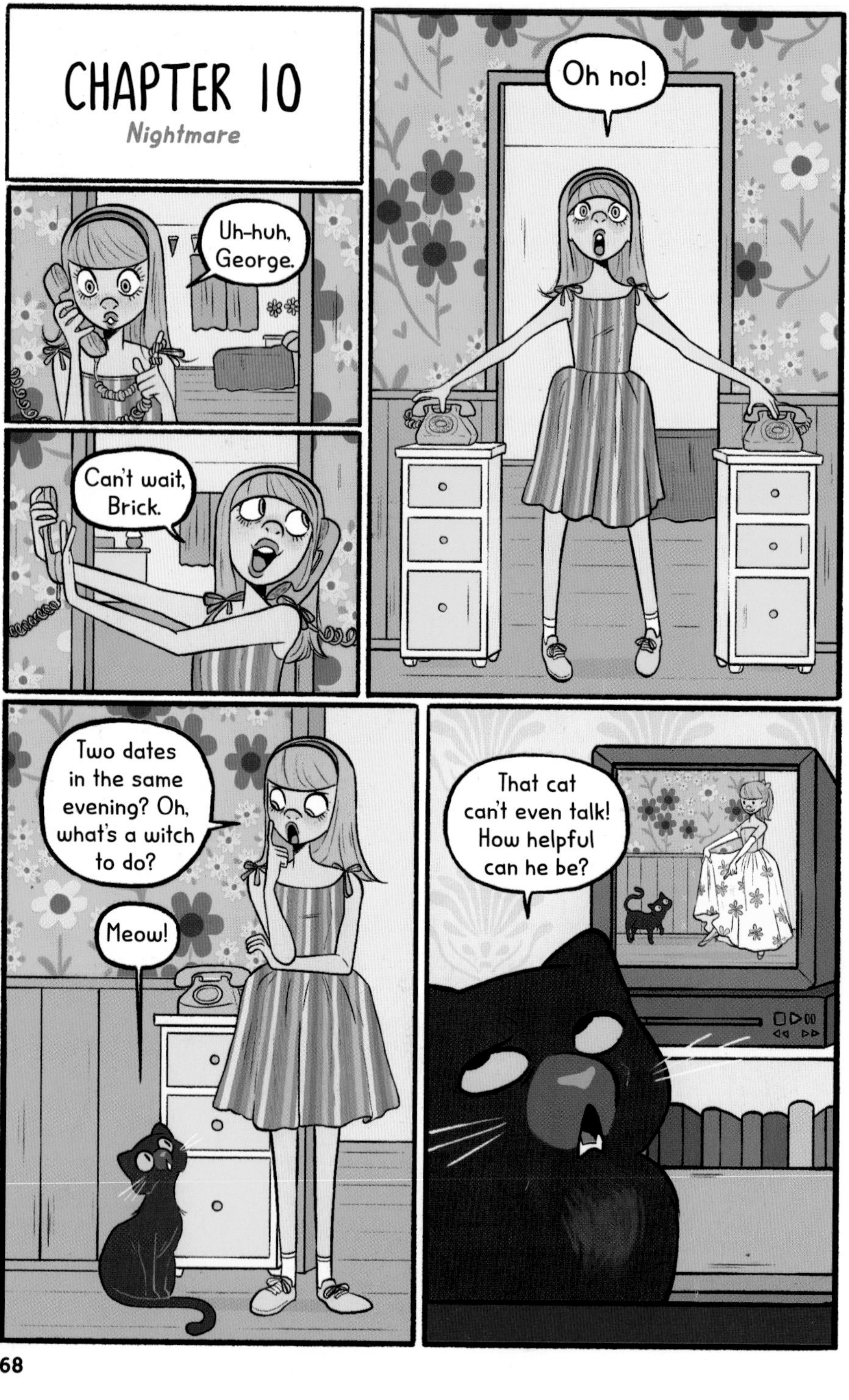
Uh-huh, George.
Can't wait, Brick.
Oh no!
Two dates in the same evening? Oh, what's a witch to do?
Meow!
That cat can't even talk! How helpful can he be?

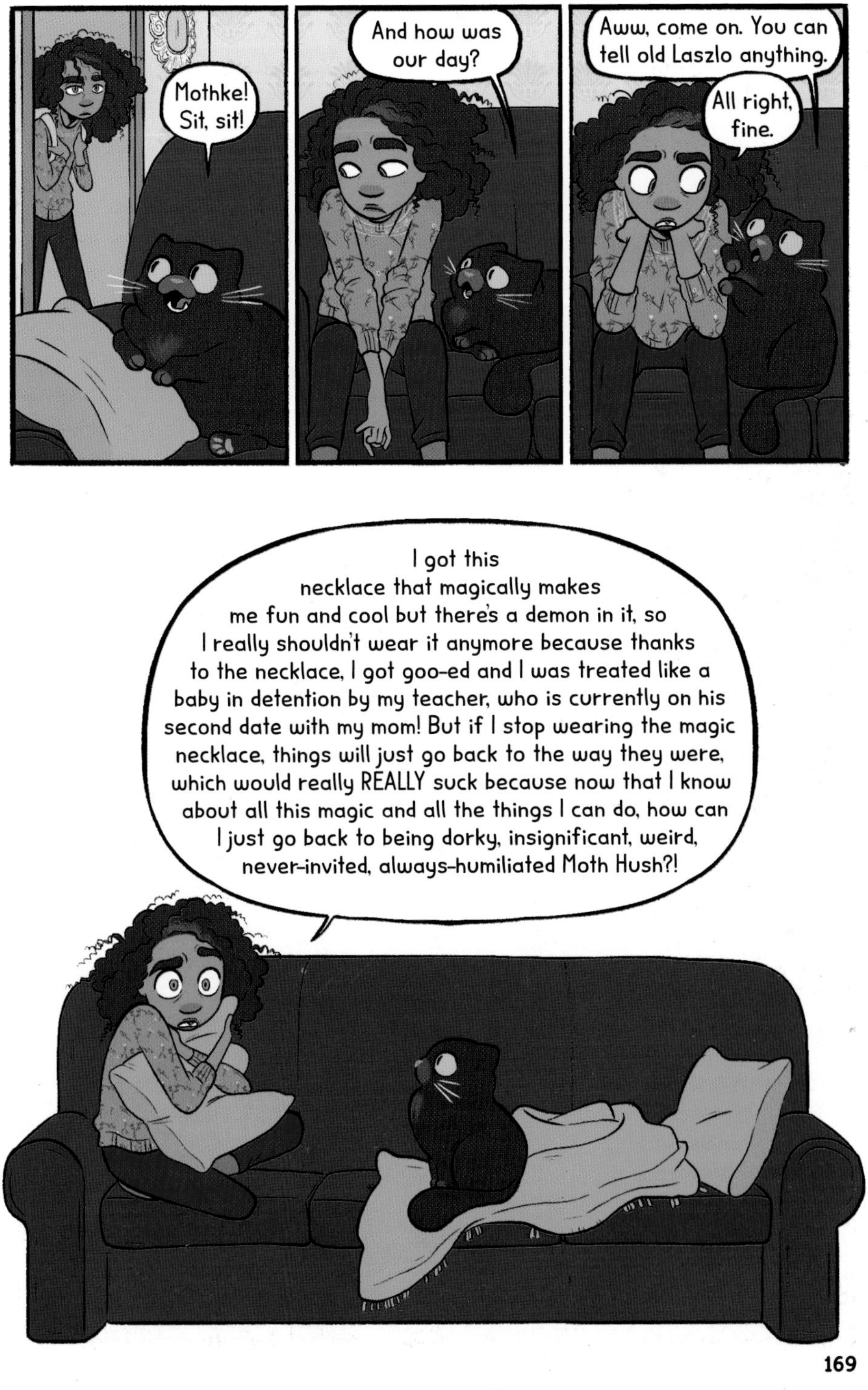
Mothke! Sit, sit!
And how was our day?
Aww, come on. You can tell old Laszlo anything.
All right, fine.
I got this necklace that magically makes me fun and cool but there's a demon in it, so I really shouldn't wear it anymore because thanks to the necklace, I got goo-ed and I was treated like a baby in detention by my teacher, who is currently on his second date with my mom! But if I stop wearing the magic necklace, things will just go back to the way they were, which would really REALLY suck because now that I know about all this magic and all the things I can do, how can I just go back to being dorky, insignificant, weird, never-invited, always-humiliated Moth Hush?!

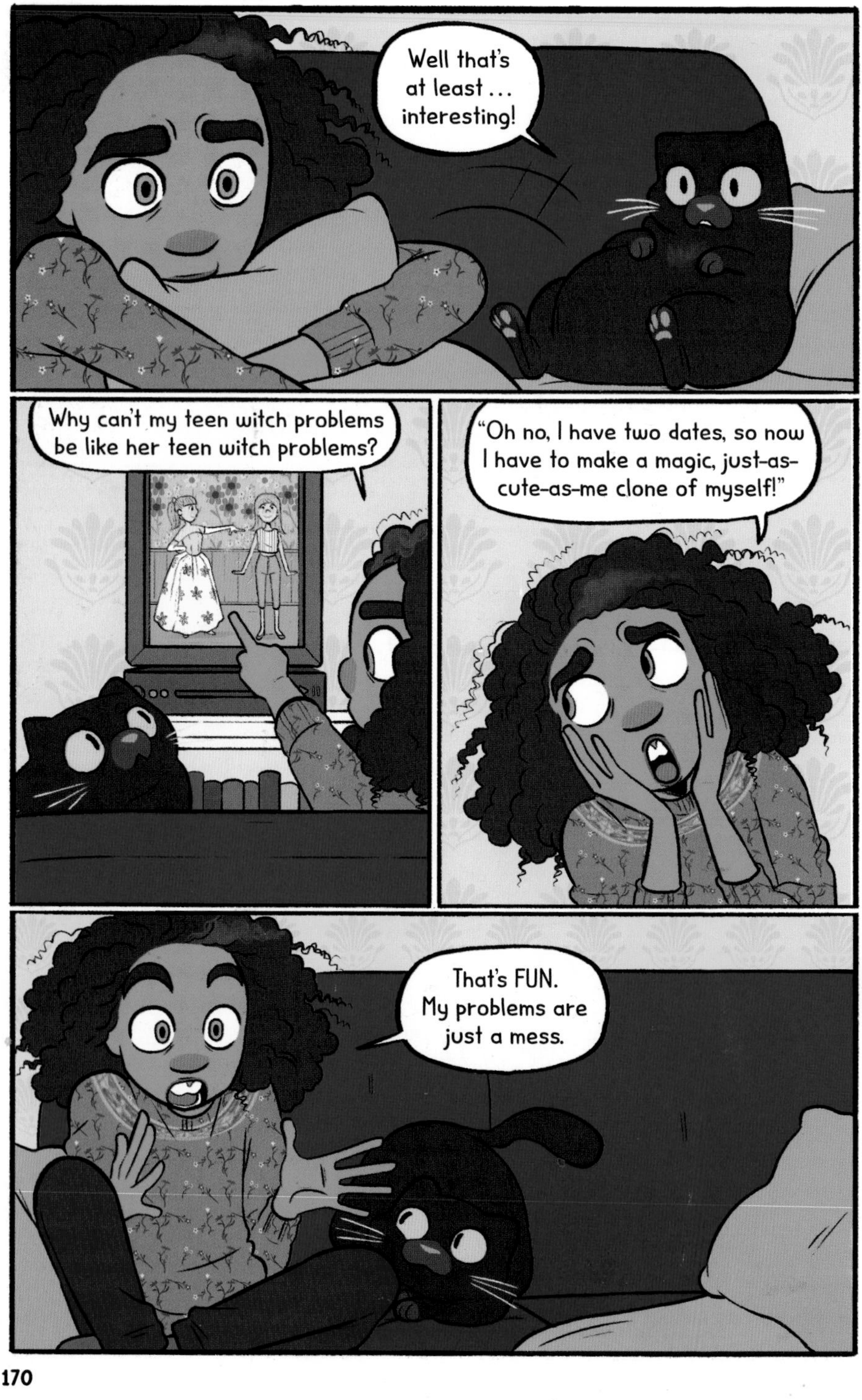
Well that's at least ... interesting!
Why can't my teen witch problems be like her teen witch problems?
"Oh no, I have two dates, so now I have to make a magic, just-as-cute-as-me clone of myself!"
That's FUN. My problems are just a mess.

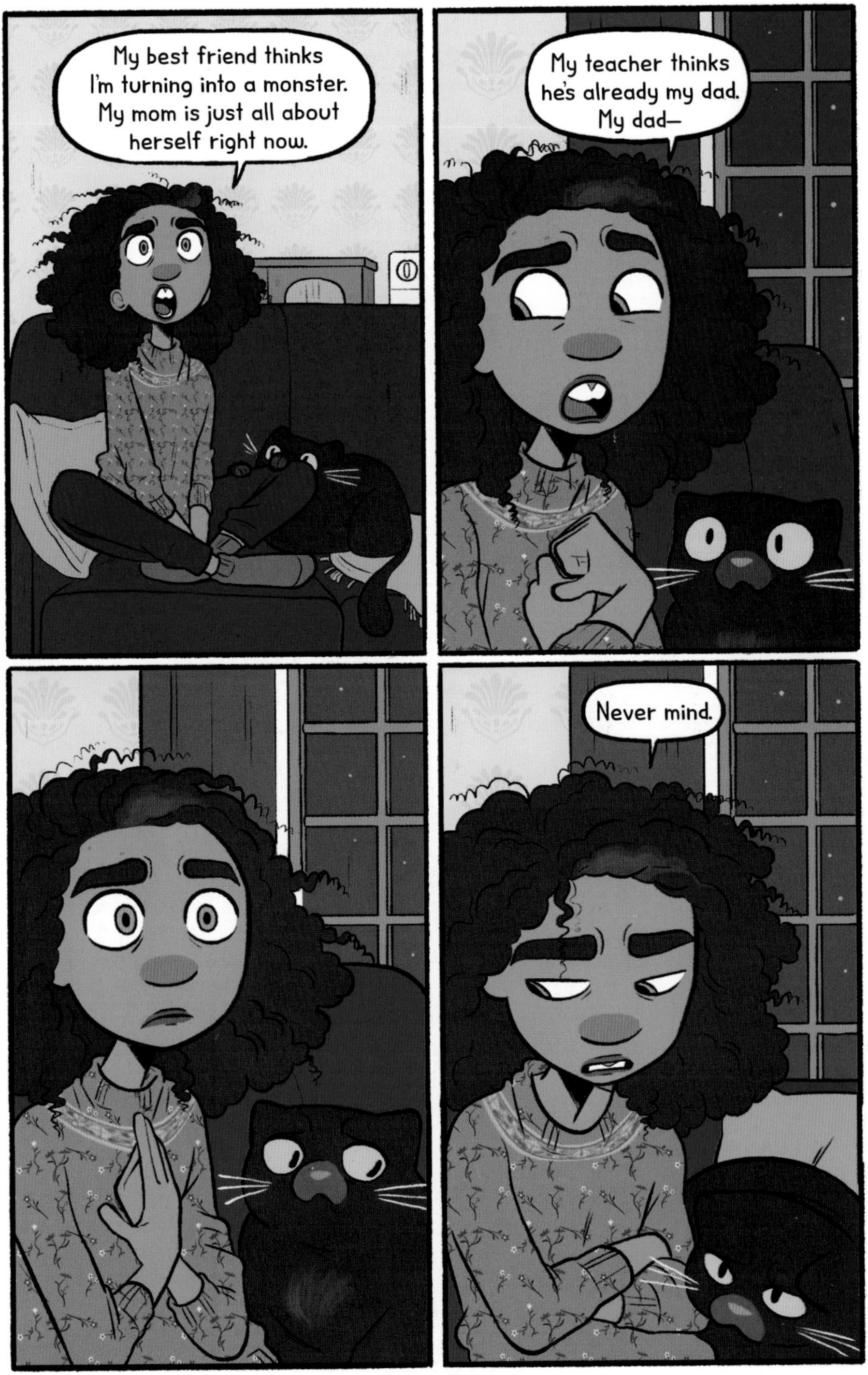
My best friend thinks I'm turning into a monster. My mom is just all about herself right now.
My teacher thinks he's already my dad. My dad—
Never mind.

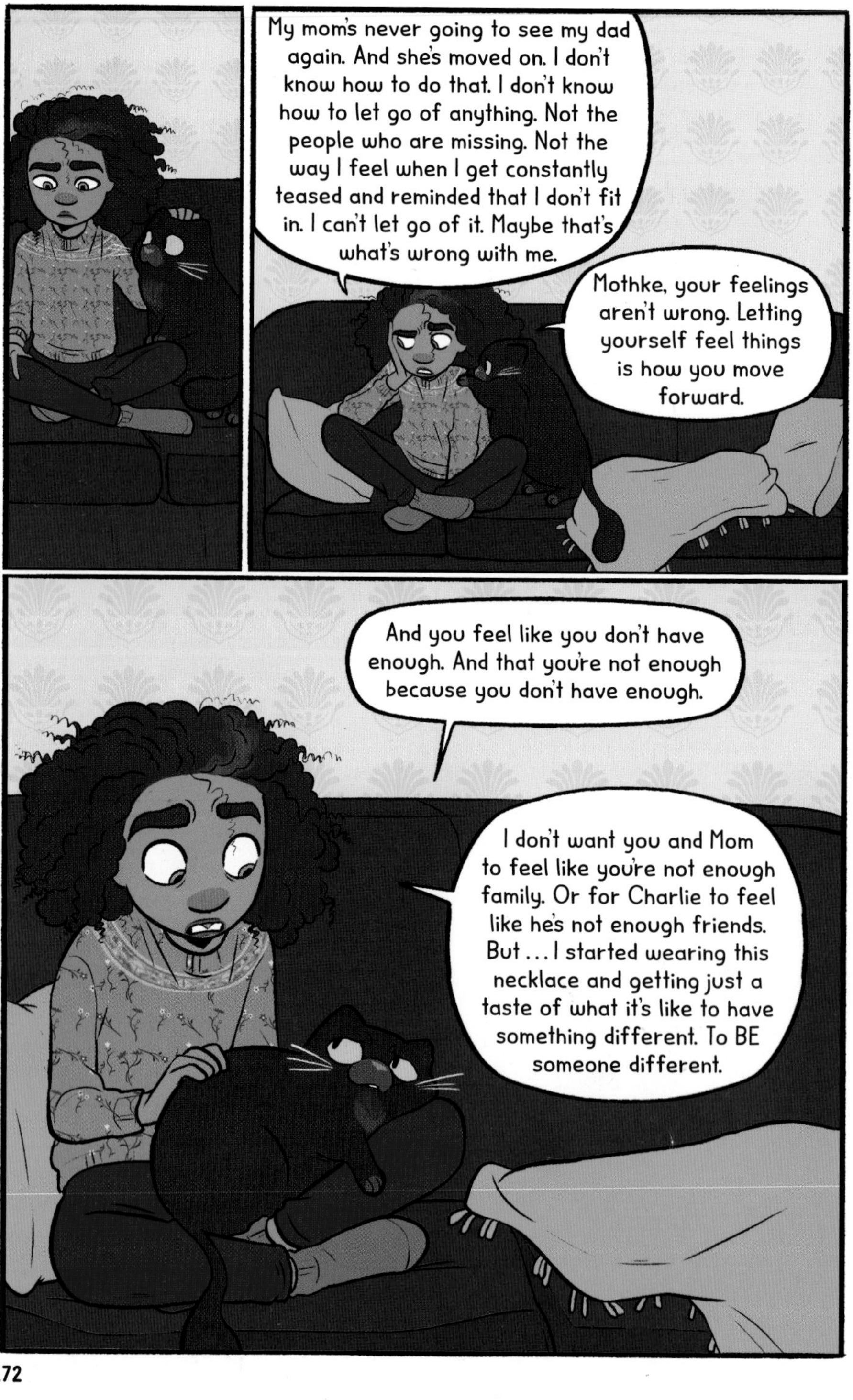
My mom's never going to see my dad again. And she's moved on. I don't know how to do that. I don't know how to let go of anything. Not the people who are missing. Not the way I feel when I get constantly teased and reminded that I don't fit in. I can't let go of it. Maybe that's what's wrong with me.
Mothke, your feelings aren't wrong. Letting yourself feel things is how you move forward.
And you feel like you don't have enough. And that you're not enough because you don't have enough.
I don't want you and Mom to feel like you're not enough family. Or for Charlie to feel like he's not enough friends. But . . . I started wearing this necklace and getting just a taste of what it's like to have something different. To BE someone different.

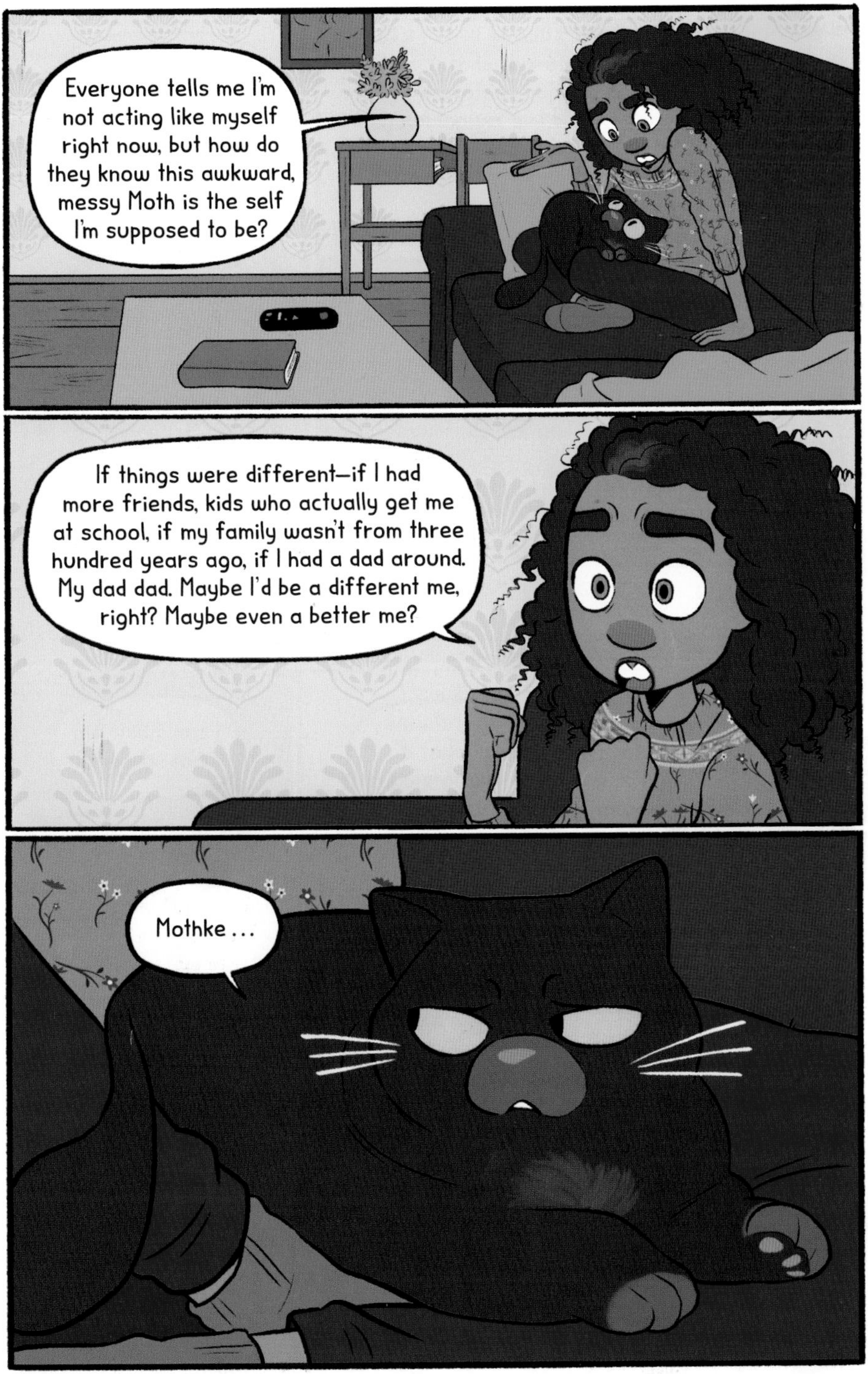
Everyone tells me I'm not acting like myself right now, but how do they know this awkward, messy Moth is the self I'm supposed to be?
If things were different—if I had more friends, kids who actually get me at school, if my family wasn't from three hundred years ago, if I had a dad around. My dad dad. Maybe I'd be a different me, right? Maybe even a better me?
Mothke . . .

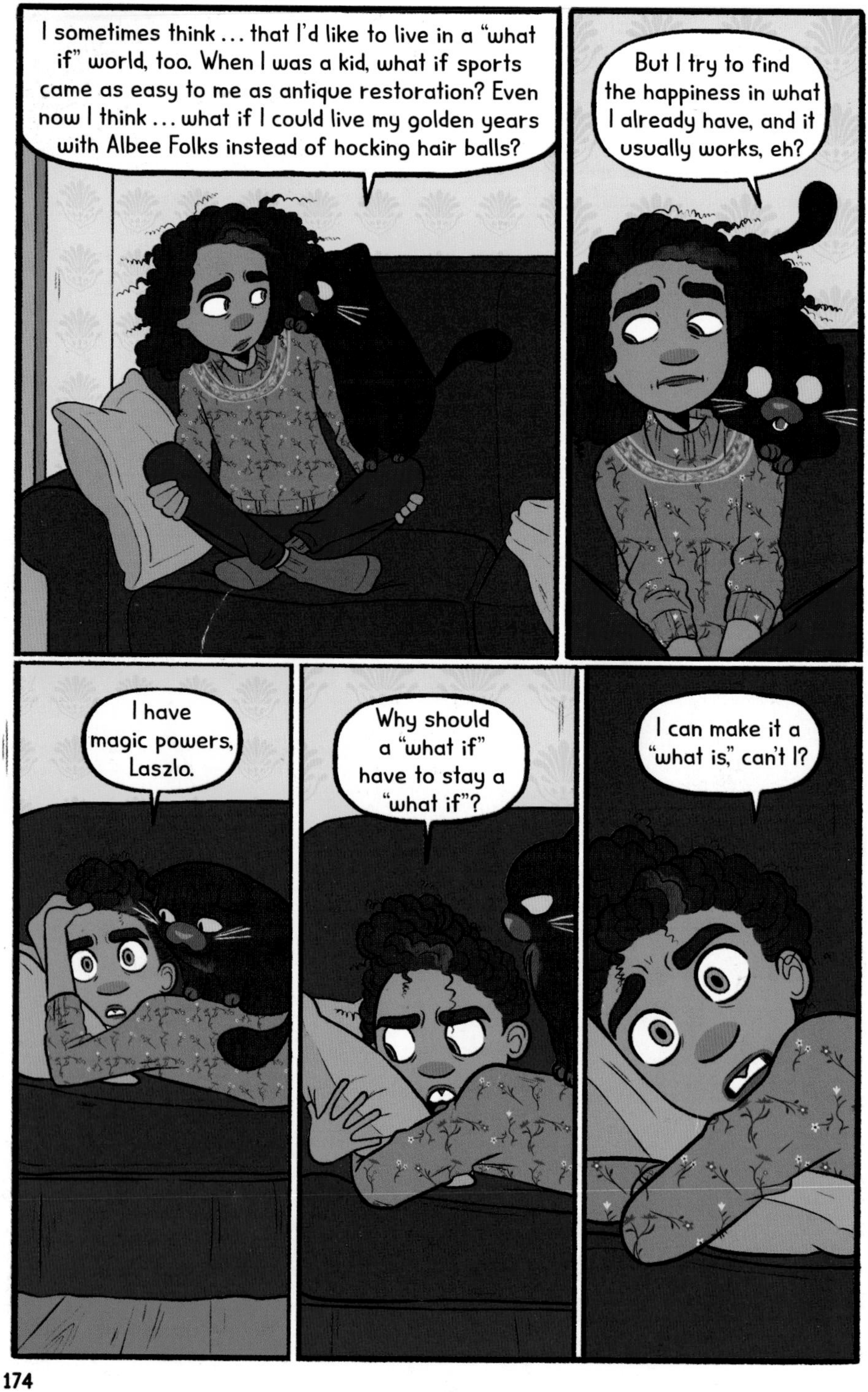
I sometimes think ... that I'd like to live in a "what if" world, too. When I was a kid, what if sports came as easy to me as antique restoration? Even now I think ... what if I could live my golden years with Albee Folks instead of hocking hair balls?
But I try to find the happiness in what I already have, and it usually works, eh?
I have magic powers, Laszlo.
Why should a "what if" have to stay a "what if"?
I can make it a "what is," can't I?

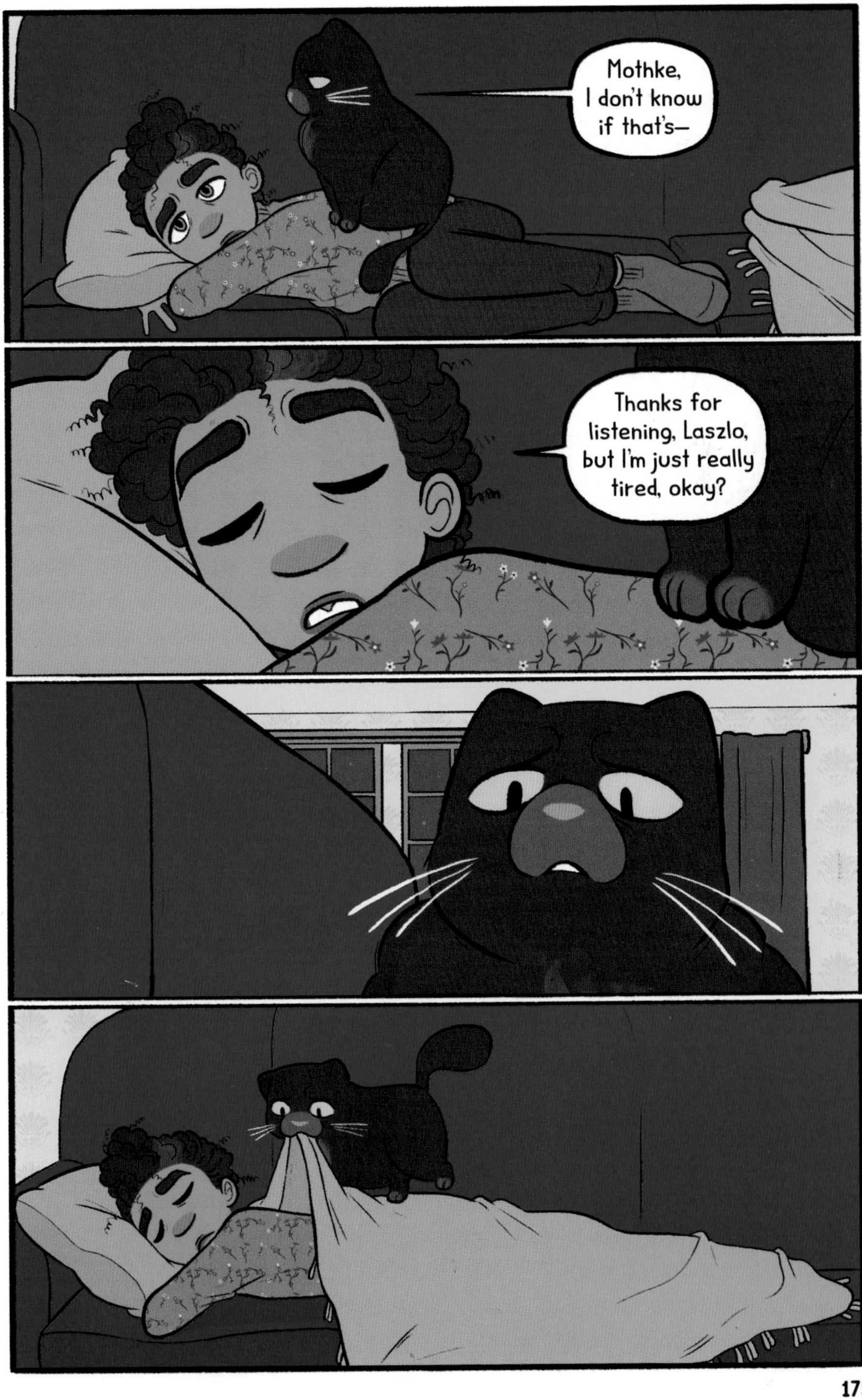
Mothke, I don't know if that's—
Thanks for listening, Laszlo, but I'm just really tired, okay?

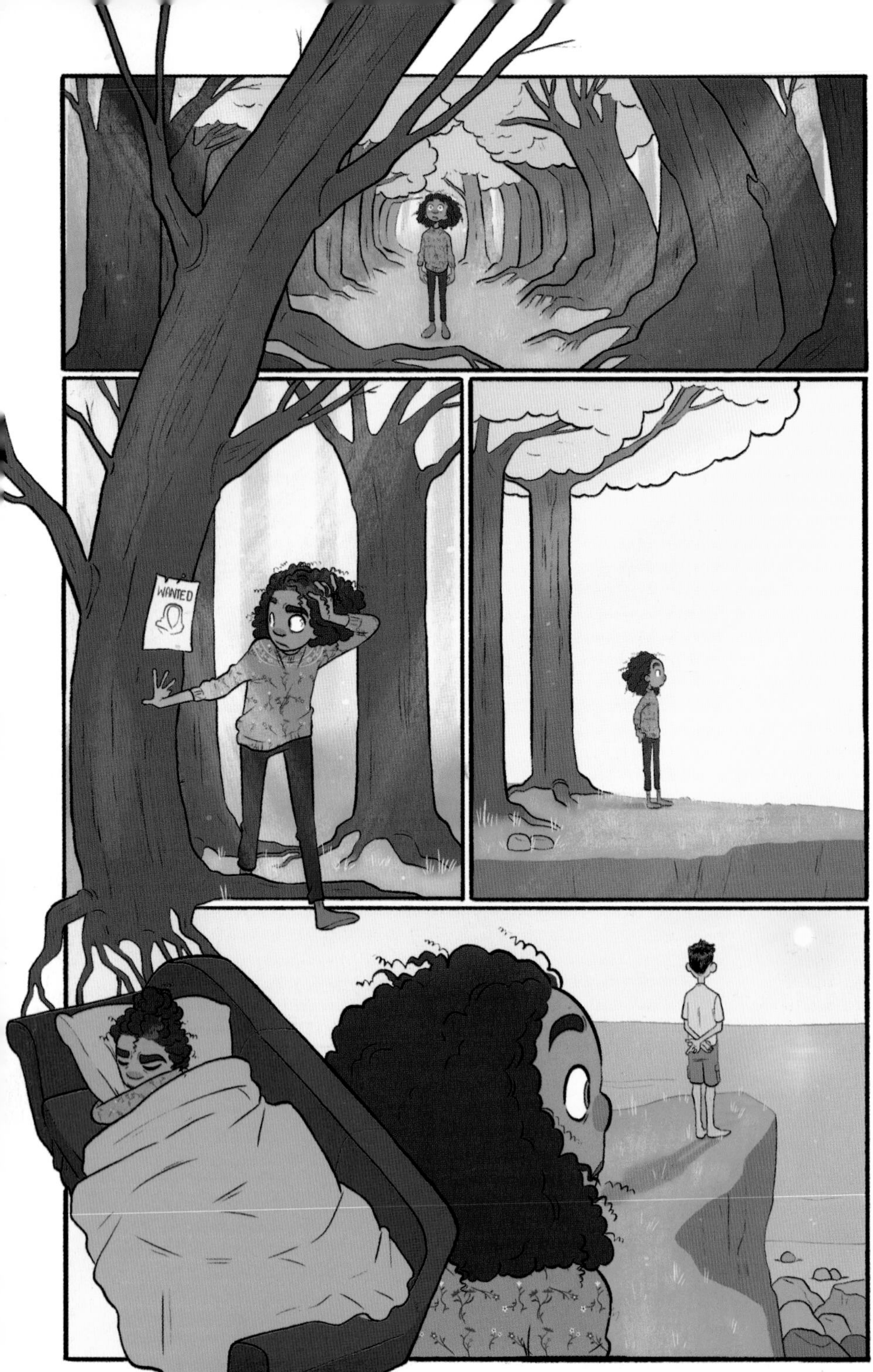
WANTED

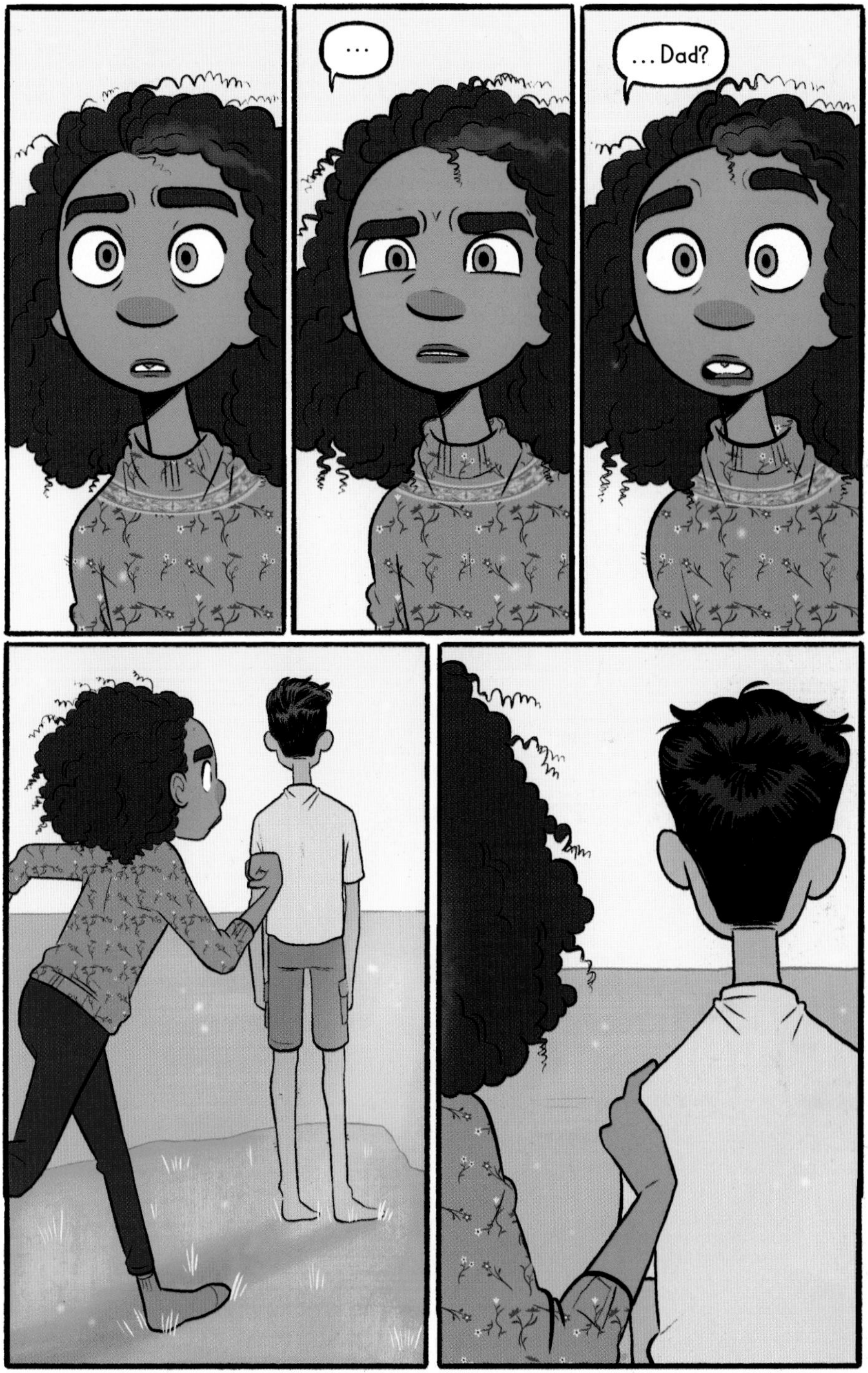
...
...Dad?

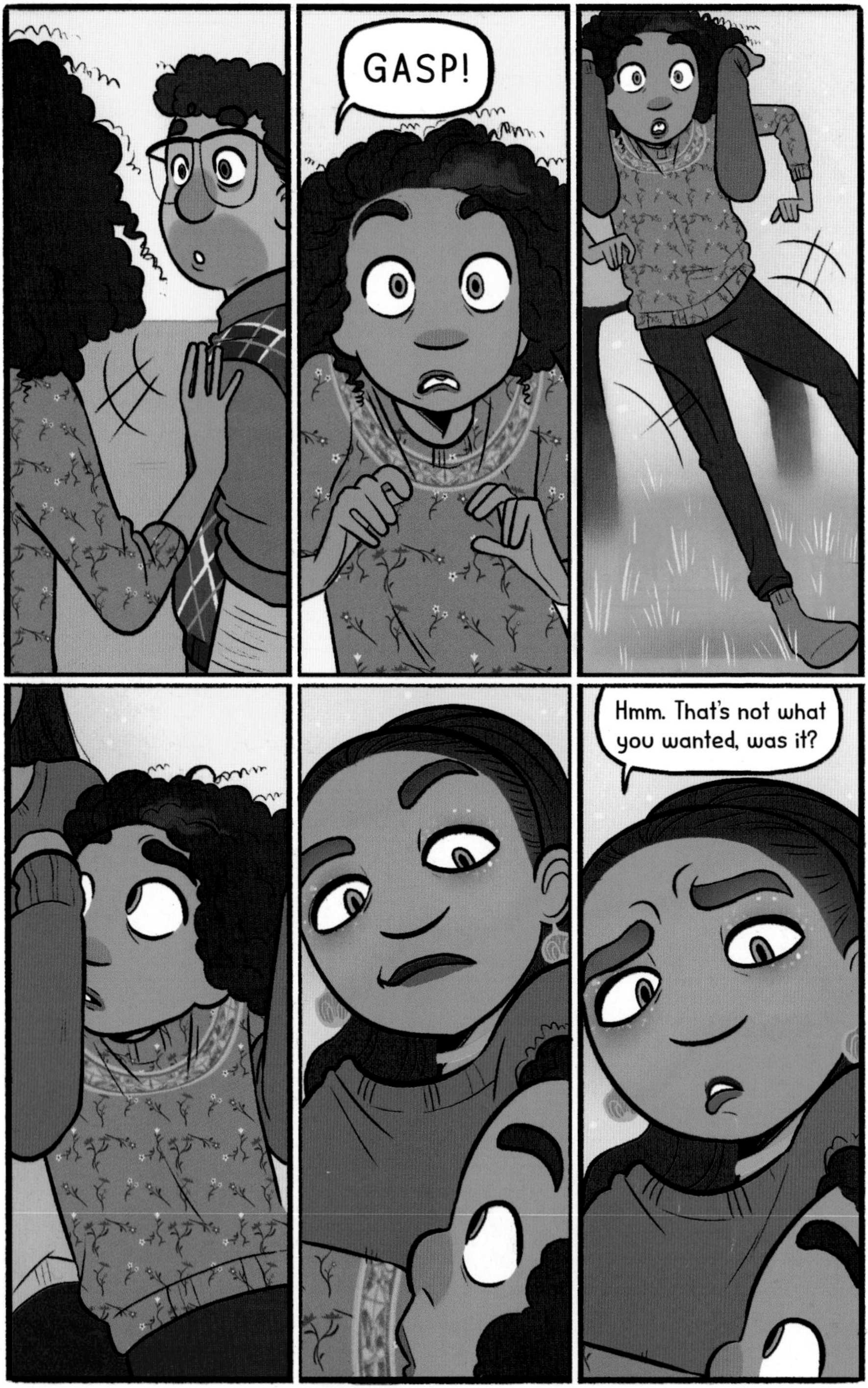
GASP!
Hmm. That's not what you wanted, was it?

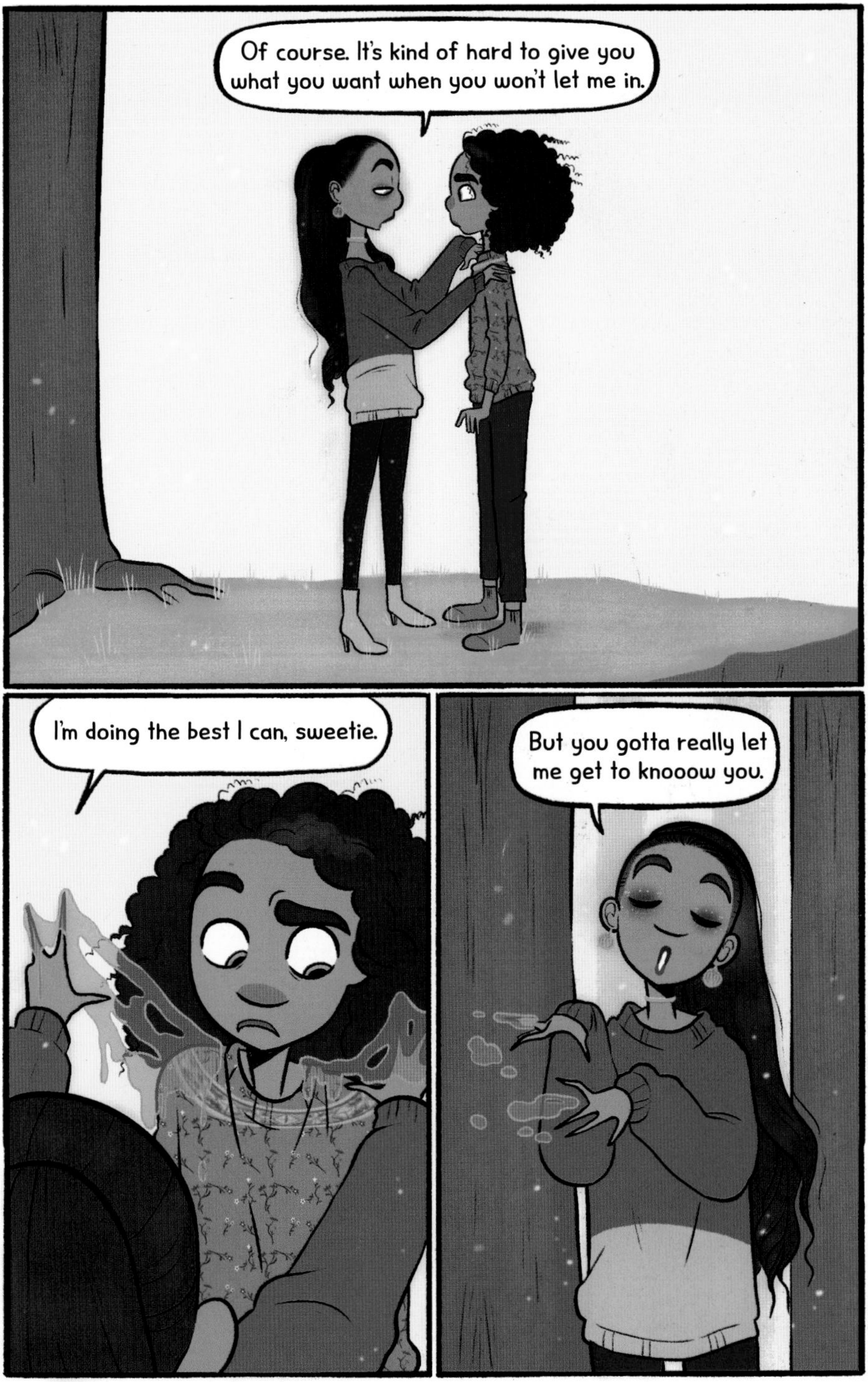
Of course. It's kind of hard to give you what you want when you won't let me in.
I'm doing the best I can, sweetie.
But you gotta really let me get to knooow you.

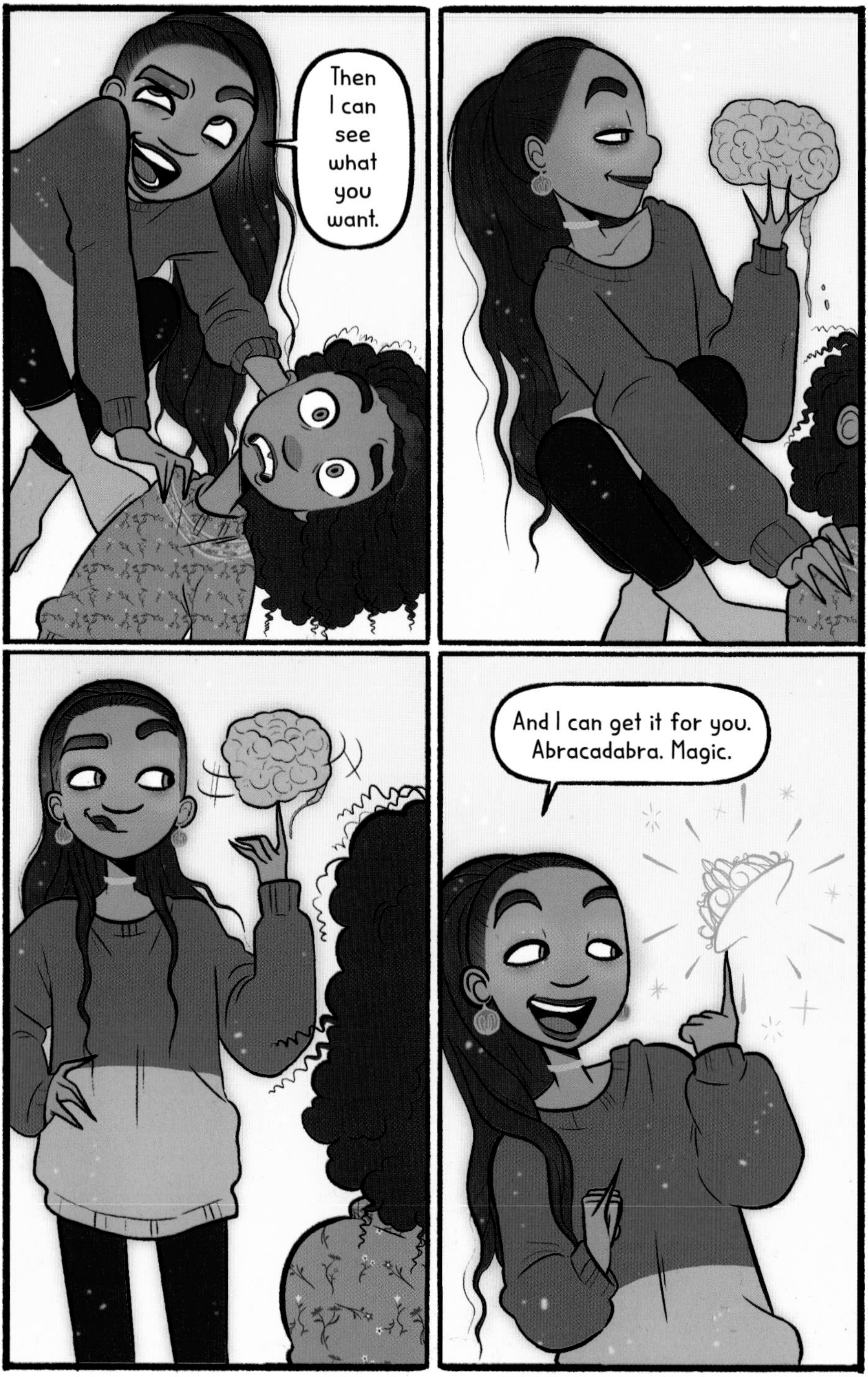

Then I can see what you want.
And I can get it for you. Abracadabra. Magic.

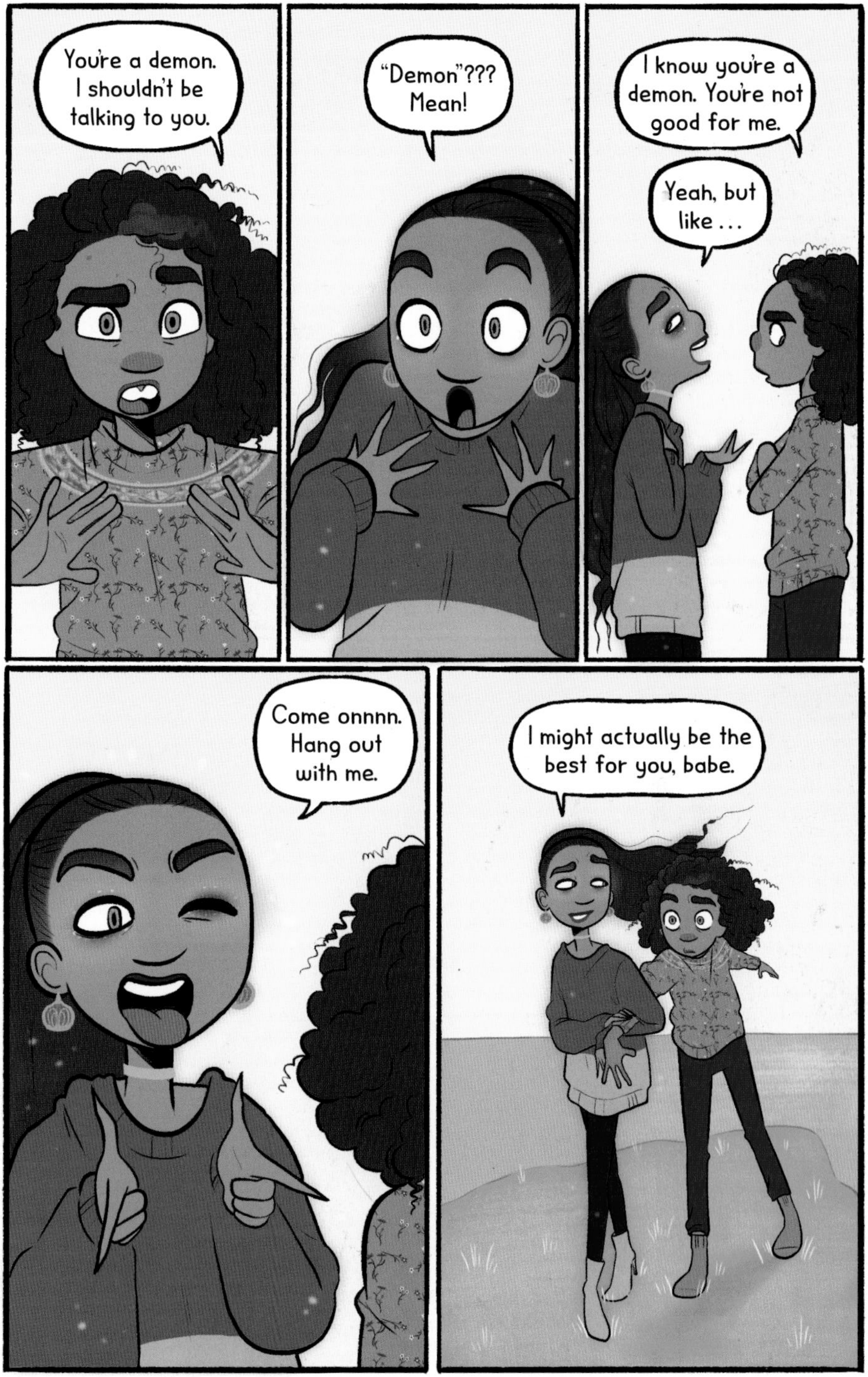
You're a demon. I shouldn't be talking to you.
"Demon"??? Mean!
I know you're a demon. You're not good for me.
Yeah, but like . . .
Come onnnn. Hang out with me.
I might actually be the best for you, babe.

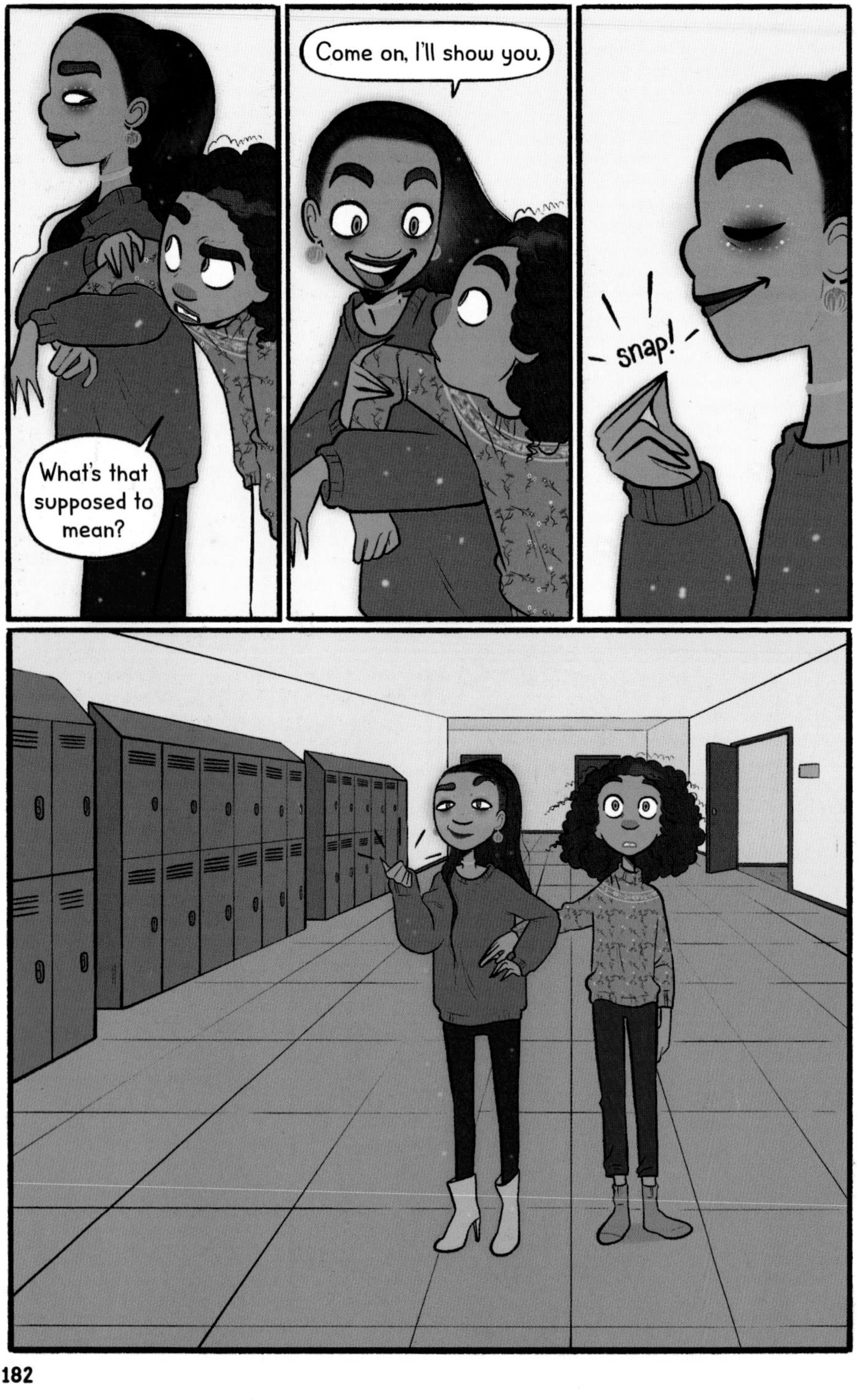
What's that supposed to mean?
Come on, I'll show you.
snap!

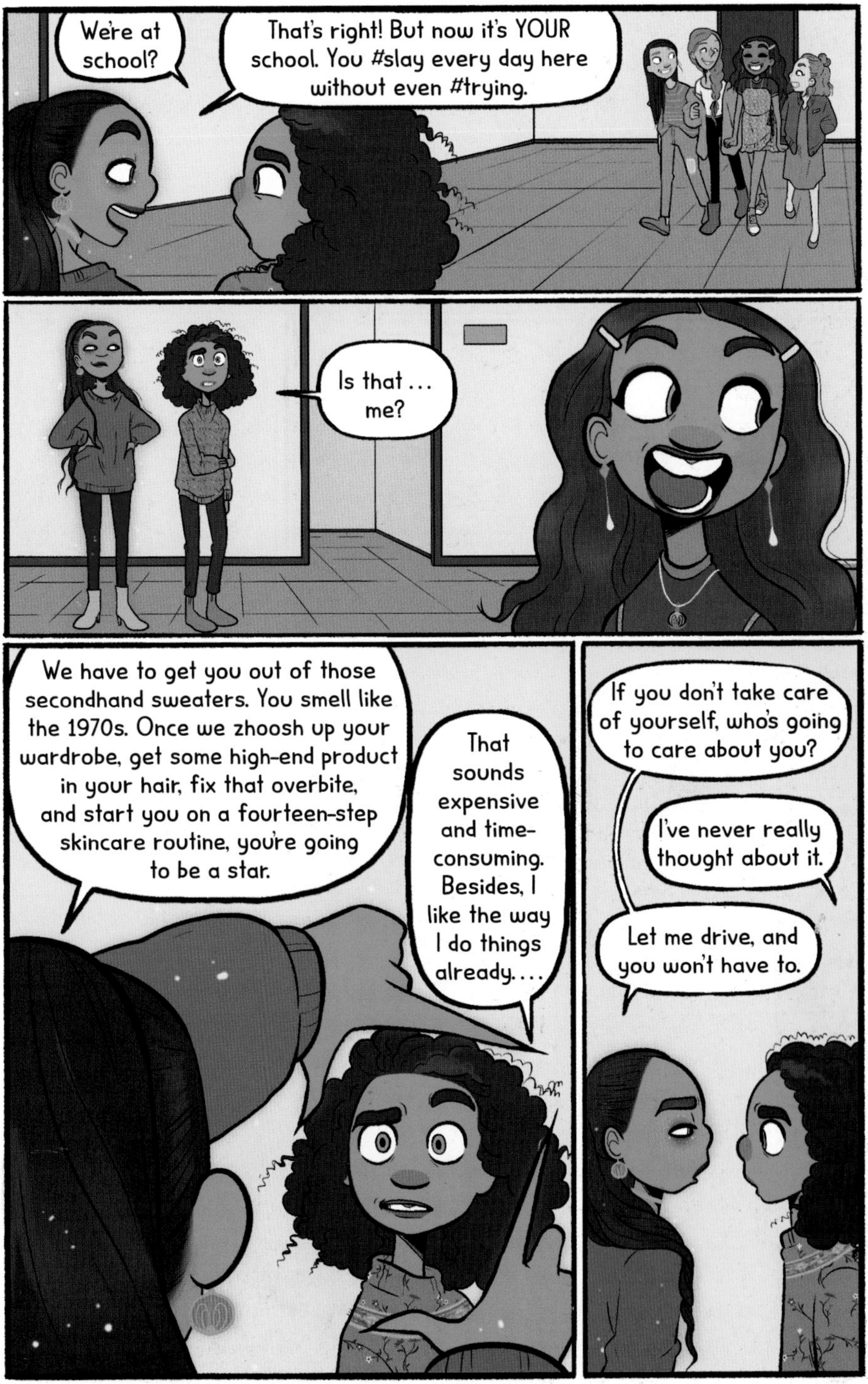
We're at school?
That's right! But now it's YOUR school. You #slay every day here without even #trying.
Is that . . . me?
We have to get you out of those secondhand sweaters. You smell like the 1970s. Once we zhoosh up your wardrobe, get some high-end product in your hair, fix that overbite, and start you on a fourteen-step skincare routine, you're going to be a star.
That sounds expensive and time-consuming. Besides, I like the way I do things already. . . .
If you don't take care of yourself, who's going to care about you?
I've never really thought about it.
Let me drive, and you won't have to.

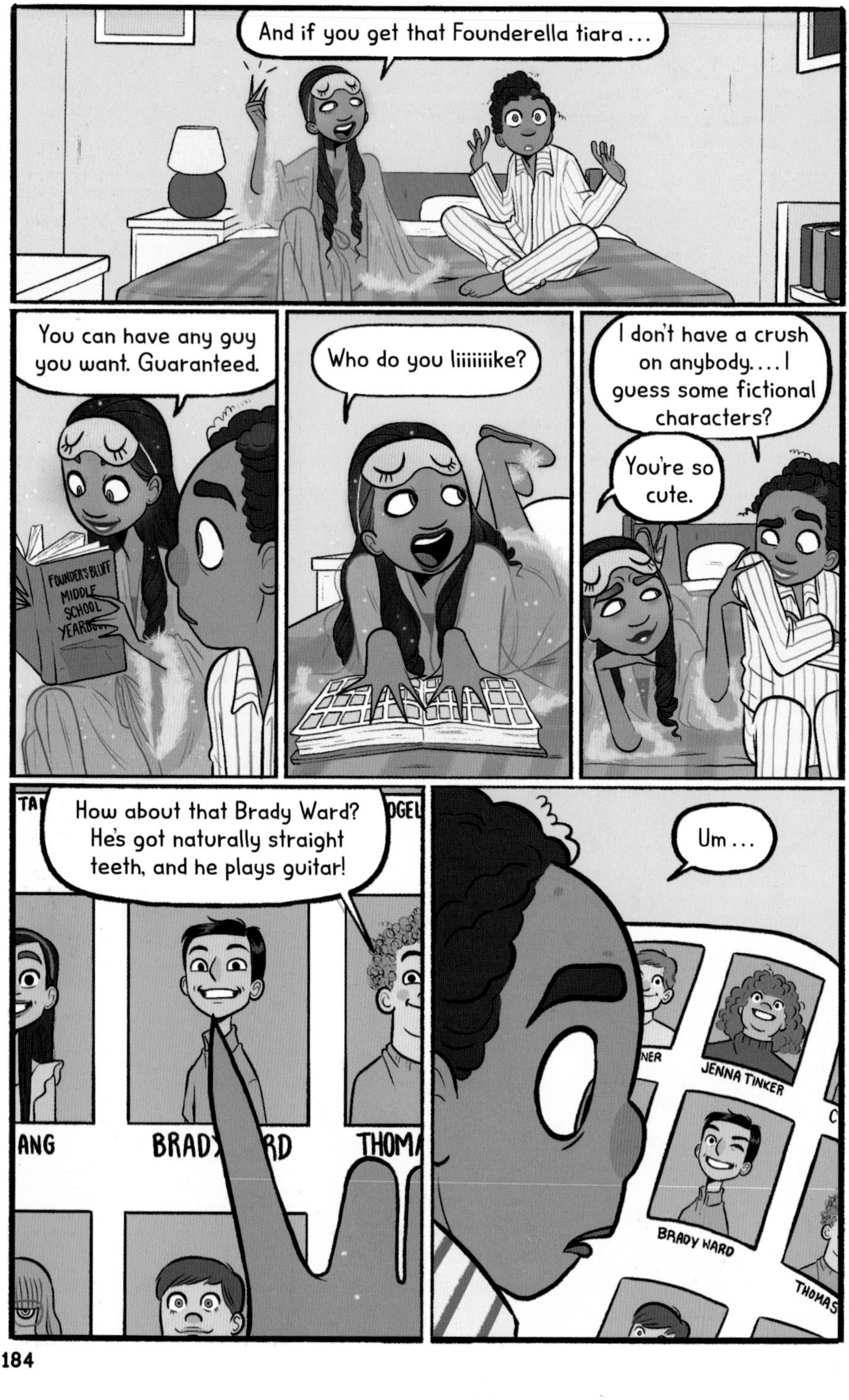
And if you get that Founderella tiara . . .
You can have any guy you want. Guaranteed.
FOUNDER'S BLUFF MIDDLE SCHOOL
Who do you liiiiiiike?
I don't have a crush on anybody. . . . I guess some fictional characters?
You're so cute.
How about that Brady Ward? He's got naturally straight teeth, and he plays guitar!
Um . . .
JENNA TINKER
BRADY WARD

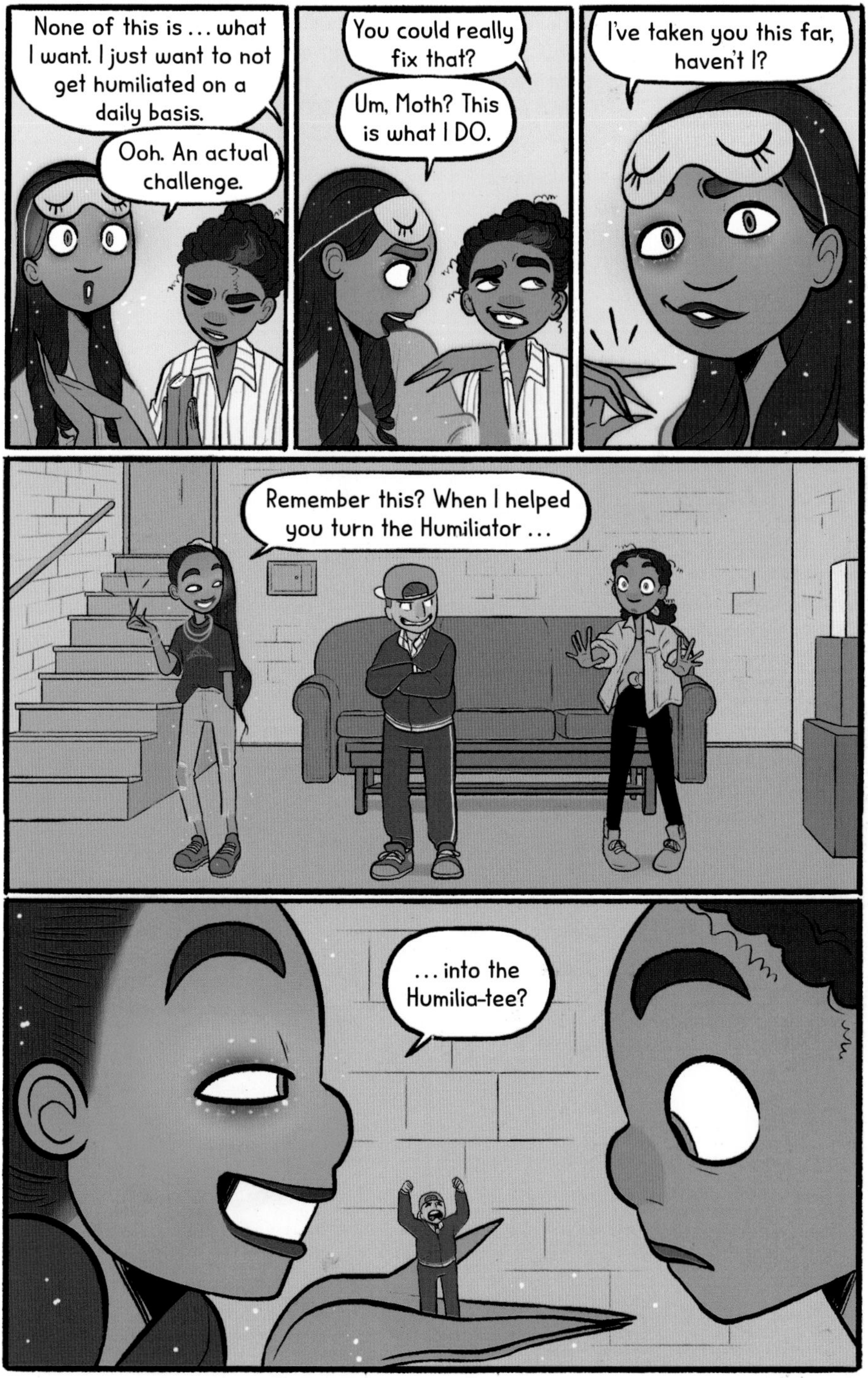
None of this is ... what I want. I just want to not get humiliated on a daily basis.
Ooh. An actual challenge.
You could really fix that?
Um, Moth? This is what I DO.
I've taken you this far, haven't I?
Remember this? When I helped you turn the Humiliator ...
... into the Humilia-tee?

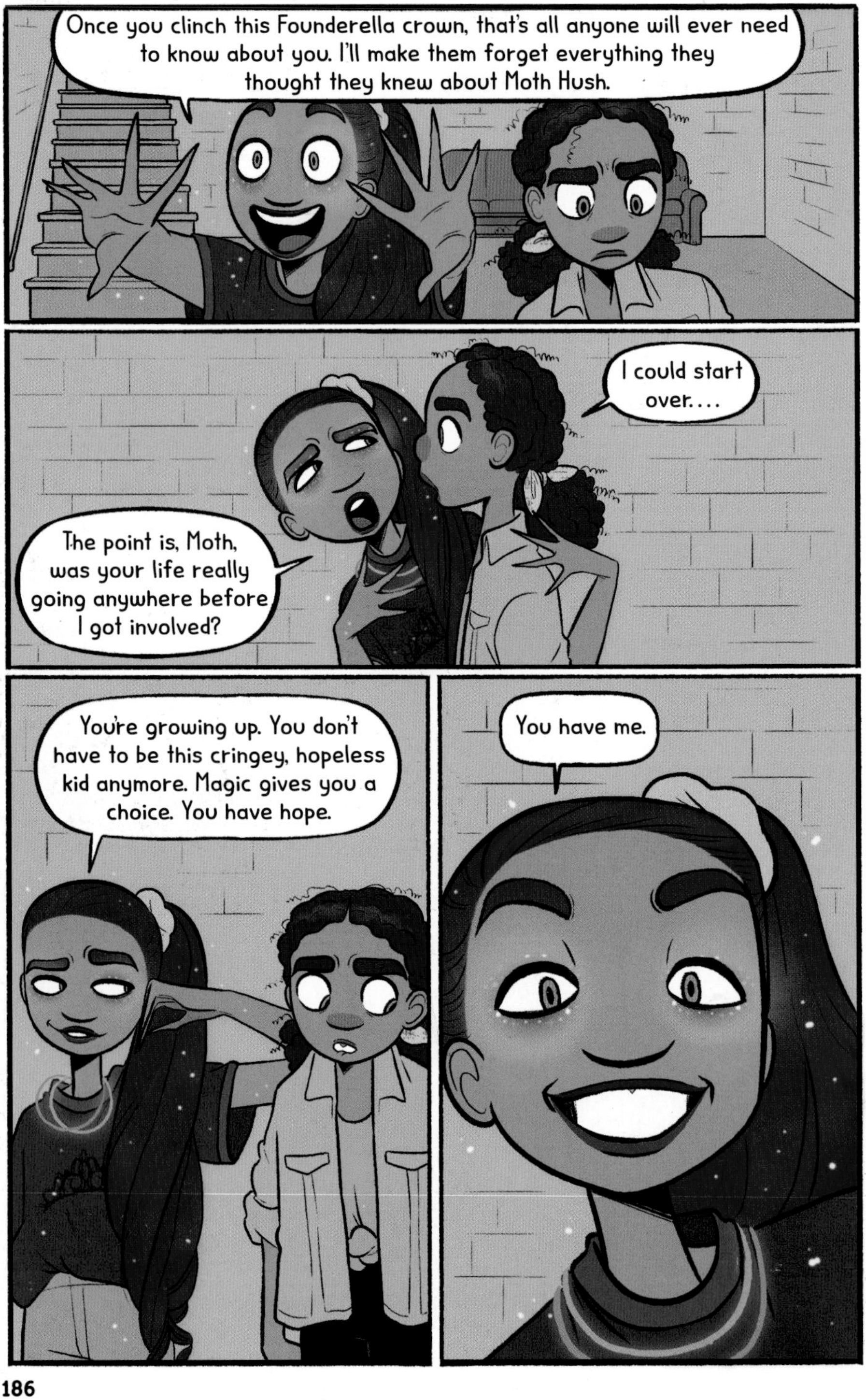
Once you clinch this Founderella crown, that's all anyone will ever need to know about you. I'll make them forget everything they thought they knew about Moth Hush.
I could start over....
The point is, Moth, was your life really going anywhere before I got involved?
You're growing up. You don't have to be this cringey, hopeless kid anymore. Magic gives you a choice. You have hope.
You have me.

CHAPTER 11

The Valentine's Ball

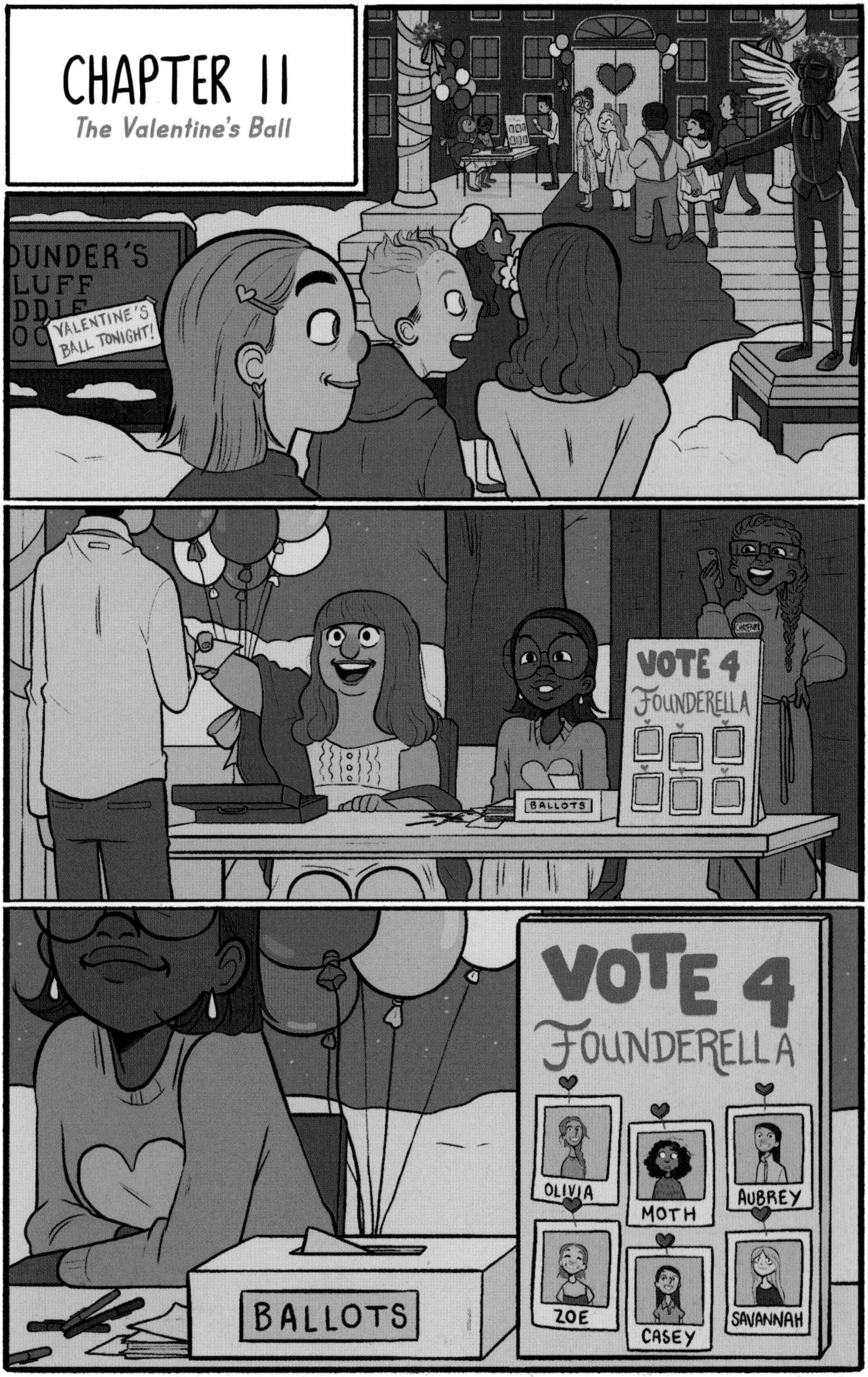
VALENTINE'S BALL TONIGHT!
VOTE 4 FOUNDERELLA
BALLOTS
VOTE 4 FOUNDERELLA
OLIVIA
MOTH
AUBREY
ZOE
CASEY
SAVANNAH
BALLOTS

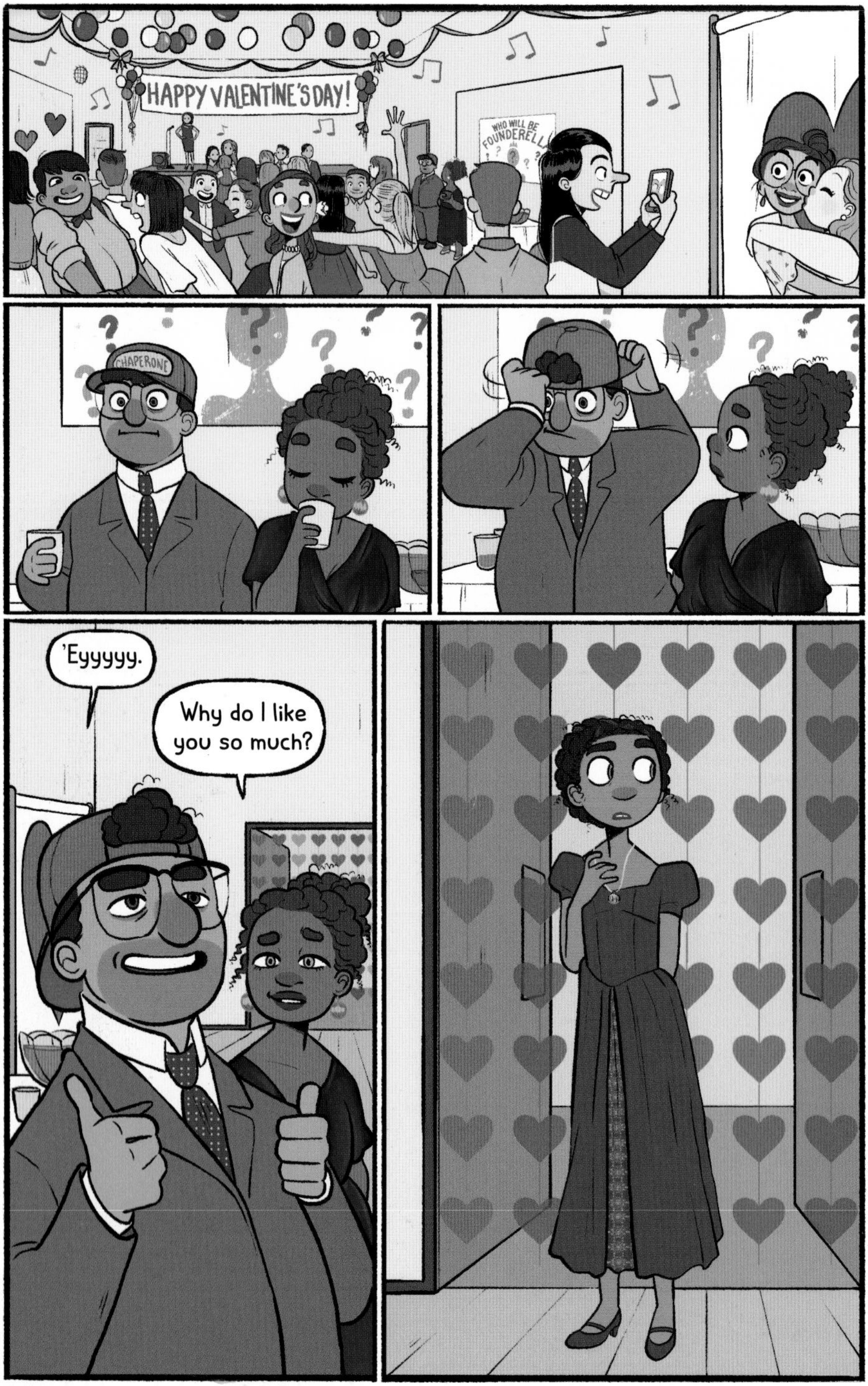
HAPPY VALENTINE'S DAY!
WHO WILL BE FOUNDERELLA
CHAPERONE
'Eyyyyy.
Why do I like you so much?

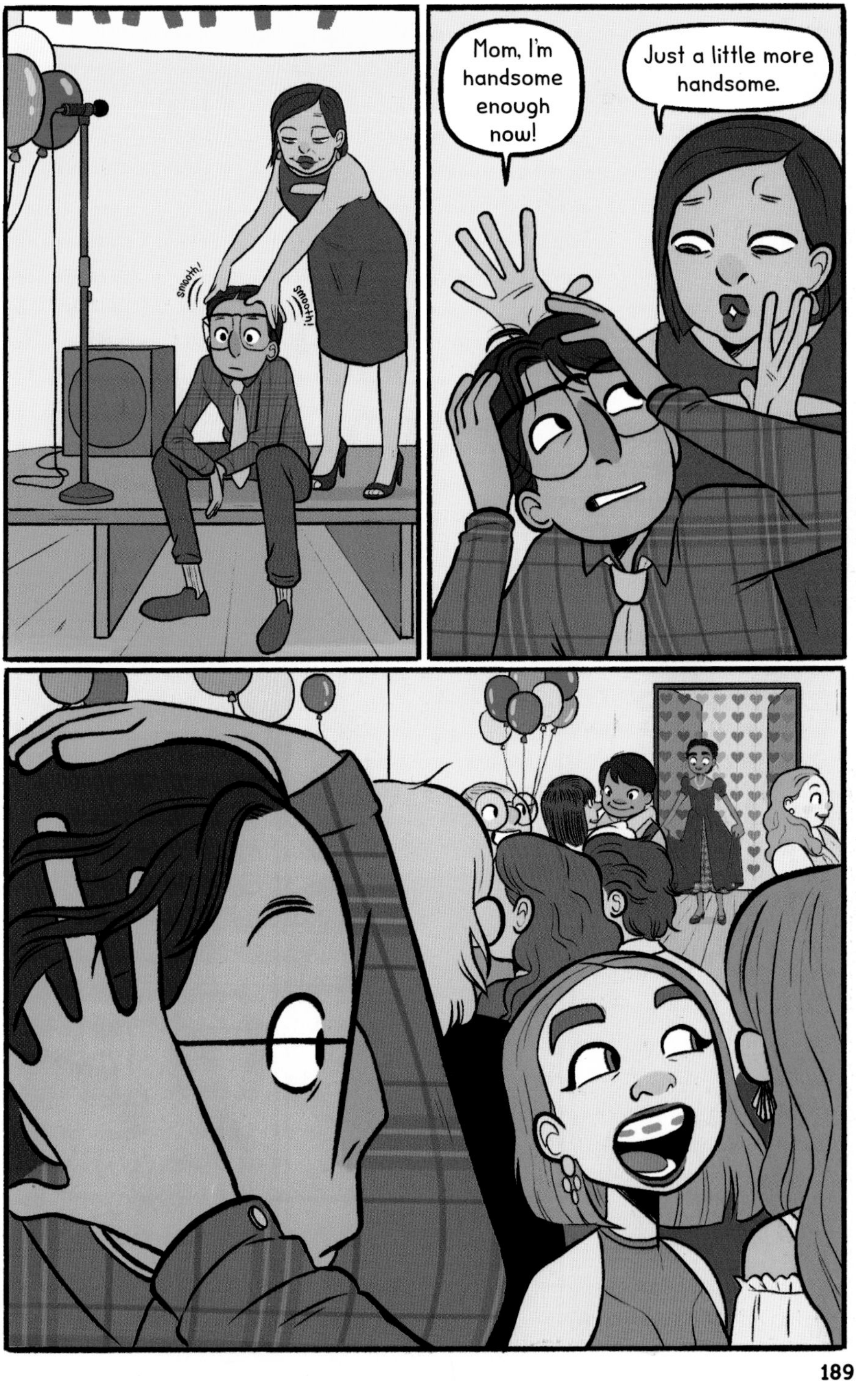
smooth!
smooth!
Mom, I'm handsome enough now!
Just a little more handsome.

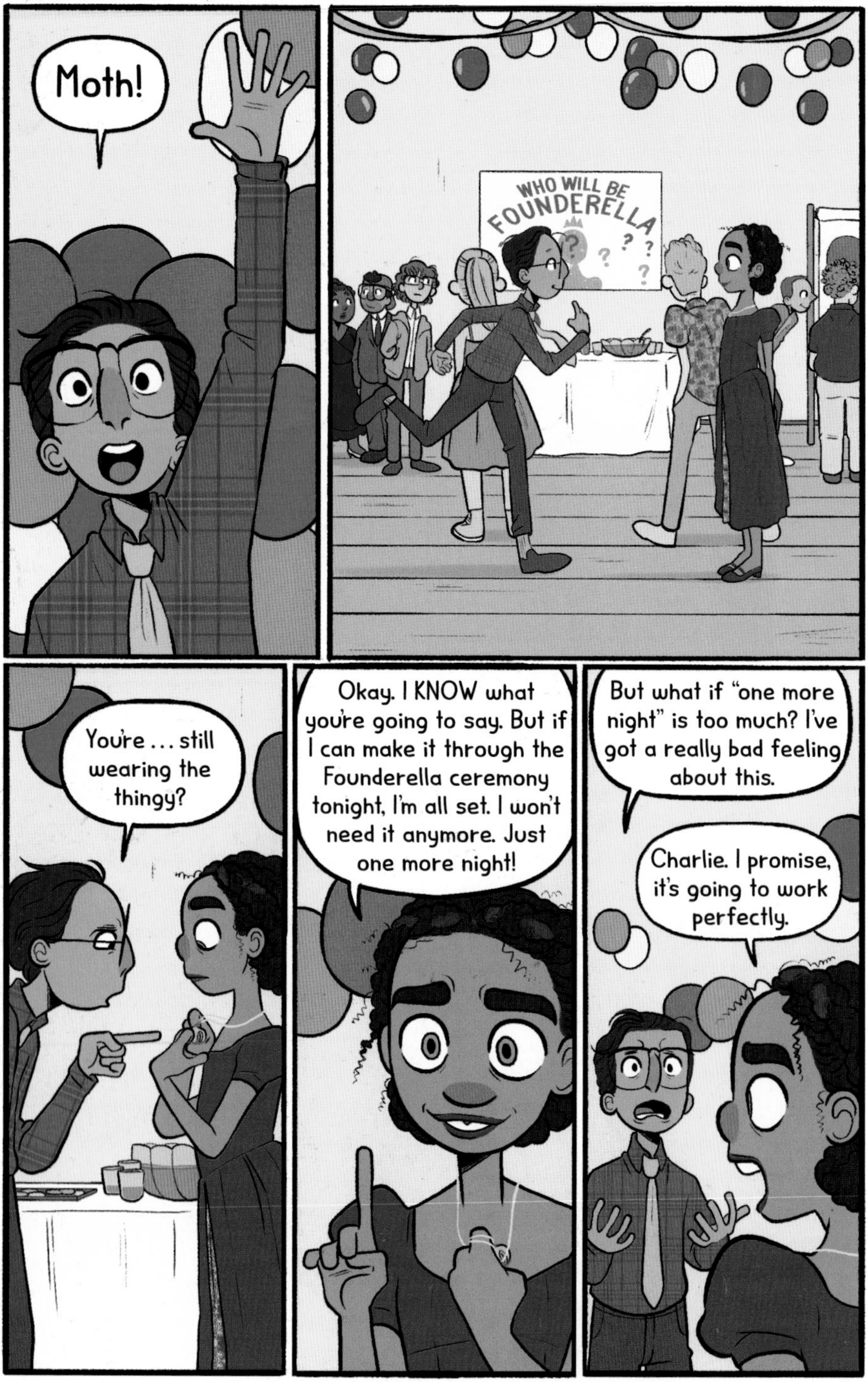
Moth!
WHO WILL BE FOUNDERELLA
You're . . . still wearing the thingy?
Okay. I KNOW what you're going to say. But if I can make it through the Founderella ceremony tonight, I'm all set. I won't need it anymore. Just one more night!
But what if "one more night" is too much? I've got a really bad feeling about this.
Charlie. I promise, it's going to work perfectly.

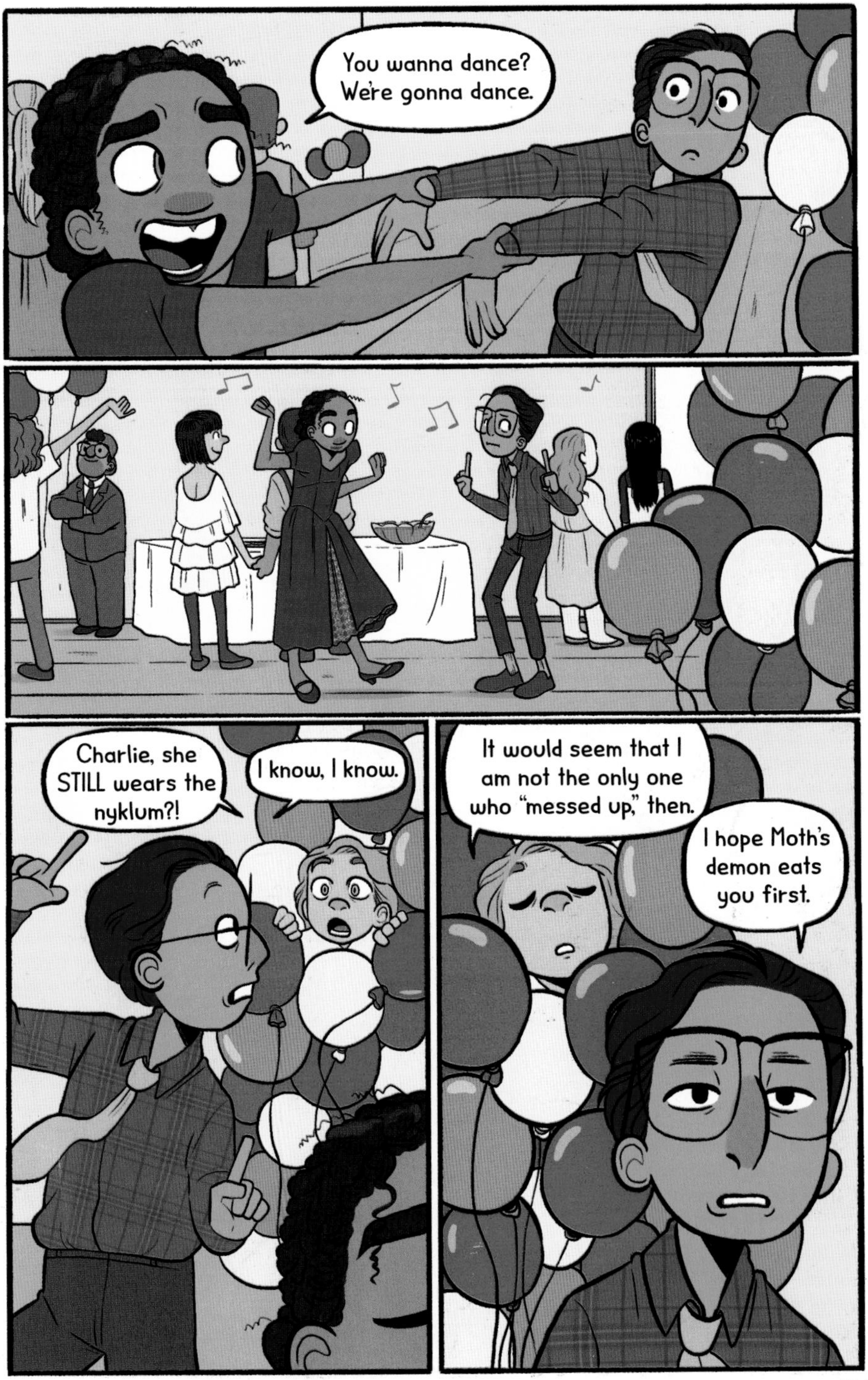
You wanna dance? We're gonna dance.
Charlie, she STILL wears the nyklum?!
I know, I know.
It would seem that I am not the only one who "messed up," then.
I hope Moth's demon eats you first.

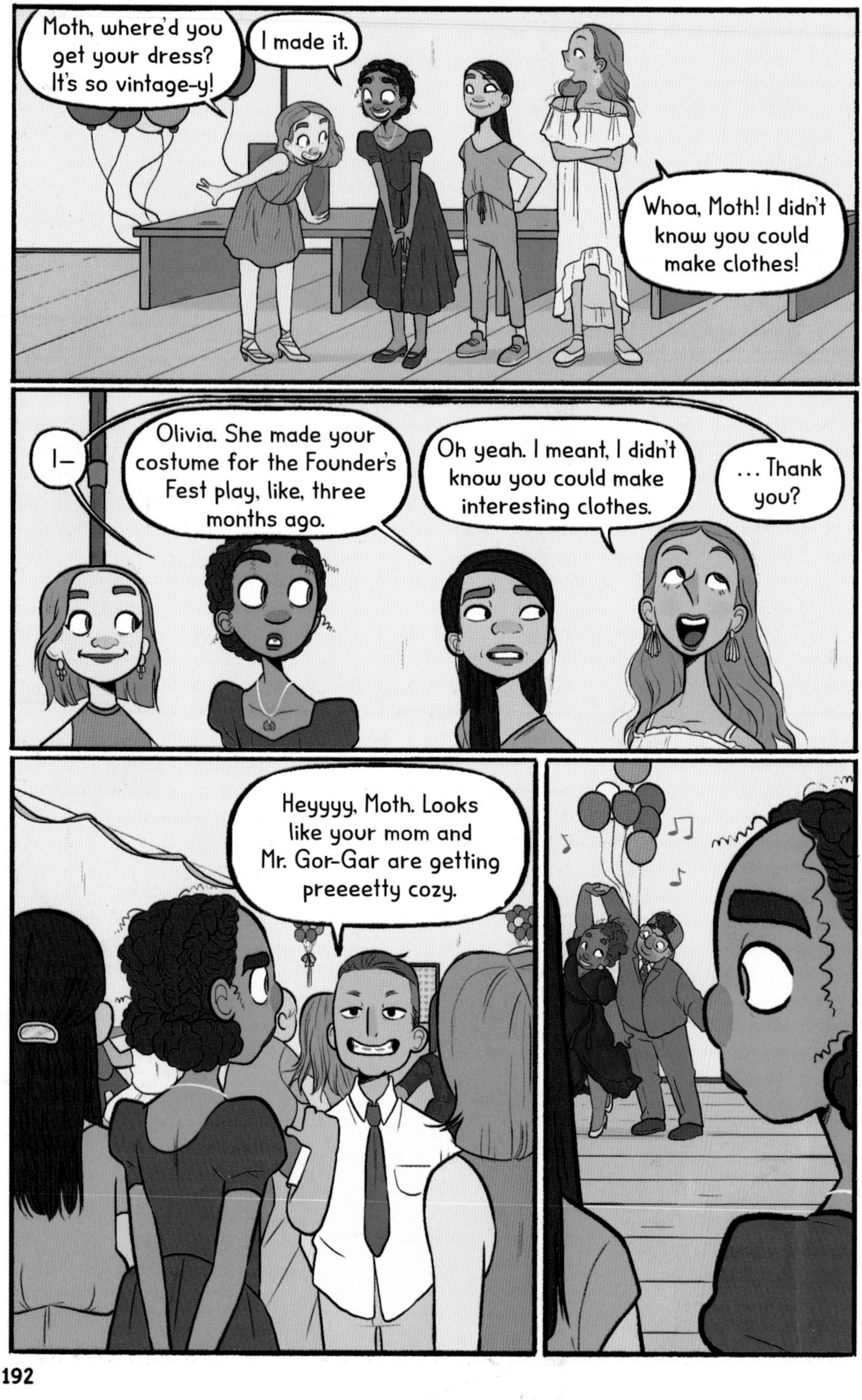
Moth, where'd you get your dress? It's so vintage-y!
I made it.
Whoa, Moth! I didn't know you could make clothes!
I—
Olivia. She made your costume for the Founder's Fest play, like, three months ago.
Oh yeah. I meant, I didn't know you could make interesting clothes.
. . . Thank you?
Heyyyy, Moth. Looks like your mom and Mr. Gor-Gar are getting preeeetty cozy.

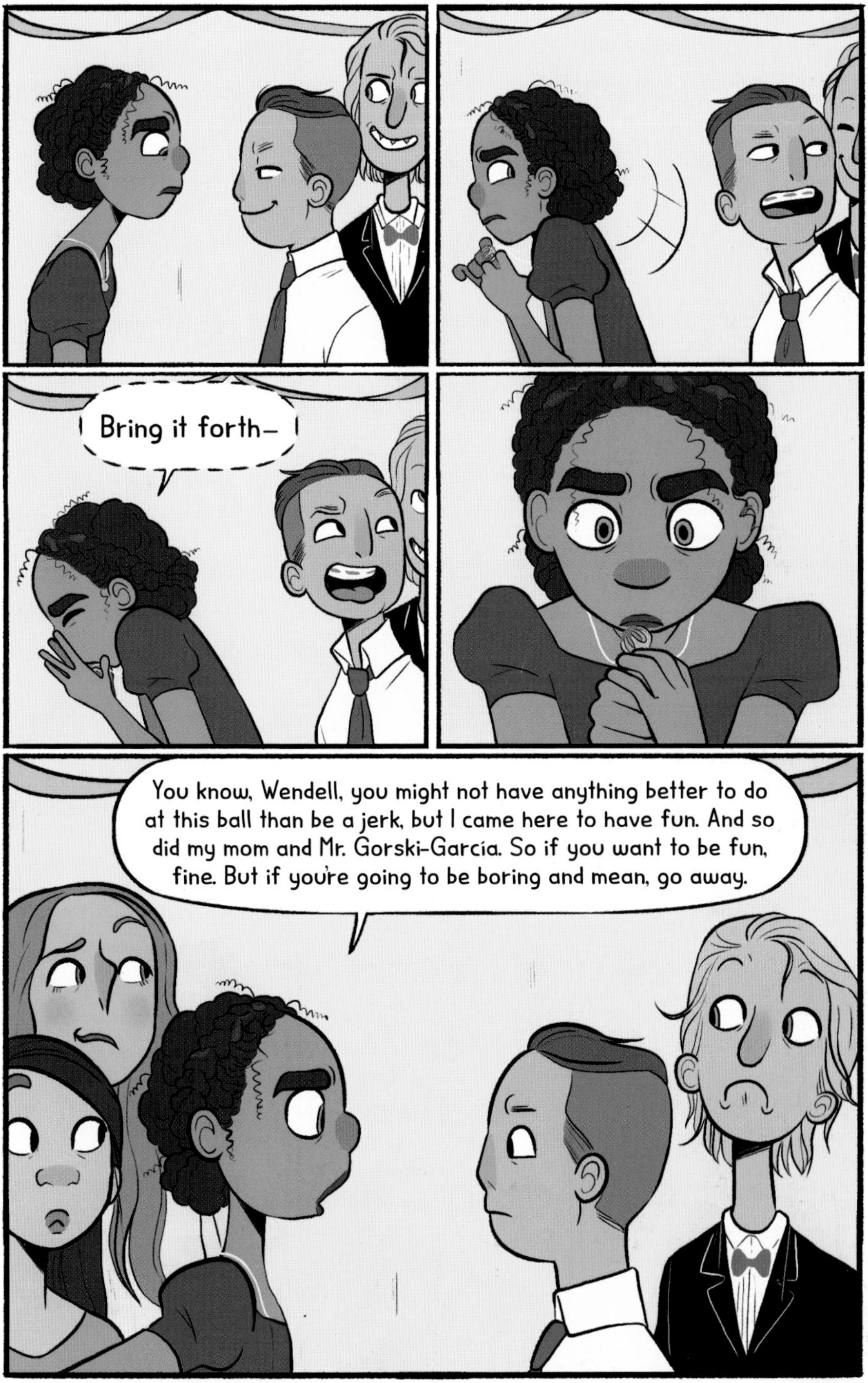
Bring it forth—
You know, Wendell, you might not have anything better to do at this ball than be a jerk, but I came here to have fun. And so did my mom and Mr. Gorski-García. So if you want to be fun, fine. But if you're going to be boring and mean, go away.

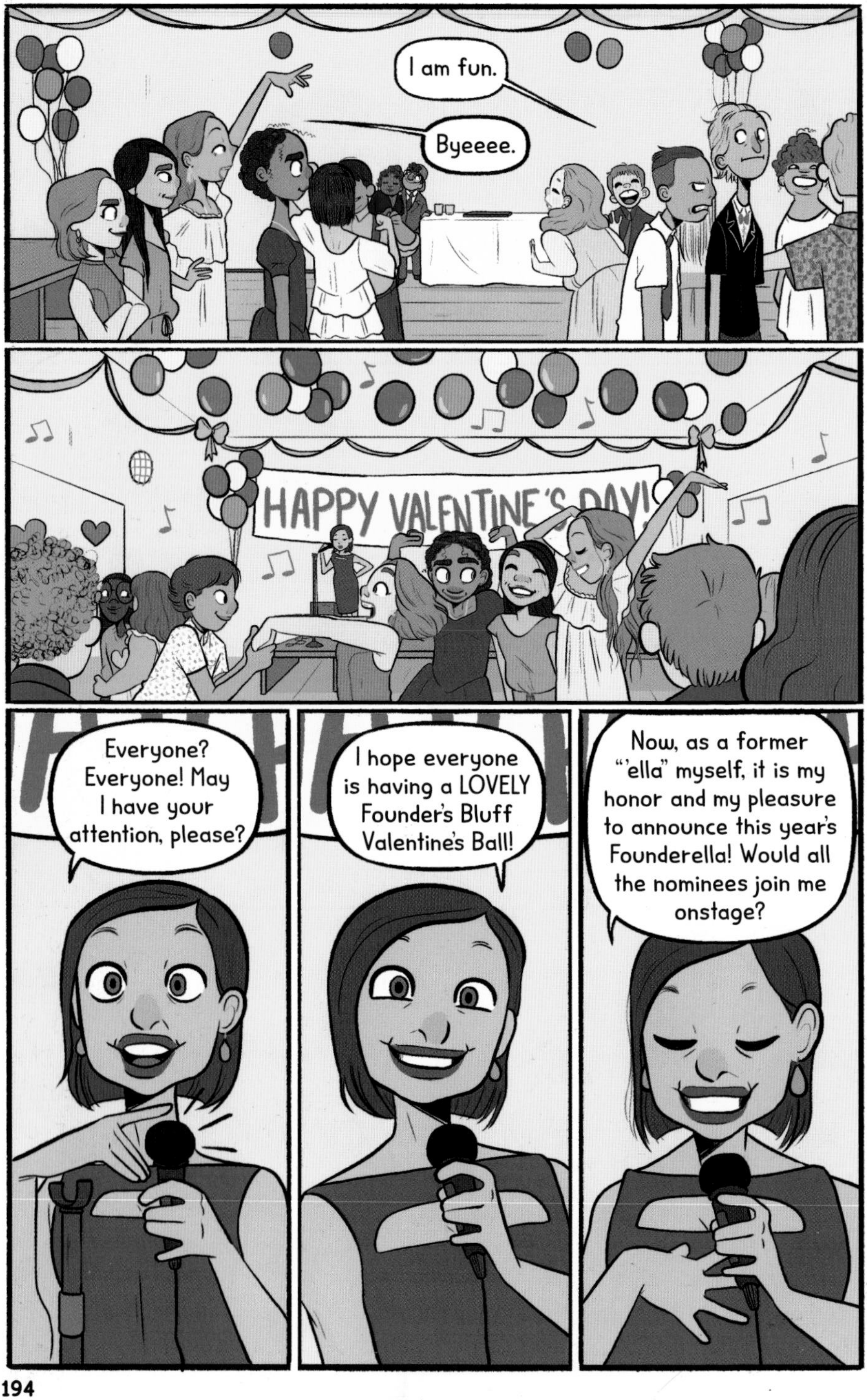
I am fun.
Byeeee.
HAPPY VALENTINE'S DAY!
Everyone? Everyone! May I have your attention, please?
I hope everyone is having a LOVELY Founder's Bluff Valentine's Ball!
Now, as a former "'ella" myself, it is my honor and my pleasure to announce this year's Founderella! Would all the nominees join me onstage?

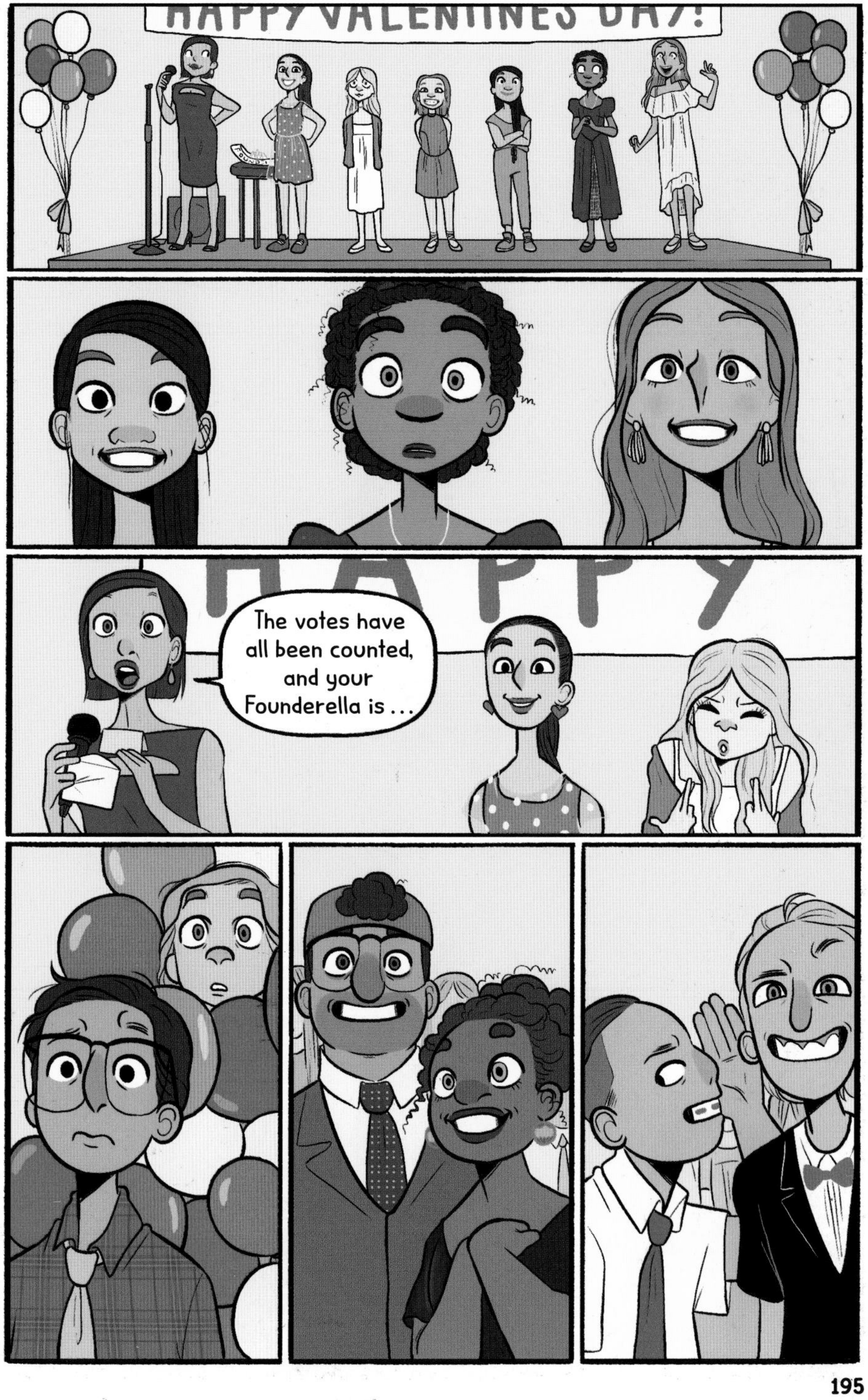
HAPPY VALENTINES DAY!
HAPPY
The votes have all been counted, and your Founderella is . . .

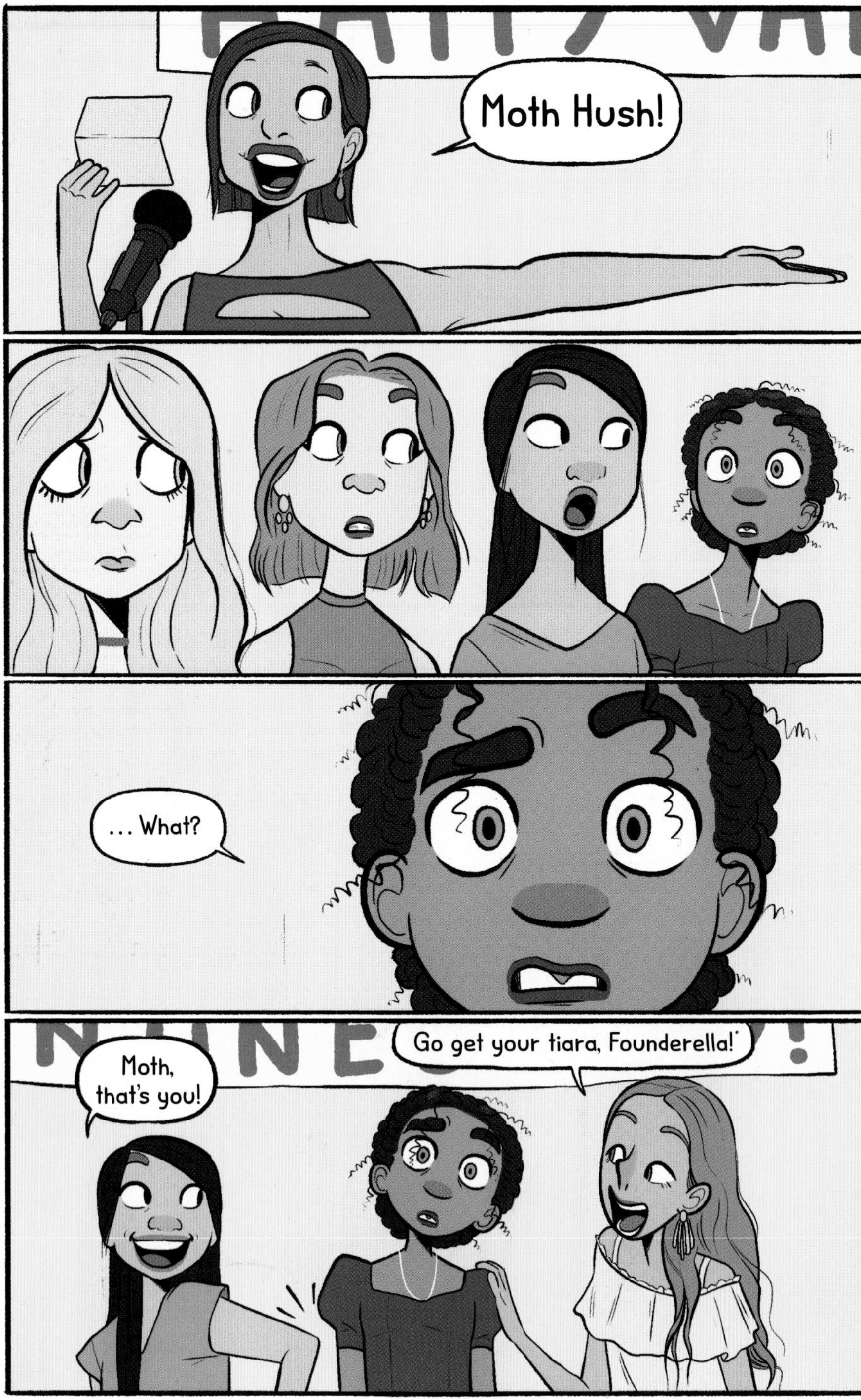
Moth Hush!
... What?
Moth, that's you!
Go get your tiara, Founderella!

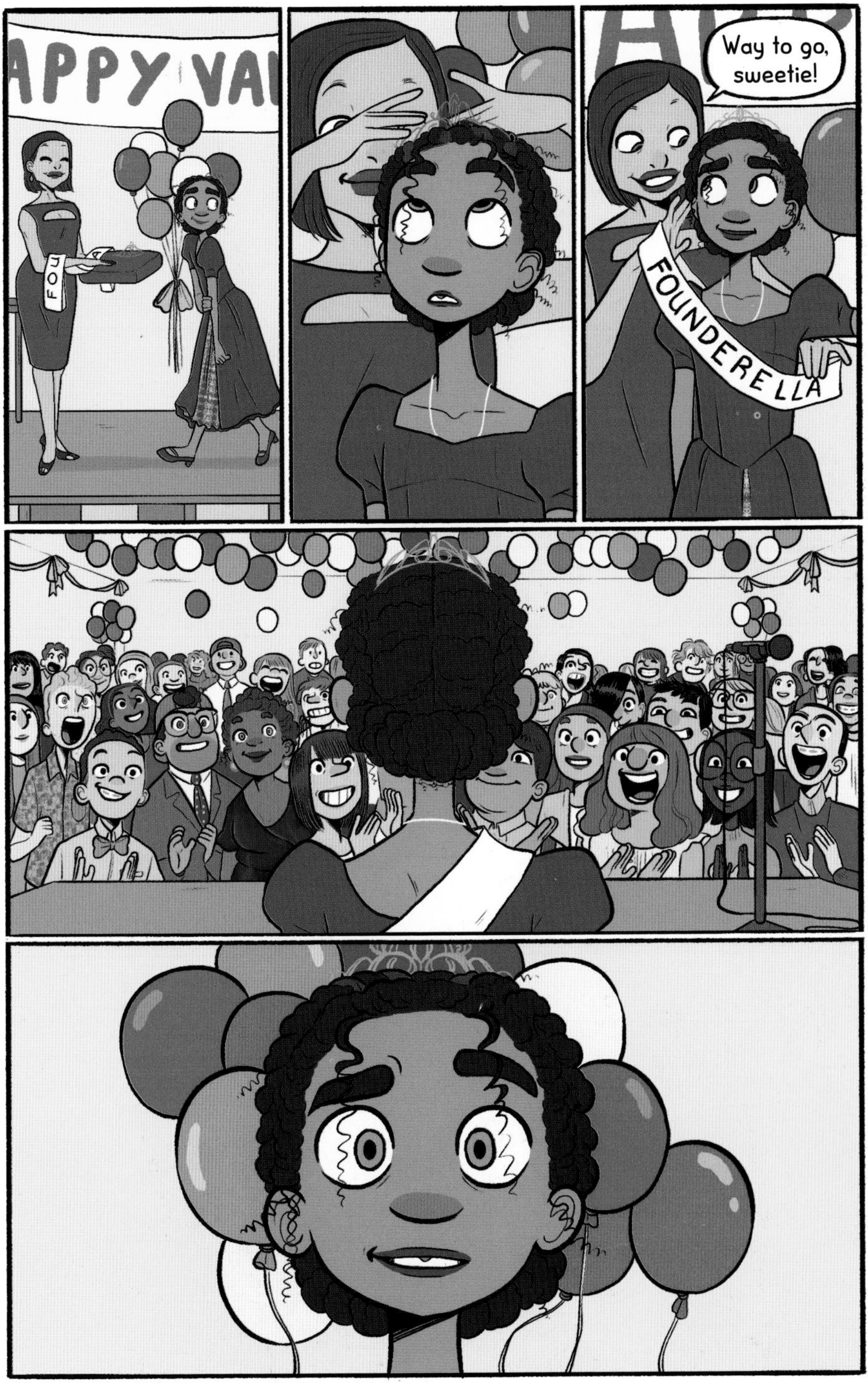
APPY VA
Way to go, sweetie!
FOUNDERELLA

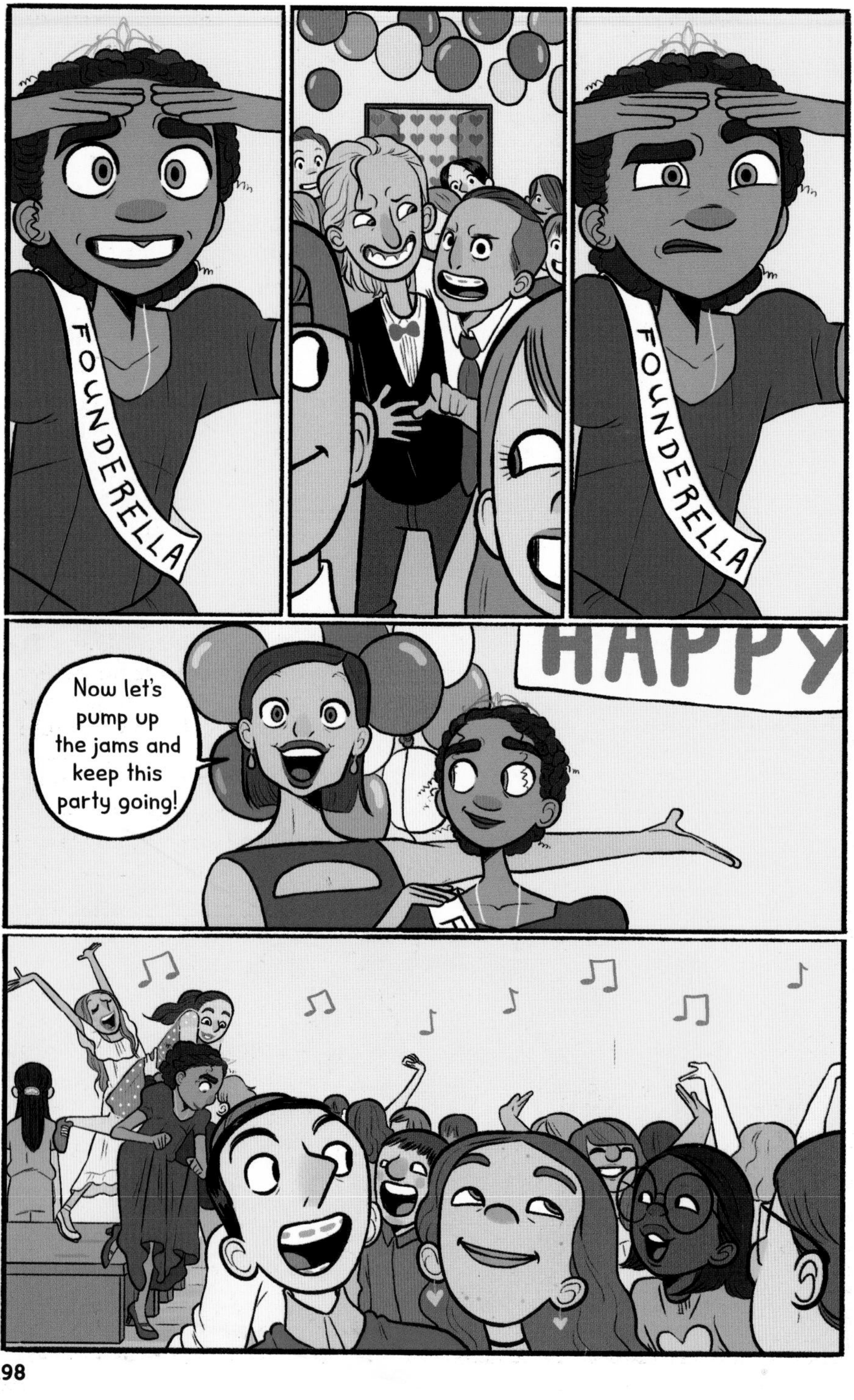
FOUNDERELLA
FOUNDERELLA
HAPPY
Now let's pump up the jams and keep this party going!

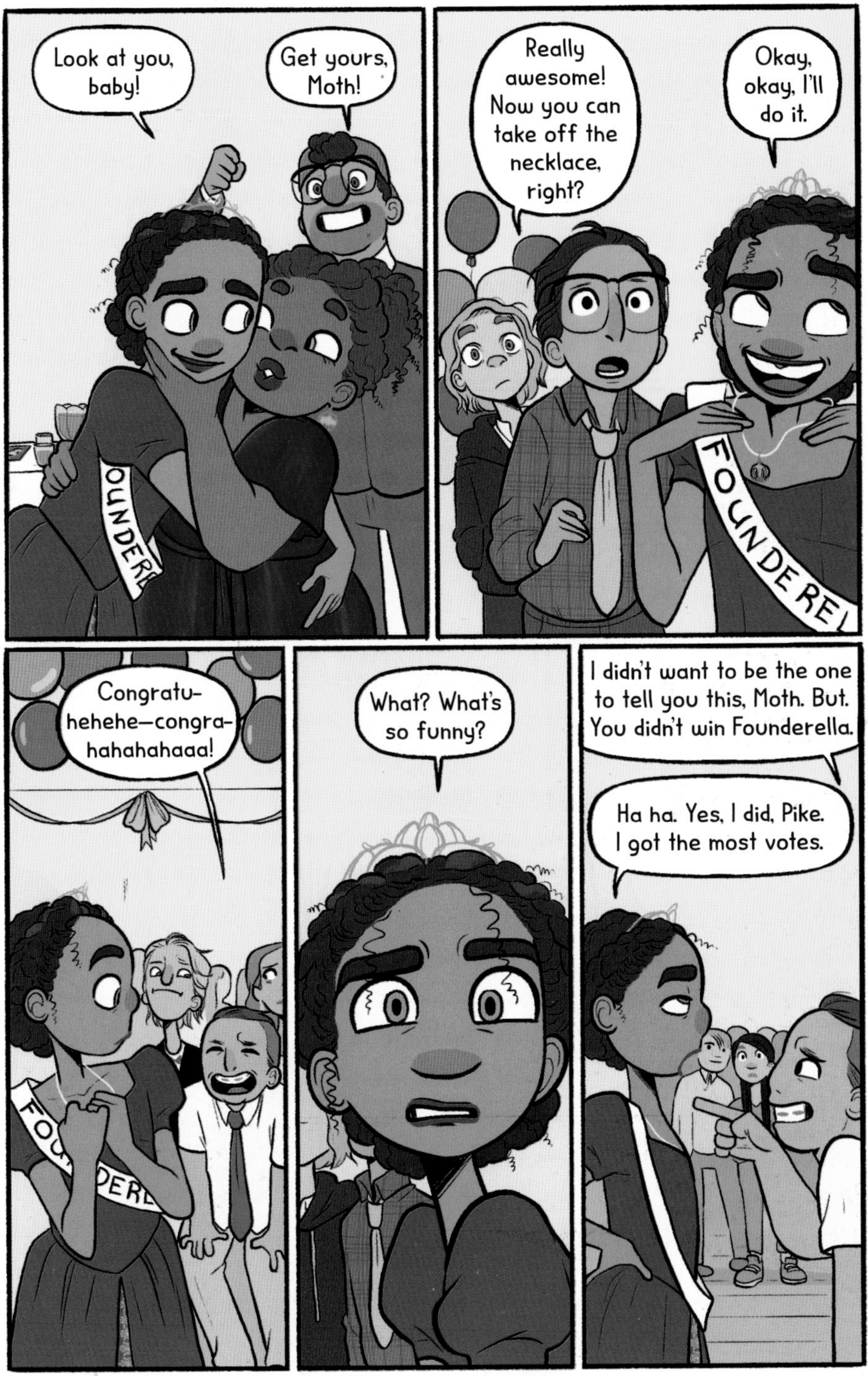
Look at you, baby!
Get yours, Moth!
FOUNDERE
Really awesome! Now you can take off the necklace, right?
Okay, okay, I'll do it.
FOUNDEREL
Congratu-hehehe—congra-hahahahaaa!
FOUNDERE
What? What's so funny?
I didn't want to be the one to tell you this, Moth. But. You didn't win Founderella.
Ha ha. Yes, I did, Pike. I got the most votes.

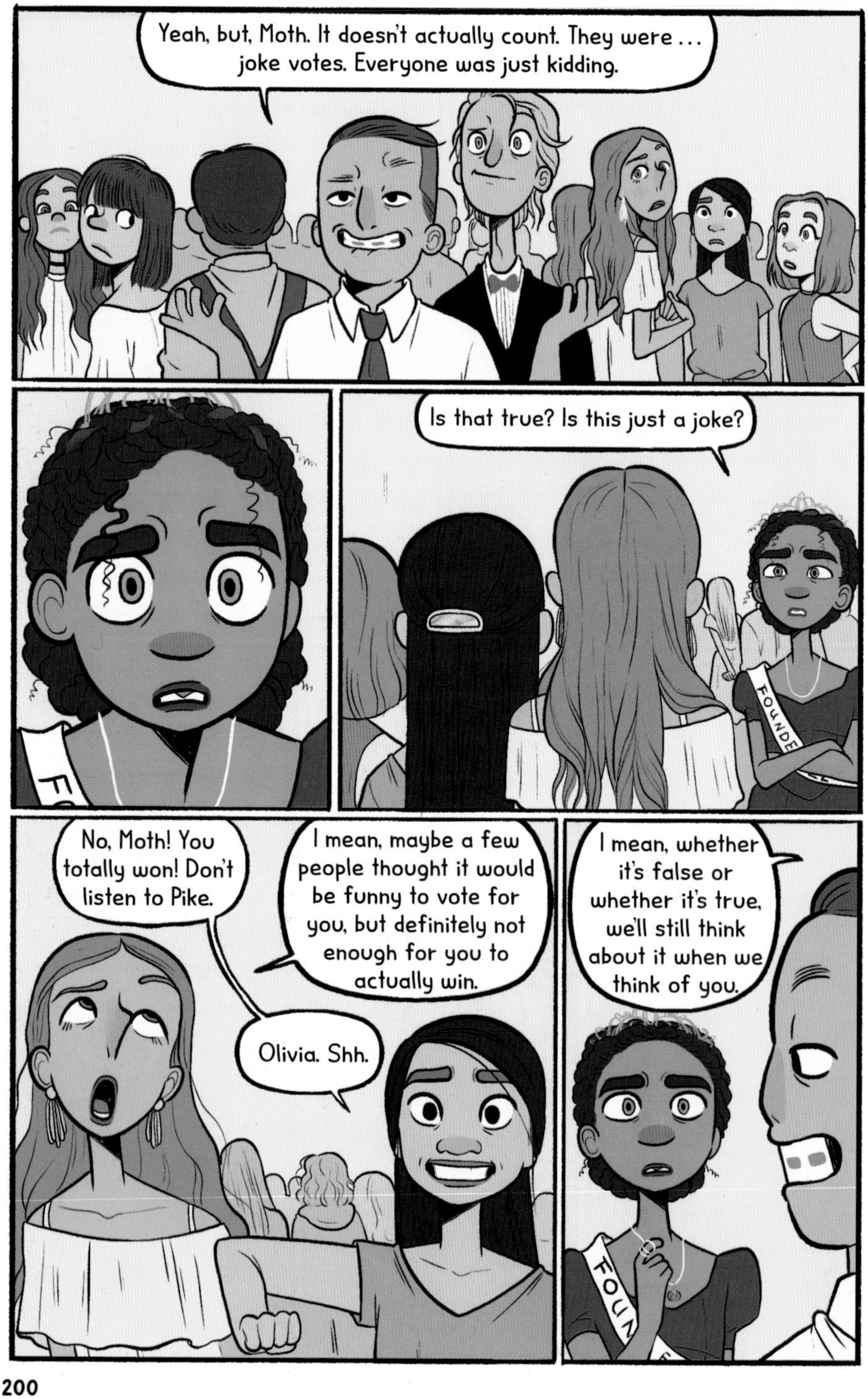
Yeah, but, Moth. It doesn't actually count. They were . . . joke votes. Everyone was just kidding.
Is that true? Is this just a joke?
FOUNDE
No, Moth! You totally won! Don't listen to Pike.
I mean, maybe a few people thought it would be funny to vote for you, but definitely not enough for you to actually win.
Olivia. Shh.
I mean, whether it's false or whether it's true, we'll still think about it when we think of you.
FOUN

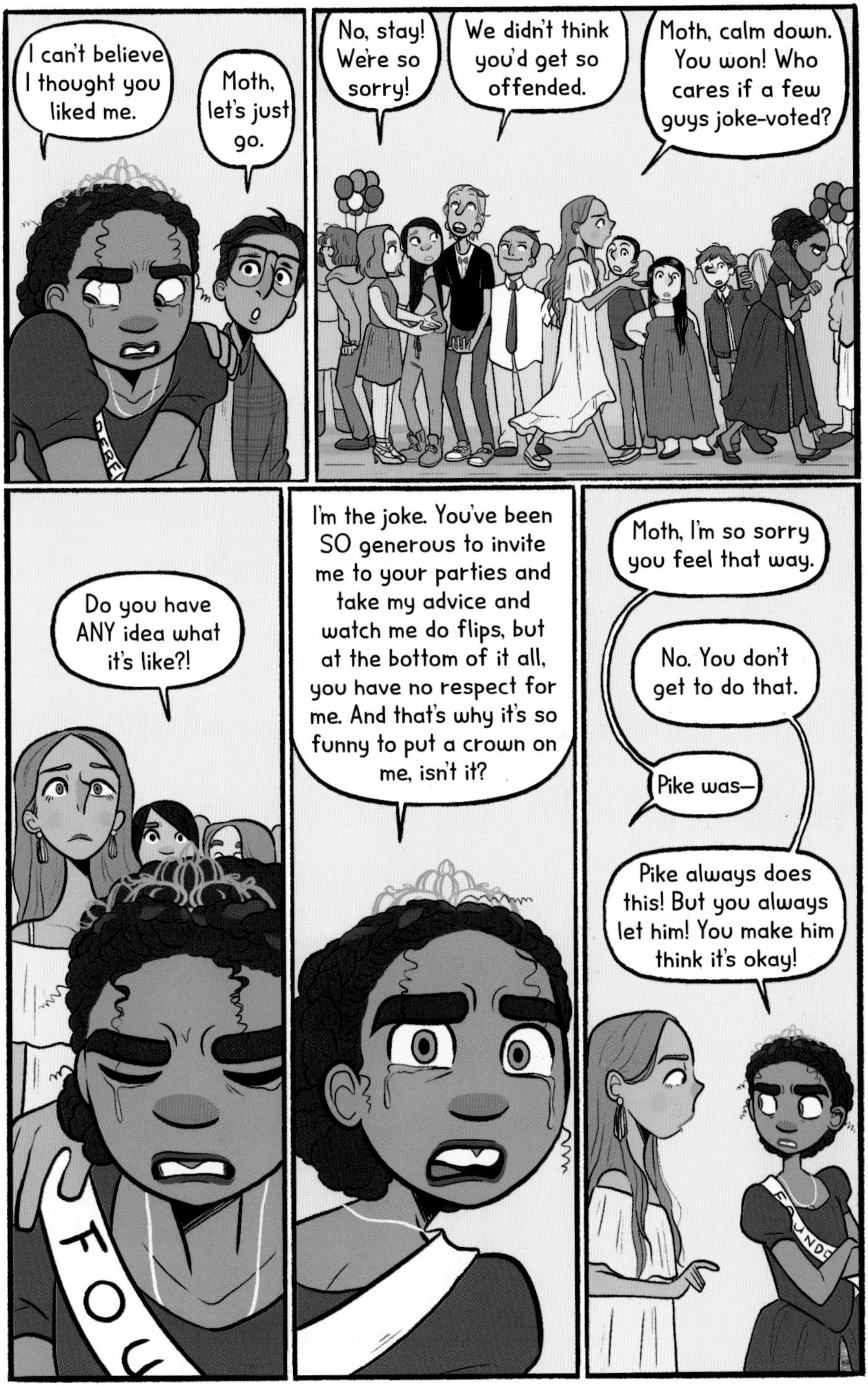
I can't believe I thought you liked me.
Moth, let's just go.
No, stay! We're so sorry!
We didn't think you'd get so offended.
Moth, calm down. You won! Who cares if a few guys joke-voted?
Do you have ANY idea what it's like?!
I'm the joke. You've been SO generous to invite me to your parties and take my advice and watch me do flips, but at the bottom of it all, you have no respect for me. And that's why it's so funny to put a crown on me, isn't it?
Moth, I'm so sorry you feel that way.
No. You don't get to do that.
Pike was—
Pike always does this! But you always let him! You make him think it's okay!

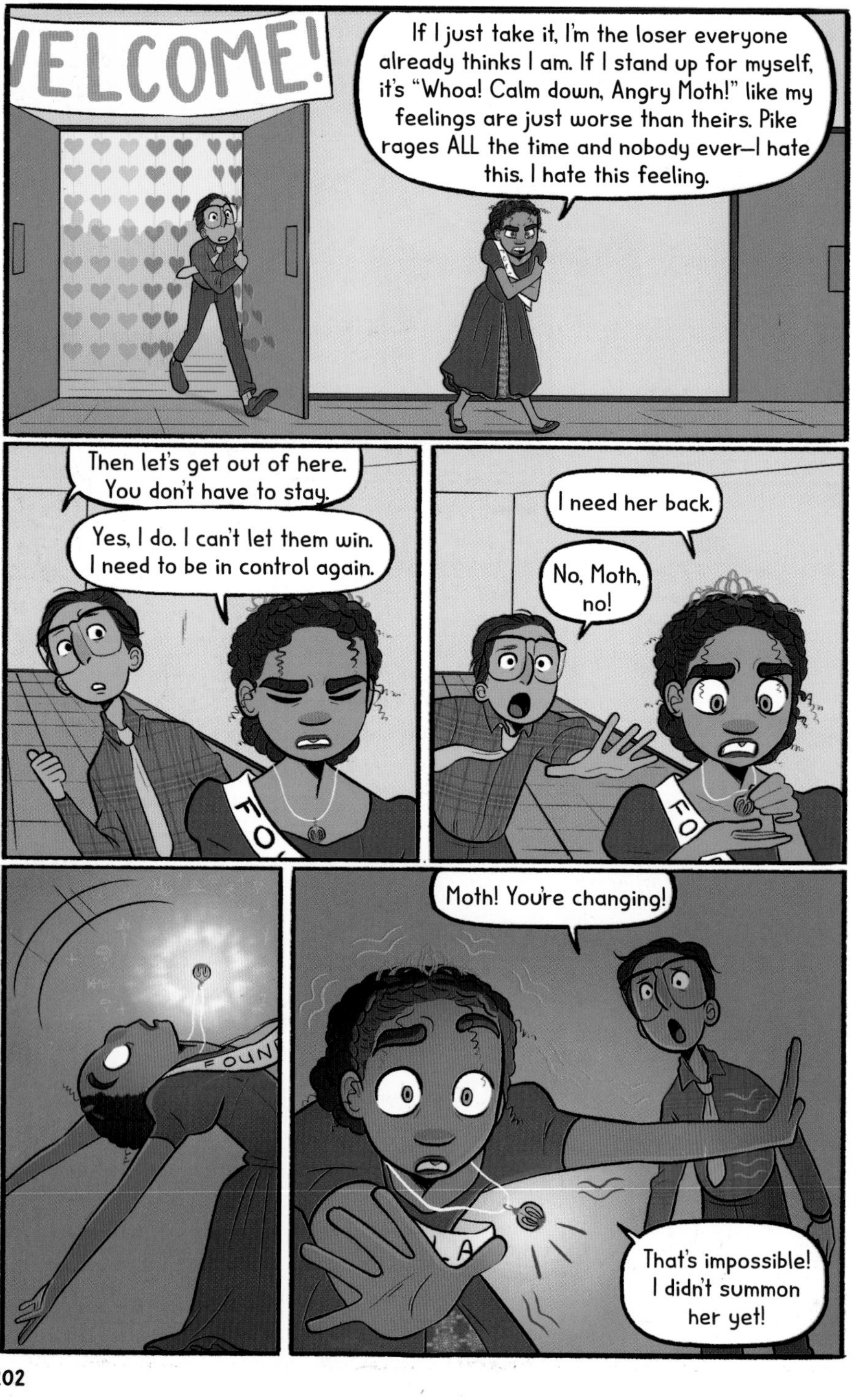
VELCOME!
If I just take it, I'm the loser everyone already thinks I am. If I stand up for myself, it's "Whoa! Calm down, Angry Moth!" like my feelings are just worse than theirs. Pike rages ALL the time and nobody ever—I hate this. I hate this feeling.
Then let's get out of here. You don't have to stay.
Yes, I do. I can't let them win. I need to be in control again.
I need her back.
No, Moth, no!
Moth! You're changing!
That's impossible! I didn't summon her yet!

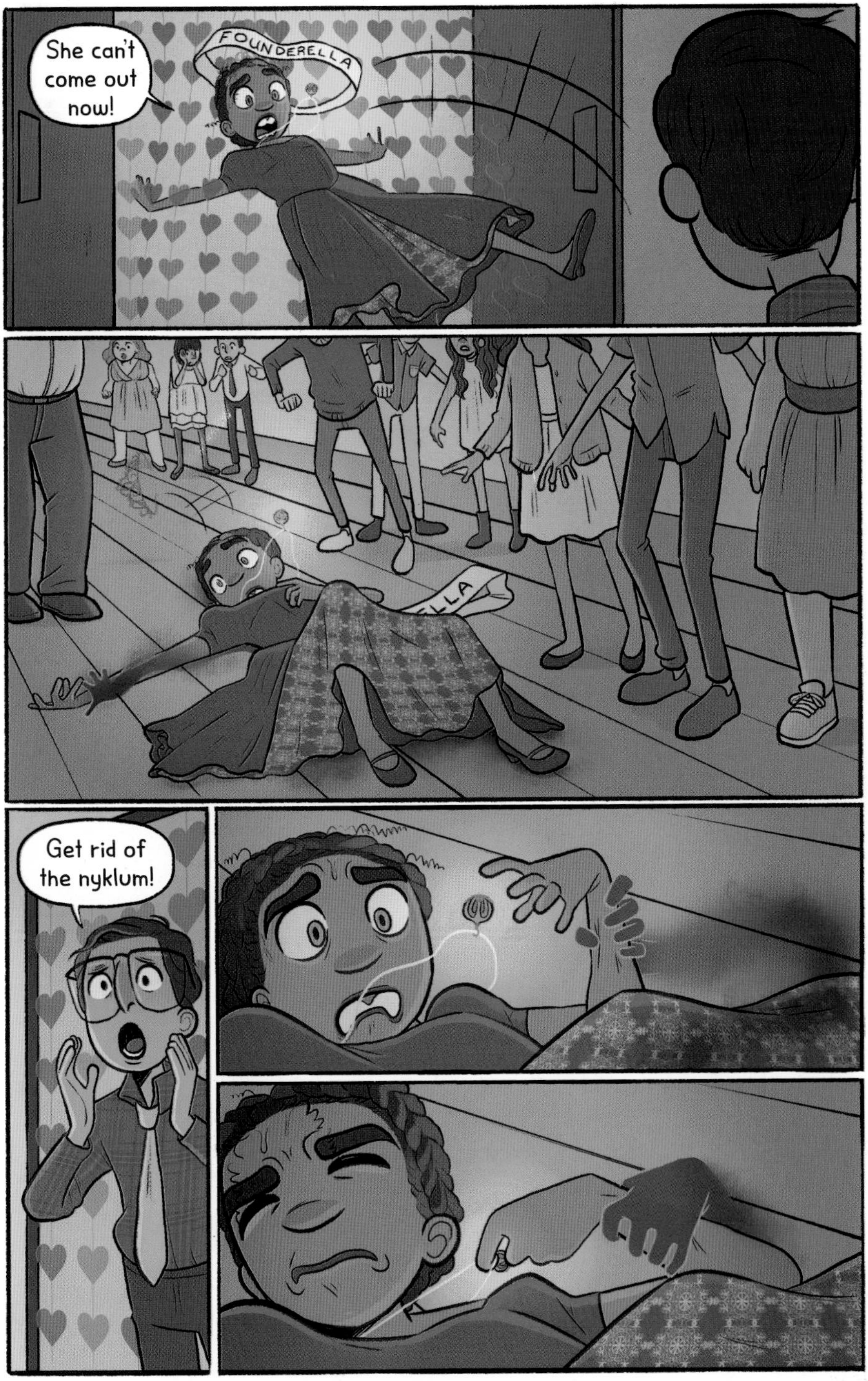
She can't come out now!
FOUNDERELLA
ELLA
Get rid of the nyklum!

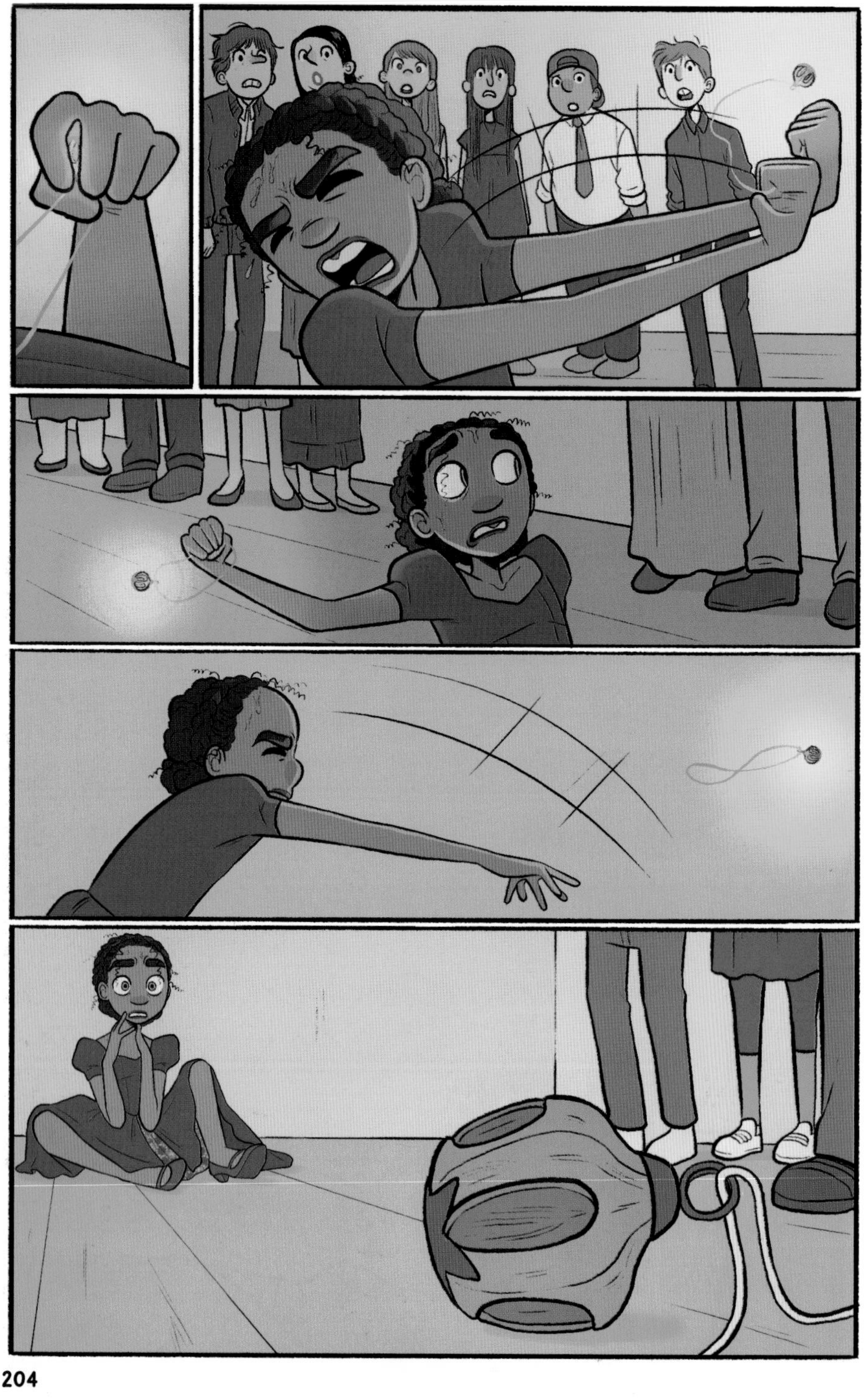

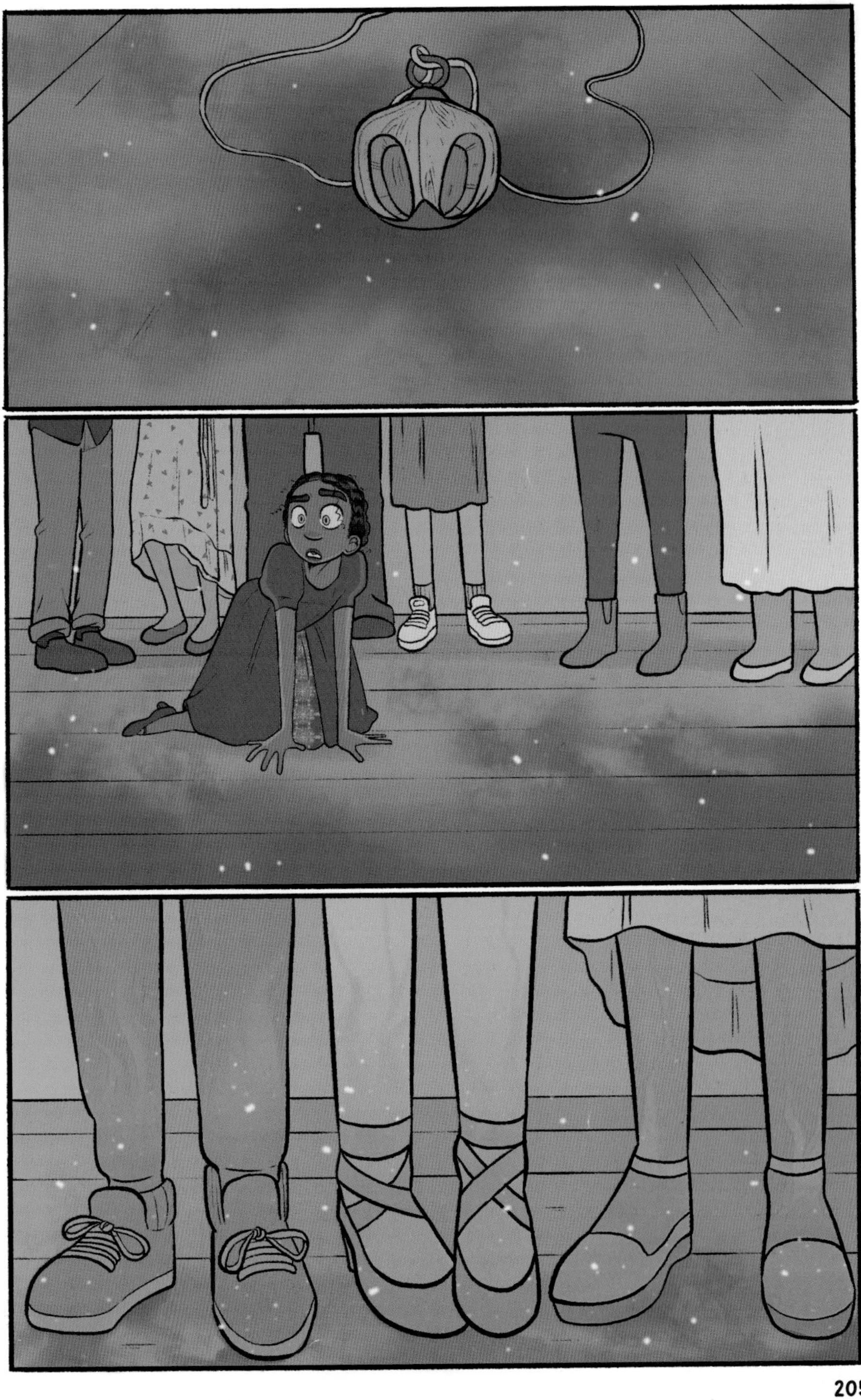

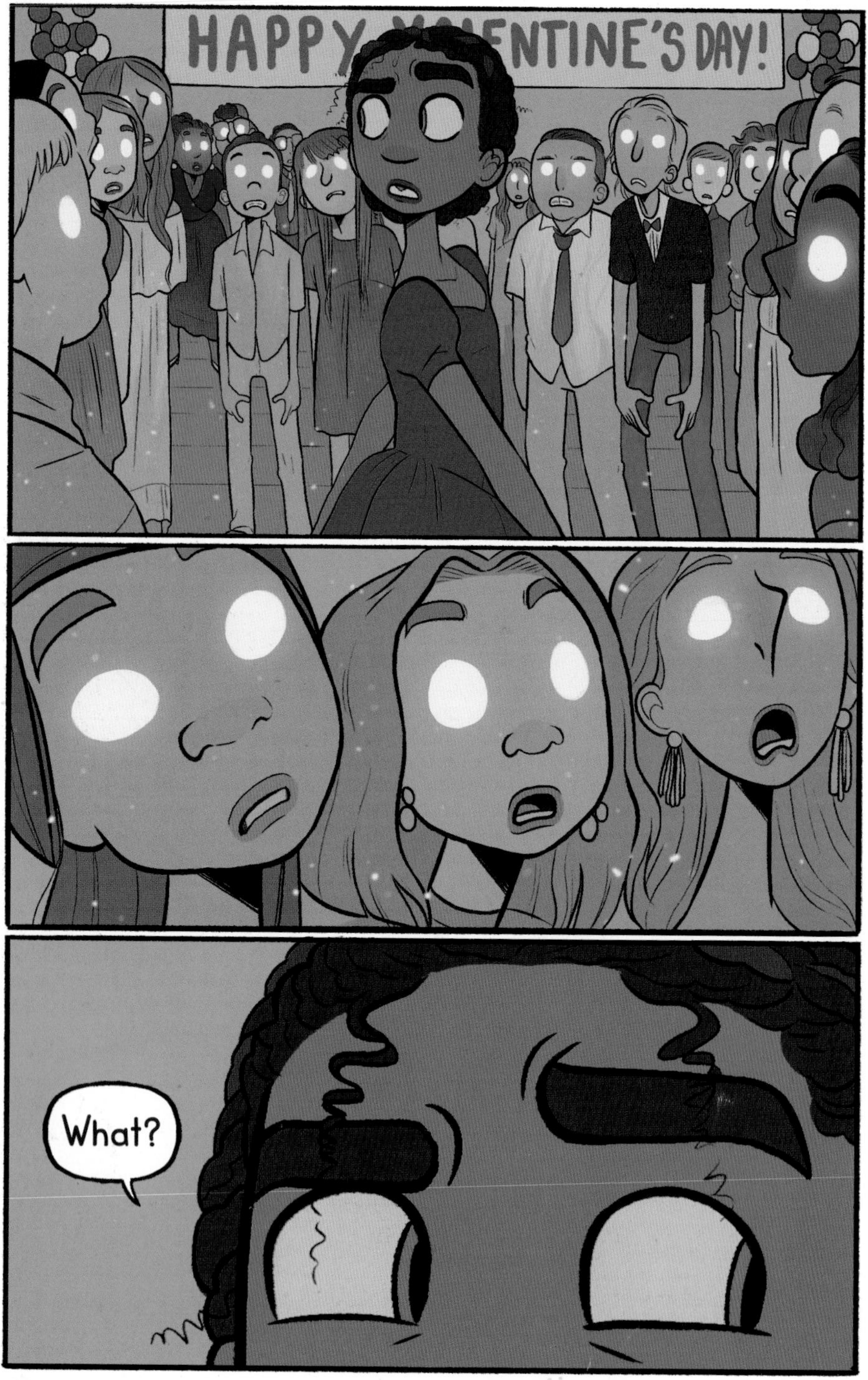
HAPPY VALENTINE'S DAY!
What?

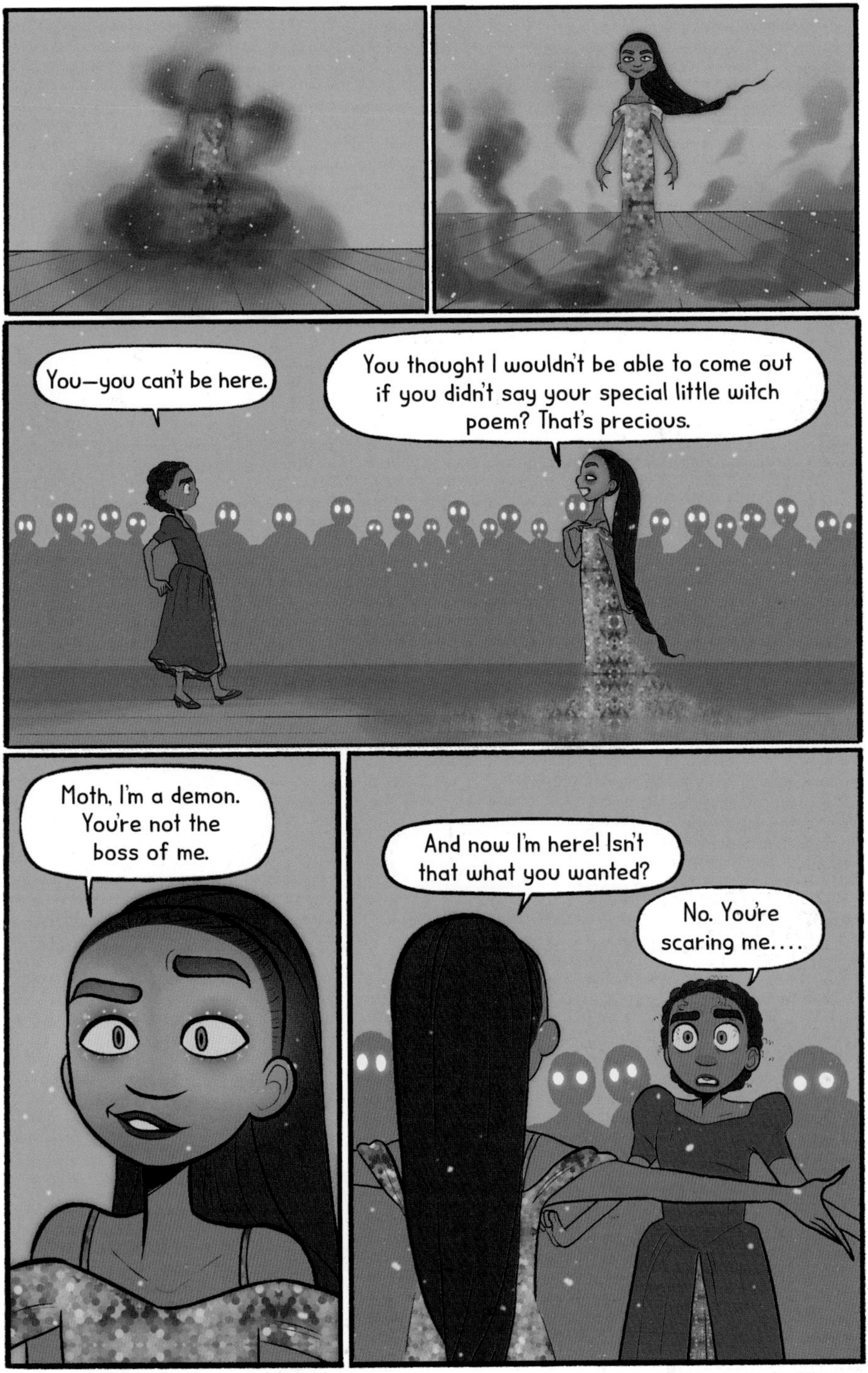
You—you can't be here.
You thought I wouldn't be able to come out if you didn't say your special little witch poem? That's precious.
Moth, I'm a demon. You're not the boss of me.
And now I'm here! Isn't that what you wanted?
No. You're scaring me....

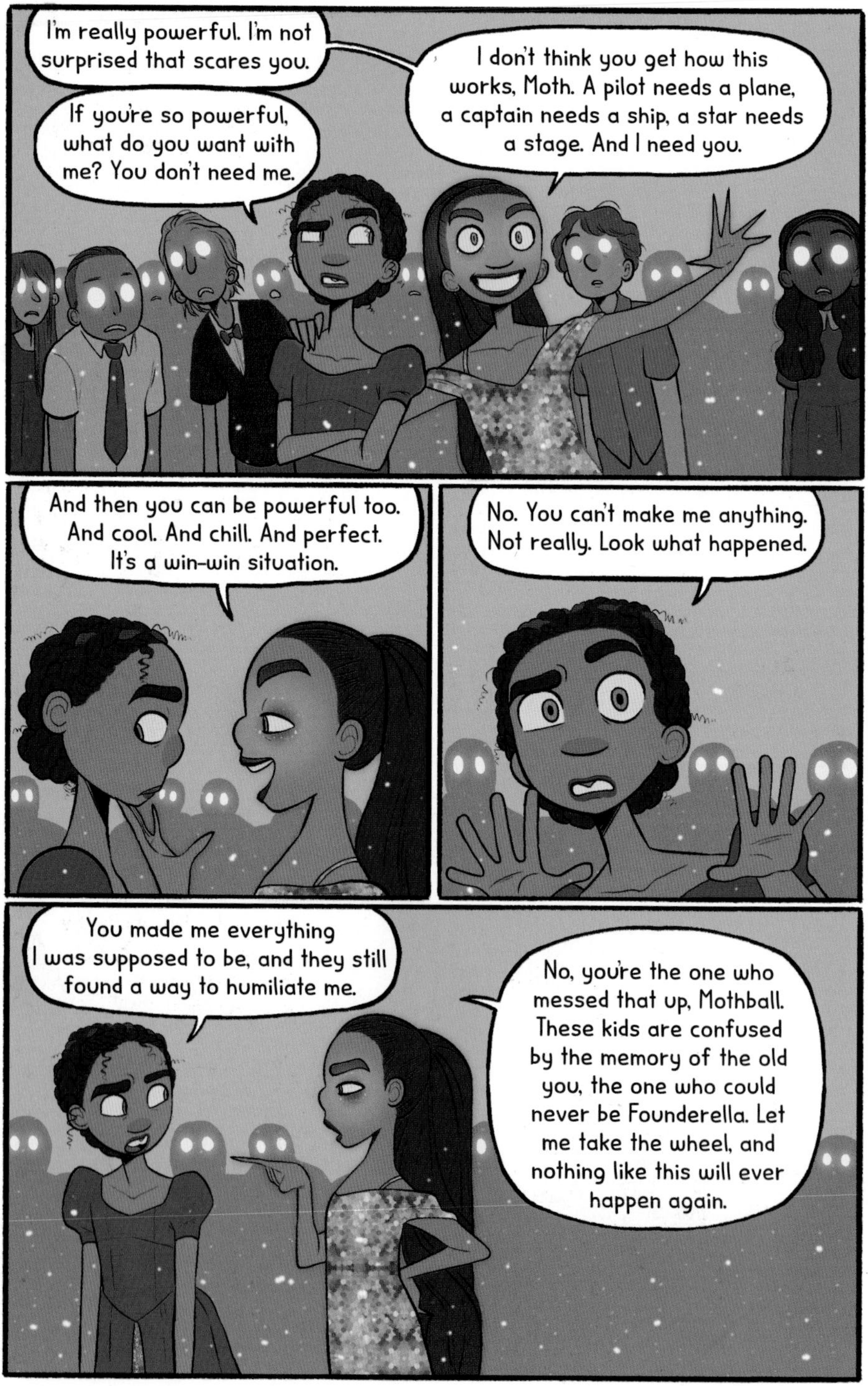
I'm really powerful. I'm not surprised that scares you.
If you're so powerful, what do you want with me? You don't need me.
I don't think you get how this works, Moth. A pilot needs a plane, a captain needs a ship, a star needs a stage. And I need you.
And then you can be powerful too. And cool. And chill. And perfect. It's a win-win situation.
No. You can't make me anything. Not really. Look what happened.
You made me everything I was supposed to be, and they still found a way to humiliate me.
No, you're the one who messed that up, Mothball. These kids are confused by the memory of the old you, the one who could never be Founderella. Let me take the wheel, and nothing like this will ever happen again.

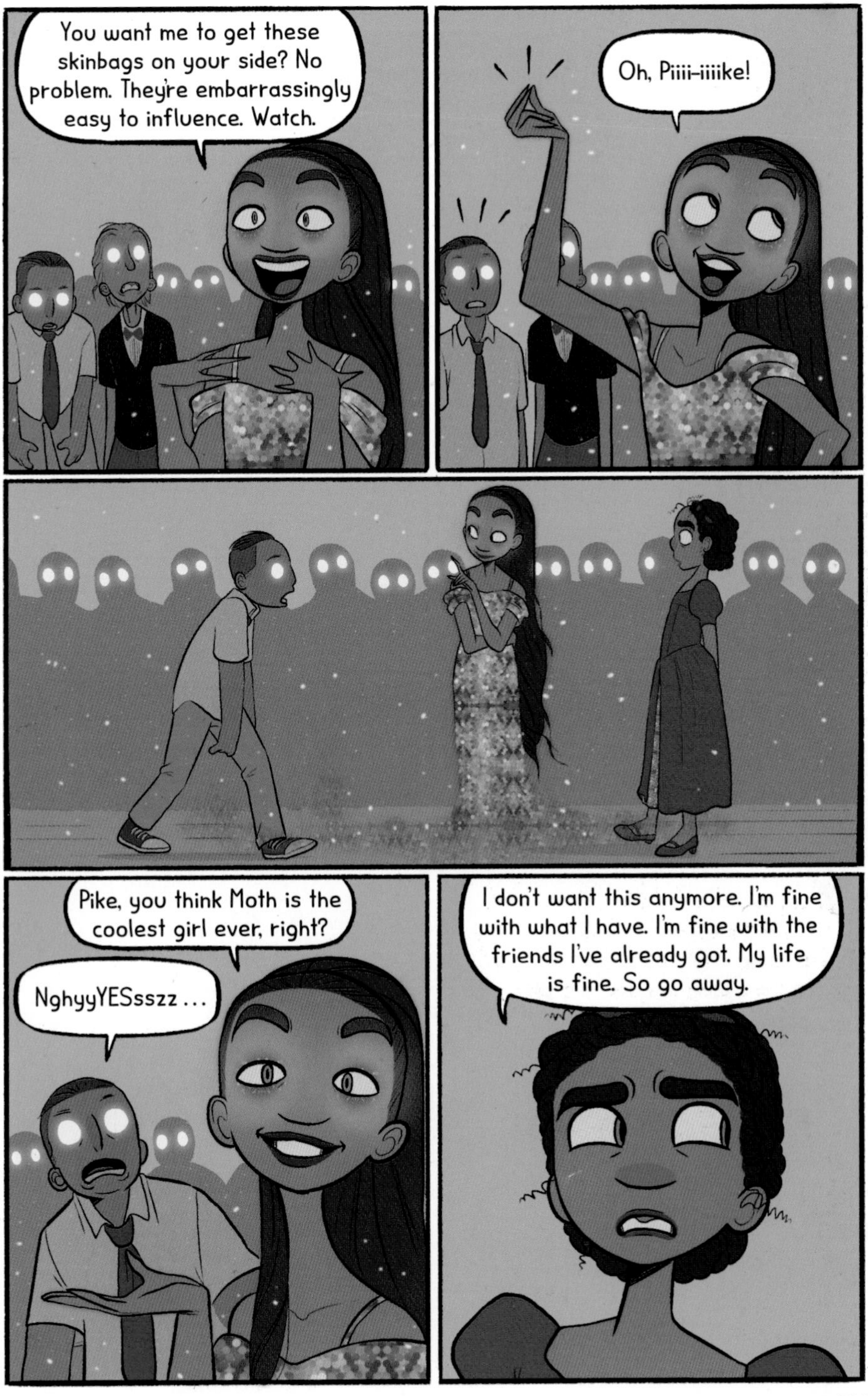
You want me to get these skinbags on your side? No problem. They're embarrassingly easy to influence. Watch.
Oh, Piiii-iiiike!
Pike, you think Moth is the coolest girl ever, right?
NghyyYESsszz . . .
I don't want this anymore. I'm fine with what I have. I'm fine with the friends I've already got. My life is fine. So go away.

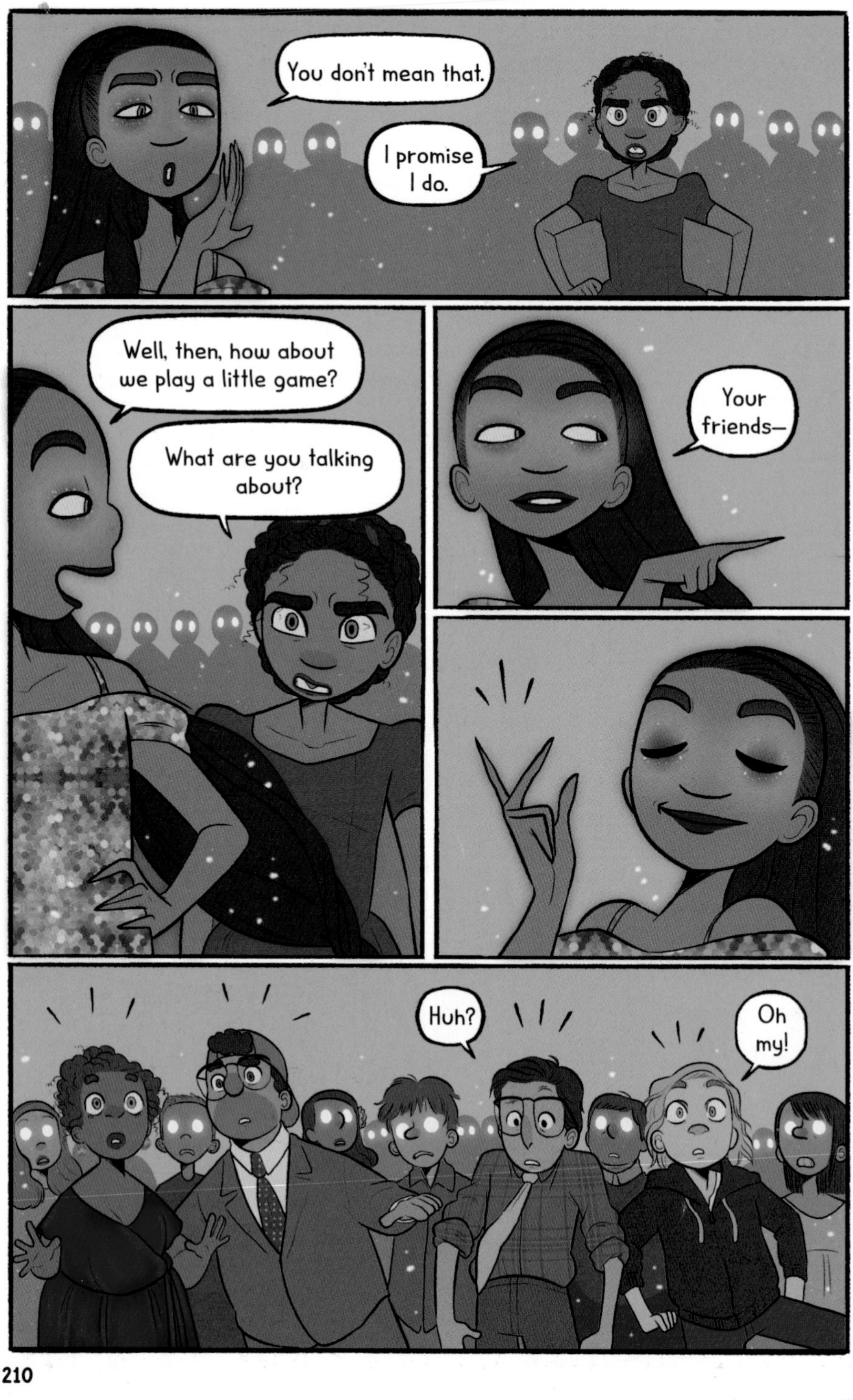

You don't mean that.
I promise I do.
Well, then, how about we play a little game?
What are you talking about?
Your friends—
Huh?
Oh my!

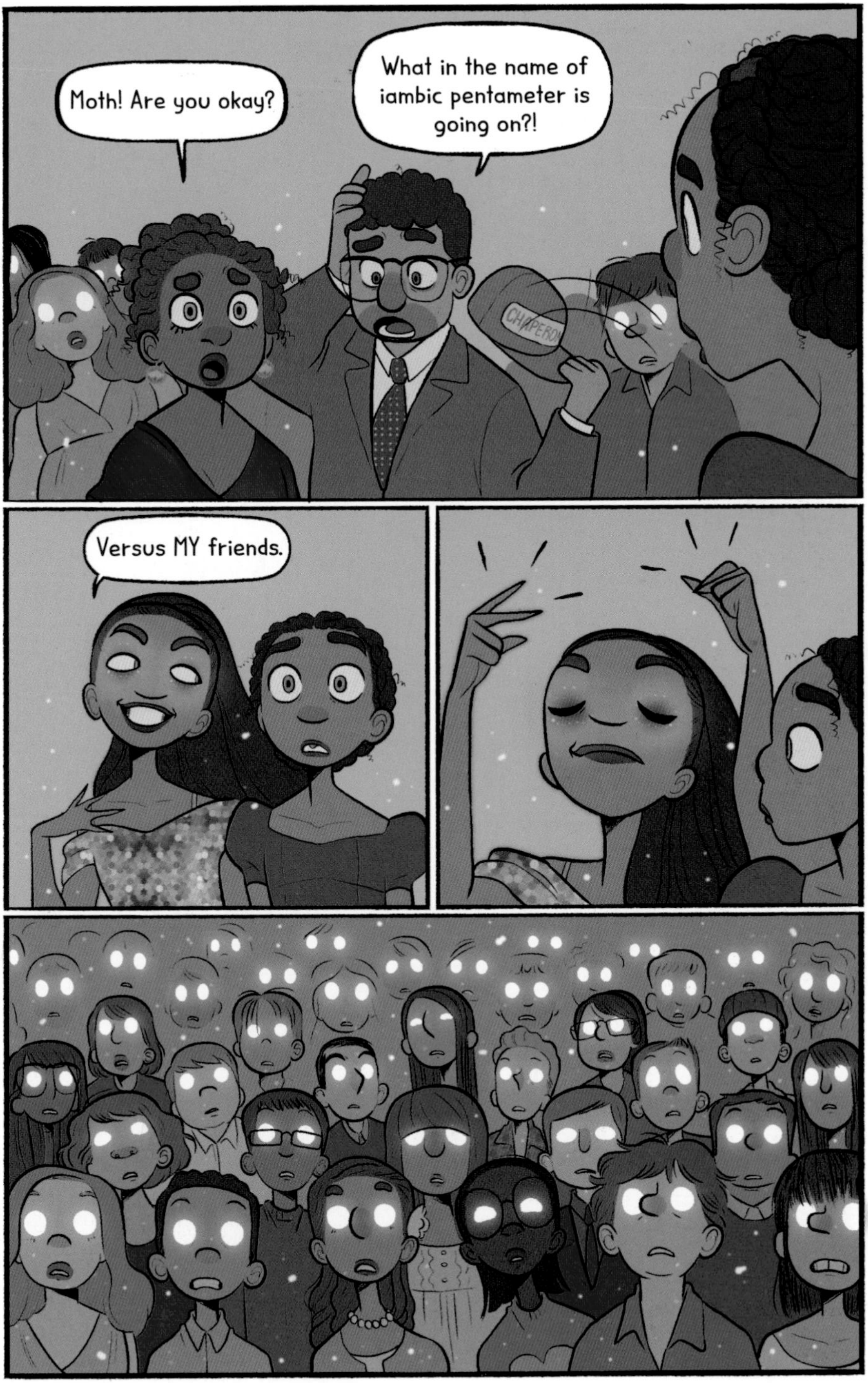
Moth! Are you okay?
What in the name of iambic pentameter is going on?!
CHAPERON
Versus MY friends.

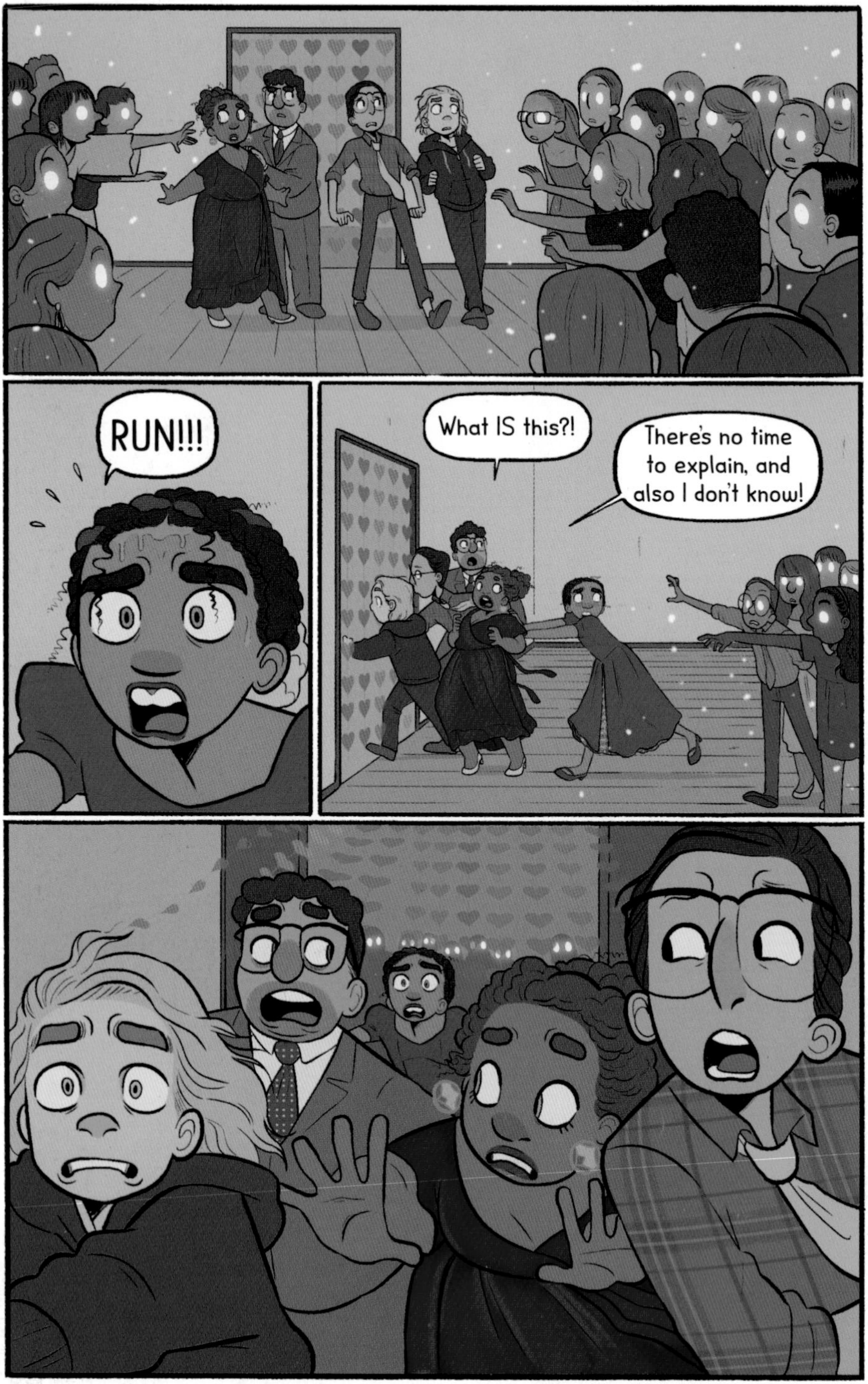
RUN!!!
What IS this?!
There's no time to explain, and also I don't know!

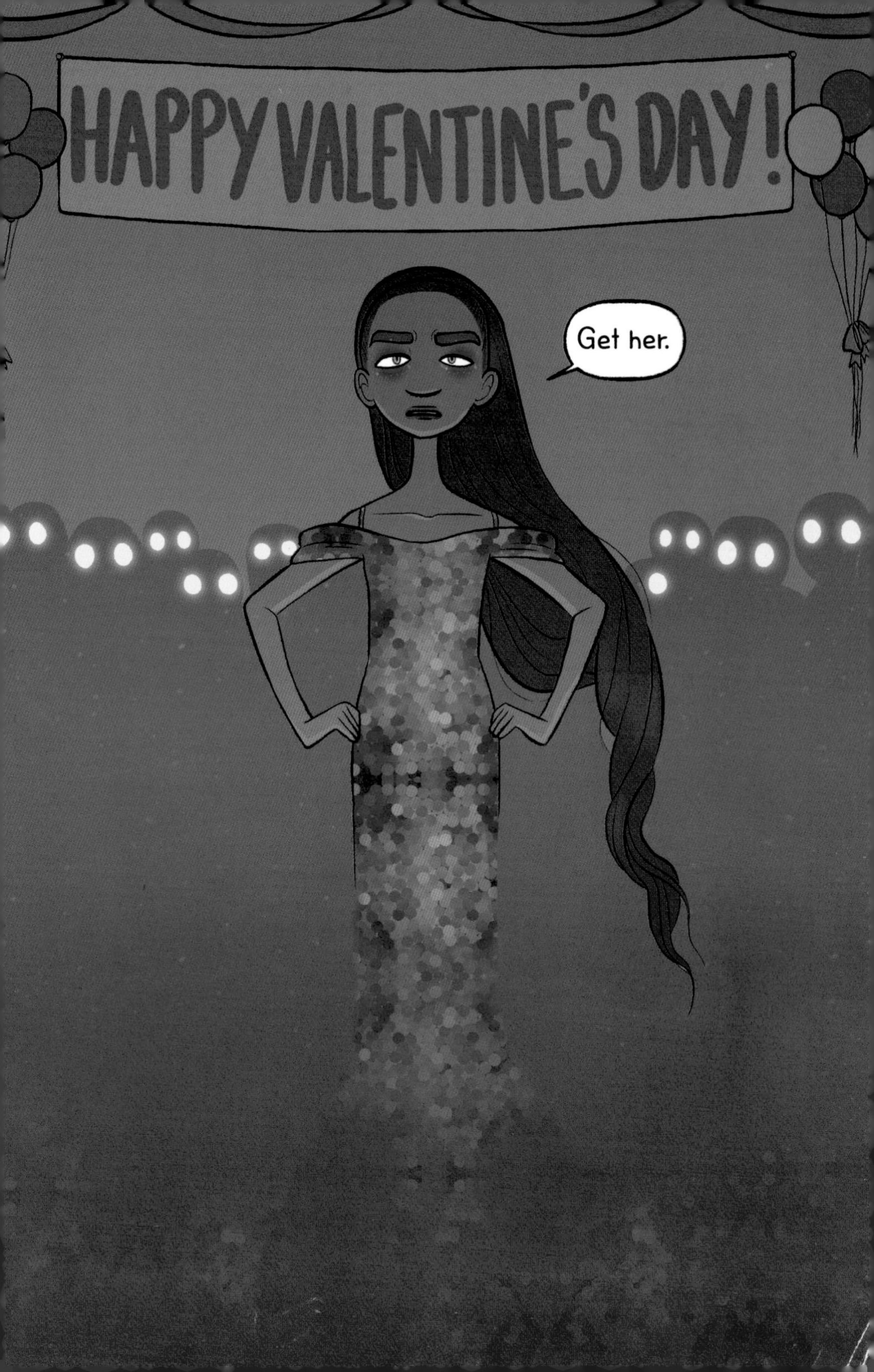
HAPPY VALENTINE'S DAY!
Get her.

CHAPTER 12

Moth and Her Shadow

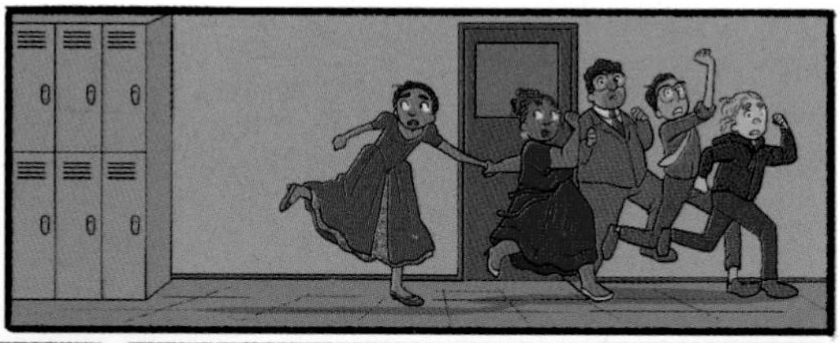

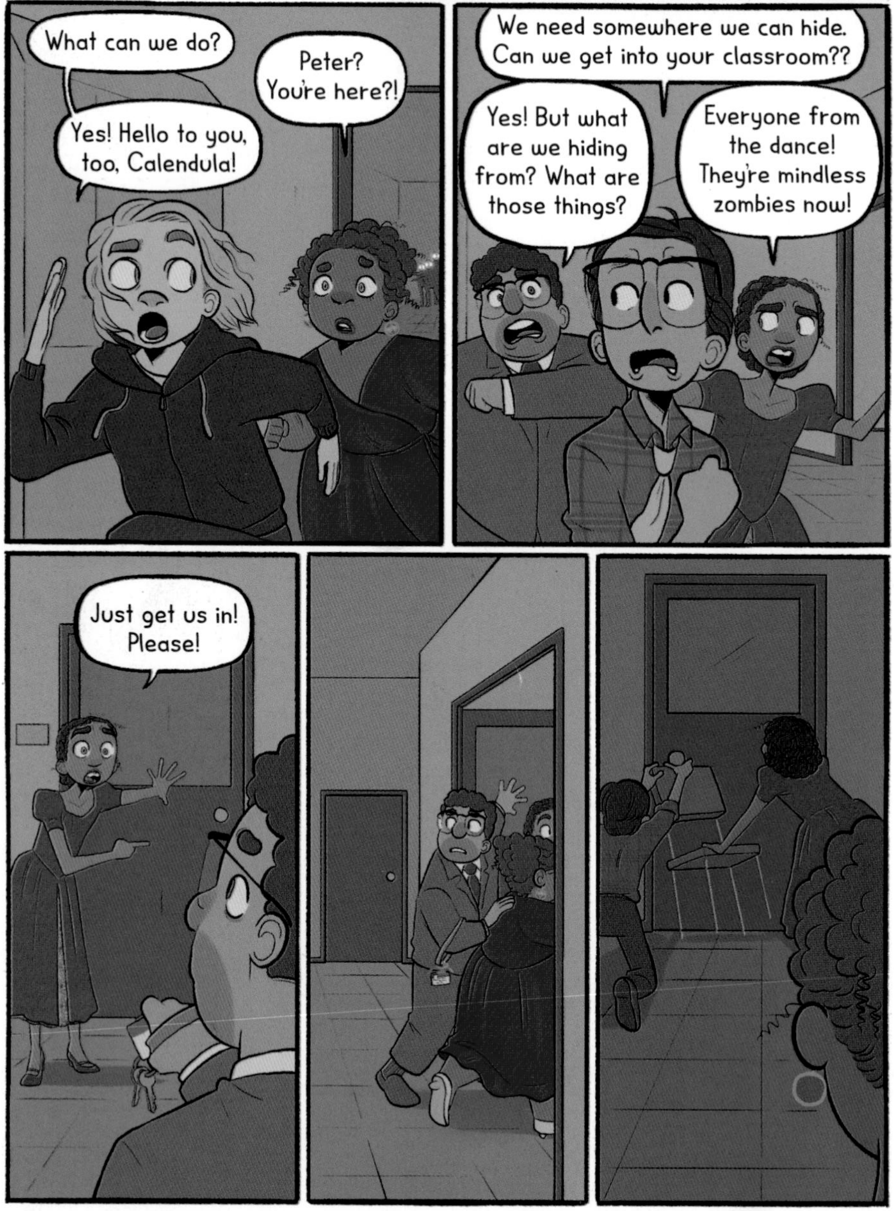
What can we do?
Peter? You're here?!
Yes! Hello to you, too, Calendula!
We need somewhere we can hide. Can we get into your classroom??
Yes! But what are we hiding from? What are those things?
Everyone from the dance! They're mindless zombies now!
Just get us in! Please!

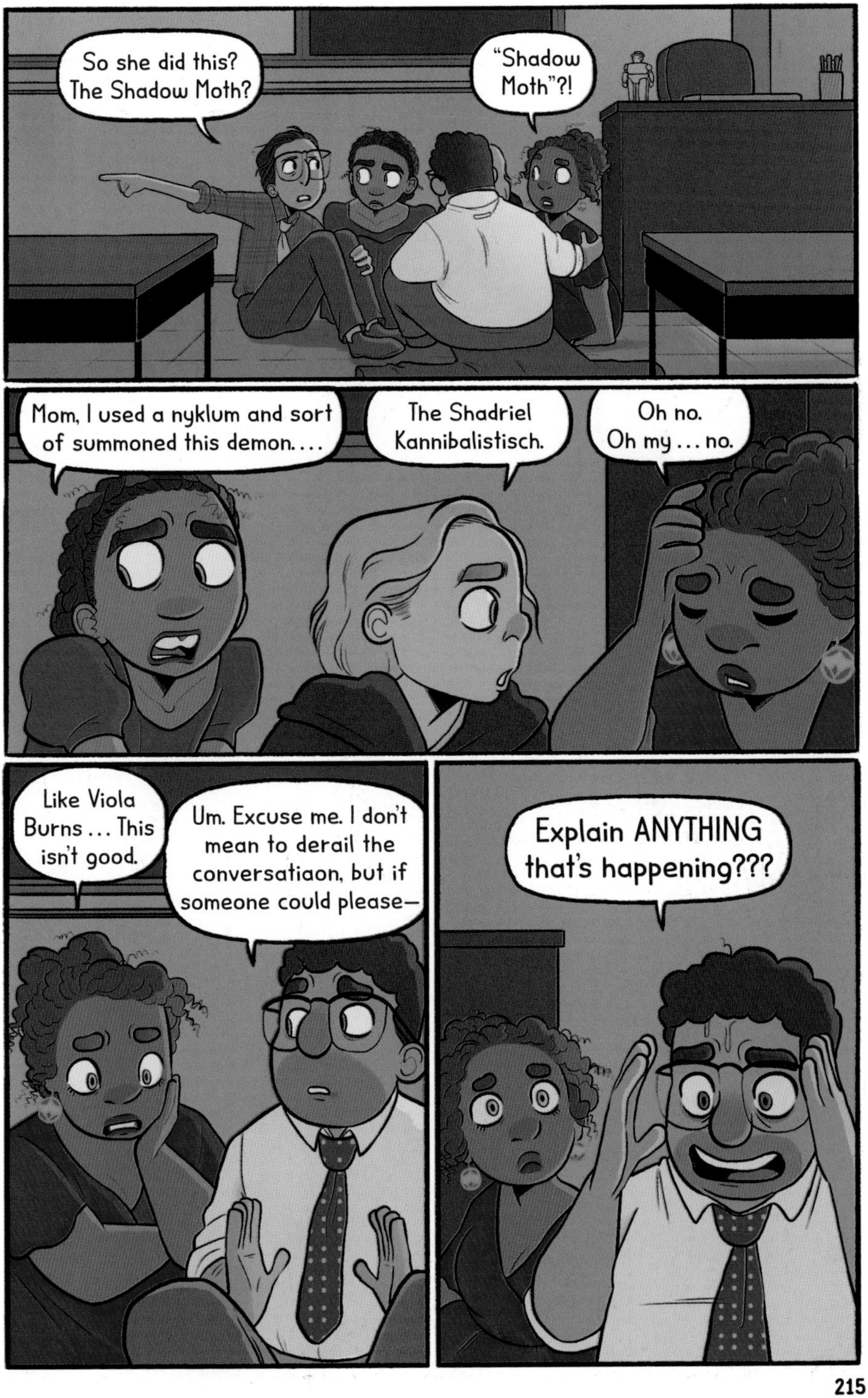
So she did this? The Shadow Moth?
"Shadow Moth"?!
Mom, I used a nyklum and sort of summoned this demon. . . .
The Shadriel Kannibalistisch.
Oh no. Oh my . . . no.
Like Viola Burns . . . This isn't good.
Um. Excuse me. I don't mean to derail the conversatiaon, but if someone could please—
Explain ANYTHING that's happening???

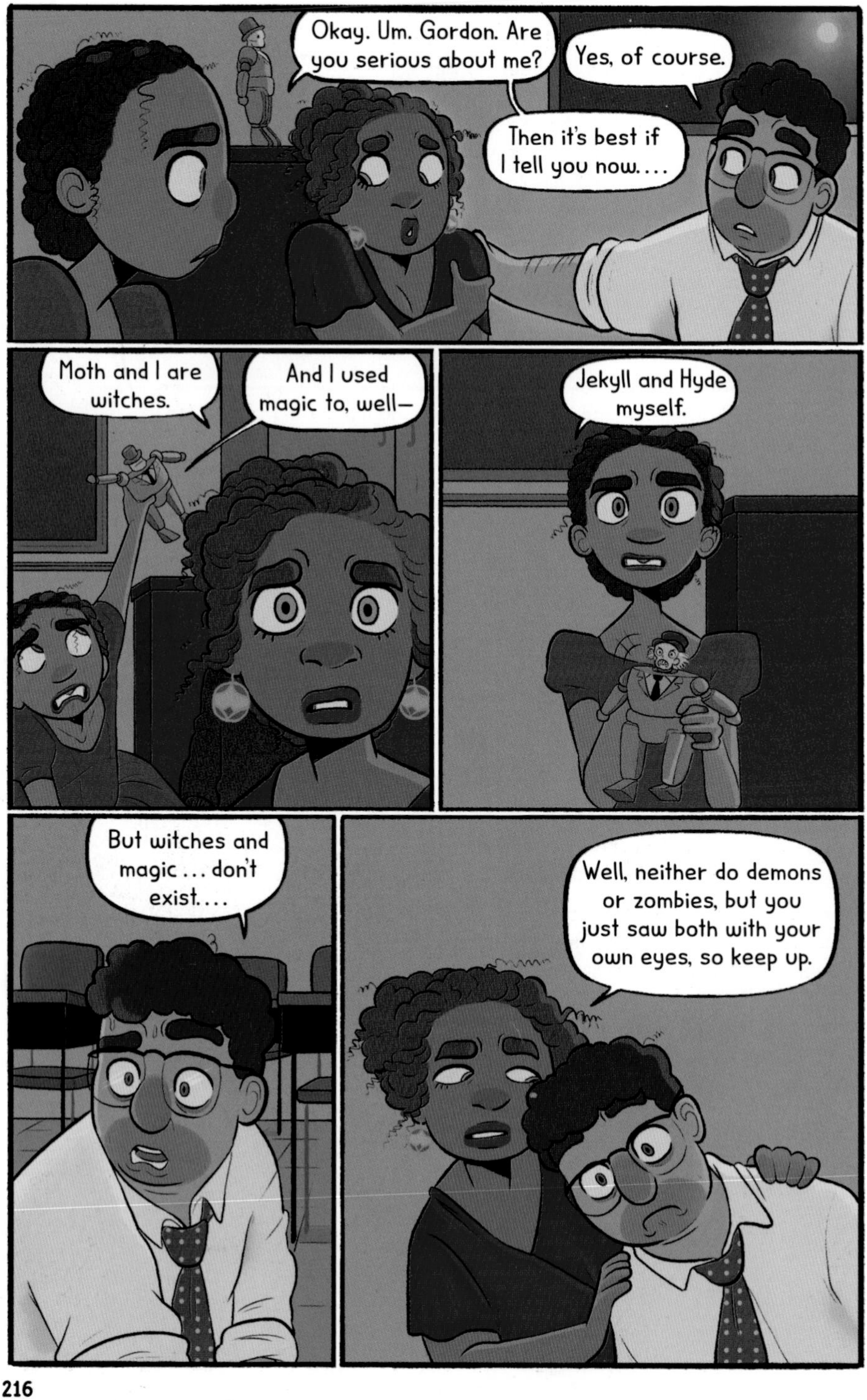
Okay. Um. Gordon. Are you serious about me?
Yes, of course.
Then it's best if I tell you now....
Moth and I are witches.
And I used magic to, well—
Jekyll and Hyde myself.
But witches and magic ... don't exist....
Well, neither do demons or zombies, but you just saw both with your own eyes, so keep up.

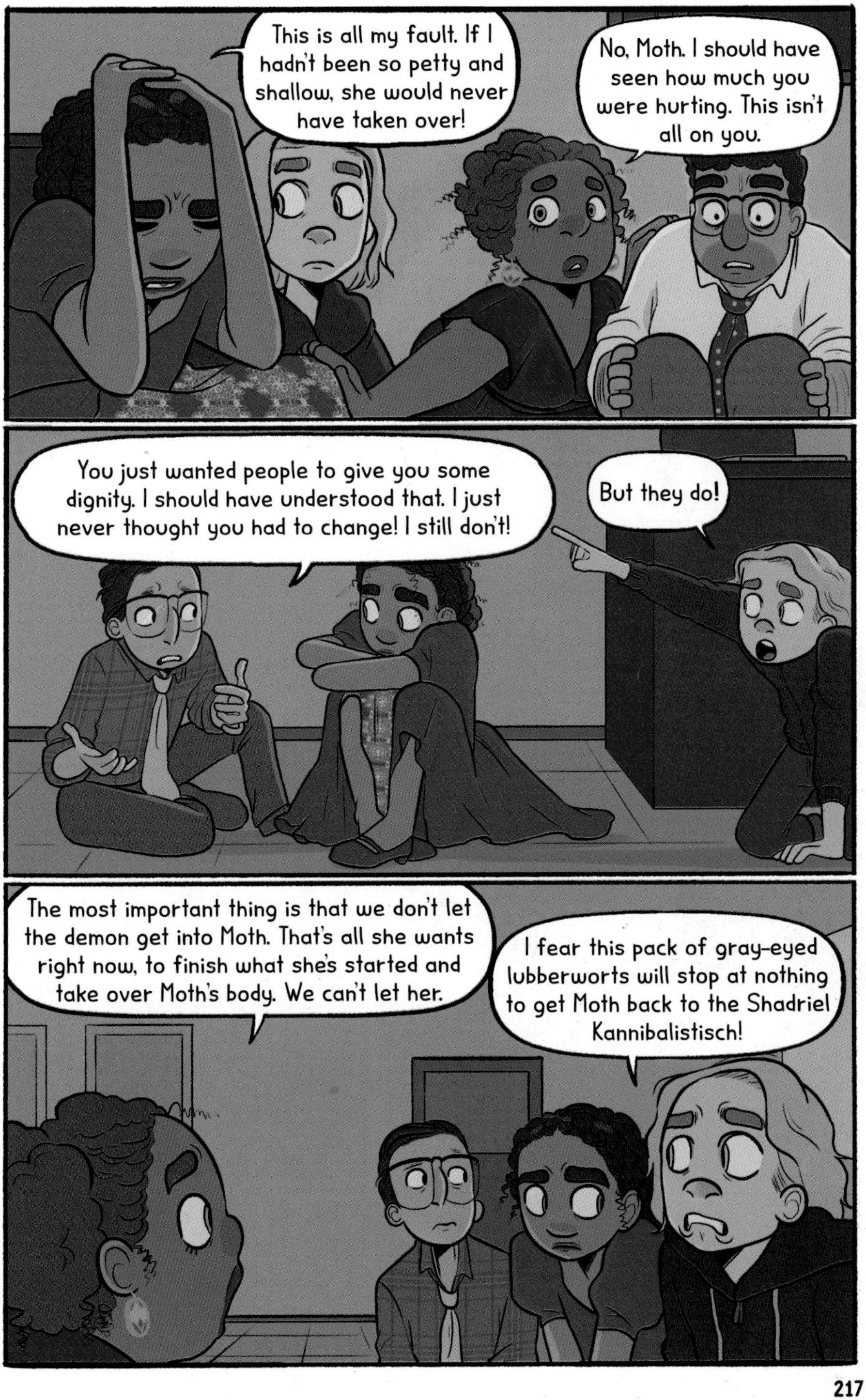
This is all my fault. If I hadn't been so petty and shallow, she would never have taken over!
No, Moth. I should have seen how much you were hurting. This isn't all on you.
You just wanted people to give you some dignity. I should have understood that. I just never thought you had to change! I still don't!
But they do!
The most important thing is that we don't let the demon get into Moth. That's all she wants right now, to finish what she's started and take over Moth's body. We can't let her.
I fear this pack of gray-eyed lubberworts will stop at nothing to get Moth back to the Shadriel Kannibalistisch!

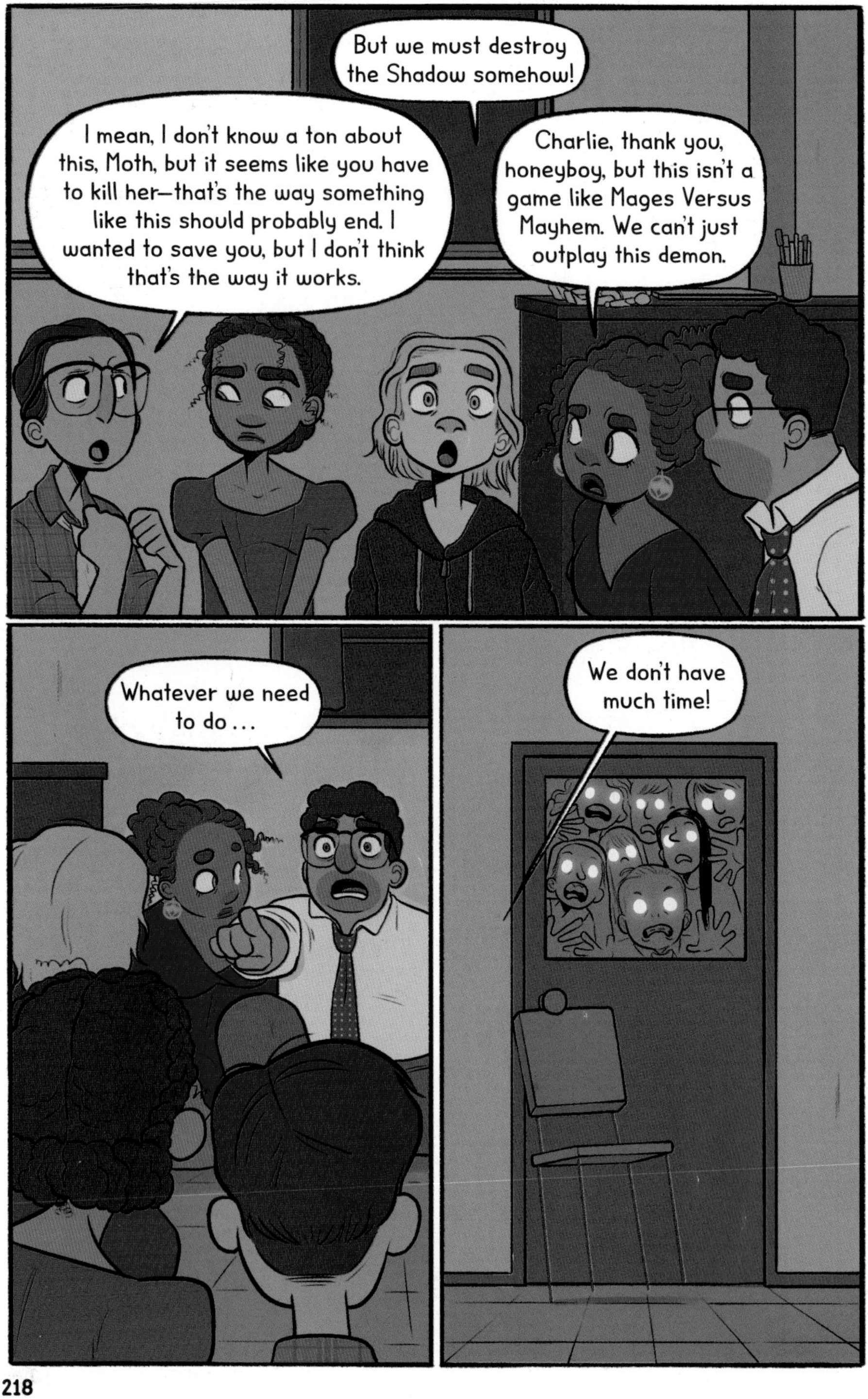
But we must destroy the Shadow somehow!
I mean, I don't know a ton about this, Moth, but it seems like you have to kill her—that's the way something like this should probably end. I wanted to save you, but I don't think that's the way it works.
Charlie, thank you, honeyboy, but this isn't a game like Mages Versus Mayhem. We can't just outplay this demon.
Whatever we need to do . . .
We don't have much time!

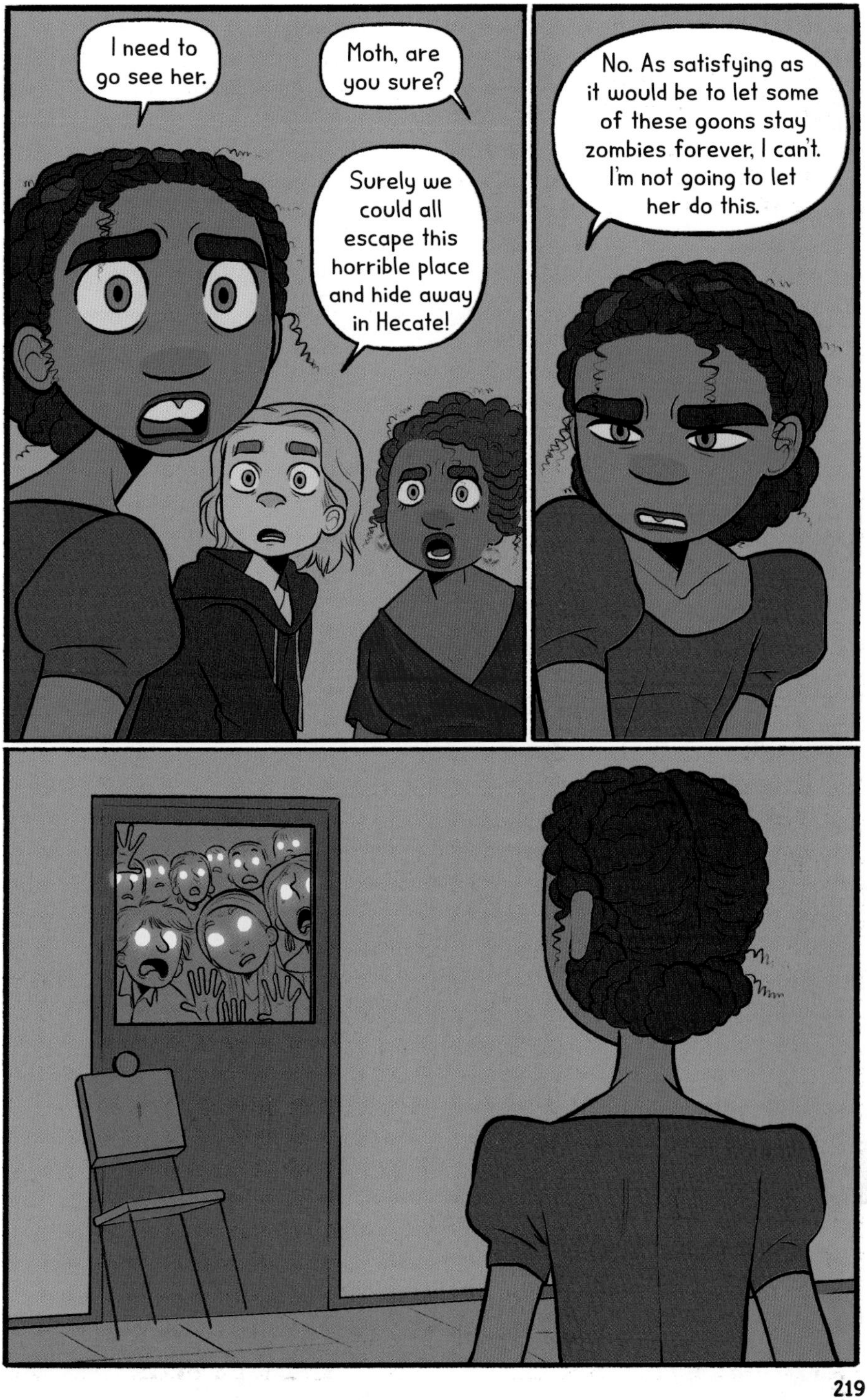

I need to go see her.
Moth, are you sure?
Surely we could all escape this horrible place and hide away in Hecate!
No. As satisfying as it would be to let some of these goons stay zombies forever, I can't. I'm not going to let her do this.

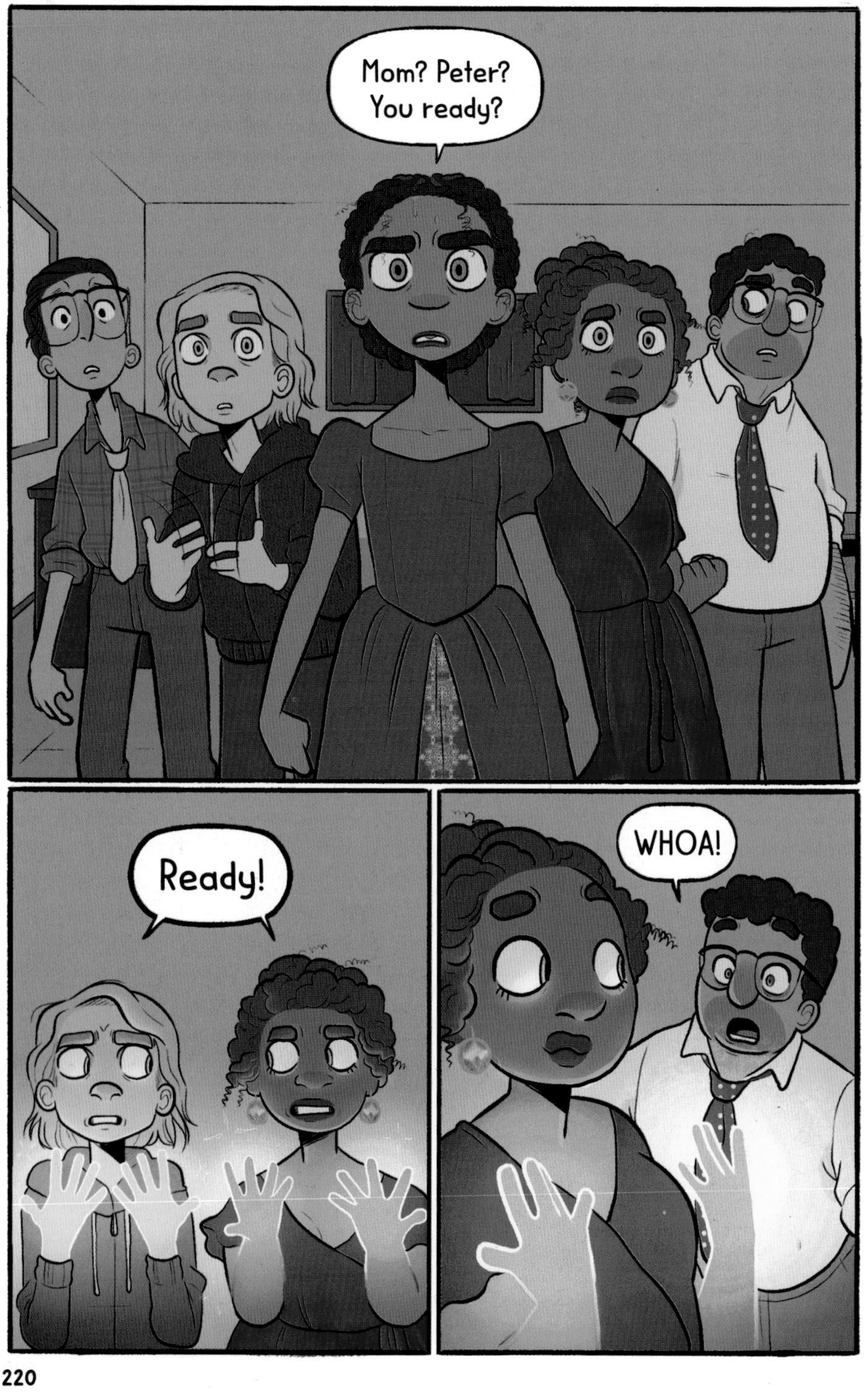
Mom? Peter? You ready?
Ready!
WHOA!

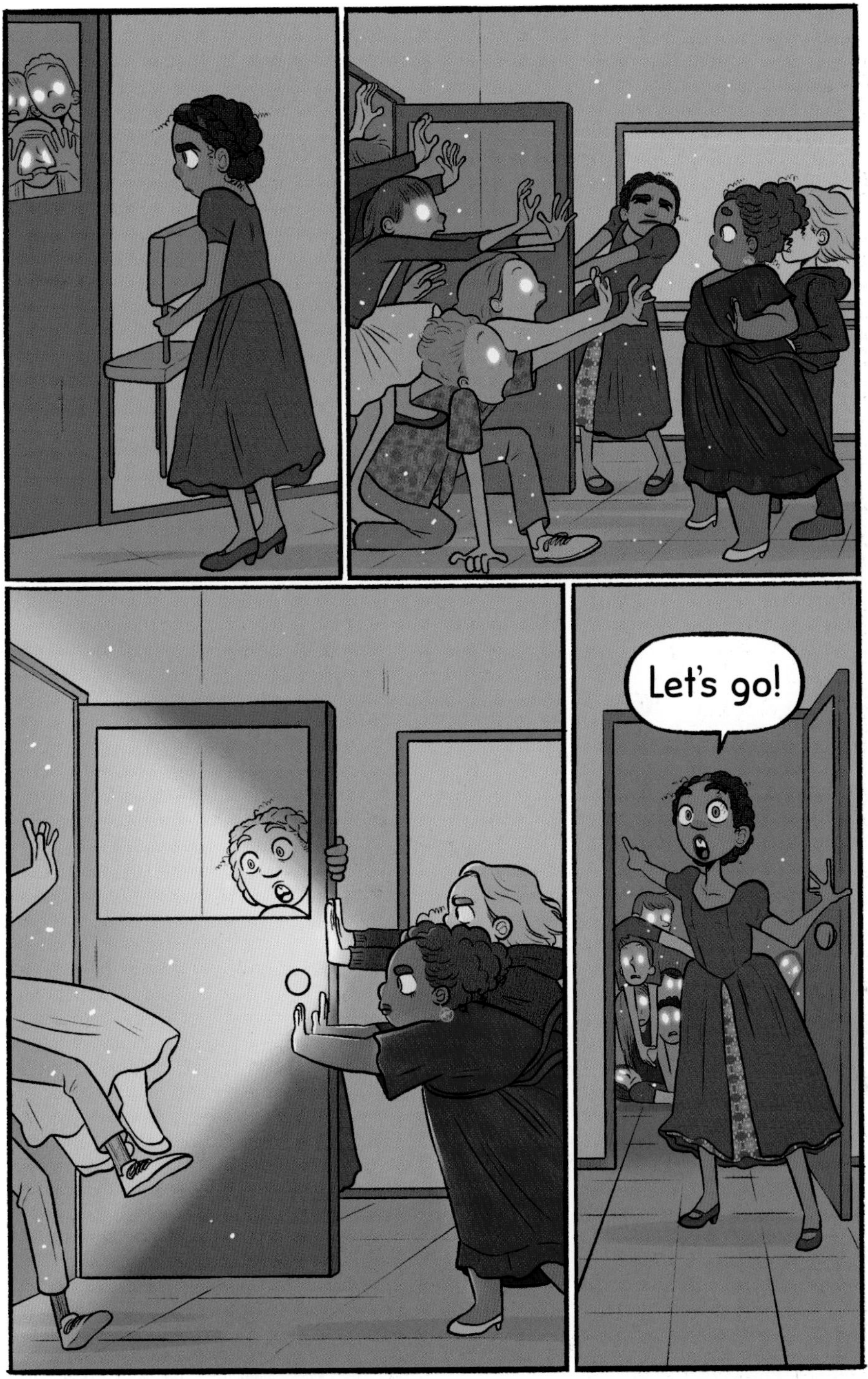
Let's go!

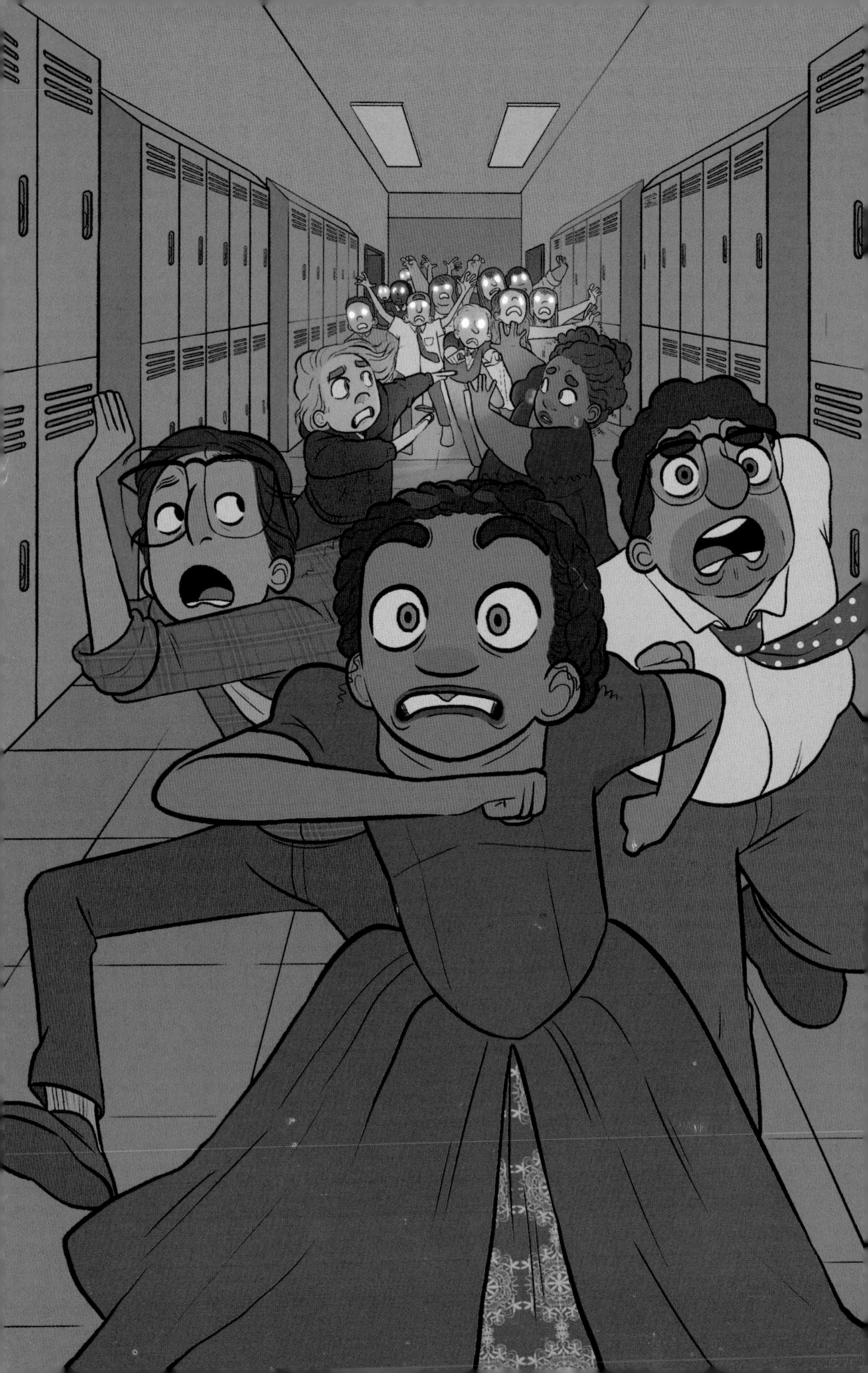

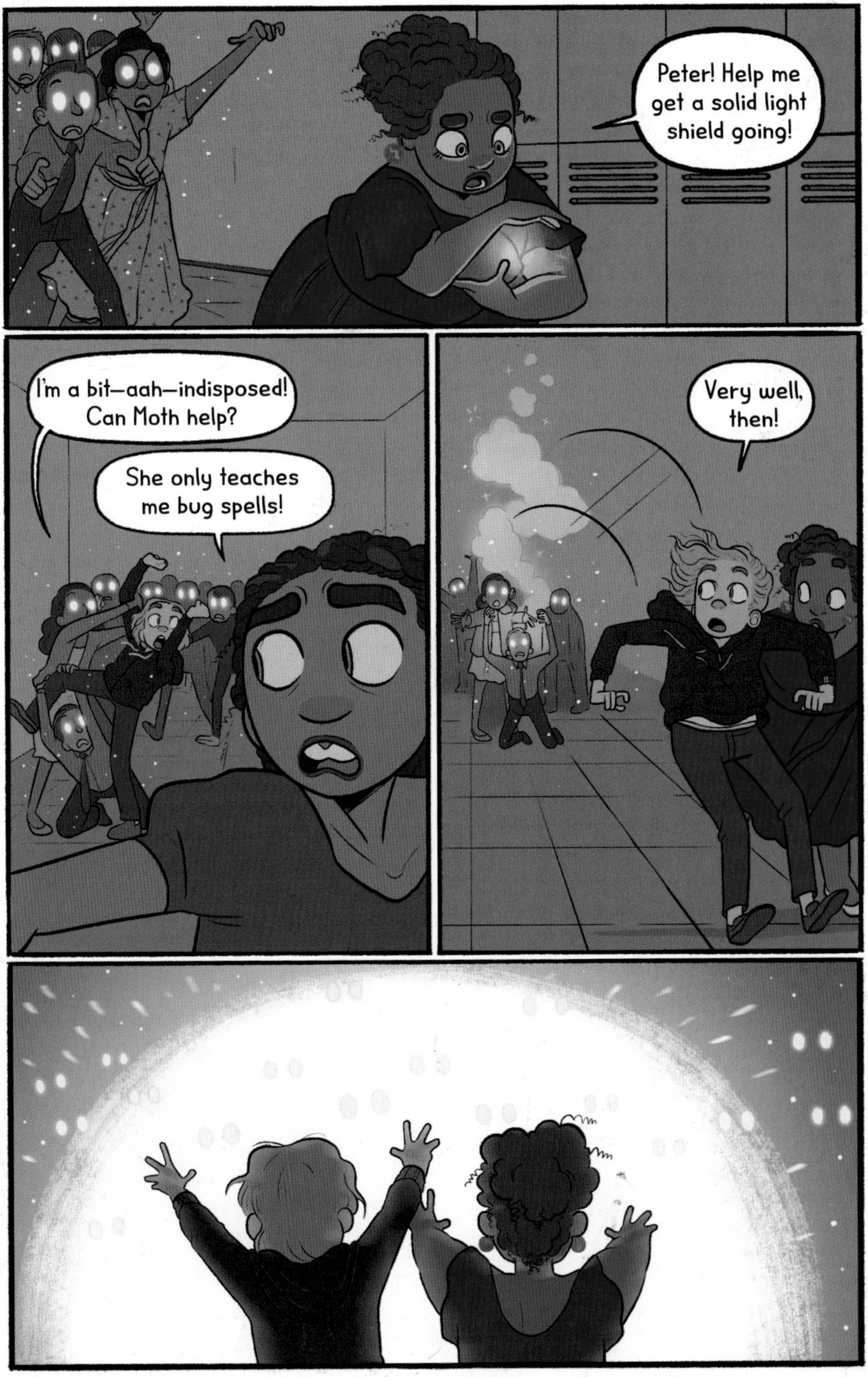
Peter! Help me get a solid light shield going!
I'm a bit—aah—indisposed! Can Moth help?
She only teaches me bug spells!
Very well, then!

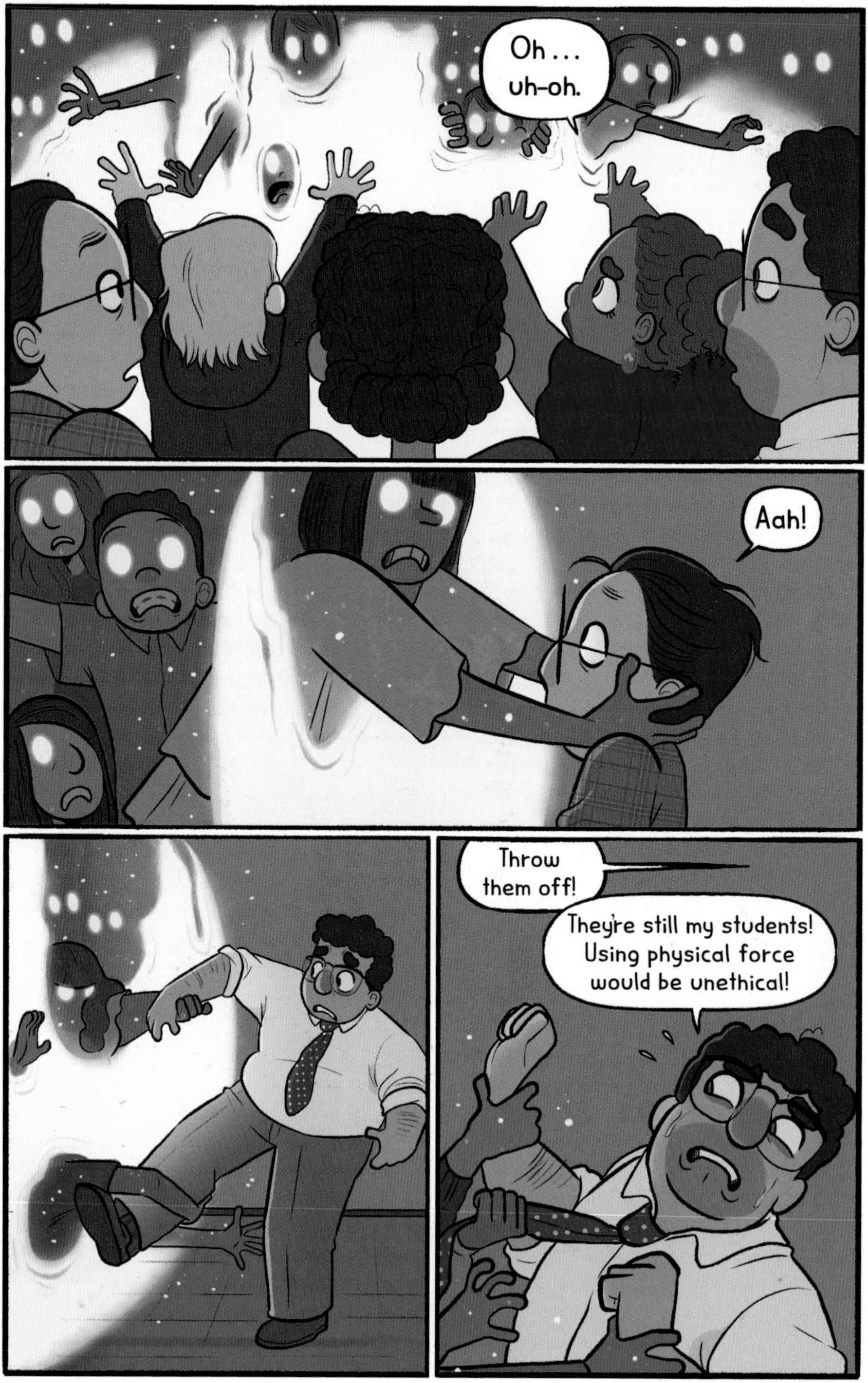
Oh . . . uh-oh.
Aah!
Throw them off!
They're still my students! Using physical force would be unethical!

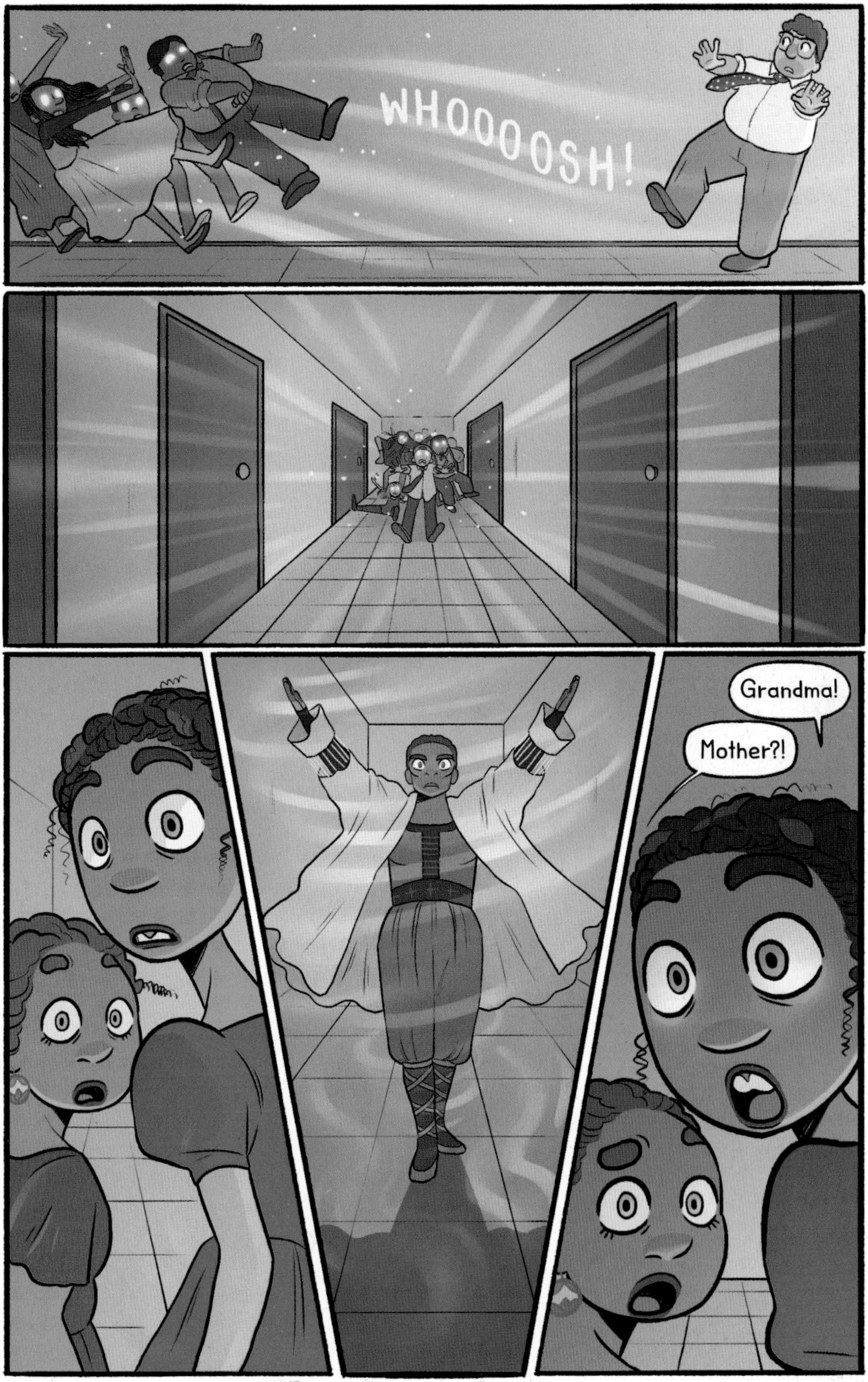
WHOOOOOSH!
Grandma!
Mother?!

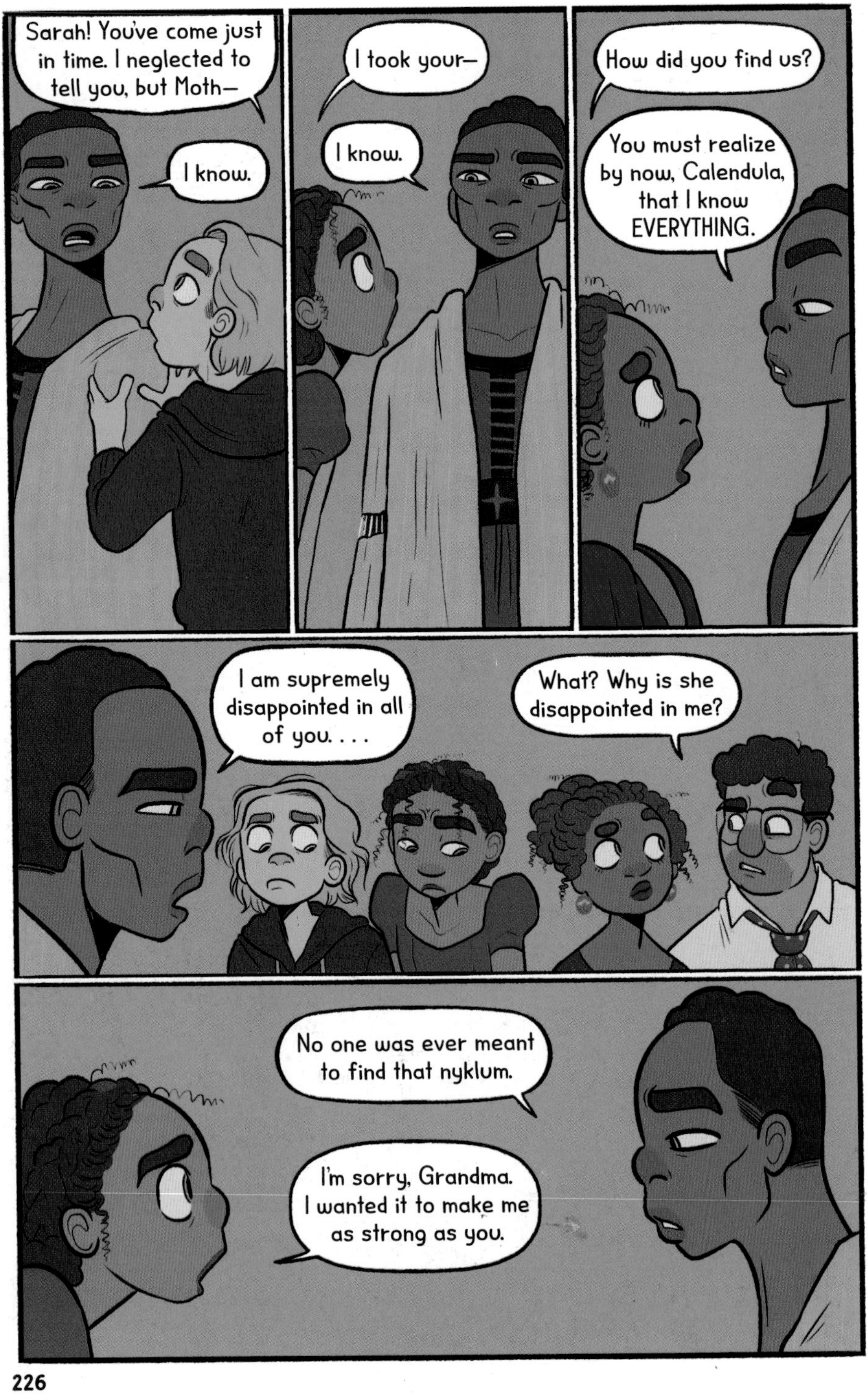
Sarah! You've come just in time. I neglected to tell you, but Moth—
I know.
I took your—
I know.
How did you find us?
You must realize by now, Calendula, that I know EVERYTHING.
I am supremely disappointed in all of you. . . .
What? Why is she disappointed in me?
No one was ever meant to find that nyklum.
I'm sorry, Grandma. I wanted it to make me as strong as you.

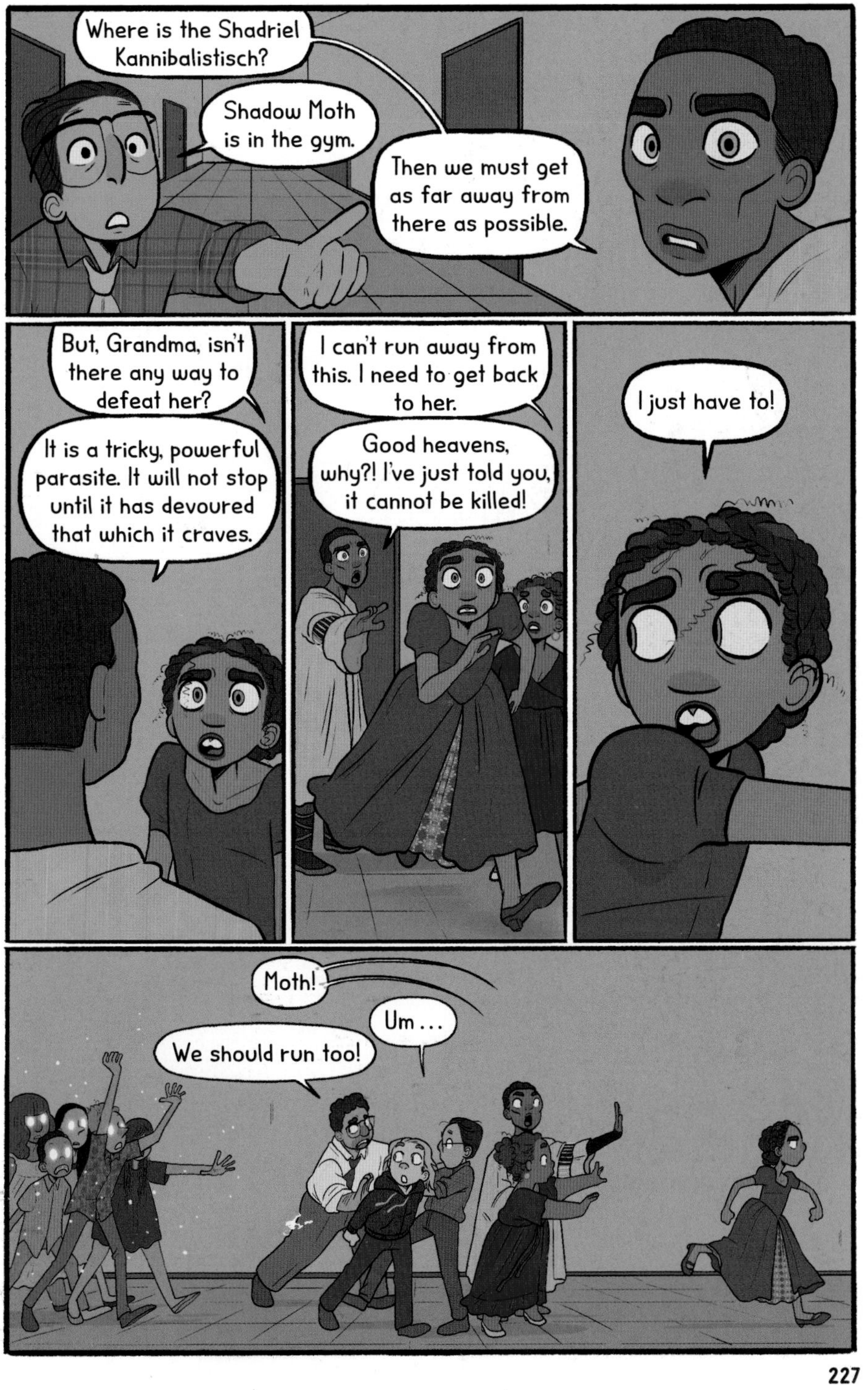
Where is the Shadriel Kannibalistisch?
Shadow Moth is in the gym.
Then we must get as far away from there as possible.
But, Grandma, isn't there any way to defeat her?
It is a tricky, powerful parasite. It will not stop until it has devoured that which it craves.
I can't run away from this. I need to get back to her.
Good heavens, why?! I've just told you, it cannot be killed!
I just have to!
Moth!
Um . . .
We should run too!

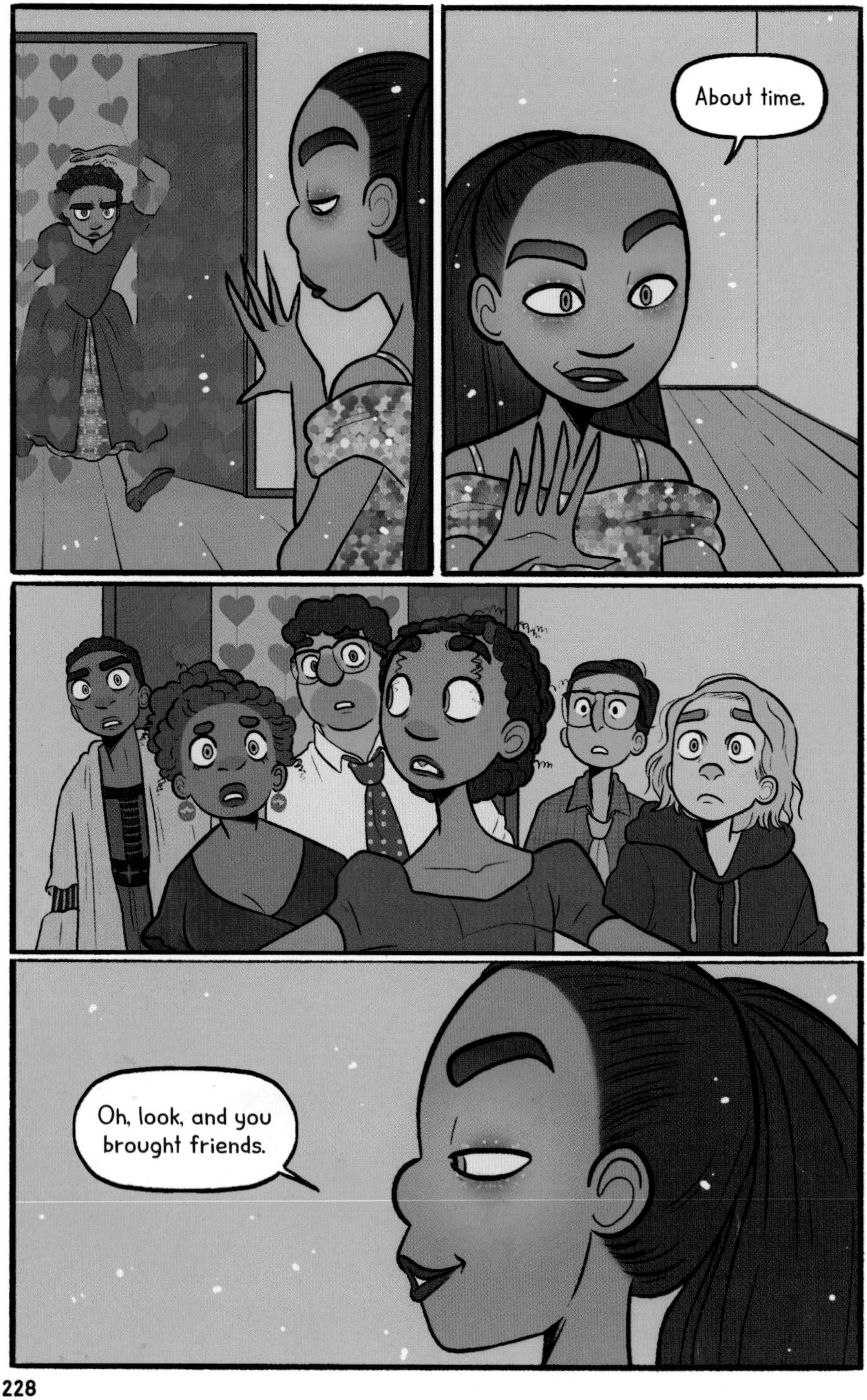
About time.
Oh, look, and you brought friends.

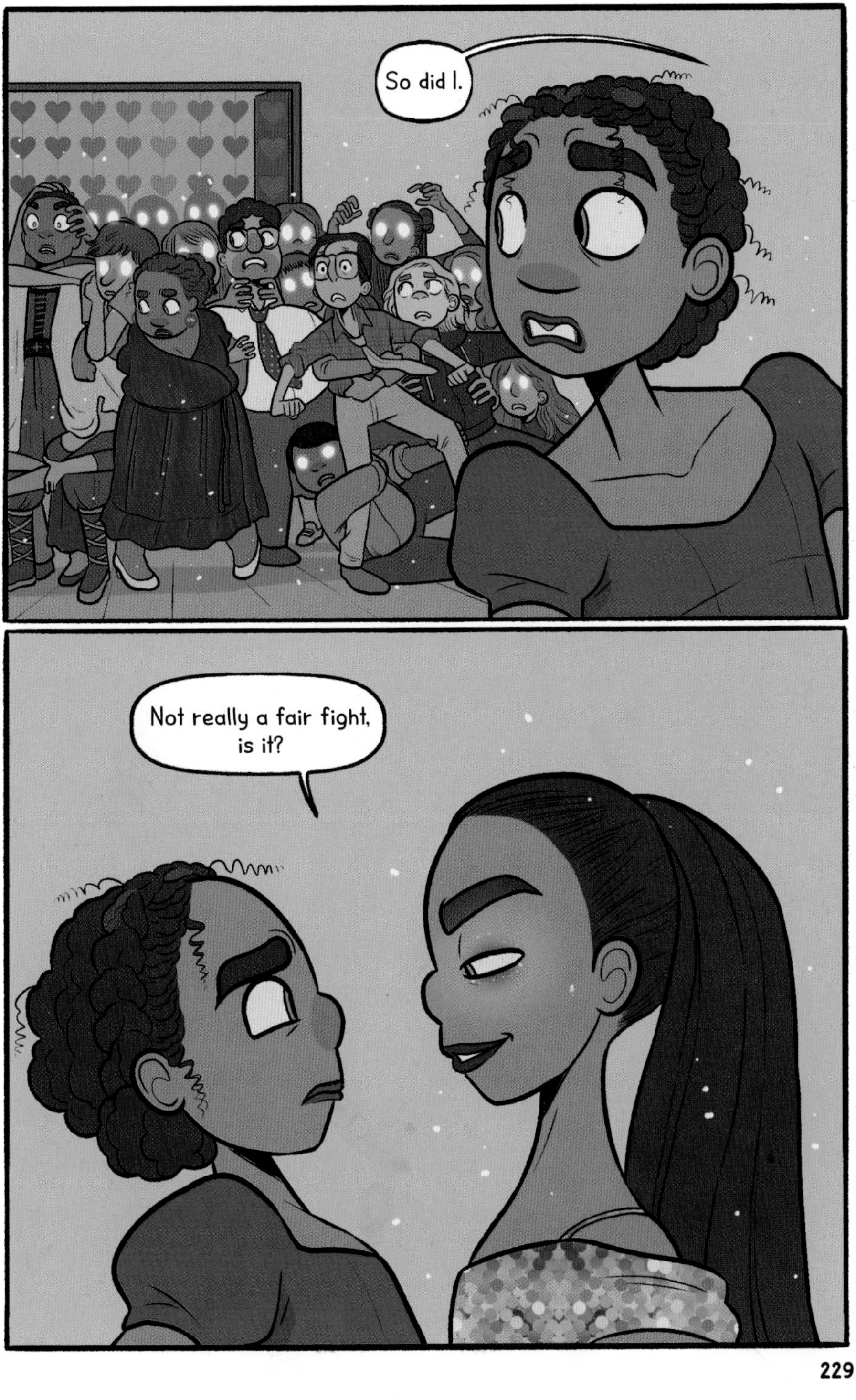
So did I.
Not really a fair fight, is it?

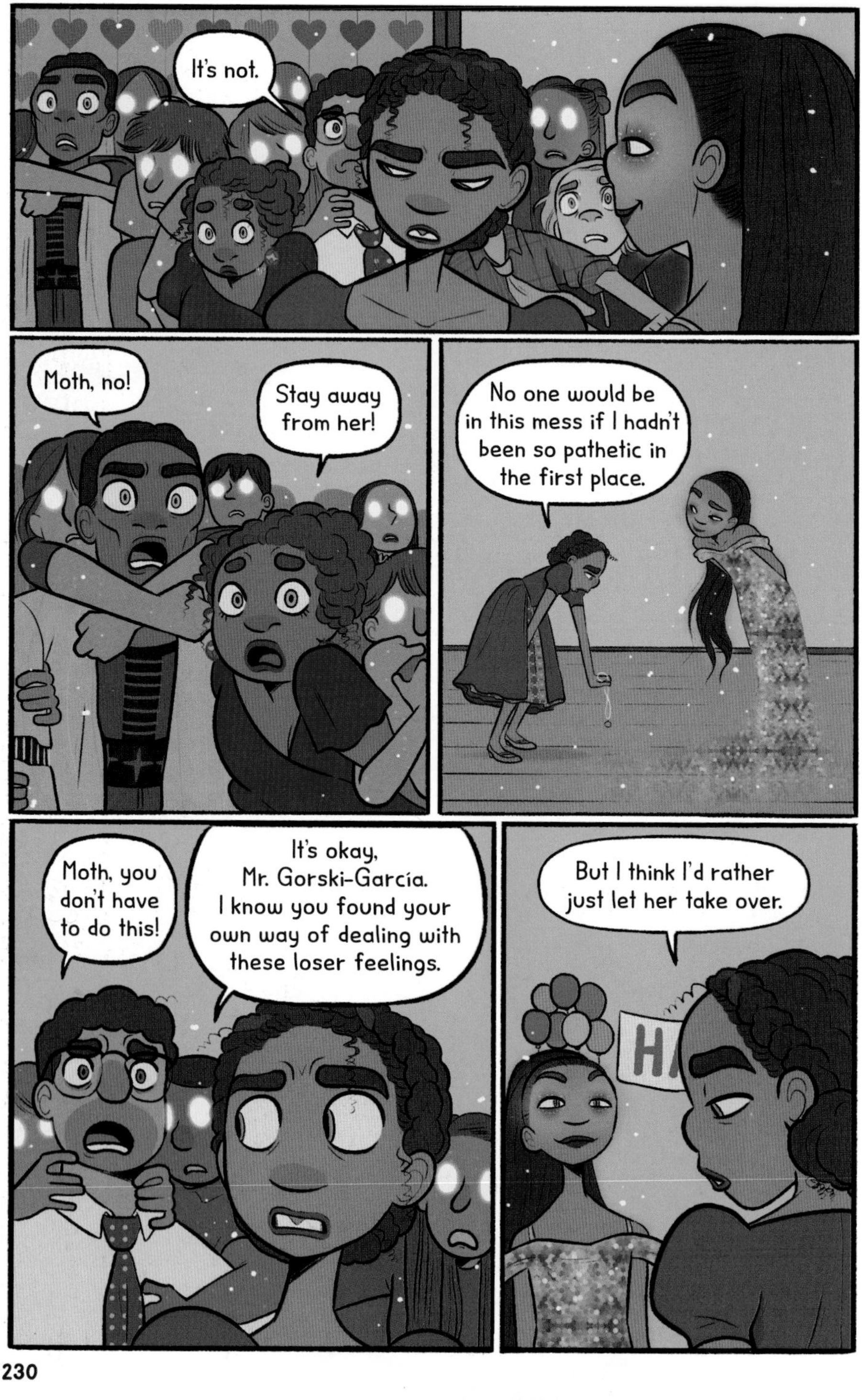
It's not.
Moth, no!
Stay away from her!
No one would be in this mess if I hadn't been so pathetic in the first place.
Moth, you don't have to do this!
It's okay, Mr. Gorski-García. I know you found your own way of dealing with these loser feelings.
But I think I'd rather just let her take over.
HA

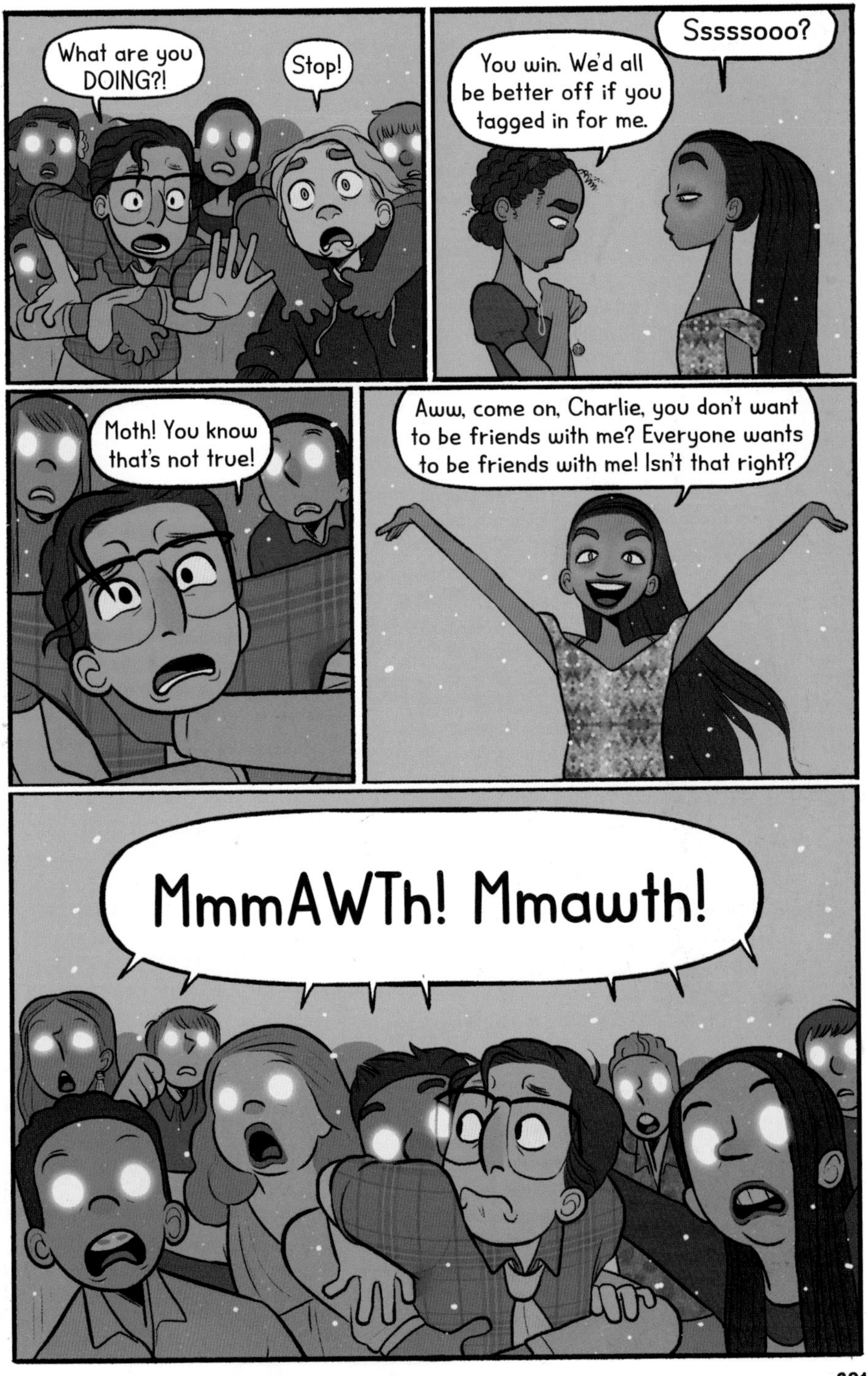
What are you DOING?!
Stop!
Ssssooo?
You win. We'd all be better off if you tagged in for me.
Moth! You know that's not true!
Aww, come on, Charlie, you don't want to be friends with me? Everyone wants to be friends with me! Isn't that right?
MmmAWTh! Mmawth!

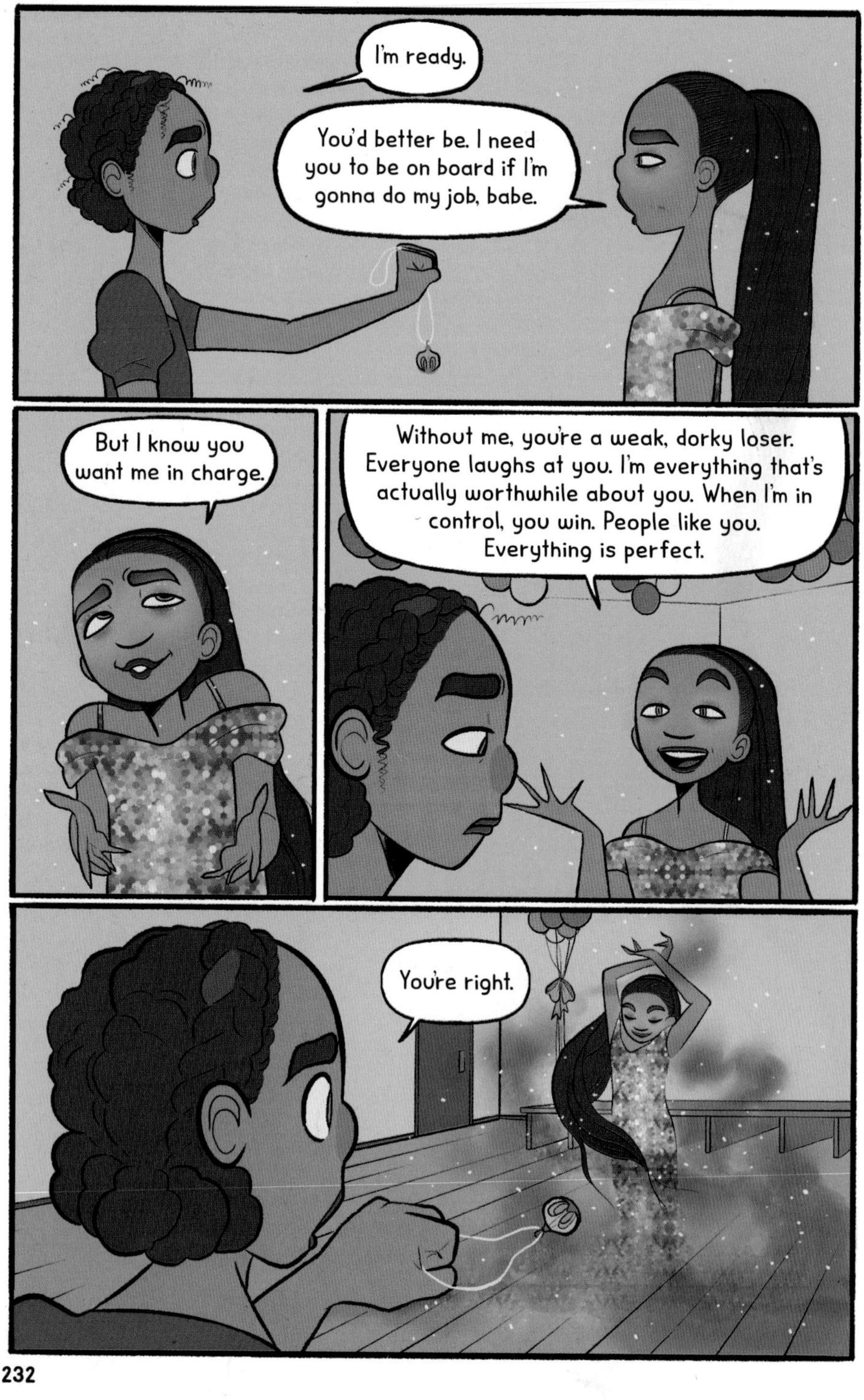
I'm ready.
You'd better be. I need you to be on board if I'm gonna do my job, babe.
But I know you want me in charge.
Without me, you're a weak, dorky loser. Everyone laughs at you. I'm everything that's actually worthwhile about you. When I'm in control, you win. People like you. Everything is perfect.
You're right.

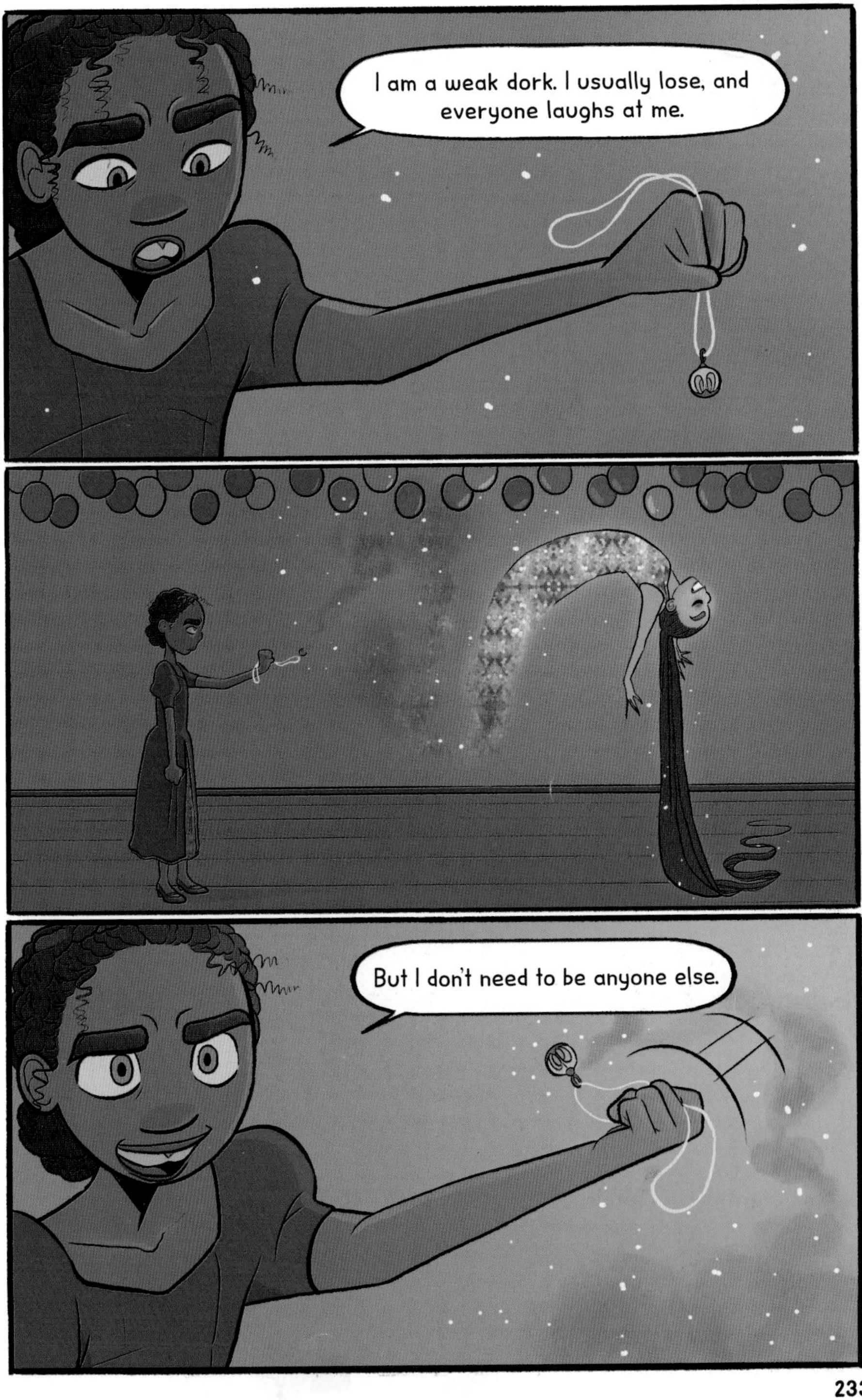
I am a weak dork. I usually lose, and everyone laughs at me.
But I don't need to be anyone else.

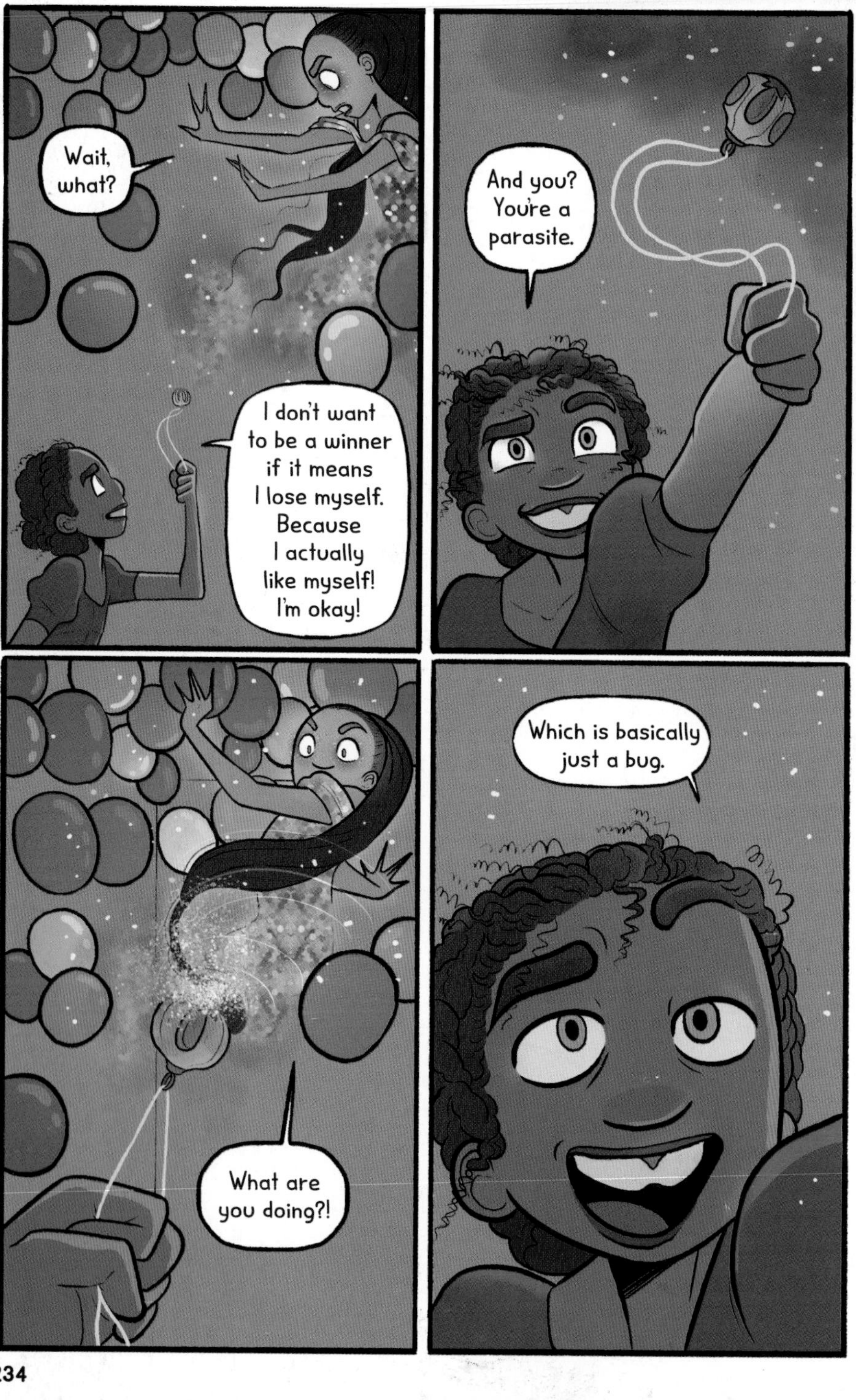
Wait, what?
I don't want to be a winner if it means I lose myself. Because I actually like myself! I'm okay!
And you? You're a parasite.
What are you doing?!
Which is basically just a bug.

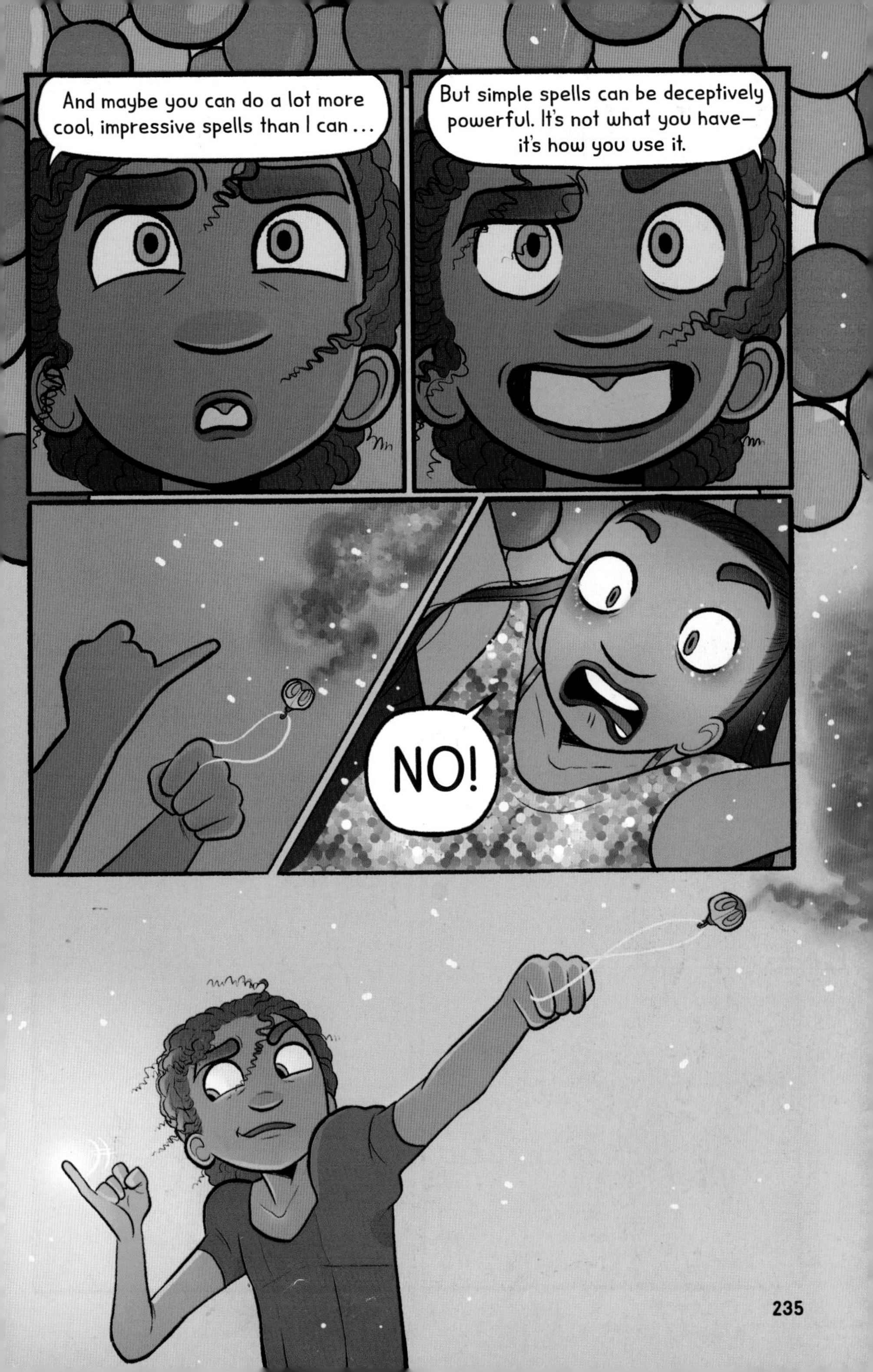
And maybe you can do a lot more cool, impressive spells than I can . . .
But simple spells can be deceptively powerful. It's not what you have—it's how you use it.
NO!

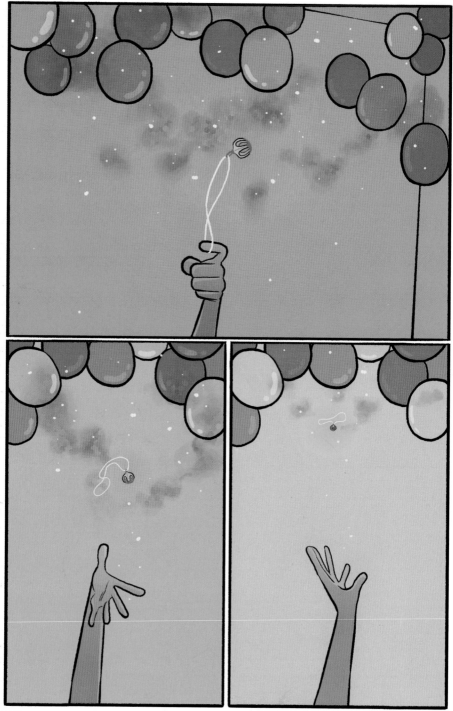

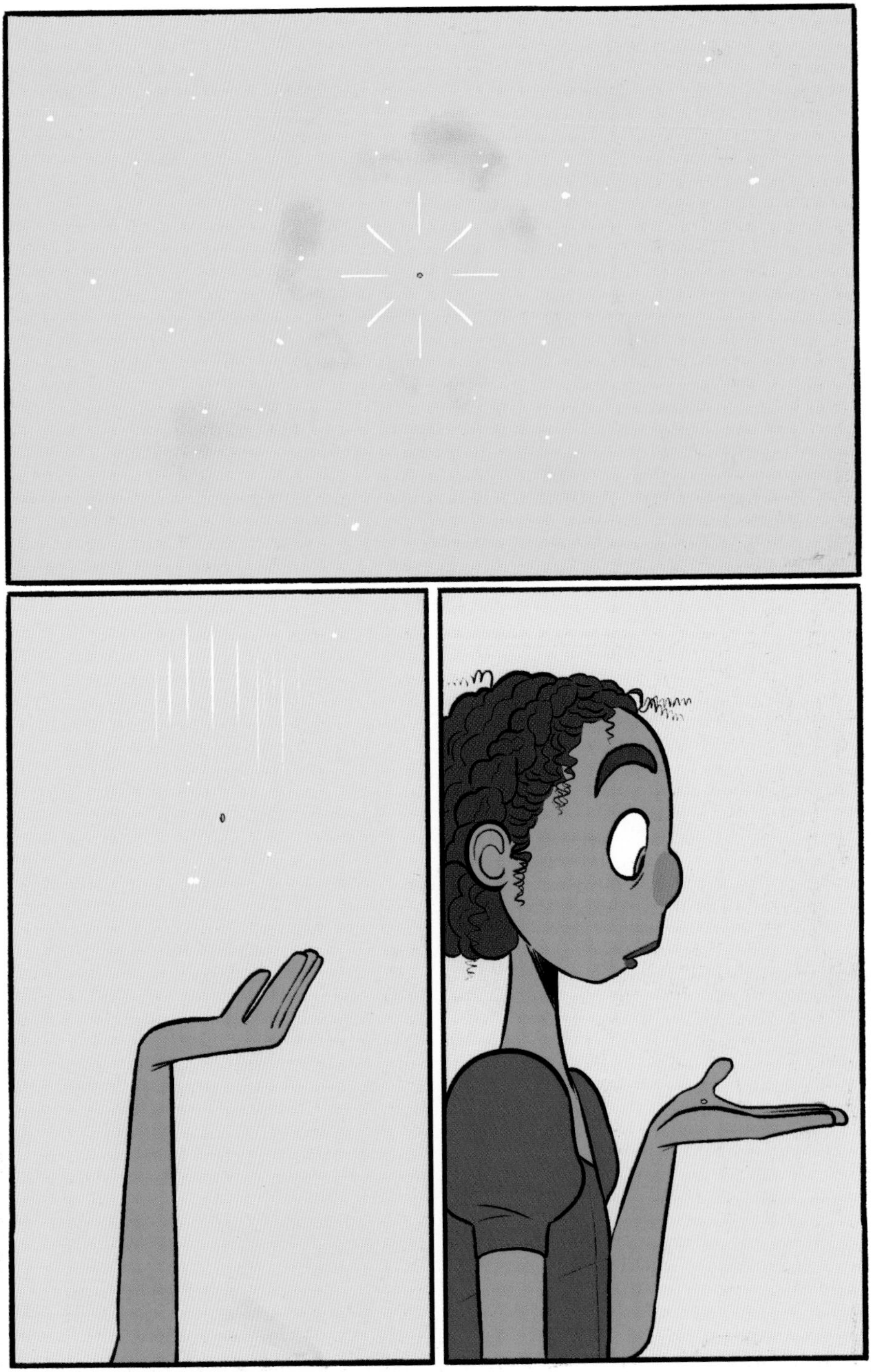

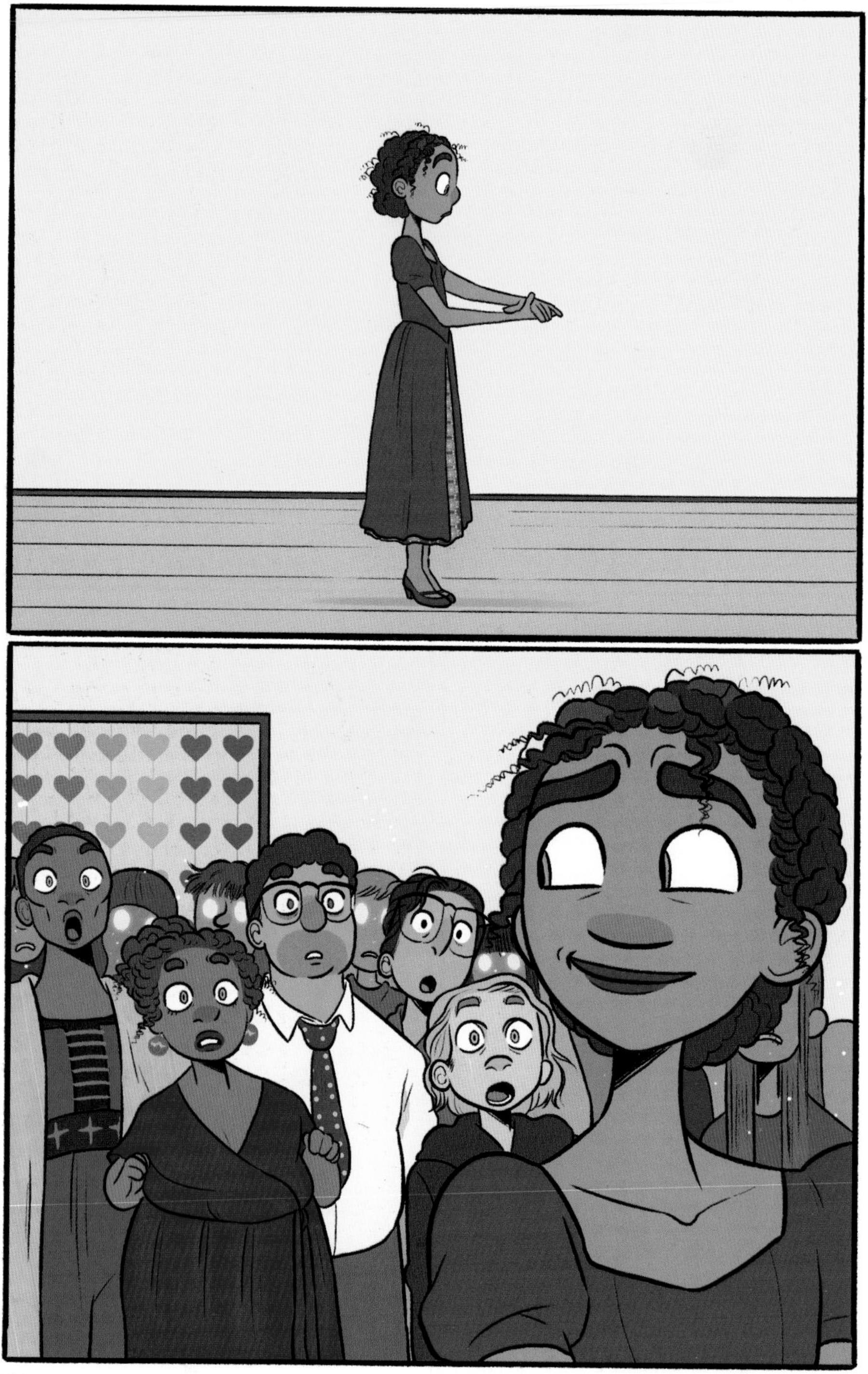

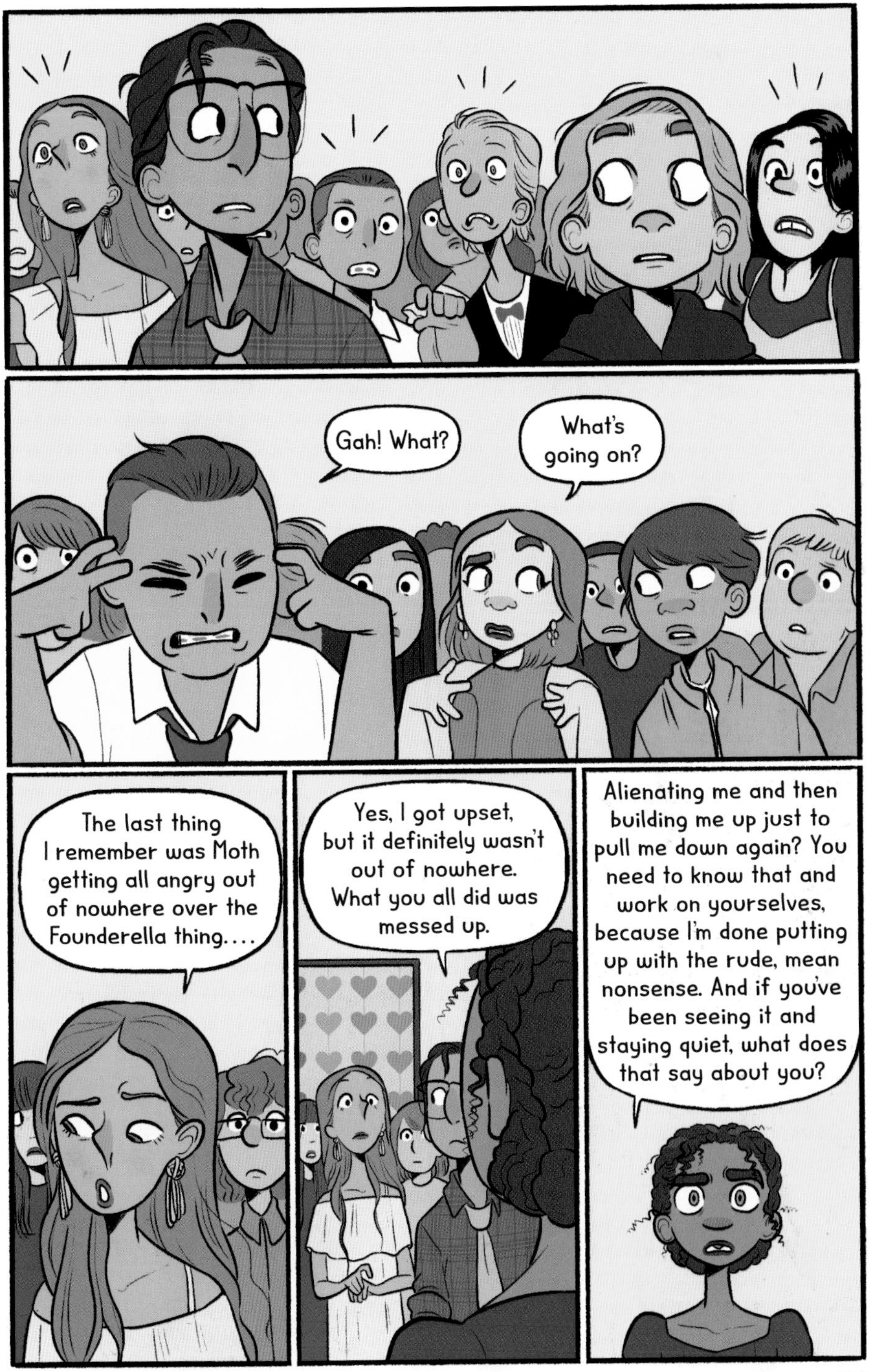
Gah! What?
What's going on?
The last thing I remember was Moth getting all angry out of nowhere over the Founderella thing....
Yes, I got upset, but it definitely wasn't out of nowhere. What you all did was messed up.
Alienating me and then building me up just to pull me down again? You need to know that and work on yourselves, because I'm done putting up with the rude, mean nonsense. And if you've been seeing it and staying quiet, what does that say about you?

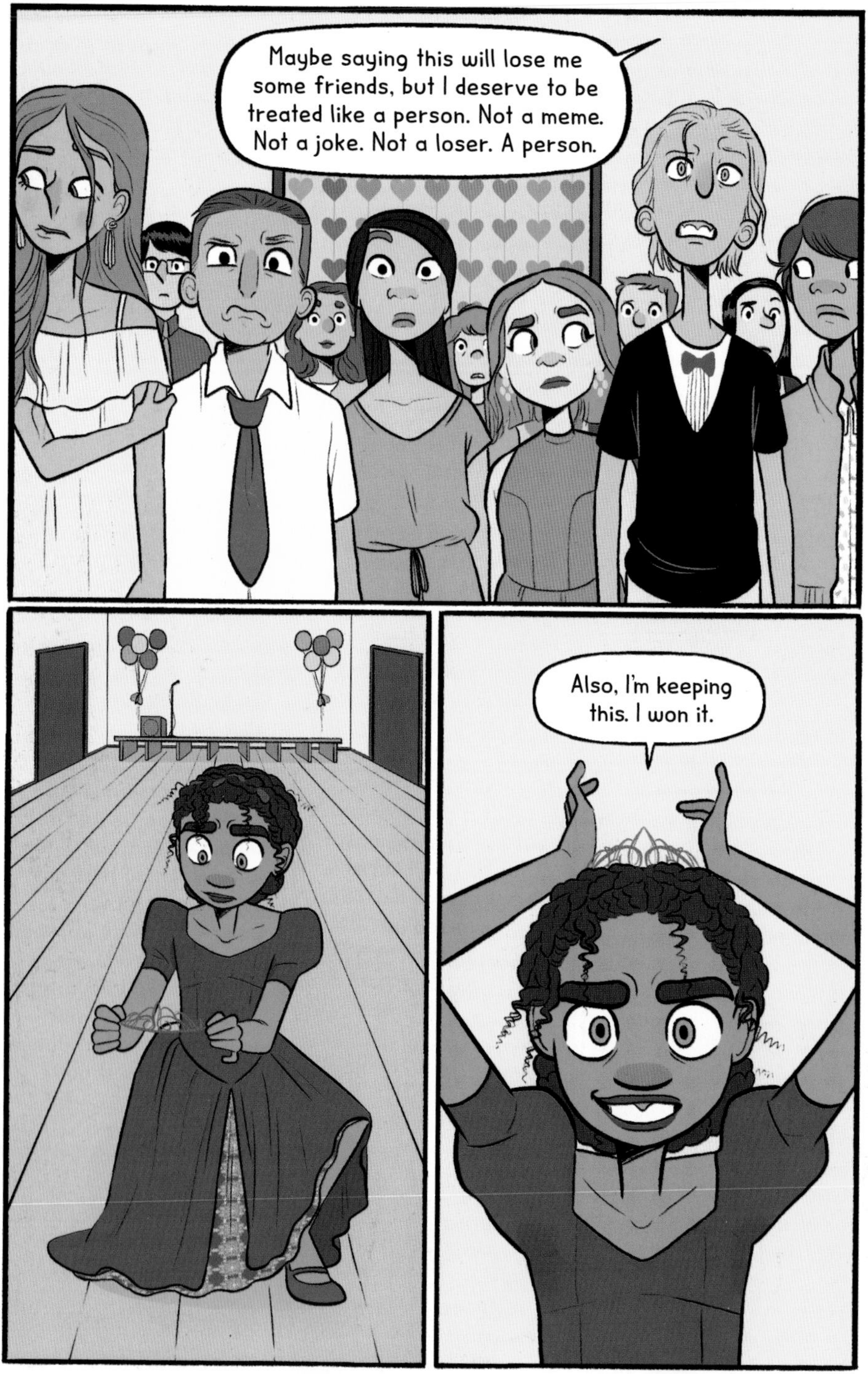
Maybe saying this will lose me some friends, but I deserve to be treated like a person. Not a meme. Not a joke. Not a loser. A person.
Also, I'm keeping this. I won it.

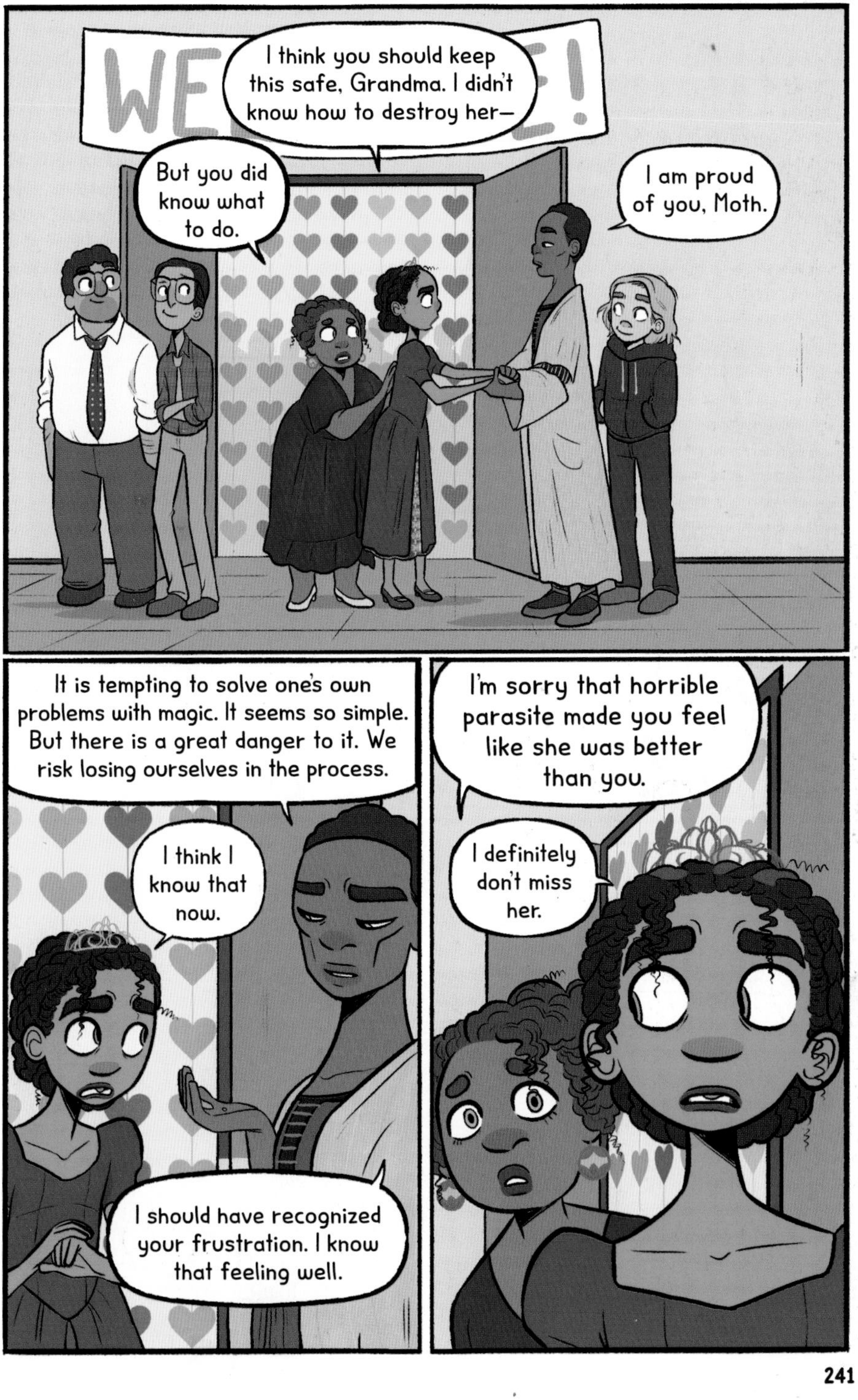
WE E!
I think you should keep this safe, Grandma. I didn't know how to destroy her—
But you did know what to do.
I am proud of you, Moth.
It is tempting to solve one's own problems with magic. It seems so simple. But there is a great danger to it. We risk losing ourselves in the process.
I think I know that now.
I should have recognized your frustration. I know that feeling well.
I'm sorry that horrible parasite made you feel like she was better than you.
I definitely don't miss her.

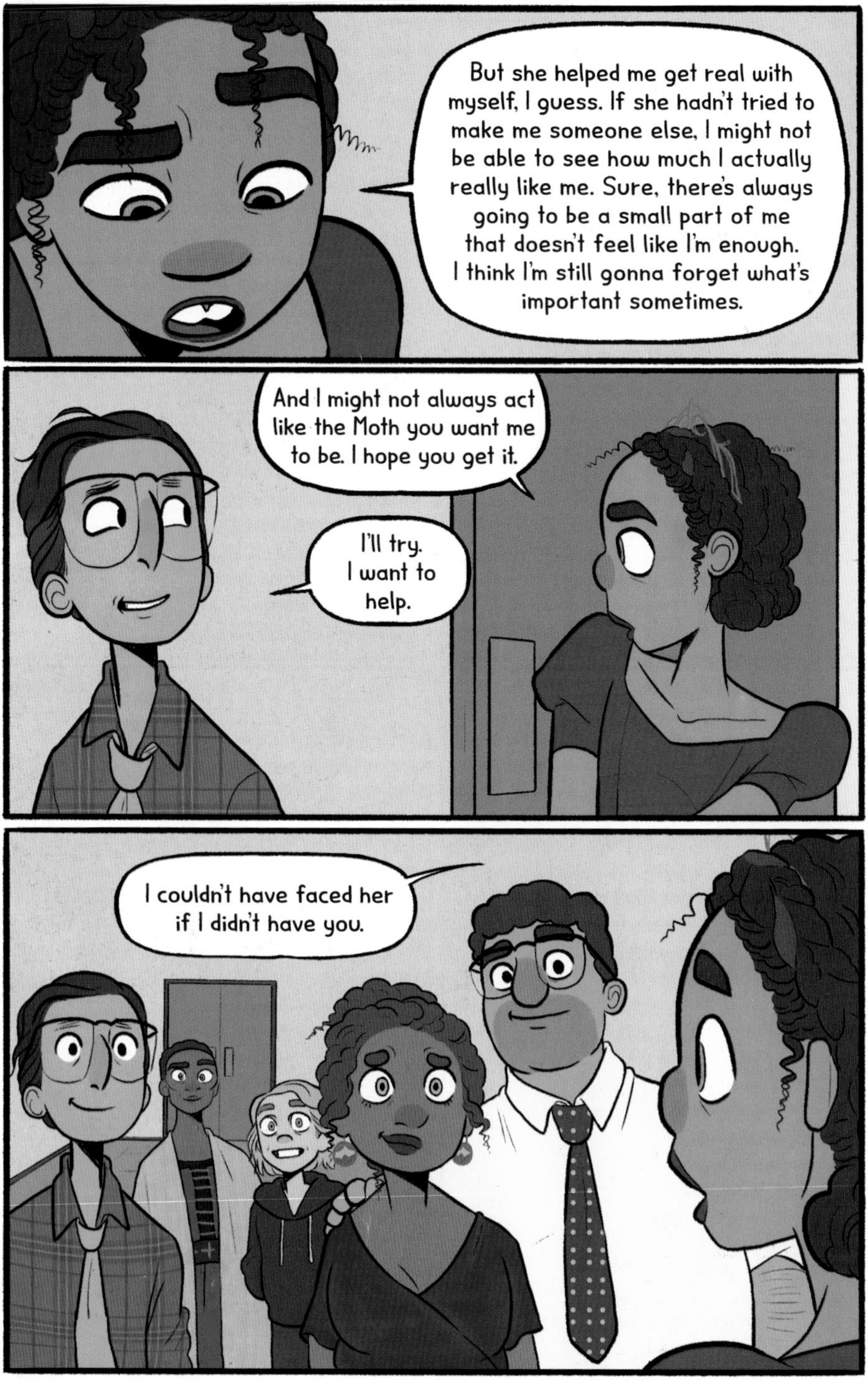
But she helped me get real with myself, I guess. If she hadn't tried to make me someone else, I might not be able to see how much I actually really like me. Sure, there's always going to be a small part of me that doesn't feel like I'm enough. I think I'm still gonna forget what's important sometimes.
And I might not always act like the Moth you want me to be. I hope you get it.
I'll try. I want to help.
I couldn't have faced her if I didn't have you.

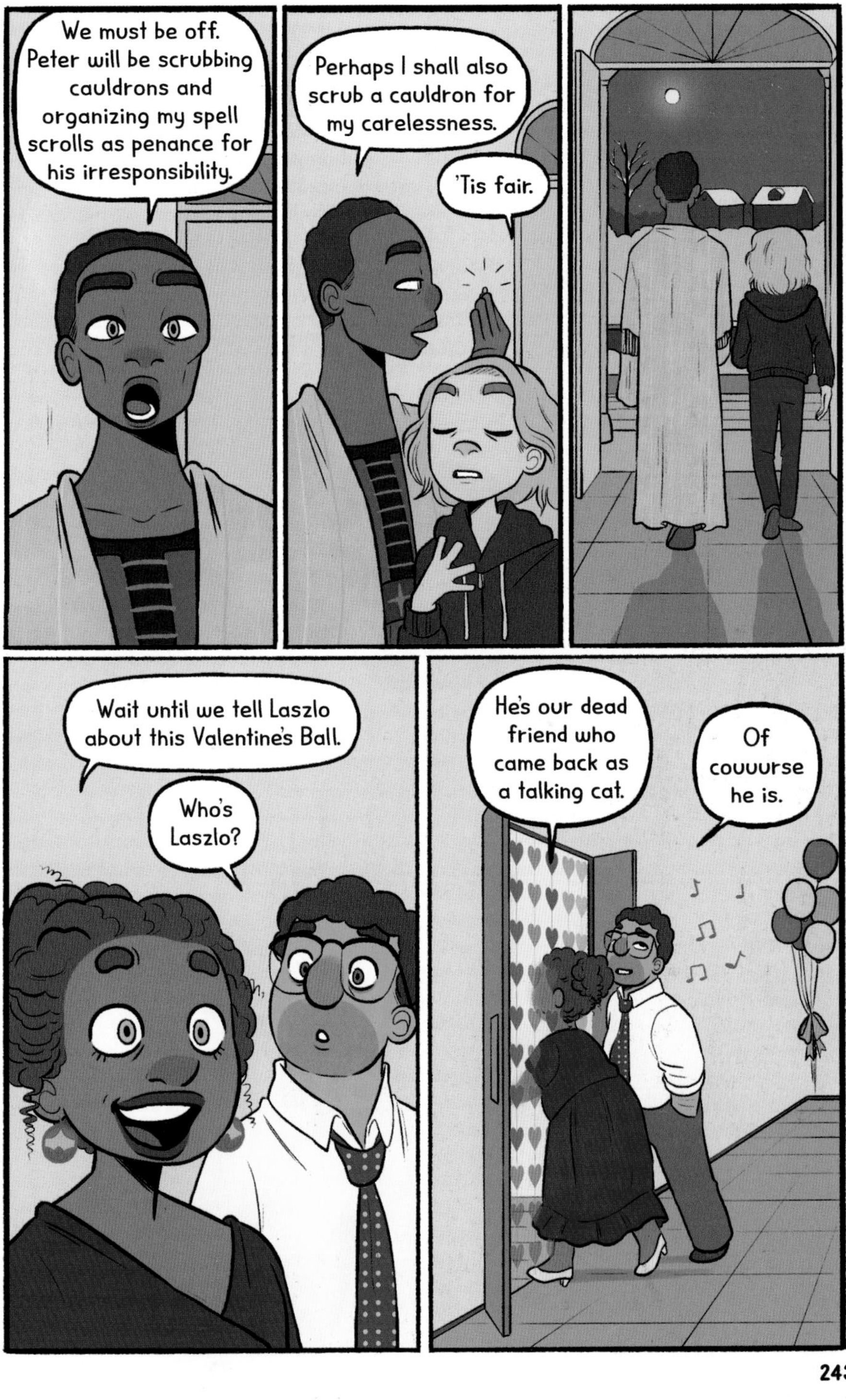
We must be off. Peter will be scrubbing cauldrons and organizing my spell scrolls as penance for his irresponsibility.
Perhaps I shall also scrub a cauldron for my carelessness.
'Tis fair.
Wait until we tell Laszlo about this Valentine's Ball.
Who's Laszlo?
He's our dead friend who came back as a talking cat.
Of couuurse he is.

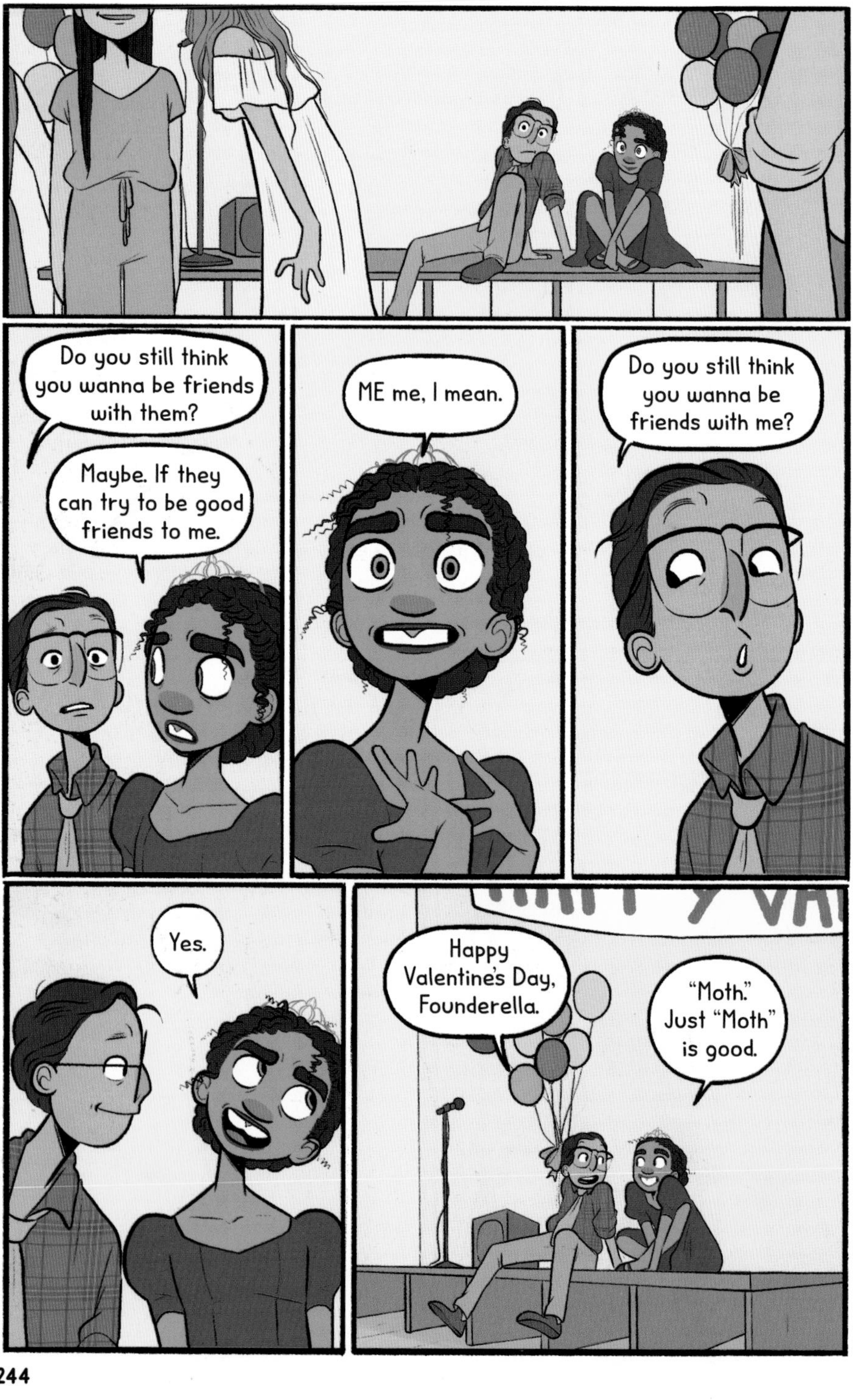
Do you still think you wanna be friends with them?
Maybe. If they can try to be good friends to me.
ME me, I mean.
Do you still think you wanna be friends with me?
Yes.
Happy Valentine's Day, Founderella.
"Moth." Just "Moth" is good.

CHAPTER 13
Okay Is Magic

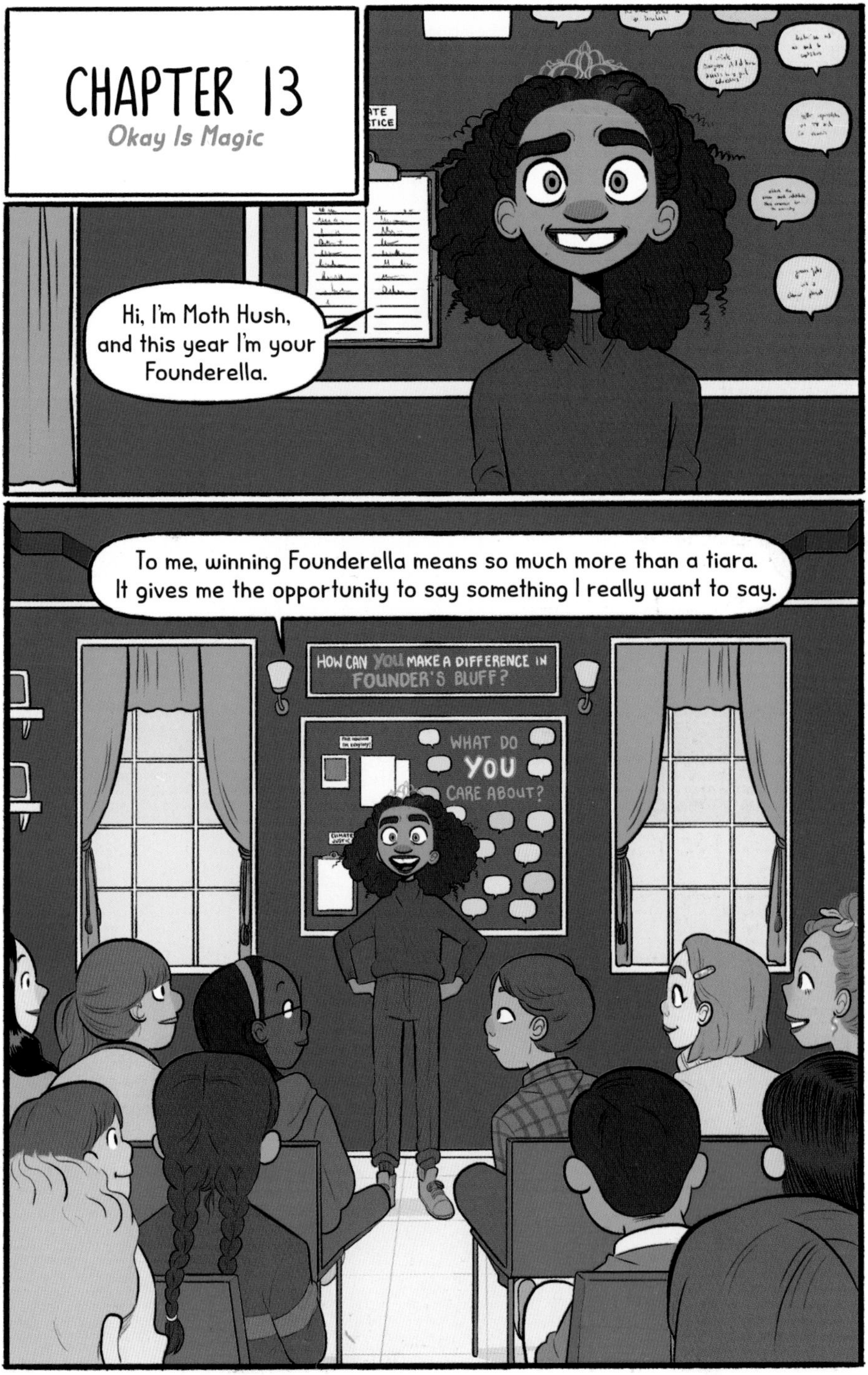
Hi, I'm Moth Hush, and this year I'm your Founderella.
To me, winning Founderella means so much more than a tiara. It gives me the opportunity to say something I really want to say.
HOW CAN YOU MAKE A DIFFERENCE IN FOUNDER'S BLUFF?
WHAT DO YOU CARE ABOUT?

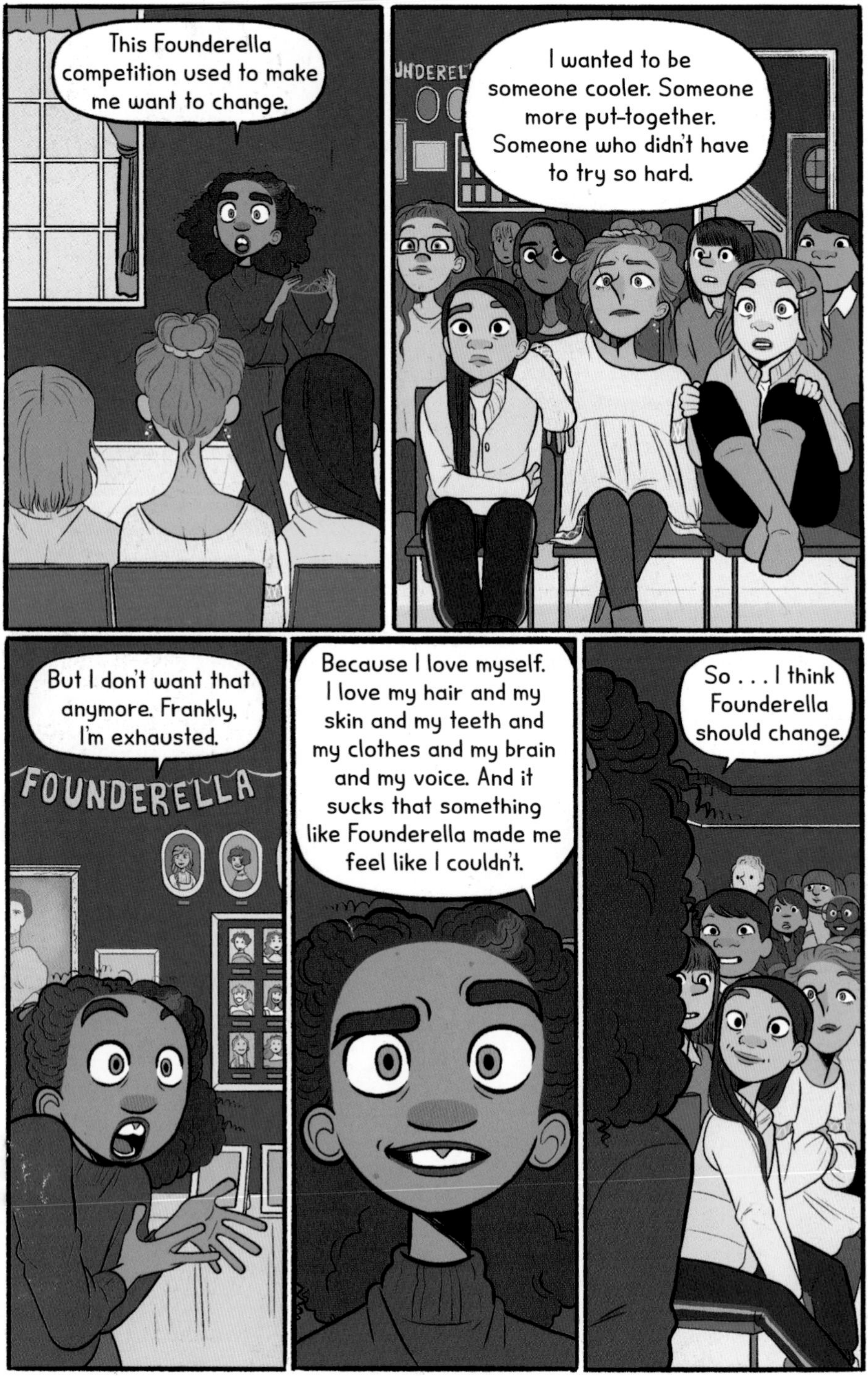

This Founderella competition used to make me want to change.
UNDEREL
I wanted to be someone cooler. Someone more put-together. Someone who didn't have to try so hard.
But I don't want that anymore. Frankly, I'm exhausted.
FOUNDERELLA
Because I love myself. I love my hair and my skin and my teeth and my clothes and my brain and my voice. And it sucks that something like Founderella made me feel like I couldn't.
So . . . I think Founderella should change.

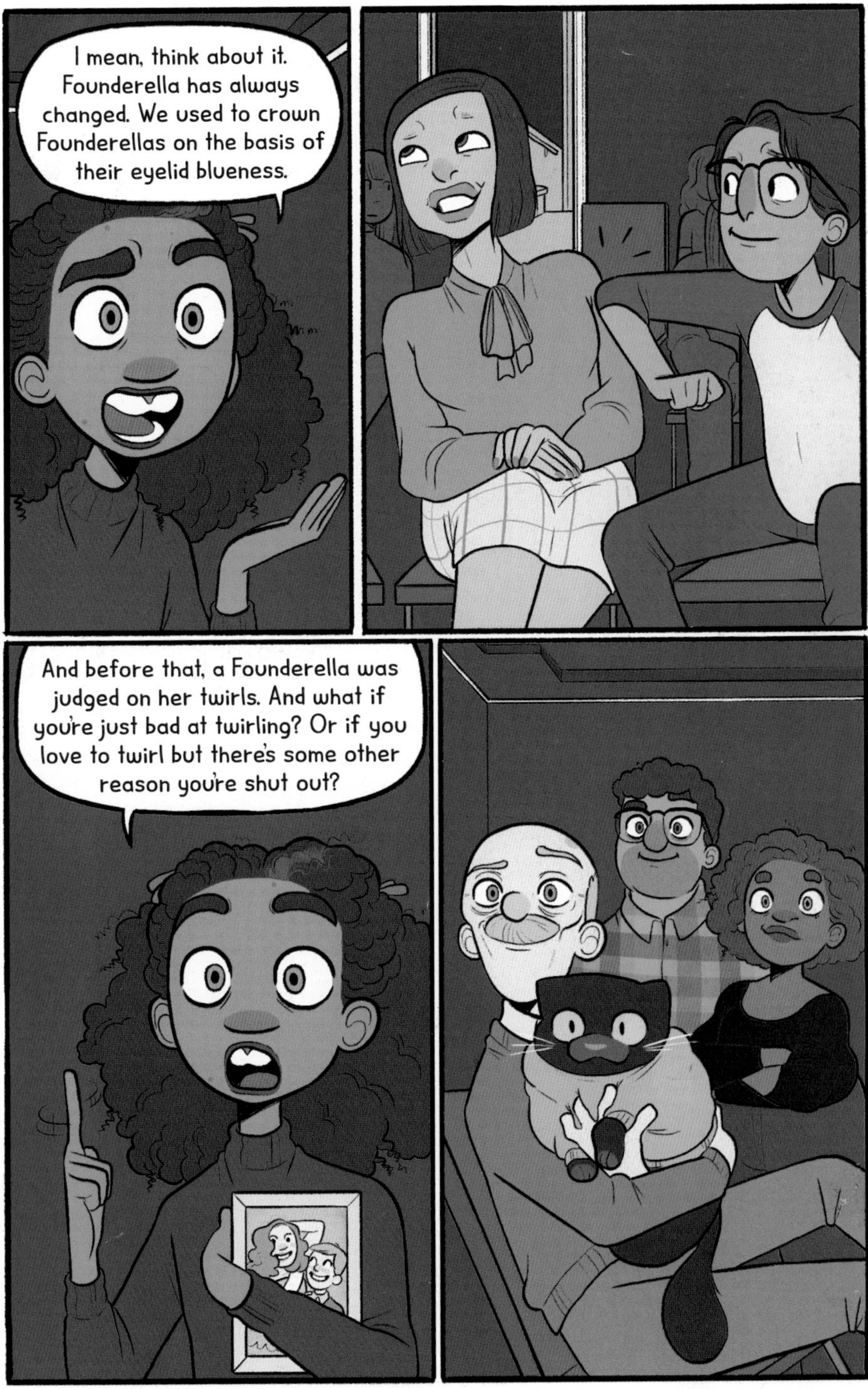
I mean, think about it. Founderella has always changed. We used to crown Founderellas on the basis of their eyelid blueness.
And before that, a Founderella was judged on her twirls. And what if you're just bad at twirling? Or if you love to twirl but there's some other reason you're shut out?

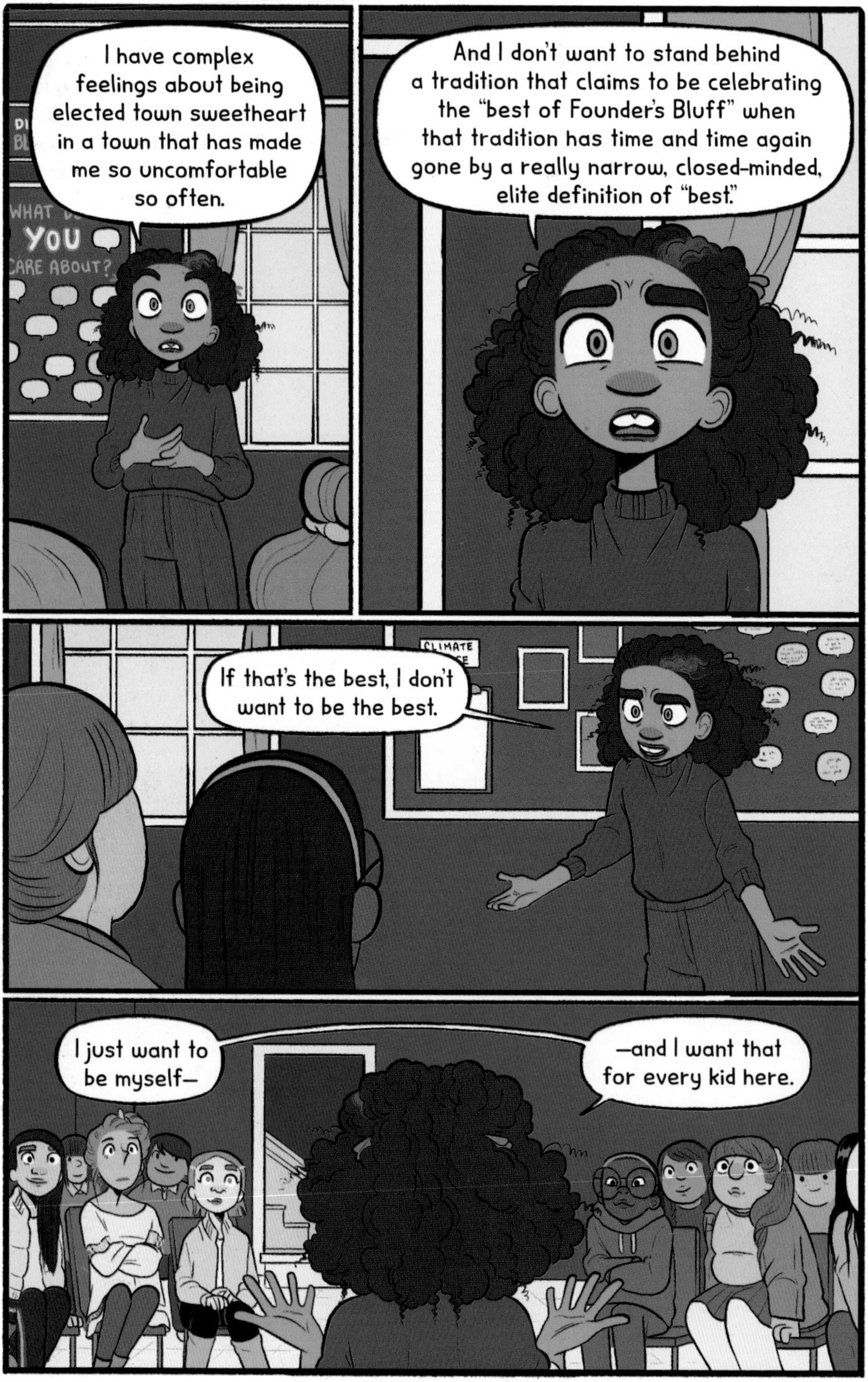
I have complex feelings about being elected town sweetheart in a town that has made me so uncomfortable so often.
And I don't want to stand behind a tradition that claims to be celebrating the "best of Founder's Bluff" when that tradition has time and time again gone by a really narrow, closed-minded, elite definition of "best."
If that's the best, I don't want to be the best.
I just want to be myself—
—and I want that for every kid here.

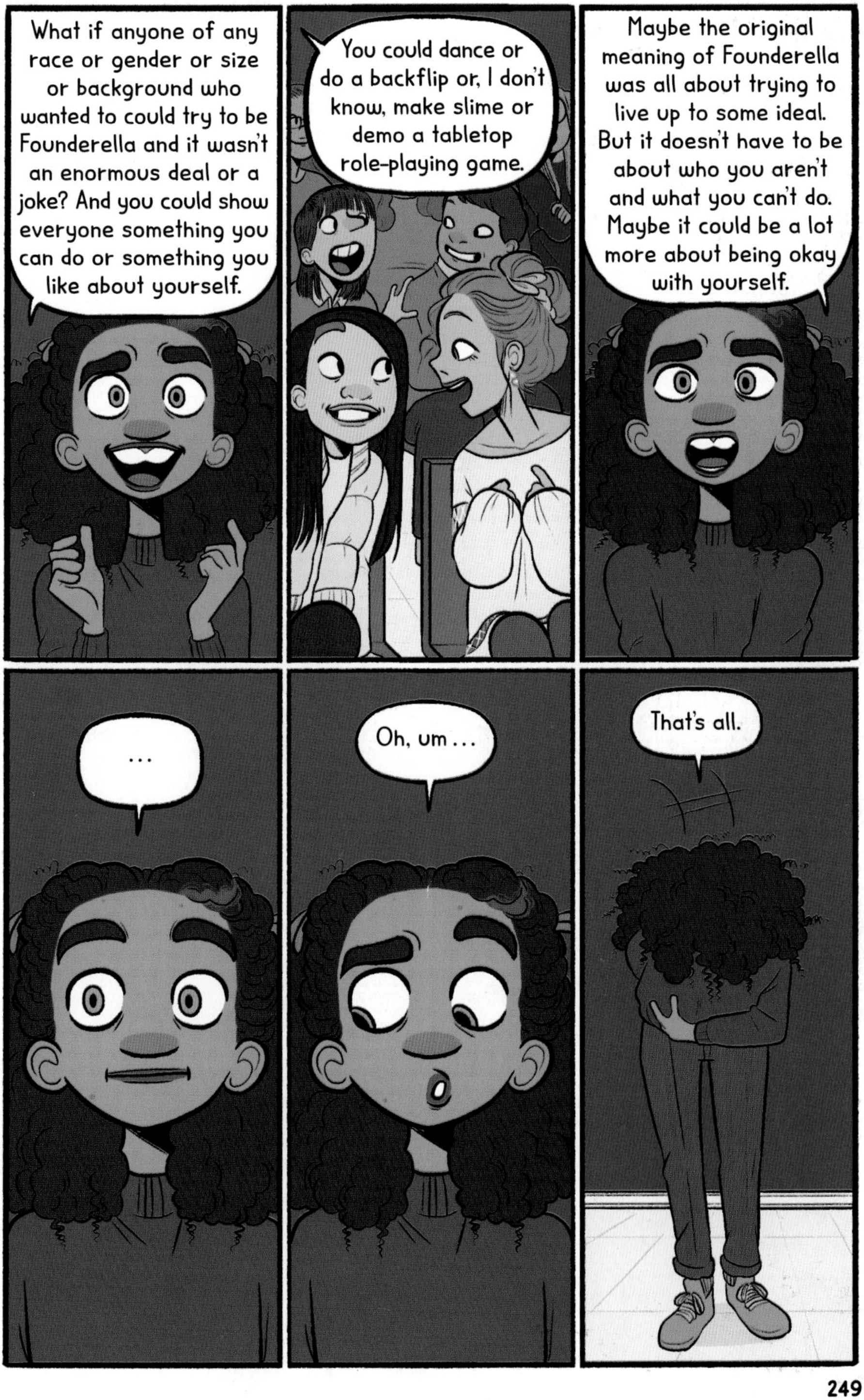
What if anyone of any race or gender or size or background who wanted to could try to be Founderella and it wasn't an enormous deal or a joke? And you could show everyone something you can do or something you like about yourself.
You could dance or do a backflip or, I don't know, make slime or demo a tabletop role-playing game.
Maybe the original meaning of Founderella was all about trying to live up to some ideal. But it doesn't have to be about who you aren't and what you can't do. Maybe it could be a lot more about being okay with yourself.
...
Oh, um...
That's all.

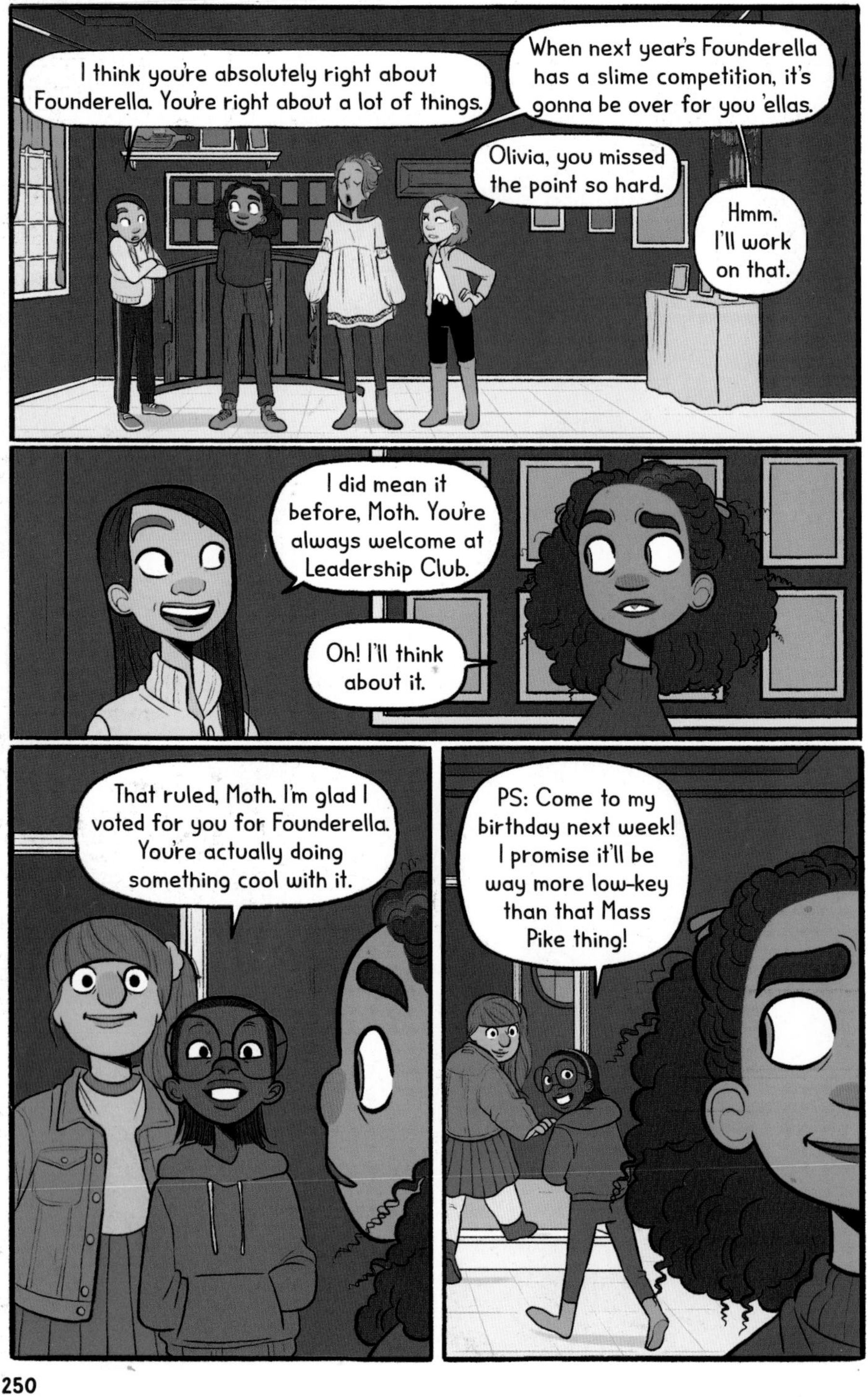
I think you're absolutely right about Founderella. You're right about a lot of things.
When next year's Founderella has a slime competition, it's gonna be over for you 'ellas.
Olivia, you missed the point so hard.
Hmm. I'll work on that.
I did mean it before, Moth. You're always welcome at Leadership Club.
Oh! I'll think about it.
That ruled, Moth. I'm glad I voted for you for Founderella. You're actually doing something cool with it.
PS: Come to my birthday next week! I promise it'll be way more low-key than that Mass Pike thing!

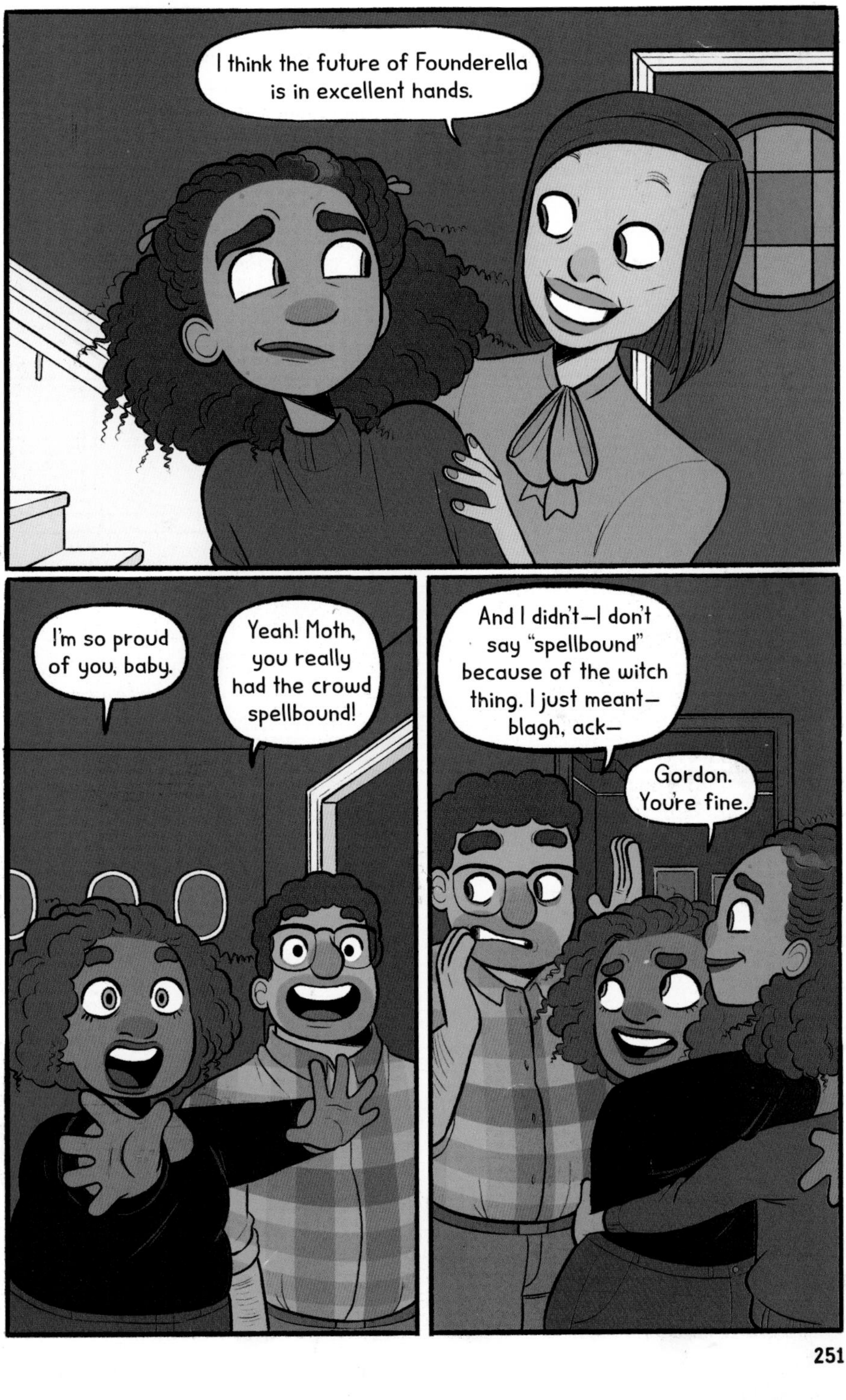
I think the future of Founderella is in excellent hands.
I'm so proud of you, baby.
Yeah! Moth, you really had the crowd spellbound!
And I didn't—I don't say "spellbound" because of the witch thing. I just meant—blagh, ack—
Gordon. You're fine.

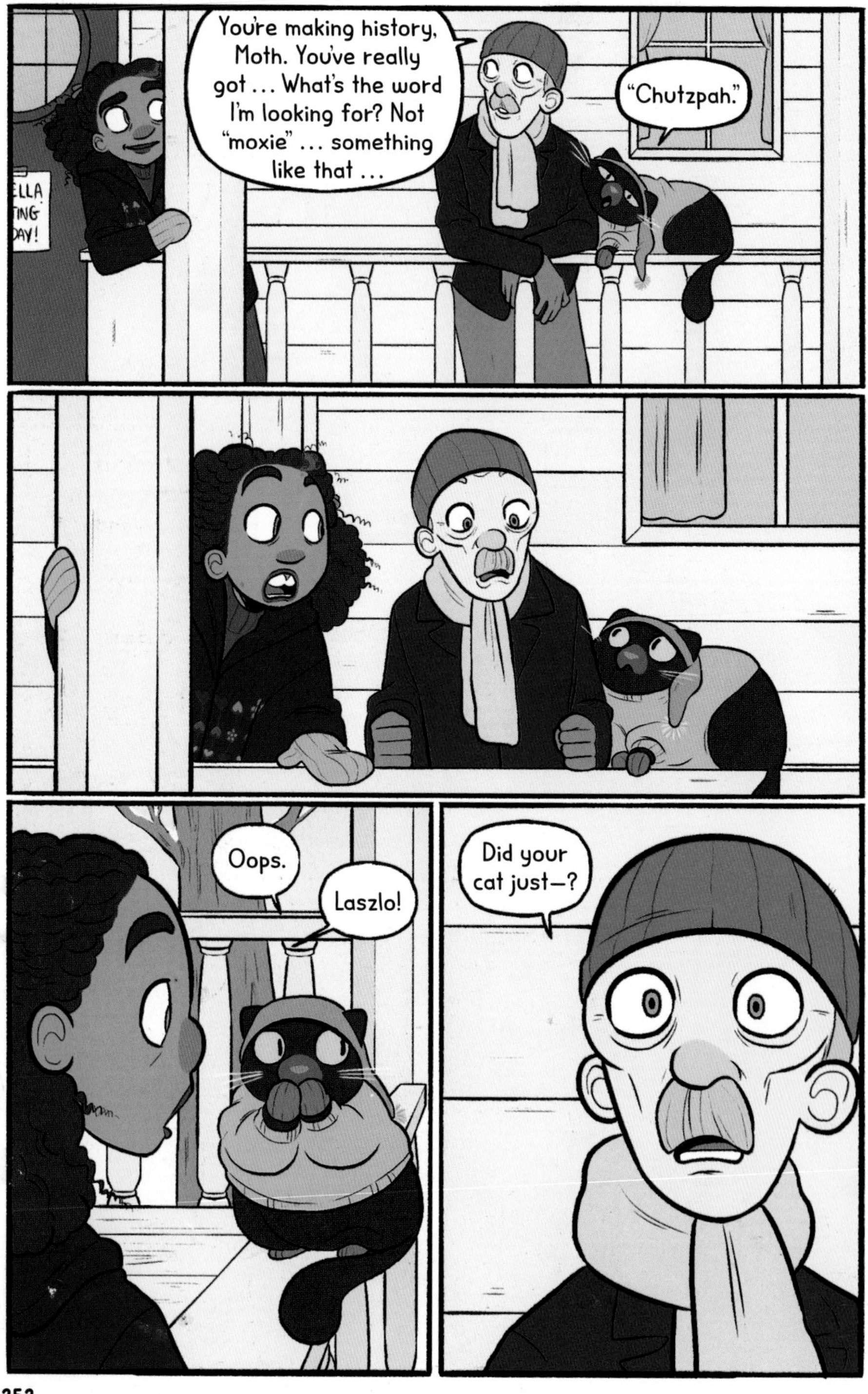
You're making history, Moth. You've really got . . . What's the word I'm looking for? Not "moxie" . . . something like that . . .
"Chutzpah."
Oops.
Laszlo!
Did your cat just—?

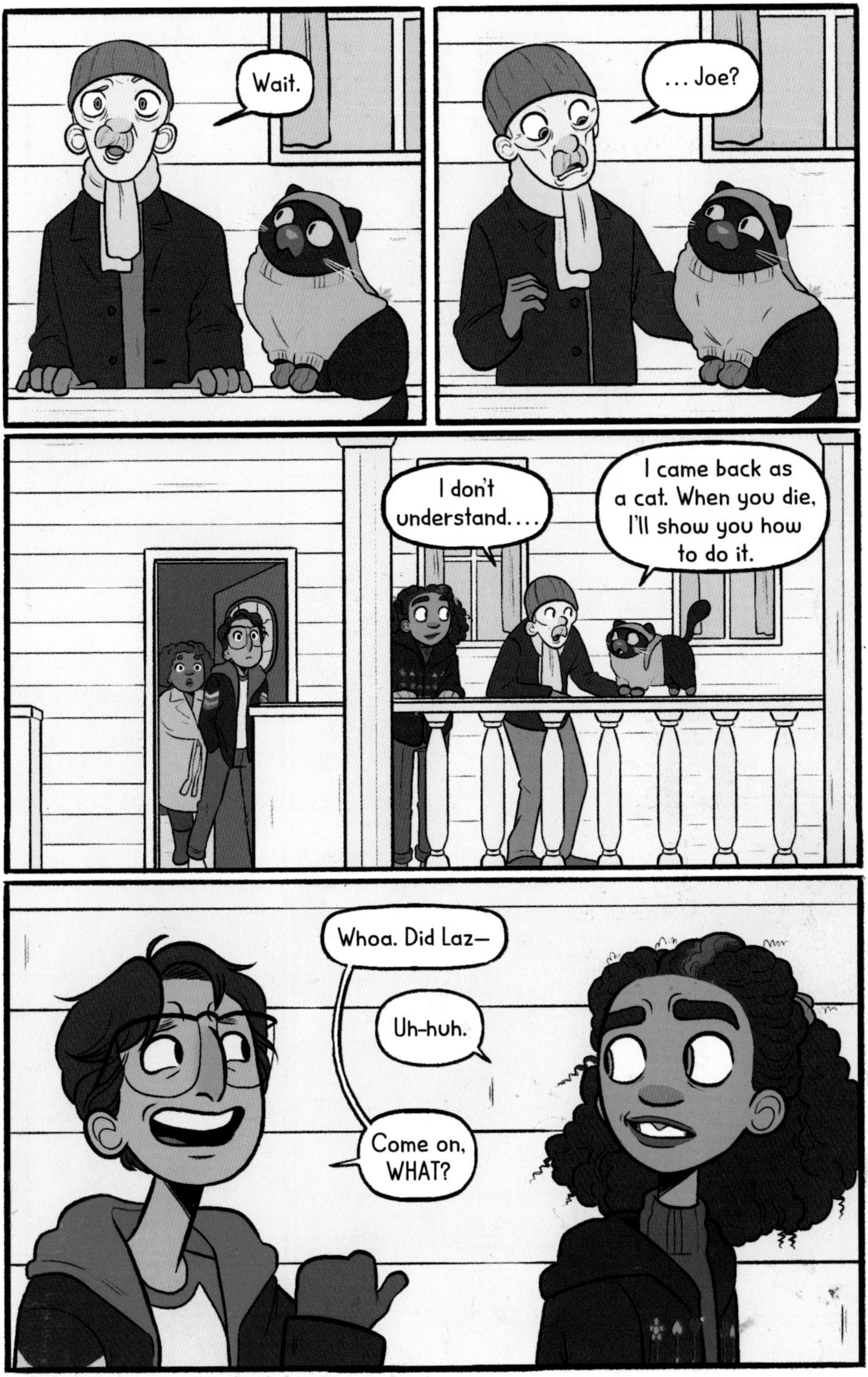
Wait.
... Joe?
I don't understand....
I came back as a cat. When you die, I'll show you how to do it.
Whoa. Did Laz—
Uh-huh.
Come on, WHAT?

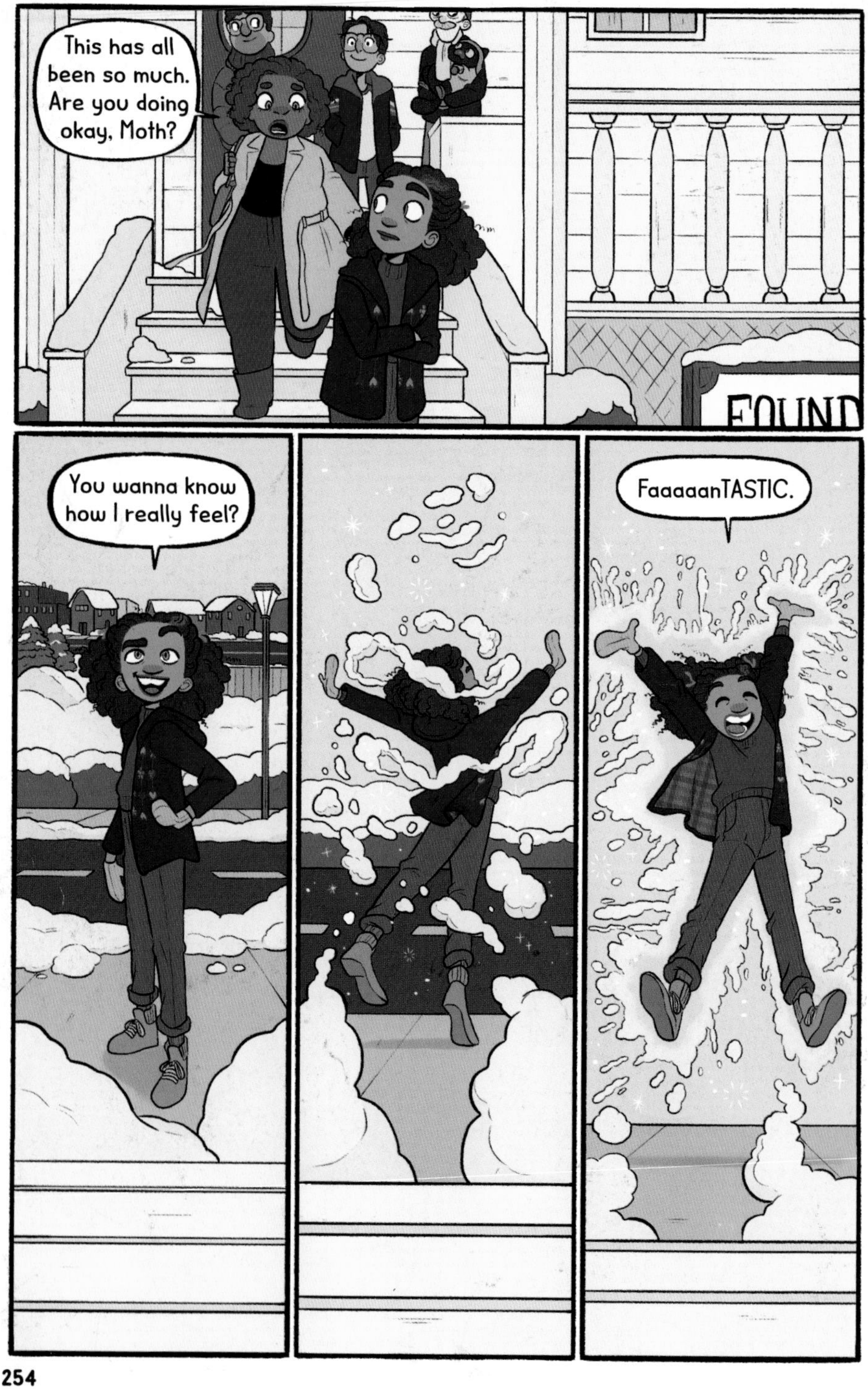
This has all been so much. Are you doing okay, Moth?
FOUND
You wanna know how I really feel?
FaaaaanTASTIC.

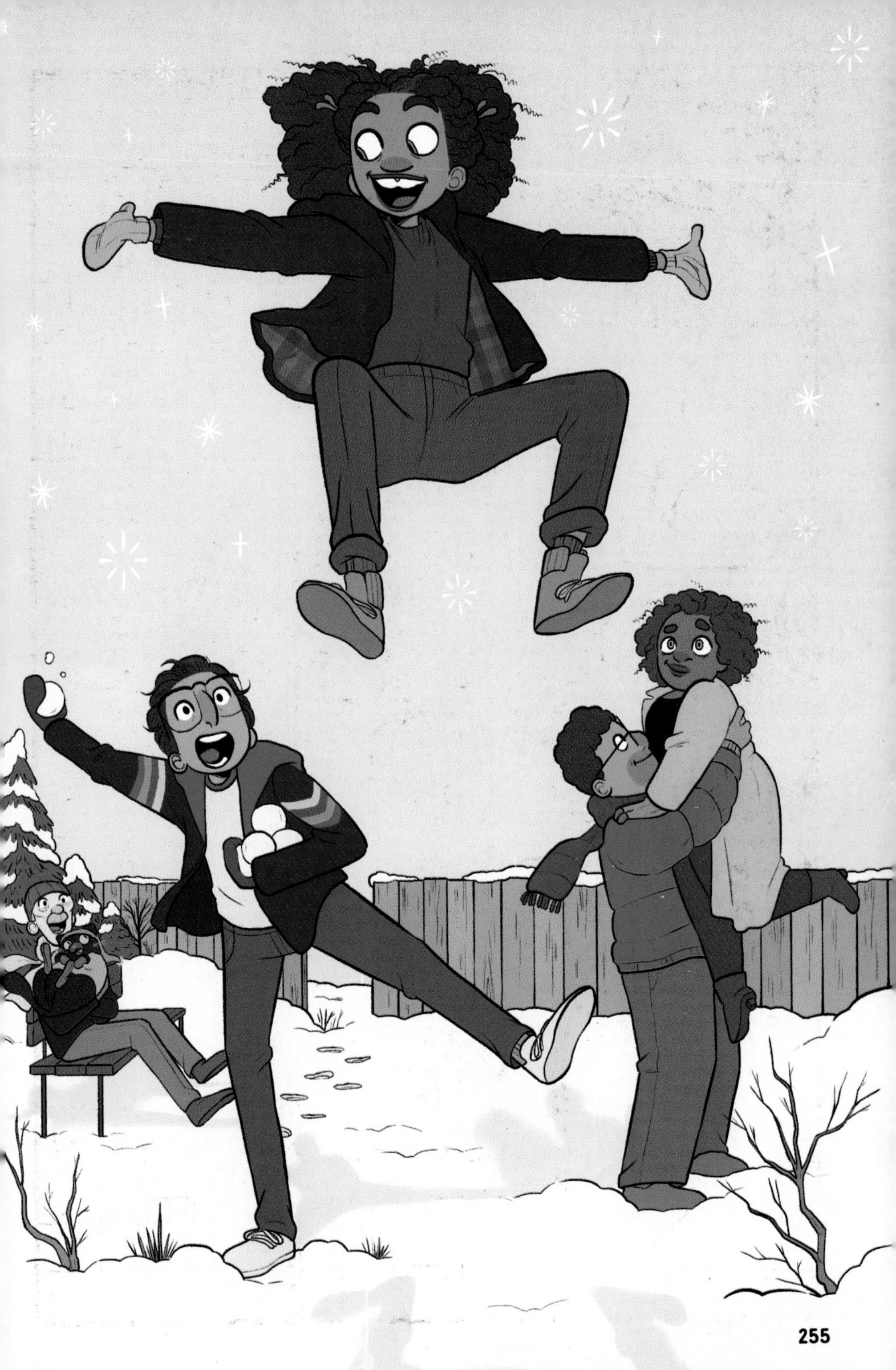

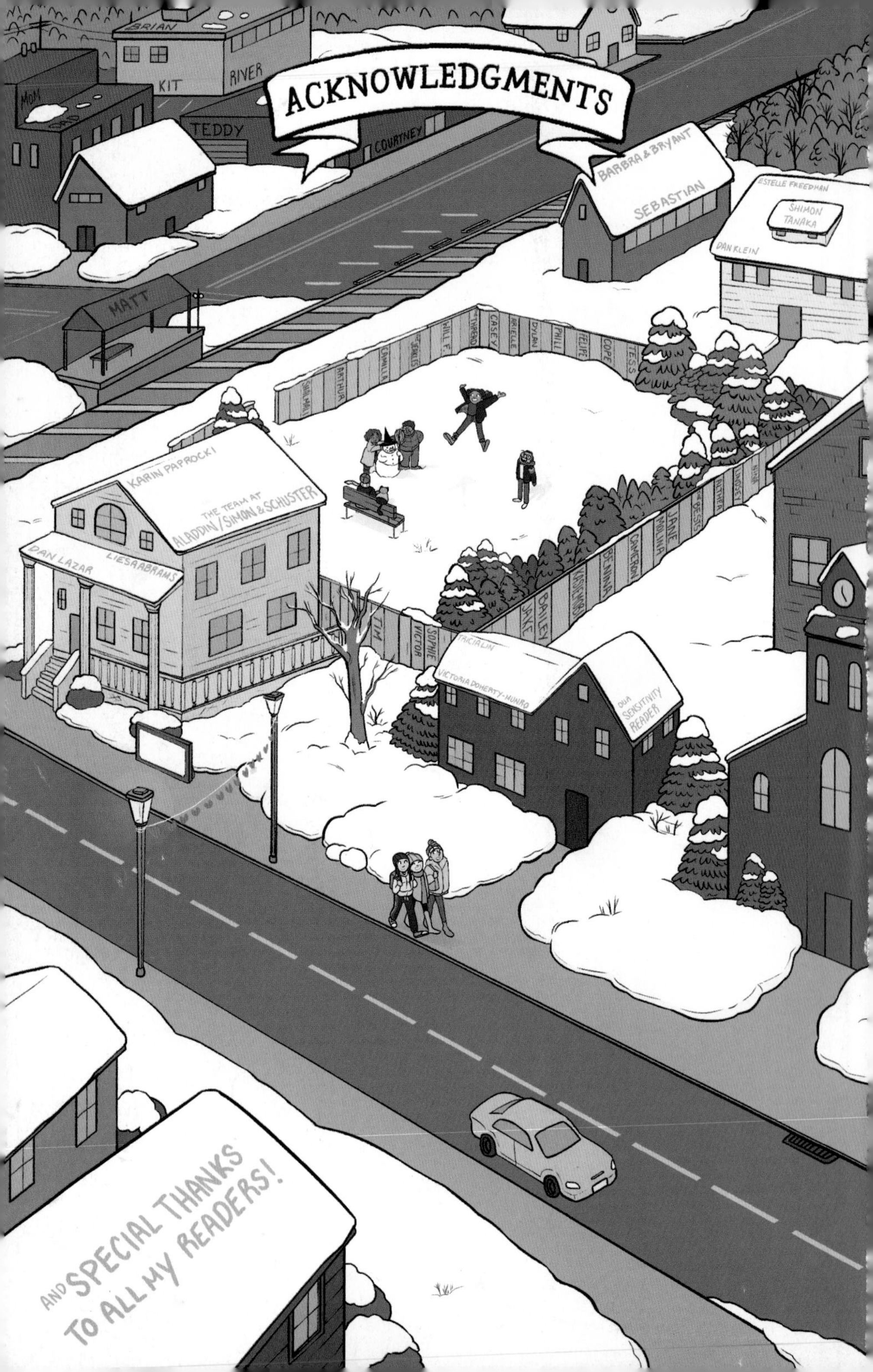
ACKNOWLEDGMENTS
BRIAN
MOM
DAD
KIT
RIVER
TEDDY
COURTNEY
BARBRA & BRYANT
SEBASTIAN
ESTELLE FREEDMAN
SHIMON TANAKA
DAN KLEIN
MATT
ARTHUR
CAMILLA
WILL F.
THREAD
CASEY
ARIELLE
DYLAN
PHILL
FELIPE
COPE
TESS
KARIN PAPROCKI
THE TEAM AT ALADDIN/SIMON & SCHUSTER
DAN LAZAR
LIESA ABRAMS
TIM
VICTOR
SOPHIE
JAKE
BAILEY
BENINA
CAMERON
MOLINA
JANE
BESTS
ALTHEA
LINDSEY
TRICIA LIN
VICTORIA DOHERTY-MUNRO
OUR SENSITIVITY READER
AND SPECIAL THANKS TO ALL MY READERS!